S0-AZB-315

From the Producer of
The Kent Family Chronicles

THE SECOND EXCITING BOOK IN THE
BESTSELLING BIBLICAL EPIC BEGUN IN
CHILDREN OF THE LION

A STIRRING SAGA OF MEN OF
DESTINY—THEIR DREAMS OF POWER
AND GLORY CAME TRUE ONLY TO BE
DASHED BEFORE THEIR VERY EYES . . .

AND THE WOMEN WHOSE LOVE
AND DAUNTLESS DEVOTION KEPT
THEIR MEN STRONG.

THE SHEPHERD KINGS

KHALKEUS
Once called Kirta of Haran, he sacrifices
wife and son to a restless quest for knowledge.

XENA
High priestess, king's daughter—and slave
to a love that her man cannot return.

HADAD
A great heart in a crippled body: artist, dreamer, lover—and hero.

DANATAYA
Courageous orphan child of the streets, she will not settle for less than love.

JACOB
An exiled king, clothed in the
robes of a shepherd.

RACHEL
To her husband she is all things—
except the mother of his child.

SHOBAI
Thoughtless, spoiled, he plays at life,
courting a savage and merciless destiny.

RESHEF
A Judas whose only god is Evil.

THE LANDS
OF THE
CHILDREN
OF THE
LION

Desert

Hittite Country

Haitusas

HALYS RIVER

Kanish

Knossos

Crete

MAEANDER RIVER

Lycia

Arzawa

Kizzuwatna

the great sea

Kittim

Ugarit

Byblos

Tyre

Canaan

Damascus

Megiddo

Moab

THE SALT SEA

Lower Egypt

Sile

Memphis

On

Egyptian Empire

Kadesh-barnea

Edom

Sinai

AREA OF INSET
"THE PROMISED LAND"

Desert

NILE RIVER

Upper Egypt

The Red Sea

0   50   100 150 200 250
MILES
Major Routes

RON TOELKE '81

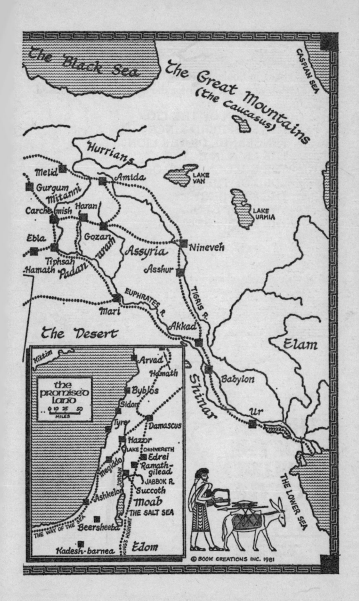

The Black Sea

CASPIAN SEA

The Great Mountains
(the Caucasus)

Hurrians

Melid
Gurgum
Mitanni
Carche·mish Haran
Ebla Gozan
Tiphsah *arah* Assyria Nineveh
Hamath Padan Asshur

Amida

LAKE VAN

LAKE URMIA

EUPHRATES R.

TIGRIS R.

Mari

Akkad

The Desert

Shinar

Babylon

Elam

Ur

THE LOWER SEA

the
Promised
Land
0 10 25 50
MILES

Kittim

Arvad

Hamath

Byblos
Sidon
Tyre
Damascus
Hazor
LAKE CHINNERETH
Megiddo Edrei
Ramath-gilead
JABBOK R.
Ashkelon Succoth
Moab
THE SALT SEA
Beersheeba
THE WAY OF THE SEA
KING'S HIGHWAY
Kadesh-barnea
Edom

© BOOK CREATIONS INC. 1981

Bantam Books by Peter Danielson
Ask your bookseller for the books you have missed

VOLUME II

THE SHEPHERD KINGS

PETER DANIELSON

Created by the producers of
Wagons West, White Indian,
Saga of the Southwest, and
The Kent Family Chronicles.

Chairman of the Board: Lyle Kenyon Engel

BANTAM BOOKS
NEW YORK • TORONTO • LONDON • SYDNEY • AUCKLAND

THE SHEPHERD KINGS

*A Bantam Book / published by arrangement with
Book Creations, Inc.*

*Bantam edition / July 1981
7 printings through January 1989*

Illustrations by Louis Glanzman.

*Produced by Book Creations, Inc.
Founder: Lyle Kenyon Engel.*

*All rights reserved.
Copyright © 1981 by Book Creations, Inc.
Cover art copyright © 1981 by Bantam Books.
No part of this book may be reproduced or transmitted
in any form or by any means, electronic or mechanical,
including photocopying, recording, or by any information
storage and retrieval system, without permission in writing
from the publisher.
For information address: Bantam Books.*

ISBN 0-553-26971-2

Published simultaneously in the United States and Canada

---

*Bantam Books are published by Bantam Books, a division of Bantam
Doubleday Dell Publishing Group, Inc. Its trademark, consisting of the
words "Bantam Books" and the portrayal of a rooster, is Registered in
U.S. Patent and Trademark Office and in other countries. Marca Regis-
trada. Bantam Books, 666 Fifth Avenue, New York, New York 10103.*

PRINTED IN THE UNITED STATES OF AMERICA

KR   16   15   14   13   12   11   10   9   8   7

PROLOGUE

*The campfire was down to glowing coals, which gave heat but
little light. To illuminate the little patch of space in the
middle of the gathering, someone had dipped rags in animal
fat, mounted them atop spears stuck into the sand, and lit
them; now the twin firebrands sent dancing flames leaping
high in the eddying, fitful winds of evening.*

*Into the space between them, suddenly and without warn-
ing, stepped the Teller of Tales.*

*The crowd's expectant murmurs rose ... and then died
away. The old man's keen eyes, a hawk's, deep-set in their
sockets, scanned the upturned faces before him. His own
gaunt cheeks glowed, like theirs, with the light of the flickering flames as he stood silent for a moment, looking down at
them.*

*The murmurs rose again—and died with the first wave of
his uplifted hand, with his first words as they rang out above
the heads of his listeners: "In the name of God, the merciful,
the compassionate ..."*

*Now he had their attention. But he wanted more. He
wanted their hearts and souls in the palm of his hand. His
voice rose thrillingly: "Hear now the tales of the Children of
the Lion," he said. "Hear of the men of no people, and of
their ceaseless and tireless wanderings among all nations—"*

*He paused for no more than the blink of an eye, hearing
the expectant sigh that rose audibly among them; then the
smallest motion of his enchanter's hand silenced every sound.*

*"You have heard of the great Armorer Ahuni, Son of the
Lion, and of his friendship with the great king Abraham,
who brought the worship of the One True God to the land of*

1

Canaan," he said. "You have heard of his great love for his wife Shepset, who bore him a son, Kirta. . . .

"Know then," he said, "that the son of Ahuni grew to maturity, a man of powerful mind and restless heart, a man who married and fathered two sons of his own, Children of the Lion but as different one from the other as night and day. And, in time, Ahuni and Shepset died, lost in a terrible gale on the Great Sea, their love for each other strong to the end. And Kirta, their son, seeking knowledge, abandoned wife and children in a quest for the dark secrets of the earth that had borne him and sustained him.

"Now," he said, his voice gathering intensity, "now hear of a time when civil strife had sundered the seed of Abraham, when his grandson, the true king of Canaan, lay captive, bondservant to a wicked man in a foreign land, far from his people and from the holy land of his fathers. . . .

"Hear of a time when the sons of Kirta, left fatherless in the land of Haran, grew up as brothers but less than brothers: the one rich, the other poor; the one tall and strong, the other small and crippled; the one great in worldly goods, the other great in heart. . . .

"Hear of a time when the Shepherd Kings, nomadic warriors from a distant land, roamed the mountains of the north, as numerous as locusts, so that no king and no army could stand before them—until the folly of a wise man was redeemed by the bravery of a coward, and the true king of Canaan came home to arm and defend his people. . . .

"Hear of the great war that shook the Lands of the Crescent. Hear of the magnificent and terrible armies of the night, and of the ragged line of heroes who opposed them.

"Hear," he said, his voice booming above their heads, "hear of the Shepherd Kings. . . ."

CHAPTER ONE

I

The wind had shifted, and smoke from the burning ships drifted across the bow of the command galley of the invasion force, anchored inside the mole below the just-captured fortifications at the head of the Bay of the Half Moon. Marineus, commander of the Cretan attack forces, brushed the smoke out of his eyes, a sour expression on his face, and turned to face the sea.

"Damn," he said again. Beyond the mole, the Cretan ships—galleys bearing the ensign of the House of the Double Axe—bore down on his command ship over choppy waves. He sighed and turned to his second in command. "Look, Tulisios," he said disgustedly. "We have company. The royal party, no less."

Tulisios peered through the smoke, his face professionally impassive. "You're right, sir," he said. "But—why? Who?"

"Damned if I know," the commander said. "Probably one or more of the pampered fops around Minos, showing up just in time to share credit for a battle already won." His brief glance at his subordinate was bright with rage. "Here we've taken the city, sunk its fleet, stormed the fortifications on the mole, and have six galleys full of fighting men cutting the rest of the population to ribbons. A perfect time for one of Minos's pretty boys to turn up. I can hear the tales they'll tell back at Knossos."

"Yes, sir," Tulisios said. " 'Ah, you should have been there when we took Rouso. . . .' " He scowled politely. " '*We.*' "

"Exactly." Marineus turned back to the bay, with its burning ships. The smoke parted now, and he could see the

3

city itself, with his own galleys beached and the men fighting before the city walls. "Exactly," he said again. "By the time we're back out to sea, they'll have a version of the battle circulating in which you and I and our captains barely had a part at all."

"Sir," Tulisios said. "Below the ensign of the Axe—there's something—I think . . ."

Marineus turned and peered through the drifting smoke. "Eh?" he said. "You're right. Oh, for the love of all the gods. It's her ship, all right. The Goddess Incarnate, eh? Her Holiness in person." He swore and spat into the waves. "I was wondering just what Minos could be sending us that might be worse than three shiploads of idle sons-in-law of the court favorites. But I've just found out."

"Perhaps she's not aboard, sir."

"Not a chance. And you know why she's here."

"I think so, sir."

"You know so. Her precious darling. She has to look out for him as though he were—for the love of heaven—as if he were her son and not her lover."

"He's not a bad chap, sir. Really. When—"

"Of course he isn't," Marineus said brusquely. "And I don't blame him for this, not at all. It's not his fault. In his shoes, I don't know what I'd do myself. Poor bastard. The Goddess Incarnate—and the daughter of Minos. Moreover, there's the way he came into the House of the Axe in the first place. Put him in a bad position right from the start. But—"

"But—" Tulisios's expression mirrored his own.

"Damn it. *Damn* it. Last thing in the world I need right now is having her bitch at me for . . ." He stopped short. "Where *is* Khalkeus, anyhow?"

"Oh. I thought you knew, sir. He transferred to the second landing ship—no, the third—when we lay off the island. I haven't seen him since."

"Ahhhh." The expiring sigh was one of resignation. "Ah, yes. I know what he's up to. Of course, I know."

"Turios of Tyre. The magician. The alchemist."

"Yes, yes. And he'll think nothing of going ashore unarmed, without even a short-sword. He'll act as though there were no danger at all. Risking that precious hide of his, and you know what she'll do to the likes of us if anything's happened to . . ."

"He's a brave man, all right, sir. To the point of foolhardiness."

4

"To my sorrow. I remember the time we took that Egyptian town. What was its name? Never mind, it doesn't matter. Anyhow, he said he had to get to the metal shop before anyone had the time to destroy anything. Well, I understand that. And he's a craftsman, a hell of a craftsman. You couldn't ask for a better. But . . ."

"But why couldn't he have turned the head of some other woman? Right, sir?"

"You have my thought exactly." Marineus turned to face the oncoming vessels again. The lead galley turned ponderously, heaving to alongside the command vessel. "And there she is, in all her mufti."

He looked down at the galley. Aft of the rowers, under a gaily painted canopy, stood Xena, daughter of the current incarnation of Minos, king of Crete—and high priestess of the Great Goddess. As he had said, she did not wear the enveloping robes of a priestess of the Lady. Instead she wore the common dress of a woman of rank at the court of Minos: a flounced skirt and an open jacket that bared full breasts whose nipples had been colored with henna like the soles of her little bare feet. In deference to her rank and sex, someone had spread a woven rug over the pitched deck, and she stood on this, looking up at him.

She did not waste words. "Khalkeus," she said in a piercing voice that carried even over the distant sounds of battle. "Where is Khalkeus?"

Marineus barked an order; a seaman stepped forward to lower a rope ladder to the smaller vessel. Then the commander turned back to the woman below. "He was with the third landing vessel, my lady," he said, his voice neutral. "He . . ."

But now she had grasped the ladder and climbed over the side to join him, and her eyes blazed as she stepped down onto his own deck. "You fool!" she said in a voice that would take the paint off a new-stained mast. "You mindless, thoughtless fool! Did you think I wouldn't hear of this? Did you possibly think . . . ?"

Marineus's face turned to stone. Only his eyes moved, nervously. He did not look at her. It was obvious that his emotions were barely under control. "My lady," he said in a strained voice. "The lord Khalkeus is his own man. He is an adult, and makes his own decisions. He—"

"Don't give me that!" Half his size, she looked up at him with searing contempt. "You're commander of the raid. As such, everyone on every ship involved in the raid is under

5

your direct command. If you'd wanted to, you could have ordered him to . . ."

Marineus glared down at her. The still-lovely face, the naked breasts—they looked to him now like the attributes of a harpy, a gorgon. "As you have reminded me, my lady," he said in an icy voice, "I *am* in command, and that applies to this precise moment. And if I choose to let Khalkeus go ashore with the landing party to seek valuable military secrets before they can be destroyed by the city's defenders . . ."

But then she turned those eyes on him: dark, almost black, flashing with secret lights. His words trailed away. He found his throat suddenly too dry for speech; his breath stopped for a moment. *The Goddess,* he thought. *She has the power of the Goddess on her, even now.*

Her smile was cruelly triumphant. "You would challenge me, would you?" she said in a half-whisper. "Perhaps you'd like a little stroke, eh? Paralysis on your right side? Or . . . what? A touch of impotence? Whatever you wish, the Lady can oblige you. If I—"

"N-no," Marineus said, in a choked voice. "Please—I meant no . . ."

And then whatever spell she had cast upon him broke, and he stood, weak as a sick child, grasping the lee rail with a trembling hand. Tulisios rushed forward to steady him. He looked up, horror in his eyes. But she was gone, over the side to her own vessel; he could hear her shouting orders to her own crew.

Hairless, beardless, his gross belly jutting obscenely above the slack loincloth which was all he wore above boots, Lukios, arms crossed over his fat chest, smirked maliciously at the Goddess Incarnate as she stood scowling at the departing crewmen. "Oh, come now," he said. "You're not *really* going ashore after him, are you?"

"I'm not, am I?" Xena said in a deadly voice. "Just watch me."

"Oh, dear," the eunuch said. "You know what your father will say. I mean, what if you're captured? What then?"

"Nobody's going to capture me." She watched the sailors overhead wrestling with the shortened sail.

"On the other hand, maybe that's what you want. Imagine falling into the hands of the sort of rough, rude types they run to in these barbaric islands." He rolled his eyes heavenward and shivered with delight. "How delightful! Why, I can remember when I was a boy in Lycia—"

6

"Keep your memories to yourself," she said resentfully. "You up there! Stroke! *Stroke!*"

The eunuch watched the drummer settle into his chair and begin to give the slaves the beat; the naked oarsmen heaved mightily, and Lukios, his eyes on the off oarsman on the starboard rail, smiled appreciatively. "Well," he said in an undertone to Xena, "if you're dead set on starting a ruckus, it's no business of mine, I'm sure. But I really can't give you any encouragement in the present matter. You're handling him all wrong, you know. *All* wrong."

Xena's expression changed, grew vulnerable for perhaps the first time. Her aggressive stance melted. "Wrong?" she said. "But . . ."

Lukios did not look at her. His eyes were still on the big oarsman with the broad chest and the long-muscled arms, pulling lustily on the long oar. "Of course. You know you are. The truth is, you don't understand men at all."

"But—"

"Not at all," Lukios piped in a smart-alecky singsong. "Not at all, at all. No man likes to think he's on a leash. No man at all . . ." The singsong ceased and he gave her his full attention for a moment, looking her in the eye. "Why, least of all, a man like Khalkeus, a man with an independent mind. A man with an inquiring and restless spirit. Didn't you tell me that he abandoned a wife and two children he loved dearly just to go searching for some alchemic formula?"

"Y-yes, but—" She hesitated; this line of talk was too close to the truth not to disarm and discommode her. "But that was a long time ago, and . . ."

"Oh, my dear," the eunuch fluted, "that sort of man is the way he's going to be in the egg. *Really.* If you had any sense at all, you'd let him have his head. With that kind the best sort of prison is no prison at all. But here you are, acting like a silly little girl, as giddy as a—"

"Prison?" she said petulantly. "Who talks of prison? Look here, it was I who freed him. A slave in my father's household, and—"

"Oh, fa la la. Don't hand me that nonsense. You took the chain off one ankle and put it on the other. Now he's beholden to you, and he hates it. He—"

"Hates? He *hates*—?"

"I'm not saying he hates *you*. He rather loves you—as much as a man like that, with his mind on other things than women and such, *can* love anybody. And let me tell you, he'd love you a lot more if you'd—well, just *let* him." He made a

7

moue. "You know. Instead of all this 'I demand' business. 'I de-maaaand . . .' " He made an epicene face, rolling his eyes again.

Now the rowers were settling into a good rhythm; the drummer increased the pace. "Hold," she said sharply. The drummer slowed the beat. "Ship oars! Anchor." The crewmen, puzzled, complied. The drummer looked her way once; then he put down his drumsticks.

"Ah," the Lycian said. "You're ready to listen to reason, I gather. Well, if you ask me—"

"You're right," she said. "We always have a dreadful scene after . . . after I've . . . well, done something like this. Something impulsive."

"Of course you do. There now. You should always listen to me. Always. If you did, you'd be a lot farther down the road toward self-knowledge than you are, let me tell you."

"I'm listening," she said. Her stance was that of a downcast pupil taking instruction. "Go on, Lukios. Please."

"Make that pretty please. But there you are. Last time I tried to tell you something you called me insolent. Threatened to have me whipped. Threatened to . . ." His mock petulance had a real note of resentment in it, but it slipped off, as always, into the whine of a giant overgrown infant.

"Please, Lukios."

"Well—last time you almost lost him. He nearly went away. There was a sea captain he met on Crete, at one of the ports. He was going to steal a coracle and row out at night and sign on as ship's armorer. He said he'd had the last of your smothering presence. But then he weakened at the last minute. He really does love you, you know—"

"And my father's money and power, and the protection of the court, and unlimited resources for pursuing his experiments." Her voice held the smallest taint of bitterness.

"To be sure," Lukios said, "with a man who has a lifelong obsession, like this one of his about discovering a new metal or whatever it is, such things are never totally out of mind. But you undervalue yourself. Really you do."

"Lukios. Don't lie to me. Don't flatter me."

He shot her a single, terrifyingly frank glance; then the hardness in his eye disappeared, and his fat features relaxed as his eye turned to the rank of oarsmen and, after a brief scanning motion, settled once again on the big slave on the starboard rail. "I never flatter you," he said, his eye still on the rower. "More often than not, I *am* insolent. I think it's what you keep me around for. Khalkeus and I are virtually

8

the only people who're not under your spell—or afraid of you. I think that's why both of us get by with so much. You keep me for a confidant, as you could never keep a woman friend. *They'd* all be angling for your position as priestess of the—"

"Lukios!"

"Of course they would. Or they'd be angling for Khalkeus. Well, you don't have to worry about me on either count. The Goddess has no use for a chap like me, who's been . . . trimmed. And as for my falling for Khalkeus, he's a bit of a cold fish. Not my type at all. Now that slave of his, Nikos, he's another matter, but Khalkeus? No."

"So—so what should I do? I mean, *now.*"

"He won't get into trouble. Let him be. Plan a victory feast instead. Oh, yes, that'd be nice." He simpered at the big oarsman. "A party. Everyone will want to unwind after the battle, won't they? And Khalkeus will have got what he wanted here, most likely, and he'll be feeling good."

"Lukios! I don't know what I'd do without you." She tried to hug the big eunuch, but he shied away from her touch, rolling his eyes. "Come, name a reward and it will be yours. You're positively brilliant. That's just the thing to do. Here, what shall I give you?"

Lukios smiled languidly, his eyes still on the oarsman, who was stretching his long limbs, the better to display their roughhewn beauty. "Oh, I'm sure I'll think of something," he said coyly.

II

Khalkeus looked down a transverse street, where, beneath a heavy wooden lintel that framed a door in the massive structure, three of Rouso's defenders gallantly battled a squad of Cretan troops. He scowled for a moment; then his features relaxed into their habitual expression of equanimity. "No," he said to Nikos. "It's blocked down that way. Let's try this alley here."

Nikos, sword in hand, looked up. High above their heads, flames danced in a second-story window. He could hear women's screams: loud, piercing. "Yes, sir," he said. "But if you'd only let me go first, sir—or let me find you a weapon."

"Time enough to think of that when trouble arrives," Khalkeus said in his dry voice. "I'm a maker, not a wielder, of weapons. But if you insist . . ." He smiled, with surprising politeness for a man addressing his personal slave. "After you, if you prefer."

"Yes, sir," Nikos said. The two men were more or less of an age; yet the slave seemed by far the younger, having retained a certain liveliness of manner and enthusiasm into his early forties. "I'll just stick my head around the corner here." He moved forward, cautiously, sword at the ready. "Yes, sir," he said. "It's clear up this way. The troops have been through here. Mind your step, sir."

Khalkeus watched him go; then, ducking under a low opening, he followed. *Curious place,* he thought. *Surprisingly modern amenities for a small city like this.* Stepping into the street beyond the doorway, he followed Nikos up a broad stairway that led to the upper city, noting the well-designed drains, baffled to slow the flow of water during the cascading torrents of the rainy season. "Admirable," he said to himself. Some real thought had gone into the design of this quarter. Whose? That of Turios of Tyre? Perhaps. The man was a genius, an engineer as well as a metallurgist. What a pity to find him working for small fry like these. Imagine what his matchless gifts could produce with the might, the wealth, of Minos behind him. Imagine . . .

At the landing, however, he'd lagged too far behind Nikos. Suddenly, soundlessly, a shape moved toward him out of the shadows: a man with a knife. Khalkeus dodged, still agile for all his forty years or more; he stepped back, moved into a crouch, raising one arm to throw back the shoulderpiece of his tunic and give more play to his well-muscled arms, the strong arms of a metalworker.

The man with the knife was fully visible now. He'd been wounded over one eye, and blood had flowed down his face, halving his vision. He had a desperate look in the other eye. "Cretan bastard," he rasped. He feinted, then lunged again. Khalkeus dodged, danced beyond his reach. "Stand, you baby-killing son of a—"

"I'm not armed," Khalkeus said. "I'm an armorer. Armorers don't fight. They don't kill babies—or women, either. Go your way, my friend. Down the stairway . . . there are some of your friends who could use a hand."

The man wasn't listening. He feinted low and swung high:

10

a wild swing that would have laid Khalkeus's face open with better aim; but, one-eyed, he had misgauged the depth. Khalkeus danced lightly out of the way. "Sons of bitches," he said. "Killed my wife and child. Killed my little son, my boy—he was only four."

A sudden wave of sympathy swept over Khalkeus. *Poor devil,* he thought. *He can't think of anything but . . .* "Go your way, my friend," he said. "While you can. If you go now, you can escape into the hills, perhaps. You have my sympathy. Go, for the love of all the gods. I won't tell anyone where you've gone. I'm a father myself."

As he said it, he realized how mealymouthed, how insincere he must sound. *Father?* he thought, feeling a peculiar pang that had become all too familiar these days. *Some father . . .*

"Khalkeus!" Nikos's voice rang out in the little gallery above the stairs. "Stay away from him! Stay . . ." Khalkeus, circling away from the open stairway, stole a glance to one side and saw the slave running toward him, sword held high. He had maneuvered the local man into a vulnerable position at the head of the long staircase. Nikos's wild rush could well force him over the edge. . . .

But somehow he couldn't cooperate. The wave of sympathy ran through him again. He shook his head impatiently, his anger directed at his own weakness. Then, in one lightning movement, he made a bare-handed feint with one hand and, reversing himself, lashed out with one booted foot to kick the knife out of the wounded man's hand. It clattered against the stones. "Now, run!" he said sharply. "Run, you fool—while there's time!"

But the despair, the bottomless despair, in the man's face turned to madness; the light of intelligence left his one visible eye. With a wild cry he ran over the edge of the wall and dived into the depths. Nikos and Khalkeus heard the dull thud of the body as it hit bottom. The man hadn't even cried out.

"Here, sir," Nikos said. "I'm so sorry. It was all my fault." There was no trace of servility in the slave's tone; instead there was genuine concern. "I got too far ahead of you."

"It's all right," Khalkeus said. "Poor devil." He almost shuddered, and an uncharacteristic look of regret swept briefly across his face. "Did you find anything?"

"I think so. We're in the right quarter. There's a row of connected houses just up the way. It may be one of those. The fighting hasn't reached this far yet. My guess is that our people have taken the quarter. All that's left is the mopping up afterward."

"I see," Khalkeus said. "Well, we'll have a look."

Now, in the lower town, fire had broken out in several houses. The basic structures were of roughhewn building blocks; the trim around doors and windows was wood, as was all the furniture inside. The arrangement of windows, open to the sea breezes against the humid heat, made each burning interior a wind tunnel, fanning the flames to unbelievable intensity. Black smoke, thick and acrid, choked the air above where Nikos and his master moved down a winding, precipitous street in the upper town, checking doors, looking inside. Twice, Nikos paused and went to one knee to catch his breath.

Khalkeus joined him the second time; down near the cobbles the smoke was not so thick; there was a pocket of relatively unpolluted air. "I wonder," Nikos said. "If he is here, now, can he still be alive inside one of these houses, choked as they are with smoke?"

"I don't know," the armorer said. "But we have to try. If there's any chance he's still here, I have to find him. The smallest chance—" He coughed—and immediately scowled at his own weakness.

"It's that important, then, sir?" Nikos said, between gasping intakes of relatively clean air.

"If it were to turn out to be unimportant, my friend, I'd know I'd wasted my life. It could be . . . I may be on the trail of the most important discovery ever made. And I have—" Here he coughed again, and made a wry face; "I have every reason to believe that Turios is ahead of me in all this. . . ."

Just then, though, the wind changed. A stiff gust blew the smoke up and away from them. The two stood, master and slave, and for a moment Nikos's face still held the surprise of hearing Khalkeus use the word "friend" with him. Surprise turned to thoughtfulness. "Ah," he said, shaking his head. "That's a lot better. I—"

But Khalkeus's dry cough turned suddenly to a deep, racking, rasping thing that shook him, doubled him over. The slave returned his sword to its scabbard and moved to his master's side, pounding him lustily on the back until Khalkeus, straightening up, his face ashen but the cough temporarily halted, said, "Hold . . ."

The armorer leaned back against a stone wall. He took several deep breaths before he tried to speak. Then, in a raw voice, he said, "Sorry there. I inherited, ah, weak lungs from my grandfather. Ordinarily, it's no problem. But in stuff like this smoke—" He gasped for air again and held one hand over his pounding heart.

Nikos's face showed concern. "Sir," he said. "Are you sure we ought to be—"

Khalkeus's icy glance cut him off in midphrase. "Of course we ought," he said. "That would apply if I thought I were going to die of this by evening." He took another deep breath or two. "Come. Let's see if we can find Turios." Nikos made a movement as if to help him stand erect, but the armorer shook him off proudly.

The first three doors opened on empty houses. At the fourth, Nikos, a step or two ahead of his master, looked in and stepped back. "Gods," he said. "If . . ." But then he moved inside the door and knelt over a huddled body. "Sir," he said. "A woman. I think she's alive. Come, let's see if we can get her out of here."

The woman's eyes fluttered open a moment or two after they'd laid her down on the cobbles outside. "N-no," she said in a stricken whimper. "No, please . . ."

Khalkeus knelt over her. "Here," he said. "We mean you no harm. If we can, we'll direct you to safety. But—we're looking for someone."

Her eyes nervously scanned the two faces: Nikos's sympathetic one, Khalkeus's matter-of-fact and businesslike one. After a moment's hesitation, she evidently decided neither face was that of a rapist or murderer. "Please," she said. "Let me go. . . ."

"My dear," Khalkeus said. "In a moment. But we need to find someone. A man named Turios of Tyre. If you can help us, we'll be only too glad to ensure your safety, offer you amnesty."

"Turios?" the woman said. "You—you mean the magus? The magician? The sorcerer?" Her eyes went wide.

"Sorcerer?" Khalkeus said, bemused. "Well, perhaps. If you prefer. But I'm trying to find him. If I can find him, perhaps I can save him from the attacking party. Can you take us to him? Please. It's very important."

The woman's eyes went from master to slave and back again. "Turios? Why, yes, I think I can, but please . . . you won't let any harm come to me? I—I've been hiding from the soldiers. I heard them grab my mother, down in the square. I hid. . . . Then, well, it must have been the smoke. . . ."

"I know," Khalkeus said in that dry voice of his. It seemed to have a calming effect on her: the dull, reassuring voice of a scribe or something like that. "I had a touch of the smoke myself. I almost passed out, too. But you're all right now." He smiled at her, a not unkindly smile. "Please," he said in a calm, strong voice that carried well above the distant sounds of battle down in the lower town. "Turios," he said. "It's urgent that I find him. If you could do no more than tell us where he lives . . ."

Nikos helped the woman to her feet. Khalkeus looked her over dispassionately. Twenty-six or so; likely a young widow—thin-faced, prematurely aged by the harsh sun of the islands and the hard life of wresting a meager living from dry soil and danger-filled sea. But no. She was no fisherwoman. Not living in the upper town. Fishermen's wives and widows lived near the water. More likely a tradesman's woman . . .

She bit her lip, looking at each of them again in turn. "Turios—he lives up that path there. He has a house above the village, on the mountainside. No one goes near there, usually. He doesn't have much to do with people."

Nikos looked at his master; then both of them looked up the hill at the winding path that trailed up and around the straggly clump of stunted olive trees past the last house. And as they did, the woman broke away and ran as fast as her legs would carry her, away from them, down the street toward the town. "Stop!" Khalkeus said. But she paid him no mind, and as they looked after her, the wind changed once more and blew across the path she had taken, blotting out their view of her escape route.

"Bloody fool," Nikos said sadly. "She'll only run into—" But his words were interrupted by her piercing scream. They heard rough male laughter and more screams, muffled this time. Nikos bit his lip, shaking his dark locks. The glance he threw Khalkeus was one which bore a deep hurt.

Khalkeus's heart pounded hard, as much from renewed hope as from the steep climb up the twisting path, as they approached the house. "Look," he said. "It's masked off from view by the grove. They won't see it from below."

Nikos reached the house first and pounded on the door with the butt of his sword. "I hope you're right, sir," he said. "If they—"

But just then the door opened. An old woman, her stringy gray hair half hidden by a dirty rag, peered cautiously out.

"Please," she said. "Leave us alone. This is no time to be—"

"Here," Khalkeus said, stepping forward. "We mean you no harm. My name is Khalkeus, and I seek Turios of Tyre, a magus like—like myself. I come in peace."

"Khalkeus?" a weak voice said from inside. "Did he say Khalkeus? Let him in, please. I've been waiting for him."

The old woman looked both of them over suspiciously. Then, biting her lip, she stepped aside and opened the door wide. "All right," she said in a resentful voice. "But you be careful now. You be careful with him."

Nikos let his master go before him, then he paused to ask the woman, "Careful? Of course we'll be careful. But why?"

"Why?" she said, her voice suddenly full of bitterness and pain. "Why? Because he's dying, that's why."

III

The room was sparsely furnished with a table, a pair of chairs. In the corner, below a window that looked out on the Great Sea, lay the bed, a wooden frame supporting a tightly laced animal hide. On it lay a man, thin, wasted, gaunt-cheeked, graybearded. He tried to sit up as the two entered, then he sank back. "Khalkeus," he said, "Khalkeus of Crete. I've been expecting you. I knew when the ships were seen off the coast that it was a raid, and I knew that when the raid came, you'd be on the boats somewhere." His voice was thin, wryly intelligent.

Khalkeus found himself fidgeting under the old man's sharp-eyed gaze. This was odd and uncomfortable; he, Khalkeus, was not one to fidget under the eye of Minos himself. "Master," he said respectfully: the guildsman's polite term of address for an elder in the craft. "My notoriety precedes me, I fear." He bowed his head in unfeigned respect.

"False modesty, let me tell you, is not the source of that, ah, notoriety," the old man said. His smile, his tone, carried a trace of irony but nothing approaching contempt. "No matter. Let us not waste words. Of course, I know why you are here," he said. A foreigner still after many years in the islands, he betrayed his origins only by an excessive caution in his diction. The words came out perhaps a trifle too precisely. *Do I sound like that?* Khalkeus wondered.

"I—" Khalkeus faltered again under that paralyzingly direct gaze. "I came to pay my respects to—"

"Nonsense," the old man said. He raised himself on one skinny elbow and looked at Khalkeus. "As my housekeeper said, I haven't long. If you were to feel my pulse for a moment, you'd understand what I'm talking about. I've had two attacks already. I know the symptoms. But take my word for it, I won't be around long."

"Sir . . ." Khalkeus scowled at himself. *I sound like Nikos,* he thought.

"No, no. Let us not beat around the bush. You're here for some secrets of metallurgy you think I'm privy to. Things which have so far escaped you. You think I can show you the way."

"Correct, sir," Khalkeus said stiffly. "If—"

"Ah," the old man said. "My friend, you have heard of me. I have heard of Khalkeus of Knossos. People in our trade tend to know something about one another. I would know more about you."

"Sir?"

"You have seen Rouso, a town to which I came as a stranger and a foreigner and which I made my own. It will have occurred to you, who work in the service of Minos and who, having his confidence, live well and have access to every amenity . . . it will have occurred to you to wonder why I spent my life in the service of a petty king of a third-rank city, when the immense wealth of Minos would not only have made me rich and admired but also would have provided me with unlimited funds for my projects. Is this correct?"

Khalkeus sighed. "Yes, Master."

"Know then—mind you, I mean no insult—I would not serve a corrupt king like Minos. A man who levies tribute against every weaker principality, who steals the sons and daughters of the gentle and peaceable islands and takes them off to make warriors and bull-dancers and whores of them— and never returns them to their families."

"Sir." Khalkeus stiffened. "It is the way things are. . . ."

"Of course. And every man of us has a choice whether or not to serve things as they are. And if we make that wrong choice—and we are never for so much as a moment in doubt which is the honorable choice to make, however we try to lie

16

to ourselves. . . ." His eyes burned into Khalkeus's soul. The younger man was silent, impaled upon that burning gaze. "Khalkeus," he said, "I would like to know what manner of man asks me for secrets of such importance."

"Sir, if you—" He stopped short, swallowed. His throat was dry. It was impossible to dissemble in front of this man. "I—"

"Come. I know what you want. You can't work the metal. You've tried and failed, just as I did for so long. You can't get the temperature high enough. Right? Am I right? But you've seen a weapon or two that I made of the stuff, and you know I can work it, can mold it to my will. It sings beneath my fingers. The weapons you have seen—you have seen with your own eyes what it can do to a copper or bronze blade. You *know* that it will hew through any sword, hack any shield to pieces. You know—"

"I have collected them. I own six. Ever since I saw the first one, I have wasted my life trying to duplicate the process. I grow past my own middle years, conscious of the squandering of my days in a futile search for the magic formula that will allow me to do with halting, fumbling difficulty what you have done with ease. It has been my life's obsession. It—"

He paused, embarrassed. Here he was, pouring out his deepest feelings to a stranger, and in front of the stranger's servant and—worst of all—his own personal slave, his body servant. . . .

Nikos recognized the problem. "I'll just step outside, sir," he said. "In case someone comes."

Khalkeus watched him show the woman out and follow her into the light. Now the two of them were alone, he and the enigmatic old man who seemed so determined to make him peel away layers of himself and bare his inmost—

He swallowed. Once begun, one might as well . . . "I—I am not Khalkeus. This is the name the people of Minos give to a smith. I—I was born in Egypt, to an Egyptian mother and a Sumerian father. My name was—is—Kirta. I am the son of Shepset of Sile and of Ahuni of Babylon. My grandfather was Belsunu of Babylon."

The old man's face was at peace now. He sank back against the pillows and regarded the younger man with something appreciably less like disapproval. "These are famous names in our craft," Turios said. "Eminent names. Names of stature. I owned a sword once, made by Belsunu. Try as I might, I've never equaled it, although I spent many a

17

fruitless hour attempting to solve the secret of the balance. It sang in the hand. . . . But do go on, my friend. I must know you. I must know to whom I give the secret you are so interested in learning."

Khalkeus's face twisted in pain. "I—I've spent more than a decade trying to become something, somebody, I'm not," he said. "What you said about—about making the wrong choice . . ."

"I understand." The old man's voice was calm and low. Its warmth and sympathy struck home to Khalkeus's soul, struck a deeper blow than had the icy obsidian of his eyes. "Please, continue. I think you need to tell this as much as I need to hear it."

"I—my father left me in Haran. He and my mother sailed to the Delta country in which I'd been born. He was an itinerant armorer, serving many kings. I am—look—a Child of the Lion, like my father, like all my line." He raised his tunic and turned slightly to show Turios the red birthmark on his lower back: the shape was that of the paw of a lion, the toes splayed.

"Yes," said Turios gently. "I have heard of the Sons of the Lion. Many kings would be overjoyed to bear so prestigious a mark. I understand it breeds true in the male half of your line."

"Yes. Both my—my sons bear it." Khalkeus's face, not the dying man's, was the one in pain now. "My sons." He drew in breath; the sound was halfway between sigh and sob. "My sons, whom I've abandoned like their mother to . . ." He could not go on. Now sigh became sob altogether; Khalkeus, the heartless, the detached, was crying like a child. And for some reason he couldn't stop. These were thoughts he hadn't spoken in a dozen years, hadn't allowed himself to think in nearly half as long. He wept helplessly.

The old man watched him, waved him at last to the chair beside his bed. "When you can," he said, "there's time. There's always time, young man, to own up to things you're ashamed of, to change them. Believe me. I haven't long. But I've spent the time I had, since I knew I was dying, to—well, to start putting my life in order. I haven't finished. But there's always time to start. And I think that the starting is the most important thing. It takes courage. It takes a lot more courage than any vain feat of arms, let me tell you. It takes a lifetime to become a fool, and only a moment to begin to become wise."

Khalkeus mastered himself for a moment, but his voice,

when he spoke, was choked with tears. "This, this idiotic quest of mine. The dark metal. My father failed to solve it, and I think it was the only failure he ever knew in his life: he, who began his life as a slave and came to be the armorer of kings. I—I was obsessed with the idea of—of surpassing him in this, of conquering the one thing in the world that had defeated him. When my father and mother sailed, and their ship was sunk in a terrible gale off the coast of Kittim, I was a young man just married. My wife was a lovely, gentle girl, as beautiful as the moon. She gave me two sons. . . ." He found he could not go on for a time. Turios reached out a weak, bony hand and stroked his arm. It was some time before Khalkeus could continue.

"I—I heard a rumor," he said. "A rumor of—well, a story that someone in the islands out here had discovered the secret, the secret of smelting the stuff. Imagine. . . ." There was now a strange unearthly light in his eyes, and the old man took obvious note of this. "Turios," he said, "I left wife and children and sailed westward. I was captured by pirates, sold to a Lydian, who sold me to a Cretan galley. Aboard the galley, I made it known that I was a man who could make things. When we docked on Cretan soil, I was taken to Minos; his daughter fell in love with me and had me freed. I—"

It had all come out in a rush. Khalkeus's eyes were clear now, and there were the barest beginnings of a hard-won understanding in his gaze. "Minos liked my work," he said. "I liked his daughter. I did not love her. She knew this. Love unrequited does terrible things to a proud woman like Xena. I have—" He almost smiled, with the terrible, aching knowledge of what his life had really been. "I have wronged her. As I have wronged wife and children. Turios, I now begin to wonder if I have ever in my life been just to any man, any woman. I wonder if . . ."

Turios, gentle and fatherly now in his fading hours, touched the younger man's hand, held it as gently, as lovingly, as if it had been a woman's soft hand and not an armorer's callused one. Khalkeus, a man who ordinarily could not bear to be touched, sighed, openmouthed, all his defenses down, and looked at the dying man. Then, impulsively, conquering his own timidity, he returned the gentle squeeze Turios had given him.

"Turios," Khalkeus said, "I have been a fool. It was not worth it. Here I am, presumably on the very edge of making the discovery, of learning the secret, to which I've sacrificed all that was good and decent in my life. And all of a sudden I—I know—damn it, I *know*—that it wasn't worth it. I wish to all the gods in all the heavens that I'd never even considered the possibility. I wish I'd stuck to the trade my father, my wonderful father, taught me. I'm a good armorer just as I am, really."

"I know, I know," Turios said with a note of genuine sympathy and understanding. "I've seen your work. Did you think I could have missed it? You're an artist. I knew that. But what I had to know was whether or not you were a man. A man of sympathy, of kindness, of responsibility."

"Yes," Khalkeus said through tears, "and I'm none of these things. I'm a cold and cruel and heartless bastard who has cheated and disappointed everyone who ever believed in me, trusted me, loved me—every one of them. And, I hid the knowledge of this from myself all those years. I never admitted any of it to myself. But—" He smiled a fierce smile of hard-won knowledge, as bitter as gall: the smile of a man with no illusions left. A man purged dry. "But, I *knew*." He squeezed the weak old hand, hard. "I knew. Of course I knew. And I loathed myself for it. I knew I'd sold myself down the river. I knew I'd sold my loved ones, and myself, and every ideal I'd ever been raised to believe in. . . . Yes, and poor Xena. I sold her as much as anyone. I don't love her. The only decent thing would have been to tell her, to let her off the hook. Instead, I've let her waste her youth, her fresh and pretty years. Now—" He was in tears again now, but he was smiling through them. It was not a happy smile. "Now—" he said.

"Ah," Turios of Tyre said in that thin old man's voice of his. He sank back on the pillows again. "Now," he said, repeating Khalkeus's last word. "Now I can tell you the secret," he said.

"Now you can . . . ?" Khalkeus stared at him, speechless, dumbfounded. "Now? When I've told you that?"

"Now," the old man said. "Now that you know how worthless it is. Now that you know what *is* worth something. Now that you know that the secret is one which means only more death and destruction, more widows and orphans, more misery. *Now* I'll tell you, my son. I wasn't sure before." He motioned Khalkeus closer; his voice was fading. "Now," he said. "You want to smelt the metal called iron, but you don't know how to get the furnace hot enough. The trouble is, you're going about it the wrong way. There's a kind of furnace you have to build, completely unlike any other you've ever seen. I learned it from a Hittite slave who'd been blinded in a war. He told me how to build it. . . ."

The old man passed away quietly, with Khalkeus holding his hand. Khalkeus, sobered, shaken, went to the door and opened it, looking out. The woman rushed past him; both he and Nikos heard her disconsolate, almost savage wail of terror and bereavement. The men's eyes met, master's and slave's. Nikos's expression was oddly different, Khalkeus thought: as though he were seeing his master with new eyes, seeing him for the first time. *A different man,* Khalkeus thought. *Well, perhaps I am. But who am I now? Khalkeus? Kirta? Who? Who?*

CHAPTER TWO

I

Spear at the ready, Ilihu, picket on the second shift at the pass which separated the military encampment from the Plain of Aram, blocked the narrow path and watched as the girl approached.

The odd thing was, she didn't really look like the average sort of camp follower. With that white headcloth demurely draped over her dark locks, she looked like somebody's sister of just about marriageable age. Her carriage was straight and dignified, and the dark eyes that regarded him now looked up at him without the smallest trace of coquetry. Her smile was shy and fleeting; yet he was sure she was not afraid of him.

He stayed put. She stopped before him. "Pardon me, miss," he said. "This road's closed. I'll have to ask you to go back."

"Please," she said, her face falling a little. "I—I have to see someone at the camp. A soldier, a young junior officer named Yassib—"

"Yassib?" he said. "Which unit does he serve in?"

Her answer was ready enough: "He's a subaltern under the lord Oshiyahu. He's a staff officer rather than a commander of troops."

"Ah," he said. "You know more than usual about the way an army works. What's your name?"

"Danataya," she said. "I live with my aunt and uncle in Haran. But my father was Nahum, who was a professional soldier. He—he died before the walls of Mari, in the days of the great siege."

"Nahum?" Ilihu said, relaxing. "You're Nahum's child?

22

Well, I'll be damned. Come to think of it, there is a slight resemblance. You've his nose, haven't you? Or at least your nose looks a bit like his did before somebody broke it in battle. Why, yes. I served under Nahum briefly. A fine soldier, if a strict disciplinarian." He smiled at her. "Here, a child of Nahum's can't be up to any mischief, now, can you?"

"Me? Oh, no, sir. But, I have to see Yassib, somehow."

"Well, I'm sure that can be arranged. But—well, you know I have my orders. I'm sure you understand. These days we've stepped up precautions, what with the reports coming down from the north." He halted for a beat, wondering if he'd said too much. But no; they'd know about such things in Haran by now. Travelers from the war-torn hills had reached Haran, "city of caravans," from all of the remaining trade routes that wound up that way.

"Please," she said. "Is it—is it as bad as people say up there?"

"I can't say from any personal knowledge," he said. "But I talked to a runner who'd come down from our scouts' camp. He was supposed to keep his mouth shut, but in such circumstances nobody ever does. And he said the nomads are like locusts in swarm, that eat everything in sight. There are more of them, he says, than ants on a hill, and they've got no more conscience or pity than ants, either. Anything that's in their way as they pass through—" He made a knife-across-the-throat sign.

"Oh, dear," the girl said. "Yassib . . ."

"Well, don't worry about Yassib," Ilihu said. "If it comes to a battle, he'll be well placed, well behind the lines where the staffs are. Besides, we haven't any idea they're really heading this way. They could strike for Mari and go down the Valley of the Euphrates. Or they could head for the coast and wipe out Ugarit. Or they could head up into Hittite country. We don't know. Their path wanders. All we know is that they came down from the Great Mountains to the north, in uncountable numbers, and that they seem to be looking for a nice fertile sort of place with lots of graze for their animals." He looked around and down, directing her eye at the green plain called Padan-aram, and sighed. "Now, we *could* turn out to be just what they've been looking for. On the other hand, there's even better land than this to the south, people say. Not that I ever served down that way."

"My father did," Danataya said. She looked where his eyes had gone. "He said it was lovely in Canaan; first, one had to

23

cross a broad desert, but then there was the richest, greenest land anyone had ever seen. But—"

"But *that* land belongs to the great king of Egypt," Ilihu finished her thought for her. "And nobody, nomads or whatever, is going to take him on voluntarily. Although," he said ruefully, "if what I hear is true, these nomads don't have any more common sense than the ants they resemble. It'd be just like them to take on Egypt. Gods, what a battle that'd be!"

"But then—" She frowned. "We'd be right in their path, wouldn't we?"

Ilihu didn't like to think about that. "Well, maybe. But look, miss. If you're going down to camp, you'd better get a move on. As it is you might have an hour at most to visit your friend, and then you'd have to get back up here and through the pass. You'd have just about time to get back to town before the city gates closed for the night."

"Thank you for reminding me," she said. Her smile was nice, Ilihu thought. White teeth, olive face, dark eyes and hair. Going to turn into a real beauty one of these days. But a trifle thin, perhaps. He wondered how well that uncle and aunt fed her. A woman her age should be—well, rounded here and there. This one had kept the slimness of childhood, although the bumps in front of her robe weren't bad. "Will you be on duty when I come back?" she said.

"If you keep to the schedule I suggested. Don't dawdle down there. Get your business done and get right back out. And if anyone stops you, tell them what you told me. About Nahum. I think a daughter of Nahum's ought to be welcome at an encampment of the Army of Haran. It's civilian memories that are short. Soldiers ought to keep the memory of an old war hero alive long enough to recognize his daughter, I'd imagine."

"I hope so," she said, smiling again. "And—thank you." He smiled and let her pass. He watched her go, her white heels peeping out from the hem of her robe. And then something made him look down at the broad plain from which she'd come, and he remembered the intercepted report the Egyptian renegade Sanehat had tried to pass back to the king of Egypt a couple of generations back, a report every young student in Haran memorized by rote: "It is a goodly land. . . . There are figs and grapes; wine is more plentiful than water. It produces much honey, and its olive groves are second to none; all manner of fruit grows in its orchards, there is barley and wheat and cattle of all kinds without end. . . ."

He shivered. It *was* a lovely country. Ripe for the picking.

24

And the forces that could at present be mobilized to defend it were weak indeed. He hoped it didn't come to war. He hoped they'd strike toward Mari instead. . . .

It took Danataya most of her hour to locate Yassib. Most of this time was spent explaining what she was doing in camp and trying to convince one guard after another that she wasn't just another camp follower.

She was arguing with the latest in a long string of these when she spotted him. "Yassib!" she said, then her heart fell at the sight of the annoyance and impatience his face registered on his first recognition of her. Worse: he looked for a moment as though he were going to try to ignore her call and act as though he hadn't heard. But she'd caught his eye, and with a visible sigh he came her way.

Danataya fidgeted. She wanted more than anything in the world to run into his arms, but from the look on his face, that was the last thing in the world she should do right now. She stood her ground, looking up at him with a nervous smile as he approached.

"Danataya," he said, "what are you doing here? Haven't I told you . . . ?"

The tone of his voice was harsh; there wasn't a bit of love in it at all. She put one small hand on his heavy forearm and looked into his angry face with eyes made suddenly misty with tears. "Please, Yassib," she said, "isn't there someplace where we can talk? For only a moment? I mean, I've come all this way alone, and I have to go back quickly."

He softened for a moment. "You're right," he said. "It is getting late. You'll just have time to head for home. You don't want to get trapped outside the city walls at sundown." There: now, at least, his voice carried a little trace of protectiveness. But he was turning her around and, one hand under her arm, hustling her back toward the road to town. "Here, I have to be somewhere very soon," he said. "But I'll walk you to the pass. We can talk along the way. What brings you—?"

But then he stopped dead. And looked at her, his face darkening. "Danataya," he said cautiously. "You wouldn't come all this way just to pass the time of day. You aren't . . . ?"

She looked at him, puzzled. Then she understood. She blushed and stammered the words out: "N-no, of course not. It's not that. I'm not pregnant, Yassib. It's just that . . ."

He smiled, relieved, and for a second she could see under

25

his changing expressions something of the warm and loving face he'd turned to her when they had first pledged themselves to each other. What a handsome man he was, with that big chest and those brawny arms! And despite her hurt and confusion, she felt a little rush of physical thrill run through her, looking up at him. But then he was turning her again and hurrying her through the camp.

"Yassib," she said, trying to catch her breath, "it's my uncle and aunt. They—they want to know when we're going to get married. They say they can't spare the space anymore. They need my room to let out to someone, someone they can charge more from. I barely pay my way working for them. They need money, and I—I've been working for barter, for my board and keep."

"Oh," he said, "it'll be soon. Tell them very soon. I—I have to know where I'll be sent once my new assignment comes down. It's a matter of knowing where we'll be living." His tone was brusque and businesslike now. She wished there were a bit more concern in it, a bit more reassurance. "You see, if we're going to be here, before the walls of Haran, it'll be one thing. But if I'm going to be transferred to one of the border outposts . . ."

"But Yassib. I don't see why we can't be—"

"Please," he said, annoyed. "It's—it's not something I can give you an exact answer about, just now. I have to find out what the future will be like." He looked across at her and saw discomfiture written all over her pretty face. "Oh, look, Danataya," he said in an altered voice, caressing her arm, "I'll be able to tell you shortly. Maybe I'll even have some idea today. I'm supposed to see Oshiyahu at sundown, when he comes back from inspecting the picket line to the east. He's doing surprise inspections these days. Anything to make sure we stay ready for combat."

"Combat?" she said. "Have things come to that yet?"

"Well, that's what a soldier's job is, after all. You of all people should know that. And Oshiyahu—well, he's the kind of commander who always takes the position that there's danger out there, waiting for the first lax moment. Now, me, I don't take much stock of the rumors that come down about the—the nomads, but the chief—he's acting as though they were right on the other side of that hill over there, ready to pounce."

"But—" She swallowed. He was hustling her along so quickly that it was hard to keep her breath. "You said you might know something today."

"Yes," he said. "Watch your step here." The path, as it wound up the hill toward the pass, was one lane; doubtless it had originally been laid out by a cow or a sheep, somewhere back there. He shooed her ahead of him. "Now step lively there, my dear," he said in that same businesslike fashion. "Not much time before sundown, and I've got that appointment, and you've got to be back in the city before—"

"*Yassib*," she said complainingly. She wished she could look back at him; but the path was so rocky, so uneven, that she had to watch her footing every step of the way. "Please. When are you going to tell me? I mean, about what you learn today? I wouldn't have come down to camp to bother you like this—I know how it annoys you—but—but you haven't been in to see me in three weeks. Surely, they let you off for a day now and then."

"Not just now," he said. "Battle preparedness. That's the be-all and the end-all of Oshiyahu's program these days. And I have to do what pleases him. He can make all the difference in my future. In our future," he corrected himself hastily. "I'm sure you understand," he said.

"Yes, but . . ."

At the top of the pass, Ilihu saluted the young officer and flashed Danataya a quick smile. He stepped back and watched them embrace, hastily—a little too hastily, he thought, watching Yassib's impatience, Danataya's crestfallen air. He looked away, but a trick of the wind carried their conversation to his ears.

". . . no time for that . . . of course, you understand . . ."

". . . uncle wants to know by the first of next week . . . I'll have to find work . . ."

". . . tell him as soon as I know . . ."

". . . I could be looking for a place for us . . . making a home for us . . . oh, Yassib, you'll like it so much. I'll make you so happy . . . really I will. . . ."

Then the wind changed, and Ilihu could hear no more. He flashed them a glance: Yassib embraced her again; his kiss was hasty, efficient—hers was hungry, desperate. The pair parted. Ilihu saluted his superior and watched him head down toward the camp. He nodded at the girl as she stood, hesitant, at the top of the downward path. She smiled once at him, her eyes blurred with tears, and then she headed downward toward the Plain of Aram.

Poor girl, he thought. If he'd ever seen a man who didn't by any stretch of imagination have marriage on his mind,

27

early or late, he'd seen one today. *What a waste,* he thought. *And such a pretty little thing.*

II

Oshiyahu, accompanied only by his orderly, rode past the inner line of pickets into camp, a black scowl on his face. Swords, spears flashed to the salute position; backbones stiffened into a more military posture instantly on sight of the commander—and each soldier's turnout leaned imperceptibly farther toward parade-ground standards once the expression on his face could be made out.

He dismounted while the horse he rode still moved; Oshiyahu's horsemanship, learned during a tour in the south in Moabite Country, was legendary in the Army of Haran. He handed the reins to a subordinate and strode heavy-footed to the command post, his thick soldier's legs churning up the ground. He didn't wait to arrive but sent a powerful bellow ahead of him. "Danel!" he cried. "Where in the name of a thousand hells in Danel! Front and center, by all the gods, or I'll know the reason why!"

An enlisted man, snapping to attention, saluted him. "Sir!" he said. "Beg to report: the lord Danel is at the commissary, buying vegetables."

"Get him here on the double!" Oshiyahu said, the edge still on his voice. "Listen to that," he told his orderly, who had caught up to him by now and walked at heel like an attack dog. "Buying vegetables. That's a job for the mess detail. A line officer doesn't concern himself directly with that sort of thing. He just keeps appointing and firing until he has a mess detail that gets it right every time without being told. One shouldn't even have to be aware of that sort of detail. Appoint a man to be in charge. Give him one mistake and chew his head off when he makes it—and make damn sure he never makes another. If he does, out he goes and not another word."

"Yes, sir," the orderly said. "Beg to report, sir: you asked me to remind you. The armorer Shobai. He's—he should be at the armory. You wanted to talk to him before he left camp."

28

"Oh, yes. And young Yassib. Is he around? I wanted to see him."

"Not here yet, sir."

"That's all right; he won't be due for another—well, hmmm. If he takes past sundown, I'll figure he's late. Anything earlier than that is all right. I didn't make the appointment totally specific as to time."

"Very good, sir."

"Hah. *Not* very good, sir. You know why I'm mad as a wounded lion, don't you?"

"Yes, sir. I think so, sir."

"Damndest mess I ever saw. I tell you, Daniel's job is on the line. When I put a man in charge of a group of pickets, I expect each outpost to be run as though it were wartime. Instead, what do I find? At two of the outposts the men are playing bones. At all of the outposts—all, mind you—at least one man is out of uniform. I won't have that sort of thing, I tell you."

"No, sir. On the other hand, sir, only one man per outpost—"

"No!" Oshiyahu bellowed. "No excuse for it! If one man's lax on picket duty, everybody in the outpost is to blame. Do they think it's not their responsibility to call somebody to account? Look here—" But the attack of choler left him almost as quickly as it had come. He was talking only to an orderly, after all. This fellow, Dushratta, had been with him for years and had learned the patterns of his master's rages. "Sorry, I forget myself."

"No, sir. Quite all right. I think you've already made up your mind what you're going to do, sir."

Oshiyahu grinned his tough soldier's grin. "Oh, I have, have I? You've been reading my mind, is that it?" He stood, hands on hips, his heavy shoulders thrown back, looking at the slim orderly.

Dushratta, used to the drill, didn't give a cubit of ground. "Yes, sir. You're going to relieve Daniel of his command."

"Ah, yes," Oshiyahu said, the mean grin still on his face. "This is good. I'm enjoying this. What else am I going to do? Have you consulted the stars about that? Have you poured out the bones? Consulted the pigeon guts?"

"You've already got someone picked out for his job, sir. You've had him picked out for days."

"I have? Well, what else am I going to do? Don't be shy. If you were going to be diffident, I'd have seen some sign of it ten years ago, wouldn't I, eh?"

"Yes, sir. Besides, you don't pay me to be bashful, sir. You're also going to relieve the mess steward, and you will very likely shake up the commissary. You were saying something the other day about crooked sutlers."

"So I was." Oshiyahu's grin turned to something a trifle closer to a frown. "All right. That's enough of the auguries. Let's go see the armorer."

When they arrived at the armory, however, both the men they'd hoped to see were there. Yassib, Oshiyahu's burly young protégé, was examining a weapon while the even younger armorer Shobai, towering a full head over him and looking as handsome as a statue, looked on.

"Oh, hello, sir," Yassib said, stiffening into a military posture. "Shobai here was showing me some of his work. Really quite extraordinary."

"Yes, it is," Oshiyahu agreed. He nodded at the armorer. "In all respect, though, I doubt if his best can match this." He pulled his own sword and handed it over, hilt first.

Shobai smiled, holding the sword high. His smile was golden, dazzling, a young god's. Oshiyahu, looking at him, thought he had never seen so strikingly handsome a young man. Yet rumor had it he was resolutely heterosexual; a bit of a satyr, as a matter of fact. "You'll get no argument from me on this, my lord," he said. "This is a collector's item, a piece of great rarity. I don't even own one of these myself, although I've handled one before." He handed the weapon to Yassib, who instantly broke into an understanding smile. "Of course I recognize it."

"I was sure you would. It's one made by your great-grandfather Belsunu. One of the last group he made. I bought it from a man whose grandfather served as a mercenary in Canaan in Belsunu's last days, in the great war against Elam. Not even your grandfather, for all his legendary skill, ever surpassed this lot of swords. Belsunu is said to have died shortly after making this one." Oshiyahu smiled, shaking his grizzled head. "I'd hate to tell you what I paid for this."

"Well," Shobai said. "I've looked for another such for years. Ever since I finished my apprenticeship. But the only other one I ever saw besides this one was the one my father—" He paused. The chiseled beauty of his features registered pain, ever so covertly. "Well, that's neither here nor there."

"No," Oshiyahu agreed, taking back his sword from Yassib. "I've seen your work. I'm satisfied. There's payment waiting for you at the paymaster's. And—Shobai . . ."

"Yes, my lord?"

"I'm afraid I presume. But—might I ask where you intend to seek work next?"

Shobai's brow raised. It was an unusual question to ask. "Why, I don't know, my lord. But I'm sure you know something of the life of an armorer. Once we've finished a job in one place, we're just underfoot there. I suppose I'll take whatever commission I'm offered, if the commissioning body can afford my fee." The banter covered a slightly strained tone; but there came that dazzling smile to bury it altogether. "I don't know. Carchemish. Ugarit. Perhaps somewhere over in Arzawa."

Oshiyahu looked at him pointedly. "You had no notion of, say, riding north to offer your services to the nomads, then?"

There was the smallest flash in Shobai's clear eye; but the smile remained in place. "Only as a last resort, my lord. It's a peculiarity of my work that mostly it comes to me. Only in depressingly quiet times do I have to chase it." He saluted both of them with the unforced politeness of an equal. "Now, sir, I'll see the paymaster, if you don't mind. I've just time to make it back to town after a fast ride."

Yassib and his commander watched Shobai go, attended by the orderly Dushratta. "He does good work, sir," Yassib said. "But—"

"But he's not his great-grandfather. Well, I'll give you some news. He's not his grandfather Ahuni either. Or his father, Kirta. He simply happens to be the best we've got. Not that it's his fault. Who knows what he'd have turned out to be if Kirta had been around to train him? But as it is, you know, he's our best. I've no complaints. Only—"

"Yes, sir?"

"I'd like to have thought a Child of the Lion, however trained in the craft, wouldn't even consider the notion of . . ." He frowned. "But, of course, he's right. I mean, sloughing off the question the way he did. Technically, it's none of my damned business. An armorer, as he says, comes and goes. An armorer bearing the paw print of the Lion can sell to both sides of a war with impunity. But—" He sighed. The frown was back on his face for a blink; then it faded. "Well, that's not why I asked you to come see me tonight." He looked once at Yassib; then he watched the fading sun on the horizon.

He did not speak for a moment. Yassib waited expectantly. Then, Oshiyahu licked his lips and said, "I'm going to break Danel."

"Sir?"

"Break him. Reduce him so many ranks he'll either quit the service—or grow up, learn from his errors, and make a better and more solid start toward the top this time."

"But—"

"Don't take up for him. You know he's slacking. Besides, I'm naming you to take his place."

"Sir!"

"Why not? You've earned it. I know, it's a step down in rank, but your staff rank isn't very real anyhow. You need some direct command just now. It'll look good on your record. And that's important, you know. I have plans for you."

"Sir—"

"Don't interrupt. I've had my eyes on you. You're bright, ambitious, and you know which side your bread is buttered on. You have it in you to rise. You're sharp, shrewd, dynamic. I wish I'd had half your assets at your age. It wouldn't have taken me half as long to get where I am today."

"You're too kind, sir."

"No, I'm not. I need good men under me. I need loyal men, able men. People I can trust. And you have to start 'em young. That's why I'm passing over a dozen officers who have seniority on you." He grinned a tight grin, his eyes on the dull orb in the west. A network of colors spread out from it, running the gamut from orange to purple. "But—I said loyal men. People close to me, people who know my mind."

"I'm honored, sir."

"More than the promotion. I'd like to . . . Look: what I'm proposing is a kind of partnership, with you as the junior partner. Junior—but a partner, one who will share responsibility and success alike."

Yassib couldn't think of anything to say. His heart was pounding fast. "I—"

"Look," Oshiyahu said. "You're young, unmarried. Any—any plans?"

His tone was so pointed that Yassib at first wondered if his tough, masculine commander was proposing some sort of homosexual liaison. Then he got the drift—and made the right, the proper, the sensible answer. "Oh, no, sir. Nothing really serious." Something cried out in his soul as he said it, but he went on. Damn the hindmost. "Just a light flirtation here and there. Nothing permanent." And his heart cried out: *Danataya!* But the cry was faint.

"Well," Oshiyahu was saying, "I have two marriageable daughters. The elder is the apple of my eye. My favorite: I nursed her through several childhood sicknesses myself after my wife died bearing the second. I hired a nurse to raise them. They look like my wife, not me. She was quite beautiful: good Amorite blood from Mari. The elder of my girls takes after her. Her name is Halima. She will come well dowered; I am not a poor man. As my son-in-law, you would find your rise steady and expeditious. My wife's relations, too, settled certain sums on her children which are not mine to touch. They have remained in trust, awaiting the girls' marriages." He put a friendly hand on Yassib's shoulder and steered him toward the officers' mess. "Now, on the day when Halima reaches her majority, she will receive . . ."

Yassib listened, not hearing entirely. His heart sank to the level of his sandals. It was almost as if he knew the entire scenario beforehand. As if he'd known all the time that somewhere down the road lay an opportunity he would not be able to resist—one which would require the betrayal of Danataya. It was as if a cold hand clutched his heart now—and began, ever so slowly, to release it. When the release was complete, he would have the new rewards, the new position, the new place in life and in the scheme of things—and he would no longer have Danataya. And what would *she* have?

He ground his back teeth together, trying to exorcise the small voice that still spoke inside him. All purpose now, he embraced the new order of things, and Danataya became just memory once and for all.

III

There was still a bit of light left by the time Danataya crossed the river at the ford, holding her skirts high, nodding politely to the women who remained in the shallows washing their families' clothing. The greetings they gave her were

33

friendly enough, but as she turned onto the main road, heading for the city walls, she knew they would be talking about her. They talked about everyone. *Everyone.*

Shapash, the barber's wife, gathered up her armload of wet clothing to leave. "I don't care what you say," she said. "There can be no good in a girl her age, unmarried and all, hanging out with someone in the army."

The widow Galmat, wet already, slipped out of her shift and, mother-naked, scrubbed it against a stone. Her ripe body, with its full breasts, glistened in the sun. As Shapash had anticipated she would, she spoke up in defense of the girl. "Look," she said with that ready smile of hers. "I'll believe the worst when she turns up with a big belly. In the meantime . . ."

"Speaking of all that," Pagat, the baker's wife, broke in, "the armorer Shobai had better keep an eye on that snobbish wife of his. While he's away, there are men going and coming at all hours."

"Oh, nonsense," the widow said. She yawned, stretching, arching her back sensually. "That's her brother-in-law, the tinker Hadad. The one who makes the little gods and goddesses of clay and metal. He's a nice boy. You know, the one with the limp."

"Oh, it's not just him," Pagat said. "There're more. In particular, there's a soldier. A man of, oh, less than medium height. He went in there yesterday—"

"And why shouldn't he go visiting the house of Shobai? He's probably ordering—oh, a dress suit of body armor, or a ceremonial sword. Shobai is famous for that sort of thing."

Shapash, still holding her clothing, seemed to have temporarily abandoned plans to go. "Well, if you ask me, I wouldn't put it past her at all to be kicking up her heels a bit while Shobai is away. She's a nasty little snip, pretty as she is. A bad piece of goods."

"Well," Pagat said, "it's not as though I'd blame her too much. I hear things. I mean about Shobai. He's quite a young rake himself. My husband had a client from Carchemish. He said that Shobai had to beat the women off with a stick when he was there. Not that he tried too hard to get rid of them. More than a few stuck to him like lice."

The widow laughed her full-throated laugh, throwing her head back. "Let me tell you—if Shobai should look *my* way one of these days, I wouldn't say no. No, my dears. For all the difference in our ages. He's as handsome as a god. He harks back to his grandfather in that. His grandfather, Ahuni, was as tall as Shobai and carried himself like a king. I remember him from when I was a child. I had a terrible crush on him, even at his age." She giggled. "Just listen to me. He must have been about the age I am now."

"Ah," Pagat said cattily. "One foot in the grave, eh?" She winced as Galmat splashed her with one hand. "Here, now! I didn't mean it."

Shapash watched silently as two of the youngest women came toward them from one of the deeper pools at the ford, their nude bodies rising a handspan at a time from the deeper water. She envied the ripe young breasts, the unlined bodies, the slimness, and the unstudied beauty of their carriage. They walked with the grace, the innocent unconcern of a pair of young mares. "Well," she said, "I'm sure we all wish for a few less years now and then."

"Ah, yes," the widow said. She looked down at her own front, one hand on her breast. "True, true. Although if going back to being young meant having to relive some of the heartache and sorrow—losing my little girl, my husband . . ."

"Oh, don't think dark thoughts," Pagat said, sympathetic now. "Think of the pleasure you've had, raising two strong boys and seeing them marry and give you grandchildren. And, Galmat, I hope I age as well as you have. I—"

She stopped. All talk stopped for a moment. Rachel, daughter of the rich livestock dealer Laban, had come down to the water well below the ford. She carried an *amphora;* gracefully, she bent and filled it. She glanced once in their direction; but, seeing them, she turned quickly and walked away, the large, oval vase balanced on one slim shoulder.

"Yes," Galmat said with a sigh, "one should count one's blessings. Now *that* poor girl . . ." She sighed. Wringing out her clean shift, she slipped it over her head. "She's had a hard row to hoe in her life."

"Well, she's certainly been a terrible disappointment to her husband," Pagat said. "I wonder what the gods are punishing her for." She thought a moment. "Or him."

"They don't believe in our gods," Shapash said. "Jacob, her husband, comes from down in Canaan where they deny the existence of any but one god. El something or other, his name is. My husband told me once that Jacob is supposed to be some sort of nobility down there. But he ran into some kind of trouble. Someone wanting to kill him."

"That's odd," the widow said. "I met him once. He doesn't seem the type. I mean, the type one would want to kill. But then he doesn't seem much like any sort of high-class character, either. His father-in-law—"

"Oh, Laban treats him like dirt. Like the very dirt under his feet. Curses him in public. Although the way I hear it," Shapash said, "he's an able enough manager of Laban's stock."

"Poor man," the widow said. "He fell in love with Rachel, there, and Laban made him work an apprenticeship to pay for her. But when the apprenticeship was up, Laban changed his mind and said Jacob had to marry his elder daughter, Leah, first, and had to work an apprenticeship to pay for *her.* Or some sort of arrangement like that."

"And then," Shapash said, heading for the shore, "she turns out to be as barren as a mule. What a disappointment."

Pagat and the widow followed her. "On the other hand," Pagat said, "it all worked out fairly well for Jacob as it was. Between Leah, the sister he hadn't wanted to marry, and his two concubines—his wives' handmaids, Zilpah and Bilhah—he has . . . what is it? Seven sons? Eight?"

"More than that," Shapash said. "Ten at least. But the way I hear it, the poor man is still in love with Rachel. Prefers her, in fact, as if it had been she who provided him with all those strapping boys."

"Well, there's no accounting for tastes," the widow said. "Although I have to admit, she's a handsome woman, even now. What would you say? Late thirties?"

"Something like that. You know, I used to think she was being snooty, avoiding the rest of us like that. But I think she's just—well, embarrassed. Afraid one of us will ask the wrong question, and she'll have to give an answer she doesn't want to give."

"Ah," the widow said. "I wonder if she and Jacob still lie together."

"Who knows?" Pagat said. "Look, the sun's going down. We'd better hurry along there."

Dinner was already on the table when Danataya came home to her uncle's house. Her uncle was gone; her aunt was feeding her two young cousins. "Where have you been?" the older woman asked. Her voice was harsh, resentful.

"I—went out to talk to Yassib, at the camp." The girl sat down and reached for her bowl. "I had a hard time finding him."

"Well," her aunt said. "What did he say?" She filled a bowl

and handed it to the younger of the children. "Has he set a date yet?"

"Well, no," Danataya said. "You see, he—"

"He hasn't? Do you mean to sit there and tell me he hasn't set a . . . ? Why, didn't you ask him?"

"Well, yes. But he's up for reassignment, and he doesn't know where he's going to be sent."

"Doesn't know?" Danataya looked up to see her aunt's expression change. There was something like panic in her eyes now. "You mean—but look, Danataya, you'll *have* to go. He'll *have* to change his mind."

"Have to?" Danataya said. "But—" Then the realization came through to her. "Oh. You—you've rented my room already. Is that it?"

"I had to," her aunt said, the panic turned to terror now. "I had to, Danataya. I—in spite of what I told your father, I—I can't charge you the same anymore. And we need the money. They've raised my husband's rent on his shop. Taxes have risen sharply in the last year." She almost sobbed the words out. "If only you'd been able to find work."

"Well, I could keep trying. Perhaps between now and the first of the month—"

"Danataya!" her aunt said, despair turning her tone to anger now. "Don't you understand what I'm trying to say? It's too late. Your uncle has already accepted the man's money. He's already *spent* it. Do you see? Can you get that through your head?"

Danataya shoved her bowl away, the light dying in her eyes. She understood, all right. All too well. As of the first of the month she had no place to live. And nothing to live on.

Oshiyahu was examining the clay tablets that the sutlers had given him—tablets bearing accounts of their dealings with the army over the past six months—when the orderly Dushratta looked into his tent. Oshiyahu looked up, his face framed in the light of the two lamps on the table. "Yes?" he said.

"The runner from the northern territories, sir. He's just come in. Shall I bring him in?"

"I'll come out to him," the commander said. "My eyes are swimming anyhow. This is fine work. Too fine for nighttime." He stood up, stretching, yawning. "So far one of the sutlers looks pretty good. Fair dealings—at least for the period under discussion."

"And the other, sir?"

"I'm going to reward him for his labors tomorrow. That is, if you can find me a tall tree with a straight limb sticking out from it."

"That bad, sir?"

"That bad? I ought to have him impaled. Which reminds me. You did notify the guards that both of them were to be detained temporarily? That nobody was to do any traveling?"

"Both of them are under house arrest. I did it as delicately as I could."

"Good." The two men walked briskly down the long row of firebrands overhead. "I take it the runner has had another look at our shepherd friends?"

"Yes, sir. But here he is. Ask him yourself."

They turned a corner and found a tall man standing by the campfire. The runner stood at attention; Oshiyahu returned his salute and bade the man stand at ease. "Now," the commander said. "You've had a look at them?"

"Well, some of them, sir. You can't get too close. Not without getting a little more trouble than you bargained for. They'll loose a flight of arrows at you on sight."

"I appreciate that. But you did see them?"

The young soldier smiled tautly. Oshiyahu found himself rather liking the youth; he had a nice, manly way of talking, deferential but not servile. *Going places,* Oshiyahu thought. "I got a look from atop a hill, sir. Their line goes on— stretches back—for as far as the eye can see. Perhaps and then some. I think you could watch them pass for days and days and they'd still be coming."

"Ah. And armed . . . how?"

"Much heavier body armor than ours. Longer, heavier swords. A curious kind of curved bow—"

"Yes, yes. They're all horsemen?"

"They've horse and foot, sir. The cavalry is well trained, sir. I'd say you'd rather admire their horsemanship. They ride like men of Moab."

"That's high praise. What else?"

"Well, sir, I—I also saw a town they'd destroyed." His face turned dark, speaking of this.

"And?"

"Well, they've some sort of machine for battering down gates. City gates. The one to this town was smashed inward as if by some terrible force. Siege equipment, too. All of it on wheels, so they can carry it from town to town." He thought a moment, then halted there. "That's about it, sir." He stood at attention. "There was probably more, but I was spotted there, and I had to make a run for it."

"Good you did. But—there's this impression that I get. That you had more to say."

"Well, yes, sir. But—well, they do pretty much of a thorough job of putting a city to the sword."

"And it made you a little ill? Well, don't be ashamed of it. It just means you're still human. Tell me."

"The men who were alive when the door came down— castrated, impaled, riddled with arrows, or simply stoned as they sat there. The women—raped, defiled in every way ... they had sport with some of them, sir. They buried a row of women up to their necks in sand. Then they'd ride past them at a gallop, it appears, and hack away at the exposed heads with their swords."

"Gods."

"Yes, sir. I ... found a man alive. He'd been wounded; they'd left him alone after he'd feigned death. He told me about the women, the games they'd played. Also about a friend of his who'd had his arms and legs hacked off, and his nose and his privates. They'd blinded him in the end, and torn out his tongue."

"Ugh. And, the man who was still alive told you—?"

"Children. They'd toss up babies and spear them on the way down. They'd rape six- and seven-year-olds and then disembowel them. Great fun, watching them run, spilling their guts ..."

"I see. I see." The commander held up his hand. "You can tell me the rest later, son. Rest easy. You did a fine job. Thank you for coming back safe."

"Yes, sir." The runner saluted and turned to go.

"Wait," the commander said. "You. I didn't get your name."

The runner half smiled: recognition. "Hoshaiah, sir. Seventh attack group."

"Ah, yes," the commander said in a gruff but friendly tone. "Hoshaiah. I'll try to remember that."

IV

Ordinarily, the gates of Haran shut tight with the last rays of the setting sun, and a man outside the gates at sundown would have to find a place to sleep somewhere in the half-world just outside the city wall, a floating market of small merchants, whoremongers, pickpockets, and thieves, as well as a stopping-place for all the great caravans which plied the trade routes to and from Haran. For such as Shobai, the armorer, a man to whom, by profession, no walls and no borders existed, such restrictions tended to vanish. Tall, erect, handsome, he hailed the gate guards just as the great doors were closing, and was waved through with a smile. He acknowledged the favor with an airy gesture, as one to whom favors were due.

Ordinarily, an armorer carries no arms, except in time of emergency; now, however, with a fat purse tucked inside his garment, the tall young man wore a long, sharp knife in his belt. The knife was of his own design and was itself worth many times a man's monthly earnings—unless, of course, that man were a wealthy metalworker like Shobai.

Wearing the knife, however, was to forget it. Shobai's commanding height was matched by his strength, and the fact was immediately evident from the broad shoulders and thick-muscled arms that hung free of his sleeveless garment. These, and his martial, fearless bearing, tended to discourage attack. Now, coming through the first of the bazaars that marked the four quarters of the city, his great frame visible by the light of the torches mounted high on the earthen wall of a warehouse that bordered the marketplace, he lightly acknowledged the greetings of the tradespeople he passed, smiling only at the people who mattered in the life of the town.

He was twenty-two and had been at the top of his profession in Haran for two years. This in itself was odd, since he had been a journeyman practitioner for no more than four; but an authentic Child of the Lion carried a lot of weight in Padan-aram, which remembered his father and grandfather as well as legends of the great Belsunu, bearer of the ancient birthmark in Abraham's time. After the death of his teacher, he quickly rose to a commanding position in his respected—and highly paid—art.

He had been raised to the knowledge of his own superiority; but the tempering influence his father might have given this sense of himself had been much missed. His father had disappeared, apparently forever, just before his tenth birthday —before his own apprenticeship had begun. Shortly after this, the merchant who had undertaken to manage his father's estate had failed and committed suicide; his mother, Tallay, had been left with two young sons to raise and a sudden, severe shortage of funds. She had sold Kirta's lavish house for a fraction of its worth, under pressure from his creditors; with the amount that remained after Kirta's debts had been settled, she had bought a modest home in a fading part of the city and had managed somehow to buy her elder son an apprenticeship. There had been no money for the second son to get an education.

Now, years later, Shobai lived in something approaching luxury. He had married the daughter of a rich merchant, and she had come to him well dowered, well enough to underwrite the first years of his now burgeoning career. Anat's money had more than tripled since their wedding; the young pair, well matched as to physical beauty, were familiar sights at every significant social event in the upper-class segments of Haran. They dressed perhaps even better than their means, and were much complimented and much admired for the fact. Few bothered to remark that Tallay, his mother, still lived in increasingly shabby circumstances in a much-decayed sector of town, or that his younger brother, Hadad, had managed no more in life than to scrape together a little business making small ornaments and trinkets of clay or metal—a trade he had picked up here and there, with no systematic training at all. As Shobai's career moved rapidly upward, mother and brother seemed, to others as well as to himself, more and more remotely related to him and his concerns.

There was little opprobrium in this. The world loves a winner, and Shobai had been an obvious winner from his earliest teens, when his body had shot upward so dramatically and his already striking features had begun to settle into something approaching their present, all but totally mature, beauty. He had been immediately recognized by one and all as a man on the rise, even before he had become a man. From the first, people had sought him out to do him favors, on the theory that by the time he had come into his own, those favors would mean something, that their value would grow with his own power and influence. Puberty came early, and women had sought him out to do him special favors of their own. In all, he accepted favors as if they were his due. It was part of his aristocratic charm. And it never occurred to him to notice how conveniently people overlooked his faults.

Now, a fat purse in his robe, he felt a bit odd—part content, part restless. His last job before this had already brought in enough to allow him and Anat, for all her own extravagance, to last out the quarter in something even better than their usual lavish style. The present sum was rich gravy on the meat, and it begged to be spent. But on what? The idea went round and round in his mind, as he made his way through the narrow streets below the characteristic beehive rooftops of Haran.

It was not a time of day for buying. The few tradesmen still on the street were tidying up their areas for the morning's business or closing up shop. Besides, the sum he'd earned would have bought out any number of bazaar businesses, and . . .

At this thought he broke stride. And an idea suggested itself to him. Rental property? Income property, purchased as an investment? The idea wasn't a bad one, all in all. He'd been offered a block of apartments a month before, and before that a warehouse. The warehouse had had little appeal. But what about a mixed block of partly residential, partly commercial properties? With his excellent financial condition, he could purchase the land beneath the buildings, and thereby gain the right to collect rents on all units in the buildings in perpetuity.

Yes: rentals were a gentleman's way of making money, after all. Anat's father, his father-in-law, had recommended his investing in this sort of property shortly after their marriage; it would, he had said, allow Shobai to retire young from a profession which, however exalted as professions went, still qualified as trade. (The older man had wrinkled his nose slightly in fastidious disdain as he'd pronounced the hateful word, "trade.") It had been good advice, if premature. But now?

Shobai smiled to himself. Yes, there was merit to the suggestion. An owner of substantial income property carried some weight in the city. The weight he carried bought him prestige, a certain power—and contracts. Contracts above and beyond the normal load he carried at present. The contracts that would come in once he'd begun to take his place among the younger generation of the city's leaders would be for gratuitous work, above and beyond the narrowly necessary. This meant more money with which to buy more property. Once you got to the point where the system started working for you, it seemed that all of your affairs started feeding one another luck, prosperity, strength.

The idea continued to fascinate as he turned a corner and headed toward his own home quarter . . . and then he stopped. This required more thought, more preparation. Once he was home, there'd be no opportunity for thought. Anat would have her own talk, and her own ideas, and her own projects. He would have little uninterrupted time for coherent and constructive thought. Perhaps it might be well to delay his return. But how? Where?

He frowned, and even his frown left those chiseled features handsome and attractive. He looked up and down the street he'd left . . . and spied, halfway down the block, the projecting sign of a tavern. Ah, yes, the Inn of the White Horse. Come to think of it, that was a frequent hangout of several of his better-connected male friends, including the merchant Aqhat, a dealer in real property in the city. Perhaps if he strolled in, he might, just by accident, of course, run into Aqhat and strike up a conversation.

He smiled, and set his steps for the tavern door.

As luck would have it, Aqhat was there, talking with a pair of friends who were evidently making ready to leave. Shobai managed to join them at their table without forcing the issue, and when they had taken their leave, he slipped the conversation around to the subject on his mind.

Aqhat had much to contribute in the way of advice. "For the love of all that's holy, my young friend, don't pay much down. And don't sink a lot of cash in a single property just now. Diversify. Buy commercial here, residential there; that way you'll be covered no matter which way the market goes. Look, you come to my house tomorrow. I can steer you to some very profitable deals. As a matter of fact, there's a good chance I can double your money very quickly on a speculative investment. I know of a block of buildings which—well, I can't say where I got the word, but it's to be bought up by the city for expansion of the constabulary. The value is way above the present owner's asking price. The owner has no idea the city is committed to buying the property, so he thinks that it isn't worth very much now." Aqhat called the innkeeper, ordered two bowls of wine. "Sound interesting?"

"If you say so," Shobai said. He kept his handsome features expressionless by a major effort of will. "How much would I have to—?"

But his words were cut off in a sudden rush of noise as the three musicians in the back of the room struck up a ringing, repeated chord of lyre, flute, and drums. Into the middle of the room, riding on the music and applause, came a young woman, her slim feet bare, the rest of her body lightly wreathed in semitransparent veils. As she reached the middle of the floor, the musicians struck up an insistent, throbbing rhythm and the wind instrument wailed a high-pitched, sensuous tune.

"Here," Aqhat said, draining his bowl and rising. He threw a coin on the table. "No, don't get up. I just have to get home; it's my son's birthday and I promised him a gift. You stay here, enjoy yourself. I'll see you tomorrow, after the midday meal. All right?"

Shobai nodded and watched him go. Then his eyes turned to the girl in the middle of the room. She had shed two of her veils already, and ripe breasts shone through the remaining veils that covered the undulating top half of her supple body. More: she had become aware of him; she was dancing for his eyes and for no other's. Her eyes sought his; her faint smile mocked him, teased him, promised him . . .

Another veil came away and was tossed to one side. Those golden breasts were naked now, their dark nipples aroused and erect. He could see, as she turned away from him for a moment, the strong buttocks under the thin cloth; when she turned back toward him he could make out the dark patch of hair at the bottom of her body, only lightly covered. Her belly shook, rolled; her eyes met his and held again.

He smiled—but his smile now was an intent and pointed one. His eyes asked her a question; her own eyes responded . . . and the undulant motions of her almost unbearably seductive body underscored her reply. Her eyes rolled once, toward upstairs. And another veil came free, and another. She was naked now, naked except for a gold stomacher that hung round her narrow waist, draped itself bewitchingly over one bare hip, dipped now and again toward the black muff of hair between her firm and womanly thighs. There was a thin film of sweet sweat all over her glistening body, and the effect was startlingly sensual, turning her into a golden statue that had somehow come alive, learned to twist and turn and quiver with a now-unfeigned sexual excitement. He could smell the musk of her; could hear, as if in his mind, the low growl of

44

pleasure in the back of her throat as she touched first one naked breast and then the other, raising their nipples and stimulating them. Her body swayed, turned, again—and then she had vanished.

In the applause that followed, he managed to slip out of the door and make his way up the outside stairs.

He awoke once in the night. The woman slept, a light, ladylike snore coming from her open mouth. Shobai stood, stretched. He stepped out onto the roof into the moonlight, naked. He yawned. It had been a good tussle, and the woman had proved to be as good as the promise in her eyes.

He thought of the previous afternoon's appointment. He smiled once. But as he yawned again, a little murmur of annoyance ran through him. The commander, Oshiyahu: what right had he to tell a Child of the Lion where he could sell his wares? Didn't he know the ancient covenant of Cain, the first armorer, his first ancestor? Didn't he know that the mark had been put on him and on all of his male issue to set them apart from all other men? That the tradition was that the mark would allow any bearer of it to cross any border, run any picket line, even go from one side to another in the middle of a war to sell his services in the making of arms? What right had he to suggest Shobai not ride northward to offer his services to the nomads? The arrogance of the fellow! Well, somebody would have to show him a thing or two one of these days.

But then he heard the woman's voice; she'd awakened and missed him. "Shobai? Shobai, darling, come back to my bed. Come, my own, my beloved. . . ." And, yawning, he followed her voice. It was easier going with the tide of things, sometimes.

CHAPTER THREE

I

By dusk, the town where Kirta had learned the secrets of working a superior metal had been taken. Its defenders were either dead or dying, and noncombatants considered themselves lucky to have escaped into the island's dry hills, where no attempt was made to follow them. The purpose of the raid had been punitive in the first place, and the orders from Minos had said to leave the civilian population alone. After all, taking the island, Minos would now levy tribute on it—levy it heavily, so that for generations to come the descendants of the survivors would still be carrying the terrible burden of Cretan taxes, and their youth would be decimated by an annual draft for the navy and the bull court.

The command force had set up a headquarters on the breakwater, and the fleet lay at anchor just inside the mole. A token complement of troops had been detailed to guard the city against counterattack, and a second unit manned the fortifications at the end of the long jetty. At the point where the artificial breakwater joined the mainland, however, preparations were already underway for a splendid victory feast. The pick of the island's spring lambs was being butchered, and the victorious raiders were carrying out big *amphorae* full of the islanders' choicest wines. The youngest and prettiest of the defeated people's girls—and boys—were herded into an improvised pen near the campfire site; they, too, would be unwilling participants in the evening's festivities.

Xena had found Nikos first. She had sent him for his master. Now, perfumed and pomaded, her bare breasts

46

rouged at the tips and laden down with a gold necklace, she waited impatiently for her lover. Lukios, by now as richly painted as she but, of course, wearing no jewelry, watched her pace fretfully before the tent the men had set up for her. A wry smile crossed his fat face.

She saw this and winced; her dark eyes flashed. "What are you simpering at?" she said. "You're getting on my nerves."

Lukios looked her up and down, dispassionately. *Well, honestly,* he thought. *She doesn't look too bad. For one of* them, *anyhow.* The hateful differences of a woman's body, with its jutting bosom and gross breadth of hip, had never attracted him; he'd been brought around to his present way of thinking well before his neutering. But he had to admit she carried her age well, and her imperious and arrogant mode had its attraction. Women, he reflected, were at their most attractive when they were being bitchy. Perhaps it was because at that time they were being less like women and more like epicene men. "Oh, come now," he said. "I'm not simpering. You look ravishing, my dear. Ravishing. You're a vision of loveliness. He'll never in a million years be able to resist you."

"I wish that were true," she said ruefully. "How I wish it were true." She patted her heavy black curls. "Lukios, I've run out of ways to hold him. And he isn't in love with me. I know that."

"Loosen your grip," the Lycian said. "That's the first step. Of course, I know it's easy to talk. I fell madly in love with a flute player once, and he led me a merry chase. I ran the whole gamut. I begged him, I—" He sighed. His eyes rolled. His hands fluttered. "Look," he said, "I've never asked. Is he a good lover?"

"*Lukios!*" she said sharply, stamping her little bare foot with its beringed toes. "What a question to ask." But she relented and motioned him closer, continuing in a conspiratorial tone: "But—since you asked—he's unbelievable. Even now, after all these years. When I can get him interested. But his mind . . ."

"Hmmm," the Lycian said. "It's a curious thing about men. Sometimes love, true love, makes them impotent. And sometimes they're at their absolute best with a boy—or," he said, shrugging, "a woman they don't feel much for. Perhaps in a way you're better off like this. I mean—"

"Oh, you know that isn't it. If only—if only I could feel he cared, really cared."

47

"You know that if you were hurt, or ill . . . well, look what happened when you had the miscarriage. He hovered over you like—"

"Yes," she said. "But he'd have done that for any woman he knew well." Her face fell. "Maybe that was the thing that did it, after all. Maybe if I'd been able to have a child for him . . ."

Lukios pursed his lips in thought. "Well, perhaps. That might have had some effect. But you couldn't. Let's face it. And now—well, you're on the edge of being too old for that."

"Don't remind me. My maids pull out another dozen gray hairs a night. And wrinkles. And—" She held up her naked breasts with both hands, "these. They're falling. They're drooping."

"Nonsense. Far and away your best feature. You know you still turn heads all around the court. You'd be besieged by every princeling from here to Libya if it weren't for the fact that everyone knows about your liaison with Khalkeus. That and the fact that—well, you're Minos's daughter, and the priestess of the Lady to boot. That tends to scare them off."

"I know. That's why I never settled on one man before Khalkeus. It unmans them. Particularly the religious thing. But until Khalkeus I never minded. I had my life. I could have any man I wanted. I valued my independence. I probably would never have married anyhow." Her voice was bitter. "I had everything planned out for myself. And look how it all turned out." There was an undertone of absolute despair in her voice that moved him somewhat, in spite of himself.

After he had her calmed down, Lukios strolled over to the slave pens for a moment (a scruffy lot, for the most part, although there was one shepherd boy who had the face of a pubescent faun) and then looked in on the preparations for the feast. The roasting lamb smelled absolutely heavenly; when no one was looking, he ducked into the cooking area and stole a little goatskin wine bottle. Slipping down the path through a grove of olive trees, he found a quiet spot in a clump of bushes, where a cool sea breeze blew through the treetops above and he had a fine unobstructed view of the sea. He uncorked the bottle, upended it, and drank. *Not bad. Not bad at all.*

He was about to take another drink when the sound of voices stayed his hand. He started to rise and look about him—and then, somehow, discretion prevailed. Instead, he shrank back into the bushes that surrounded him and cautiously corked the bottle again. What were they saying?

". . . told me about this a month ago, I'd have told you to go play with yourself. But after today . . ."

The voice was familiar. Whose? But of course: Marineus, commander of the expedition! Lukios silently slipped even farther back into the bushes. His eyes were wide now.

". . . planning for quite some time . . . some of the most respected men at the entire court . . . not the sort of people to do anything rashly . . . but there comes a time when things simply can't go on that way anymore. Do you agree?"

"I'm not saying I do; I'm not saying I don't. But . . . go on. You have Amphimedes, you say? And Orestes? And Klumenos? That's remarkable. Klumenos is the most conservative man alive. If he's come to the conclusion that Minos and his family have to go . . ."

What was he hearing? Lukios sat upright. The other voice—it was Tros of Phaistos! And the two were sitting there calmly discussing—what? Revolution? Assassination?

". . . not the first to come aboard, I'll grant you. But once he was convinced, he became the strongest one of us. 'I'll put this foot of mine as far as any man's,' he says. 'You can count on this hand of mine.'"

"Remarkable. You are serious. Really serious."

"Well, you can't speak as though it weren't justified. Fully justified. You know you can't. And you can't say it is without precedent. The grandfather of the present Minos himself came to power in the same way."

"But—the priestess of the Lady . . ."

"Ah. Superstition still has you in its thrall, has it? Tell me, do you know any man in your command above the rank of subaltern who actually believes in the all-powerful Goddess? Give me the gods of the mainland. Male gods, I remind you. Male gods, who understand a man's concerns."

"Sad to say, everything you say is true."

Lukios's eyes bulged out of his head. His fat lips hung open. His breath came in labored gasps. This was—this was nothing less than treason! Here were two of the highest-ranking men in Minos's mighty fleet, talking calmly and—on the one side, at least—purposefully, and of what? Of deposing the greatest king north of the Nile Delta? And of . . .

He scowled. Of removing Xena as well. His, Lukios's own mistress! And—would they then remove her slave, too?

Would they then find it expedient to get rid of everyone around her, large and small? Would they?

He bit his heavy lower lip. *Look here,* he told himself. *You're panicking. Get hold of things now.* After all, this was actually an opportunity. He'd had a chance to hear it all beforehand. He'd be the only one expecting it. He'd be in a position to head things off. He'd just go to Xena and . . .

No, wouldn't it be better to take it to Minos directly, and . . . ?

". . . Plouteus, too. He was one of the first to join us."

Lukios sat bolt upright. Plouteus? Plouteus, who had seduced him at a drunken party not six months before? Plouteus, who continued almost weekly to tell Xena, however jokingly, that he was going to buy her slave from her one of these days? Plouteus? What if . . . ?

He listened eagerly. A slow smile began to spread over his thick features. Yes, yes. He'd do what he could to get close to Plouteus, who'd expressed such thorough satisfaction with him after that last divine evening, when Lukios had stretched out their pleasures until the first rays of dawn had begun to break over the eastern hills. He'd find his way somehow into Plouteus's bed before the week was out. And he'd plant the suggestion that if anything were ever, all the gods forbid, to happen to his beloved mistress, how happy he would be to . . .

Yes, yes. And Xena? Well, let the poor woman fend for herself.

He lay low while the party below him broke up. Then Lukios cautiously slipped out of the little grove and strolled thoughtfully down the path toward the bluff, where the land dropped off toward a small, seaweed-clogged rock beach. Only when he came to the cliff itself did he realize that he'd left his stolen wine bottle behind. No matter: he had, by chance, been given something appreciably more valuable, more satisfying, than any wine could be.

Plouteus—yes, he'd go about getting on the right side of the courtier as soon as they'd returned to Knossos. In the House of the Axe it was always an easy thing to contrive an "accidental" meeting with someone—particularly someone you'd had a little liaison with earlier. Perhaps at a party— there was a festival coming up, and there might even be a general celebration of the successful raid on the great island itself. And—

He stopped dead, bemused. A small smile played over his fat lips. And, his mind running in several channels at the same time, he looked down to the waters of the blue bay and noted where the last of the raid ships was beaching. The royal family of the island had escaped during the heat of the battle, and two of the Cretan boats—small, fast boats that maneuvered well on the water—had been dispatched to catch them and bring them back. Now, looking down, Lukios could see the results of their hunting: the king's head, and his son's, had been struck off and now decorated the tops of the fighting ships' twin masts. The queen and her two young daughters, naked, their pampered skins white against the sunburned brown of their captors, were being led up the beach. The queen was trying to maintain whatever dignified hauteur she could manage, but that wasn't much. *Relax and enjoy it, darling,* Lukios thought cynically. *And forget the old pleasures. You're going to have to learn a whole new way of life.*

He smiled more broadly now. His plan was taking shape. He was enumerating the ways of ingratiating himself with Plouteus and his friends. One of them stuck out immediately.

Their little murder plot hadn't quite hatched yet. An attack on Minos and his daughter would have to be planned with great care. And it would require help. Help, for instance, from informers in the camp of Minos. Informers like himself —he, Lukios, who came and went with almost complete impunity within the royal apartments, who had his ear to the ground, and who was the master of every scrap of stray gossip that came to hand within the House of the Double Axe. He'd be in a unique position to know the comings and goings of guards, the weak moments in the day's schedule. He'd be in an absolutely pivotal position to supply information as to the proper moment to strike. And then . . .

Lukios smiled. He wouldn't be a slave for long.

II

The sun was almost down. Nikos, looking for his master, ran into a friend near the slaves' campfire: a man called Ekhinos—"the sea urchin"—because of his mop of unruly hair. Ekhinos was the slave of one of the raid's commanders and had spent a busy afternoon running messages between his master and the onshore commander in charge of land operations. Now, a skewer of lamb chunks in one hand, he smiled and welcomed Nikos. "Here, my friend," he said. "Break your fast. There's enough for all."

Nikos hesitated—but then his belly reminded him of the inescapable fact that he hadn't eaten a thing since morning. "All right," he said. "I was looking for my master. But I think that if he is proving difficult to find just now, it may be because he does not want to be found."

"Ah," Ekhinos said, handing his friend another skewer from the fire and indicating with his free hand a wine bottle which stood propped against a tree stump nearby. "Woman stuff, I gather. I hear the priestess—"

"Something like that," Nikos said. His tone indicated that the inquiry would stop right there. No sense gossiping here, when you couldn't tell who was listening. There was already quite enough talk, most of it disparaging, about his master's relations with Minos's daughter without his muddying the water by adding to it. "My master and I found a man who appears to have some sort of alchemic secret which is very important to him. His mind is probably working pretty furiously, trying to absorb what he's heard and make sense of it." He took a bite of the lamb; it was succulent and bore the pungent taste of the smoke. He nodded appreciatively, chewing. "I think it was something Khalkeus had been looking for all his adult life."

"Well, good for him. Minos will be pleased. He'll be well rewarded. Who knows? Maybe there'll be something in it for you."

"Khalkeus is generous," Nikos agreed, watching the last sliver of the blazing orb sink into the dark sea in the west. Almost simultaneously, a light wind struck up, stirring the flames above the hot coals at their feet. "He's also more thoughtful than before. He watched the man die, the man who passed the secret along to him. They seem to have had a conversation of sorts. After the man died and Khalkeus came forth, I could see he had been weeping. And for a stranger."

"Well, you never know what's going to set someone off," Ekhinos said. He picked up the wine bottle, squeezing a stream of the liquid into his open mouth. Then he passed the bottle to Nikos, who drank deeply. "Perhaps the man said something that reminded him of something. It's curious: I wouldn't have pegged Khalkeus for being the weeping kind. He's so—well, composed all the time."

"Yes. He has the reputation of a cold fish. But I think

that's unkind. I have had many worse masters. Many. He's not unfeeling at all compared to the lot of them."

"Ah," Ekhinos said. "How long have you been a slave, Nikos?"

"Ten years," Nikos said in a hard voice, "six months, and four days." The sudden sharp edge to his voice surprised Ekhinos. "Let me tell you: there isn't a moment of my waking life when I'm not aware of the running count, to the last day. And—" He swallowed a moment, and when he spoke again his voice was husky. "There's not a moment of that time when I'm not aware of—" He couldn't go on, though. The skewer dangled from his hand.

"Here," Ekhinos said, putting a hand on his shoulder. "Here, now . . ." His voice trailed away. He couldn't find anything to say. "I—I know. Most of us don't talk about what—well, what we've lost, but—"

Nikos mastered himself. He stood straight and tall. "I had a wife, over in the long strait between the mainlands, an island woman like myself. We had a little girl-child, as beautiful as the sun and the moon put together. She was—what? Eight at the time? She had big brown eyes, and silky brown hair, and she sang like a bird. She—she'll be grown now. If she's alive. She won't remember me, most likely. My wife was still young; she'll have found another man. I hope he's good to her. I hope . . ."

Ekhinos put down the wine bottle he'd retrieved, this time without drinking. He threw the long metal skewer into the fire. "Yes," he said. "I was a fisherman and I had three boys. My wife died giving birth to the last, peace to her shade. I saw all three of my sons killed in just such a raid as this." He tried to speak; his mouth worked convulsively. He sighed. He shook his head, looking down at the coals and seeing nothing.

"Just such a raid as this," Nikos said. "Only it was not on a raid on my hometown. I was on business across the island. I was captured in the raid; they needed strong backs to man the oars for an assault on the mainland. I was a scribe, a man of some small affluence. My hands were soft, my muscles weak. Well, that condition didn't last long. And as I pulled on the oar, my palms and fingers bleeding and blistered, blinded by the sweat in my eyes, I thought every moment of my wife and child. And I have not stopped thinking of them at least once every day. It's foolish of me. It's always foolish to dwell on things you cannot change. And—for the love of all the gods—the image I have of them is as they were, not as they are. I probably would hardly recognize them now."

"That part doesn't matter, does it?"

"Not at all." Ekhinos listened. Nikos was a quiet man normally, and here the words were coming out with a rush, carrying a dizzying confusion of emotions. "You know, I—as I was being carried off my native island, I put a stone in my mouth. A stone from my native soil. I wanted to have something left that was mine, that would remind me. I had nothing else. I was naked, bleeding from a dozen cuts. My hands were bound behind my back. But I purposely took a spill, my face in the dust. And before I got my legs under me again I had spied a little round pebble, something a boy might throw at a sheep. A smooth little pebble that had been polished in a stream in one of the rivers that come down from the hills on my island in the thaw season. I moved my face a little, and my lips closed around it." He looked at Ekhinos with thoughtful eyes. "I have changed hands many times since then, as a chattel. Each time, I have had that little pebble in my mouth when my body went on the block for sale. They always reduce you to nothing, selling you without any garment to show such blemishes as you may have. Not always do they check your teeth. I always smiled broadly to show how healthy mine were. Nobody ever found the pebble. By now it is a source of great pride with me." He reached inside his tunic and pulled it forth, holding it in the light of the glowing coals. "It doesn't look like much," he said. "But I think that by now I would kill to keep it." His expression had a peculiar intensity about it that Ekhinos could not completely identify. "It is all I have that is mine. To this day."

Ekhinos's hand went to Nikos's shoulder and squeezed hard. There wasn't much need for further words between them.

From the darkness nearby, seated on a ragged tree stump, Khalkeus watched and listened. His own eyes were wet again, and his heart was full of a thousand feelings that clashed violently with one another. Nikos . . .

This was the side of a slave that the master never saw, the part that revealed itself only to another bondman. And—why hadn't he seen? He, Khalkeus, who had once been a slave himself? Why had he remained insensitive to the feelings of the most constant companion he'd had in years? Of course: it was his own self-absorption, his own damnable selfishness. It was this which had cheated all the people in the world that he knew of anything he could possibly have found in himself to give them.

But then—of course, of course. He had deliberately

avoided learning these things about Nikos. They would have reminded him all too well of what he himself had lost: a good and true and virtuous wife whom he'd loved after his fashion —cold comfort that *that* must have been, he thought bitterly —and who had loved him dearly; two sons, one strong and handsome, the other small and . . .

Yes, and a home. For all that, as a Child of the Lion he was a wanderer by trade, he'd known a home with her for a number of years. A warm and welcoming and accepting place where he was loved and honored. Friends in the city. And plenty of work to do, plenty of call for his services. In the warrior country between Hittite lands and the Land of the Two Rivers there was always plenty of call for an armorer. He'd armed proud Mari during one year-long stay away from wife and family, and his work had helped the king there stave off a fierce siege from Assyrian lands. He'd done respected and highly rewarded work arming Ugarit.

Yes, but there'd always been that sweet and warm home to come back to, the warm fire in the hearth and the meal simmering in the pot and the two happy, dusty little boys tussling good-naturedly at his feet as his wife, smiling, looked on. A place of his own . . .

Ah. And what had he now? He was a rich man—and still as much a chattel as he had been when he was a slave. He was at Minos's beck and call, in a palace not one stone of which could be called his own. He owned, perhaps, his own clothing; but that was it, for all practical purposes. Minos owned the tools; Minos owned all that his skill fashioned. And Xena . . .

Yes, Xena. If he was anyone's chattel, he was hers. She owned him as completely, now that he was technically free, as she had when he was a bondservant. She did everything it was in her power to do to assure him that this was not the case—and then her own fierce jealousy would drive her to reassert her own domination over him, time after time.

The terrible thing about it was that he did not hate her. He did not even dislike her. She was a fine woman: a fit consort for any king in the lands of the Great Sea or beyond. Take her features one by one, she was as beautiful, still, as any courtier's woman or daughter in the domain of the Axe. Why? Why couldn't he feel more for her?

But, in all sobriety, he knew the answer. Because in everything Nikos had said a moment before, he had heard the virtual echo of the things which had begun to tear his soul apart during the last few months.

This damned fool quest of his. Meaningless, meaningless. Today, he had learned the secret of the smelting of a new and impossibly potent metal. His father, Ahuni, had told him when he was a lad that his grandfather, Belsunu, who had armed the great patriarchal leader Abraham for the great war that had for once and all broken the power of Elam and Shinar over Canaan—that Belsunu had once found in a market in Ashkelon, a sword made of the stuff: dark, incredibly hard metal that, some said, fell from the sky. How the unknown worker had worked it had been a secret neither Belsunu nor Ahuni had ever mastered. But the fact that someone had mastered the metal had haunted him, Ahuni, all his life.

And this had been the obsession of Kirta, son of Ahuni. And he had left home without even a commission in his pocket, to sail away in search of the secret that had eluded his father and his grandfather. To be sure, he'd left wife and children with money enough to live in comfort, and even to pay for the boys' apprenticeship once they came of age. But even then, in his heart of hearts, he'd known he would likely never see them again.

Lost them. All for—what? Now that he had the secret, his moment of triumph was empty, echoingly empty. In some ways he not only didn't feel better for having the knowledge, he felt worse—infinitely worse. Wasted. His life had been wasted. And he'd cheated so many people, beginning first of all with his wife and children, who deserved more of him, who deserved having a husband and father with them all those years, to care for them and protect them and to help the boys grow up healthy and strong, in spite of the younger one's—

No, that wasn't totally true either. The first person he'd cheated had been himself. Unquestionably, himself. The middle years which others found so rewarding, so happy and fulfilling, the years of watching two fine sons grow to manhood, the years of accepting and returning the sweet and forgiving and enduring love of his wife, all of these he'd lost. Cheated himself of having. And for what? For a meaningless formula. A method of building a cookstove out of ceramics. A method of getting a work-fire to burn hotter, more brightly . . .

Dross. Chaff. Offal.

Well, he told himself. *You've made a fine mess of a lot of lives, haven't you? First of all your own.* And what was he going to do about it?

Good question. Thinking about it, Khalkeus sat bolt upright on the tree stump. It would be a worse folly than he'd ever committed if he took an insight such as he'd had today and threw it away, failed to act upon it. This was the sort of insight, of augury even, that changed a man's life. If he took the wrong fork of the path at this point, he knew his life would sicken and die on him. After that, it'd be all grindwork, empty gestures, going through the motions, marking time until merciful death. But if he took the right path, perhaps he could rectify—perhaps he could remedy . . .

But what was the right path? Should he leave Xena, slip away in the dark of night, and stow away on a boat bound for the Ugarit coast? Make his way back to a family which must by now have given up wondering what had happened to him? Go back to Haran?

Well, there was merit in the idea. There was a particular responsibility he'd had and that he'd skirted. His sons were Children of the Lion. They should have been trained in the craft by their father, by another Child of the Lion. And he'd left them to be trained by—whom? By the sort of bumblers and fumblers that had remained in Haran when he had left all those years ago? He shuddered. How could he have abandoned them to that? Yes, he'd return and . . .

And—look at him. He was proposing abandoning Xena, just as he'd abandoned his wife and sons.

Khalkeus stood up and moved out of the shadow, heading slowly down the point toward Xena's tent. There didn't seem to *be* any right thing to do. Everything he thought of managed somehow to hurt someone a little more. And he was tired of hurting people. He wanted to change the direction of his life. But in the meantime, there was all this cleaning up to do. He set out, leaden-footed, his mind as preoccupied as ever.

As he passed, Tros of Phaistos turned to his fellow conspirator Amphimedes and said in a low voice: "Another of them. I'm sure he can't be trusted. If our coup takes Xena with it, surely he—"

"I'm not sure," Amphimedes said. "There's been trouble between them. And he's an independent sort. I think he'll go to work for anyone who rules. And *think,* Tros. Khalkeus has useful skills. When we strike, we'll have to arm ourselves to defend ourselves. Minos has friends, allies, relatives we'll have to deal with. If we spare Khalkeus . . ."

Tros's angry scowl was faintly visible in the dancing light

of the campfire's flames. "No!" he said in a tight voice. "I say kill him. . . ."

III

Slaves from her galley had erected a tent for Xena not far from the officers' campfire, and a small fire now danced merrily in the middle of the enclosed space. By the light of the flickering flames she completed her devotions to the Lady, whose gaily painted image adorned a corner of the tent.

But as she bowed toward the little statue and turned away from it, she was acutely aware that her supposed communion with the Goddess had been an empty thing, almost totally devoid of meaning for her. These days the Lady's power came upon her less and less frequently, and the moments when she felt the thrilling possession of her body and mind by the Goddess were rare indeed.

When, she wondered now, had she begun faking it? Going through the motions? It had been some time back, that was all she knew. And how long since the last time the Lady had deigned to visit her, to inhabit her body? Why, it must have been a matter of months now. She shivered at the thought. This would be—yes, it'd be the longest absence yet.

The thought came as a shock: *Has the Goddess left me forever? Am I then no more than an ordinary woman now?*

The thought stopped her dead. She stood looking into the dancing flames, seeing nothing at all. If the Lady left her altogether, she was *less* than an ordinary woman. An ordinary woman, at her age, would have a husband and children by now. And she would have . . . ?

Xena, a flash of panic running through her heart, reached for the little table the men had brought inside for her and, for the twentieth time, retrieved the bronze hand mirror that went with her everywhere. *Oh, look at those lines. Crow's feet around my eyes . . . my face is beginning to fall. . . .* Stricken, she let the mirror drop lightly to the ground at her feet.

If she lost the Goddess . . .

If she lost Khalkeus . . .

It was, she reflected, no good telling yourself you were a

king's daughter. That was little comfort in the small hours of the night. And while, as a princess of the blood and sharer, to some extent, of Minos's power, she could have her choice of virtually every available male in the court and some of those not officially available, she knew that there was little in this to console her in the event that Khalkeus ever made good the threat he'd made twice in the past to run away. She knew good and well how that would affect her. As it was, if Khalkeus spent a night or two away from her bed, visiting some magician at the far end of Crete or even working day and night on one of his experiments, she couldn't sleep a wink. She'd tried every nostrum, and none of them worked. By the time Khalkeus came back to her, she'd be a wreck—a pitiful, whining, babbling wreck, red-eyed and haggard. Worse: she'd *look* a wreck, not just feel it. At the very moment when she needed him most, she'd be in the worst position for attracting him.

And—look at her now. Right now, when he could drop in at any moment. She shivered again and retrieved the mirror. Well, perhaps there were things cosmetics could do to salvage her looks for now, what with it being night and all. She sat down before the little table and, propping the mirror up against her ointment box, made hasty repairs to her appearance. She grimaced at herself in the mirror, baring her teeth. Well, at least *they* were all sound. Losing a tooth would age you faster than anything if it were a front tooth that showed.

She arched her back, forcing her breasts out. She inspected them clinically in the mirror, holding them up, turning this way and that. It was as Lukios had said; they were among her best features. They still stood high, their rouged nipples sensuous and their skin still white and delicate, almost to the point of transparency. She'd taken pains to stay under the canopy during the sail from Crete, and now she congratulated herself for having done so. Direct sunlight aged one so.

Well, she thought, *so much for the inventory of assets. What about liabilities?* She frowned—and then forced the frown from her face. Frowns made wrinkles; so did smiles. *All right, Xena,* she thought. *Calmly now. What about yourself could you improve? What changes for the better would please Khalkeus most? What?*

But the frown returned, and turned to a fidgety look mirroring her despair. That was the trouble. She could look her prettiest; she could look her worst. He always treated her with the same maddeningly thoughtful, almost polite respect. When he complimented her, it was in the same tone of voice he'd use to compliment the gardener of the royal apartments for competent work pruning a floral arrangement. It wasn't that he didn't notice; that in itself would have been bad enough. He just didn't care very much. That was the part that hurt the worst. It meant that whatever it was that he felt for her after all this time, it wasn't love.

Perhaps—perhaps it was that that had begun her slow—and now possibly permanent—disaffection from the Lady. She'd prayed to the Goddess virtually nightly ever since she'd fallen in love with him, begging the Lady to make him return her love. But always, the Lady had turned a deaf ear to her complaints, her prayers, her despairing pleas. Small wonder, then, if her own belief had faded. Small wonder if the Lady, sensing Xena's disbelief, had slipped away from her and taken virtually every vestige of Her awesome power with Her. Look at today, for instance: her tiff with Marineus. In the old days, she'd have been able to force Marineus to his knees before her, feeling the might of the Lady flowing through her. But today—today there had been no feeling of possession. She had tweaked Marineus's nose with a mere trick of the mind, one that any unbeliever could learn. Whereas before, when she had had the full force with her . . .

Oh, she was losing it all. Losing everything. If only the Lady, leaving her forever, would compensate her by giving her, if only for a time, the love of Khalkeus. If only . . . But she shook her head. One of the things she was losing, little by little, was her own belief in the Lady and Her power to intervene in such matters. She who had been so faithful for so long, surely the Goddess could have given her that one thing.

She sat toying with the mirror, looking idly at the fire, her features falling once again, insensibly, into the same expression of near-despair that had become almost habitual with her in recent weeks. Perhaps—the thought horrified her with its blasphemy, but had been forcing itself into her mind for some time—perhaps gods and goddesses, like men and women, had their allotted time, and when it was gone, they began to fade, as men and women did. Tales had begun to drift across the sea from the mainland about new cults, new gods—male ones, which denied the female principle, the female mystery, the source of all life. There was the cult of the Earth-Shaker, a god who produced earthquakes and volcanic eruptions—a cult which, by some odd alchemy, had begun to merge into the cult of the Great Father of the Sea. These were rude barbaric cults, concerned with masculine power and destruction rather than the feminine gift of existence. . . .

With a sigh that was almost a sob, Xena slumped further in the chair, and the lines of worry once again appeared on her still-lovely face.

Khalkeus, silent still, stood in the tent doorway watching her, watching the increasingly somber expressions play across her features. That last look of despair was like a knife stabbing at his heart; poor woman, she'd been looking at the mirror, counting the wrinkles, reflecting on the lost years. . . .

He sighed silently. And what had brought her to this? Only his own callousness. Only his own indecision. Somewhere along the way, he could have gone to her and told her the truth: *Xena, I do not love you. You are a beautiful and passionate woman who deserves to have a man who loves you as I cannot. Let me go. This thing between us is bleeding you white. Go, seek a healthy love, something that will bring the youth back into your heart, the bloom into those lovely cheeks again.*

Khalkeus pursed his lips. And you, Khalkeus who was once Kirta, if you told her all of that, what would you do then? Where would you go? Would you stay here, under Xena's eye, reminding her of things that couldn't be, torturing her? Would you sit there in your lavish apartment in the House of the Axe—the palace of her father and your benefactor and master—and content yourself with working the dark metal whose secret has eluded you until today? Would you be content, after the day's revelations and confessions, with a sterile life in which human concerns are absent?

As he thought this, he knew that would be impossible. The day's meeting with the dying Turios of Tyre had changed his own life, permanently, irrevocably. Everything would be different from now on, his life would have new direction, new action. Sooner or later, Xena must see the change. Early or late—and early would be better for all concerned—something had to be done to break the stagnation into which his life had fallen.

He sighed in resignation. "Xena," he said.

She didn't react for a heartbeat's length, lost as she was in her own thoughts. Then her face changed as she turned to him. The warmth and passionate abandon of her hopeless love for him came across the tent-framed room in all its power and force. "Khalkeus!" she said. "My darling!"

Then she was in his arms, and he was not responding as he had intended to respond, pulling her arms away from him and keeping her at a distance. Instead, to his surprise, a wave of deep empathy ran through him. He understood her. He felt for her. He knew what she was going through. And now his own defenses against that empathy were down, and he could no longer keep himself from feeling. Indeed, could he ever again mask away his feelings from himself? Likely not: Turios had given him two gifts today, and both of them were two-edged swords. The one gave knowledge—and the ability to kill. The other gave feeling—and the inability to hide it anymore. He held her close, and suddenly found himself weeping, the deep racking sobs shaking his body as he clutched her to him.

As luck would have it, Xena, believing what she wanted to believe, misread the source of his sudden and baffling tears, his heartfelt sobs. "Oh, my darling," she said. "My own sweet darling." Her hands caressed his back, his neck, drew his head down to hers. Her lips burned on his face, his eyes, his lips. As the chemistry of misunderstanding wrought its bizarre spell, the hot flush of sexual need came upon her just as the violently mixed feelings within him tore him apart. She drew his face down to her naked breasts; her thighs trapped one of his between them, and her wet pubis ground lustily against his hard-muscled leg.

"Khalkeus," she said. "Take me. Now. Now, my darling. I want you . . . I've missed you so. . . . Here, my own. Here, my beloved. Please, darling, please. . . ."

The emotions within him hopelessly confused, Khalkeus found his own passions rising to meet her needs. His strong armorer's hands gripped her, lifted her; suddenly and thoroughly aroused as he had not been in months, he lifted her slight weight easily and carried her to the pile of pillows in the corner of the tent. Silently, he took her, to a chorus of low animal moans that grew and grew in intensity to fever pitch and climaxed in a piercing scream.

He awoke in the night. There was a chill in the air; a low-lying night fog hung on the little peninsula. Slipping away from the sleeping Xena, he stood up, first covering her with a fur against the cold. Still naked, he walked to the open door of the tent and stood in the doorway, looking out over the moonlit sea, ignoring the goose bumps on his bare skin. He sighed, for perhaps the hundredth time this day. Here he'd had one thing in mind—and he'd done another. Worst of all, she had seen his despairing passion as a sign of newly awakened love. In the heat of his own ardor, he'd ignored this—and ignored the consequences that would follow.

He felt cowardly, spineless, utterly vile. Swine that he'd become, he'd cheated her again—cheated her of the truth that might cure her of her passion for him. And he'd cheated himself.

Nikos's words came back to him. *My wife was still young; she'll have found another man. I hope he's good to her.*

Yes, yes. And his sons. His two adorable little sons, each so different, each so precious. How could he have left them? How, given the numerous opportunities he'd had to escape, could he have forgotten his wife, his boys, and stayed on in comfort in a foreign land? Now, too far away, years too late, the thought went through him like a red-hot spearhead. *My darlings,* he thought. *Flesh of my flesh, souls of my soul, I abandoned you.*

Now the resolve grew in him, strong and unwavering. He knew what he had to do, whatever the price. He had to return. He had to go back to Haran and find them. If there were any way in the world of making up to them for the neglect they'd suffered in his absence, he'd do it, whatever it was.

Yes. He'd begin making plans immediately. As soon as the flotilla found its way back to Knossos. No matter that it meant cheating Xena again. He had other priorities. He had responsibilities he'd been evading too long. He had to go back, for the good of his soul. He'd set his affairs quietly in order back in Crete, telling no one his plans. And then, when Minos and Xena least expected it, he'd go down to the harbor, having first cashed in some of his little treasures to get his fare, and bribe one of the Phoenician captains to let him stow away on a ship bound for Kittim, say, or Ashkelon or even Ugarit. *Yes,* he thought. *Yes.*

As dawn broke, Marineus woke and slipped on a battle tunic against the cold. He shook his head, sat up, and saw, to his surprise, Tros of Phaistos sitting across the guttering embers of his tent-fire, looking at him, his gaunt face intent and full of purpose. "Tros," he said. "What are you doing here?"

"I couldn't sleep," his coconspirator said. "My mind was racing. One of your captains captured a Lydian soothsayer who'd been in the service of the king of the island. He told him some details of the—the plan you and I discussed earlier. The soothsayer read the bones. He consulted the stars. He . . ."

"Yes?" Marineus said.

"He said, 'You must strike soon. When the stars are right.' " His voice had an edge of excitement in it.

"Hmmm," Marineus said. "And this is . . . when?"

"Within the next cycle of the moon. The auguries are favorable for—" He paused pensively.

"Come on, man, get it out."

Tros hesitated, then smiled. "Three weeks from tonight."

Marineus felt a quick pang of fear. Then, it was replaced by an answering rush of excitement. And, his eyes locked to Tros's gaze, he committed himself once and for all to bloody revolution. "All right, then," he said. "Three weeks it is."

IV

Beneath the fire-scarred walls of the once-white houses of the city on the bay, the fleet drew anchor in time to catch the morning tide. Two ships' complement of men, freedmen and slaves alike, had been left behind as a token force of the overlord nation, to administer a town now chattel to Minos. The vacated places on the oars were taken by brand-new slaves: men who had been free a day before. Their women were divided, living spoils of the battle, among the captains of the attack ships, although additional provision had been made, as Marineus had expected, for the noncombatant hangers-on who had accompanied Xena's vessel to the port and arrived after the battle had been fought and won. These, too, took slaves home with them. The port city had been decimated, not once but twice: both war and impressment had taken their deadly toll. The town would not recover for a generation, if at all.

Nikos stood by the lee rail and looked out, bitterness in his heart. He remembered the island town that he himself had seen razed and enslaved on the day when he had lost his freedom. He could see it now in his mind's eye. And if he worked at it a bit, he could also conjure up a picture of the town he'd lived in: a town probably equally subject to Minos, although in all his years of servitude, he'd never heard another word about the place he'd called home. He could see his wife, his child, falling prey to the same sort of slavers he'd seen this day, carrying away women and children, separating woman from child. He shut his eyes against the sight, but darkness only sharpened his mental picture. And, in despair, he looked north toward his home isles, his heart yearning, a great emptiness inside him. Would they even remember him now? Would they sometimes wonder what had happened to husband and father when he went away? Or had they, in fact, suffered the fate he'd pictured in his mind so depressingly a moment ago?

Tight-lipped, he brushed a salt tear from his eye and breathed a silent prayer to gods he no longer believed in, the harsh masculine gods of his home isles. *Please,* he begged. *Let them be free now, free and healthy. Even if they have forgotten me, make them free.*

Xena, her eyes bright again, hope burning in her heart for the first time in years, stood by the right hand of the man who manned the huge rudder of her own galley and looked toward Crete, toward home. For the first time in many months, she felt she had a future. She felt vibrantly alive. Never mind the years; a woman was as young as she felt. And Khalkeus, the night before, had—well, he'd seemed something like his old taciturn self, but his actions had spoken more loudly than any words could have done. He'd wept over her; he'd shown emotion before her. His arms, strong arms of a metalworker, had held her close, and he'd made love to her with the vigor of a stripling and the expertise of a man of mature years. She'd never experienced such divine abandon, such complete physical union with anyone, not in all her life, not even during the frenzied, drug-induced times of the festivals of the Goddess, when a woman consecrated to the Lady might make love to a dozen men a night.

The night's dear pleasures had given her hope again. Surely, the emotions that had poured forth from Khalkeus— not in words, but in so many other ways—betokened a change of heart in her once-reluctant lover. Perhaps now he stood perched unsteadily on the brink of real, enduring love; perhaps for the first time she'd begun, by some magical means she still could not put a name to, to reach forth into his heart and dislodge the specters that she knew had always dwelt there: the wife abandoned, the half-forgotten boy-children. . . .

Yes! She'd never been able to drive them away before, the ghosts that had walled him away from her. And now, by some incalculable alchemy, she'd been given for the first time a small corner of his heart. How had she doubted the warmly maternal, protective heart of the Lady? How could she have doubted her great Mistress for so much as a moment? Surely, it was the hand of the Goddess that had brought him back to her—and surely (here her heart beat fast and her blood quickened), surely, the great Lady would help her to win over the rest of him. But for now, casting her thoughts to the clouds above the dark sea, all she could think, was *Thank you, Great Mother. Thank You. . . .*

Tros of Phaistos also bent his eyes toward Crete, far across the white-dappled waves. His thoughts were similarly of gratitude, but toward the Earth-Shaker, source of all power. *I pledge you a cock by the morrow, Great One,* he thought, his pulse quickening. *You've given me Minos, in the palm of this very hand.* With the thought, smiling, he looked down at his palm and closed it.

What a coup! Marineus, mightiest of all Minos's admirals, coming over to his side! Until now, he'd had mainly bureaucrats, courtiers, landowners, men of influence in the city but not, he reflected, the sort of men to organize the kind of operation needed to depose and murder Minos and those close to him. Now, with a military man—and him the greatest warrior on Crete—in charge of the physical aspects of the revolution. . . .

He smiled again. His heart pounded furiously. Yes! And if that weren't enough, that fat eunuch Minos had detailed to follow Xena around and keep her company, he'd volunteered his aid, leaking secrets out to the conspirators from the royal camp. That could prove very useful indeed. He'd have to congratulate Plouteus when he saw him next. There was no telling what sort of new loyalties might arise from a casual dalliance that went perhaps a bit beyond the casual. And Plouteus's chance seduction of the fat capon had made a new and useful conspirator, slave or no, of him. Truly, Tros thought, the Earth-Shaker was looking out for him. His smile became broad and all-embracing. He was happier than he'd been in years. In three weeks, he'd have a hand in the killing of a king. And in the making of a new one, one who would remember in times to come who his friends and allies had been in the great days when Minos was overthrown.

The eyes of Kirta, son of Ahuni, who had gone for more than a decade under the name Khalkeus, looked back from the bow of the ship in which he'd come across the seas—one of the ships of the conquering flotilla. He looked to the east—toward the Great Crescent, toward hidden Ugarit and mighty Carchemish and busy Haran. And seeing nothing, nothing at all. His face somber, he closed his eyes the better to see. But no faces, no places rose in his memory. *Oh, gods,* he thought in despair, *I've lost them. I've forgotten what they looked like. And if I've forgotten them, they'll have forgotten me. I might as well have been wiped from the face of the earth.* And his soul, which had so seldom prayed since childhood, prayed now, to gods equally forgotten: *Let me find my way to them before it's too late. Let me, please let me....*

His eye rose, following the soaring flight of a gull, high above the mast. The bird, its great wings spread wide, drifted eastward, ever eastward, toward the lost lands of his, Kirta's, birth. His sharp eyes focused now, Kirta followed the gull until it was a mere dot in the blue sky, flying above the trackless sea, toward the mysterious East.

CHAPTER FOUR

I

The blind beggar Bahirum awoke in the chill fog of the dawn hours, his head throbbing with pain, his torso aching with a dull discomfort. When he tried to move, there were, in rapid succession, stabbing pains in his chest and in his left forearm. He tried to cry out—and felt the pain in his throat as his cry became an almost inaudible croak.

Despite the pain, he forced himself to a sitting position, using his right arm. Here he sat, gasping at the exertion, trying to remember. . . . Yes, yes; there had been three of them, from their voices, and they had taken much wine from the sound of things, and—

"Oh, no," he said, his voice breaking. He lurched forward, feeling again the stabbing ache in his chest. He fumbled around him with his good hand and located his begging bowl. Empty. Empty—after the best day he'd had in months and months. Empty, after two days' starvation.

He sat back, disregarding bodily pain. The pain inside his mind was worse than all the aches of his bruised and broken body. How would he take his place in the bazaar now? He was sure he had at least one broken rib, and his left forearm was certainly broken as well. He wasn't sure he could even stand up. How could he . . . ?

Now he heard footsteps, coming near. Were they coming back to finish him off? He cowered against the wall, his good hand held up to shield his face. "No, please," he croaked in his hoarse voice, terrified. "Don't hit me any more, please. . . ."

"Why—what's this?" said a youthful voice. There was a note of concern in it, in what might normally be a cheerful sort of voice. "Here, sir, did you take a spill? Let me help you up."

But when the helping hands touched him and tried to lift him, the beggar turned his face up to his benefactor with a whimper of pain. "No, please. My ribs . . . I've got a broken arm, I think. Please . . ."

The newcomer knelt beside him and put one comforting hand on his right shoulder. "Goodness, my friend, someone really worked you over, didn't he? And robbed you, too, I'll bet. No, you don't have to talk yet if you don't want. Hmmm. Does it hurt—here?" The blind man winced. "I see. And that arm—yes, I think you've got a bad fracture. Don't move, now, stay still. You've got a bad cut on your forehead. If you'll promise to sit still here for a moment and not move around, I'll just step over to the well and get a little water and wash you off. I'll bet you could use a drink of water, too, couldn't you? Now—stay right there. . . ."

Bahirum wasn't about to move. He sat back against the wall, breathing hard. Well, at least they hadn't returned. And this stranger seemed to want to help—but why was his voice vaguely familiar? He must have come into contact with this person somewhere.

The footsteps returned. "Here. I borrowed your bowl for a moment. Have a drink of this, and then I'll wash your face and your forehead and see how bad that cut is." There were new footsteps in the distance. The young man, swabbing his head gently, lifted his voice. "Here! Abirapi! Over here! Give me a hand, will you?" The footfalls stepped up their pace.

"Hadad!" a new voice said. "What's the matter? I—why, that's the blind man, isn't it? The one from the Bazaar of the Twin Oaks? I saw him only a week ago."

"Yes," the younger voice said, right by Bahirum's ear. "I think so. Somebody's beaten him up pretty badly. He's got some broken bones. Look, could you do me a favor? Could you step over to the barber's? And tell him we've got somebody hurt here? He'll know what to do. Perhaps he can set this gentleman's broken arm."

"No, please," the blind man said. "I have no money. I'm a beggar, and they robbed me. I can't pay the barber."

"Please," the person called Hadad said in that cheerful and friendly voice. "Go ahead, Abirapi! Look, you owe me a favor. You know that. Go get the barber. Tell him it's an emergency." The footsteps receded now. The voice spoke more quietly to Bahirum: "Don't worry about it. The barber's a good sort. I'll slip him a coin or two and settle with him later. But look: do you know who they were—the people who attacked you, I mean? Because, well, we can't have that sort of thing happening in this quarter. I'll take it to the magistrate. He'll take steps to—"

"No—no magistrates." The beggar's professional instincts took over, overshadowing all his worry and pain. He didn't want any police sticking their noses into his life. Not for any reason.

The barber led him away to his little shop. As they turned to go, the blind man said, "You, sir—Hadad. I know you. You're the—the sculptor, at the Bazaar of the Well—"

"That's right," the young man said. "Now you go along with my friend here. And don't worry about anything. Here." He pressed a coin into the beggar's hand. "That ought to last you for a few days, until you feel well enough to take up your position once again. And—good luck."

The barber loosed his grip on Bahirum's arm for a moment. "Hadad, for the love of all the gods, you take this back. I know how much you make. This is your dinner money. What are you trying to do?"

"Ah," the young voice said. "There, my dear friend, you're wrong for a change. It just so happens that I made a sale yesterday. I'm going to collect today at noon, as soon as I've delivered a little anniversary gift to my brother and sister-in-law. By midafternoon I'll be flusher than I've been in months. The merchant's paying me not in base coin, but in gold."

"Well, good for you!" the barber said, approvingly. "But, nevertheless, you take this and—"

"Let our friend have it," the cheerful voice said. "He'll need it. He doesn't look as though he's eaten well lately. You, my friend: you buy yourself a good meal with this. You hear? As a favor to me, eh? You owe me a favor, you know. Well, the only way you can pay me back is by taking care of yourself. You hear?"

"I—I hear," the blind man rasped. "And—bless you. Thank you and bless you."

The blind man hesitated for a moment, pulling against the barber's hand. He listened for the footfalls of his benefactor, leaving. He wanted to memorize the sound, so that he could recognize the man's gait if he ever ran across him again.

And then his face fell, as he heard the halting, lopsided gait of his young savior, limping awkwardly down the street. *Gods!* the blind man thought. *Poor devil, he's lame.*

The girl slave Tanuha answered the door. Hadad smiled at her, looking into the washed-out eyes and the dull face. *Ah,* he thought. *Poor girl!* And he shook his head once again at Anat's vanity. Who but his sister-in-law—the most beautiful girl in Haran, and the most vain—would buy a girl slave for the household on the basis of her plain face, just to increase the contrast? He chuckled to himself—but the humor in his thought was sympathetic, even admiring. After all, the most beautiful girl in the city could afford a few minor faults, couldn't she?

"My mistress is bathing, sir," Tanuha said. "My master hasn't returned from the encampment yet. But I'm sure my mistress would want to see you, if you'd like to wait."

"Fine," Hadad said. "Thank you. I'll wait in the garden, if that's all right. Flowers. I never get enough of flowers. And I get to see them so seldom in my part of town."

"Yes, sir." The girl showed him in. Her eyes, dull or no, took him in: the dark, unruly curly hair, the warm, good-natured face with its friendly pug nose and broad humorous mouth, the thin body, and the beautiful, expressive hands, long and tapered. *Artist's hands.* She smiled at him, wishing she were free, wishing she were rich, wishing she were pretty. She turned and preceded him, wanting to avoid the sight of his ungainly limp. *The poor man . . .*

The flowers in Shobai's garden were as expensive as everything else in his sprawling house, and as showy. They were ornamentals brought in seed and bud and cutting from far away, along the trade routes. Yellow flag, moluccella, roses of Sharon, even the rare Nazareth iris, brought up by traders from Lake Chinnereth down in Canaan. Hadad's smile grew wider and wider as he limped down the aisle between the rows, cool under the overarching trees, sniffing the exquisite bouquets of each delicate bloom, his color-sensitive eyes glorying in the delicate balance of hues. *How pleasant this is,* he thought. *It restores your soul.* Particularly, he reflected, after a terrible incident like this morning's. Imagine people beating and robbing a poor, defenseless blind man! Imagine stealing the pitiful earnings of a beggar!

He stepped closer to the little pool with its bright explosion of hyacinths. How lovely . . .

"Hadad?"

71

The voice was cool, a little harsh. Hadad smiled. But that was his sister-in-law, Anat, for you. His grin full of admiration and affection, he turned to greet her. She stood tall and statuesque, her perfect features composed, her dark hair exquisitely coiffed, her soft white robe falling over high breasts. Hands and feet alike, peeping from the robe's fringes, were of uncommon delicacy and beauty. All negative thoughts left his mind immediately as he looked at her, his eyes full of bashful and innocent puppy love. The only sight that might have seemed more beautiful to his worshiping eyes would have been the sight of the two of them, Shobai and Anat, standing together.

"Hello, Anat," he said. "I—"

"We're going to be pretty busy this morning, Hadad," she said, extending her hand regally. "I don't have much time. What can I do for you?"

Hadad blinked, swallowed. "Well, I—I remembered it was, uh, your wedding anniversary. And—well, I'd been working on a little something as a remembrance of it. I—I wanted to give it to you. And, uh, Shobai. If—" He swallowed again and reached inside his garment. "Well, here it is. Uh, here. I—I hope you like it."

He handed it over. It had cost him two weeks' labor in his spare time, although you couldn't tell to look at it: he'd spoiled it over and over again and only after a dozen tries had he managed to come up with a finished version of the little statue that embodied the particular kind of grace he'd had in mind when he'd begun. Now he was proud of it. It was the best that he could do, however little *that* might be. "It's, uh, it's the goddess Anat. Your namesake. I worked very hard . . . I hope you and Shobai . . ."

She took it, looked it over. Her expression changed minimally several times in the course of two blinks of Hadad's clear, green eyes. The first glance dismissed it; the second, as dispassionately as any jeweler might, weighed its virtues and defects—and found it impressive, expensive, a small work of art worth many times what she'd paid for some of the artifacts in their parlor. Her final expression was one of near-dismissal. It wouldn't pay to betray any enthusiasm, she thought. He might get to expecting things. "Why, thank you, Hadad," she said, as if he'd picked a handful of flowers from the gutter and handed them to her with dirty fingers. "That's so nice of you—"

"Anat? Anat, where are you?"

Hadad's half-deflated expression changed to one of happiness. He looked past his sister-in-law to the door. "Shobai!" he said. "We're out here. In the garden."

Shobai came out to meet them. Hadad looked at him, then at Anat. Her expression turned as cold as the ice in the northern mountains. "Good morning, Shobai," Anat said stiffly. "Where have you been?"

"Uh, I got held over at the encampment," Shobai said carelessly. His face was flushed, his hair tousled; his garment was smudged. It wasn't the usual Shobai at all. "Hadad: what are you doing here?"

"He brought me an anniversary present, Shobai," she said pointedly. "For our anniversary yesterday. I missed you last night, Shobai. So did the guests we'd invited."

Hadad writhed inwardly, his anguish painful in the extreme. "I—I can come back later, if—"

"No, no." Anat's voice was cool and collected. "It was kind of you to remember our anniversary, Hadad. It was very thoughtful of you. I'm sure both Shobai and I are very grateful." Her words weren't directed to Hadad at all. "That is, if Shobai remembers what an anniversary is. Or what it means."

"Remember?" Shobai said, his voice full of anger and annoyance. It was transparently obvious that he'd forgotten the whole thing. "Anat, you forget yourself. For your information—" He cleared his throat, groping for an easy out, stalling. "For your information, I was talking to the merchant Aqhat. I was talking about . . . buying you a new house. A new house over in the neighborhood of the Temple of Ishtar. A better neighborhood. A place where one can really entertain. I've picked out a couple of places," he improvised, remembering the real estate market report. "There was the home of Yahila, the king's vizier: it has the roof garden and the little pool with the waterfall. . . ."

The change in Anat was remarkable. "Oh, *darling!*" she purred. She stepped into his arms, forgetting Hadad altogether. As she embraced Shobai, her voice cooing in his ear, her throat full of the peculiar huskiness that only money, possessions, riches could bring forth in a woman, Hadad's little gift slipped from her garment and fell onto the stones. Hadad looked down; the head of the goddess Anat had broken off. He winced, but smiled over her shoulder at Shobai's triumphant face. Shobai did not notice either his discomfiture or his gently reassuring smile; he led Anat back into the

73

house proper, leaving the little statue in two pieces on the tiles.

After a couple of moments, Hadad walked forward and, stooping, retrieved the little pieces of fired clay. Perhaps he could fix them back together again. Or . . . Well, perhaps it didn't really matter all that much after all.

II

Hadad continued to finger the two little pieces of clay all the way through the house, out into the street, and down the avenue. There was a hurt disquiet within him which had not yet reached, and might not get around to reaching, resentment. His hand probed within his garment where the two hunks of clay reposed, feeling the shapes, feeling the wrongness of them now that they were not a single organic thing but a pair of disconnected lumps. "Well," he said in a resigned undertone, "maybe I was premature. After all, the statue was just—well, something that *I* did. Who am I to go putting on airs? Why should anyone treat something of mine as something special? Now, if it were Amitanu, the court sculptor, the man who did the statue to Dagon before the Temple, that might be another thing."

His face, as always, mirrored his feelings; he had developed no talent at all for dissembling. There was still the look of shocked hurt there when he passed the brown-haired man with the drawn face and the haunted expression; the man turned, after a beat, and looked after Hadad as he limped down the street, his heart a desolate waste but his mind set on not admitting it to himself. The man moved forward, followed him. Halfway down the block he caught up with Hadad easily, his normal steps outdistancing Hadad's ungainly, crooklegged pace. "Excuse me," the man said. Hadad blinked, saw him at last. He stopped and looked at the man, the hurt in his eyes real. "Excuse me," the man said. "You looked as though—it's none of my business, but—" He started to withdraw, embarrassed; then he looked into Hadad's eyes again. "Is there something I can do for you? To help? I mean . . ."

Hadad sighed. Then he saw the expression of honest

concern in the man's face and his own expression changed. "Oh, I—I thank you, but—I was just preoccupied. I wasn't feeling well, and I wasn't thinking of what I was doing or where I was going." There was warmth and gratitude in his voice now. *How nice of the man to think of—why, a stranger and all!* "How kind of you to say that," he said. "I'm all right. It was just—"

The man had a worn face and large, compassionate eyes that had known some hurt of their own. There was an air of decency, of comradeship, about him. Instinctively, Hadad's heart went out to him in friendship. The man seemed to understand. "Well, if you're sure. You see, you looked as though you'd lost your best friend, or someone close and dear to you. I—I've lost friends. I've lost dear ones. I know how such things can hurt." He put a hand on Hadad's shoulder. "I realize you don't want a stranger to pry. But if there's anything I can do to help—well, my name is Jacob. I live in the street of the aqueduct. Ask for me there; everyone there knows me. If you need help . . ."

Hadad impulsively took his hand. "Well, thank you. Thank you very much. I'm quite taken aback. I'm not used to people volunteering acts of kindness. Jacob, you say? I'm Hadad. I have a little shop in the bazaar down the road there, just past the well. I'm pleased to meet you."

"Well met," the man said. He smiled his guarded smile; only the eyes expressed him totally. "I couldn't help noticing. Are you in pain?"

"Oh. The leg? No, no. That happened when I was a child. There was no money to have it fixed. The leg never grew any longer. I don't feel it, I assure you. But thank you for asking. Now I'm happy. I've made a friend, haven't I? That's always a happy occasion. I'll remember: Jacob, in the street of the aqueduct. And, look, I'd be happy to see you at my shop sometime, if you're free."

"I'd be delighted," Jacob said. Hadad tried to guess his age. Forty? A little less. There was something about him, something special. "But—I'm on my way to somewhere, and I'm late. Well met, I say, and good fortune to you. God be with you."

"And you." Hadad, still smiling faintly, watched him go down the street and turn a corner. What an odd, what a nice meeting! But what a strange man. His accent wasn't the local one, that was certain. Something southern, most likely. And that strange farewell: "God be with you." Which god? Bel? Dagon? Baal? He shrugged it off; the important thing was the kindness. It would be nice to run into this Jacob again sometime.

Hadad's appointment was short and sweet. The merchant complimented him on the work he'd done and handed him a small purse. "You're a fine craftsman, young man, for all that you're not a member of the guild. If I'm not being too nosy, why not? Get in trouble with them?"

"No, sir," Hadad said, hefting the purse. *Even more than I'd hoped for!* he thought, excited. "No, I lost my father young. There wasn't money to buy me a place in someone's shop to learn the craft formally. I just sort of picked it up. You know, here and there, keeping my eyes open."

"Well, that isn't the worst apprenticeship, you know. It's how I learned business myself. I started out poor too. 'Ibalum the Shabby,' they called me at first. But you've a real knack. Any artists in your blood?"

"Oh, yes, sir," Hadad said proudly. "My father was a metalworker, and my older brother, Shobai, he's the best smith in town. He does work for——"

"Oh. Shobai. A good worker, but look, you've more of a talent for this than he has. By far." He shook off Hadad's horrified protests. "No, let me have my own opinion, young man. In many places the word of Ibalum the Merchant would not be disputed in such matters. Don't you dispute me."

"You're too kind."

"Nonsense. Look, my young friend. How do you live? I mean, what's your main source of income?"

"Sir? Oh, for the most part, I make—well, little images of the gods. For use in worship. I sell them."

"Yes," Ibalum said, his smile satiric. "For a pittance, I'm sure. And then the priests of Dagon, or whoever, charge your customers six times as much for blessing them. I know the routine. Don't tell me." Again he waved away Hadad's protests. "Well, that's neither here nor there. You've given me full measure, and not everybody in Haran does that, let me tell you."

"Well, sir, I did my best——"

"Yes, and not everybody does *that,* either. Young man, I'm afraid you don't know your worth. If I had time, I'd do something foolish and teach it to you. That shows you how senile I've become at the end of my long career in trade."

"Senile, sir? Oh, no . . ."

"What else would you call it? Now, if I were to pay you the absolute bottom price on everything, and let you go on thinking you're just a hopeless dub, a hacker at this trade, *that* would be good business. Yet here I am wanting to sing your praises. Raise your prices. That sort of thing."

"Well, thank you, sir."

"Thank you. And—look, young man. I'll be out of the city for some time. You stay in touch with my brokers here, though, and find out when I'm due to return. I don't want to lose touch with you. I want to see you again. I hope to give you further business. Maybe steer a friend or two your way, people who appreciate nice things."

"*Thank* you, sir!" Hadad's heart was light again. The bad mood had passed.

The feeling lasted all the way through town. And then he was back in his own bazaar, greeting old friends again, being greeted. His heart lifted all the way, as it usually did in the bazaar, among his friends; it was only on the way home to his cluttered but empty single room that he ever got lonely. Here—here he had such good friends, such dear friends. Marsatum, the greengrocer's wife, whose children he'd helped to nurse through an attack of the lung disease; Bunu-ishdar the blacksmith, whose wife he, Hadad, had helped to midwife through a difficult breech birth; Yahila, the butcher's wife; Uzziya, the spice merchant . . .

As he came through the square, however, his leg, dragging at its usual grotesque angle, got in the way of a passing customer; the man tripped and went down on one knee. He turned and cursed Hadad for a damned shabby cripple. His voice was strong; it carried. There was a momentary hush in the little square, and suddenly the visitor found the mammoth bulk of Bunu-ishdar blocking his path. The blacksmith towered a full head over the entire crowd, and his mammoth fists were the size of two leather bottles of wine.

"Look here, friend. Perhaps you'd be happier at one of the other bazaars," the giant said. "If so, I'll be glad to escort you to the edge of this one and point out the way to you."

"Why . . . ?" The visitor was speechless for a moment. Tradesmen were supposed to be servile. They were in business to curry your favor. "Why, who are you to tell me where to shop? I've half a mind to call a guard."

The big man looked down at him with a triumphant smile. "Call away—once you've left us for good. You'll find that not only does every merchant and tradesman in this bazaar owe enormous, unrepayable personal debts to that damned cripple, as you saw fit to call him—but that the guard who works this quarter is a man named Ishi-dagan, whom the damned cripple saved from a bad beating or worse when he'd been attacked by a gang of thieves. Hadad doesn't look like much to a swell like you, perhaps, but he's got a good hand with a slingshot. And let me tell you, my friend, we value him a great deal more than we value your business. Now if you'll be so good as to leave? Or am I going to have to tuck you under one arm and . . . ?" But the visitor had thought better of the matter by now and was beating a hasty retreat.

The whole matter had been hardly more than an embarrassment to Hadad, who didn't like people to make a fuss over him. He yearned to change the subject and turned to the greengrocer's wife for diversion. "Say, Marsatum," he said. "Look what I just came by." He pulled out the little purse he'd been given by Ibalum the merchant. "I sold a little statue to a rich merchant. He was very complimentary about my work, and—" He stopped. He'd opened the purse and was astounded. "Why, look at all that! Good heavens, who'd imagine he'd pay that much for—"

"And in gold, not base metal," Marsatum said. "Oh, Hadad. How wonderful. Now you can buy that winter coat you wanted so much. We all worried about you so last year, when the weather stayed so raw for so long."

"Coat? Uh, oh, yes. Yes. But look! Not coin gold; *lump* gold. How much could that be worth, now? And—oh, Marsatum. Here's my chance. I never get any gold to work with. If I can make myself a little ceramic stove for working it, now . . . Wouldn't my mother love a little Ishtar, made of this? And, look, I can afford the wax now for the casting."

"Hadad!" her voice showed her exasperation. "Here you've been given enough money to cover your winter expenses, maybe even to move to a better room, and what do you think of but . . . ?" She couldn't find words to express what she felt; it came out as a wordless cry of something rather like anger. But there was no real fire in it. "Hadad, why in the name of all the gods don't you ever think about the future? Think about yourself, about taking care of yourself? We all worry about you half the time. You've no common sense at all."

"Common sense? Me?" he shot a blank glance at her. He wasn't listening; he was just being polite. His mind was elsewhere; it was shaping a delicate little image of the goddess.

"Yes, you, you dummy! Look, with that money I know what I'd do if I were you. For one thing, I'd go out and find a girl. I'd do something in the world to cure my loneliness. Here you are, eighteen, nineteen, whatever—there's no sense in a nice young man like you going home every night to an empty room, sleeping alone . . ."

"Girl?" Hadad said. Incredibly, he blushed. *Just as I thought,* she said silently to herself. *A virgin.* "But Marsatum. I mean, who'd have somebody like me—shabby, skinny, with this silly leg of mine jutting out like this, all stiff and ugly? Marsatum, I've no illusions. I know what girls want—even if their fathers *don't* get into the picture. Their fathers, now, they want a man with a future, somebody who can afford to raise them a batch of fine healthy grandchildren. The girls— well, even the girls of the quarter, who haven't any fathers to think about in the first place, they want somebody handsome and tall and strong—someone like Shobai."

"Shobai?" Marsatum's tone was incredulous. "Shobai? For the love of heaven, Hadad. You're talking the wildest-eyed nonsense I've ever heard in my life. A woman wants a man who'll come home every night, not a man whose eye is always wandering. Not a man who'll stick it in virtually anything that comes along, just out of vanity. Not a man who's going to bring home, one of these days, a nice case of some disease or other."

"Marsatum!" Hadad's face was red. "You shouldn't speak that way of Shobai, just because—"

"My goodness, Hadad. Do you think the quarter hasn't got eyes and ears? Why, only last night—"

Hadad put his hands over his ears. "I won't listen. Look, Marsatum. He's my brother. Besides my mother, he's all I've got, him and Anat—"

"Anat? That cold fish? Look, I could tell you some nice tales about her, too." Hadad pushed his hands against his ears even harder, but the words still got through. "Well, cold fish or no, she knows that husband of hers is tripping around behind her back. And she's got her own ideas as to how you pay a husband back for that kind of foolery. She—"

"Marsatum! Please don't go on! Stop right there, please! I don't want to hear anymore!"

"Just watch her doorstep, Hadad. Watch her door, the next time Shobai goes out of town. Just watch. . . ."

III

Jacob stood in the street, trembling with rage and mortification, watching his father-in-law Laban's great gross bulk recede down the avenue with the skinny form of the scribe Ishiluna at his side. His fists clenched and unclenched; he tried to swallow, but found his throat was dry.

How *dare* Laban speak to him that way in public! How *dare* he curse his son-in-law in front of a third party, a man not of the family? How *dare* the great bloated buffalo accuse him of dishonesty, of mismanagement, simply on the word of a shallow-minded fool who idly dipped into his accounts and found an apparent discrepancy in the receivables? He, Jacob, who had put in thankless years of work in his service, working always on his behalf and taking nothing for himself?

Worse: how dare Laban berate a man in front of his sons? Levi and Dan had been standing there talking to their father when Laban had come up; they had witnessed the whole thing—and they had seen that Jacob made no move to defend himself from the older man's attacks, where another man might have struck Laban for such talk. This could only increase their already entrenched disrespect for their father.

But there you were. They were his sons—but they were not the sons of a love match, either of them. Levi was the third son of Leah, his favorite Rachel's older sister. He had never loved Leah for so much as a moment and had only taken her—quite against his will—as part of the bargain with Laban that had eventually won him Rachel, the true and only love of his life. Dan was the son of Jacob's concubine Bilhah. He had not loved the concubine either. The boys' mothers had known this—and had raised their sons to know it, their sons and the sons of Zilpah, the other concubine. All of them resented him. All of them felt contempt for him, mired in debt to a man who treated him like the very dirt underfoot.

And all of them—the elder wife, the two concubines, and his ten sons by them—all of them treated poor Rachel abominably. This hurt, somehow, much worse than all the other burdens he had to bear. Poor barren Rachel! She'd kept most of her youthful beauty through all the years of disappointments, false pregnancies, the single miscarriage that had killed their hopes in the one pregnancy she'd had in all these years. Only now was she beginning to show lines of care, of unhappiness, in her lovely face. . . .

But that wasn't what he'd loved her for, anyway. The streets were full of pretty women. It was just that the time he met her, those many years ago, he'd known—known somehow in his heart—that this was the soul mate he had yearned for all through his youth and young manhood. His heart had gone out to her then, open and unguarded. And she had returned his love from the very first. It had been true love, once and forever.

He sighed, and turned his weary steps homeward. The years had gone by so quickly—and they'd left her barren; barren in a home in which three other women had lain with her husband, and each had borne him strapping sons with which they taunted her, as women tended to do. It was a terrible thing, in this society, for a woman to go barren like that, to fail again and again to give her husband a child, even a girl-child. It did terrible things to a woman's heart to see everyone else outstrip her in what was considered a woman's basic function.

How could he reassure her? He tried night and day. His love had been constant and all-embracing. He'd told her of his love, showed her, and still she was beginning to grow apart from him, sealing herself inside her protective shell like one of the forbidden creatures of the sea. But no matter how many times he told her, no matter how gentle and persuasive his caresses had been, she had begun to withdraw from him in her unhappiness. How could he reach out to her? How could he get through to her?

He didn't know; but he did know that he had to try. He himself needed her terribly, isolated as he was from virtually all other sources of solace: a stranger even after all these years in Haran—a stranger in a strange land, an exiled ruler in a foreign clime.

Ah! The pain of it! Now he thought, as he'd begun to think recently, of his old father, Isaac, wrinkled and blind; of his fiercely protective mother, who had preferred him to his slightly older twin brother, Esau; of Esau himself—redheaded, terrible-tempered, impulsive—and of lovely Canaan itself, the beautiful Land of Promise that his grandfather, Abraham, had been given by the One True God, whom some called El-Shaddai and others called by the mystic names no man should speak aloud . . .

A pain went through his heart: *The God of whom he, Jacob, was the hereditary priest and prophet, and whom he, Jacob, had served so ill by leaving Canaan that way, whatever his reasons for doing so. The God who had spoken to him, Jacob, so memorably on his way northward into exile, and who had never spoken so much as a word to him since his foot had first touched foreign soil not consecrated to Him. The God who had deserted him, and would likely continue to desert him until . . .*

Jacob quickened his steps. There it was again: the thought that had been preying on his mind all this week. If only he could get back to Canaan, taking his wives and women and sons . . . if he could once and for all settle his debts with Laban, and be a free man again and not a bondman . . . would not all of his troubles begin to settle themselves? Would not the God of his fathers cease His persecution of him, and put new life in Rachel's loins? If he could get back to Canaan and settle his accounts, too, with his fiery-tempered brother, Esau, whom he'd wronged so . . .

Oh, Isaac! Father forgotten! Rebekah, mother neglected! Oh, forsaken Land of Promise!

But now he spotted Rachel in the street. She had gone to the bazaar to shop, and she bore a packet from the greengrocer's. "Rachel!" he said, his voice rising. She turned, waited for him, that hurt smile on her face, her eyes downcast after a first glance at him. "How nice to run into you, my dear. . . ."

She turned away from him when he approached, though. "Rachel?" he said. "What's the matter, darling?"

He looked down at her drawn face. It was full of undisguised self-loathing. "Nothing, Jacob. It's just that . . . well, I've got my period again. Once again I've failed you. Will it never end?"

He took her hands and agonized for her. And again she withdrew from him. What could he tell her? That it didn't matter to him? That would be small comfort to her, when the evident truth was that it mattered the world to her, Rachel. *Oh God of my fathers! Forgive! Forgive!*

Oshiyahu had brought Yassib to town. In the morning, Yassib had been presented to Oshiyahu's dark-eyed daughter Halima, an olive-skinned beauty with wide-set eyes and full lips that curved warmly in a bewitching smile. The dowry was set, the marriage had been arranged. Oshiyahu, with a soldier's immediacy of mind, did not believe in putting things off. If you're going to do something, do it now. You never know when you'll go to war and die.

Yassib's head was swimming. Overnight his entire life had changed. One day you were a young soldier, engaged to a girl—or at least promised; there had never been anything formal between them, after all, just a sort of understanding—and wondering about your future. The next day you were promised, engaged, formally committed to another girl, one you'd barely had a chance to meet—and your future was assured. You were now on the rise, and at a devil of a clip. It was the sort of thing to leave you in a daze.

Now, walking through the city streets, coming home from the visit to the city scribe's office where the formal agreement between them had been posted, the two men slowed their pace to an amble. It was mainly Oshiyahu talking now; Yassib's replies had begun to confine themselves largely to murmurs of assent or agreement. He couldn't quite think straight. Naturally ambitious, he couldn't get used to the idea of ambition being a thing so easily gratified.

Oshiyahu was talking:

". . . a fine city, all in all. It's had its troubles, of course: wars, that outbreak of plague a couple of generations back. But all in all a city favored by the gods, I'd say, if there *are* any gods. Oh, come now, man, don't look shocked. When's the last time you saw an old soldier who believed in those phantoms they prate about in the temples?

"But look: a favored city. A city where the living's good. A man can get rich here quite easily. All he has to do is have his wits about him and be the type who lands on his feet—and converts his mistakes to strokes of apparent genius. I tell you, that was the main thing I had to offer as an officer, coming up: the ability to cover my errors. And let me tell you, I made plenty of them. Although, in my own defense I have to say I haven't made a hell of a lot of them lately. That's because I'm acting on experience now. I wish to heaven I could impart some of that experience to His Royal Highness right now, or to some of the addlepated pacifist advisers who've been leading him up the garden path recently. Those damned fools have never been to war; they've never even seen what happens to a city which *has* been to war—and lost.

"Look up there. Do you see a full complement of guards on the walls? The hell you do! You see a skeleton force. And the town garrison is at half strength right now. And my own army—*our* army. You've no idea how much of a fight I have to get into every term, trying to get the money to stay in operation at all, much less increase our strength against the threat from the north. They don't think there *is* any threat at all. If I could only get across—"

"Sir?" Yassib broke in now. "I meant to ask. How bad is it up there? I mean, what if they *did* turn our way?"

"Huh." Oshiyahu broke stride to look him in the eye; it was a stern and serious look. "Look, son, if they come this way, why—according to the intelligence reports I receive almost daily, they'd wipe up the ground with us. The city of Haran, after three days' siege, would be a burned-out hulk. The men would be—gods!—lying in pieces in the streets. The women—damnation, better not even think about the women. They'd have it worst of all, they and the children. I've run into people like these before, across the Great Sea when I was a boy, doing a stint as a mercenary, learning my trade. We happened upon a town that had fallen prey to the likes of these. Not the same people, of course, but savages of exactly the same stripe. I've never seen such wretched, bastardly butchery in my whole life, not even after the Assyrians attacked the towns east of Mari. These people up north—whoever they are, wherever they come from across the Great Mountains—they're the same kind of people. They make the Assyrians look softhearted by comparison. I know. I've got runners all over that country up there; whenever a runner comes in, I send another man out the same day. And the reports I get—"

"Yes, sir?" It was occurring to Yassib, at last, that these barbarians his commander was talking about were people he might well have signed up to fight. Savages!

"Well, you might just not believe them. You might not. But you'd have to, eventually." His tone changed suddenly. There was something wistful, almost elegiac about it. "Look around you. A lovely city. Sober, decent people. They can't imagine it, and their leaders don't believe me either. They even talk of disarming. Of sending message-bearers up into the north country to tell the barbarians that we ... uh, what's the phrase ... greet them in peace and mean them no harm. This sort of garbage is supposed to turn them aside."

"And you're sure it won't?"

"Gods! What it'll do is convince them we're a bunch of milksops who won't fight. It'll draw them the way the smell of honey draws a bear. Why, look, Yassib: you've seen a lion pull down a gazelle. But they only go after a gazelle in an emergency. A lion would rather eat a coney, weak and defenseless, than a gazelle any day. A gazelle, frightened, panicky, can shake you up with a well-placed kick, putting you out of commission for days on end. You may even starve to death, even if you are king of beasts. As long as there's a plentiful supply of coneys, no lion is going after a gazelle. Do you get me?"

"Yes, sir. But what are the chances that—well, if we don't send them any messages at all, and strengthen our defenses, and all—what are the chances that we can survive all this?"

"Fifty-fifty, my friend. No more. The only chance we have is if they decide to pass through some other region, not ours. Whatever region they pass through will be a wasteland a month later. A wasteland. A place even the vultures will shun, for want of something to eat. It will be a valley of skulls and bones. Haran, you, me—we'll be a distant memory, a heap of stones beside the trade route. And if that happens, the gods help the people to the south. A lush green place like Canaan? It won't stand a chance."

Yassib swallowed—and tried to hide the shudder that ran through him. But then he shook himself free of his fears and straightened his back. Surely, he thought, surely it couldn't be *that* bad.

Danataya, crushed, said, "I—I don't believe it. It can't be true. It must have been someone else."

Her uncle shook his head. "Not a chance. I was there, do you hear? I was there paying my taxes for the quarter. I heard it all myself. They've announced the banns, your Yassib and this girl, what's-her-name, the daughter of the commander. Your boyfriend has picked a better way to rise in the world. That's why he's been stalling you."

"But—no. He would have told me. He would have—"

"Look, Danataya. As far as I'm concerned, that finishes it. We've been keeping you on partly as a favor to my brother, the gods give his soul rest. But partly—well, to be brutally frank, as long as you'd some hopes of making a good marriage and perhaps repaying some of your debt to us. But now? Now I'm afraid I have to be—well, realistic about things. You'll have to be out as of the first. I've got someone moving in. . . ."

"I have no job yet—no money—"

"I'm sorry. I'd like to make the sentimental choice. I'd like to do you a favor. But things have been tough on your aunt and me, and we've no other choice but to do as I said. I'm sorry, but look, even if Yassib changed his mind, Danataya, we've already committed ourselves. The room's been rented." There was an annoyed embarrassment in his voice now; a hard edge. "I'm afraid you'll have to go."

He turned away, went out the door. Danataya stood looking at the bare walls, seeing nothing. *It can't be true,* she thought desperately. But in her heart she knew it was. Her life had changed. Permanently.

IV

In the morning, Hirgab, commander of Haran's northern force and second-in-command in the army to Oshiyahu, rode out to the far outposts with his adviser Reshef. The air was cool, the weather pleasant and mild; the soft wind sang over the steppes. They made good time.

For many leagues the path wound single file, or scarcely better, through the foothills. Then, as they came down out of the rolling country onto the flat plains, the trail widened, and Reshef pulled up alongside his leader. Hirgab nodded at him: recognition without affection. Reshef, he'd decided earlier, was a rare piece of goods. What you saw was a human fox, crafty, alienated, cunning: a man who saw other men not as creatures like himself, but as members of some inferior species. His feral smile was deadlier than another man's scowl of rage.

Hirgab looked at him once again. "As long as there's no scandal I suppose it's none of my business," he said in a matter-of-fact tone, "but word is getting around about you and what's-her-name. You know, the smith's wife."

"Ah?" Reshef said. His smile was a jackal's. "I thought I'd covered my tracks. Well, no matter. She's a discreet little piece, and she knows his goings and comings better than he does. Little chance of his coming home to surprise us."

"Well, watch yourself. He's a big bastard. He could break you in half." Hirgab stole a quick look at his adviser. Well, perhaps he shouldn't use the word "bastard" that way, just tossing it off. Reshef was touchy about his birth, the result of a wrong-side-of-the-blanket liaison between a nobleman and a pauper's daughter; it had hampered his rise at first, but had whetted his ambition.

"It's all right," Reshef said. "I've that which makes all men equal." He patted his sword hilt. Well, true, Hirgab thought. Reshef had a rare hand with the blade. "But look," the ferret-faced man said. "We're there, aren't we? That would be Balami's signal fire." He pointed out across the steppe. "Here, you stay behind and I'll ride ahead. We're pretty far ahead of our lines. You never know when somebody's going to take over your post. Can't have the second-in-command of the army riding into a trap. I'll check it out and signal back to you when it's all right to come on."

"Good," Hirgab said. "I'll wait here." He watched the sharp-faced little man spur his horse forward and break into a gallop across the prairie.

Reshef broke stride coming into Balami's little camp. The picket greeted him, spear at the ready, and the pair exchanged salutes as Reshef dismounted, all styleless efficiency. Balami indicated the prisoner. "Here's a real find, sir," he said. "I found him wandering, half-dead with thirst, a bit north of here. He seems to have been the sole survivor of a raid by the nomads on a little Hurrian city to the northwest."

Reshef looked down at the prisoner. The man was emaciated, bloody, his clothing tattered. "Can he talk?" he said. "Here, let's sit him up. Whatever he's got to tell us won't wait."

The two of them propped the gaunt man up against a rock. "Here," Reshef said, "who are you? Where do you come from?"

The prisoner blinked, tried to speak. Balami uncorked a leather bottle of water and gave the man a drink. "Thanks," the prisoner said. "I—I'm from Ditana. Ditana is no more. The barbarians—"

Reshef knelt next to him. "Tell us about them," he said. "We need to know. We may be forced to fight them ourselves. Every scrap of information will come in handy."

"The—the siege went on for days," the prisoner said. His eyes looked through the two men and saw nothing. He was remembering, and the memories registered on his face in a stunned expression of pain. "The old, the children, were dying of thirst and starvation. Then—then there came a runner from the nomads' camp. No: runner isn't the word I

87

was looking for. In—in fact, he seemed to be a man of some substance among them. He said his name was Manouk. He came under a flag of truce. He spoke well. He brought greetings from his commander, a man he identified only as 'the Leader.' He didn't give this 'Leader' a name, then or ever. He said only that this 'Leader' was a king of kings—leader of the Shepherd Kings who rule over the nomads. He said that if we laid down our arms and swung the gates wide, it would mean the end of bloodshed. Our women and children would be spared. We—our king made them an offer, a qualified surrender. This Manouk, he took the message back to his 'Leader,' and when he returned, it was with the news that our terms had been accepted." He paused, closed his eyes. The expression of pain on his face was acute now.

"Yes?" Reshef said. "Go on, man. Get it out."

"We—we opened the gates. Stacked our arms. And—"

"Damn it, you!" Reshef shook him by the neck. The picket Balami cried out in protest. Reshef turned a savage face to him. "Keep out of this," he said. He shook the prisoner again. "What happened?" he said. "Go on."

The prisoner's first words came out in a half sob. "They fell on us like butchers. They slaughtered us all, all. Me, somebody brained me with a rock. I awoke later under a pile of dead men. Somebody must have thought I was dead, too. They had piled up the bodies, intending to set fire to us, and then somebody—perhaps the 'Leader' fellow—had called it off. They had simply left. I walked the streets. They were full of . . . pieces of bodies . . . of dead babies, dead children, hacked and gutted by their spears . . . and the women . . . my own woman, Tasuba . . ."

"I see," Reshef said. "And this Manouk fellow. He seems to be the one to deal with, then?" The prisoner turned his face away, his eyes still closed. "Damn your eyes!" Reshef said savagely. "You answer me, or I'll—" But as he shook the gaunt man, his prisoner gave a last giddy shudder and seemed to faint dead away. "Here!" Reshef said in cold rage. "Don't do that! Come alive there!" Then, in disgust, he threw the prisoner away from him and stood up, wiping the blood from his hands.

Balami bent over the prisoner, touching him here and there. "There's no pulse," he said. "He's dead."

"Well, good riddance," Reshef said. He was looking off into the distance, thinking. His face slipped into a small, crafty smile. *Well*, he thought, *you've come upon a little windfall, haven't you? One too good to share with anyone—*

except perhaps on your own terms. He weighed the matter for a moment and then came to a decision, a commitment. "Balami," he said. "Reach me that water bottle, will you?"

The guard turned his back. As he did, Reshef drew his sword and, in one quick movement, buried it in the picket's back. It protruded from the man's front; Reshef had to kick him in the middle of the back to free the blade. The guardsman fell heavily on his face. Reshef bent over him and finished him off with a mighty slash across the neck. Then, a thoughtful look on his face, he stepped over to the prisoner and stabbed the dead body in several places. Then he wiped his blade clean, and in an afterthought, he dirtied the guardsman's sword in his own fresh blood.

"Very well," he said to the two dead men. "You grabbed Balami's sword and killed him. Then I killed you." He thought about it for a moment and remembered to dip his now-clean swordpoint in the dead man's blood. Only when he was totally satisfied with the little scenario in his mind did he mount and ride to the top of the rise to signal Hirgab.

Waiting for his commander to approach, he smiled his weasel's smile and pondered the information he'd received. Manouk, eh? The man to deal with—unless one could get through to this "Leader" of theirs.

His smile widened. He squatted and drew his stained sword. He drew a rough map of the northern lands on the dry sand with his swordpoint. Here were the High Mountains, just so—and here was the known route of the nomads so far, due south. . . .

But no, that was wrong. South? But Ditana—that was no more than a couple of days' ride from here. And it was well to the west of the original route of their southward march. Well to the west . . .

Reshef bit his thin lower lip. His heart beat fast. His eyes shone with a glint that was part excitement, part apprehension, part wild panic. With a trembling hand he sketched in the site of dead Ditana, far off the earlier route of the barbarians.

The route had changed. They'd turned.

Turned toward Haran . . .

"What a shame," Hirgab said. "You relax for a moment around some of these people and they'll do you in." He prodded the body of the prisoner with one boot. "Good thing you were there," he added. "Good work."

"Yes," Reshef said. "No sense spoiling Balami's good

name, though. He did a good job capturing this chap. I'd just—well, put it down that he was killed defending his post. That way the widow will get her pension. Right?"

The suggestion was so unlike Reshef that Hirgab looked hard at his subordinate; on Reshef's face, however, there was no more than the usual guile. "I suppose so," he said. "Did he say anything about the prisoner? Who he was, where he'd come from? Those are fairly recent wounds—a couple of days at most."

"No, sir," Reshef lied. "Perhaps he was injured in one of the border wars." He was improvising quickly now, and a bright idea began to glow in the back of his mind. "I did hear him speak. He had an accent. An accent I've heard before— in the hills north of Mari."

"Mari, eh? Then what was he doing this far west?"

"I don't know. But he said something about the nomads."

"Ah. That's interesting. Perhaps he came from a town that had been in battle with them. Mari, eh? That means the nomads are heading south, over to the east of us. . . ." He shook his head. "Well, Mari's loss is our gain. Those damn fools down there won't know how to handle the nomads. They're all hotheads, just like Oshiyahu. You know him. He'd have us fight them to the death. A wiser man would figure out some way to deal with them. You don't just put your head down and charge, not when the odds are like those."

Reshef looked at his commander, the small vulpine smile playing on the edges of his thin lips. So that was the way the wind was blowing, eh? Deal with them? A pacifist in the second spot in the army? And—he reminded himself pointedly—a pacifist who, rumor had it, had the ear of the king; Hirgab was distantly related to half the court.

He helped Hirgab mount and then turned to his own horse. He stood there looking at the animal, his hands on the reins.

He'd done right silencing Balami. He'd known that at the time, although he couldn't have come up with an immediate reason for it. What Balami had heard had meant that he had to die; he, Reshef, had to be the only person in the entire domain of Haran who had access to this new information. The nomads were heading their way—and nobody but him, Reshef, had any idea of this. It gave him some lead on everyone else. It gave him time to think.

He mounted, the same pensive look on his face. Of course, Haran was doomed. That went without saying. It also went without saying that he, Reshef, wasn't going to go down fighting for his beloved city. He was going to figure out some way to—well, not only to escape this fate, but to profit from it all. He was going to survive the fall of Haran without a scratch on his precious hide, and he was going to get out with a purseful of money. And somehow, he was going to milk the situation for power as well as money. But how?

Ah, yes. In the meantime he had to improve his situation vis-à-vis the city, the army, and the king. He looked over at the not-too-bright Hirgab. With Hirgab's connections, he could rise quite quickly. It would take some time for the nomads' column to work its slow way here; they tended, from all reports, to camp in a newly won area until their livestock had grazed the available greenery down to the dirt line. This would give him time to work out a plan. But first, he had to begin cultivating Hirgab. Cultivating him very carefully . . .

That evening, far to the northeast, Manouk, the man of no tribe, second-in-command to the great chieftain of chieftains who had been born Karakin, in the High Mountains, but whose name no man dared pronounce now, strode down the long row of firebrands that stood like a colonnade to either side of the path that led to the tent of the Leader. Guardsmen snapped to attention one at a time as he passed; finally the last of these barred his way to the tent.

"Manouk," he said. "To see the Leader."

"Yes, sir." The guard stepped to one side. Manouk walked inside. A central fire burned before him; past it, he could see the twin guardsmen, huge and heavily armed. Between them, the two perfectly paired slave girls, both naked and chained, stood ready to serve their master food and drink at a command. Manouk gave them a glance and for the fortieth time wondered if even the Leader could tell the girls apart.

And between them . . . the Leader of the Shepherd Kings.

He was twice the bulk of either of the two guardsmen, with massive shoulders and a barrel chest. His unruly hair and tangled black beard were both flecked with gray, but there was little other hint of age about him. He looked, if anything, like a great bear—until you saw the eyes. The eyes were those of a reptile.

"My Leader," Manouk said. "The prisoner made his way to the outposts of Haran. Our men saw him captured. Word will have reached Haran of the fall of Ditana by now."

"Good," the rumbling bass voice said. "Woman: wine for the captain."

The slave on his left reached forward to pour wine into a

bowl—and stumbled. The red juice splashed on the dark boots of the Leader. He looked up at her with those basilisk eyes. His face contorted in rage. His eyes went to the guardsman beside her. He nodded, a low growl rumbling in the back of his throat.

"No," the girl said, shrinking back. Her slim hand went to the collar around her neck. The other instinctively went to her naked loins. She started to turn toward the guard—and the wild swing of his heavy sword caught her just below the chin. Blood spouted. Her slim body swayed. The sword swung again, a mighty backswing.

Her head rolled at their feet. Her body crumpled to the ground.

The Leader looked around, the mad rage still upon him. He looked at the girl's twin, cowering beside him. His voice was a cavernous snarl, full of hatred and animal rage. "They were a matched pair." He spat the words out. "Now they are worth nothing." He nodded to the second guardsman. "Yes," he said to the man with the sword. "Yes. Now!"

This time the guardsman's bloody errand required but a single swing.

Manouk had watched, silently, straight-faced. One did not show emotion around the Leader. Now he reached down for the fallen wine bottle. He shook it; there was still wine in the bottom. He held it up, a question in his eye. The Leader nodded; Manouk drank. He avoided looking at the slaves as they cleaned up the results of the Leader's murderous wrath.

The Leader settled himself back against the cushions. "Now," he said. His voice still trembled, but with what emotion, Manouk could not say. "You said Haran," the bass voice said. "What is in Haran? What should I know about Haran?"

CHAPTER FIVE

I

"Khalkeus! Khalkeus, let me in!"

Xena's voice was high-pitched, nervous, nasal; it carried through the oak door, through the interior of the large apartment Minos had set aside for the metalsmith in the great House of the Double Axe. Nikos stood near the door, his manner showing his hesitancy. He looked at Kirta, the question in his eyes.

Kirta scowled. "What a time to—" He sighed. "Tell her to—but no. She won't listen to you." He put down the bellows and went to the door. "Xena," he said in a voice that reflected his annoyance. "Please, for the love of heaven, I'm not only busy, I'm right in the middle of something difficult and delicate."

"Please, Khalkeus. Only for a moment. Please . . ."

He looked at Nikos, his face going blank for a moment. He shook his head. Then, reluctantly, he unbarred the door. "Xena," he said. "If only you'd—"

But she rushed into his arms, burying her tear-stained face in his chest. He stepped back, trying to avoid her. "Please, Xena. I'm filthy as a hog. I'm covered with soot—you'll get yourself all dirty."

She pulled away from him for a second, her little hands still on his thick biceps, her face already stained by the black matter that covered his naked torso. "Oh, Khalkeus, I had to see you. I had such a dream—"

"A dream? You break into my work because of a dream? For the love of all the gods, Xena."

"But this one—it was so real. Just like the one I had a

93

week ago. There were people plotting to kill me, and—and Minos—and you. I ran and ran, but they caught me, and . . ." She reached for him again, but he pulled away. Then, with reluctance, he put one arm around her.

"Xena," he said. "My dear, it's only a dream. There's nothing more to it than that. Go back to your chambers. Here, Nikos will take you back. I'll be along soon. I have one thing left to try."

"What's the matter?" she said, concern in her face. Lukios had been coaching her; she now went to some pains to show interest in his work, where she had always let him know of her resentment of it before. "Is something wrong?"

"Well—" His brow knotted. "The formula Turios of Tyre gave me—it's not quite as simple as it sounds. All the information is there, but the firing process is much more delicate and exacting than one would think." His face relaxed as he talked about his work, and Xena took note of this. Lukios had been right: this was one way to his heart, after all. "Look," he said, leading her over to the workspace he'd carved out of the apartment.

"*Two* furnaces?" she said. "Why two of them, Khalkeus?"

Kirta winced at her use of his Cretan name; he'd asked her repeatedly to begin calling him by the name he'd been given at birth. But he softened his voice, speaking to her. "One of them is for smelting the ore," he explained. "The other is for reheating the smelted metal to soften it for hammering." The heat in the smelting oven had gone down; he opened the little door cautiously. "See?" he said. "The ore has to be completely surrounded with charcoal. I use up a lot of it. That's why the extra charcoal mounds outside. That's why we've all but leveled a forest just west of here."

"But the problem?" she said. It was difficult figuring just what sort of vague question to ask. The important thing was to keep him talking. And listen to how his tone softened when he explained it all to her!

"The problem is—well, if I expose the ore to too much carbon, the iron becomes hard and brittle. If it's exposed to air, it oxidizes again. So far most of the iron I've produced— what little there is of it—has been porous. I have to hammer the hell out of it to get anything. And the result doesn't resemble the best work of Turios in any way."

"Oh, dear." She looked up at him, smiling, careful to look as though she were hanging on his every word. She hadn't the smallest notion what he was saying. "I thought you said you had a few pure bits of it the other day. The day you came in singing like that."

"Well, yes," he said. "But we've always been able to come by pure bits of it—even while smelting copper. Or lead. The iron combines with the silica in the ore to form slag. From time to time, if you get the furnace hot enough and the atmosphere's right, the process produces small bits of fairly pure iron along with the lead. But it's all accident. What I'm trying to work on now is a process which will take the accident out of things, allow me to predict the quality of the stuff I produce with some sort of accuracy."

"Ah!" she said. "It's like magic. Alchemy."

"No, no," he said with minor impatience. "Alchemy isn't magic. It's just the application of principles. Anyone can do it if he's patient enough. I could teach you to do it, Xena. Anyone."

She ignored the inadvertent slight. "Could you, Khalkeus? Could I at least watch sometime?"

"It wouldn't bore you?" he asked. He wiped the sweat from his brow with a sooty forearm. "Oh, but look: I've ruined your dress. Go change it and get ready for supper. I'll get clean and come to you. Minos will want to see me and ask how things are going. I wish I had better news for him."

"Oh, don't worry about him. I'll handle him. You just teach me how to describe what's happening, in simple words one doesn't need to be a magus to understand. I'll be your intermediary." Her heart stopped a beat at the smile that broke out on his face. "Yes!" she said enthusiastically. "Oh, that's a *good* idea, Khalkeus—"

"Kirta," he said. "Please."

"Kirta, then. Oh, my darling, I don't care what I call you. But look: I'll handle Minos. Just give me a daily account of what's happening and coach me in how to explain it. I can handle him better than you anyhow. I've lived with him for longer."

"So you have," he beamed. "Ah, Xena. What a wonderful idea." He hugged her with one grimy arm, and she thought her heart would stop altogether. Wonderful indeed!

The stone risers towered on both sides high above the bull court. It was afternoon, late afternoon, and the sun seats were still uncomfortably warm; only a scattered gathering, mainly court hangers-on of low degree, sat there. The shade seats were two-thirds filled with people chatting, walking from one seat to the next to speak to friends, flirting, gossiping. It was a fine place to see and be seen.

It was also a place to go unnoticed. The closer one sat to the end of the court, near the exits and entrances where the dancers and the great bull entered, the less attention would be paid to one's goings and comings. Coming down the far aisle, Amphimedes had a difficult time spotting Tros of Phaistos; when he did notice the thin-faced man sitting there in the deep shade, he deliberately looked right past him. Instead of joining him immediately, he went down four rows, crossed to the far aisle, and sat down below.

In a moment Tros joined him in the aisle seat deliberately left open. "Greetings," he said. "Did you notice? That fat weasel of Xena's is sitting down front as if he were royalty. Disgusting toad! And him a slave. Gods, he comes and goes with a freedom few nobles of the blood enjoy."

"But you will remember," Amphimedes said, always the reasonable man on the surface, "he is useful to us—for now. Let him go and come. He will continue to bring us tidings of this and that." Amphimedes had brought a warm bottle of wine and made as if to pass it along; Tros shook his head. Amphimedes drank, watching the fat slave below them as he shamelessly flirted with one of the slim young male dancers who were limbering their long-fibered muscles with exercises in the court. "I saw him this morning," he said. "He says Khalkeus and Xena seem to be patching up their differences."

"It's as I told you," Tros said sourly. "I said he'd eaten Xena's bread and he was Xena's man. Never mind Minos. For Khalkeus, Minos is no more than a source of funds for those endless experiments of his. But his attachment to Xena is stronger than it looks. There was a time when he might have left her. But now—"

"Now, I'm afraid, the difference doesn't seem to be Xena, really." Amphimedes smiled at him mildly. "It seems to have more to do with these mysterious experiments that have been going on ever since Khalkeus came back from the raid on Rouso."

"I don't understand."

"Well, the slave says that Khalkeus thinks he came across some earth-shattering secret while on Rouso. Magic swords that will bite through armor like a sharp knife through butter. That sort of thing. I don't pretend to understand all this alchemic gibberish. Anyhow, you know the smith. He lives for this sort of thing the way Minos lives for power, the way you yourself, my friend, live for revolution."

"And you? Are you cooling on the revolt?" Tros's eyes flashed.

"Not at all. I continue to regard it as absolutely necessary. Minos's policies have reduced the value of our coin in all foreign lands. My own status has suffered. So has the trade that supports me—in a reduced style from the one I'd prefer. But when Minos falls, my hand will cut off his head in cold blood, not hot." He studied his hand as if it had already committed the deed, his expression detached. "It does not matter," he said. "Cold blood can kill as quickly and as decisively as hot. And cold blood makes fewer mistakes."

"Whatever you say," Tros shrugged. He didn't like personal talk like this, as if Amphimedes were accusing him of something. "What else did the fat hog say?"

"Well, that there was a time when Khalkeus first came back that Lukios thought he was going to leave, was going to stow away on some vessel somewhere and set out for whatever backward, landlocked town he hails from, far off to the east. He was really fed up—with everything."

"But what changed his mind?"

"The experiments started working. And when they did, he couldn't leave them alone. Day and night. Apparently, they're still giving him problems, but the problems are not the insoluble kind."

"But what has this to do with Xena?"

"She seems to have figured out the way to Khalkeus's heart for the first time. And the way seems to be in supporting, not competing with, his passion for experimentation. At supper last night, she gave an impassioned speech before Minos and the familiars of the inner court. Something about Khalkeus being on the edge of a discovery that could make Crete an undisputed power in the upper reaches of the Great Sea. That could challenge the might of Hittite and Egyptian alike, and that could drive away the influx of the new peoples who have been moving into the mainland to the north of here in recent years."

"Xena? Talking politics? That's a new wrinkle all right." Tros frowned nervously. "Khalkeus must have convinced her."

"Right. And think you, my friend: what if Khalkeus *has* discovered something new? Something that would make our warriors mighty?"

Tros's face took on a worried and thoughtful look. "Gods. If he armed Minos with this new secret before we struck—"

"Ah, yes. Disaster. But the word is, he's not ready to begin production. There are still problems with the process. It's almost there, mind you; but the point where he could begin making weapons with the new stuff is some distance away. This affects our plans, doesn't it?"

Tros stared at him. "Go on."

"Well, what do the auguries say now?"

"That—that we should strike on the day appointed. The same day we'd planned on."

"Ah. Perhaps we need some new and better soothsayers. A new astrologer, to read the heavens for us. Think, Tros. No man is indispensable. Am I correct?"

"I don't understand—" But the light dawned on him at last. "Or, perhaps I do. We need to step things up. Correct?"

"Exactly. The coup must take place before Khalkeus masters his new process and has a chance to apply it. Before he can arm our enemies with it."

"Yes, yes."

"And if we strike at the right time, if we seize Khalkeus at the right moment, we can learn his secret, and apply it for ourselves. Then he will be of no further use to us, and he, like Xena, will have to be disposed of—for political reasons." Amphimedes paused, smiling, watching as the dancers consecrated themselves for the entrance of the bull in the court below. "Yes, Tros," he went on, "it must all happen soon, sooner than we had expected."

"Yes." Tros got the message. "And—"

"And you must get me a new astrologer. Immediately. Get a new man to cast the pigeon guts and the bones. You and I don't put much credence in this stuff—but our fellow conspirators do."

Tros smiled his dark smile. "Yes," he said. "And what would it be convenient for the stars and the bones to recommend?"

Amphimedes took another leisurely drink of wine before answering. "Next week begins the Festival of the Moon. As it winds down, Xena and her women will be doing their usual drug-induced whoring in the sacred grove. It's commonly an occasion for the royal guard to slip into the grove and sample a taste of what ordinarily goes only to the sons of the rich."

"Amphimedes!" Tros said, shocked. "During a religious festival?"

"They'll be at their weakest. And look you; among our friends are many who would replace the worship of the Goddess with that of the Earth-Shaker anyhow. To whom, mind you, such action would be no sacrilege at all." He smiled almost smugly. "Minos will be more weakly guarded than at any time in the year." He stopped, let the idea sink in. Almost as an afterthought, he added, "But Tros. The astrologer? The magus?"

Tros grinned his hard grin. "They're as good as dead," he said.

II

One week exactly before the day set aside as final day of the three-day festival, Xena purified herself and prepared to ride up through the passes to the east to Lato, a site particularly sacred to the Goddess. Having little patience with the managing of animals, she brought Lukios along to drive the beasts that drew her little cart. Almost immediately, she wished she had not. This day of all others Xena wished for peace and quiet, for a chance to commune with herself and organize the thoughts she would share with the Lady; but with talkative Lukios along, this peace was not to be had.

At the top of the high pass, she looked back to see stately Knossos on its rolling plain below the massive, overshadowing bulk of Mount Ida, still bearing its cap of white although the equinox approached. Vineyards and olive groves dotted the land, climbing the soft pastel hills; the only jarring note was the devastated little forest of hardwoods, below the city, which had been cut down to fire Khalkeus's furnaces night and day while he continued his frenzied attack on the secrets of metallurgy.

It was a lovely land—*her* land. The land of her fathers. A land made green by the blessing of the Lady. The sacrifices which took place at the four festivals of the solar calendar had been accepted and blessed by the Goddess, and the land remained fertile and friendly. The winters were not long or unduly harsh; green vegetables grew much of the year, and the livestock always found fertile graze on the hills' verdant slopes.

She wished Lukios would stop chattering. She wanted time to think.

What if . . . ?

But no. It was impossible. It would be foolish, wasteful—and a sacrilege of the worst possible kind.

But, what if . . . ?

"Lukios," she said. "Do they know the Goddess to the east of here? Is she revered? Worshiped?"

The eunuch looked at her, his brows high. "Why, what a question!" he said. "Why? Are you thinking of leaving here?"

His question was too close for comfort; she winced and lied unconvincingly. "Just curious. People speak of the cults of the Earth-Shaker taking over here and there—"

"Well," the eunuch said, rolling his eyes, "I suppose you'd say something rather like the Goddess, as you know her, reigned over much of the east at one time or another. There are still cities which revere her. But, you know these isolated cults. They start introducing variants." He sighed and shrugged half-comically. "I'd suppose you'd say I myself had been a sort of novice of the Lady at one time. That's how I got—well, trimmed."

"You?" she said. "I can't believe it. Men don't . . ."

"Not here," he said. "But I wasn't talking about here. Do you want to hear or don't you?" he said waspishly.

"Please."

"Very well. It was at—why, as a matter of fact, it was at this selfsame festival we're coming up to right now. How curious." He yawned. "They did things differently. On the first day, a pine tree was cut in the woods and brought into the sanctuary of Cy—of the Lady, I suppose you'd call her. There was, as I recall it, a sort of sacred guild of tree-bearers, whose job it was. They'd swathe the trunk with woolen bands as if it were a man, and deck it with wreaths of violets. They—"

"Violets?" Xena said, her interest quickening. The Goddess loved violets—particularly at this time of year.

"Yes. Violets, the folklore had it, were what sprang up from the blood of Attis, the Goddess's consort. Then they'd tie an effigy of Attis himself to the tree. On the second day . . ."

"Please. Go on." Her heart was pounding. It was not the sacred ritual, not by a lot; but she could recognize it.

"On the second day, was a day of music. Mainly horns as I remember. The third day . . ." He looked at her oddly. "You know, I haven't thought of this in years. It sends chills up and down my spine."

"Please, Lukios."

100

"Please, is it? I like please." He simpered at her; but there was dead seriousness in his eyes, and his tone had sobered appreciably as he continued. "My memory of it all is rather vague. I was so young. But there was a lot of dancing, and then we, the novices, and the priests too—we were all invited to eat of the sacred mushroom. It was all very exciting. My head reeled. The priests danced around and cut themselves, their arms and legs and chests, with potsherds, offering up the blood to the altar and the sacred tree—" There was an odd ring about his voice. The cart slowed as his hand on the reins slackened. She looked over at him. His eyes were glazed; there was a thin film of sweat on his fat face.

"The high priest drew blood from his own arms and offered it to the altar. The music was in a frenzy. I was drunk on the mushroom—I didn't know what I was doing. The dance moved faster and faster. . . . They cut away our robes, mine and the other novices'—we were naked. All the priests were naked, and their bodies were running with blood—only our young bodies were white and clean—and we knew, we knew, even in the middle of our drunken stupor, as we whirled giddily around in the dance and the cymbals clashed and the trumpets blew and the drums beat, beat, beat. We knew what it was we were supposed to do. . . . And as we danced they—one of them, I don't know who—handed me a knife, all gleaming and clean in the light—and I saw my friend Daos, his eyes rolling back in his head, grasp himself by the privates with one hand . . . and the knife was in his other hand . . . and it flashed . . . and my heart was beating fast, and I was so excited, and I grabbed myself the same way and—"

"No. Please. Lukios . . ."

The cart came to a stop. Lukios touched himself once in the crotch—gingerly, as if in pain. Then his hand shrank away. He moaned. His eyes closed. He wept, in terrible shuddering sobs.

She put one hand on his broad back. "Lukios," she said. "Lukios?"

He straightened. He looked ahead. He swallowed. He wiped his eyes. "I—I'm sorry," he said after a few moments had passed. His back straightened. "I'd forgotten. But of course it doesn't matter now. It was something that happened when I was a boy. It happens to many people where I come from. It made little difference in my life. I never became a father." He shrugged airily. "So what? I didn't want to be a father." His mood changed; some of his old insouciance came back. "I didn't want to be a priest either. Most likely it was a good thing I was captured soon after. I think I like even my present life better than that of a priest of Cybele."

"Cybele?"

"The Mother's name, back where I come from." His eyes cleared and looked right into hers, an equal's. "So you see your Lady *is* honored in that part of the world. Or was, when I was a boy. Who knows what changes have taken place?" He clucked at the animals, and the cart lurched forward. "I *am* curious about all this interest."

"Well," she said, some caution creeping into her voice. "This is absolutely not for other ears. I'll have your tongue cut out if you breathe so much as a word of it. But—" Still, she hesitated.

"Oh, come now. You know you can trust me. If you can't trust me, whom *can* you trust?" The words fell oddly on his tongue. They might have been true once.

"Lukios," she said. "Khalkeus—Kirta, he insists I call him now—he wants to go back to his own country."

"Ah," he said thoughtfully. This was news.

"He has this terrible feeling of guilt. Not so much about his—his wife, whom he abandoned. She must, of course, have found a man by now; she was young and pretty when he left. But—it's his sons. The two boys. He feels he's cheated them in life. You see, he's a member of this dynasty of armorers; it's famous in the Land of the Two Rivers."

"Ah," Lukios said. "I've heard something of this. It has to do with the birthmark he bears. You remember I used to attend Khalkeus at the baths."

"Yes. But the business about his sons—it's preying on his mind these days."

"So send him back. He'll never find them. They'll be grown by now."

"I'd never see him again. Let him out of my sight but once . . ." She paused and sighed. "But there I go, acting like my old self. Of course, it *has* changed. This happens, this terrible attack of guilt on his part, at the very time he has begun, I think, for the first time to fall in love with me." She held up one slender hand. "No, no. It's true. I should know. Having done without Khalkeus's love—"

"Kirta's, I think you said."

"Yes. Having done without it all these years, I can tell a difference in our relationship. Now for the first time, he truly begins to care for me. . . ."

Lukios stared at her as her words trailed off. "I don't

102

believe what I am hearing. Do you really propose to—?" He gaped at her openmouthed. "By all that's holy," he said, "I think you're actually serious. You are. You *are*."

She just looked at him. The cart slowed down again.

"But, to abandon all this—the House of the Axe and your position in it, your position as priestess of the Lady—"

"The Lady will desert me if I am dishonest with her. Perhaps I can be most true to her by leaving the House of the Axe."

"But how will you live, the two of you?"

"I haven't even suggested it to him yet, and *you'd* better keep my secret, or I'll—" She gripped the rail hard. "An armorer always finds work."

"But he'll—you'll—both be captured and enslaved."

"Who would enslave Minos's daughter? The priestess of the Lady?"

"But . . ." He forced his eyes back to the road. And for once he couldn't think of a thing to say.

It wasn't until they had reached the half-ruined Temple of the Goddess at Lato and Xena had stepped down and gone alone into the great house, with its broken columns and its still-standing altar, that the full enormity of what she had suggested came through to him.

He wondered now what her timetable was—the timetable for her defection, her desertion of Crete, of Minos, of the House of the Double Axe, of the Goddess herself as people in Crete knew her.

Could she possibly be thinking of deserting them *before* the final night, known as Blood Night, even though the Cretan version was a tame and pale thing compared to the rituals of the Goddess in Asia Minor?

He swallowed hard. His heart recoiled at the horror of it. If she escaped—if she managed to be out of Knossos, and on the way to this mad destiny of hers—if she slipped through their grasp just as they made their way to purge all Crete of her father and his influence—

Lukios's fat hand went to his heart. He had to get closer; he had to hear what it was that she was saying to the Lady, there at the half-tumbled stones of her altar. . . .

He slipped around to the side of the wrecked temple. On all fours, he crawled closer to the Holy of Holies and managed to catch a word or two between gusts of wind through the mountaintop shrine:

". . . forgive me for what I am thinking of doing . . . worse

103

sacrilege to continue, feeling as I do . . . know that your great woman's heart, Beloved Mother, will see into my mind and know that I am sincere in what I say . . ."

But then the wind picked up. And in a moment she had made the ritual signs and was backing out of the temple. Lukios scrambled back to the front gate and reached his former place just in time. To his delight, she didn't even notice him. Instead, she strolled to the high cliff beside the shrine and stood looking down at the dark sea far below, her back to him, her eyes looking out, far out, over the vast blue expanse toward the dark and secret lands where Kirta had been born, where his destiny now led him, and perhaps her as well.

Her foot dislodged a stone. It rolled over the cliff. The wind died suddenly. After a long wait Lukios heard the stone hit, far, far down the mountainside.

The wind picked up again. It blew her skirts around her slim ankles. Her hair blew with it.

Lukios's heart was pounding, pounding. If she left Crete— if she escaped the purge, alive—the blood of Minos would still be out there to menace his killers, his successors. The blood of Minos, and the anointed Goddess Incarnate. The new throne would never be safe, and he, Lukios, would be unsafe with it.

He hesitated. Then he crept forward.

It would take no more than a little shove. With her standing on the edge of the abyss like that, with a terrifying, yawning drop before her—

He raised his hands . . .

. . . and then she turned. Her eyes dismissed him. The moment passed. "Here, Lukios," she said matter-of-factly. "Let's see if we can get home before dark."

III

Nikos, standing atop a small rise and looking down at the devastation the slaves' axes were making of the little grove of trees below the western wall of the House of the Axe, could see the man approaching. He wondered what errand would bring to his, Nikos's, side a slave of the great house of Klumenos. He watched the slave's approach with some interest.

At ten paces, the slave stopped and hailed him. "Greetings, Nikos. I am Alektruon, slave to Klu—"

"I know whom you serve," Nikos said with equanimity. "What may I do to serve your pleasure? Or your illustrious master's?"

The slave looked him in the eye. "My master would have a word with you."

Nikos looked around. "I see. Here? Or—?"

Alektruon made an inconclusive motion with his hand. "At his apartments. At your convenience, of course. But the sooner the better. If you are free to come with me now, I can take you to him."

"I'm supervising some work for my master," Nikos said. "On the other hand, it's not pressing, and my presence is not really needed. If you'll wait while I send a message back to Khalkeus, telling him where I am—"

"Ah," Alektruon said. One dark brow went up in an expression of veiled significance. "That is just the thing my master would prefer that you not do. He would like to speak with you away from the eye of Khalkeus."

Nikos hesitated. He looked at Alektruon, trying to read the slave's expression—and could make out nothing. A meeting Khalkeus was not supposed to know about? This was unusual. More than that: there was something vaguely sinister about it. "I'm sorry," he said. "I'm accountable to my master for my whereabouts at all times. I can't just . . ."

Alektruon's smile took on an air of something disturbingly menacing. "My master would like you—would urge you—to lay aside certain considerations for an hour or so. It has to do with, ah, certain conditions affecting the safety of your master." Alektruon looked around cautiously before continuing. "Between us—your master's life may be in danger."

"Ah," Nikos said. "From whom?" But he knew the answer. "I see. This is for Klumenos himself to tell me. Am I right?"

"Right. Now if you'll be so kind—"

The sumptuousness of Klumenos's huge suite on the top floor of the House of the Double Axe became evident even before Nikos entered it. For one thing, it had its own patio, open to the sun, sharing it with no other apartments. For another, it had its own similarly open stairwell leading up from the second floor, where the royal family of Knossos transacted business and welcomed visitors from foreign courts. These were something like royal appointments in their exclusivity, and the furnishings of the court onto which the staircase led were of a comparable luxury. Nikos nodded to the slave Alektruon, impressed. Alektruon, however, took it all in his stride. "Please, wait here," he said.

Nikos complied. He looked about him, marveling at the expense to which the decorators had gone. Here was a fresco worthy of the king's rooms; quarried tiles, hand-cut and hand-fitted by a master builder; a miniature pool with water lilies and hyacinths, and exotic fish darting below the surface.

There was a noise behind him. Startled, Nikos turned—to receive an even greater surprise. Klumenos stood before him, his robes put aside, wearing only the kilt and codpiece the nobles wore in the privacy of their own rooms. The nobleman's body was still slim and supple in his middle years, with a hard belly and powerful legs. His hair was beginning to show flecks of gray, but there was a look of hard-won vigor and strength about him.

"Nikos," he said. "I brought you here because it's more private than other places. I have to tell you: your master's life is in danger. But—" Here he held up one restraining hand. "You must not tell him as yet."

"I don't understand, my lord," Nikos said.

"Mind you, this is just between us. But, your help can save your master's life. And, I might add, preserve the peace of the court of Minos." He looked over Nikos's shoulder, gestured. "Alektruon. Bring wine. For me, and for our, ah, guest." The subtle distinction was not lost on Nikos, but his face betrayed nothing.

"Now," Klumenos said. "I'll tell you right off—and believe me, if you tell anyone about this, including your master, it will mean your life as well as his."

"My lips are sealed," Nikos said lamely.

"Very well. There's a palace revolt of sorts afoot. An attempt will be made shortly to assassinate the king, and with him the Goddess Incarnate, his daughter."

Nikos's face registered his surprise and shock. He remained silent.

"A number of us," Klumenos said, "have found out about this in advance. Never mind how. We have decided to step in

106

and head it off. But"—he held up one finger—"it's no good breaking it up if we don't have all the conspirators when we make our arrest. So far we know of only a few of them."

"Sir," Nikos said. "I know my master. He'd never have anything to do with that sort of thing. He lives entirely for his work."

"I know," Klumenos said. "Please. Sit down. Relax. We're aware of your master's political neutrality. We're also aware, however, of the fact that he is, shall we say, uncommonly close to the Goddess Incarnate."

Nikos shrugged. Everyone knew of this.

"Since, according to our informants, the Princess Xena is to be one of those assassinated, we may assume that if that, ah, closeness continues, Khalkeus will also become a target for the assassins. Can they strike at Xena—this is an act of unforgivable sacrilege, mind you, as well as one of political murder—and leave Khalkeus behind as a witness? Ah, I see you understand."

"What can I do, my lord?" Nikos said simply.

"All right. Now, we can't tip off Khalkeus beforehand. We feel reasonably sure that the first thing he'd do would be to take immediate steps to protect Xena, and this would let our conspirators know that they're being watched, that a trap was being prepared for them. Xena would go to Minos. And the revolt would be crushed—except that some of the conspirators would remain free, ready to strike a new blow in some future time."

Klumenos paced back and forth, shooting Nikos a glance now and then. "You see the problem. What we need now is information. Information as to Xena's every plan. And Khalkeus's every movement as well, since we can be sure that where he goes, Xena will go. And if they wander to places where we cannot protect them—"

"Pardon me, sir," Nikos said. "Then, you have no idea of the schedule for all this? You don't know when they intend to strike?"

"No. That's the hell of it. All we know is that it's to be soon—very soon." He looked Nikos in the eye and stopped pacing for a moment. "That's where you can come in handy. Minos and I—we have quarreled. A minor spat, mind you—ordinarily we're as close as brothers—but enough to ensure that at the moment I am not privy to his inmost thoughts. It is a damnably inopportune time for this to happen, mind you. Just when I need to know the most I can know in order to protect Minos from harm, we have this ridiculous little falling-out. Over nothing. Over the disposition of a trifling franchise in lamp oil."

"Yes, sir?"

"Well—what we need to know are things like this: have Xena and Khalkeus any plans for any new activity of any kind on the days to come? What are they going to do? When are they going to do it? Has there been any change in their relationship lately? Have they—?"

"Well, sir, I think—well, that last. Their relationship. I think I could say with some confidence that relations have improved radically between them. The lady Xena has spoken in my presence of—of, well, sailing away with Khalkeus."

"Ah," Klumenos said. "Now that's just the kind of information we can use. Sailing when? To where?"

"I don't know, sir. But I could find out."

"Could you do that, please? Because—mind you, it could make all the difference in the world. Because if they get off like that, all isolated from our protective influence, and the assassins hear about this before we do, and head them off—"

"I see, sir. Very bad."

"Disastrous. And another thing. There is rumor about Khalkeus's having discovered some sort of alchemic formula or spell."

"Oh, sir, it's not a spell. It's a process for making—" But here Nikos's earlier pledge of silence to Khalkeus came into play. "I'm afraid I'm not supposed to say what it is, sir."

"Good man. You keep that secret. You guard it well. It's none of our business just now anyhow. Khalkeus will tell us everything when the time comes. I admire your circumspection. If you keep my secret—*our* secret—half as well as you're keeping that one, I'll be satisfied. But look you: what I need to know is not the nature of the discovery. It's the timetable, once again. Has he perfected the process? If not, how close is he? And can we perhaps be notified on the very day when he announces that he has, in fact, made the breakthrough?"

"I—I'm sure I can do that without breaking my oath, my lord. Yes, sir, I'll be glad to."

"Fine, fine. Of course, you understand what's going on: the enemy—the conspirators—have discovered that Khalkeus is onto something. And they think it important, as important as you do. Word got around back on Rouso, mind you. The

108

people there knew that the magus—what was his name? Turios—that he'd discovered something important. And our conspirators know—or think they know—that Khalkeus shared in Turios's confidences in his last hours." He stopped and looked at Nikos. "But perhaps *you* were there, as well?" He cast a sharp glance at the slave.

"No, no," Nikos said hastily. "No, my lord. I went outside, at Khalkeus's bidding, while the conversation took place. It would have been improper for me to overhear."

"Ah," Klumenos said, holding up one forefinger again. "Perhaps it was *then*. But now? Now, when Khalkeus's life may hang in the balance? When your circumspection and loyalty may result in your master's death?"

"I understand, my lord."

"Ah, so. Anyhow, our conspirators will presumably not kill Khalkeus until after he has perfected his new process. They want it for themselves, for the subsequent reign of whatever usurper they choose to place on the sacred throne of Minos. And, Nikos—there's one more thing."

"Yes, my lord?"

"We have reason to believe that the conspirators have already planted a spy in the inmost circle surrounding Xena."

"But no! You can't mean it, my lord! Who?"

"That's neither here nor there. Suffice it to say that Xena—and Khalkeus—are being betrayed, and by someone who knows every thought of Xena's mind."

"Lukios! Lukios, the lady Xena's slave! Why, that fat swine . . ."

"Now, now. I won't confirm it, I won't deny it. But let me add this: if it is the person you've described—do you now begin to understand the terrible and immediate danger your master and the lady Xena may be in?"

"Yes, sir."

"Very well. All the more reason for our tightening our noose quickly around the necks of the would-be assassins—once we know precisely who they all are."

"Yes, sir!"

"With this spy informing the conspirators of everything Xena knows and thinks, you can see why it's absolutely essential for us to have a reliable informant feeding us the information, as it develops, even before their informant has had a chance to do his dirty work?"

"Yes, sir! Yes, my lord." Nikos shook his head in near-disbelief. But his face bore the visible signs of acceptance. As the conversation wound down into trivia and Nikos was dismissed, his face took on a profoundly serious, even solemn, look.

Alektruon came in to take up the wine cups. "Then he's our man, sir?" he said.

"I think so," Klumenos said. "Thinking he's protecting Khalkeus, he'll report to us, and we'll at last have a representative—a spy, if you will, inside their camp. Frankly, I think it'll be an improvement. Xena, after all, acts only in reaction to something Khalkeus has said or done. Finding out her reactions gets us the information a day later than it would have taken if we'd had a line into Khalkeus's rooms. Besides, I hate that fat toad Lukios. I don't trust him at all."

"As you say, sir. I'll take pains to keep in the closest touch with Nikos from now on."

Nikos slipped back out of the House of the Axe just in time to see the woodcutters breaking off work early. He cursed them and ordered them back to work until sundown. Then he sat down and, cross-legged on a flat stone, watched them work, his mind working like lightning.

One thing he knew: Klumenos was a liar. He was in fact one of the conspirators. He and his friends were plotting to kill Minos, and Xena, and Khalkeus.

The question was, what was he—Nikos—going to do about it? He fingered his home-stone in his pocket, his fingers running back and forth over the smooth, polished surface. If they won, he'd be a slave. If they lost, he'd still be a slave. Under which faction would he be better off?

His mouth a grim line, he looked out over the rolling country below the House of the Axe, seeing nothing. The little stone, the badge of his years of exile and slavery, rolled over and over between his fingers.

IV

Early the next morning, Kirta sent Nikos out to two of the villages that lined the road across the spine of Crete to Inatos. The day before, a charcoal mound used to provide charcoal for Kirta's furnaces had collapsed, killing the two men walking atop it; Nikos was dispatched to take money to the men's widows.

When Nikos was gone, Kirta stood looking at the now-cool furnaces. Was it worth starting them up again for the limited kind of work he'd be able to do alone? He had almost made up his mind to fire up one of them anyway when he heard a familiar knock on the door. He looked; sighed. "Yes?" he said.

"It's Xena," her voice came through the heavy door. "Please: may I come in?"

He made a wryly amused face. Somehow, quite recently, Xena had acquired a politeness he'd have sworn was foreign to her nature altogether. She'd used the word "please" before, to be sure; but always in a context of begging. In the old days it had been a drearily predictable oscillation between begging and demanding. Now she asked—and courteously. It was a rare thing for a woman her age to learn anything new on this everyday level. How much more rare for a king's daughter, a religious leader, a woman used to having her own way?

He walked to the door, opened it, and stood, astonished, looking at her. "Xena," he said. "I—" But speech failed him.

She didn't look like Xena. She looked years younger. Her dress was the short, tuniclike garment of a peasant, baring one lovely breast and trim thighs. She wore simple leather sandals and her feet were bare of the usual anklets and golden toe rings. Her hair was up, piled high atop her well-shaped head, and the effect was to draw attention to the slender beauty of her long neck. Her face, usually heavily made up, was scrubbed clean, and her smile was bright and sunny. All the drooping lines of her face were gone; only the tiny crow's feet at the corner of her eyes betrayed her age.

"Xena," he said again. "I—I don't know what to say."

"Well," she said with little coquetry in her tone, "you could start by saying 'Come in, Xena, my dear.' And then you could tell me how nice I look."

He took her hands. "You do look lovely," he said. "What a surprise. What a pleasant surprise. But this mode of dress. Why? I don't understand."

She squeezed his hands, once, and then drew his face down for her kiss. "Oh, Kirta, my darling. All this time you've been here, and you don't remember a one of our holidays. No one works the day before the festival begins. You know that."

111

"But—"

"Look," she pointed to the workspace in the other end of the room. "Something must have spoken to you, though. You're honoring our custom in spite of yourself. Your furnaces are cold."

"I *was* debating whether to try to get in a bit of work—"

"And deciding not to. Well, perfect. What better time than this for a day in the open air? After all, here you've been, all cooped up inside like this, for days and days. Come: I've a pair of horses saddled outside the gates, and the saddlebags carry wine and cheese and bread and fruit and olives. I have some coins; we'll hire a boat down at Amnisios and sail east for an hour to a tiny cove I used to know when I was a girl, a place you can't reach from the land. There's a lovely little beach, and all the privacy in the world, and we can swim, and—"

"Xena. Please."

"—and lie in the sun, naked, and—"

"Xena, I haven't got time for—"

"—and make love like a couple of striplings. Come, Kirta. See how nice I can be, darling? I haven't called you 'Khalkeus' in days, have I? Come, the day's wasting. Please, Kirta. It's not a day for sitting inside getting all sooty from burning coal. It's a beautiful, warm spring day, with just the right touch of nip in the air, and we haven't done anything like this in a long time. Too long."

He started to protest again, but then he looked in her eyes. This was a new Xena: a creature free of guile, a person with a clear eye, a ready smile. An *attractive* woman, damn it. A woman who'd turn your head as she walked past, pauper's tunic or no. He smiled. "You know," he said, "I like you this way. I really do."

"And why not?" she said. "*I* like me this way. Oh, Kirta: now I've finally caught your eye, do you think you're ever going to be able to ignore me again? Ever? I'm going to surprise you. Just you wait and see. I'm going to grow younger, not older. I'm going to become the most fascinating woman you've ever met in your whole life." She patted her hair in a proud and defiant little gesture, and Kirta beamed at her. There was such suddenly unselfconscious charm in the gesture!

"Perhaps you're right," he said. He looked down at his roughly woven work clothes. "I'll just change—"

"No, don't," she said. "That's part of the fun of it. We'll

112

just be a couple of working-class people out for a holiday. Here—bend over so I can reach—" She stepped up to him, and as he bent forward, drew his garment over his head. She dropped it on the floor beside him. Now he was naked except for his codpiece—a thin cup of cloth secured to his body by a belt and by an almost invisible string that went between the buttocks. "Oh Kirta, you're such a lovely man. You ought to go around like this all the time. With that big chest and that flat belly you look like a man half your age. Here, put on your sandals. You'll need them in Amnisios, with all those sharp rocks underfoot." But before she let him go, she embraced him once again, her face soft against his naked chest.

By the time they reached the port, Kirta had begun to get used to the idea. They stabled their horses and borrowed a small sailboat from a fisherman in the harbor; he wouldn't take their money. There was no pretense about not recognizing them. Court people—the nobility—sometimes liked to dress as common folk when they went out on a lark, and these could sometimes pass unrecognized as specific people, although their lighter skin and haughty bearing immediately betrayed their origins. But the Goddess Incarnate? Her double status as priestess and king's daughter picked her out of any crowd, in whatever clothing.

Kirta boarded the little boat first, helping her down. This was the last help she required, for once on board, she took over, requiring from Kirta nothing more than the shifting of his weight as the vessel got under way and tacked around a headland. Of the two, Xena, not Kirta, was the born sailor. Kirta, raised inland, marveled at her miraculous rapport with wind and wave as she piloted the little craft into a narrow little bay whose arms were steep cliffs that rose from a seductive strip of beach. Well back from the land, though, she raised the sail, yanking lustily on multiple brails to bunch the square sail securely against the yard. Then she dropped anchor.

"Here," Kirta said. "What's this? We'll get our food wet bringing it in. . . ."

Xena pulled her tunic over her head and stood, slim and deliciously naked, in the stern. "No we won't," she said. She stood up on the tiller seat and stepped daintily overboard, coming up a moment later blowing water out of her mouth. She pulled herself up on the gunwale of the boat and took the lunch parcel in one hand; then she eased herself back into the water, holding the parcel high. She lay back in the water, her white body flashing through the blue, the dark patch of hair in her lap winking at him. Her hair, unbound, spread about her head in the water like a nimbus of shiny black. "Come," she said. "Off with your loincloth and into the water. I can beat a landsman like you to the shore swimming on my back, with one hand."

Kirta stripped and dove in, splashing her lightly. "No fair!" she said, as he struck out for the shore. Having lost a stroke on him, she set out after him, her strong legs kicking powerfully, her one arm cleaving the water. Despite the head start, Kirta was little match for Xena, who had grown up in the water. They pulled up onto the shore in a dead heat, laughing, and sat gasping for breath on the pebbled strand. "I won!" she said, tossing the parcel to a safe spot high and dry behind them.

"No, you didn't," Kirta said. But there was a twinkle in his eye when he said it, and his glance looked her up and down with a new interest. "Here, I'll show you what we used to do to cheaters back where I come from." He reached for her leg.

But she was too quick for him. She was on her feet in a moment, sprinting down the beach, hands holding her full breasts to keep them from jouncing on her chest. Kirta raced after her, laughing lustily, feeling young, feeling like a child again, a child free of guilts and regrets alike.

Then he tackled her, and she was sand and grit all over, and so was he. They had to go back into the blue water to wash off, and she led him, paddling easily, out to the deep water past the moored boat. She dove and dared him to follow; she went deep, deeper. His lungs bursting, he pursued her as far as he could, but then had to admit defeat. He surfaced, spitting up water—and worried for her for a moment until her dark-haired head broke the surface, and he saw her merry smile. He swam to her and let his hand caress her face softly, just once. Then they were drifting back into the shallows again, feeling the warm sun on their faces as they floated lazily to shore.

She was swimming up to him just as he stood up, chin deep in the water, feeling his soles touch the pebbles underfoot. Her hands went to his shoulders, and drew him close. Her legs wrapped around him. In the water she weighed nothing, nothing at all; her cool bare body was silky against his; he found himself becoming aroused. And she knew it, and adjusted herself until he could enter her, and there, in the cool water, they made love for the first time that day.

They swam. They ate. They played, as children play. The whole long day slipped by as they toyed idly with a day's brief life, naked as First Man and First Woman. The only sign of civilization, by the time they'd buried the leavings from their luncheon, was the little square-rigged boat bobbing lightly at anchor way out in the water.

Then the cliff threw its long shadow across them, and they felt the chill of evening coming on. Kirta stood up, all goose bumps. "Here," he said. "Back to the boat. We'll just have time to get in." They embraced, and set out for their little vessel. It had been a priceless idyll.

The water was choppy. Xena, still naked, lowered the sail and steered their way expertly around the point. There was a strong, dangerous tide, and the fitful wind made navigation difficult. Still, she tacked wildly this way and that and brought the boat in little by little. He marveled at her skill. But the journey was long, and they docked in the last rays of the setting sun.

There was a sliver of a moon, but clouds drifting overhead blotted it out more often than not. A squall was rising offshore, and the wind was rising. As they reached the stable, dressed now, the rain began: softly at first, then a driving hail of needles. Soaked, with Kirta nearly naked, they shivered in the chill. They sought refuge in an inn. There, before a roaring fire, they took a leisurely meal from an innkeeper who—seeing them wet, bedraggled—really couldn't recognize them. It somehow made their meal more intimately satisfying. Under the table, their knees touched; they smiled a secret smile.

"Innkeeper," Kirta said. "Have you a room for the night?"

"Why, yes, sir. Above my own. I'll send my wife up to tidy things up a bit." With a deferential bow, he disappeared through an open door.

Kirta smiled at her. "You know," he said, "I feel wonderful. I'm so relaxed. I wonder when I've felt relaxed at all in years."

"Oh, I'm so glad. My darling—"

"There's so much I haven't known about you all this time. It was all there, and I—I was too busy to notice it."

"Oh, Kirta, it's never too late. We've still time for all the love in the world—"

But she stopped. Quick expressions of fear and hurt flashed

across her face. "What's the matter?" he said, taking her hand gently between his own.

"I—I'm afraid it'll all go away. You still worry about— your wife, your sons. You'll be wanting to go to them still."

"Xena, I—"

"Please, Kirta. We have to talk about this. I know how you feel. How could I not know? But what I fear is that one night I'll awaken, and you'll not be there."

"Xena."

"Kirta—can I go with you when you go? Just to be with you? Just not to lose you? If only—"

"You'd do that?" he said, unbelieving. "You'd give up everything you have here—betray your relationship with your father, your religion?"

"It's awful. I'd give up everything. Everything. But don't leave me. Please, don't leave me."

His hand touched her cheek gently, softly. It was the tenderest, most delicate gesture she'd ever seen or felt, and quick tears of emotion sprang to her eyes. Such gentleness, from so powerful a man . . . "Xena," he said. "I couldn't go anywhere without you. Not now. I know there's no reason in the world for you to believe me after all these years of neglect, of insensitivity, of callousness. But—Xena. I love you. I didn't know it, but it must have been coming on me for some time. And today I really knew it for the first time. Today you made me happier than I've been in years." His hand smoothed her still-damp hair; his fingers traced down her cheek to wipe away a tear. "Xena. My Xena."

And all of a sudden her heart was full of such a wild and uncontrolled mélange of emotions that she felt it was going to stop altogether. She reached for his big hand and squeezed it, held it to her cheek, kissed it again and again.

"You damned fool! How could you have lost them?"

"I don't know, sir. But by the time I got to Amnisios they'd taken a sailboat and gone—out to sea. Nobody knows where."

Tros of Phaistos looked the servant up and down, his face a mask of rage. "I told you not to let them out of sight for so much as a moment!"

"I had them, sir, right up to the point where they took the short cut across the fields. They were on horseback, sir. I was in a goat-cart. A cart can't jump hedges, sir. I had to stick to the main road."

"Gods! And you say they didn't return?"

"No, sir. I waited until dark. Not a sign. And sir—"

"Yes?"

"You asked if there were any foreign ships in port to-day."

"And there were?"

"Two mainland merchantmen. A Lydian galley. And sir, a Phoenician . . ."

"Phoenician? Are you sure?" Tros's heart was in his boots. At the servant's frightened nod, he turned and strode away. The servant had ridden a borrowed horse into the ground getting here, risking his own life in the process. He was hardly to be blamed under the circumstances. But what rotten luck! The pair had escaped—and nearly on the eve of the revolt. This meant that they would have to change their plans. There was no longer any reason for delaying. Better to strike now and consolidate their newly won power while they could. There'd be time later for sending out assassins in search of the missing Xena. But the time for seizing that power was now. . . .

"Quickly," he said, turning to the servant. "Take a couple of good men. Round up for me Marineus, Klumenos, Amphimedes, Plouteus, and Orestes. I'll get the rest myself. Have them here as fast as you can."

"Yes, sir." The servant turned to go, but then he looked back. "Sir?" he said. "Does this mean we won't be striking during the festival?"

"Damn you!" Tros said in a hoarse croak. "It means we strike tomorrow! Do you hear? Now—go!"

V

Dog-tired, dusty, hungry, Nikos stumbled up the hill in the dark to the south entrance of the House of the Double Axe. As he sometimes did, he marveled at the sheer bulk of the great edifice, as much small city as palace—and, unlike any city or palace he'd ever seen in other lands, undefended by high walls or exterior guards.

Somehow, it looked even bigger than usual in the dark, with the intermittent moonlight lighting its high roofs and the flickering lights of lanterns glowing warmly in the upper windows. Its mammoth bulk was evidence of the sophistication of the high culture that had taken root on Crete; its lack of walls or gates spoke vividly of the stability of the Cretan rulers' reign.

Or did it? Did it instead, perhaps, speak of the vulnerability of the throne of Minos? After all, even the present king's recent ancestors had come to the throne through usurpation, and here there was some sort of plot hatching right now, one big enough to draw the attention of a powerful (and, until this point, conservative) man like Klumenos.

It *could* work. He knew it. The plot as outlined by Klumenos—who, of course, had only been telling as much as he thought necessary to convince Nikos of its validity—could succeed under the right circumstances. It would take careful planning—but it appeared they were doing quite a bit of this.

Now the road ended, and the peripheral path around the great edifice began. His eyes on the torch above the south door of the palace, he tripped and stumbled—and fell squarely into the path of another man, coming upon the entrance ahead of him. Nikos picked himself up painfully and stifled the impulse to speak sharply to the man he'd tangled with. After all, he was still a slave, and you never knew whom you might run into in the dark here.

But his own face had caught the light. "Nikos!" a voice said. Nikos squinted through the darkness, trying to make out a face. "Nikos, it's Alektruon."

"Oh," Nikos said. "Sorry. I couldn't see anything out here." He set his foot on the first step and climbed toward the flickering torch's light, hearing the footfalls close behind him. "What are you doing out at this time of night?"

"Out?" Alektruon said. "Haven't you heard?"

Nikos turned. "Heard what? I've been out in the country all day."

"Tros of Phaistos. He tried to assassinate the king."

"Gods!" Nikos said. "You don't mean it." His mind was racing. Had the plot been tried prematurely—and failed? And if Tros talked, and implicated his coconspirators—how long would it be before he, Nikos, would be called before Minos? After all, he'd agreed to spy on Xena and Khalkeus; no matter that the agreement was one made only to save his own hide. He hadn't reported the offer. That would be evidence enough of his own implication in the plot. "What have they learned from him yet?" he said. "How is Klumenos?"

Alektruon looked at him sharply. "I see. You didn't buy

118

that roundabout version of all this that my master was trying to sell you. Well, the truth is, nobody knows. I mean, everybody knows how Klumenos is. He's all right. He wasn't in on it. Tros took it upon himself. He must have panicked." He sighed. "You'll have noticed the southern door, here, is unguarded. That's because all the guards have been drawn away to guard specific places, like the staircase to the second floor—the one off the central court near the throne room. That area is crawling with guards."

"Then the upper floors are sealed off for now? I *thought* there were an unusual number of lamps lighted."

"Yes. The theory is that if there are any collaborators, they'll turn out to be insiders, people close to Minos." Alektruon's brows raised significantly. "And—but listen. They'll be putting Tros to the torture right now."

Sure enough, a piercing scream came from the inner rooms of the first floor. It echoed and died; then another followed it. "Gods," Nikos said. He wiped his brow, slick with cold sweat. "If that means what I think it means, it won't last long. Either he'll talk—or he'll die."

Now they came out upon the hallway that led to the inner court of the great castle, and Tros's anguished screams grew suddenly louder. As they looked, they could see the ring of soldiers around something in the middle of the court, and they could see the commanding bulk of Minos, topped by his unruly gray hair. Ropes had been thrown over beams; from these, Tros hung spread-eagled, his feet off the ground, his body naked and bleeding from dozens of cuts. Minos faced him, hands on hips; an overseer stood at his side. Tros's bloody body dangled in a great, fleshy X, dripping blood onto the grass. The ropes had been pulled taut. By Minos's side a brazier burned; something dangled from his hand.

They could make out the king's words now, some of them: ". . . daughter? What have you done with *her*? Now, don't you lie to me. . . ."

The figure that hung there from the ropes said in a hoarse voice, "Got away . . . escaped . . . running away with the smith . . ."

"Running away?" Minos roared. "The daughter of a king does not 'run away.' The priestess of the Great Goddess does not steal away with her lover. . . ." His hand lowered the thing he was holding into the open brazier, stirred the white-hot coals around. And now the two slaves, looking on from above, could see what he held in his hand: a pair of tongs.

"I swear ... I had them followed. They went to ...
Amnisios. They disappeared." He gasped for breath; he was
in terrible pain. "People in the ... the port said they'd sailed
away."

"You've killed them," Minos said in a voice full of hatred.
"You've killed them, you miserable cur." He picked a white
coal out of the brazier; he advanced on the man hanging
from the ropes. The glowing coal came closer and closer to
the midpoint of the human X. ...

Nikos had never heard a scream like this one. He shut his
eyes, held hands over his ears. It continued until Tros's breath
ran out; ended in a sobbing gasp for breath; began again. And
now he could smell the horrid searing. ...

"I can't take any more," he said, white-faced. He turned
and fled into the first available room, a storeroom flanked by
giant *pithoi*—huge jars full of lamp oil. He had hardly
entered the room when he vomited onto the tiles.

In a moment he was enough in control of himself to walk
unsteadily across the room to sit down on a stone bench.
Immediately the screams began again, though, and again he
fled, putting as much distance as possible between him and
the terrible sight he'd seen.

A long hall cut across the row of storerooms in the western
half of the building, running north and south. He ran north,
wobbly-legged, hearing the hideous shrieks fade. At length, he
found himself near the north entrance, behind the complex of
rooms and suites that surrounded the ceremonial room in
which Minos sometimes held court on local matters.

Another bench presented itself; again he sat. Weary, terrified, he stared dead ahead, seeing nothing—until his eyes lit
on a pair of booted feet, sticking out from behind a standing
oil jar. And he focused upon them.

"Here," he said to the man standing in half-darkness.
"Who's there?" His hand went to the little knife he'd stuck in
his belt before heading south on the highway that morning.
"Come out—"

But it was only Xena's fat slave, cowering behind a jar. He
took one timid peek out into the hall and stepped out.
"Nikos?" he said. "I—I thought it was the guards."

"Don't worry," Nikos said. "They're already occupied with
Tros. Look, I just got here. How did all this happen? Tell me,
quick. I haven't any time to waste."

"Well, Tros found out Xena and Khalkeus had gone into
the city, and he lost them there. He thought they'd—you

120

know, done what Khalkeus has been threatening to do. Up and leave."

"What would make Xena want to leave with him?" Nikos said. "Why would Tros think this? Why—?" But his eye caught the fat eunuch's, and he knew. "You! You cowardly, double-dealing bastard. You've been spying on them, have you? And reporting back to the cabal?"

"I had to—they threatened me."

"They threatened me, too. But I didn't sell anyone out. How could you?" His lip curled in rage; but then he thought better of it, and sighed heavily. "Well, no matter. Give it to me in a hurry. You knew better, didn't you? And you didn't tell Tros this. And—"

"It was the only way I could save Xena," the eunuch wailed.

"Save her? You were selling her out."

"Look. She—they think she's gone now. It's the best chance she has for getting away. It's not my fault that Tros panicked and started things off too early."

"Look, we've got to save them. There's only—"

"Save them? But who'll save me? Why, the moment Tros talks, he'll mention me. I was the last one he talked to."

"Gods! If you—"

But he stopped dead in the middle of his thought. Tros's screaming had stopped. But now there was another sound. A louder one, and from the throats of many men. "Wait here," Nikos said. He ducked through a labyrinth of doors and hallways to a window which opened on the central court. There he could see the guards battling with men who had come up the great staircase from the private apartments located on a lower floor to the east of the central court. As he looked, an arrow flew through the air and struck Minos in the chest. The king fell to one knee; two guards rushed to his side, fending off an attack by two swordsmen from above. But another arrow flashed and struck Minos in the neck. There was a dark spurt of blood; Minos's great body wobbled. . . .

Gods! They'd done it! They'd begun the revolt!

Nikos hesitated. What could he do now? Minos was dead, or would be in moments. He himself would be in terrible danger, now that he'd betrayed himself to the fat capon, Lukios. They'd dispose of a double agent without even giving the matter a second thought.

There was only one thing to do. He had to get to Amnisios and tell Khalkeus and Xena. Tell them to fly, to escape, before the rebellion reached them. He was certain that the rebels would want to do away with every drop of royal blood that flowed in any veins at all, to make sure no descendant of Minos or close relation of Minos remained alive to cast doubt on the legitimacy of whatever successor they'd picked.

But just then a guardsman, sword in hand, came around the corner. Nikos took off at a dead run around a suite of storerooms—and slipped on a wet spot and fell heavily to the stones.

He rolled out of the way as the guard charged him; his arm lashed out, the knife clutched tightly in his fist, and slashed at the guard's leg. The knife bit in; the guard cursed and fell . . .

. . . and Nikos, staggering to his feet, was astonished to see the eunuch Lukios, coming up behind the soldier, raise a small *amphora* high and smash it down on the guardsman's head. Wine splashed all over him. The broken pieces fell all over the tiles.

Nikos reached down and retrieved the guardsman's sword. "Lukios," he said. "I thought you were on their side."

"I was," the eunuch said. "But no matter who wins here, you and I are marked men. The only thing we can do is go to Amnisios, as fast as we can—"

"Ah."

"—and warn Xena and Khalkeus. And pray to all the gods, beg them to take us along, wherever it is that they're going."

Nikos thought about this. "You'll only slow me down," he said.

"Not so," Lukios said. The terror in his eyes was under control now. "There's a cart stored down the hill, and a pair of asses to pull it. They're sure-footed and swift—"

"So?"

"—and they respond to my hand only."

"I see. Well, let's go. We—"

But the fight spilled into their hallway now. One of the rebels spotted them. "You! Stop there!" Another shot an arrow their way which missed Nikos by no more than a handspan.

"Away!" Nikos said, and sprinted for the northern door, the fat slave at his heels.

VI

"Kirta! Kirta of Hara-a-an . . . !"

Kirta sat bolt upright, suddenly awake. He blinked twice, wiping the sleep from his eyes. Pulling free of the warm arms of sleeping Xena at his side, he slipped out of bed to put on his loincloth.

"Ki-ir-taaa . . ." the voice said again. Kirta went to the door, stepped out onto the little balcony at the top of the staircase.

Who knew his real name? Who here on Crete except . . .

But then he could see the two of them, coming down the little street in the chilly dawn, past the fishermen heading for the wharves to begin their day's work. Nikos! Yes, and the fat slave Xena was so fond of. "Here!" he yelled, waving his arms. They saw him; Nikos stopped the outcry. The two jogged toward him, the fat eunuch puffing loudly.

By the time they reached the stairs, Xena had awakened, slipped on her brief tunic, and come to the head of the stairs to join them. "Kirta," Nikos said, forgetting protocol, all breathless. "There's been a palace revolution . . . Minos is dead or dying . . . they've taken over."

"Gods!" Kirta said. He looked at Xena. Her eyes were wide—but there was no panic in them. She was a king's daughter after all, a warrior-king's child. She'd been trained to the acceptance of this moment since childhood. The only sign of her distress was the drawn look around her mouth. "Who's taken over?"

"It's been in the planning stages for some time," Lukios said, catching his breath. "There was—hmm, Plouteus, Orestes, Amphimedes—yes, and Klumenos, too. I suppose Klumenos will become king now: the new Minos. And—"

"Klumenos," Xena said, an edge to her voice. "Klumenos, my father's *dear* friend. Who supped with Minos not two days ago . . ."

Kirta put a hand on her arm. "Please," he said in a low voice. "Go on, Lukios."

"Yes. Well, they added Marineus at the battle of Rouso, I believe. And Tros of Phaistos."

"*That* swine!" Xena said.

"Please, Xena. What set this off, though?"

"Tros—he had the two of you followed. They'd got wind that the two of you were thinking of going away—that Kirta wanted to return to the land of his birth, and that the lady Xena might accompany him."

"Got wind, eh?" Xena said, her eyes flashing. "And precisely how, might I ask? Considering you were the only one who knew . . ."

"Please, Xena. Time enough later for recriminations. It's obvious Lukios is in this with us now, up to his neck. Go on, Lukios."

"Thank you, sir. I *was* feeding them information. I regret it terribly. They threatened me. . . ." He looked at all three of them and decided not to pursue that lie any further. "But anyway: the intent had been to wait until the festival reached its peak of frenzy and then attack while Minos was lightly guarded. Both of you were to die as well."

"But when Tros's spy lost you here in town and heard you'd sailed away, he waited until dusk and then rode for Knossos. Tros heard that you'd apparently escaped, as he saw it—" Nikos interrupted himself with a cough.

"Yes," Lukios said. "He panicked. He lunged at Minos at a dinner party, a knife in his hand. He was captured and tortured—but while this was going on, his friends attacked and apparently took the palace. As we rode down the hill in the dark, we could see the upper floors of the palace burning."

"The House of the Axe—on fire?" Kirta said, unbelieving. He looked at Xena. "There's no time to lose. You're safe only so long as they think you dead. And unless I miss my guess their men will be here in Amnisios in a matter of hours, maybe less. One of their first concerns will be to secure the port."

"Kirta! But—what . . . ?"

Kirta slammed the door shut after ushering them inside. "No time to talk much. There's a merchantman in port from Cyprus, which my people call Kittim. I saw its sail and banners as we came in last night. You were too busy playing the skipper to notice, I suppose. Well, Kittim is close enough. From there we can find passage to Ugarit."

"But how? We don't have any money."

"A smith can always find work. And these two can pull an oar, if it comes down to that."

"Gods!" Lukios said in horror, looking down at his baby-soft palms. "Me? Rowing a—?"

"But—Kirta." Xena took one of his hands. "Can I leave my country? My people—when they need me?"

Kirta's voice was firm. "There's nothing left that you can do for them—except die. And I won't have *that*. Look, you two: you're armed, right?" He looked them over. "Well, a knife, a sword—it isn't much but it'll have to do. I want the two of you to guard the lady Xena—and guard her with your lives, you hear? If she's hurt or captured, I won't let either one of you survive. I'm going down to the waterfront to arrange our passage. My suspicion is that the merchantman will sail on the tide."

Lukios whimpered, but stood firm. Nikos handed him the short knife he'd carried and took up his stolen sword. "Yes, sir," Nikos said. "But—hurry. They'll be on us before you know it."

"I understand," Kirta said. His voice had a new edge of purpose in it. Xena looked at him, startled. She'd shown him a new Xena the day before; now he was showing all of them a new and powerful Kirta. Or an old one, perhaps: maybe this was the man he'd left behind in Haran all those years ago—the firm, decisive man he'd be when first his foot touched his native soil again. She put a hand to her breast and felt her heart pounding. He was exciting, this way!

But as he stood and made for the door he passed the open window and stopped for a moment. "Look," he said. And their eyes followed his pointing hand to where the morning breeze carried over the hills to the south the thick pillar of dark smoke that marked the fall of the House of the Axe.

The captain was a broad-bellied, spade-bearded bullyboy named, appropriately, Poliwos. As the name suggested, wherever hair appeared on head or body it was as gray as a squid. His eyes twinkled with cupidity when Kirta began bargaining; metalworkers trained in Egypt under the hands of a Sumerian were rare in these parts. More: he'd heard vaguely in his youth of Ahuni of Babylon, and while some doubts obviously remained in his mind—could this loinclothed, clean-shaven Cretan be the son of the famous Ahuni?—he apparently decided early on to take a chance. "But make haste. We draw anchor in—hmmm—when the sun's above this mast, just so."

"I understand." Kirta thought furiously for a moment. "What? An hour? All right. We'll be there."

And as he turned away, he felt a sudden surge of something in his blood. Excitement! Anticipation! He was going to sea again—going back to the lands of his birth! It was a heady and utterly delicious feeling. He hadn't felt this way in years. Vigorous. Alive. Young again.

His path led him along the breakwater that extended out into the bay to form a protected mole. The blood sang in his veins; after the little squall the night before, the weather had cleared, and the sun beat down on his mostly bare body with a pleasant warmth. The waves battering the breakwater sent a delightful spray cascading up against his legs, his sandaled feet. It was a good day for sailing, a *good* day.

But now he looked up to the hills, where they sloped down gently to the ocean. To the road from Knossos.

There was a large party of riders winding its way down the narrow road toward the little seaport.

The rebels! And they'd be in the little town in a matter of minutes!

He broke into a trot, then a run. He had to get Xena and the others aboard the ship as fast as possible. If he could get them there, that far, he'd be able to explain to Poliwos the danger in remaining in port any longer. There'd be new people swarming over the boat, wrecking things, impressing seamen for shore duty, appropriating cargo. It would be a disaster if Poliwos remained a moment longer than necessary.

He turned into the little central street, long and straight where the ropemakers backed down the strand, braiding their lines. He turned the corner and sprinted to the little inn, with its outside staircase to the second-floor guest room.

Then he missed a step and nearly fell on his face. His heart almost stopped.

The door was standing wide open.

"Xena!" he said. He went up the narrow stairs two steps at a time, panting, and paused at the door. "Lukios," he said to the fat eunuch, who sat in the middle of the floor, his eyes red from weeping. "Lukios—where are they? Where are Xena and Nikos?"

"Khalkeus," the slave said. "Don't blame me—it wasn't my fault. She has a mind of her own. I could never control her. She . . ." He let the words trail off into a sob.

Kirta yanked the slave to his feet, slapped his face once, twice, back and forth. "Damn you! Where did they go?"

"At—at first she was happy," the eunuch blubbered, his voice rising to an epicene alto. "She wanted to go away with you . . . and then she got to thinking aloud . . . about her responsibilities . . . about how her people still needed her . . . needed her to intercede with the Goddess on their behalf. She said they'd erred . . . the Goddess would be angry."

"Enough of that! Has she gone back to the castle?"

"Y-yes—and Nikos said he couldn't let her go back alone. He took the sword, and the knife he'd given me, and he went with her. . . . They've gone for the—the horses you brought with you."

Kirta released him with a curse. The slave fell to the floor and tried to embrace Kirta's legs. Kirta struggled to break free. "Please, Khalkeus, don't go with them—you'll be killed, just as they will. Go to the ships instead. Please, please—and take me with you—Don't go, I implore you. . . ."

Kirta thrust the eunuch from him with a curse. He sprang to the door and bounded down the stairway. As he did, he could see the line of horsemen coming down the hill. "Nikos!" he said, heading for the stables. "Nikos, wait! Don't go—"

But now the two of them were riding toward him, and Xena's pony broke stride as she saw him. "Xena!" he said in an anguished voice. "No, please! They're coming—the troops are coming—"

She stopped, looked at him. As she did, Nikos swooped down on him, pulled the horse to a halt, and held a hand down to him. "Kirta!" he said. "Get on."

Kirta sprang onto the horse behind Nikos. "Head her off, Nikos! Don't let her get away!" Nikos spurred the beast forward, cutting off Xena's route. Kirta reached over and grabbed her reins. "Xena," he said hoarsely. "I can't let you go . . . the soldiers are coming down the hill . . . there's just time to make it. Quickly—"

She looked him in the eye, hesitated, and touched his hand. In that moment she committed herself to him forever. And, biting her lip, she wheeled and drove the horse back toward the harbor. Her trot became a gallop; the horse, its rider crouched low over its neck, streaked along the breakwater toward the tall mast of the merchantman on the dock.

Kirta looked over Nikos's shoulder. The soldiers were pouring into the streets of Amnisios; the riders fanned out, spreading into the empty streets. "Ride, Nikos!" he said, and the horse turned and galloped along the mole toward the ship.

127

Looking ahead, Kirta could see Xena dismount and point back where she had come. Poliwos was clearly in view, listening to her, watching where her finger pointed. "Faster, Nikos!" Kirta bellowed in the slave's ear—and then the horse tripped, fell, tossed the two of them over its head to the ground.

Kirta hit and rolled. He made it to his feet. "Kirta!" Xena's shrill voice cried, up ahead. He looked around, saw Nikos lying inert on the mole. "Kirta!" Xena screamed again. He looked back; the riders were spurring their mounts toward the breakwater—toward him, toward Xena and the ship!

He gulped—and abandoned poor Nikos with a sigh. He sprinted toward the ship, seeing Poliwos ahead of him, shouting orders; seeing his sailors casting off from the shore. He put on an extra burst of effort—and as the galley pulled free of the dock, its oarsmen stroking powerfully, he vaulted the last two steps of empty air and landed precariously on the open deck.

Xena helped him to his feet. On the docks, the soldiers dismounted and shouted after them. "Come back! Come back, in the name of Minos, King of Crete!"

"Minos is dead!" Xena cried. With a shiver of—what? Relief? Happiness?—she turned her back on the dockside scene and embraced Kirta. "Oh, my darling," she said. "I was so afraid you wouldn't make it. How could I have thought for a moment of leaving you? I didn't mean it, really—you're my life, my whole being." Her arms, winding around his body now, had a fierce strength in them; having found him, having lost him and regained him, she wasn't about to let him go. Kirta, still gasping for breath, held her close with one arm, his face buried in her dark hair, tears in his own eyes now. . . .

Then there was a powerful shock. He felt it the way one feels an aftershock in an earthquake—only he felt it through her small warm body. She went limp in his arms. He looked up. Bowmen on the dock were loosing another rain of arrows. He saw one land on the deck beside him and stick, its bronze tip sharp and shiny.

He held Xena to him. She did not respond. He moved his hands around on her back, and his fingers clasped a hardwood shaft that protruded from her left shoulder. With a sob he eased her down. Her eyes were closed; her breathing was labored.

"*Xena*," he said despairingly, feeling the life leave her. He

128

tore with aching fingers at the wooden shaft in her back and managed to withdraw it from the wound. As he did so a spurt of blood followed it. "Oh, gods," he said. "Help me. Please help me." But in his heart he knew it was too late. He touched her limp wrist but could feel no pulse, no answering beat at all. He looked blindly at Poliwos, his face a mask of defeat and despair. And little by little, as the strong stroke of the oarsmen shifted tempo and the ship beneath his feet pulled out to sea, his eyes focused on the slender shaft between his fingers.

Its feathers were those of an eagle. He knew that style. Its wooden shaft was long, graceful, polished. He knew the woodworker whose patient hands had formed it.

The bloody head of the arrow—the metal point that had pierced Xena's heart—was a crude, fledgling effort, made of iron.

It was one of his own.

VII

They laid her out in Poliwos's own cabin. Once the galley had cleared the headland and set out to sea, the oarsmen settled into a long, powerful stroke that soon left the harbor of Amnisios far behind. After a time, even the mountains behind the town disappeared, and Poliwos, looking astern, could see no other sign of Crete than the cloud bank that hung today over an invisible Mount Ida. He set a course, barked a couple of orders to snub-nosed Simon, his second-in-command, and strolled forward to his cabin.

There on his own bed he found Xena, wearing only her short tunic, bare feet side by side, her slim hands crossed over her breasts. Her eyes had been closed; her face had a look of peace on it. She looked young, lovely, a woman not many years past puberty. A woman recently slipped off to a sleep full of tranquil dreams.

Kirta sat facing her, his great shoulders slumped in fatigue and defeat. He looked up as Poliwos came through the open door. Then, his eyes dull and bloodshot, he turned back toward her.

"She was a beautiful woman," Poliwos said. "Gods! And a king's daughter, and a priestess." He shook his gray head. "She doesn't look old enough to be a novice," he said.

"She was nearly my age," Kirta said. "She was nearly too old to have a child—if she could have had one." He bit his lip. His voice was as dull as his eyes. "I've never seen her looking so young. So lovely." He shook his own head slowly from side to side. "All her cares are gone now. The lines, the wrinkles she worried about so—they were things I put there, with my neglect of her. Well, now she's spared my carelessness, my thoughtlessness. . . ."

"There, now," Poliwos said, taking a seat near her bedside and looking at Kirta. "You did what you could. I'd say you saved her. Then a lucky shot from the mainland—"

Kirta looked at him, eyes red. "I *made* that arrow. It carried as well as it did, struck hard the way it did, because the head was made of a heavier and better metal than the others, one which—despite my wretched ineptitude at it—took a sharper edge. I couldn't have killed her more surely if I'd shaped the stuff into a knife and stabbed her to death with it."

"Don't be a fool," Poliwos said.

"I'm not. I'm facing things. Things I should have faced a long time ago. Twelve years I've been here. Twelve years, in which I not only neglected my responsibilities to my wife and two boys, but . . ." He lowered his head, held it between his hands.

"Tell me about it," Poliwos said in a softer voice.

"I . . . landed here a slave. In Crete, I mean. Xena saw me and—well, I never believed in love at first sight. But it must have been that in her case. She had her father free me, put me to work. Minos liked me; most of all, he liked the fact that I could have no ambitions to marry his daughter. He also came to believe my crazy story, that one day I'd learn the secret of the making of iron. He knew that if I ever mastered this, and armed his navy with it, he'd be virtually invulnerable. Look: I had notions of arming the front end of fighting galleys with the metal. You know: put a sharp point on the bow, just below the waterline at battle strength. You'd ram an enemy vessel, and the iron would cut through the sides of the enemy ship, sink it right there. I had all sorts of schemes."

"It ought to work at that," Poliwos said mildly, thoughtfully. "Especially if this iron stuff is what you say it is."

"Meaningless," Kirta said. "A great stupid child playing with toys. That's what I was. And Xena . . ." His sigh was audible in the little room. "The years went by. I neglected her. Her youthful years passed, and she began to fade. But these things, I didn't notice. I slept with her, lived with her—but it was following the line of least resistance. It was less bother to go along with things. I lived for the work I did, and Minos threw vast sums into my research."

"I see little to blame oneself for in this," Poliwos said. "If—"

"Blame? What does blame matter? But regret—" Kirta's voice took on a harder edge. "She was a lovely and brilliant woman. Any man on earth would have envied me. How could I have failed to see what they saw with ease? And then at the end—I finally found the answer, the secret, of the dark metal. I suppose I'd expected some sort of divine vision. But instead, what I found in it was not a revelation, a vision—unless it was a vision of emptiness. Or the worthlessness of the foolish game I'd played, of the prize I'd sought. Of the vanity and waste of my own life, and of the suffering my self-centered behavior had caused. And—all of a sudden I could see Xena in a new light. Could see in her what all men but I had seen all these years."

"Yes?" Poliwos didn't want to halt the flow. He threw in the single syllable more as punctuation than anything.

"A woman who is loved grows younger, not older. When my glance first fell on her with love, Xena began to bloom like an orchard. It was the most amazing thing I'd ever seen. I thought: *It isn't too late. The things I have done in life I can undo. If I revisit the sites where I have harmed people, perhaps I can . . .*" There was naked yearning in his eye now as he looked the captain in the eye. "Do you know what I'm talking about?" he said.

Poliwos rolled his eyes upward ruminatively. "Ah, yes," he said thoughtfully. "I think so." His gaze came down to meet Kirta's in a hurry. "But it doesn't always work. And it isn't always necessary. People make their own lives. Your boys, now. They're probably doing all right without you. They've got good blood in them, after all. They're probably both rich as Minos himself by now. Who knows? Perhaps your going back and looking them up might only complicate their lives in a way you hadn't intended. You might do more harm than good."

Kirta looked at him, thunderstruck. This was a thought that hadn't occurred to him. It *could* be true, he was thinking. His return could mean nothing better than pain and confusion. What if Tallay, his wife, had remarried? What if the

131

boys had been raised as the sons of this other man, the man who'd remarried their mother? What if . . . ?

Then he frowned. That was a perilous road to follow. It led back to his shirking responsibilities. He'd done just that for over a decade. It was time for him to face up to everything he'd ever done: stare down all his oversights and faults and do something about their results.

His eye once again fell on Xena, though, looking so fresh and young and sweet there. How heavily he'd leaned on her, all of these years! And how weak and cowardly he was now, with her enduring woman's strength taken from him forever! Where would he get the strength to go on? How could he do it all without her?

But in all of his heart and mind, he could find no answer.

There was no time for a real funeral; the merchantman was due in Kittim and no excuse but bad weather would suffice to explain delay to Poliwos's factors. Kirta kissed the cold lips once; then one of Poliwos's sailors sewed her statuelike body for all time inside a length of sailcloth. They gave her a sailor's funeral, dropping her over the side as befit a great seafaring king's daughter, a woman whose hand sang upon the tiller of a sailboat, who knew every last nuance of a seaborne wind and could sail as well by night as by day. Kirta, his heart empty, watched the little bag of canvas slip below the waves, watched the broad wake of the galley spread across the spot. Watched the spot recede. Watched a gray cloud slip over the sun's disk, and the light grow dim. Watched the first signs of a squall strike up at sea, many leagues aft. Watched twelve years of his life begin to fade, now seen as though shadows in a distant dream. . . .

Farewell! Farewell!

CHAPTER SIX

I

With the lump gold out of circulation and untouchable, Hadad's little purse soon ran dry. After he'd paid his own landlord and, surreptitiously, his mother's, there was only bare subsistence money left in his little hoard. *Well*, he told himself, *you didn't want to get fat this summer anyway*. He began skipping his midday meals. His face grew thin, drawn; his ready smile now had wrinkles at the corners of his mouth and eyes. As he labored to shape the sacred images for the festival trade, his friends in the little bazaar took note of his gaunt frame and clucked to themselves. One noontime, Uzziya, the spice merchant, came over to give the little sculptor some strong goat cheese and flat bread. The following day, by arrangement, Marsatum, the greengrocer's wife, made him a gift of some figs and olives that, she said, had fallen from the cart and been bruised too badly for sale. It was a flagrant lie, and nobody believed it. But Hadad, his heart brimming with love for his friends, honored her deception. It would have hurt her feelings to do otherwise.

On the third day, Yahila, the butcher's wife, came to him with two delicious-looking strips of dried salt meat. Finally, having looked over her lavish gift, Hadad said: "Yahila. You're not going to try to tell me *this* fell off a wagon. This is prime meat. It'll be salable at top prices a month from now." He pressed it back into her hand. "You know how grateful I am," he added, an extra warmth in his voice. "But I can't take this. I know what kind of business you've been doing lately. How can I take from you something which, sold, will help you and my good friend Abisuri out of your present debts?"

133

"Please, Hadad," she replied. "If you don't take it, Abisuri will be angry with me. He told me this morning, before I came to the bazaar: 'Give Hadad—'"

Hadad sighed. "I see. Well, we can't have Abisuri getting mad at you, can we? All right." He took the meat. "But look: I'm doing fine. You and the rest of my friends here don't have to worry about me. If I get desperate I can always melt down some of the gold—"

"Hadad! If only you would—"

"Shush. Please. I'll tell you what. I'll share it with my mother. She seldom gets anything like this to eat. It'll be a particular treat. We'll make a party of it."

Impulsively, Yahila put a hand on the cripple's thin arm. "How is Tallay, Hadad? I haven't seen her in quite some time. Abisuri was asking. So was Marsatum. . . ."

Hadad sighed again, and smiled sadly. "Sometimes she's just fine. Sometimes, it's just like old times, when Shobai and I were boys and he was still coming home weekends during his apprenticeship. She'll laugh and remember old times. Sometimes she'll tell me ancedotes about my father, and there'll be that old gleam in her eye." He took a deep breath and let it out. "And then other times—"

"Oh, Hadad. Is it really that bad?"

He smiled ruefully. "You can read it from my face, eh? Well, I suppose I ought to be—" He shook his head, the sad smile fading. "I try to tell myself otherwise. But she's slipping away, a week at a time. I—I hate to admit it to myself, Yahila, but sometimes I dread going over there. I—can you believe someone would admit to feeling that way? But there are times when I actually dread it. Because—because I'll know. I'll know even before I've arrived that—that she'll have slipped a little farther away by then." His eyes sought hers, abrim with tears. He tried to smile reassuringly, but the smile was an even sadder sight than the unshed tears.

"Hadad," she said. "Does Shobai know of this?"

"Shobai? Oh, no—at least, I don't think so. I—well, I try to keep it from him as much as possible. It would just upset him."

Yahila shot a sharp look at him. *Upset Shobai?* she thought. *You couldn't upset Shobai with an earthquake.* But she kept her own counsel. "Then he doesn't go to see her?" she said, in mock innocence.

Hadad's thoughts were far away. He didn't notice the quiet irony in her tone. "I—I don't know," he said. "Of course, he does, but, hmmm, it must have been two months back. She told me. No, three. No, as a matter of fact it was ..." His voice trailed off inconclusively. "Yahila," he said. "The thing that breaks my heart is—she's so young still."

"I know. She's not my age. The poor dear."

"Yes. And it's as if she were—oh, a great-grandmother or something. An ancient, ancient woman. Yet her face is still young, unlined, except for the lines on her forehead. . . ."

"Lines of care," Yahila said with a slight undertone of bitterness in her voice. "Lines of worry. The gods preserve the poor woman, she's had enough to put up with. A husband disappeared. All her property lost in shady deals, while you and your brother were too young to help defend her against the sort of jackals who descend on a woman alone in this city—"

"Please, Yahila. It doesn't pay to bring up the past. It really doesn't. All that's gone by. If I were to sit here thinking of what might have been—"

"Hadad, for the love of all that's holy! You and your mother and that thoughtless, heartless brother of yours were taken like a bunch of gulls! Can't you at least show some human resentment? So help me, if anyone had done anything like that to me—"

Hadad let out a lungful of breath in a single, despairing blast. "Please," he said. "That's like saying to me: 'Hadad, can't you at least grow angry at the boys who picked on you when you were in school, learning to cipher, learning to read?' What good would that do, for heaven's sake? What earthly good would it do for me to hate them? They don't know any better. They didn't then. They didn't mean to hurt me. They were just playing games. Stupid childhood games."

"And I suppose the people who swindled your mother out of your house, the house your father had built for her—they were just playing games? Simple, harmless childhood games?" Her tone carried an exasperation which almost—but not quite—approached resentment. Yet her glance, as she looked Hadad in the eye, was one of love: warm, protective love, almost a mother's. "Hadad. For the love of heaven." She scowled; reached into her basket. "Here. Here, take it. No, take it! If you don't, I swear I'll tell Abisuri. And he'll take time off work and come down and call you sixteen kinds of dim-witted fool."

"Yahila! Five pieces of meat? No, six? I can't take this."

"It's not for you, you dummy!" she lied. She knew on what

135

level extra food had to be pressed onto Hadad when he was being like this. "It's for Tallay! We're worried about her—with nobody but a phantom like Shobai, a man who only comes home when—"

"Yahila, please! I won't have you speak of Shobai like that."

"—and an improvident fool like you, who scarcely knows when to come in out of the rain or snow."

"Yahila, take that back! Shobai is a busy man. He has work to do. He has business in—"

"Yes, and if I had a son like him, I'd take poison. But you, you foolish one! You won't take decent nourishment when you're starving. You won't cover your bare backside even with the winter coming on. You—"

"Yahila, the winter isn't coming on. It isn't even summer yet."

She stood up, hands on hips, blowing. Her eyes flashed sparks, as bright as any that ever leaped from Bunu-ishdar's forge. "You dummy!" she said. Now all the people in the little bazaar were looking at the two of them, artisan and tradesman and customer alike. "Take it! Take it and good riddance! You fool! You silly, improvident fool!" She turned on one heel and strode away, leaving him holding the long dried strips of jerked beef.

Hadad, a sad half-smile quivering on his lips, looked after her. *Nobody understands,* he was thinking. *Nobody understands at all. . . .*

II

Bahirum, the blind beggar, deserted his post by the great wall late in the day. The traffic in the streets of Haran was unlike any he'd known, and its strangeness seemed to be increasing rather than returning to anything like normal. He tapped his way along the narrow street, seeking the bazaar. As he did he ran smack into Hadad, limping down the street, lost in thought.

Hadad, recovering, held the beggar by the arms to steady him. "Here," he said. "My apologies, friend. I wasn't paying—" Then he stopped. "Say," he said. "We've met before."

The blind man's brow knitted for a second; then he smiled. "Yes. Yes, you're Hadad the sculptor, aren't you? The young man who helped me?" He put one hand on each of Hadad's shoulders, noting the crooked stance forced upon Hadad by his game leg.

"Why, yes," Hadad said. "Here: you're away from your corner, aren't you? Can I take you anywhere? You'll make better time going with me, wherever you're headed, even if I don't move as quickly as the next man."

"Thank you," the blind man said. "I was going home. I live down behind the Temple. I was going to the bazaar to ask a question."

"Fine," Hadad said. "That coincides perfectly with my own plans. I was just going to visit my mother, who lives down that way. And maybe I can answer your question, if it isn't too hard for me."

"Thank you," the beggar said, leaning on Hadad's arm on the side nearest his strong leg. They began a slow progress back up the narrow alley to the main cross street. "I was wondering—the city's so full of people speaking strange tongues these days. Others with odd accents. Sullen, quiet people who pass a beggar by, leaving nothing in his bowl."

"Oh. I've seen a few of them myself, I guess. But perhaps not as many as have passed you by. They tend to avoid the bazaars except at opening time in the morning, when they come by begging for scraps from the greengrocer's—" Hadad's tone changed a bit. "How did your own day go, Uncle? Did you do well?"

"Nothing," the old man said. "Hardly anything at all. I'll have a poor supper this evening, I will. But you were saying—"

"I'll tell you what," Hadad said in an improvisatory tone. He grappled in his garment for something and withdrew it. "Look," he said, "I just came by a real windfall. Somebody gave me some dried meat. Look, why don't you take a piece of it, now? I'm sure the people who gave it to me would approve." Hadad shrugged off the insignificant twinge of conscience that followed this bald-faced lie. He pressed the jerked meat into the beggar's hand.

"Thank you, my young friend. You're very kind to an old man. But, I was asking. About the strangers—"

"Oh." Hadad steered the blind man around a corner and

137

up a narrow side street. "Well, the way I hear it they're from up north somewhere. They, or people much like them, seem to have been coming into the city for over a month now. First a trickle, then—well, their number seems to be picking up some."

"Some! Of course, I can't see them, but I can judge how many there are from their voices—and I can feel much that I can't see. There'll be over a hundred that have passed me by, at day's end."

"Goodness," Hadad said. "That many? Anyway, the way I understand it there's been a war up that way fairly recently. These folks were burned out or something, driven out of their own lands by somebody. People tell me they're living in terrible poverty outside the walls now—and coming inside the walls during the days, looking for work. It hasn't made anything too easy for the local folks. These people are penniless, for the most part. They don't spend anything, most of them. The ones who managed to bring a little money away with them, or who have skills easily marketable, they move into the city and drive the rents up in the poorer quarters of town. I wouldn't be surprised to have my landlord raise my own rent, or my mother's, one of these days."

"Gods. Then they'll be raising mine. How will I live?"

Hadad stopped their progress to let a heavily laden donkey pass by them, its master yanking fiercely on its reins. "It's going to be hard," he said. "And, imagine if you're looking for work, and these people come in from outside, willing to work cheaper than you can afford to."

"But—why do we allow them in? I don't understand."

"Well, my friend Bunu-ishdar, the smith, says that the people who make the rules here tend to profit from new sources of cheap labor. But that's Bunu-ishdar for you. He's very cynical, more so in recent months. He tends to look for the worst possible interpretation of people's behavior. I don't know that I agree with him in this—but on the other hand, I understand your question, and I don't really have an answer ready myself."

But now, as they came around a jutting building that blocked their way, a group of the strangers passed by on a side street. Hadad stopped to watch them pass. They were thin, ragged, with haunted eyes. Their faces had deep lines down their cheeks, and their mouths were grim slashes in the gaunt faces. They spoke in unintelligible monosyllables. "There go some of them now," Hadad said. "Poor people.

138

They must have suffered greatly. I hope they don't let their troubles embitter them."

"I don't understand," Danataya said, clutching her little parcel to her chest. "You promised *me* the room. You said if I came back today, I could have it for only—"

"I don't care what I said," the owner of the hostelry said. "These people paid in advance. They live five, six people to a room, and they can pay, among them, twice what you offered. These are difficult times, girl. I have to make the best bargain I can."

Danataya saw the obduracy in his face—and the guilt. And she understood. Times *were* rough. Who knew this better than she? In a way she didn't blame him entirely. If she'd been in his place, she might have been forced to do the same thing, and her face would have shown the same shamefaced signs of self-loathing. She turned away without another word, her little shoulders slumped.

"Here," the landlord said. "Look, I'm sorry, but . . ." He followed her into the street, calling after her. "Look, if you find nothing else, I know where you might find a room. Try at the Inn of the White Horse. They might even let you work it off. . . ."

The trade name registered on her mind, but her thoughts remained glum. The day was almost over—and she didn't have a job. Worse, her uncle had asked for the room back today, to clean it for the new tenant. *He* hadn't been able to look her in the eye either.

She had no place to sleep. No place at all . . .

Of course, there was the woman in the Street of the Two Gates. She'd vaguely promised work. If she *had* a job, now, people would look at her differently when it came to renting her a room.

She looked up. The sun had disappeared behind the city wall.

A kind of panic ran through her for a moment until she had recovered herself. Her pace quickened; she almost ran down the long alleyway, holding the parcel that contained all she owned in the world close to her chest.

At first nobody answered. She knocked and knocked again, rubbing her knuckles half raw in the process. Finally, the bolt was drawn inside the house, and a face appeared in the crack. "Oh," the woman said. "It's you."

139

"Yes, ma'am. I hope I'm not too late. You said by sundown and it's not quite—"

"Look," the woman said, exasperatedly. "The job's been filled—an hour ago." She started to close the door, but Danataya jammed her parcel in the crack and stopped her.

"Here!" the woman said, indignant. "I'll call my husband. You can't go forcing your way—"

"Please," Danataya said. "I'll work hard. I'll work harder than anyone you could find. I'll—"

The woman was shoving at the little parcel, trying to get the door closed. "You asked too much. Too much for a scullery maid. I found someone who would work for less. One of the women from the northern settlements. Her husband does gardening work. I can get the two of them together for what you asked." She finally freed the door and slammed it. Danataya could hear her annoyed voice through the thick wood. "Now go away, and don't come back!"

Danataya stepped down into the street, her face drawn and her mouth hanging open. She stared at the door for a moment; then, her heart almost stopping, she looked again at the growing darkness in the eastern skies. Night was coming on—and she had no place to go.

The messenger caught Shobai just as he was preparing to go out. He talked briefly with the man and then dismissed him after giving him a small coin. He went back into the house, where Tanuha was attending her mistress. The slave knelt at Anat's feet, and as Shobai watched, Tanuha reached for Anat's bare left foot and held it. Then she began gingerly buffing its pink nails, her movements as delicate as a sculptor's. Anat looked up at him, her gaze cool and uninvolved. "I thought you were going out," she said.

"I was, but I thought I'd better tell you: a messenger came from Carchemish—I met him in the street. We'll have to change our plans. I won't be able to go to the party at the chief scribe's."

Anat withdrew her foot angrily, narrowly missing kicking Tanuha in the face. The slave rocked back on her heels and sat patiently, awaiting notice to continue. "But Shobai! I bought the new robe especially for this party! I had my hair fixed."

"I'm sorry," Shobai said, in a tone that said there'd be no further argument. "The offer is quite good. *Quite* good. If I take it—and of course I will—we'll have no problem at all buying that house I showed you. You know, the one with the reflecting pool, and the garden . . ."

Anat's face remained tranquil, a statue's. Only her eyes showed emotion—and this was mixed. There was a brief flash of icy hatred, then a calculating look. Then she smiled for the first time. It was a chilly smile, a polite one. "Very well, Shobai. I'll forget the party. When do you leave?"

"In the morning. It was an urgent call. I'm to arm the city guard—and supervise the refurbishing of the city's defenses. They're pretty jumpy over there. They take this supposed threat from the north pretty seriously. Well, that's the sort of thing that fattens my own coffers." He yawned. "I'll be up quite early. There's a caravan leaving just after dawn."

"All right," she said. She sat primly, knees and feet touching. "It sounds as though you'll be gone quite a while this time."

"Several months. But just think of the money. I'm sure that if you think of the money, you won't be bored." He turned as if to go again, but stopped and looked at her. "Don't sit home and be bored. There's plenty to do here. You have your friends. . . ."

She smiled the tiniest smile, her face utterly composed. Her tone was cool and musical. "Oh, don't worry about me, my darling. I won't be bored. I'll find some way to pass the time." Her eyes narrowed only slightly. "Where are you going now?" she said mildly.

"Going to arrange transport," he said. He yawned again and stretched; his huge chest strained against the cloth. "I don't know how long it'll take. Don't hold up supper for me."

"I won't," she said. She watched him go. Then she looked Tanuha in the eye and smiled a very different smile. Tanuha almost flinched, feeling its heat. "Tanuha," she said.

"Yes, my lady?" the slave said. She held out her hand for her mistress's foot; but Anat remained in the prim posture.

"You heard my lord and master. *Don't be bored,* he says." Her voice was a silky purr. "To hear is to obey. I want you to take a little message for me."

"You mean to—"

"You know who I mean. Tell him your master will be leaving with the morning caravan. Tell him—but that's enough. He'll get the message, I think. And I'm sure that between us we'll figure out some way or other of avoiding boredom. Who knows?" she said with delicate irony. "I might not regret missing that party after all."

The woman was gone quite a while. When she returned, she brought the innkeeper with her. He was fat, black-bearded after the southern fashion, sharp-eyed. The woman looked at him, then at Danataya. "Here she is," she said.

"Huh," the innkeeper said. "And she wants . . . ?"

"Please," Danataya said in a tiny voice. "Someone told me you have a room. . . ."

He looked her up and down. "Well, I did, but I don't anymore. Have you any money?"

"N-no. Not much, anyhow. But I'm looking for work, and I'm sure I'll find—"

"Huh," he said again, dismissively. "*I'm* not so sure you'll find." He grunted and looked her over again. "What do you think, Admuniri?" he said to his wife, ignoring Danataya. "A little skinny? Undernourished?"

"She looks strong enough. She's young and she'll fill out some. Try her."

"Look, you," the man said. "Your name is . . . ?"

"Danataya, sir. If you know of where I can find work, or a place—"

"Maybe," he said, interrupting her. "I could use a girl to—well, entertain the men. You know . . ." He waved his hand ineffectually. Danataya looked at the woman and blushed when she recognized her expression.

"Oh, no, sir. Please. I couldn't. I haven't ever . . ."

The woman laughed. It was a mean laugh. "I didn't think you'd get the answer you wanted on that one, Abi-samar," she said to her husband. She looked at Danataya and said, not unkindly, "Look, little one. You're presentable enough, skinny or no. We could use a girl of all work here for now. It won't pay much but it's better than nothing, and nothing is very likely what you're going to find waiting for you out in the night there. Nothing—or something rather worse than nothing. Take it from me. I've been there." She put a hand on Danataya's arm. "Don't be frightened. He's just a gruff old man."

"Damn it, Admuniri, if I'd wanted you to butt in, I'd . . ."

She ignored him. "I'd advise you to take the job for now," she said to Danataya. "The work's hard and the hours are long, but it could lead to something better. And look: you sign on here—and come to work tomorrow morning—and I'll recommend you to a friend of the house who may just have a room for you, fairly cheap."

Danataya still hesitated, looking from one to the other. The woman Admuniri smiled at her. It was a friendly smile, a little amused. She had been very pretty once. "But—will I have to—I mean, with the men . . . ?"

The woman's full lips curved in a striking smile. Her eyes were dark and knowing, but there was no malice in them. "Not if you don't want to," she said. "Nobody does, at first."

III

Next morning a minstrel, a man who had arrived with the caravan from Mari, came to the Bazaar of the Well. He was assured, sophisticated, a man of much surface charm. His skill with the many-stringed lyre was considerable, and his voice was pleasant—if his diction was that of a foreigner.

His repertoire was pleasantly varied. He sang love songs of Dumuzi and Inanna; he sang the "Honey-Man" song, and the funny song about the Sated Lover, who begs his girl to let him go, he has done enough loving for one day. His songs echoed the classical patterns of Sumer: the *sagidda,* the *balbale,* the *tigi*-song. There was a studied perfection about his performance, a learned guildsman's skill. But the market was full of poor people this morning, poor people and beggars who had drifted into town with the refugee migration, and the minstrel did not make much money on his morning's stint. As time for the noon meal approached, he looked over the dwindling crowd and made a wry face.

"Come, minstrel," Marsatum the greengrocer's wife said. "You've given us, at least, a good morning's entertainment, even if none of us has made much headway. The least we can do is pitch in and give you something to eat." She brought out a bowl and filled it with grapes and fresh fruit. Bihira, wife of the goatherd, provided cheese, and flat bread was brought forth by Pagat, wife to the baker. "Here," Marsatum said. "Cheer up."

The minstrel turned to her a face whose expression stopped just short of haughty disdain. "Thank you," he said lightly, as one to whom all this was no more than his due. He took a bite of Bihira's cheese and raised an eyebrow appreciatively. "I thought Haran was supposed to be a prosperous town," he said. "If I'd known this morning what I know now, I'd have gone off on the caravan to Carchemish." He gauged the effect of his words, then decided to palliate them. "Mmmm. This isn't bad. Not bad at all. You people do know how to eat."

"Ordinarily things are better than this," Marsatum said. "But—well, the town's all full of people from the north. Apparently, there's some sort of war going on up there. And they're all coming to town impoverished and starving." She shook her head. "I suppose some of them had money. But if they did, they're spending it in some bazaar other than this one."

"Well—perhaps after the noon meal I'll try elsewhere." He looked up and saw a pretty, dark-haired young woman, wearing the rough shift of a servant, her face smudged from a morning's dirty work, dipping a water jug in the well. "Hmmm," he said. "Or then again perhaps I won't."

Marsatum looked up. "Oh, her?" she said. "Forget about that, my friend. She's the new servant at the Inn of the White Horse. Went to work this morning. And if I know Abi-samar, he'll work her to a frazzle way, way into the night. Even if she were inclined that way, by the time she gets off work she'll be so bone-tired she won't have any thoughts of dalliance in mind." She watched the girl walk away, bearing the heavy weight of the full jug, the movements of her hips graceful and pleasing under the thigh-length shift. "Pretty little thing. I suspect she'll wind up upstairs above the inn," she said without malice. "Most of them do."

"Ah, well," the minstrel said. "I wondered. She's been by here three times getting water."

"If I know Abi-samar, he'll have her down on her hands and knees scrubbing the steps between trips," Marsatum said. "My, that's a lovely instrument you have there."

The minstrel dismissed it with a glance. "It's not bad. A copy made for me in Shinar. It's a copy of a lyre once owned by Shulgi himself. You know: the musician-king of Ur. Some generations back."

"Oh, we know of Shulgi," Marsatum said. "Hadad the sculptor sometimes sings a song or two of Shulgi's. His great-grandfather was the famous armorer Belsunu, who was trained in Ur before the Fall."

"Oh?" the musician said. He bit lustily into Pagat's fresh and chewy bread. "I heard one of those in my youth. But like a damned fool I forgot it. Who is this Hadad? I take it this Belsunu is someone I should have heard of." He threw grapes, one, two, three, into his open mouth. "But you know the minstrel caste. We never pay any attention to anything outside our trade. Unless, of course, we're hired to write a song celebrating the virtues of some rich man's ancestors."

"Hadad!" Marsatum called out. "Come over here!" She watched as the young sculptor hobbled crooklegged over to where they sat. "Hadad, meet the minstrel—here, I didn't get the name, sir?"

"Ninshubur," the musician said. "Well met, my friend. The lady tells me you know some of Shulgi's songs. A minstrel is always on the lookout for new songs. Or old ones of merit, which the popular taste has let pass into forgetfulness."

Hadad smiled his guileless smile, his wide mouth open, his eyes full of enthusiasm. "Well, I know only the ones my grandfather knew. He did not learn them from his father, because they were separated by ill fortune. But—well, he took some pride in his Sumerian background and blood, and took pains to learn them. I may not have all the words right."

"That's all right," the minstrel said. "A singer subtly changes a song to fit his personality. It's inevitable. If you're at all musical, you'll add to it rather than subtracting. Do you play?"

"Yes, sir. A little. But I wouldn't presume to play an instrument owned by a professional like yourself. What a beautiful piece of wood."

"No, go ahead. Just be gentle with it. Please. If you know any of Shulgi's songs, I can sing them at court next time I'm in Shinar."

Hadad took up the lyre, handling it in a gingerly fashion. He turned it this way and that, and then settled it in his lap, his game leg sticking out awkwardly before him. He tested the tuning and looked at the minstrel. "Please," he said. "My grandfather taught me the old tuning, the tuning of Ur. It was different from this. It fits the songs better. May I?"

"Well . . ." The minstrel's brow went up. But he sighed and sat back to watch. "You seem to know what you're doing."

"This far anyhow," Hadad said good-naturedly. "Now: this one goes up a step—and this one goes down three steps." He suited the action to the word. As the tuning progressed, the musician sat up and watched with interest. "It's the old way," Hadad explained. "Virtually nobody knows how to do it now. Maybe only me, in all of Padan-aram." He tested the final tuning, playing a note on each of the strings in turn. Then he played a chord or two. The strings rang in the warm afternoon air.

"All right," he said. He hit a chord, setting the pitch. Heads turned all over the little bazaar to hear, and conversations came to a halt. "This is a song in which the great king, Shulgi, sings of his power and exploits. Don't mind, now, that it's only me, Hadad the cripple, singing this. Close your eyes and imagine that it's the great king himself, and he's strong and tall and handsome, with powerful legs that run swiftly into battle, with strong arms that strike fear into his enemies. . . ." He hit the chord again and sang:

I, the king, a hero from my mother's womb am I,
I, Shulgi, a mighty man from the day of my birth am I,
A fierce-eyed lion, born of the *ushumgal* am I,
King of the four corners of the universe am I. . . .

Marsatum, proud, looked at the minstrel. He was watching wide-eyed, his sharp ear taking it all in. Hadad's magical young voice, which could do anything in the world he asked it to, became the strong, utterly masculine baritone of the warrior-king, singing his manifesto of liberty and justice backed by the swift sword of the benevolent tyrant; it had a thrilling ring to it. And now the minstrel smiled with pleasure, undisguised pleasure, as Hadad's voice shifted moods:

I widened the roads, made straight all highways of the
    land,
I made the roads secure, built there great hostelries,
Planted gardens alongside them, established resting-
    places,
Settled there friendly folk,
So that whoever comes from upriver or down
May refresh himself in the trees' peaceful shade;
The traveler who travels my highways at night
May find refuge there as in a well-guarded city. . . .

The song wound its way down after a thrilling climax in which the singer-king made secure his kingdom. At the end it came to rest on a long-held, ringing note of praise. Hadad finished with a rapid flourish on the beautifully tuned strings.

"Gods!" the musician said. "You're a fellow member of the craft!" He stepped forward to wring Hadad's hand as the applause rang through the little bazaar. "More: you're a genius! What are you doing squatting here in this shabby bazaar . . .?" He looked around him at the suddenly hostile glances from all sides, and backtracked hastily. "Look, I

146

mean no harm, my friends, but this man should be singing for kings, queens, the nobility of the earth! He should—"

Hadad put one hand on the minstrel's arm. He smiled his gentle, self-deprecatory smile. "My friend Ninshubur," he said, "these *are* the nobility of the earth. I could travel the world over and never find people I'd have more occasion to love and respect. Look, I'm an amateur. I sing for fun."

"But—but—" The musician sputtered, confused, frustrated, unable to finish his thought. "I—I've worked at this trade my whole adult life. I'd give anything to be able to do what—" He let out an exasperated sigh. "Play, my young friend, play. I just hope I can remember some of this by the time I get back to Shinar. Even then, I'll always be comparing my performance with yours, and telling myself I'm a fraud, who shouldn't even be trying to . . ." He shook his head, half-angrily. "Play! Sing!" he said.

"All right," Hadad said. "This is a lullaby Shulgi wrote for his firstborn, the light of his life and the joy of his age. . . ." He struck a different chord and sang. This time his voice was a gentle crooning, the voice of a father looking down on his baby's cradle, his heart bursting with love:

> Come Sleep, come gentle Sleep,
> Come to this my son,
> Hurry, Sleep, to my much-loved boy,
> And put to sleep his restless eyes. . . .

The little bazaar, buzzing with idle chatter a moment before, was quiet as a tomb now except for the gentle tinkling of the lyre and the lulling, half-hypnotic lilt of Hadad's voice. The musician's eyes shone with unfeigned tears as he watched Hadad, hearing the perfect pitch, the power, the deeply felt, superbly controlled emotion behind his singing. Marsatum, herself enthralled as always, smiled to see this. And the thought ran fleetingly through her mind: *Yes, this was the real Hadad. Not the one with the weak and crooked body. Close your eyes, your senses to all but the sound of his voice and you'd see him in your mind's eye: you'd see a man strong in heart and body, with powerful legs and strong arms. . . .*

Danataya stood at the well, the empty jug dangling from her hand. It was the most beautiful thing she'd ever heard. The powerful young voice rang effortlessly, throbbing with emotion, across the square; the chords came in, exquisitely spaced, behind his words, a perfect complement to the seamless grace of his performance. Her own heart was full at the sheer loveliness of the sound.

She could see his face now, over the assembled crowd. He seemed to be sitting on a tradesman's counter, the better to be seen and heard, but she could make out no more than his face. It was round, likeable, good-humored, with a wide generous mouth and warm brown eyes, and its mop of curly hair was a careless child's. Something in her heart went out to him.

But there was work to do. Still listening, she filled the jug, her eyes on her work, as his song came to a gentle close. She heard the applause and looked up just as the crowd broke up. Her eyes went to the singer, to his simple, expressive face, as he put down the lyre and thanked the minstrel for letting him play it. Then the crowd parted and she could see him as he stood, awkwardly, and limped away, his bad leg sticking out at an angle that it pained her to watch. Her heart sank. *Oh, the poor man. The poor dear man. Gods! Gods above! How could you do that?*

Reshef, passing the bazaar, also heard the singer, and grinned his ferret's grin. *The cripple,* he thought. *Sometimes the gods do compensate somewhat.* He shrugged. He'd heard the boy was a celibate. Well, a pretty singing voice was small comfort in a lonely single bed.

He dismissed Hadad, and looked around him at the sparse crowd of customers in the little square before turning into a side street. *Refugees,* he thought. *A damned lot of the rabble.* There'd be plenty more by the time the year came to a close. Scuttling through the streets of a strange city ... eyes haunted, fearful ... wondering where their next meal was coming from ...

It served them right, the damned fools. Letting themselves be driven from their home towns. Fighting it out instead of negotiating with the Shepherd Kings, as any sensible person would do. Faced with an enemy of superior strength, you looked about you for whatever you could sell to him to keep him from eating you alive. Or whomever. More likely whomever.

One thing was sure, that sort of thing wasn't going to happen to *him.* If Haran were attacked, he'd find something, or somebody, to sell. He'd wind up running things, owning it all. And if Haran fell, he'd be out in time, with a sizable fortune in his keeping, and with a whole skin. He'd ...

Ah, but here he was. He looked up once at the big house, at the ornate door. And, a lecherous grin on his foxlike face, he stepped up and banged lustily on the door. The little slave answered, beckoned him inside. He took his time, looking around, stretching, yawning. What the devil did he care who saw whatever? It didn't matter in the slightest. Not to him, Reshef.

"Reshef!" came a sharp voice from inside the door. "Get inside! For heaven's sake, the whole street is watching."

He smiled that same cold smile and stepped inside. She was waiting for him, exquisitely dressed and coiffed, as lovely as a king's woman. Only her face showed her anxiety, which faded as he approached.

"Good morning, Anat," he said blandly. Then his hands were on her, and he was kissing her, and he could feel the shivers of delight run through her body, already beyond her control.

IV

By the time two-thirds of that first terrible day had passed and the sun was low in the western skies, Danataya was sure she'd never last until getting-off time. Her back and every joint ached; her feet hurt horribly; her shoulders were bruised and raw, both of them, from carrying water from the well. An inn used a lot of water in the course of an average day; all of it had to be hauled by hand from the well—and the only person free to do this was the new servant girl, Danataya.

Worse than the aches and pains, however, was the treatment she got from the inn's less civilized customers during the peak hours. She was patted and pinched like a prize cow, and by late afternoon she was sure she was black-and-blue from all the prodding fingers. She'd learned to ignore the salacious things the men said—and in some ways she was glad when, the better clientele having moved on, her employers made room for the refugees, people willing to eat other people's leftovers. The refugees for the most part were broken and secretive men, men whose spirits had been so thoroughly shattered by their experience that there was little thought left in their minds for harassing a woman.

There was even a way in which the best work was the most physically degrading, the least absorbing: when you were on your hands and knees scrubbing the tiles, the front stoop, at least your mind was free to think.

Scrubbing up after the noon customers, she thought about the wretched room Admuniri had found for her, and her brutal, insensitive new landlord Horon. He'd at first demanded payment in advance; then he'd made insulting suggestions as to how she might work out the rent by barter. Only when Admuniri had intervened would he agree to wait until her first pay came due to get his money. Even then, the moment Admuniri's back was turned he had made one more insulting remark. Gods! She'd thought her earlier life with her aunt and uncle hard; now she was beginning to realize that she'd led a sheltered life all those years.

Most of all, she tried not to think of Yassib and of his betrayal of her. To think along those lines was to despair, to hate—and, worst of all, to indulge in wild, half-suicidal bouts of self-loathing. Because, of course, there was a way in which she could not blame Yassib. If he'd been offered a chance of rising in the world and if the world really was the cynical, hateful place it now appeared to be, how could she blame him, really, for preferring the daughter (the *rich* daughter; it would not pay to forget that) of his boss if she was offered to him? Over a pauper like herself? Besides, she'd seen Oshiyahu's daughters. She'd even seen them naked at the river, bathing. Their figures were full, lush, womanly; hers was skinny, the body of a woman hardly past girlhood, for all the fact that she'd left puberty and virginity behind shortly after she'd met the handsome and persuasive young Yassib, with his winning ways.

And, of course, if she couldn't hate and loathe Yassib, whom could she blame for her predicament, since blame seemed to be called for under the circumstances? Only herself. Fool that she was, she'd presumed above her station. What a fool she'd been to trust Yassib, to expect him to honor promises made to a girl without a fortune, without family or dowry. Him, a rising young soldier with a future (but only if he managed his career well).

No; that was a bad line of thought to pursue. She forced her mind into other channels. Yamam, the dancer, for instance, who'd greeted her at lunchtime. Yamam was a woman in her late twenties, full-breasted, beautiful, with lovely, graceful hands and feet and wide, womanly hips. Her smile was bright and knowing, and much enhanced by the lovely mole on her cheek, perfectly placed. She'd been quite friendly to Danataya on their first meeting: kind, understanding, treating her like an equal rather than a slavey who cleaned the floors, the lavatories. She'd said, "I hope we can get to be friends—when you have the time." And she'd kidded Admuniri about "giving the girl some time off to watch the show. You never know: she might get some ideas."

But Admuniri had snorted and shooed her away, and Danataya had gone back to her work. Nevertheless, the pleasant feeling remained that she'd made a friend. And—the thought still shocked her a little—she rather looked forward to being able to see a bit of the show, when the musicians played away furiously in the corner while Yamam came out and—well, what *did* she do? She danced for the men in the tavern. She took off her clothing. And . . .

It was a little exciting, in a way. She wondered about it. Nobody but Yassib had ever seen her body—and then only fleetingly, their meetings having mostly taken place at night and by bad light. No man had looked at her naked. She was even a great deal less shameless than most of the women at the ford, who would skin down to nothing and not worry at all whether a passing man could see them from the shore, or from the place upstream where the horses crossed. When she bathed she tended to go to the deep water, more often than not, and go in up to her neck. She was still ashamed, just a little, of her slim young body. Particularly in a world which valued ripe bodies like Yamam's. (Would she ever, ever look like that? With those marvelous breasts, those wide hips?)

And, of course, her thoughts went to the strange and moving experience she'd had during the noon hour: hearing the young man sing, with his strong, beautiful voice—and seeing his likable, kind, vulnerable young face, and adjusting her thinking so as to fit that voice to that face. She had found that they fit together ever so much better than she'd have imagined possible when first she had heard the voice and had thought it to be that of a big, strong, masterful man.

Then she'd had to adjust her thinking once again as he stood and walked away, dragging that poor crippled leg behind him, sticking out to one side the way it did. Gods! What injustice! Things—and people—should be all of one piece. What good was it when beautiful young men like Yassib should prove so false at heart! What justice was there when a young man who sang so beautifully had to walk around looking like . . . ?

And then, thinking this, she stopped scrubbing the steps for a moment and looked unseeing at the far wall across the street. There was a way in which the young man with the bad leg *was* beautiful. His simple, open, trusting face, a stranger to all guile, had about it a sweetness, an unspoiled quality that she'd never seen in a man before. She'd longed for him to look about him just once as he sang; to notice her; perhaps, for no more than a moment, to look fleetingly into her eyes. To recognize her existence, and take note of it, and let her know that he'd taken note of it.

But now she thought of his ungainly walk, his weak and skinny body, his . . .

The thoughts fought within her. And from the chaos a strange new feeling was beginning to grow. The thoughts of Yamam, dancing naked in the tavern, began insensibly, as she returned to her scrubbing and began to put her back into it, to merge with her thoughts about the crippled young singer. Then a small, frightened, utterly vulnerable fantasy crept for no more than the blink of an eye into her mind. A single picture flashed once before her eyes, and then turned black as she recoiled from it in fear and embarrassment. The picture was of her, Danataya, with her girl's body with its rose-tipped, girlish breasts, showing her body to the young singer, naked as the day the gods had first made her: seeing the desire grow in his warm brown eyes, the lust spring to life on his sweet, good-humored young face as he saw her, as his broad mouth hung open with happy astonishment to see her—her, Danataya, dancing on bare tiptoes, her whole slim body on display for him, her narrow loins and belly exposed to his gaze, her arms held high the better to indicate her openness, her vulnerability to him, her invitation to his appreciation of the all-but-unspoiled young womanhood she had to offer him. . . .

But then Abi-samar came up behind her and saw her idling. "Get to work, girl!" he bellowed. "The evening trade will be along any moment now, and we've got to be spotless for them."

Hadad pounded once again on the door. "Mother!" he shouted. "Mother! Are you there? Please, open the door."

He'd been banging away at Tallay's door for several minutes now. He was almost ready to give up and go ask one of her neighbors what had happened to her when the door opened a crack and he could see an eye, no more, visible in the dim dusk light. "Mother!" he said again. "It's me—"

"Shobai?" the madwoman said. Her tone was wistful,

half-happy. "Shobai, my darling, is that you? I—I don't dare open the door. There are strangers about—people speaking strange tongues. . . ."

"Mother, it's me," Hadad said. "Hadad. Your son—"

The door opened another crack. "Who? It isn't Shobai? No—no, you're not Shobai. Shobai is tall and strong, and you're—" Her face fell. Then she smiled, somewhat. "Oh. Hadad. Hadad, you've come to see me." She opened the door another slit. He could see her face now, with its stringy, uncombed hair.

"Mother," Hadad said. "Please. Let me in. I've got food for you. See?" He opened his garment, drew forth the strips of jerked meat, the fruit his friends had given him, the bread and cheese. "Mother, please. Please let me in, it's growing dark."

Now, at last, the door swung wide. The empty eyes flashed signs of intelligence, of sentience, for a moment; then they faded. *What year will she be living in this time?* Hadad thought despairingly. The last time she had been reliving, after her limited fashion, the last week before Kirta had left and disappeared forever. She'd treated him as if he were the little boy he'd been, only she'd continued to call him Shobai again and again, even when he'd reminded her. "Hadad?" she said. "I thought it was Shobai."

"I'm sorry it isn't, Mother," Hadad said. "He had to go to Carchemish. It was quite sudden." He went inside, and found a candle, lit it, placed it in a plate outside her reach. "I didn't hear about it myself until I went by Anat's house today and she didn't answer my knock. One of the neighbors told me he'd left early this morning."

"Dear Shobai," Tallay said. Her face was empty; her eyes went in and out of focus, and her mind went in and out of focus. Hadad looked her in the eye once and, flinching, looked away. "Dear Shobai," she said again. "He came by to see me, you know. It was—why, it was just the other day. It was—why, it was just—let me see, it was the solstice festival, I remember it because . . ."

Hadad winced again. She was probably talking the truth. But that was—what? Four cycles of the moon ago. Poor dear, she waited so patiently for Shobai's infrequent visits, and who could blame her if she tended to blank out the intervals between them? After all, she was much too far gone to understand Shobai's business, or the fact that the nature of it made it impossible for him to take the time to come by to see her. After all, he had appointments with the great people of

153

the city; he had to stay in their favor, or his business would dry up. In such a trade, he had to keep up the important contacts, and that meant being quite social, throwing parties and dinners and whatever, and attending the ones others put together. And then there was always the need to travel, once the local markets had been exhausted. How could you explain this sort of thing to a poor woman whose mind was beginning to go?

No, he thought now. *Not beginning to go; going. Sometimes—more frequently every time he saw her—gone altogether.* His heart sank, looking at her as she arranged and rearranged—whether in his honor or that of the absent Shobai he had no idea—dried-out weeds in the vases before her as though they were flowers in bloom. "Mother," he said again, "I—I brought some food for you. Look: dried meat, the finest quality. Figs, olives. See? It's for you. My friends, down at the bazaar, gave it to me for you. Wasn't that nice of them?"

"Very nice, Shobai, my darling," she said. "It was very nice of them. Please be sure to tell them how glad I was to get it. But you'll need some of this yourself, when you go back to your apprenticeship. Here, my dear, take some of this. I won't take no for an answer. Hadad and I won't mind. We'll get by. Everyone is so kind to us. And Hadad's small. He doesn't need much to eat. While you, you're a growing boy, big and tall like your father. Here, you *must* take this. More: more, please. I know your master doesn't feed you. Poor darling, you work so hard. Believe me, Shobai, we can spare it. Hadad and I—why, we do just fine here in the neighborhood. Only the other day, someone gave Hadad a whole bag of day-old bread. We lived very nicely off that for quite a little while. Didn't we, Hadad? Hadad! Why, where is that boy? You never can find him when you want him! No, wait, Shobai. I'll find him, it'll be just a moment. . . ."

Hadad looked at her, puttering ineffectually with the dried weeds in the dusty vase, and he could not find a single word to say to break into her foolish, heartbreaking monologue. He began what seemed at first a sigh, and then felt it turn into a sob. He wiped his eyes. He gulped. He tried to smile as she turned her face toward his—and then he knew it didn't make any difference. She wasn't seeing him, Hadad, at all. She had slipped further into her dreamworld, a world in which she could pin her hopes on her elder son, who would save them all from the terrible poverty into which they'd sunk after they'd been swindled out of the little money Kirta had left

154

them. A world in which she and her younger son had but the one function, to keep Shobai, who couldn't handle the gray reality of the life to which she and Hadad had sunk, from knowing what the world was really like. And to hang on, hang on with terrible tenacity, until the end of Shobai's expensive apprenticeship could liberate them all at last from the fear and worry she'd lived with daily since the day Kirta had left.

Hadad shook his head, angry at himself. *What a way to think!* He bit his lower lip and looked at his mother as she fiddled with the dried leaves. "Come, Mother," he said as he'd said so many times before he turned ten. "Come. The sun's about to go down. We've been having some very pretty sunsets lately. It'll be quite lovely. Come see it."

And as he led her out the door, he scourged himself inwardly. *That's right, Hadad,* he thought. *Give her a pretty sunset. Heaven knows you don't have much else to give her. . . .*

V

Yassib walked through the streets of Haran below the torchlights, adjusting his pace to avoid puddles, slops, and scurrying rats. It was a bad quarter to be going through at this time of night, and he was glad he'd come armed and in uniform. As it was, he'd narrowly escaped being challenged by one group of ne'er-do-wells in the Thieves' Quarter; he'd clapped his hand on his sword hilt and barked an order—and, after some hesitation, they'd retreated to a dark corner to watch him pass. In the present climate, it didn't pay to mess with an army man; one soldier hurt in a brawl in the city could lead to a whole squad of troops coming into your quarter to break heads indiscriminately.

He stepped into a puddle and cursed as he felt the wetness on his sandaled foot. Gods! These people lived like pigs down here! But on the other hand, it was either take this route to the house of Shobai—or pass the Inn of the White Horse, where a friend had told him Danataya had come to work this very day. He would gladly step in slops, and worse, to avoid running into her just now.

After all, what could he say? *"I'm sorry, Danataya, but somebody made me a better offer"*? The words would die in his throat, sour and unpronounceable. And what would she do? What would she say? What sort of reaction could he expect from her? It would even be better if she were the type who could curse at him and call him names; he at least knew how to defend himself from all that. But tears? That was something he had no idea how to handle. And worst of all, Danataya would blame herself. She'd say things like, "I know it's my fault. I'm not pretty. I have no money. I can understand how you'd want to . . ." Well, he couldn't have stood *that*. All the better to get away, avoid her and her whole part of Haran until things had blown over a bit.

Now, turning into the better quarter, he breathed a sigh of relief. Here, where the monied people lived, the guards were on duty all the time rather than just now and then. Not that he feared a scrap, but—well, why waste it? A soldier, Oshiyahu said, was paid to fight the moment he had to, for money, in defense of his city and people—and not a damned moment before, if he could help it. That was good thinking.

He fingered the tablet Oshiyahu had given him, with its neat cuneiform markings. This, now, was disquieting news, however Oshiyahu had tried to palliate it in private conversations with him. Obviously, the commander had been keeping his scouts busy, coming and going constantly, in order to have found out this kind of information. Oshiyahu had spoken highly of one of the runners—who was it? Hoshaiah —yes, he was the one. Well, according to his reports, and those of his fellows, the great column had turned. The vandals were headed *their* way! That meant that the army might well have to fight, unless some sort of accommodation could be made with the nomads.

It wouldn't pay to talk *that* kind of talk with Oshiyahu. He didn't believe in accommodations of that kind. Compromises, truces—they weren't the old fox's style. Trick 'em or lick 'em, he said, and if neither of these worked, go into the damndest strategic retreat you can possibly manage, as long as you can manage it. And sell your retreated-from land as dearly as you can possibly sell it. Make 'em die for every handspan of land they force you to retreat across. Bleed the bastards white. And burn everything you retreat from. Foods, trees, houses, whatever; burn everything you can't carry. Don't leave anything at all for 'em to live off. After a while you'll have the supplies, and they'll be stretched out over a long, long line of barren ground.

Take the nomads. They were sheepmen, herdsmen led by chiefs whom they called Shepherd Kings. They rode horses. And horses pulled those newfangled chariots they rode, that the scouts had made so much of. Sheep and horses need graze. When you draw back a league overnight, set a prairie fire the moment the wind's blowing the right way. The wind in a valley usually reverses its direction at sundown. Pick a spot to face 'em where the wind blows your way in the daytime; then, at sundown, fire the whole line in front of you and let the evening wind carry it their way. It'd not only give them a hell of a time putting out the fire and dealing with it; by the time the fire was put out there'd be a league of worthless, scorched earth before them, and grazing animals to drive across it.

Well, the old fox was brilliant. It was easy to see how he'd stayed alive all these years—and here he was, proposing to teach him, Yassib, everything he needed to know about soldiering. It was a wonderful opportunity. Nevertheless, Yassib reflected, there were rumors—rumors of disapproval of Oshiyahu and his hard-line approach to soldiering, in the city government, in the court. There was also no secret that Hirgab, his second-in-command, hated Oshiyahu's guts.

He'd asked Oshiyahu about this. After all, he'd known Hirgab for an enemy for quite some time—and then he'd given him the crucial promotion himself. Why? Why? Oshiyahu had laughed coarsely and said, "If he's an enemy, better to have him out in the open, in an exposed position. In peacetime, he can't do me a hell of a lot of harm anyhow—and in war I still outrank him. If he's too big a pain in the ass, I can always send him into battle on the front lines, in a situation in which we're going to lose that particular battle anyhow. If he does well, you have a victory against odds and all the better. If he does as you expect him to, well, what the devil, there's one less enemy." He'd smiled a knowing smile and snorted loudly. "Hell, many of my greatest victories have been won for me by people—subordinates—who hated me and who'd have cut my throat for me if I'd ever given them the ghost of a chance. The secret, my boy, is never to give them that chance."

What a wise old fox! Yassib, thinking about the commander's cynical remarks and don't-give-a-damn tone, had to smile. Nonetheless, it wouldn't pay to get himself too totally identified with Oshiyahu, just in case. It would definitely pay to make friends with some of Hirgab's friends, people who would carry back to Hirgab the welcome news that Oshiyahu's young companion wasn't totally, unhesitatingly, in the other camp.

Reshef, for instance. There was little doubt that, given a choice between Oshiyahu and Hirgab, Reshef would come down on Hirgab's side. Some even went so far as to call Reshef, the wily jackal, the real force behind Hirgab's little power-move at court. Well, perhaps not the power—not yet—but the brains at least. And perhaps even the initial impetus. Hirgab, for all his aristocratic connections, wasn't that smart, that calculating. Reshef was. It might pay to cultivate Reshef a bit, for all that the very sight of him inspired fear and distrust.

Which house was it that he . . . ? He stopped, turned around. Ah, there it was. He strode toward the ornate door and rapped upon it. Inside he heard footsteps coming his way. Then the door opened a crack. "Yassib, adjutant to the lord Oshiyahu, commander of the garrison at Haran—to see the lord Reshef," he said in an efficient-sounding military voice.

"I'll see if—" a girl's voice came from the crack in the door. But a familiar male voice crackled in the evening air. "Let him in," it said. The girl opened the door and Yassib came inside.

To his great surprise, Reshef greeted him in a thoroughly unsoldierly deshabille: he wore only a soiled loincloth which he was unhurriedly belting about his middle. His hair was tousled. Yassib looked at the girl, a slave. And *she* showed no signs at all of recent roughhousing. Whomever Reshef had been cavorting with, it had to be the mistress and not the slave. But this? This was the house of Shobai, the rich armorer, the man who'd armed Oshiyahu's army. And Shobai was known to be a big, strong, very physical sort of bastard who could, and would, break your arm for you without giving the matter a second thought. Gods! he thought to himself. Reshef was really taking his chances.

"Here," Reshef said, stepping into his sandals. "I gather you've got some sort of message for me. Well, time enough for that." He yawned elaborately, letting his face settle afterward into the usual wolf's grin. "Here, Tanuha: call your mistress. There's a good girl." He slapped the slave on the bottom, audibly.

"But—sir—she's—"

"Damn it, do as I say! Do you want your brains scrambled?" Reshef shot her a threatening glare. Then he turned to Yassib, suddenly affable. "I'll send for some wine. This military talk is dry stuff." He slipped into his tunic and belted it with his sword-belt. "You," he said to Yassib, his eyes crafty, "you've risen quite a way very quickly. I hear you're marrying the commander's brat."

"Sir, I—" Yassib stood at attention, stiff and angry.

"Oh, come on. Don't play the dummy with me. It's as good a way to rise as any. Why get your back up about it? Well, how do you like your father-in-law-to-be? You know, of course, that you're marrying trouble. That is, if you creep under his coat like a body louse and expect to rise all the way with His Excellency."

Yassib stayed more or less at attention. "I understand the commander *has* made political enemies," he said grudgingly, "but he—"

"Enemies? Damned right he has. They'll be the undoing of him one of these days. If he thinks—" He turned, angry. "Anat!" he bellowed coarsely. "Tanuha, where the hell is she! Tell her to get her ass out here and—"

But just then, an interior door opened and a woman stepped out. Her eyes were frightened-looking, annoyed, but too fearful to express it; they went from one soldier to the other. "Reshef, please. Not so loud. The neighbors—" Her voice was subdued, pleading. Yassib gaped shamelessly. She was stunningly beautiful even in her dishevelment—barefoot, her hair down, wearing only a short shift. He could see the bruises on her arms where Reshef had handled her roughly; the cherry-red bite mark on her neck.

"Loud?" Reshef said, raising his voice. "You want loud? I'll give you loud—unless you get your ass in step and bring the two of us some wine." His voice was cruel, brutal. She winced visibly—but she obeyed, tiptoeing out of the room on silent bare feet. "Damned bitches," Reshef said. "You've got to stay on top of them. The moment you start treating them any better than you'd treat a stupid, sullen pig of a brood-mare, they start giving themselves airs. Now, take that one: her ass of a husband spoils the hell out of her. She hates his guts, can you imagine? And who does she come running to the moment the old man is out of town? Me, that's who. Me, who treats her like the slut she is at heart."

Yassib, embarrassed, fingered the tablet inside his garment. "Sir," he said. "The lord Oshiyahu told me to deliver the message as quickly as possible. I'd better report—"

Reshef scowled, annoyed. He scratched his crotch and yawned cavernously again. "Oh, well. If you feel you really have to...."

"Well—" Yassib drew forth the tablet, handed it over. Reshef, yawning again as he read, looked it over and threw it back to him. He barely caught it in time, juggling it in the air precariously. "But—but, sir—"

"So the nomads have turned our way?" Reshef said, rubbing his eyes and his nose, making the faces of one who has just climbed out of bed. Scratching his head. Stretching. "Well, it's no more than any fool might have expected. We're smaller, weaker, more poorly defended. So is Carchemish, for that matter. Mari, on the other hand, is rich and powerful. And if you anger the king of Mari, you anger the kings of Shinar and Elam, and perhaps throw enough of a jolt into the Assyrians to get them interested in you. If I were the nomads, I wouldn't go tackling Mari either. Matter of stirring up a hornet's nest. Damn foolishness."

"If you'll excuse me, sir," Yassib said, "aren't you taking all this—well, rather lightly? If—"

"Oh?" Reshef said, opening his eyes wide for the first time, looking directly into Yassib's face. "You're taking a personal interest in all this? *Personal?* What kind of a soldierly attitude is that, my young friend? Gods! The next thing you know I'll be hearing you extol the virtues of patriotism, seeing you wave the banners of Haran. Don't tell me you've developed a sentimental attachment to this grubby backwater town? *Really.*" The eyes were a vulture's, cold, calculating, chillingly detached.

Under that basilisk gaze, Yassib fidgeted and flinched. "Well, no, sir—I mean not really—I mean, after all—"

"Look," Reshef said. "You look like an intelligent chap. And I've heard stories about you. You have the reputation of having your wits about you. If I'm right about you, you'll have gauged just how much you could get out of a maneuver like marrying Oshiyahu's spawn. And you'll know just about when it'll be time to cut loose the parental apron strings. Right?"

His smile was a terrible thing; his eyes dug into Yassib's vulnerable young soul. Somehow, he could not lie to this man, could not dissemble. No matter that he had already learned precisely how much, and how outrageously, one might lie to Oshiyahu, and could perform with a virtuoso's grace and skill at this difficult and dangerous art. Lying to Reshef, himself a liar who understood liars, who could sniff them out of a huge crowd, was another matter altogether. "I—I defer to your greater and more mature judgment, sir," he said, his throat dry.

Reshef cackled cynically. "Well spoken!" he said appreciatively. "I could hardly have come up with a more diplomatic answer myself. You're championship material, young man, if you don't weaken. Do you know the principle you've just put into action, young fellow? It's one of the most important you could possibly come up with. I can state it in a single sentence. *When in doubt, answer every question with another question.* Splendid, splendid. And if you can work in a little dollop of nice, greasy flattery, all the better. My compliments. You'll go far. *If* you don't weaken."

The woman came in now with wine: a jar and two bowls. She flashed half-angry looks at the two of them and withdrew. Reshef made no move to thank her. "Now," the senior officer said, "I'll pour, here—there. Drink up, young man." The two of them drained their bowls of wine in identical motions, then set them down again. "Here," Reshef said. "Now that you've had your wine, get along with you. Tell His Excellency I'll be right along in the morning, blah blah blah. You know the routine. Tell him what he wants to hear. Tell him I'm, ah, 'gravely concerned.' That sort of thing. If I've read you right, you'll know the kind of flowery language to couch it all in. And in the meantime, well—" He yawned again, and this time the yawn, ending, turned into a lecherous, heartless grin. "Go along with you. And keep in touch, eh? I think you and I will have more to talk about as time goes by. Eh? Am I right?"

"I—I suppose so, sir," Yassib said, feeling acutely conscious of having committed himself to something the outcome of which was perhaps dark and shady—but feeling that there'd been no other choice. Then, as he turned to go, he saw that Reshef's mind had turned definitively from his affairs to other matters. Making his way to the door unattended, he heard Reshef's nasal, sarcastic voice say, "Anat! Where have you gone to? Come to my arms, my dove, my angel! Anat! *Anat!* Damn your eyes, come here or I'll—" The tone carried neither love nor respect nor any positive element Yassib could identify. It sent chills up and down his spine. His ears burning, he beat a hasty retreat.

VI

In the morning a messenger came from the Temple of Ishtar, bearing a commission for two dozen small figures of the Goddess. They were not to be inlaid or ornate in any way; there was a certain house style that was to be followed, and the pay was nothing special; but it was pay, after all, and Hadad's meager reserves—he would not touch the lump gold—had long since been exhausted. He was glad to get the commission and set to work immediately, humming happily as his deft fingers shaped the clay.

This wasn't by any means his favorite kind of work, even leaving aside the question of price. There was far too little opportunity to individualize the work. It would be a great deal more fun to do secular figures, which could be personalized; this one with a big comical belly, that one with a hump on its back. Or faces: faces with squints, faces with broad smiles, old people's faces with wrinkles that delineated character. This above all he enjoyed: Hadad's keen interest in people made the shaping of faces a real joy, and everyone who had seen his work had commented on his ability to find exactly the proper means to bring out personality in the clay sketches he made of his subjects.

But this? There was a house style and you followed it. And, strictly speaking, virtue did not enter an image of the Goddess until the moment it had been blessed. That was why the priests and priestesses could charge so much more for his work, passing it on to the rich, than he could, passing it on to the temple. Hadad accepted the situation and thanked his lucky stars for the work.

Still, he remembered the merchant Ibalum, and wondered if anything would ever come of their meeting. "Stay in touch with my brokers," the man had said. "Find out when I'm due to return . . . I hope to give you further business. Maybe steer a friend or two your way, people who appreciate nice things."

His hands kneading the clay, he mused about this now. Of course it wouldn't pay to go counting on anything. A big man like Ibalum couldn't be expected to remember every shabby ragamuffin who happened along, artist or no. But—

how nice it would be to see him again, to meet more "people who appreciated nice things."

He decided it wasn't just the money. There was ample reward in the look that came into people's eyes when they saw his work and really liked it, and could appreciate the little nice touches that had occurred to him while he was shaping it. The tone of their voices changed subtly as they discussed his work, sometimes not so subtly. To share that joy with them was reward enough. Any money they happened to give him afterward was sauce on the meat.

And, of course, the truth was that people who gave him the reward of appreciation—people of substance, educated in the ways of art—usually tended to reward him more handsomely where money was concerned than the others did. To be sure, there were exceptions—he'd even been swindled outright once or twice—but on the whole, people had been honest, even generous. Some of them, Ibalum among them, tended to value his work more highly than he did himself.

Ibalum—how nice it would be to have a steady customer like the merchant, a man who liked his work and knew how to seek out the people who would also like it and who would pay him handsomely for it. It was a pleasant dream, but of course dream was all it was, and there wasn't much sense in pursuing it further. If it happened it would happen, and if it didn't—well, there was no use speculating about things like that.

But . . .

That was the trouble with hackwork like this. There wasn't much in it to occupy your mind, and as a result you tended to let your mind wander. You started daydreaming, you dreamed about having enough money to get by comfortably, not a great deal but enough, and having a nice house in a clean, safe part of town—perhaps a place with a little spot of garden, and with a room for Tallay, and perhaps even someone to look after her so that she didn't fall and hurt herself. And—well, if you were daydreaming this way, why not add things like maybe a little fishpond in the garden, with bright little fish swimming around in it, and lily pads? Why not a cook, to prepare the food? Why not . . .

"Well, for goodness' sake, Hadad. Look what you've done." Marsatum's voice broke into his reverie. He looked up, startled, and saw her amused face, eyes crinkled with humor. "Look," she pointed to him. "Look what you've got in your hand."

He looked down. He almost dropped the clay in surprise.

He hadn't been paying attention to what he was doing—and the image in his hand was not a house-style image of the Goddess, cold and abstract, at all. It was a highly realistic depiction of a real woman's torso, with a sensual belly, ripe buttocks, and round womanly breasts whose nipples stuck out like little thumbs. He shot another glance at Marsatum; then he looked away, embarrassed. "Please," he said hastily. "I—I wasn't thinking."

"Yes you were," Marsatum said, tolerant affection in her voice. "And I approve. Hadad, you're a member of the human race after all."

By early afternoon he had better than half the work done. He'd skipped his midday meal—he was broke until he could collect from the temple for the work he'd done, and in fact he owed for the clay—and worked straight through. Now, however, he looked up and saw a man approaching: a man recognizably of the upper class, but sober, businesslike. "Hadad the sculptor?" the man said.

"That's me," Hadad said smiling. His hands continued to work; he didn't need to look at them to know what he was doing. "How may I serve you?"

"My name is Arusian," the man said. "I work for the merchant Ibalum."

"Oh?" Hadad said. "I was just thinking about him."

The man was uninterested in this fact. "Ibalum has asked me to get in touch with you and remind you of his interest in your, uh, work." He looked skeptically at the hackwork in Hadad's hands.

"Oh," Hadad said, looking down. "Don't mind this. This is just a quick commission from the temple. I do this to keep body and soul together. Meanwhile, when I have time—"

"Ah, yes. I understand. I'm sure Ibalum knows very well what he's doing. He told me that I was to remind you to get in touch with him the moment he returns from his current business trip. He left with the caravan for Carchemish the other morning."

"Oh, yes. My brother went on the same caravan."

"I see. Well, he'll be trading there and in Ugarit, and in the southern cities along the shore of the Great Sea: Tyre, Ashkelon. At any rate he'll be back in a while. When he returns, he has a proposition to make to you. If you're interested, that is."

"Me? Interested?" Hadad said enthusiastically. "Of course I'm interested. Who wouldn't be interested?" But his thoughts now caught up with his enthusiasm. "What sort of proposition?" he said.

"I think it has something to do with his acting as your agent in selling your work here and abroad. Let me tell you too, young man, that's an unusual thing for him to do. The usual method of dealing with a maker of—things like this—is to buy his work cheap and sell it dear somewhere else. He's proposing something altogether different in your case."

"Different?" Hadad said, putting the little statuette down and looking his visitor in the eye. "How different?"

"Well, he's thinking of helping pay for your materials, for one thing. And then selling your work on commission only."

"I don't understand. I've never worked except on an outright-sale basis before. This is all new to me."

"He'll go out and sell it for the best price he can get—and then, after subtracting the cost of the materials he's advanced you, he'll take a certain percentage of the total and give you the rest." The man shook his head. "Most unusual. I've never seen him do this with a—a common tradesman." Arusian backtracked almost immediately. "I—I didn't mean to offend, of course; what I meant was . . ."

"That's all right," Hadad said. "I understand. I'm absolutely amazed. How very kind of him. How very nice."

"Yes. And do you know, my young friend, you may wind up quite well-to-do if his interest in you continues? His patronage has made a lot of difference in the careers of a number of artists of various kinds. Painters, musicians, mummers. But particularly in the lives of people who make things, the way you do. I was at his house the night before he left; he gave a party for various well-placed guests. He showed every one of them the work you did for him. He spoke in praise of your work, mentioning you by name. But—and I would ask you to take note of this—he did not tell them your whereabouts. For all they know, you could be living and working in Carchemish or Mari."

"Why? I'm afraid I don't under—"

"Because he wants to represent you exclusively. He wants them to have to come through him if they want your work. And a good thing too, my friend. Because if they came to you directly, you'd get only a fraction of what he can get for you, dealing with them himself. Even after his commission, your fee will be—well, I don't know what you make now." Hadad gave him a figure. "Is that all? Let me guess that you'll be able to command a fee at least ten times that. More."

"Gods!" Hadad let his breath out. "You have my head

spinning. I'd better not even think about it. I—would you please send Ibalum my thanks? Next time you send a message after him? And—and thank you, too, for coming."

He finished the day's work in a daze, and as dusk approached, he climbed the tall stairs of the temple to deliver the images. He collected his small fee and turned back to look down at the city spread beneath him, looking down on houses and streets, on gardens, on the walls of the city itself.

He looked down at the little purse in his hand. It was sparse, and the payment had been in base coin. It wasn't a great deal, but it would come in very handy right now. He was broke. He'd even had to skip the evening meal the night before after leaving the fruit and cheese and meat with his mother (having bribed a neighbor to store it for her and portion it out to her). Now at least he was sure of the rent and could eat for—oh, perhaps a week or more, if he didn't splurge anywhere.

But . . .

His heart beat a little faster. What if this Arusian fellow were telling the truth? What if Ibalum had taken that kind of interest in him—and had decided to work only on commission, in his behalf? Why, what an extraordinary thing this would be! He could—he could get rich! He could *have* that house with the garden he'd daydreamed about only today. He could *have* the cook, and the servant or slave to look after his mother. It *wasn't* just an idle dream.

He sighed. The thing was, it all sounded so plausible, given the very friendly treatment Ibalum had given him earlier. It didn't sound like the sort of foolish and unrealistic expectation you got stuck in your head when you'd had a trifle too much wine. Not after you'd actually talked to Ibalum, heard the tone of his voice when he talked to you, looked him in the eye. It all seemed so . . .

But now his eye, roving over the rooftops, roved also over a garden wall, and there was something oddly familiar about the garden, about its arrangement of trees and flowers, and . . .

It was Shobai's house! Shobai's garden! Who would have thought you could see into the back garden from here? How curious! And you could—

His heart almost stopped.

Into the garden came a woman. She wore only a simple shift; no sooner had she moved into view than she loosened

166

the cinch around her waist and let it fall to the ground. She stood there, half facing him, naked, her whole long slim body on view. He tried to look away and found he couldn't. He couldn't shut his eyes either, no matter how he told himself he should. But you shouldn't, he told himself, you shouldn't look at your brother's—

Anat. Anat . . .

He wiped a sudden cold sweat from his forehead. The woman beckoned to someone out of sight. A man moved into view. A soldier, uniformed. She embraced him, her nude body pink against his clothed one. The embrace was sensual, passionate. His knee went between her bare thighs.

Anat! Please! Please don't . . .

Now she was undoing the man's belt and drawing off first his sword, then his tunic. He stood nude except for a narrow loincloth; she removed this, too. Her hands ran all over his naked body. She sank to her knees before him, her hands gripping his hairy thighs. Her face disappeared behind his body. His hands came around and buried themselves in her dark hair as he stood before her.

Hadad was almost crying, looking down at the scene below. He put his hand to his mouth, bit into its flesh hard to keep himself from crying out. He found he was trembling uncontrollably. The worst, the worst part about it was that he was not only mentally shaken by all this but, but— Yes. He was aroused by it as well. Painfully. He balled his hands into fists, tried to control the shaking fit that had come upon him, tried to make himself look away. His brother's wife, with a stranger, a soldier—no, it wasn't a stranger either, was it? It was the soldier Reshef. The one with the bad reputation. How could she? And so shameless about it! So—so low, so vulgar! What could bring a woman, a good woman, to such a—?

But now the soldier's body was shivering just as his own was, and his hands gripped the woman's head hard, and his body quivered, grew rock-hard . . . and then relaxed. And her dark head waggled slowly, almost sleepily, from side to side as her hands ran sensuously up and down his flanks, caressing him, caressing him. . . .

Anat!

VII

Danataya was up before dawn the next day, and by the time it was light, she had scrubbed the walls of the Inn of the White Horse until they virtually shone. Then she climbed atop a chair and scrubbed the sign until the white form of the prancing pony stood out against the background. She was still working on this when Abi-samar came in from his home in another quarter and saw her. "Good work!" the innkeeper said, cheerier than usual. "Keep that up and you'll hear no complaints from me. Have you eaten yet?"

"No, sir," she said, climbing down carefully. "There wasn't time. Not if I was going to get down here and get all this cleaned up before the people awoke and started coming to work."

"Well, go inside and have a bit of something. You're too skinny. You'll have me worrying about you. Ask the cook for something. Tell her I sent you. You hear? I want to fatten you up a little bit. Not a lot, but some. Put a little weight on your bones and you'd be quite pretty, you know?"

"Thank you, sir," she said. But as she turned to go, she and Abi-samar saw the woman coming. She was thin, thinner than Danataya was. She wore a drab headcloth, and the face below it was drawn with care, but had been pretty once—and could be again, if something happened to erase the pervasive impression of unhappiness she gave.

"Well, Rachel," Abi-samar said. "What can I do for you?"

Danataya could have left, but somehow the woman's expression so mirrored the worry within her that she stayed for a moment. Perhaps there was something she could do to help. The woman spoke: "It's Jacob," she said. "He didn't come home last night. I asked everyone. Nobody seems to know where he could be. And—I'm afraid to ask Laban. If my father learns he's missing . . ."

"I understand," Abi-samar said. "Not that I'd want my opinion to get back to him, my dear, but—well, Laban is a hard man. And he rides Jacob hard—too hard. A number of us here in the quarter have thought about mentioning it to him. Jacob's a fine manager of your father's herds. Gods, I wish the man who looks after my own stock were the tenth part as good. I'd hire him in a minute if your father—but no. If Jacob can ever get out of debt, he'll be his own man. He won't want to work for anyone."

The woman Rachel had listened patiently to this rambling discourse. Now she said, "But—he's gone. It isn't like him. And—Abi-samar. Someone said he saw Jacob down here last night. At your inn."

"Jacob? Here? Well, I was out for a good portion of the evening, but I didn't see—"

Danataya spoke. "Excuse me, is he a man of medium height, with big, intelligent-looking brown eyes? Looks very sad? And—and has long lines by the corner of his mouth, and a sort of tense look?"

"Yes!" the woman said. Her eyes grew wary, her expression intense. "That's him. Where did he—?"

"I don't know, ma'am. But—he has such a distinctive face, as if he were—oh, a wise man, a magus or a priest or something, only as if he'd read the auguries, the stars or whatever, and had learned that things were bad and getting worse. . . ."

"Yes," Abi-samar said, concerned. "That's Jacob, all right. Why?"

"Well, he took note of me. I spilled something, and he helped me pick it up. That's why I remember—"

"Where? Outside? In the bazaar?"

"No, sir. In the inn. It was something else I noticed. He seemed desperately, horribly unhappy."

"He is. Go on, please."

"Yes. Well, he ordered wine, and—"

"Wine? Jacob? Drinking in an inn?" Rachel was horrified. "Look, I don't mean to hurt your feelings, but that's impossible. Jacob's religion—our religion—forbids that sort of thing. Drinking, things like that . . ."

"Yes, ma'am. That was the strange thing. He ordered wine, and then he just sat there looking at it. As if he were trying to decide what to do. As if he had some sort of insoluble problem to solve. Some impossible burden to bear. And looking as if he couldn't make up his mind what to do because all the choices available to him were bad. . . ."

"You see much," Rachel replied. "You're a bright and observant girl. And—you have a bit of heart about you. Thank you for noticing. But, afterward, what happened? No, wait"—she put a soft hand on Danataya's arm—"I think I can add to what you've told me. His horse—the one he uses to ride out into the farthest fields Laban uses for grazing his herds—well, it was gone this morning. But none of his sons has seen him, and they've sent word back that he has not been seen at any of his normal places." She looked at Abi-samar now and withdrew her hand—but not before caressing Danataya's arm thankfully. "I'm afraid he's just, well, gone off somewhere. Laban—father—humiliated him shamefully yesterday, and two of his older sons, sons of my sister Leah, were there to see it. They're a shiftless and sarcastic lot, I'm afraid, and they seem to have taunted their father for his inability to fight back when Laban cursed him. As if it weren't Jacob's forbearance under the heavy burden of father's rages that had supported them and their brothers all these difficult years."

"Ah, yes," Abi-samar said. "Ungrateful puppies." He spat scornfully into the street. "Jacob's had a hard row to hoe all this time. Me, I'd have put a knife in Laban long ago. He has a tongue on him, Laban has. But—you think he's just up and gone? You mean, last night?"

"There's enough moon to ride by. Jacob's known at the gate. He could find his way out. Maybe he needed to—oh, just get off by himself and think things out. But in this unsettled time, with the area all full of desperate strangers from the north... with the threat of war hanging over Mari, to the east... with bandits said to be roaming the hills wherever the guards are sparse..."

"Well, I wouldn't worry about that. Jacob's a man of sense, of resources. He can take care of himself. He'll be back in a while. Don't worry, my dear. He'll be all right. I'm more worried about you than I am about Jacob. You don't look well. Too skinny, like young Danataya here. Oh, I didn't introduce you. Rachel, daughter to the wool and beef factor Laban, wife to Jacob. This is Danataya, who's come to work for us."

"I'm so glad to meet you," Rachel said, and the real spark of friendship in her eye for a fleeting moment showed Danataya the beauty the woman could be again. She touched Danataya's arm once more and then smiled at Abi-samar. "Please," she said. "If you hear anything..." And then she was gone.

As Danataya turned to go, she spotted another figure coming down the street. She'd have bet half her wages that she could not, in the space of one morning, see another face as unhappy as Rachel's; but now, she conceded, she would have lost the bet. Hadad, the young singer, came limping painfully down the little street, his face a mask of pain and suffering, his leg dragging awkwardly. He looked through her and saw nothing; his eyes were red-rimmed. (From crying? From loss of sleep? She couldn't say. Maybe both.) One hand wrung the other miserably; his mouth worked as if he were speaking, but no words came out. Abi-samar looked at Hadad, shook his head sympathetically, nodded at Danataya. "Here," he said in a kind voice. "Go get yourself something to eat. Forget everyone else's troubles, girl. You've got a lot of work to do today. Get some food in you to do it on."

Jacob reined in his animal at the top of the ridge and looked out at the hardscrabble scrub toward the east. The horse on the far hill saw him, whinnied, and turned to run away. He wished the animal had come closer, even if he'd remained unable to catch it. It would have been a nice thing to catch a stray—but he'd have settled for a closer look at the unfamiliar saddle and rig on the beast. It wasn't something he'd ever seen before.

One thing was sure: the horse had had a rider. But where? How long ago had the rider been thrown and abandoned by the animal? And who, in an area like this, would be riding alone? Could there be two such damned fools as himself, riding out beyond the farthest scouts' camps, where bandits prowled the mountains to prey on hapless passersby and even on caravans whose leaders had been so stupid as to under-arm themselves?

And now that he thought on it, the more fool he, Jacob, seemed to himself. At least when he'd had the impulse to get away, he'd had the prudence to fill a leather bottle with water and to throw bread and cheese into a saddlebag. Well, that was Jacob: the man of prudence. All the real rashness had gone to his twin brother, Esau. Yet—look at him, acting as Esau might have acted, riding out, taking chances.

He frowned. Self-recrimination was a waste of a grown man's time and spirit. He'd do no more of it. But it did feel good to get out by himself, as he'd done so many times as a boy in Canaan, riding on one of Isaac's Moabite horses out across the enormous domain God had given to Abraham and his seed forever, rejoicing in the length and breadth of the land of his fathers.

(*Oh, Canaan! Will I ever see you again?*)

Now, however, with the sun getting high, it was time to return. He'd work to do, and it wouldn't pay to have Laban come by and see him missing and no one able to say where he was. It would lead to another scene, and he, Jacob, wasn't sure just how many of these he could put up with any longer without telling Laban off. He—

Jacob cut off his rambling thoughts abruptly. He held his head high, one hand on the horse's neck, calming the animal. He turned his head, his ears, this way, that—

"Aihee!"

The cry was from some distance, but it was clear and unmistakable. It was a man's voice. Jacob patted the horse again, listening. Once again the cry rang out. He rode forward, reached the top of the hill, looked around. This time, when it came, the sound was closer.

Now he turned back along the path that had brought him to the top of the ridge. He led his surefooted pony's steps down the trail . . .

. . . and all of a sudden saw a flash of metal, visible in the rays of the morning sun. He rode down to the edge of the cliff. "Here!" he said. "Where are you? I—"

Then he saw the man. He was on his back, halfway down the slope. He was waving, crying out. Jacob couldn't make out anything he was saying. He remained mounted, but rode nearer the edge. Then he took a coil of rope from his saddle. "You!" he said. "I'm going to throw something down for you! Do you hear me . . . ?"

Neither the stranger's clothes nor his accent (he spoke a halting, heavily guttural version of the language common to Haran and Mari and all the northern towns) was familiar to Jacob. When Jacob had managed to haul him out of the ravine into which he'd fallen, he learned the man had sprained one ankle badly. He offered to help the stranger up onto his own horse; but the stranger, shaking off his aid, threw his head back, put two fingers to his mouth, and let out the loudest, most ear-splitting whistle Jacob had ever heard.

To Jacob's astonishment, the horse he'd seen, the one with the strange saddle, appeared over the top of the hill and headed their way. In a moment, the limping rider had his hand on the animal's bridle and was rubbing its neck with rough affection. He turned to Jacob. "I—thank you," he said haltingly.

"Here," Jacob said. "The least thing you can do is stop for a moment and share a meal with me." His smile was open, accommodating. "After all, you owe me something. Why not pay off the debt in company?"

It took a few more words to explain this. After some

circumlocution, Jacob got the message across. He did this mainly by pulling the saddlebag down from his now-hobbled horse and pointing to bread, cheese, water bag. The man looked Jacob in the eye and nodded. He hobbled his own animal and limped to a clearing atop the hill, where the two of them sat down cross-legged on the bare ground, after the fashion of outdoorsmen the world over, and broke bread together, passing the water bag back and forth and drinking guardedly.

"You are from . . . where?" the stranger said.

"I am from Haran," Jacob said. "At least I live there now. I was born far to the south. And you?"

The stranger ignored the question. "South?" he said. "How is like, down there? Is green? Much grass, much—mmmm—much figs, olives?"

"Very much so," Jacob said. "Not so much so as Goshen, our name for the delta of the Nile River. *That's* a land of milk and honey. You throw a seed at the ground and you must jump back or the plant will spring up so fast it will knock you down." He smiled at the mild joke. "But Canaan —that's my own land—it's quite good. I'm sorry I'm not there now." He passed the water bag. "And you?" he said again. "You come from . . ."

"Ah," the stranger said. "From far north. Beyond high mountains. Everywhere . . . dry. No water. And . . . what you call? Grass . . . sick. Sick."

"You mean blight? Something killed off the grass?" The stranger nodded. "That's too bad. Well, if your herds are not too numerous, you should find graze for them somewhere along here. How many do you have?"

The stranger's gaze was impenetrable. His eyes sought Jacob's, lit up for a second. "How many?" he said. His voice was chilling. "How many grains of sand?" He picked up a handful of dirt, let it sift to the ground. "How many stars in sky?" He softened that dry voice for a moment. "You are called . . . what?"

"Jacob," he said. "If you come to Haran ask for me. We have broken bread together."

"Yes," the stranger said. "Bread, together. Is good. You . . . friend."

"Certainly," Jacob said. The stranger seemed to want to say more. Jacob waited patiently, one adult listening while another adult gathered his thoughts.

"You . . . friend. Help me. I . . . help you." He illustrated his meaning by pointing first at Jacob, then at himself. "If I

173

come to Haran, I say, there will be no Haran. Gone. Everything gone. I send for you. You, Ja-cob. I say, Ja-cob be gone. You go away. I . . . spare you. The Shepherd Kings, their armies, spare you. *Your* family. *Your* herds. You hear? None else. Only Ja-cob. His wives, his sons and daughters. His herds. You hear? I . . . owe you, Ja-cob. As you say. Break bread. Friend. I come, I call to you, you go away. You go away soon, Jacob. Everybody die. . . ."

After the stranger had mounted and ridden away, Jacob, astride his own beast, watched after him. He rode east, and a little toward the north. Jacob pondered what the man had said, wondered how seriously he was to take the man's words. Herds like the stars in the sky? Shepherd Kings? It all seemed farfetched. And then again it didn't. There *were* all the stories the refugees had brought into the city: gigantic nomad armies led by great chieftains, sweeping the land clean of all life.

Well, he had a warning. And he had, within limits, a friendship, one which would save him from whatever harm the stranger's people might bring with them if they should come to Haran.

And he had a name to remember: the stranger's name, which the stranger assured him would mean the difference between life and death for Jacob and his own kind some day. A strange name, short and pungent. Jacob rolled it on his tongue now. *"Manouk,"* he said. . . .

VIII

It was impossible for Hadad's friends not to notice the difference in him. He was morose, uncommunicative. He looked off into space; his hands trembled and mauled and mutilated the clay. Worst of all, when they approached him, one at a time, to say hello and try to draw him out of himself, he would lapse into a vague smile, shallow and unconvincing, and "make conversation." It was the worst conversation they'd ever heard.

Several of them gathered in a corner of the bazaar to discuss him. Then, after the midday meal, Marsatum, whose stall was closest to his in the square, approached him again. "Hadad," she said. "Something's wrong. Now don't lie to me and claim it isn't so. Do you take me for a fool? Something's bothering you terribly, and it has all of us worried. You'll be doing us all a disservice if you keep it to yourself and let it tear away at you like this."

Hadad looked at her; his eyes filled with tears. "I—" He gulped and tried again. "Marsatum," he said. "I can't."

"Is it your mother?" she said. "Because—look. We can help you take care of her. We can pool our resources. Each of us can volunteer one day a week. Do you understand? That way it won't become a burden on any—"

"No, no. She's all right. I mean—no, she isn't all right, that's not true—but, well, that isn't what's the matter."

"Is it something that's happened to you? Did anyone hurt you? Insult you? Make you feel bad about . . . ?" Her eyes went to his twisted leg.

"No, no. No, thank you, but—Marsatum. What would you do—I mean you yourself—if someone—someone you loved and admired and trusted . . ."

"Who? Some friend of yours? Your brother?"

"No, no. If someone, well, if you saw someone . . . doing something . . . that was going to ruin him and . . . make other people's lives miserable and—"

"Hadad. Is it someone close to you? Is that it?"

"I—I'd rather not say, but—"

"Hadad, how can I answer if you don't tell me? How can I help you if—"

"I can't say!" he cried out in a voice full of torment. "Please! Please! Just leave me alone!"

The guard stopped Jacob at the outer edges of the vast army encampment. "I'm sorry, sir, I can't let you in unless you have some sort of pass, or unless I can have the approval of—"

"Look, my friend," Jacob said, still the reasonable man, "if you'll just try calling one of your officers. I've met the lord Oshiyahu a couple of times, selling him mutton for the army. If you'll be so good as to call him . . ."

"He's gone on an inspection tour," the guard said. "His orderly and his adjutant went with him. I can't—"

But then the guard looked up and saw someone coming behind Jacob. Jacob wheeled to see a man in military uniform dismounting. The face was familiar, unpleasantly so, but he couldn't tie a name to it. The man handed the reins of his horse to the guard and faced him. "You," he said. "What are you doing here? What's your name?"

Jacob lifted a brow but did not react quickly. Prudence, always prudence. "My name is Jacob. I'm a purveyor of mutton stock. I've sold to your sutlers, and—"

"Sold to our sutlers, eh? I suppose you know one of them is in danger of hanging? For swindling the army, working in cahoots with crooked dealers and—"

"That may be as it may be. I have also sold directly to the commander of the garrison. Perhaps you would like to tell me how much trouble *he's* in."

The soldier smiled a crooked smile: unpleasant. "Ah, you're a smooth one, aren't you? All right, state your business. But make it quick. I haven't much time."

Jacob was thinking. *The name? What was the name? Yes: Reshef. What a name. Who would name an innocent child after the god of plague?* "Last night I—I took a ride out past the pickets. I rode until morning. I saw something—someone —who perhaps shouldn't have been there. Who should be called to the attention of someone in authority." *Keep it cool and correct now.*

The soldier's eyes narrowed. "Here," he said. "Come with me." He waved to the guard. "It'll be all right," he said. "He'll be with me." He led Jacob to a clear space and looked around. "I gather that what you have to say is not for the ears of just anybody," he said. "Go on."

"Whose ears this is for is not my affair," Jacob said equably. "I just thought I should share what I saw and heard with someone in a position of authority." Quickly, he told the whole story: the accident, the brief sharing of bread, the man's threat and promise. "That's all," he said. "I don't have any idea whether this Manouk was telling the truth or not—"

Now, however, the soldier stood back, hands on hips, and laughed aloud. "You don't have any idea," he said. "Have you any idea whether he wore horns on his head or not? Or whether he had leathery wings and a face like a pig's snout? Friend, go home and sober up. And stay away from the taverns. Last night I saw you sopping it up at the Inn of the White Horse. You—"

"That's not true," Jacob said. "I did order wine—but I did not drink it. I sat looking at it. I was troubled."

"Sure, sure. Look, friend. Go home to your wife and sleep it off. You've had yourself a little hallucination."

"I know what I saw," Jacob said. The equability was gone from his voice but had not yet been replaced by anger. "I have discharged my civic duty. I have passed the information along to someone in military authority. That's all I am required to do as a citizen of Haran. Now that I have done my duty, I will take my leave of you." He looked Reshef once in the eye, hard, smiled a smile as cold as Reshef's own, and turned on one heel to go.

Reshef watched him depart. *You're a cool one,* he thought. He nodded appreciatively as Jacob went out past the guard and mounted his horse. It was always a pleasure dealing with someone whose intelligence approached your own, someone who couldn't easily be stampeded or prodded into senseless (and spirit-wasting) rage. Dealing with anyone else was a game whose odds were fixed. This at least provided a bit of seasoning to the stew.

His face assumed a thoughtful cast. Manouk, eh? And scouting the Haran approaches himself, all alone? He must be quite a fellow, this Manouk. It would pay to make some sort of separate, private contact with him. Perhaps something could be worked out. Perhaps it might be pointed out to the Shepherd Kings—particularly if they had an intelligent and sensible man like this Manouk out front, scouting things, testing the air for this "Leader" of theirs—that it would be useful to leave untouched a town like Haran: rich, productive, the nexus of a network of trade routes. As a sort of way station and warehouse, it could give them supply along their route to the rich lands of the South.

And if they were to leave such a city untouched—untouched, say, except for subjugation—it would pay them to have a friend there running things for them, wouldn't it? And what better sort of friend than himself, Reshef, a man after this Manouk fellow's own heart?

It was dusk by the time Jacob rode past the ford toward the gates of Haran. To his right he heard giggles, splashing. Through the corner of his right eye, he could see pink flesh in the water, jumping, bouncing. He looked straight ahead. Other men's women did not interest him much. He had two wives and two concubines. Among the four of them, they covered most of the range of female conduct and psychology. Womankind had few secrets from him by now, at least so far as women's relations with men were concerned. One woman loathed herself and wanted you to punish her. Another liked

177

to play the winsome coquette long after she'd grown as fat as a hog. Another resented any and all men just because they were men; she built her whole life around the business of trying to get men to react to the things she said and did, and the more she did to attract attention, the less attention was paid her, which only fed the whole foolish cycle. And then—only once in a man's lifetime, if that—a woman came along who really *was* an equal, a partner, a person you could tell the truth to all of the time, a person who didn't play games with you. *Rachel* . . . The thought of her unhappiness was a knife in his heart.

He had put the discomfort of the meeting with Reshef from his mind; but now the results of it, inconclusive, frustrating, came back to him.

There'd been something surpassingly odd about the meeting. First off, whether he'd admitted the matter or not, Reshef *had* believed his story—but for some inexplicable reason of his own had decided to deny it. The added insults had been gratuitous, impersonal. They'd been added for no reason other than to discourage his pressing the matter further.

But why?

That was the odd thing. He couldn't come up with a single reason why a soldier, a man whose life would be laid on the line first, long before the war reached the city, should ignore and deride warnings of a possible conflict to come. He'd have to inquire around, about this Reshef. God of plague indeed . . . !

Danataya wiped the sweat from her forehead and tucked a straggling tuft of hair up under her headkerchief. She'd finished the front room; it was ready for the first guests of the evening. Now what . . . ?

"Danataya?" a voice said behind her. She turned to see Yamam, prettily robed in a garment of expensive purple. "Here," she said. "You're killing yourself. Come. I've got some cheese and figs. If I know you, you haven't had anything to eat since morning. Come, there's plenty. We'll go sit by the fountain."

"Thank you," Danataya said. "But Admuniri said—"

"Forget Admuniri. I've already cleared it with her. What's more, I've told Abi-samar. That way neither of them will come looking for you and get mad if you're not there. Come!" She held out a hand to the girl, a friendly smile on her face.

"But I'm—I'm dirty. . . ."

178

"That's all right. We'll wash you off at the fountain. I even brought a robe if you want to change. We're more or less the same height."

"That's too kind of you."

"Not at all. Come *on,* now." And Danataya let herself be led by the hand through the streets to the all-but-deserted bazaar where Yamam helped her comb out her stringy hair, wash her face and arms, and—shielding her from strangers' gazes—change into the new robe.

Danataya took off her sandals and washed her feet. "Oh, you don't have any idea how refreshing this is," she said. "The worst part is feeling all sticky and dirty."

"I know," Yamam said. "How do you think *I* started at the Inn of the White Horse? That's how we all start. From that grubby job of yours, some of the best careers in the city have begun. I know one girl who's now a courtesan to the king. She lives in an apartment twice the size of the inn and has people to wait on her hand and foot. Although that's not going to last long if she doesn't watch her weight."

"Goodness," Danataya said. "And you, too, and—"

"Oh, I haven't leveled off," Yamam said. "Not yet. I'm looking for a nice situation in life where I'm assured of position even when I'm an old crone. I want a husband, or I want a lover who'll settle money on me, money his heirs can't take away."

"Husbands? Do husbands come out of—*your* job?"

"My job? Don't act as if it were something nasty, my dear. Try it and you might find yourself enjoying it. *I* certainly do. And—you'd be surprised at the offers you'll get. The gifts. I've got to show you a pair of earrings somebody gave me last week. Why, a couple more like that and I could retire. If I wanted to. But why *should* I retire? I mean, before my body begins to go?"

"You mean—you don't have to—to work?"

"Heavens, no. You won't either, after a year or so of it. Look, I'll let you in on a little secret. I've had a proposal of marriage. A rich merchant. I'm thinking it over. He wants to make me respectable, he says, and I may well let him. Of course, I know that isn't what he wants. He wants me to stay just the same as I am, but to go naked for his eyes alone, share his bed only. That's what they all want, darling. And it behooves a girl to let them have just that—after making the best bargain she possibly can."

"But—"

"What I'm saying is that I'd like to train you to follow in

179

my footsteps. I mean, Abi-samar and Admuniri are my friends. I don't want them to be left out in the cold when I announce my, uh, retirement."

"But me? Oh, Yamam, I couldn't. I really—"

"Don't be so sure. There's a little bit of the shameless slut in all of us, my dear. You too. Just wait and see. And if you can indulge the shameless slut in you and still stay respectable, somebody that a rich man will want to marry and have children by—"

"But how could I—?"

"Look. Don't go prejudging things. You've done enough slave labor for a day. Just take a break, a little while from now, and come watch the show from the wings. Later, if you like, we can go over to my place and I can show you a step or two, just to get you started. Tomorrow's a holy day. You don't have to get up early."

"Yamam, that's very sweet of you, but—"

"No more buts. I insist."

IX

The innkeeper's wife came over to Hadad's table herself. "Excuse me, sir," she said. "Could I perhaps get you something to eat?" She looked down at the array of empty wine bowls before him, scattered across the table. "I wouldn't recommend, well, so much wine on an empty stomach."

Hadad belched softly and looked up at her, trying to get her face in focus. "I—I know you," he said. "Your name is Admu—Admuni—"

"Admuniri. Why, yes. And you're the sculptor who works in the Bazaar of the Well. But, are you sure you want—?"

"Here," Hadad said. He dropped a little purse on the table, the purse he'd earned on the statuettes for the temple. "If you're worrying about whether I can pay—I can pay." He smiled. His smile was an even sadder thing than the sad look his face had borne through most of the evening. "Please," he said. "Wine. More wine."

She looked at him skeptically, wondering what Abi-samar would do if he were here. "Well—I'll tell you what. I'll get some more wine for you if you'll take some bread and cheese."

But just then the music began, loud, insistent. Admuniri straightened, looked up at the players, looked back down at Hadad's wine-blurred features. Well, perhaps the show might distract him. If he got to paying attention to what was happening in the middle of the floor, to the jolly sounds of the three-piece band, perhaps he might forget his desire for more wine at any expense. She looked back at Hadad, saw him beating time with one hand, humming along with the tune in a husky but truly pitched baritone. Yes; she'd try a little neglect. Perhaps he'd forget. She moved away across the floor.

Hadad, recognizing a tune, laughed a terrible laugh. "Well played!" he bellowed. He held his wine bowl high, sloshing it onto his head and shoulders. And he sang in a hoarse croak made sour by drink, by hours of weeping, by the torments of a mind that could not handle the things it had learned in these terrible last two days:

Praise the goddess, most awesome of goddesses,
Let us revere the people's Mistress, the greatest of the
    Igigi;
Praise be to Ishtar, most awesome of goddesses,
Let us revere the queen of women—

"Here!" someone shouted. "Shut up back there!" But Hadad continued until his tongue tied so badly that he could not get the words out. He contented himself with banging on the table. He kept the time tolerably at first, but even his natural feel for rhythms had deteriorated horribly under the brutal beating he'd given his system in the last hour or so. He fell behind; someone grabbed his arm and made him stop. He let his head fall on the table and rest there for a moment in a puddle of spilled wine; then, as movement drew his attention across the room, he pushed himself up to a sitting position.

At first, he could only make out the motion; swirling cloths, a flashing arm here, a pointed foot there, shaking bronze anklets that tinkled in time with the music. He blinked, trying to get everything in focus. It didn't work at first. He had never before drunk in one day more than a single bowl of wine, and that diluted with water from the well. So this was drunkenness? he thought. He had thought its palliative power would be stronger than this, somehow. All this many bowls and he could still feel the pain? Well, perhaps he hadn't had enough. He started to bellow for more, more wine. And then something stayed his hand, stilled his voice.

His eyes went into focus and picked out the swirling, circling figure of Yamam, lush-bosomed, ample-thighed, as she shed the third of her veils. There was a coarse animal quality about her movements—but also a professional grace that pleased. He was a performer himself, of sorts; he couldn't go interrupting a performer's turn, now, could he? Better to watch her, to applaud when it came time to applaud.

This was a lovely dance, now. And—gods! She was naked above the waist now, with big, beautiful, dark-nippled breasts. Her round belly, with its deep-set navel, caught his eye, churning round and round as it did. Her lovely hands beckoned, beckoned—and now she removed another of her veils with a flourish. . . . She was almost naked—naked here before him, before the rest of these men. . . . Her eyes caught his, moved to another's. . . . Her smile was wise, dark, tantalizing. . . .

Danataya looked on from the wings, her own breast heaving with a mixture of feelings and sensations. Her hand went to her bosom—and felt there the excited state of her little nipples. Her eyes went again and again from Yamam's beautiful womanly body (nude now and made all the more lovely by the light film of sweat that bathed it, picking up the light from the flickering lanterns that surrounded the little dance floor) to the ring of male faces whose eyes remained fixed on Yamam's dance.

Her own little body was afire. She had hardly felt this way when Yassib had made love to her, with his rash young soldier's ways and his untutored haste. She'd often wondered what this passion was that the women at the ford talked about: this excitement that made them unable to resist the advances of the men they romanced. Now—now she was beginning to understand, a little. It was as if someone had cast a spell on her and turned her, almost, into some sort of rutting animal, her and all the men who watched as Yamam's bare body undulated sensually, buttocks rotating and grinding.

She pressed her thin legs together; covered her own fully clothed lap with one narrow hand, as if it were her own nakedness on display out there. Her eyes went from one end of Yamam's golden body to the other, from the soft hair that fell over her shoulders down to the slender ankles and the flashing metal bangles that encircled them, and that were now the only articles of clothing she wore . . .

. . . and then her eyes scanned the men's faces again, and stopped on one. The young singer—the one with the crippled leg; what was the name, now?—he was watching Yamam with the same rapt interest as the other men. His eyes were bleary and his face slack-jawed with drink. There was the same helpless lust on his face as there was on the others'—and yet—and yet—there was something else too. A sorrow beyond all solace, a pain beyond all mending. A hurt self-loathing that rejected all that was good in him, all that could ever be good in him.

Yamam swept off into the wings now, passing her, smiling, reaching for a cloth to wipe the sweat from her face and bosom. She caressed Danataya's neck affectionately as she passed. "Here: you are coming to my place after work, aren't you?" she whispered.

"I—I'm not sure," Danataya said. "Abi-samar said—"

Yamam swabbed down her belly, then her thighs. "Here," she said. "Do my back, will you? There's a dear."

Danataya's hand trembled as she took the cloth and wiped down the glistening sweat on Yamam's nakedness. "Really, Yamam, I couldn't ever—"

"Oh, come now," Yamam said, her voice full of tolerant good humor. "Of course you could. It's just a matter of getting your feet wet that first time. Besides, I asked Abi-samar. He said you'd worked like a cart-ox today and could take off a little early. And think: no getting up early tomorrow morning! Look, stay over with me. It's got to be better than that little hovel Admuniri found you. We'll have a couple of drinks and go to bed and sleep till noon. It'll be fun. I haven't had a girl friend here in such a long time. I can teach you the steps. . . ."

Danataya wasn't listening. She was thinking of the young singer with the bent leg and of the terrible succession of expressions that had come across his face as he'd watched Yamam do her dance. Something, somebody, had hurt him terribly. She wondered what. He had seemed like such a sweet, likable young man, and everyone at the bazaar had seemed to like him so. And there was that beautiful, haunting voice of his. And here he was, drunk as any soldier, ready to fall on his face—and for what? What had led him to this? Was this the way he usually was? Could her instincts possibly have deceived her so?

A squad of soldiers had come in. Hadad had managed to get his hands on another bowl of wine and was banging on the table with it, singing a cacophonous song about a flea who wandered into a house of ill repute. His face twisted as he uttered every coarse word; his voice slipped down one tone, wavered. "Here, shut up, you!" someone yelled close to his ear. "You sound like a jackass in heat!"

Hadad tried to stand up but found he couldn't—not on the first try, at least. He held his wine bowl high and tried again, just as two half-drunken young soldiers tried to push their way past. The bowl was joggled; the wine spilled on the first soldier's face, his clean uniform fresh from the parade ground. "Why, you—" the soldier began. He grabbed Hadad's garment and tore it across at the chest. He grabbed again at the torn parts and wrestled Hadad to his feet.

"Excuse me," Hadad said. "My apologies; I didn't—"

"Let him go," the second soldier said. "He's drunk."

". . . teach the drunken bastard to spill wine on *me*. Damn civilians think they can get by with . . ."

". . . here, let him loose, you can't . . ."

". . . sorry I got in your way . . ."

Now, somehow, a new flash of red rage went through the soldier. He'd had a hard day; he'd been yelled at and penalized and called sixteen different kinds of blundering, incompetent fool, and he had to take it all out on someone. He drew back a fist and smashed Hadad in the face. Hadad went back, tripped over a bench, and fell on the ground in an ungainly somersault. The soldier vaulted the bench and came after him. Hadad held his arms over his face ineffectually as the soldier stood him on his feet, the better to rain blows on his head and arms and upper chest. The soldier drove him back, back; he backhanded Hadad across the face, drawing blood; his knee came up and caught Hadad in the groin, doubling him over. The soldier's hand grabbed Hadad by the hair and straightened him up again. He wrestled Hadad to the door and threw him bodily out into the street. Then, his friend in his wake, he followed the young sculptor into the street and kicked Hadad into the gutter, where he fell and did not rise. His crooked leg stood out at a ghastly angle; one arm was pinned under his body. His face lay half submerged in a puddle of slops, his nose and mouth barely out of the vile water.

Inside, in the Inn of the White Horse, the band began to play again: jolly bouncing music, fit for dancing. "Come on,"

184

the second soldier said. "He's learned his lesson. Let's go. The dancer's going to be going on in another moment or two."

One show came and went, then another. As the music struck up for the third and last show of the night, Hadad's one good eye blinked—once, twice. He moved his head a trifle—and got stinking, befouled water in his mouth and nostrils. Coughing, he scrambled to his knees. His head hurt; it spun round and round—he almost fell on his face again. But then, his gorge rising, he vomited up his guts into the puddle of slops he'd been lying in.

He tried to stand, but his muscles seemed to have turned into gelatin. Finally, he managed to rise to his knees and look around. One eye was closed and hurt terribly. His nose had bled down over his face, and he could feel scabs forming over cuts on his neck and chest as he moved one hand here and there. One tooth seemed to be loose.

He tried to stand again, and this time he got to his feet; but dizziness overtook him and he fell heavily against the rock wall across the street from the tavern. He stood there, weaving, unable to stand without help, his good leg and the crippled one alike refusing to bear the battered burden of his skinny body even as far as the bazaar, where he could at least sit down in safety and put himself back together.

The inn emptied behind him; nobody paid him any mind, except a drunken foreigner who laughed at him and threw something that shattered on the wall above him, raining down scraps of plaster. He tried to move his bad leg one step. He followed it with one ungainly step with the good one; but then he had to pause exhaustedly for breath, holding onto the rough wall desperately. . . .

Jacob, coming in from the encampment, found him there, hanging onto the rock, gasping, his one good eye blinking like a Cyclops's, his face and his torn garment covered with blood. He looked around, saw the two young women come arm in arm out of the inn together. "Here, please!" he cried out in a gentle and courteous voice. "Please, could you two help me here? There's someone—he's been hurt. Yes, please, over here."

And as Yamam and Danataya rushed to his side, Jacob managed to catch Hadad just as he fell.

185

X

Among them, they managed to walk Hadad back to the inn, where they roused Admuniri just as she was closing up shop. She protested for a moment; but then she got a look at Hadad's battered face. "Ah," she said. "I just knew something was going to happen. He isn't the kind to drink a lot, or to know how to handle it."

Jacob eased him into a sitting position in a chair against the wall. "Are you all right?" he said. "Where does it hurt? Here? Or perhaps here?" He prodded Hadad's chest, arms; touched his bad leg. "Nothing broken, I'd say." He turned to Danataya. "You, my dear," he said gently. "Could I trouble you to get a wet cloth or something like that? I mean, to sponge him off? And—Yamam? Did I get the name right? Thank you—if you could perhaps bring a couple of candles so we can see what sort of damage has been done."

Both women disappeared, concern showing on their faces. Jacob turned to Admuniri. "How did this happen?" he said. "He's drunk. This young man, I'd wager, has never had too much to drink in his whole life. For one thing, he can't afford it."

"Yes," Admuniri said in a chastened voice. "I'm ashamed that I served him. When I saw he couldn't hold what he was drinking, I refused him more. But by that time the damage was done. How was I to know? After all, his brother is well known here. His brother is rich. Why shouldn't he be able to afford it? And his brother drinks heavily and hardly shows it."

"Ah, Admuniri. I think you know more than you're telling me. I've inquired about this boy. He's shy, awkward with women, innocent. And for heavens' sake, he works at the Bazaar of the Well, just up the street from you. You should know him by now."

"Well, I—Jacob, I just didn't think. I'm used to the kind of people who come here. People who know their way around. There was some sort of scuffle, but it wound up outside so quickly that I didn't bother to look. It's my fault the boy got

186

hurt. Abi-samar will scold me when he hears of this. And he'll be right."

"All right. Think no more of it. Let's get him cleaned up." He looked up to see the two younger women approaching. "Ah, thank you, ladies," he said. He placed the two tapers where they would do the most good and dipped the proffered cloth in the water bowl. Working with fatherly tenderness, he gently sponged Hadad's bruised face, wiped the grime away from his bulging black eye. "Hadad?" he said quietly. "Hadad, can you hear me?"

The boy groaned and turned his head away—and in a great heaving rush, vomited the remains of what was in him onto the floor. Danataya rushed out for a mop. Jacob, all patience, propped him back up and washed him off again. As he did, he spoke in a low tone to the three women. "If there's a single person in Haran who'd be out of place getting drunk in an inn, I think it would be this boy here. As I said, I've been inquiring after him. Asking questions of his friends in the bazaar and elsewhere. He hasn't any enemies, not a one in the world. They all say he's got as good a heart in his breast as anyone who ever drew breath. Kind, generous, warm-hearted—manly," he said, looking the three of them in the eye one at a time, "manly in the best sense of the word, for all his weakness and his innocence. I've a mind to make friends with him myself, if he's amenable. A man never has too many friends, whatever their ages. And I've no reason to doubt the word of the people in the bazaar; on their say-so, I'd say I wish that I had a son like him myself. I've many sons; they've all been one kind of disappointment or another, every one."

"Oh, by the way, Jacob," Admuniri said. "Rachel was looking for you. She was worried. Disappearing like that wasn't like you."

"No, it wasn't, was it?" Jacob agreed. He pulled off the rest of Hadad's ruined garment, wincing as he saw the bruises on the boy's battered torso. He cluck-clucked at the young man's skinny body above the patched loincloth. "Admuniri: surely Abi-samar can spare some sort of thing for the boy to wear? That's a good girl, now." She went into another room.

He looked up at the two women who remained. "He's the sole support of a mother who's gone mad from care and worry," he said quietly. "The two of them live apart, in great poverty. He's an artist, and a fine one—but he's never qualified as a member of the guild because the only education

187

his mother's pittance could provide went to his older brother. The older brother is rich, careless, self-centered. It's never occurred to him for so much as a moment to try to provide for his family." He sighed. "I suppose the older boy takes after his father. I met Kirta once when I first came to Haran: a cold sort, all business. He up and deserted wife and boys shortly after that. Nobody ever heard of him again. Well, like father, like son. I'd wager the younger one—this one here— gets his humanity, his decency, from his mother. Poor thing. Poor things, both of them."

Danataya had stolen a glance at Yamam while Jacob had been speaking of Shobai. She took note of how Yamam winced with embarrassment. Then she looked back at the young man sitting against the wall. Her heart was full of mixed and inchoate emotions. The boy's battered face made her want to cry; to turn away; to go to him and comfort him; to wreak her own terrible vengeance on everyone who'd ever hurt him, let him down.

Jacob looked up at Admuniri. "You mentioned Rachel. I've wronged her," he said. "In a moment of weakness I went off to be by myself. In a way, the God of my fathers must still be looking out for me, false though I may have been to Him. Having done a foolish thing, I learned a useful thing." He looked at Hadad and put a kindly hand on the boy's shoulder. "Maybe two. But I must now make it up to Rachel. I understand this boy's fool of a brother, I suppose, more than you'd imagine. Like me, he always intended to get around to doing something responsible, to cleaning up after himself, to putting his affairs in order. But he continues to put it off, put it off, thinking that one of these tomorrows the proper time will come. Well, I've made the same mistake for many years. I've put off the decisions I should have been making, the actions I should have done. I'm in no position to rejoice in my blessed superiority and preen myself on how much smarter or better I am than Shobai, the boy's brother. In a way I'm worse. I'm older; I should be wiser. I see the problem clearly; he may not, not yet."

"I don't understand," Admuniri said. "If—"

But Hadad chose that moment to open his one good eye. He spoke through bruised, puffed lips. "Shobai—Shobai is good," he said. "Please—don't say things about Shobai."

Jacob put a hand on each of the boy's shoulders. "Yes," he said in a gentle and wonderfully calm voice. "Continue to look for the best in people, my young friend. It's the only way

188

you are ever going to find it. If you don't look for the good in Shobai, who will?" His own eyes were misty with unshed tears, but his voice was strong and deep, the voice of a father speaking to a beloved son. "Keep that stout and generous heart, my son. Don't let the hard ways of the world soil it. It's more important than anything, any quality you'll ever develop. I could use more of it myself.

"But maybe you've put some heart into me. Hadad, I think you and I will become friends, great friends, in the time that remains to me here in Haran. Perhaps what experience of life I do have can help you understand how to handle the burdens you have to carry in your world. Call for me if you need someone, will you? Well, no matter. Your mind may still be clouded by all this. Don't worry. I'll come to you. I've failed to be a father to my sons, and in a way I've cheated them as thoroughly as your father cheated you. Maybe I can learn from you what it is that a son needs. Maybe that way I can learn how to give my sons back the thing I've failed to give them."

"I know you," Hadad said, blinking the one good eye. "You're—Jacob. I met you in the street."

"Yes," Jacob said. A sudden happiness shone in his lined face. "I can't say how pleased I am that you remember. Well—well met. Hadad, you're not the man to drink to excess or get in brawls. Something has disturbed you greatly in the last day or two, I think, and perhaps it's a burden best borne by two." He looked up at the women. "Admuniri," he said. "Go up to bed. I'll sit with Hadad here, and I'll lock up when I leave to take him home. Don't worry; I'm known as the most prudent man in Haran. Abi-samar himself said so. I won't leave a door unlatched or a window cracked. It's all right. I'll take care of things."

Jacob turned to Danataya and Yamam. "My thanks to you two," he said. "You've been very kind—but, come to think of it, it's late, isn't it? I quite forgot. Listen, if you can help me get our friend back to his room, I'll walk the two of you home. Young women shouldn't have to go through the dark streets at this time of night. Come: help me get him to his feet."

Jacob, Danataya, and Yamam managed to half guide, half carry Hadad back to his room, where they laid him gently on his wretched little bed. As they departed, closing the door behind them, they could see him, in one last moonlit glimpse,

189

staring at the ceiling with his good eye. "He won't sleep, poor devil," Jacob said. "In other circumstances I'd stay with him; but you need me, and my family needs me." He steered them down the narrow street.

"You said somebody had hurt him," Danataya said. "How . . . ?"

"Oh," Jacob said, "I guessed something. He's learned something, the kind of something that hurts as it teaches. And he has some adjusting to do before he can use it. Perhaps he has more pain to experience before he can use it. If that's so, I'll be there to help him if I may. There's good stuff in him, the best. He'll make some woman a good man one of these days." He stole a sly, sidelong glance at Danataya.

"Him?" Yamam said in gentle reproof. "Friend Jacob, a woman needs a man of position, of property, of future."

"And what do you know of Hadad's future? I tell you there's good stuff in him. He may just be starting off slowly. I'd say he had it in him to make a woman rich—if she knew how to show him how to do it. Maybe the right woman is all the boy needs. Like the right herb that makes the stew. You get my meaning?" he said in a friendly raillery.

"Perhaps," Yamam said. "But you don't buy a cow in the dark, Jacob. A woman would rather know what she's getting up front, from the very beginning. A woman doesn't like gambles. That's for men, not women."

"One woman speaks, and she thinks she speaks for all women," Jacob said. "I live with four women, and the four of them can't even agree on whether it's going to rain tomorrow. Why should women speak with one voice when the men don't? Why shouldn't women show the same diversity of opinion and taste that men show? Eh, Danataya? Did I get the name right? Danataya?"

"Yes, sir," she said. "And—I *would* say that I'd value a good heart in a man. I trusted one once who was tall, strong, handsome, ambitious. He had a good job and was on the way up. He was as beautiful to look upon as the sun and moon. But the heart was bad, and he hurt me as no man—no, nor woman either—has ever hurt me."

"You see?" he said to Yamam. "One woman is thin, the other plump and voluptuous. They cannot wear the same garment with grace. Why should they need the same man?" Jacob was in a good mood now. He took their arms and, a new and merrier note in his voice, struck up a jolly sheep-shearing song they all knew. They sang together, and as they

190

did, the years fell away from Jacob like the tattered remnants of a rotten robe.

Jacob let himself in quietly. Moonlight shone through the open window; in its light he could see Rachel sitting asleep in a chair, her body bowed over a table, her face resting on her arms. He stood over her, looking down at her with love. It was some moments before he spoke in a soft whisper: "Rachel—"

She stirred in her sleep, moved her head slightly. His hand brushed her hair with a caress as soft as a feather.

"Rachel," he said again. "Rachel, my darling."

Now she stirred again, and her head came off the crossed arms. She looked up, blinked, her face sweet and indistinct in the soft light. "Oh. Jacob. I—I'm afraid I drifted off. You—it's dark. Why, it's dark. Where have you been? I've been so worried."

He sat down across from her, smiling. His hand went to her cheek; she raised her own hand to hold his to her. "Rachel," he said. "Dear Rachel. A household full of people and only you are sitting up waiting for me when I come home. Only you, of all the others, have kept your faith in me all these weary years. I've been a poor father to all my sons. I've been a poor mate to wives and concubines alike. The others have given up on me, and I don't blame them. But you? The one true North Star of my life? You alone sit up to wait for me."

She smiled, her face still puffy from sleep—but with beauty shining from it as her mouth opened to speak and then did not speak.

"Rachel," Jacob said. "I'm home. I'm home to stay. And I'll tell you something. From this moment, Laban no longer holds the reins. I've taken them away from him. From now on, I run this family, and Laban can scramble around for my leavings. It'll take time to work things out; it'll take time to reassert myself around this household. But from this moment, I swear to you by the One True God of my fathers, I am the man you thought you'd married. I am the man who will lead this family. I am the patriarch here, not Laban."

She stood and rushed into his arms. "Oh, Jacob," she said. "Oh, my own darling."

"Rachel," he said. "One thing more. We're going back to Canaan. We're going to Canaan, where I'm a king. I'm going to face down my brother, and make peace with my father, and come into the kingdom that's mine. I'm going to be everything I've been refusing to be all this time. It won't be overnight. Preparations will take time. Getting away from Laban will be hard. He thinks he owns me. But hear my words, Rachel—"

"I hear you," she said, and now he could hear the dark musky note in her voice. "Oh, Jacob, I've needed you so. . . ."

There were no more words. Jacob picked her up, feather-soft in his strong arms, and swept her up the stairs to their bedroom. And when he took her a moment later, it was with an adult's control, perhaps, but with the passion of a man half his age.

XI

"You can't really mean it," Yamam said. She sat cross-legged on her own bed, watching Danataya try on her dancer's costume. "You really think so?"

"You haven't heard him sing," Danataya said. "Goodness. You fill this thing out so wonderfully. On me it just hangs. And I'm not that flat-chested, really I'm not."

"No, you aren't," Yamam said. "All you need is regular meals. Well, you'll get those at Abi-samar's. I have to say that for him. If I didn't watch things, I'd be as fat as a hog. Now throw your chest out a bit. Yes, that's more like it. They're little, perhaps, but that'll change. They're certainly pretty enough. By the time you've teased the boys a bit it won't matter. Do the beforehand stuff right, with the right amount of tantalization about it, my dear, and all you'll have to do to please them, by the time you've taken your clothes off, will be not to be a boy. And goodness knows, for a thin girl you're quite nice naked."

"Oh, you're embarrassing me. Does this go this way, or—?"

"Over the other shoulder. When it comes off, it comes off with a swirl, like so." Yamam poured herself more wine; drank; let the good feeling circulate through her body. She made a funny ticklish motion, half shrug and half shiver, and laced the fingers of her left hand between the toes of her right foot. "Oh, my. I'm getting a nice feeling. This is good wine. If Abi-samar knew who it was that had taken it—"

"You know he wouldn't mind. You make a lot of money for him. Now, I think I've got all this stuff on. There's actually quite a bit of it."

"Seven layers. You never wear that many layers of anything out in the street. Actually, when the show begins you're downright overdressed. Now, take a step or two, the way I showed you. No, the tummy rotates—well, you know. You have to get into it more. Back when I was a girl, they used to teach this dance to pregnant women. It helped them get the body ready for having a baby."

"Really?" Danataya said. She stopped, looked Yamam in the eye. "Incidentally, Yamam: I'm *not* pregnant."

"Congratulations. The soldier you told me about?"

"No. There is no problem there—I found that out weeks ago."

"I see. Well, I'll drink to that. Danataya: you're not drinking the wine. And I went to such pains to steal it."

"I will." The girl turned, twirling the veils around her slim body. She took off one veil—then paused, embarrassed. "Oh, I could never do it. Never."

"That's what I said. You try working as hard as you've worked today for a month or two. You'll be ready to do headstands atop the Temple of Bel to get out of more of that backbreaking labor." She drank again, licked her lips, smiled. "Mmmm. You're missing something good." She spilled wine on her breast, wiped it off with one hand. She was bare-breasted now, wearing only a short skirt. "This crippled fellow," she said. "You really think he's—well, got something? He looks like no more than a boy. I'll bet he's a virgin. Jacob as much as said so."

"Virgin is a lot different from impotent. Or incompetent. That's what my aunt always said."

"Perhaps. But—that *leg*."

"You haven't heard his singing. It made me tingle all over. I've never heard anything so lovely in all my life. Besides, Yamam, straight legs aren't everything." Danataya removed two veils in a decidedly utilitarian fashion, freeing her legs. She took up her wine bowl and drank. "Oh, this *is* lovely. But—goodness. I shouldn't drink it so quickly."

"It's stronger than most. Sit down. Take off the rest of those clothes. You were saying?"

Danataya removed all the rest of what she'd been wearing,

down to a thigh-length skirt. She looked at Yamam, blushed, covered her breasts with one arm. Then she put on a shift. "Well, I don't find him so ugly. He has a nice face. A nice, expressive face."

"Huh. Now if it were that brother of his—" Yamam drained her bowl and poured again, wiping her mouth with her free arm. "You want to know a secret? I went to bed with his brother last week."

"The rich one? What's his name? Sho—"

"Shobai. And he's handsome as a man can get: big and strong and tall. And rich as the king of Egypt—"

Danataya's eye caught hers. "You stopped. There's more."

"Well, you're right in a way. There *is* more to it than being big and tall and handsome and rich. Shobai labored to please me. But—it was a performance. A nice professional performance. My dear, I once went to bed with the lover of the queen. She kept him, the way a man keeps a woman. Only once in a while he'd sneak out and—"

"And?" Danataya said, wide-eyed. She'd never heard such frank revelations before.

"And—well, my dear, I appreciate all the technique. And I appreciate all the diligent attention. Goodness knows I do. But, we had this little affair. The queen was out of town: an affair of state, a royal funeral in Carchemish. And it took two weeks for her to get back to town. I had a great time. But—"

"You sighed, as if it had all been a great disappointment to you."

"In a way it was." She drank again; refilled Danataya's bowl. "After two weeks of him, I felt drained dry. I'd never felt such passion. But I kept wishing just once he'd behave like—oh, like an ordinary *man*. Mount me like a bear. Nice and hard, until my teeth shook. Do you know what I mean?"

Danataya blushed. She hid her face behind her wine bowl. "I—I'm not sure," she said. "Yassib—he was the only man I ever—"

"Ah. And he was young and eager and . . ." She sighed, drank again. "Well, my darling. You have a lot to learn. Some of it good, some of it bad." She sighed again, more deeply this time. "I—I wish I could spare you the bad part. But nobody can spare anybody anything. We all have to learn for ourselves, and the best a friend can do is comfort us when things aren't going well." She smiled a friendly indistinct smile, her face beginning to be blurred by drink. "I like you,

194

Danataya. I want so much for us to be friends. My life's all men—"

"*My* life's all work."

"Exactly. All the more reason why both of us could use a good friend just now. And look: I *want* to give you my job when I go." Her speech was beginning to be slurred. "I think I may actually marry this rich goose. He's no prize in bed, mind you, but he *is* rich, and he thinks the sun rises and sets in my—"

"*Yamam!*"

"Well, you know what I mean. And you: I don't want you going off on a tangent and getting your blood up over some pauper with a crooked leg, somebody who gets drunk and lets a bunch of soldiers beat him up and—"

"I wonder who—I wonder what hurt him so. I mean, the way Jacob said. You heard him. The man—Hadad—he isn't the type to do that sort of thing. He's gentle and thoughtful and generous and—"

"Oh, what's the use of talking to you?"

"Yamam. When you—when you go naked before the men, how do you handle it? I mean, what goes through your mind?"

"Hah! I think of how much money I'll be making!" Yamam, her eyes half out of focus already, smiled wryly, looked Danataya in the eye. Her expression changed. She put a hand on Danataya's bare calf, ran it down her leg, caressed her foot; then she sighed audibly. "No. If we're to be friends, I have to be honest with you, don't I? Well, let me tell you. What I do is pick one face out of the crowd. I may look at all the rest, but there's only one face I'm playing to. One set of eyes. I work at making that one man fall in love with me, even if it's only for an hour or so." She smiled. Her hand went back to Danataya's bare knee. "Do you know what I mean? Perhaps you don't." She drank again, smiled; her eyes were indistinct now. "Perhaps you don't—"

Danataya patted her hand chastely. Her thoughts were far away. "Perhaps I do," she said in a voice almost too soft to hear.

After a time, Yamam rose, yawned, drained her last bowl of wine, kissed Danataya—a cuddly, sisterly kiss—blew out the candle on her side of the room, and turned in. In a moment she was snoring softly.

Danataya studied her own bowl; then she finished it in a series of short sips and put it down. She looked at Yamam's broad bare body, decided against envying her, and blew out her own candle.

Once in bed, though, she found herself staring at the ceiling. She'd envied people like Yamam all her life: people who could just turn over and be out like that. With her, sleep came slowly and sometimes not at all.

Yamam was nice. A little calculating, perhaps. A little coarse. But a good person, and one who might well make a good friend. Goodness knew she, Danataya, would need all the friends she could get in the time to come. She stretched, feeling the ache in muscles and joints. What a lot of work she'd done today! Well, that was all right; tomorrow was an off day. Perhaps she could catch up on her rest then. Yes! She'd sleep till the sun was high, and then perhaps she could go down to the ford and get a nice bath and wash some clothes. Then come back and . . .

Again, she found herself wanting to look up the young singer and see how he was. Poor dear, he'd taken such a terrible beating the night before. What a pity. Who would want to hit him like that, a nice gentle boy like . . . ?

She closed her eyes and almost immediately saw his face. Not the broken and beaten face she'd seen by candlelight that night at the inn, but the open, honest, likable face she'd spotted at the bazaar the day he'd sung. Was that only yesterday? Was it only yesterday she'd come to work? Why, it felt like months ago. How strange . . .

And as sleep crept into Danataya's mind she heard his voice again: gentle, fatherly, manly, singing a much-loved child to sleep:

> Hurry, Sleep, to my much-loved child,
> And put to sleep her restless eyes. . . .

The rays of the moon crept past the edge of the window and fell full on Danataya's soft-featured, peaceful face. She slept, her mind moving effortlessly from gentle reposeful images to other images that mingled jumbled feelings: child-like longings, eroticism, fear. She cried out softly in her sleep, but Yamam, lost in her own dreams, did not hear.

Anat awoke in the hours before dawn. She moved out from under Reshef's hard, intrusive, possessive arm and found a space on her side of the bed. She smelled his foul breath and shrank away from him. The cruel, insensitive bastard! How could he . . . ?

She felt up and down her own naked body. She felt the dried musk on her belly; the scratches and bites; the bruises. She felt—soiled. Ugly. Dirty. That was the way Reshef left her feeling, virtually every time.

Well, perhaps it was what she deserved for being such a fool. Perhaps it was what she had coming for having such low and vulgar tastes. But no, it wasn't that, was it? She'd gone after Reshef in the first place to spite Shobai. Knowing that the one thing that would puncture his rotten vanity would be for her, his beautiful and highly prized possession, to give herself freely and willingly to the ugliest, meanest, most universally despised . . .

But no, *that* wasn't it, either. She'd rather admired Reshef's style from the first. In a world of men with soft spots, vulnerable spots, Reshef had yet to betray by any act or word the very existence of a vulnerable place in his makeup. Other men might be hard here and there, but they all had the soft spot. Shobai's was his boundless, endlessly self-centered vanity. She could always get at him through that. But Reshef? Not a soft spot anywhere. He was hard, hard all over, through and through.

And there was a way in which this was exciting. She'd always been able to do anything she wanted to with men, to wrap them around her finger, to make them jump. She couldn't do anything at all with Reshef. And for once she did not feel with him the contempt she always felt with softer men, men she could push around. Instead, with Reshef it was like pushing a stone wall. He was harder, stronger, less vulnerable than she was.

Surreptitiously, she reached over, thinking this, and touched his arm. Thin, stringy, it was rock-hard, all muscle, all unyielding hard flesh. A little thrill of excitement ran through her. Hard! Unbending! Cold and cruel! All the things she herself was! All the things she loathed! And the only things in the world she respected.

A cool breeze came in the window. Rachel stirred, lying in the cradle of Jacob's comforting arms. She turned slightly to look at his sleeping face in the moonlight, lost in peaceful sleep for the first time in—how long? She couldn't say.

Her own heart was more at ease, too, than it had been for a long time. Her body, now, felt calm, composed—satisfied. Jacob had made love to her tenderly, passionately, masterfully, as he had not done in a decade. Best of all, he'd come home to her—*really* come home, once and for all.

His arm moved in his sleep, pulled her closer. Happily she snuggled into his embrace.

And Hadad slept fitfully, and his neighbors of the bazaar slept, and the soldiers and officers of the garrison, and the refugees and the townspeople all across Haran. Some slept in peace, some in fitful dreams. Late spring, a balmy time in the foothills, lay on the whole of peaceful Padan-aram in its last year of peace and prosperity.

Far to the northeast, another small city fell to the nomads in a dawn attack. The great advance slowed, the better to savor the joy of victory, plunder a dead town, rape its women, kill its old and weak, enslave its children. The livestock of the invaders—as numerous, indeed, as the stars in the clear, semidesert sky above—were turned loose to graze the green grass of the foothill lands down to the dirt's edge. Only when the land had been made brown and bare would the nomads move again: slowly, surely, inexorably, to the southwest. Toward Ugarit. Toward Carchemish.

Toward Haran.

CHAPTER SEVEN

I

"So, Ibalum. What brings you to the court of King Hagirum?"

Ibalum turned to his neighbor at the long table, a look of mild amusement on his face. "Why, the same as usual," the merchant said. "Business. And you, friend Yasihamu? What could bring you to desert the bazaars of Aleppo? The women of Carchemish, for instance? I can't believe Aleppo has run out of courtesans."

"Oh, yes, in a manner of speaking," Yasihamu said with a sigh, sprinkling salt on his rice. "Let's face it, my friend, from time to time the pleasures of home begin to pall. At such times I do, I admit it, manufacture occasions to come here to Carchemish. Of course, there's always sound reason for making the trip anyway."

"Agreed. For one thing, I have good reason—as do you, my friend—for wanting to hear what Hagirum's advisers have told him about the threat from the east."

"Oh, that? You don't take that seriously, do you?"

The merchant poured sauce on their meat: first Yasihamu's, then his own. "How can I not take it seriously?" he said. "The trade routes are closed to the northeast of Gozan. I have not received goods from Nineveh in months and months. And look you: there are rumors that the route of the nomads has turned. Turned *our* way, my friend. Toward Haran," he ticked off the names dourly on his fingers, "toward Carchemish, toward Ugarit, toward Aleppo."

"Huh. If this is the truth, why haven't *I* heard of it?"

"Perhaps the same element reigns in Aleppo that reigns in

199

Haran. Haran, it appears, has lost the knack of self-defense. The reigning monarch is advised by pacifists who think the proper way to deal with a warlike enemy is to bring him a bouquet and hope he'll fall in love with you. The ruling party in the city consists of business-as-usual people who simply discount any news that they don't want to hear."

"Hmmm. I can see the truth in what you say. We have our problems in Aleppo. Bandits attack my own caravans regularly in the hills. Getting the city to organize a party to get up and wipe them out is like pulling the teeth from a crocodile."

"Exactly. And how much worse it would be if it were not bandits, but an army which, some say, is mightier, and more awesomely armed, than that of the king of Egypt?"

"Ah. Is it so bad?"

"I've talked with people to the east. I've also talked to the refugees who pour into our own city daily. Not beaten-down peasants, with no understanding of things. Men who once were men of substance, men of rank. Not gullible people, but people whose powers of observation I have come to trust as I would trust my own."

"Ah." Yasihamu pondered that, chewing. He looked down the long table, at the varied list of faces: men from Ugarit, Arvad, Byblos, Tyre, Damascus, Megiddo. "It seems others share your curiosity."

"Yes. Hagirum has called these people—leading men of their cities—to discuss the threat. I suspect he'll be calling us to order in a little while. Well, I'll say this for him: he acts with dispatch. Imagine Shemariah of Haran acting decisively—on this or on any other matter, large or small."

Sure enough, at the end of the meal the trumpets blew, and Hagirum was announced by an aide who called all to silence. The aging king stood, looked around the table, his eyes solemn below dark beetle brows.

"My friends," he said. "I have called you together to tell you what my scouts have learned of the great migration in the east and to announce the response of Carchemish to the threat."

He cleared his throat and went on. "I'm sure you have heard of this by now. An immeasurably large migration of nomadic pastoralists, led by fierce chieftains and armed with fearsome weapons, has begun to move down from the High Mountains north of Lake Van. They are rapacious, bloodthirsty, and without either pity or fear. And—they have come to stay."

There was a general murmur at this. Ibalum, his eyes bright with interest, leaned forward the better to hear him. The king continued: "Twenty towns have fallen to these Shepherd Kings," he said. He paused for a moment to let that sink in. "Some are simply no more. They are broken stones, their people dead—or worse. Other cities—those that lie athwart important trade routes, and which, because of this, will form a line of supply—have been fortified and manned by the invaders. The fortifications, from all reports, are now well-nigh impregnable. The captured cities cannot be retaken by those who once held them." He gestured to an aide, who signaled to unseen people in an adjoining room. They came in bearing a flat board on which a model of a fortified city had been constructed of clay.

"Their fortified cities look much like this. This, for instance, was a town near the headwaters of the Tigris, far to the north of Nineveh. Here was the old city, the one that fell." He pointed to a tiny clump of buildings in the center of the construction; its low-lying walls and small gateways were dwarfed by the construction that surrounded it. "Now here," he said, pointing to the encircling ramparts, "is the fortification built by the nomads to guard the taken city. Massive embankments and sloped ramparts—here—surrounded by deep moats, impassable on foot or on horseback. You can see immediately: we are dealing with a whole new way of war."

The massive sigh that went up around the table was broken by a single voice. The king recognized a delegate from Haran. "Your Majesty," the delegate said, "this is most impressive. But as none of us is at war with these people—"

The king snorted, interrupted him. "None of us is at war with anybody—yet. I grant you that. But look: I haven't called this meeting hastily. The moment the trade route closed north of Nineveh, I started sending scouts into the area. Some of them," he said portentously, "did not come back."

"Oh, well," the delegate from Haran murmured, "there's always a certain incidence of desertion. . . ."

"Desertion?" the king said, his eyes flashing. He gestured to another aide, who brought a sack. "When a later scout went into the area, the contents of this bag were sold to him by one of the barbarians—*sold*, mind you, for copper coins—in a town on the fringe of the migration. A town, let me remind you, which no longer exists." He untied the string at the top of the bag and rolled the contents of it out onto the table. There was an outcry, an outburst of horror and loathing.

It was the head of a decapitated young warrior, a man hardly past boyhood, that stared open-eyed up at them.

"Please," the king said. "Remove it." An aide cleared the table. "This, mind you, was one of my most trusted young men on the far borders. Though he, poor devil, didn't make it back, others did—and told of scenes of unbelievable brutality and cruelty. They also told of talking with some of the nomads themselves: men spoken with in the cities they were soon to despoil and destroy. Before each battle, there is some influx of individual members of the tribe who come in to trade—and to spy and memorize the fortifications of the city and disarm public opinion. 'Why should we fear these nomads?'" he said, mocking an imaginary milksop of a pacifist. "'Why, I met one the other day and he seemed so nice. Just like you or me.'" His tone was savage as he continued. "I daresay you've the same kind of dim-witted fool in each of your own cities."

Some of the murmurs were in assent; others were in resentment, from people who obviously shared the pacifists' opinions.

Hagirum ignored both. "Well, it would please me to hear that you, the men of influence and substance in the cities which lie—as Haran and Carchemish lie—in the Shepherd Kings' path . . . that you, my friends, would join me in deciding to oppose the calls to inaction, to pacifism, to disarmament. To—let's put it bluntly—to loss of our ability to defend ourselves.

"But however you may choose to think and act, be it known that Carchemish will defend itself. That Carchemish will arm. That Carchemish will fortify. That Carchemish, in the next three months, will order conscription of the young males, no fewer than one son per household, and will triple the size of its present standing army." He waited for the ripple of surprise to subside; then he continued in a firm voice: "That I have already hired the master armorer of the area, Shobai, grandson of the great Ahuni and a Child of the Lion, to supervise the arming of our expanded army." He indicated the tall young man sitting two seats to his left, who stood and bowed, making a striking impression on the crowd.

"Moreover," he said, "I have been studying the Shepherd

Kings' plans for fortification. It is an axiom that nobody ever builds a fortress that he himself could easily breach. Therefore, I am setting several thousand workers to the immediate construction of fortifications for Carchemish which are closely based on what we have learned of the nomads' plans. The nomads may take Mari. They may, for all I know, have taken proud Nineveh itself by now." He scowled at the representative from Haran. "Oh, my friend," he said, "they will go through poor quiet peaceful Haran like a white-hot knife through soft cheese. Unless you rearm—why, you've less than a year to live at the most. I'd say . . . what? Nine months? Ten? By this time next year, if Haran has not done as I am doing, your city will be knee-high rubble that even the vultures will have deserted and forgotten." He ignored the flustered reaction this produced.

"But," he said, "they will not take Carchemish. Not while I am alive to breathe air. Carchemish will fight! Carchemish will stand! And Carchemish will prevail!"

In the street, Ibalum circulated easily among the men who had come out of the great hall moments before. "Well, Ibalum," said Imnah of Byblos. "How did you like the fire-breathing speech?"

"Me?" Ibalum said mildly. "Oh, I love oratory. Any kind. But look, who wants to talk politics on a night like this? You, Imnah. You, Gera of Ugarit. You, Elon of Tyre. All of you: the night is young. Who will be my guest at the Inn of the Four Palms? I've a room reserved. There'll be music, a dancer, pretty serving girls. . . ."

He had no trouble getting a party together. He pointedly ignored the representative of Haran, and his group went away down the moonlit street, chatting and laughing. The night was indeed young. There remained plenty of time yet for both business and pleasure.

After the first show had ended and the little dancer had scurried from the room in a tinny tinkle of ankle bells, Ibalum called for more wine. When the faces had all turned to the table again, Ibalum said, almost too casually, "I rather thought that, as businessmen—merchants—you might be interested in this."

He reached into his garment and pulled out a little leather bag. Opening it, he withdrew and laid on the table the lovely little ornament he'd bought from Hadad in Haran. All the faces lit up; the piece was passed from hand to hand, and approving adjectives flew thick and fast. Ibalum sat back with a benign smile.

"Splendid," said Elon of Tyre. "Where the devil did you get *this*, old man? I didn't know the trade routes to Hittite country had reopened. You sly old fox. I'll be damned. You've got a new source of supply. This is from Hattusa, isn't it? Come on, now. How did you get it?"

"Hattusa?" Ibalum said, turning the corners of his mouth down in a negative gesture. "You'll never believe in a million years where I got this. And let me tell you, I'm not *going* to tell where I got it. No, my friends. There's more where this comes from, and I've got the exclusive rights to it." It was a minor lie, and one easily remedied once he was back in Haran. He blithely absolved himself of sin and went on. "The truth is, through my representatives I've discovered a genius. One of the greatest hands at the trade I've ever run across. And hardly anyone but me knows anything at all about him."

"But how can this be?" said Gera of Ugarit. "How can there *be* an unrecognized genius at a guild-regulated trade? The guild knows with great intimacy the styles and skills of every one of its members, in any city."

Ibalum smiled with the pleasure of his secret knowledge. "But my dear friend, who said my undiscovered genius was a member of the guild?"

"But how—he can't—"

"He never even had an apprenticeship. His family was too poor. His father disappeared some years back, probably dead now. He left the family destitute, for all I hear. The boy's brother was trained to a trade; the boy himself picked up the remnants of a trade in the streets, living from hand to mouth. As I speak to you, he's living in something approaching indigence. But my representatives have instructions to keep an eye on him and make sure he comes to no harm before I re—before I go back to the city where he lives."

"Well," Gera of Ugarit said, fingering the little piece. "If he can produce more like this, he won't be poor for long. Not if I know a clever merchant like you." Then he stopped, let the new understanding seep in. "Ah," he said. "I see. This is why you brought us to the inn. This is why you're footing the bill. We're outlets—once this genius of yours goes into production."

"Correct. You and others here in the city this week. I have people to talk to from Lydia, from Egypt, from Elishah, which you southerners call Kittim. From Lycia. From Crete, and from the island kingdoms to the north. By the time I'm done, I'll have a network of markets all around the borders of the Great Sea. But you, my friends, are my oldest acquaintances in the trade. I have been doing business with the likes of you longer than I can adequately remember. I thought I'd approach you first, before your competitors . . ." But now the servant girl brought the wine and was pouring it into their bowls. Then, shy, she skipped nervously away.

Ibalum held up his bowl in salutation. "Now, I understand that you need more proof. You'll get it. In the meantime— always providing that I know what I'm talking about and really do have a genius on my hands—do we have a deal? Will you represent this material in your markets?"

They were tough-minded businessmen; they seldom agreed easily on anything. Now, however, their roar of agreement virtually shook the timbers of the building.

II

"I'm sorry, Annuta-aram," Shobai said. "I really have to go." He stood, straightening his garment, looking back abstractedly at the wife of King Hagirum's ranking minister in charge of foreign affairs. She still lay in a provocative pose, naked on the coverlet, her ripe body adorned only by a priceless gold necklace that he, Shobai, had made for her to her husband's specification—this and the routine rings on fingers and toes, gleaming in the late afternoon light.

But the expression on her face was not an erotic one. It was the look of a woman deflated, disappointed. The body spread out so enticingly before him was certainly pretty enough; but the disheartened look on her still-young face made her look old. "Shobai," she said, her words coming out in a thin unattractive wail, "you can't leave now. I'd planned dinner for the two of us. Just us alone. It'd be so lovely; we could eat out in the garden, with the smell of the lilies in the air, and—"

"I'm sorry," Shobai said. He ran his fingers through his rumpled hair, fluffing it up. Even this gesture, a woman's, did not seem effeminate from him. It remained essentially masculine, but appeared a function of his boundless vanity, like his habit of picking up her mirror from time to time and looking himself over. "You should have told me beforehand that you were making these arrangements. I've a business meeting this evening, a dinner engagement at someone's house. No party; just something small. And in the morning I have conferences with the leaders of the Army of Carchemish, to discuss their needs. I'll spend the afternoon recruiting journeymen armorers, smiths, whatever. People who can do the blanks, the roughs, which I and the advanced journeymen can finish. I'm afraid this is more of a business trip than the last one was."

"But, Shobai . . ." She was on her hands and knees now, her lovely breasts hanging like ripe fruit beneath her. Her plump, well-rounded behind stuck up gracefully behind her. Shobai's eyebrow rose for a moment, and the thought of another amorous tussle with her slipped fleetingly through his mind; she *was* a lusty piece, for all her middle years. . . . But he remembered his business.

"I'm sorry," he said firmly. He stood tall and statuesque, neatly robed, as she pressed her naked body against him, embracing him not just with her arms but with her whole soft-fleshed frame, her skin still warm and tender from the time they'd spent in bed together. "Please, Annuta-aram. I do have to go. If I had my choice, of course I'd stay. But it's business. This is perhaps the biggest job I've ever done. It's so large that when they pay me off at the end of it, I won't be able to take the money back with me. It would require too large a guard. Instead, Hagirum will send a royal messenger ahead to Haran to arrange for an appropriate amount of credit for me with the government of my own city. From that moment on, when I need money, all I'll have to do will be to take out a stylus and tablet and write myself a draft on that credit."

"How nice for you," she said in a petulant voice. "How nice for that frigid wife of yours, the one you were telling me about. . . ."

"Oh, don't be like that," he said. "Anat will share the money, to be sure. We're buying a bigger house, for one thing. Then I'll invest the rest in land and in ground rents. But the big house is mainly for show, just as Anat herself is mainly for show. She's devastatingly pretty, in her own way. . . ."

"*Shobai*," she said, pressing herself more closely to him.

"Oh, you know what I mean. She's an ornament. It's like having the prettiest slave in town. It makes you look the richer, the more prominent. All that contributes to your stature in the community—and raises the prices for your work."

"Shobai. She can't bear you a child."

"I suppose not. I can always take another wife."

"Shobai, how horrid!"

"There'll come a time when I'll want an heir, I suppose. But why should I grieve at Anat's inability to produce one? It would just spoil that perfect body of hers. And with blemishes, with fat on her, with her looking like an ordinary sort of woman, why, what good would she be to me then? She's poor company: whining, petulant. I'd have nothing to show off to visitors."

"You men are so cruel, so calculating."

"Are we?" he said. "And you? You women? You're not that way at all, are you? You never think a practical thought, do you? You don't examine a man's financial worth through intermediaries before you allow your doting fathers to let him come courting? You do nothing at all for show, eh?" He frowned and held her at arm's length. "Look, my darling. You've no intention of walking out on your husband, and you know it. You know what the penalties would be for that. Let's face it. You have your life here, your place at court. You wouldn't swap places with Anat. I'm tolerably rich, perhaps, but your husband has riches *and* power. And you wouldn't think of losing that."

"Sho*bai.*"

"Ah. You're ready to admit it, are you?" He smiled tauntingly. "You like things to go on just as they are going. But you just want to make me feel guilty for leaving before *you* give me leave to go." He turned her a quarter turn and slapped her playfully on her naked rump. "I know you. Don't you think I'm onto all of your little games?" He bent and kissed her. "It's all right," he said. "I'm only teasing a little. You know I love you. It's just that I have to move along. This is an important trip for me."

"But Shobai, darling. When will you be back?"

"I'm not sure. It'll depend on my work schedule. I'll be at the camp for around two weeks, supervising the training. Then I'm off to the northern hills to buy copper and to secure the trade route for delivery, with a troop of soldiers at my command. And in the meantime, I'll try to keep track of your husband's activities, his comings and goings."

"I'll send a message to you when he's gone."

"Yes. But for the love of all the gods, my dear, keep it discreet. Do it through intermediaries. Or, at worst, send a trusted slave. But no: the slave will be recognized as coming from your house. Send a third party, someone not known to be associated with you. Have a slave hire him for the job." He playfully reached up and cupped her bare breasts in his hands, as if weighing them. His thumbs touched the erect nipples, teasing them. Then he released her. *Always leave them wanting a little more,* he thought. "Good-bye, my dear. We'll get together as soon as we can. I promise you."

But as he went to the door, not looking back this time, he knew he was lying. She was becoming importunate. Continuing the affair would only jeopardize his chances at the court of Hagirum. Best to break it off. There were always other women. There always had been, from the first days of his puberty: ripe-bodied, erotically inclined older women whose husbands were more business than not and who left them at home, bored and unsatisfied. . . .

It wasn't the first lie he'd told her that day, he reflected as he strolled, unhurried, through the crowded streets of Carchemish. There was, of course, the one about his "business" that evening. He had business all right, but . . . He smiled to himself. After the dinner meeting last night, in the halls of the palace, he'd run into a fetching little thing who was the new wife of a merchant of the city and whose husband had left her alone while he touched ground at a dozen markets around the borders of the Great Sea. She'd as much as seduced him right then and there, and she'd been a hot little thing, guiding his hand inside her garment like that. He was looking forward to the encounter, even after a morning's tussle with an experienced woman like Annuta-aram. In love as in all else, the newness wore off things and they grew tiresome. Variety. Novelty. They did count for something, after all. With that little thing he'd met last night . . . he wanted above all else, right now, to get the clothes off her and look her over, and see what her response would be like if he . . .

Ah, yes. There *was* such variety in women. Why should a man be tied to one of them, anyhow? Any more than a bee should be restricted to one flower?

And—who would want Anat for long, with no relief? Anat, who bored him to tears most of the time? Anat, in whom he had never for so much as a moment been able to wake the ghost of passion? Who would want a self-centered, frigid woman, no matter how pretty? Better to do as he did: keep her on the shelf, available for taking out and showing off before people of rank who appreciated beauty and knew how expensive was its upkeep. Trot her out for occasions. And in the meantime, all of her ills and complaints could be cured by putting a poultice of money on them. She was shallow, after all. Dangle a bauble in front of her nose and she'd forget all of the complaints she'd piled up, ready for reviewing before him.

Still thinking all this, he looked up ahead and saw the jutting sign of an inn—the Inn of the Crawfish—hanging over the crowd in the street. An inn—he patted his hard flat stomach. After all, he hadn't eaten since the noon hour, and Annuta-aram had this pathological fear of getting fat; she'd underfed him terribly. His stomach was growling. Better ease the hunger; then, this evening, when he had his little assignation, he'd have the strength to go a bit longer. . . .

Inside the inn, he took an empty table next to one occupied by a group of soldiers, obviously on leave from their duties. The mistress of the inn, a stout, jolly creature, brought wine. He ordered food: lamb from the spit, cheese, flat bread. And with nothing better to do, he took out of his robe the tablets he'd been given the night before by Hagirum, the tablets which outlined the schedule for the work he had to do. He ignored the noisy talk behind him—until, in a particularly salty exchange, he heard his own name spoken.

Instantly alert, he sat up—but then slumped again into the same position as before. No need to choke off the source of new information at the very beginning. But now? What was it they were saying?

". . . came in with the caravan last night from Haran. And he told me the damned little devil has latched onto the most gorgeous piece of . . ."

". . . but—who is Shobai? I don't understand. You act as though I ought to have heard of . . ."

". . . fellow who's here to arm the army against the people who've been causing such a fuss to the east of here. He's apparently been away from Haran for some days, and while the cat's away . . ."

"Oh, I see. This Shobai—he has the kind of job that leads a woman into temptation, I gather. Out of town all the time, and . . ."

"Yes, yes. My friend tells me Reshef told him she'd been playing around behind the old boy's back for some time. Regular city gate, through which everybody gets to pass. Everybody above a certain rank anyway. . . ."

"But . . . what happens if the husband comes home?"

"That's the beauty of it. He won't. She knows his schedule

209

before he leaves. And once he has a big job like the present one in hand, can you see His Highness letting him off for a few days to go home and check on his wife's comings and goings?"

"No, but . . ."

"Still, the word I hear is that this Shobai fellow is a big devil, strong as a seed bull. You know what a stringy little bastard Reshef is. If Shobai ever did come home, I'd say Reshef would have his hands full. Smiths run to size and strength. And my friend says he's a big 'un. Big as that chap behind you, from the description."

"Ah. Look out, Reshef. But—this randy wife of the smith's. What the devil would she see in an ugly, mean, low-down little bastard like Reshef? I mean, a woman who had her wits about her would rather lie with a jackal."

"Who's to say what is going to please a woman? Their minds don't work like ours. Maybe she likes it dirty. Or mean. Maybe that's the way Reshef gives it to her. I can't imagine him being the soul of tenderness, when you come right down to it. Or the romantic lover, kissing her toes for her."

"Well, I'll agree. Women are perverse. But—*Reshef.*"

"Yes, I agree. And—he's *mean.* He's the type you'd better never turn your back on, ever. He'll carry you along until the moment he doesn't need you anymore. Then, the first time you show a weak spot anywhere, in goes the knife and out goes your life. Oh, I wouldn't be too damned surprised if Reshef could take care of himself, even against a big chap like this smith fellow. After all, he's pure hell with the sword and the short knife. Fencing champion of the Army of Haran, and he used to do exhibitions at the great astrological festivals. I remember one time at the solstice festival in Ugarit . . ."

"Well, I'll tell you. *I'm* in no hurry to tangle with him. Even if he didn't outrank me and we were equals, I'd still give him a wide berth. But—imagine Reshef. A lover? A lover capable of seducing the beautiful wife of a rich man? I can't believe it. You'd easier imagine him in the stews, shoving it into some drunken slut with tangly hair and a dirty face. Well, as you say, there's no accounting for tastes with the ladies. Sometimes I think they've nothing between their ears more substantial than barley or wheat chaff."

Shobai had little by little pulled himself upright, despite himself, to listen to the bawdy conversation. Now, his face drained white, he sat, stiff and rigid, his hands motionless in his lap. His eyes looked at nothing. His mouth was a white, bloodless slash across his rock-hard face. He sat thus for several minutes, not moving more than an eye. Then the innkeeper's wife came with his food. He stood and paid her. "I'm sorry," he said. "I'll pay for the food, although I haven't the time to eat it. Give it to the help. I—I remembered a pressing engagement."

"But, sir . . ." the woman said. Then she looked down at the too many coppers in her hand and smiled. "*Thank* you, sir," she said. "Thank you and come again."

But she said it to his back. Shobai, as quickly as he had come, was gone.

III

Scarcely an hour after the caravan had arrived in Carchemish, Ami-malik—beggar and cutthroat—found his meal ticket for the day. The stranger was short, powerful, black-bearded, and dressed somewhat in the fashion of Mari; but his hair and beard were arranged in a different and slightly exotic style. He spoke the local language, haltingly and with a heavy accent. But it was plain to see that he knew nothing of Carchemish or of local customs. Such a man might well need the services of an experienced guide.

Such a man, well and expensively dressed for a long journey such as this (Where was he from? He never quite said), might also make a fine gull for an experienced cutpurse, confidence man, and sometime assassin. Ami-malik kept this sort of information stored at the very edge of his thoughts as he showed the stranger around, and it never quite left his mind. The point was in finding out how much of his money the stranger kept on him and where he kept it. Then, perhaps, at the end of a long day and after a few too many drinks at an inn—maybe even after a drink that had been sweetened to Ami-malik's order with drugs—the stranger could be steered to a likely quarter, where his faithful guide had friends who could be trusted to look the other way. . . .

The trouble was, he didn't really look like anyone's gull. His habitual expression was mild enough, but the eyes were sharp and all-seeing above that bland smile. And he was solidly built, with powerful-looking forearms, and carried a wicked-looking knife. He might prove trouble if one went after him clumsily. Well, all the more reason to drug him a bit before trying something. With his head reeling, he'd be an easy enough mark.

Now the stranger was moving about the city at a brisk enough clip to make his faithful guide pant slightly at the unaccustomed exertion. His curiosity was boundless: *What is this building? That one over there?* He marveled aloud at everything: at the recently doubled guard detachment high atop the stout walls of Carchemish, at the thickness of the inner ramparts, at the size and construction of the great gate through which all entered the city. *I am, how you say, maker of houses, back where I come from. Maker of walls.* Did he mean an engineer? *Yes, en-gi-neer. Is good word. En-gi-neer. I study ways all men makes these things. . . .*

That was understandable. A professional man would want to keep up with what other people in his field were doing. And—yes, an engineer might well become as prosperous as the stranger appeared to be. Some lines of work were horribly overpaid. The system wasn't fair.

Now the stranger stopped up ahead and waited for him. "Here," he said in his thick voice. "What is this? This is house of king, no?"

"Oh, no," Ami-malik said. "That's the temple of Anat, the goddess. The king's palace is over there. The big place, with the tower."

"Ah, I see." The stranger laughed at himself—but Ami-malik noticed that the laugh did not quite reach his eyes. *He's a smooth one,* he thought. "I make many mis-take," the stranger said. "You are, how you say, kind. To cor-rect me."

"Oh, think nothing of it, sir," Ami-malik said. "We're friendly folk here in Carchemish. We like to give guests a good welcome when they visit our city for the first time. But—sir. Perhaps you're growing hungry. You haven't really broken your fast. Perhaps one of the inns . . . ?"

It was a good time to ask this. The stranger had arrived at the outskirts of the city well after the gates had closed on the previous night. He'd been let into the city along with the rest of the huge and varied party the first thing that morning. Surely he was hungry? And surely he could afford to foot the bill for a meal for his faithful guide?

"No," the stranger said. "No, I thank you. No inn. Maybe one of ba-zaar? Maybe fresh fruit? Olives? Cheese?"

"Oh," Ami-malik said, crestfallen. This was something of a comedown. Well, perhaps he could make the most of things. At the Bazaar of the Fig Tree he had friends—friends who might well be willing to discuss a bit of business. Business that would come to fruition later that night, after the last inns had closed, when the stranger had had his nice strong drink of drugged wine. "Certainly, sir. I know just the place. A good international sort of place, full of foreigners like yourself. You'll feel right at home."

The Bazaar of the Fig Tree served two quarters and was perched midway between them. The Quarter of the Artisans used the bazaar to vend their wares. On the other side lay the Quarter of Thieves, an unsavory rabbit warren of narrow winding streets where a man would have been a fool to wander at night without a weapon. Its denizens, too, plied their trade in the big bazaar.

Now, with the sun high, the bazaar was full of people. Ami-malik sought out the area where fresh foods were sold and rustled up a light meal at the stranger's request; the stranger sat near the well and ate, watching the busy scene around him. Ami-malik, meanwhile, threaded his way through the crowd to the fringe that bordered on the Thieves' Quarter. He skirted a busy discussion of artisans over the work of a fellow craftsman, paying little attention to their eager and excited exclamations.

At last he spotted a friend: burly, hirsute Yadinim, perhaps the most accomplished and reliable assassin in the city. "Yadinim," he said. "Would you step over here behind this stall with me? We may be able to do some business together. . . ."

Ibalum, showing his wares at the craftsmen's stalls in the bazaar, spotted Ami-malik speaking to Yadinim and shook his head disapprovingly. Now there was a pair for you, he thought. The little weasel and the big bear. And two of the slimiest creatures that worked the stews of Carchemish. What could they be planning together?

He shrugged and turned back to his business. He made it a point to know the territory wherever he traveled, and that included learning as much as possible about the local criminals. But he also knew that he was well known enough in Carchemish, and well connected enough, for any thief with

213

his wits about him to give him a wide berth. Thieves in Carchemish, where the guards and the courts alike were sometimes startlingly severe, usually took pains to restrict their attacks to strangers and people of little or no standing. Otherwise, an attack on someone in the king's favor could bring down a general raid on the Thieves' Quarter in which everyone would suffer alike.

Ibalum turned back to his presentation. "Now these, gentlemen, are my summer goods from Mari. Look them over carefully and ponder the fact that caravans are beginning to avoid the trade route between Mari and Haran these days. You may not get another chance at goods from Mari for a season or more."

"Bosh," one of the bazaar traders said. "Surely you don't believe that guff everybody's putting out these days? Look, that's the sort of nonsense people talk when they're trying to raise their prices to otherwise unacceptable levels."

"You accuse *me* of this tactic?" Ibalum said mildly. There was a cold glint in his eye when he said this.

"Well, no, but—"

Ibalum did not wait for an apology. "In the meantime, my friends, I was going to give you a preview of the sort of thing I'll be importing in my next trip." He unwrapped Hadad's little ornament and laid it gently on the big bench. "Please tell me what you think. My judgment may be faulty, but I think I'm onto something."

The ohs and ahs rose above the general hubbub. Several of the merchants lined up to handle the little piece, examine it.

"Why, you old fox," one man said. "I've been trying to do some trading in the upper Hittite country for two years. And here you've beat me to the punch. How did you ... ?"

"It isn't Hittite," Ibalum said.

"Nonsense. This is the biggest coup of the season."

"Look, I tell you, it isn't Hittite. What it is is the work of an untutored genius I've discovered. A young man who isn't even a member of the craft guild."

"I don't believe you. Let me see that thing again."

"Believe what you will. I've been trying to open trade with the craft guilds in Hattusa for years myself. I sympathize totally with your sense of frustration. But I haven't solved the problem any more than you have. What I have done is—well, I've gone around it. See before you. This is the work of a young discovery of mine. I'll have him under exclusive contract by the time I see him next, and I'll be representing him exclusively to the trade."

"But—can he produce like this in any volume?"

"If I keep him well enough paid for it, he can. And if I provide him with the gold he needs to work with—and I will. I intend to make this young man rich. I'll tell you how much I believe in him: I'm not buying his work outright from him. I'm selling his work on commission only."

"Gods! A sharp operator like you? Why?"

"The happier I keep him, the better work he'll do. Most of us go our whole lives without realizing this. I've finally got it through my thick skull. I'm going to make this boy rich. The richer I make him, the richer he'll make me. Believe me, I can't tell you his name until we've signed and registered the tablets that bind us together on an exclusive basis. But let me make this one prediction. Within five years, his name will be famous in the trade over the whole world as we know it. And justly so."

"Justly so indeed, if he can produce work of this quality on a regular basis." A second merchant handed the piece to his neighbor, smiling at Ibalum. "Well, if you're not bluffing, I'm willing to concede you've made something of a coup. I'll represent you here, if nobody else will."

"Done," Ibalum said. "I'll have the tablets drawn up." His smile—the one the world could see—was small and cautious. Inside, it was as wide as a smile could get. His heart was beating fast. He had! He had discovered a genius! He couldn't wait to tell the boy, to see the expression on his face.

Shobai's face was like stone. He sat across the table from the man with the eyepatch, looking at the scarred face and seeing nothing. "You can trust me, Kihilum," Shobai said. "I won't report you to the guards."

"Well, I don't know," the man said in a wheedling voice. "What you propose is highly irregular. I could get in a lot of trouble—"

"So could I," Shobai said. "Keep that in mind. Once we enter into a contract, either one of us can put the other's head on the headsman's block. But I'll chance it. And I'm willing to pay—probably better than you've ever got for the work."

"I'd have to subcontract," the man said. "I don't know exactly whom I'd use. It'd have to be an expert. He'd have to be discreet, extraordinarily discreet. There are—well, ticklish political overtones involved in any operation we attempt to carry out over at Haran."

"Damn your political overtones."

"Ah, well you may say that. But the truth is, relations

215

between Carchemish and Haran are chancy enough as it is. Our Hagirum has been openly ridiculing your Shemariah for his damned fool pacifist stance. Shemariah has responded openly to this. Relations between the cities could break down."

"What is that to the matter at hand?"

"A lot. You talk of an offense against a public figure which could be viewed as—well, political. Military, even. That could be real political trouble."

"It needn't. Find men who can do the job. Men who can be trusted. Men who won't bungle it and whose faces are not known here well—or there at all."

"You're really obdurate, aren't you? A real blood-drinker. Hardheaded, too—"

"You're insolent." Shobai's eyes blazed. "Keep your tongue to yourself."

"Go to the devil," the man with the eyepatch said. "You're going to bring up rank? Here? Sitting across a table from me planning violence? Bah. Go peddle your high-and-mighty notions elsewhere." He started to rise.

Shobai put a big hand on his arm. "Pardon," he said. "That's anger speaking. I shouldn't take it out on you."

"Quite right," the man said. "Or on anyone else either. Anger makes a man careless. Better to keep it collected, calm. Violence planned or executed in an excitable state is violence bungled. Only when you're totally in control of yourself can you do the thing right." His smile showed broken teeth. "Smile, and smile—and nail the bastard."

"Right. That's good advice." Shobai breathed deep, calmed himself. "Now," he said. "Can you do it?"

"Let's find out," the man said. "You don't want him killed, you say? Killed would be better. Dead men can't tell anyone about the faces they may have seen in a stray shaft of light."

"If it can be avoided, I'd say avoid it. Dead men also feel no pain. I want this man to feel pain. If possible, I want to know that he'll feel pain the rest of his life. And spoil his face for me too, spoil it for good. Take out an eye, perhaps. I want him so ugly that nobody but the lowest drunken whore from the worst whorehouse in Damascus, desperate for money, would look amorously at him again."

"I see," said the man with the eyepatch. "Got after your wife, did he? Or was it your mistress?"

"None of your damned business."

"Ah, touchy, touchy. But you're right. The comment was

216

gratuitous. I'll stick to business. You want him lamed. Maimed. What else?"

"That should be enough. Except of course that I don't want either you or me ever to be connected with it in any way. You were going to subcontract?"

"Of course, of course. Now as to payment—half now, half on delivery. Meaning when you have proven to yourself by whatever means you choose that I've fulfilled my end of the bargain."

"All right. How much?"

"A thousand."

"Done. And a bonus if I like the results."

"Good. A man should be paid for good work."

"But remember. He's said to be a master of the sword. He's an instructor for the army."

"We won't use a sword. There are other ways." His smile was crooked and cold. "And no man is a swordsman in the dark. Leave it to me, my friend. Leave it to me. . . ."

IV

Now it was dusk, and the long shadows covered everything. Ami-malik had found the stranger lodging with a friend in the trade (a friend who would look the other way when the time came, and who had a short memory). And now he steered his stranger to an inn at the edge of the Thieves' Quarter, an inn where the innkeeper owed him favors.

The stranger ordered a lavish meal for the two of them. Frugal by day, he appeared to unbend a bit in the evening. All the better; Ami-malik would see the color of his money— and see where he kept it. There was a purse hanging on a cord around the stranger's neck; once he was incapacitated it would be no trouble to . . .

Ami-malik excused himself just as the dancer came on. Time enough later for staring at a well-rounded rear end. Time enough, for that matter, for arranging a more private performance, with a fat purse in his hand. He slipped outside and whistled soft and low.

"Ami-malik?" a voice said so close by his elbow that he jumped for fright.

"Quiet, damn it!" Ami-malik said in an angry whisper. "No names. You know that—who the devil are you?"

"No names, you said." The assassin's grin was faintly visible in the moonlight. "But—I was sent by Yadinim. He'll be joining us in a bit."

"All right. When he comes, you tell him that we'll be staying through the second show, perhaps the third. I'll try to get him out as soon as possible. He'll have to be a little drunk in the first place before we can slip him the drugged drink and not have him suspect."

"I understand. Is he armed?"

"A knife. Be warned: he looks as though he could use it."

"I thought this was going to be easy."

"Well, it could be. But only a fool takes on a job like this with no notion that anything could go wrong. Be warned."

"All right, all right. You didn't imagine Yadinim would be sending some beginner, did you?"

"No, I didn't. Don't talk like one."

"All right." The assassin slipped back into the shadows. "Yadinim said to steer him down by the bridge. . . ."

"I hear. The bridge it is."

Back inside the inn, the innkeeper was chatting with a new employee, a bondman, about the ferocious-looking stranger who was finishing his meal and watching the dancer.

"You're sure?" the innkeeper said, glancing at the stranger. "It could be someone else, someone who looked like him."

"I am sure," the new bondman said. "Can be no mistake. I see with these eyes. You think I forget? I forget man who kill my son? My father?"

"But he could come from anywhere. He could have come from Haran."

"No Haran. You hear him talk. Go: you talk to him. See if he speak like man of Haran." The bondman's voice quivered with emotion. "Is no man of Haran. Is murderer."

"Those are strong words, for a man who—"

"Look. I spill wine near his foot. I bend to clean up. I hear him talk. Is different words. But is same man. I hear voice before."

"Well, be that as it may, it doesn't concern me. As long as he pays his bills—and mind you, he's been doing that,

218

promptly, all night—as long as his cash is good it's no affair of mine."

"But—"

"Or of yours."

"But please, if—"

"Or of yours." The innkeeper's voice was firm, his tone final. "That's all there'll be of that. Now get back to washing up. The bowls are piling up. There'll be a new crowd coming in in a little while. It's up to us to be ready for them."

"But if only—"

The new bondman stared at the innkeeper's retreating back. His heart was pounding fast, and the hot blood boiled furiously in his veins. *Murderer! Murderer!* And as his eye scanned the kitchen, his gaze lit on a sharp knife he had used to cut the cheese for the evening meal. Sharp—and long. His hand trembled as he picked it up.

Ami-malik, coming back inside, spotted Kihilum. What was *he* doing here? Ami-malik wondered; but before he could speculate further, the man with the eyepatch came over to him.

"Good to see you," Kihilum said softly. "Can we talk? I may have some work for you."

Ami-malik flinched a little under the hawklike gaze of that single eye. "Not now," he said. "Maybe later. I have something of my own going."

"Ah. The foreigner? Someone told me you'd found a new victim. Well, won't it wait a few moments while we talk? There's good money in what I've got going—*very* good money."

Ami-malik sighed. "Look, it's no good. Get someone else. You—" He sighed again. "What kind of thing is it? Something quick?"

"No. Not at all. Take perhaps a week at the least. But the money is, as I said, exceptional. Two men—good with weapons. Perhaps three hundred each."

"Three hundred? That's not bad. But a week?"

"Well, perhaps three-fifty." Kihilum frowned at the notion of seeing his own finder's fee diminish. "But I doubt I can get more. Look, if you can't do the work yourself how about somebody who's on the run? Somebody who could use a few days of lying low right now—out of town."

"Hmmm. I'll have to think. I'll see what I can do for you. If I can't do it myself, I'll try to send you someone."

"Well, don't wait too long. Time is important. My client has had his, uh, happy home invaded."

"He wants the man killed?"

"No. But he wants him to remember the encounter. The more painfully, the better. You know: a hand, an eye. Broken bones."

"Ah. And how well guarded is the quarry?"

"Only by himself—when he's in town. He's an officer in the Army of Haran." Kihilum's eye narrowed. "A good man with the sword."

"That lets out a few people I would otherwise have recommended."

"What about Yadinim? He's both strong and quick."

Ami-malik paused, ruminated. "True. But look: I have him in this thing with me just now. When we're done with it—if it comes out the way we hope it does, praise be to the gods—I'll talk to him. But—a week?"

"Yes. In Haran."

"That's chancy. And political problems, too."

"Right." Kihilum's eye narrowed even further. He wasn't about to give away any more of his commission. "Think of what three-fifty each would buy. Or—tell you what. Does Yadinim have to know what the price is? You'll split seven hundred. Take four; give him three."

"You're beginning to talk my language. But—could I get back to you in the morning? Meet you—oh, say, at the bazaar? Or, better, by the canal?"

"Shortly after the gates open? I'll be there. Meanwhile, if you want to talk to me tonight, I'll be at the Inn of the Lion Rampant until it closes."

"That pigsty? What for?"

"Closing a deal, my dear friend. Delivering a shipment of choice Hittite females for the whorehouse upstairs. I bought them at the market yesterday. Captured in a raid, and juicy and plump as ripe figs. The markup isn't much, but it's a quick six hundred for a night's work."

"I see. The Lion Rampant. We'll see how it goes tonight."

"Very well. Until then . . ." The one-eyed man's nod was almost courtly until you took note of his bleak smile.

The stranger had put away a fearsome amount of wine, yet he did not show signs of drunkenness. Ami-malik was beginning to wonder if the evening's work would be the simple thing he'd thought it. Now the stranger's hand beat time to the drum as the little dancer, nude and glistening with sweat, gyrated below the flickering flames. "How much this woman?" he said, indicating with his hand. "How much any woman?"

Ami-malik looked at the dancer's trim behind. "I don't know," he said. "I could ask if you like. Ten coppers, perhaps less."

"Ten?" the stranger said, pursing his lips. "So much?"

"I'll find out," Ami-malik said. He stood and slipped away from the table with a single deferent nod to his charge. He made his way through the dim, crowded back corner of the room to the kitchen. Inside, he signaled to the innkeeper, who came forward. "Now," he said.

"You're sure?" the innkeeper said. "I saw him a moment ago. He looked as cool as if he'd been drinking goat's milk."

"I'm sure," Ami-malik said, his tone full of more confidence than he felt just now. "Do it. Go ahead."

"I don't want to get in trouble, now——"

"Do it!"

The innkeeper turned. "You!" he said. "Damn it, where's that new bondman? These bowls are supposed to be clean, and if——"

Ami-malik watched the stranger drink, slowly, savoring each sip. *Can he taste the difference?* he wondered. He wiped the cold sweat from his own forehead. The stranger's eye left the naked girl, went to his bowl; an eyebrow rose. Then he drank again.

Then he put the bowl down. He blinked his eyes.

He's feeling it, Ami-malik thought. His own heart was beating fast. *He's feeling it already.* . . .

"Strange," his table partner said. "All of a sudden I no feel good." He put his hands to his temples, closed his eyes.

"It's close in here," Ami-malik said. "Perhaps too close. Maybe what you need is a little fresh air."

"Yes," the stranger said. He stood, weaving. Ami-malik supported him, helped him out into the air. There, in the moonlight, he stood in a pool of light in the middle of the road, shaking his shaggy head. "Strange," he said. "Drink taste bad . . ."

Ami-malik looked into the shadows. A pair of eye-whites gleamed out at him. "Come," he said. "Down by the bridge. The air's cleaner over running water. . . ." *What were they doing here, of all places?* he wondered, his mind in a panicky

221

turmoil. The arrangement had been to meet at the bridge, not here. Not here, where customers came and went, where the guards checked in three times a night to make sure order was being maintained.

He reached out to take the stranger's arm—and found his own wrist grasped in a grip like a wrestler's. His heart almost stopped. He tried to pull free and couldn't. Suddenly, a knife flashed in the stranger's other hand. "And what would happen by bridge?" the stranger said. "You have friend there, waiting? You and friend, they kill me, drop me in water? No? Take money and kill me? Eh?"

"N-no," Ami-malik said. His knife was on the wrong side. He couldn't reach it with the other hand—not and maintain his current arm's-length distance from the stranger. "You're all wrong. I had no—"

"You put bad drink in wine. You think I not know." The powerful grip was now pulling Ami-malik to him, slowly, tantalizingly. The moonlight glinted on that long knife again; Ami-malik cringed away, groping for his own weapon back-handed, not finding it . . .

. . . and then behind the stranger there was a choked scream of rage and a figure lunged out of the darkness. A second knife gleamed. It struck the stranger somewhere in the back. He recoiled, let Ami-malik go, and turned, circling away from the new attacker.

Ami-malik, released, fell to the ground. He rose to one knee, trying to get a good look at the new arrival. It wasn't Yadinim at all—and it wasn't his sarcastic assistant either. It was nobody he'd ever seen before . . .

. . . but yes it was! It was the new bondman the inn had taken on, the refugee—the one who had spilled the wine and had to clean it up! Every instinct told Ami-malik he had to run for his life; but something equally powerful seemed to be holding him there. He watched as the newcomer feinted with his blade, swung it in a wide sweep. The stranger parried the blow and lunged, catching the bondman a glancing blow.

"I know you," the bondman said, his voice choked with anger and helpless rage. "You led army that kill my city. You come in peace. White rag on stick. You open gates, kill all people. My father, my son. You! You! I know you. Now I kill you—"

"You are mis-taken," the stranger said in his deep voice. He parried another blow. "Now go. I do not wish to kill—"

"*I* kill *you!*" the bondman said. He was beside himself now, totally out of control. Blood stained his robe where the blow

222

had caught him. "I kill you—for what you did! You, murderer! You—*Manouk!*"

To Ami-malik's eye the stranger seemed to sigh, as if to say *I'm sorry, my friend, now you've forced me to kill you.* His hand swept up, down—the motion was literally too fast for the eye to follow. The blade sliced into the bondman's face; there was a gout of blood. The bondman dropped his weapon, put his hands to his mutilated face. The weapon stabbed—once, twice. The bondman fell first to his knees, then on his face.

The stranger turned.

Ami-malik got his feet under him and took to his heels. There was no pursuit. It didn't matter. He wanted nothing more than to put as much distance as possible between him and the stranger. But—the bridge! He knew they'd be waiting for him at the bridge! He raced to the water, calling out in a terrified voice: "Yadinim! Run! Run! It's no good—"

And now there were feet pounding the ground after his, two pairs of them. He raced deep into the stews, into the Quarter of Thieves. He had no idea where he was going; he simply wanted to get away, away.

He stopped at last in a street of brothels, with the whores sitting in the windows calling out to him. He ignored them, waited for his friends to catch up. When he could get his breath, he led them to one side, out of earshot of the raucous-voiced, foul-mouthed women, and told them what had happened, as much of it as he could make out.

"Then you're in trouble," Yadinim said. "He saw you. He knows you. And as long as he's in town—" He whistled low. "You'd better get out of town, my friend. And in a hurry."

Ami-malik, still panting, stared at him. And at the thought of meeting that cold, controlled fury again at the end of a knife he shivered and nearly befouled himself. "Out of town?" he said. "But how . . . ?"

Then he remembered his conversation with Kihilum. And, small comfort though it was, he drew comfort from the fact. "Yadinim," he said. "I—I *do* know where there's a week's work out of town, well paid. If we start immediately—"

"How well?" Yadinim said. He turned to his assistant. "Go away," he said. "How well, Ami-malik? And where?"

The assistant left with a scowl, cursing them. Ami-malik watched him go before continuing. "In Haran," he said. "If we hurry, we can make a deal tonight, down at the Inn of the—"

"How much?" Yadinim said. His giant shoulders bunched. "Haran's a long way—"

"Two hundred fifty," Ami-malik said. "For perhaps an hour's work in all."

Yadinim looked at him from under dark brows. "Make it two hundred eighty," he said.

Ami-malik, still gasping for breath, held his hand to his pounding heart. "Done," he said.

V

"Can the boy work in other styles?" Imnah of Byblos said, reaching for another olive. "I mean, Cretan, Lycian . . ."

"My friend," Ibalum said, looking at the trader over his wine bowl, "I think this young man of mine can do whatever I hand him to do. He makes a living doing the most insultingly stylized work for the temple—for a pittance, of course—and his own work in that line is at least the equal of anything anyone else does. It's when he has been allowed some room for self-expression that he really begins to come into his own, though."

"That's not what I was asking," the trader said. He watched a small bird fly down into the garden where they sat and pick up a crumb from their table. "In Lycia, for instance, there's a certain style for representations of Cybele—or images of Attis. If he can—"

"I see," Ibalum said. "Look, that's how the boy learned the craft. Somewhere along the way, he picked up the knack of making workable clay from the right kind of soil. With no formal apprenticeship to guide him, he learned everything by copying. He copied everything. Absolutely everything. There's a way in which this was better for him than the standard apprenticeship would have been. I think perhaps a master might have cramped his hand, making him do things the recognized way. But—well, you show him a style and he'll have it down in a week's time if he has no other work to do."

"Good. I have a market for religious pieces in Lycia. I have one—or *had* one—for images of the Goddess and of the

224

Kraken in Crete. Of course, with the palace revolution there nobody knows what the market will be six months from now."

"It'll all blow over. The new Minos will be much like the old, where trade is concerned. No king of Crete will let anything interfere with business for long."

"Perhaps. I'm more likely to take the pessimistic view. But as you wish. Since we're talking about only the most expensive material, in the most severely limited quantities—"

"Oh, mind you, I've nothing against having my young man train an apprentice or two to do work for the lesser markets—"

"Of course. But in the beginning, before we give them the lesser copies, we must release into the high-pay markets only examples of the most exacting skill and artistry—"

"Oh, I couldn't agree more. We begin at the top. At the top we sell only to kings—and to the fabulously rich."

"And for the most fabulous prices."

"Which will go up in a while."

"Many times, before we're done. Many times, before the young man has gray in his beard."

"We limit the supply, of course. Only so much to Lycia, only so much to Crete, only so much to Egypt—"

"I agree. After a time, it will make a newly rich man feel poor indeed if his household does not contain at least one staggeringly expensive item by your young man—"

"Ah, castles in the air. But let's face it, my friend: if a businessman doesn't dream, if he doesn't project into the future—"

"Of course. He remains a trivial sort of drummer, working the minor bazaars, content with what he has."

"He remains just a peddler with a pushcart, and no matter that he may be selling to royalty—"

"I see we understand each other. Well, have we a deal?"

"We have. Now let's talk prices."

Shobai paused at the door as an unseen hand tugged at his sleeve. "Psst! Sir—if you please—over here—"

He looked around, annoyed—but saw Kihilum beckoning. He looked to right and left. Nobody seemed to be looking his way. He stepped into the alley with the man with the eyepatch. "What is it?" he said curtly. "You know, I'd rather not have anyone following me right to the door of . . ."

". . . to the door of the wife of the general whose army you are arming?" Kihilum said with sly insolence. "Never mind that. When you hear the news I have—"

Shobai reached for the one-eyed man, his eyes flashing; but Kihilum shrank away from him, his face twisted in a greasy smile. "News?" Shobai said. "What news?"

"I've got your men," he said. "Two of the best in Carchemish. Quiet, competent, discreet. Now: do we talk business?"

"Hmmm. They're strong? Adept? They work well together?"

"None better. They're ready and waiting. This business matches their needs perfectly."

"Needs?"

"To—ah, let us say, get out of town for a bit. Shall we say the weather is getting a bit hot for them right now in Carchemish."

"Well, that's not my affair. How quickly can they do the job?"

"Who knows? The first consideration is not speed, of course; it is to get the job done in such a way that it can never be traced back to you."

"I see. And what is it that they're waiting for?"

"Your approval. And—ah, some financial—"

"Yes, yes. I'll tell you what. Come to me tonight, at the Inn of the Four Palms. At dinner time."

"Ah, sir, that's too rich for my blood. They won't let me in there."

"Send in a messenger. Bribe someone at the door. You know how to handle these things. Don't tell me you don't."

"Well, all right, but—"

"Don't worry. When the messenger comes in, I'll come right out and talk with you. Drop whatever I'm doing."

"And—you'll have the first payment?"

"Don't worry."

"In gold, as I asked? Not in base coin?"

"I'll arrange it. I have almost unlimited credit here."

"You'll have to. But," Kihilum said in his old wheedling tone, "I'm sure you have all that arranged, sir. I'll see you tonight. And sir—"

"Yes?"

"The men will leave in the morning for Haran. On the first caravan out. I've already taken the precaution of arranging their passage."

"Good. Now leave me." The one-eyed man, with a slimy grin, turned and disappeared into the street. Shobai moved back to the door, looked both ways again, and knocked, once, twice. Then, after a calculated pause, he knocked two times rapidly.

He clenched his big fist in anticipated triumph. He'd show the damned little bastard to fool around with his, Shobai's wife! In a way it was worse than stealing property. Reshef had sullied his bed, befouled his wife, his lovely and ornamental chattel. He must be made to pay, and dearly, for the insult and dishonor. Tonight he'd give Kihilum specific instructions for the two assassins: Reshef must lose his nose, perhaps, or an ear. No, an eye. An eye would be better. . . .

The door opened a crack. A lovely brown eye peered cautiously out of the doorway. "Shobai?" a soft voice said.

"That's the one over there. The one with the beard."

The young officer squinted into the setting sun. "Looks harmless enough to me," he said. "You're sure, now? You don't want to go making false accusations against people. You never know when someone is going to turn out to be somebody important. Or, just as bad, related to someone important."

"Just ask him a question or two. Listen to him talk. He's not from anywhere around here. He's not from Mari either, or Nineveh. I tell you I saw—"

"But look, you just said he's leaving. On the morning caravan, eastward bound. What more harm could he . . . ?"

"Gods! Are you listening to me? I got suspicious from the first. No sooner had he come inside the gates than he took up with a scoundrel named Ami-malik, a common criminal. He had Ami-malik give him a grand tour of the city."

"No harm in that. I know the little rat you're talking about. I've arrested him once. No, twice. But still: there's no law against letting him make a few coppers showing someone around."

"But he was showing him things like the city's defenses. The guard posts. The—"

"You're a little on the nosy side, aren't you?" the young officer said. He looked at the man who'd drawn him aside: an ordinary-looking fellow, not particularly well dressed. A busybody. The sort of person who's always trying to run somebody else's life for him. "You followed them around like that? Don't you have anything better to do with your time?"

The informant drew himself up. "You're insolent. I'll report you to your commandant. I'll—"

"Go ahead. But in the meantime, perhaps I'll check the man out. Hmm. That's odd. There's a bloodstain—if that's

227

what it is—on the back of his robe. I wonder how he came by that. Yes, and a rip. Looks as though someone stuck something in him recently. I could ask."

"Do that. Yes. But when I talk to your commander—"

"Oh, be quiet." The soldier left the officious citizen behind and approached the stranger. He was adjusting the saddle on a high-spirited black horse, a tall and lusty animal which pranced proudly as its master fiddled with the cinch. "Excuse me, sir," he said. The man didn't hear. The young officer looked up at the high walls of Carchemish above them, at the guards on the ramparts. *But what if he* were *in fact a spy?* the young soldier thought suddenly. To be sure, the man's clothing was unusual. He couldn't place it at all. *What if . . . ?*

Some little tickle of apprehension, below the conscious level, made him put one hand on his sword hilt as he approached. "Excuse me, sir," he said in a louder voice. "I'd like to ask you some questions—"

The dark head turned his way; the eyes flashed. The gaze shot downward to the soldier's hand on the hilt of his weapon. The man's whole posture stiffened. Instantly alert, he held the reins of the horse.

"Excuse me, sir," the soldier said again. Now his own stance was full of tension. A citizen up to no harm didn't act this way, approached with routine questions by authority. "I'd like you to come with me—"

But the stranger stepped back one step and, suddenly, leapt upward into the saddle. The soldier sprang forward, reached for the reins. The stranger yanked them free. And now, with a motion almost too quick for the eye to trace it, the stranger's free hand had reappeared with a sword in it. The soldier drew his sword and lunged; the blow was parried swiftly, deftly. The stranger's blade swung backhand; the flat of the blade smashed the young soldier on the side of the head, knocking him to his knees. Dazed, he bellowed in a choked voice: "You! Guards! Stop him! Stop that man there!"

But the stranger had spurred the black horse from trot to gallop, and he was past the guards, past the first ring of the great caravan, beyond the range of an arrow. "After him!" the young soldier cried, holding his hand to his bleeding head. But by the time anyone could mount, the stranger was a dwindling black dot at the head of a great column of dust.

"You don't mean it." Ami-malik sat back and gaped at Yadinim. "Gods! How did we escape with our lives?"

"I don't know. That's one you owe to the gods, I'd say. I talked to two of the refugees, people who knew the dead bondman. He mentioned it to both of them. From what he told them, the stranger you were squiring around was second-in-command of the entire nomad force. No, that isn't quite what they said. He was—well, one of them called him 'the Executioner.' He said something like, 'You have a king, and he says, "Kill him!" about somebody or other. And there always has to be somebody right there to see that it's carried out. Usually he doesn't do the killing himself—but he's not above it if—' "

"Executioner, eh? And here he is, spying on Carchemish. The gods help poor Carchemish. . . ."

"I wonder," Yadinim said thoughtfully. "I wonder if something of this shouldn't be passed along to the authorities somehow. If it were known that the nomads had had a spy in the city, looking over the defenses—"

"No!" Ami-malik said, horrified. "What are you thinking of? Tell the authorities? And put my own head in a noose? There's the dead bondman, after all—and the city's been trying to find something to frame me with for the longest time."

"Ah. I see your point. Well, all right. We'll keep it to ourselves. But, it doesn't look good for Carchemish."

"No, it doesn't. But look, my friend. Once we've done the present job and collected the second half of our payment, I'm thinking of shaking the dust of Carchemish from my sandals soon anyhow. I'm too well known here—"

"Ah. And once we've maimed this Reshef fellow and got our money—what new frame of action do you have in mind?"

"Hmmm. Carchemish is doomed. So is Haran. Perhaps Ugarit? Byblos?"

"All right with me. At worst it would put off the date when we have to make a decision to leave there, too. He and his friends—this Manouk fellow and the nomads—they'll not stop with Carchemish and Haran from what the refugees say."

"No. That's true. So where shall we go next? Ashkelon? Tyre?"

"All right with me. I can stay alive in any seaport. If worse comes to worst, you just go down to the docks and make an arrangement with a couple of ships' captains. Then you go in business as a press gang. There's never a time when they don't need warm bodies manning an oar—and the captains pay

229

well for every man you bring 'em—if you haven't hit 'em too hard before bringing 'em in."

"Sounds good to me. But that's all in the future. Let's get to bed early. The caravan leaves at dawn. The faster we get this over with the better."

"I'm with you, my friend."

CHAPTER EIGHT

I

Yamam stopped by the Inn of the White Horse at noon. "Come, Danataya," she said. "I've some cheese and bread. Let's go eat down by the canal. The air's cool there over the water. I have something to tell you. Something exciting." There was an amorous twinkle in her eye.

Danataya wiped her dripping brow. "Thank you, Yamam. It was nice of you to think about me, but—"

"But nothing," the girl said. "Come along. Surely Abi-samar won't begrudge you—"

"It's not that. I—I've got a problem. I want to try to see if I can stay on Abi-samar's good side just now. I—need to ask him a favor."

"Oh, let me ask him. He wouldn't dare refuse me."

"I—I can't. I just can't."

"Well, is it something I can help with?"

Danataya looked at her friend. For a moment she thought she'd be able to get herself to say it: *Please, Yamam . . . I have to have thirty coppers by sundown tomorrow. Could you please . . . ?* Please what? she asked herself. Please lend me the money? Then how would she pay it back? Please let me move in with you? That would really be too much to ask. . . . "No," she said after a moment's hesitation. "No, thanks—"

"Well, at worst you can come down and have lunch with me. I need to talk to someone, and you're the best friend I have."

"Maybe," Danataya said. She bit her lip. "If—look, Yamam. Could you wait for me for a moment? I mean, I have to go talk to Admuniri. Maybe she'll be easier to approach. If I'm going to talk to Abi-samar, I'll have to wait until nightfall."

"All right. Maybe I can spend the time down at the bazaar. Not that I can buy anything right now. I'm broke. I just spent every copper I had on the most wonderful robe."

"Ah," Danataya said. Well, that settled that. So far as the loan was concerned, anyway. "Yes," she said. "You go to the bazaar. I'll meet you there. One of the dry-goods booths? All right. I won't be more than a moment. I can wash my face and fix up my hair first—"

"Oh?" Yamam said. "I forget. That's where that cute little singer with the bad leg works, right? You don't want to look anything but your best for—"

"Yamam, *please.*"

"All right. But he was so beat-up the last time we saw him, I'd be surprised if he had any thought of girls. He probably won't even notice."

"You go on," Danataya said with a harried smile. "I'll be right along." She watched Yamam go, then went back inside, pinning up her dark hair. She caught Admuniri on the way out. "Please," she said. "Ma'am—"

"Oh, it's you. Did you finish the floor yet?"

"No, ma'am. It's noontime. I want to go join Yamam at the canal."

"All right. But be back soon. And be sure to clean off the tables."

"Yes, ma'am. I will. But Admuniri—"

"Yes? Please, make it quick. I've got to go—"

"Yes, ma'am. But—it's Horon. He says if I don't pay him by tomorrow at dusk, he'll throw me out."

"I'll talk to him. He can't be serious."

"He is, I'm afraid. He has another tenant. He says the other tenant has cash in hand. He thinks I'm too skinny and weak, that I won't last. Besides—"

"Abi-samar will talk to him."

"I don't think that will help, ma'am. If I could only get an advance against my—"

Admuniri looked at her with exasperation and embarrassment. "Gods. Danataya, if it were any other week in the history of the world—you know of course that it's tax time."

"No. I didn't."

"That's probably why Horon is being so impossible. He has to have the money by the day after tomorrow, bright and early. He knows that if you don't have it to pay him with by dusk tomorrow, he may as well never have it."

"And—and you and Abi-samar—"

"Yes. We can barely meet it ourselves. Otherwise, you know we'd be glad to help. You know we would. But business has been bad, very bad, and with the city full of refugees, people who can't afford an inn themselves and who scare away the good solid substantial people who can—"

"I understand. I sort of thought things were slow. I mean, except on the weekend."

"Very bad. It's all we can do to pay the help, and meet the tax assessment, and buy provisions for the paying guests."

"I understand. I really do."

"Well, I hope you do, child. If it were any other week—"

"Yes, ma'am." Danataya turned away with a deferential bow of the head, trying to hide the terror on her face. There went my last hope, she thought. Unless—

Yes. At worst, Yamam could put her up. She'd even suggested it a few days before. Yes, she'd have to swallow her pride and ask. Not that Yamam would do anything to hurt her pride in any case. She'd probably insist on it.

She washed her face with water from a basin she'd drawn at the well an hour before. Then she tucked her hair up under a headcloth, brushed the dust from her brief garment, and went out into the street.

At the bazaar her eye went cautiously to the space where she'd seen Hadad sing the song; but the little cripple was nowhere in sight. Gathering up her courage, she approached the greengrocer's woman. "Please, ma'am," she said. "I was one of the people who found the young man—Hadad, I think the name is? Anyhow, I found him the other night, and I was wondering . . ."

The woman looked her up and down. "Ah. You're the new maid-of-all-work down at Admuniri's place, aren't you?" she said. "Thought I'd seen the face before. No, Hadad didn't come in today, or the day before. I went to see him yesterday. Poor dear, he was pretty bad looking. Someone really beat him badly. How did he get to drinking like that, anyhow? Hadad's never had two unwatered bowls of wine in a row in his life."

"I don't know, ma'am. He was too ill the night we found him and Jacob took him home. . . ."

"Jacob, eh? He was by here this morning asking about Hadad. He's a decent, well-spoken man. You a friend of his? Or . . . ?" The woman's eye took on a suspicious glint.

"Oh, no, ma'am. I'd never seen him before. Well, yes I had, but—" She flushed with embarrassment. "It's not that way, ma'am. Jacob was passing by on his way home, and—"

"Well, that may be as it may be. However it happened, we're all glad you and he happened along. We're fond of Hadad here. More than a little protective of him, in a way. We more or less raised him, the rest of the bazaar and me. We're all the family he has, really. His mother, poor dear, is mad. His brother is a bigwig who doesn't come to see him because he isn't important, as he sees it. Anyway, if you helped him, you're all right with us."

"Thank you, ma'am. But—is he all right? Was he badly hurt?"

"Not that much—physically, anyhow. Something's hurt him badly inside, though, and we can't seem to find out what it was. Otherwise, what would he be drinking for, he who never does that kind of thing even on the rare occasions when he can afford it? But he won't say. As for his poor body, I think there's nothing broken. I'm going to check on him this evening, though. If you stop by here tomorrow, I'll know more." Her smile was friendlier this time. She looked Danataya up and down and apparently didn't disapprove too much of what she saw. "Come back tomorrow," she said again. "Come back any time you like. Hadad needs friends. If you're a friend of his, you'll find friends at this bazaar."

"Thank you," Danataya said. She turned to see Yamam coming, the parcel of food under one arm. "Yamam," she said, wondering how to put it. "Could you . . . ?"

Yamam's free hand took Danataya's; she led the girl out of the bazaar. "No," she said. "Let me tell my thing first. I'm bursting with excitement. I've met the most marvelous man. He won't last long, mind you, and I'll have him only for a month or so at most, but while my rich old man—remember? the one who wants to marry me?—while my rich old man is gone, this fellow is going to make me very happy."

"A new one?" Danataya said. "But I thought you were being faithful to . . . ?"

"Well, I *am*, darling," Yamam said. "After my fashion." Her grin was conspiratorial and irresistible. "But when the old man's away on business, I figure there's little reason to sit home and mope." She caught the crestfallen look on Danataya's face. "Oh, look, sweetheart. I didn't mean to say that I haven't enjoyed *your* company." She gave Danataya a quick impulsive hug. "But—well, youth won't come again. And if I'm going to lock myself up with an old man for the rest of my life—or," she said with the same wicked grin, "for the rest of *his*—I'm going to kick up my heels a little first, whenever I can. And this new one, oh, my! He's beautiful! Just beautiful! He's a soldier, and he has the *strongest* arms!"

Danataya bit her lip. She knew what the answer would be before she asked, but she asked anyhow. "And—he's staying with you while the old man is away?"

"Why, yes, darling; where else would a soldier stay? I mean, I couldn't very well go join him in a tent up at the army camp, could I? Not and keep any reputation at all. Goodness knows it's bad enough just taking up for a bit with a soldier in the first place. If I were to go where he goes, I'd soon have the reputation of a camp whore who puts out for every man jack in the whole army."

"I—understand." Well, there went her last hope. First Admuniri, then Yamam. What was she going to do? Where could she go? Perhaps Admuniri would let her sleep at the inn—on a table, perhaps, or off in a corner somewhere. Perhaps . . .

Jacob had come home for his midday meal. Now he watched, a small smile playing on his lips, as Rachel cut the cheese, her every movement a thing of grace that brought joy to his heart. "And Leah and the boys?" he said. "They're at Laban's, I suppose?"

"Yes," she said in her sweet gentle voice. "Jacob, you're sure you can handle them, when the time comes? I mean—"

"I know what you mean," Jacob said. "And I think I can. Up to now, I haven't tried. I've let it all get away from me, let the reins slip out of my hands. Well, no more. I'm taking the control back. As of tomorrow."

"I couldn't be happier, darling. They're not bad boys, really. Just undisciplined."

"Certainly. And that's my fault. But mind you, I'm not going to indulge myself in idle recriminations. I'm just going to grab the reins and take over. Once they've got used to the idea, I think they'll actually like it."

"I'm sure. After all, they're your children." She set the cheese on a tray and turned to face him. Her smile was warm and loving. "And you're a good father. You've just been—distracted. My father is such an ogre. . . ."

"That's another thing. Did you realize we're almost paid up? I mean, the debt to Laban? The apprenticeship debt, and—"

"Oh, Jacob," she said. She sat down quickly and took his big hand in her two small ones. "You mean it? Really? After all this time?"

He smiled happily at her. It was so good to see her like this. Well, that was what several consecutive nights of tender passion could do for a woman—and a man too, for that matter. "Yes. And not only that, my portion of the herds is stronger, healthier than Laban's."

"The God has been looking out for you," she said.

"Yes. But I've been looking out for myself, too. Wait until I tell you about how I've been handling the breeding of the ewes—but that can wait. Look, my dear. I want to let them know that we're leaving. Do you think Leah will tell Laban before I want her to?"

"Not if you do it right. Look, darling. Leave it to me. I'll work on Leah and the others. When do you want to leave?"

"Ask me rather when I can afford to. That'll be some months from now. Of course, I'm impatient. I wish we could leave—yesterday. The idea of staying away from the soil of Canaan another year fills me with . . ."

"I understand." She squeezed his hand again. Her eyes were full of love—and full of self-respect for the first time in many months. The realization sent a lump up into Jacob's throat that he couldn't get rid of no matter how hard he tried. He smiled, his eyes misty with tears. "Look, don't rush telling them. I'll work on them little by little," she said. "They're good boys, really. And Leah and the servants—they'll pretty much do as I want them to when I put my mind to the running of their affairs."

Now it was his turn to squeeze her hand. She was wife and more than wife, he thought. Partner. Equal. Life-mate. He felt a little thrill surge through him. He felt he'd never in his life loved her more, not even the first day he'd seen her and fallen in love completely and forever.

Hadad sat up, holding his ribs. He groaned when the stabbing pain shot through him. With his one good eye he looked up at the open window. It was midday, he supposed. The shadows fell just so at midday. He had to get up.

But the effort tired him half to death. He gasped for breath. And sighed, his heart full of a great sadness. Maybe he wouldn't be able to do it today after all. Maybe he was still too weak. . . .

He sat back against the propped-up pillow on his bed, looking around his bare little room. Tomorrow, he thought.

He'd surely be well enough to do it by tomorrow. But no later than that. He couldn't put it off any longer, this business of confronting Anat. It had to happen. He simply had to get the guts to do it. And he would. Tomorrow. Tomorrow, without fail. . . .

II

In the morning, Danataya was up even earlier than usual. She hadn't slept a wink for worrying, and her eyes were red-rimmed from crying. She threw herself into the work, cleaning up tall stacks of bowls and scrubbing the tabletops clean, and had the inn nearly spotless by the time Admuniri came in. The innkeeper's wife looked around her and lifted a brow in pleased amazement. "Good work, Danataya. But why . . . ?"

Then she saw the look on the girl's face: drawn, desolate. "Oh, yes. You didn't find anything, did you?"

"No, ma'am. Nobody will take me on without money in advance. If only I could—"

"Danataya, I'd love to be able to help you. Really I would. I talked to Abi-samar about it last night. I sat down with him and figured what we actually had in hand. It's barely enough to purchase provisions for sale here at the inn. Now, if this were a week from now—but it isn't. You see, we *could* borrow the money for you. But if we did, then it would become taxable, too, and—I'm sure you understand, dear."

"Oh, yes, ma'am," Danataya said bitterly. The worst part about it was that she really did understand. She understood everyone's reasons for not being able to help her. And she couldn't blame anybody. This left the enormous void of rage and bitterness and fear inside her unfilled; this left nobody to blame but herself. She could feel the self-loathing already stirring within her. . . .

The situation continued through the morning. All this time, Abi-samar did not show his face at the tavern. All this time, Danataya worked as though she were preparing a place for one of the gods, attacking each smudge on the walls with a fanatical frenzy, as if trying to rub out the stains left on the fabric of her young soul by her self-loathing and shame.

At noon, Abi-samar came in, all bustle, all business. He got together with Admuniri for a moment, talking of taxes, talking of assessments, talking of matters that concerned only husband and wife. Then he came over to Danataya. "Look," he said. "I had a talk with Horon. And he said—"

"Yes?" Danataya said. She put her broom down and wiped the sweat out of her eyes. "He said . . . ?"

"He said he'll give you another day's grace. One more—out of friendship for me and Admuniri. But no more." He sighed, embarrassed. "I tried to get more of a concession out of him than that, but . . ."

"Then—dusk tomorrow?" she said. "Well, that's better than it was. Although I don't think I'll be able to find anything by then."

"I gave some thought to that, coming back from talking to him. Look, why don't you take the afternoon off to look? You've done a fine job here today. You've done enough work for one day. No, take the evening off too. You look as though you hadn't slept for days. Go down to the well and make yourself pretty. Wash your hair. Change your robe. Make yourself look your best. And see what you can promote. Eh? Doesn't that sound like a good idea?" He clapped her on the shoulder with a friendly hand. "Here now: get along with you. The day's wasting. . . ."

At the well, though, she ran into Yamam, who embraced her as though they hadn't seen each other in a month. "Darling!" Yamam said. "How delightful to find you—I've found a solution to your problem."

"You have?" Danataya said. "You mean your boyfriend isn't moving in, and—"

"No, no. He'll be here for two weeks. Then I'll have to kick him out, to my great displeasure. My old man will come back then, bless his gray old hairs. But Danataya, I have a way for you to make money. Not just the money for this month's rent. Enough money for the quarter. And for some pretty clothes too."

"But—how?"

"Look," Yaman said, turning her around. "See that man over there? The one with the bald spot? He's a merchant from Aleppo. He used to look me up when he was in town. He's a nice man, not mean or nasty. He's a free spender, too. He came to see me this morning—and although I said no, why, look—he's taking me shopping." She indicated her string bag. "You should see the robe he's buying me! Gods,

238

it's the loveliest thing I've ever—" Her eyes caught Danataya's now. "But darling," she said. "What's the matter?"

"You mean . . . I'd have to . . . with him? That man there?"

"Why, darling. Of course. And look: I wouldn't steer a mean one to you. Somebody who'd leave you with bites and bruises all over. This one's a real sweetheart, I promise you. He's kind and gentle." Her voice turned conspiratorial. "He's also—well, not very vigorous. If you don't like—well, the way he is in bed, my dear—grin and bear it. He won't trouble you more than once tonight, and then not for long." Her smile was tolerant and calculating at the same time.

"But, Yamam—I couldn't. . . ."

"Darling. That's what I said myself when I was at your stage of life. But I did, and look at me. Am I the worse for it? Am I the worse for making my own disposition of my body and of the things it means to a man? I mean, rather than letting my father make it for me? Look, if I'd followed the traditional path, I'd be living in a grubby hovel by now, up to the hips in squalling brats. Instead, I'm having the time of my life. Soon I'll be rich. And soon my old man will pass on—he's already too old to marry, you know; he can't last long—and I'll have his house and his fortune and a lot of years left to have fun in."

"I understand," Danataya said. But she didn't, really. She was hurt and frightened and confused. She looked at the man. He seemed to have a nice face. It was the face of a man grown old perhaps before his time. Some people's faces did that—aged too soon. This man's face was lined with care. And what was he? Forty, perhaps?

"What's his name?" she said tentatively. Her heart was beating fast with fear and worry. "I mean, would I have to . . ."

"Ah, now you're talking sense. Just leave it to me. You've the afternoon free? That will be fine. You can use my room. I'll drive a bargain that will make you fat and rich. Well, relatively. At least you won't have to worry about the rent for another quarter. And you and I can come down to the market on the weekend and shop for a pretty new robe for you."

The caravan had made good time—exceptionally good time. The great gathering began before the walls of Haran in the early afternoon. Tents rose; pens were constructed for the animals; the smell of cooking meat rose over the little community outside the walls of the city.

And the two assassins, Ami-malik and Yadinim, paying off

the caravan's master, left to stroll easily into town through the great gates. They passed through the bazaars, walked the quiet streets of the city, relearning the town they hadn't visited in some years.

They paused for a bowl of wine at an outdoor terrace in one of the better quarters. The tavernkeeper gave them a suspicious look, taking note of their clothes and dusty boots; but when he saw the color of their money, he took their orders grudgingly and went away.

Ami-malik beckoned an urchin of the streets over to him. "You, boy," he said. "How well do you know this quarter?"

"None better," the boy said. "For a copper I can find anyone and anything you want."

"And how much would it cost me to buy your silence about what I asked you to find for me?" Ami-malik said, with a solemn wink at Yadinim. "Eh, boy?"

"Hmmm," the boy said, looking the two of them over, mentally figuring what the traffic would bear. "I'd say five coppers, sir."

"Make it four," Ami-malik said. "We're, uh, emissaries of the Army of Haran. We're checking up on a captain named Reshef. We understand he frequents this quarter."

"Yes, sir. What's he done? Are you going to arrest him?"

"That's neither here nor there. But you understand—this involves grave matters of security. Nobody must hear of our mission—nobody. Least of all Reshef. It may make the difference between life and death here in Haran." He leaned forward and continued in a conspiratorial whisper. "Reshef is suspected of being a spy."

"A spy?" the boy's own voice slipped to a whisper. His eyes went wide.

"Yes, boy. For the government of Mari. And we've been given the commission to follow him around and learn what we can of his goings and comings. You know, everything about him." He caught the boy looking over their clothing again; they were manifestly not of the proper class for all this. "That's why the lower-class disguise, boy. If we dressed too well, he'd notice us. See us coming. That sort of thing. You understand? We have to stay as inconspicuous as possible."

"Yes, sir. I understand, sir. But—how can I help?"

"Well, we want to know all about him. Where he spends the day, the night—when he's not in camp. Where he stays. Who he sees. We may actually be able to trap other spies in the process."

"Yes, sir!" the boy said, still in the same whisper. "Well,

sir—you know the armsmaker Shobai? A big tall man with broad shoulders? Like this?" He held out his hands, far apart.

"Yes. Everyone knows Shobai. What about him?"

"Well, he's out of town, you see, and everybody is talking about—"

"Yes, I've heard. His wife. She's one of them."

"She *is*?"

"Yes . . . but you mustn't tell a soul. You understand. Nobody. Nobody at all. Not your mother, your—"

"My mother's dead. Nobody knows who my father was. I live with my uncle. He's drunk all the time. He wouldn't even know to ask."

"All the better. I knew I had come to the right boy. Now—this Shobai's house. Where is it?"

Danataya, naked, drew away from him. She reached for her robe, held it to her front. "No, please—I can't. I can't go through with it."

"But, my dear, I wasn't going to do anything you didn't want me to." He was a quiet, sad man. She rather liked him. That only made it worse. He put one gentle hand on her arm. She shivered and drew away.

"But, you see, I just can't. It's not that I don't like you. But—oh, I'm sorry. I've let you get—all aroused. I've led you along. I've been such a fool. It's cruel of me, but—"

"But no. Not at all." His arousal had come to grief by now, and he was all patience and understanding, even fatherly. "Look, I can understand. This is your first time, isn't it? I wish Yamam had told me. I'd have gone more slowly. I know a girl can't be rushed. . . ."

"But I can't do it. I can't do it at all. I—I like you. You're a nice man. But this—not like this. I have to feel something."

"I understand. There, now."

"Please. Please don't . . . I want to put on my robe. I want to—"

"Whatever you wish, my dear." His voice now carried an undertone of quiet resignation. It made her feel even worse, if anything. "Here, I'll help you dress." But as she stood and held out her arms for the robe, he looked her up and down again, in an almost involuntary motion, and she covered breasts and lap, blushing. Feeling shamed. Feeling simply horrible. She reached for the robe and put it on, her back to him now. She could feel—feel!—his gaze on her, lingering on

241

her slim back and firm buttocks. Her flesh crawled. And the terrible surge of guilt ran through her again. Guilt, self-loathing, despair. She had ruined everything again. The afternoon had passed, and she still didn't have the money. And Yamam: would Yamam ever speak to her again? She had to go to her right now. Go to her and apologize. Otherwise, she'd lost the only friend she had, just because of her own stupidity.

"One other thing," Jacob said mildly, but with a new note of authority in his voice. "I don't want any of you hanging around Laban's house anymore. We have to be there quite often enough as it is, on matters connected with work, with our livelihood. There'll be no more hanging around there after we're done working for the day. Laban knows entirely too much of our affairs as it is."

"Why, I never heard of such a thing," Leah said with indignation. "My own father and mother? I'll visit them any time I want. And the boys—"

"No, you won't, my dear. Not anymore. You may try defying me once. You won't try it twice." His smile was gentle, but it had a stern finality about it.

"You can't talk that way to mother!" Reuben said. He stepped forward, his fists bunched. "I'll tell grandfather! I'll—"

"No, you won't," Jacob said. "You won't speak to your grandfather again unless you're spoken to. And then, when he asks you a question, you will consider every word I've said today before you utter so much as a word in return, my son. And," he said with a gentleness that masked a granitelike immovability, "you'll lower your tone when speaking to me. Or Leah. Or Rachel. You'll be kinder and more understanding with Bilhah and Zilpah, too. We're all one family, by the laws of my people, and the father stands at the head as the patriarch of the house and the priest of its God. And a loving father and patriarch does not let dissent in his family turn to bitterness. Gad and Naphtali are sons of mine too, and your half brothers. You will treat them as such, and not as hangers-on, as second-class members of this household. You will not pull rank on your brothers. There is no rank here. There is only the will of the One True God of our fathers, yours and mine. And a family sundered, bickering and backbiting, is an offense in His sight." He looked out over the gathered throng that was his own family: wives, concubines, offspring. There was a strange disoriented look on most of the faces—all, really, except Rachel's, which glowed with pride.

"We have been a sundered family," Jacob said in a quiet voice that carried the whole length and breadth of the large room. "This has been my doing. I tried to avoid the commands of the God, and He has punished me by not speaking to me in all the years I have been in Haran. I have decided to make whole all that was broken. Perhaps the God will speak to me again. But whether He does or not, we *will* become a family again. One that solves its own problems under its own roof. We *will* work together. We *will* love one another, and respect one another. This is not my own will speaking, but the God's. We will all respect it, you and I." He smiled, and his steady gaze was a man's now, not that of a servant of Laban's. "Am I heard? Am I understood?" He placed his palms together before him in an attitude of something like prayer. "Then hear me. I obey the will of the God, from this moment. And I will be obeyed."

III

Yamam knocked once more on the door. "Danataya?" she said. "Danataya, are you there?"

Danataya sat on the bed, staring disconsolately at the wall. More than anything in the world she wanted not to answer; more than anything she wanted Yamam to give up and go away. But now, in a choked voice, she found herself answering. "I'm here, Yamam," she said.

"Danataya, don't you want to talk to me? Open up, please. I know how you feel."

"No you don't. Don't say you know when—when you don't," she finished lamely with a half sob.

"Darling, let me in! Please! Look, I understand. Really I do. You have to let me help you. Please. Please, Danataya."

Danataya stood up and walked barefoot to the door. Her sandals still lay where she'd kicked them off when the man had been there. Easy enough to take off your shoes, she thought. It's the rest of the taking off that isn't so easy—including the taking off of your inhibitions, and all the habits you've been raised with. She pulled the bolt and let her friend in.

Yamam was expensively dressed, exquisitely made up. "Oh, Danataya," she said, pressing the girl to her in a tentative sort of hug, sincere but don't-muss-the-hair. "Darling. I'm so sorry. My friend told me—I mean, you have no idea how sorry he is, too. He's mortified, poor darling. He didn't mean any harm, you know."

"I know," the girl said. "I know." Her voice was full of self-loathing. "I let him down, didn't I? He was expecting me to be—something I'm not. Something I don't know how to be. I seem to be letting everyone down."

"No, no. Please. Sit down here, darling. Look, I left a bottle of wine under my bed here. There it is. Yes, it's still half full. Look. You have yourself a good drink of this now. No, I insist. I absolutely insist. There—there, now. Let it go down slowly, warm your innards. It'll cheer you up."

"It just makes me feel more depressed."

"You haven't let it work yet. Here, have another. No, I insist. Now, darling..." She sat down beside the girl, her voice low and reassuring. "Look, I rushed you along too fast. I did. It's all my fault. I've apologized to our friend. I'm the one to blame, not you."

"You don't have to apologize. It's me—"

"No, no. It's all right. Forget it. Time enough for that, perhaps, later when you're not under pressure. Right now we have to think of a way to find the money for Horon." She bit her lip, thought. Then a large sunny smile appeared on her face. "Oh, Danataya," she said, grasping the girl's hands in hers. "Maybe this is our chance. Look, my new boyfriend's coming by this evening. He's been wanting me to see if I could get off early. He doesn't want to wait until after the show."

"So? How can that—" But then it dawned on Danataya. "Oh, no, Yamam. Not—not that. I couldn't. I really couldn't. No—"

"Sure you could, sweetheart. Any girl can, if she has the figure for it. And you'd do it better than any of them. Haven't I coached you in the art myself?"

"But I couldn't."

"Would you rather be thrown out into the middle of the street? Is that better? Is that something you could live with more easily?"

"No, no, but—"

Yamam rose and went to the chest at the foot of her bed.

"Here's an outfit that ought to fit you. I wore it the first time I worked at the inn. I wasn't much bigger around than you are now. Here, take off your clothes."

"No, Yamam—"

"I said take them off." Yamam helped her; with one flip over the girl's head she had her single garment in her hand. "Oh, you look sweet enough to eat. Even a little sexy, my dear. If I weren't the type who liked men more than women . . ."

"Oh, Yamam, please—"

"Now. Get into this. Wrap it around here, so—"

"If only you'd let me—"

"Now." She stood back, looked Danataya up and down. "Next the second one. Over the breasts, just so."

"Yamam, *please!* I can't. I just can't."

"Well, of course you can't, with that hangdog expression. Goodness, I'd fire you in an instant if I were Abi-samar. All down in the dumps—"

"No. No more. Look, I'm taking this off."

"No, you're not. Not yet anyhow. Here, have another drink. It'll loosen you up, help you relax. Try relaxing into it and it'll go just fine. There. Isn't that better? It's very good wine, you know. It was a gift from that sweet, rich old man of mine. Now where were we? Yes, just stand still. I'll wrap it so—and when you want it to come off, you just twirl and—see? See? Neatest trick in the world. But let's put it back in place now, and I'll fasten the other."

"But Yamam. You need the money yourself."

"Sure, but I'd give it to you if I had it, darling. But tonight's the first night after the caravan arrives. You know what that means? Why, the floor will be full of tips, so much you'll trip over them. If you can't clean up enough for the next two months on the first two shows, it'll be because the caravan from Carchemish sent us nothing but boy-lovers this time. And that isn't very likely, let me tell you. Men from Carchemish have much more conventional tastes, and thank goodness for it, I say. Here, don't wiggle so. Now! That looks just fine. Just like an old professional. But let's see what we can do with that hair."

"Yamam. What'll I do? I could—well, maybe if you were there in the wings, for moral support . . ."

"But darling. If I show up at all, Abi-samar will have me out in the middle of the floor in my pelt in nothing flat. And that'll spoil everything, won't it? Look, darling. A girl's always alone out there. It's a matter of getting your feet wet.

Hmmm, feet. You can't wear *those* sandals. Barefoot is all right. But look, take a couple of my anklets, with the little bells. And maybe this pretty little gold stomacher a trader from Ugarit gave me once. It'll hang low on those slim hips of yours and draw attention to your little what's-its-name," she giggled. "And touch up the nipples with a little henna before you go on. Yes . . ."

"Yamam, I can't. . . ."

Yamam sighed resignedly and looked the girl in the eye. "But darling. You *have* to. I mean, I've run out of everything else. So has everyone else. It's that or—"

Danataya looked at her, despair showing over all her face. Her shoulders slumped. Then she squared them. She threw her slim shoulders back. "I—I'll try to do my best," she said.

"Sure you will, sweetheart." Yamam gave her another careful hug. "Just remember what I said. Pick out one pair of eyes. Dance for those eyes alone."

"I'll try," Danataya said bravely.

Hadad watched the soldier swagger down the street away from him, a strutting cock of the walk. His face twisted; he shook his head back and forth as if to clear it. So brazen! So open about it! No attempt at all to hide anything!

Yes, and he'd walked past Hadad, dismissing him with a single glance as one unworthy of notice, a battered and bedraggled nobody. And this right in front of Shobai's house, with the neighbors coming and going, as shameless as you please.

His hands shook as he approached the big door of the house. He stood on the step, took a deep breath. His heart was in his boots. He felt simply livid with shame.

He knocked, timidly at first, then with more authority.

The door flung open. "Look, if you think I'm going to—" a shrill voice said. But then Anat stopped and stared at him.

He looked back at her. She wore only a torn shift. Her hair was in disarray. There were scratches on the parts of her skin that showed through the tears in her garment. "Anat," he said. "What's wrong? Can I help? Please—"

Her eyes took him in—and chewed him up and spat him out on the tiles. "What are you—you!—doing here? Get out!" She tried to push the door shut. But Hadad, reacting instinctively, was too quick for her. He stood in the way, and then, looking at her half-naked, disheveled state, moved inside and closed the door behind him.

"You—*get out!*" she said. She came at him with her nails out, cuffing, clawing. Hadad gave ground, trying to protect himself without hurting her. "You sniveling little pipsqueak—can't you mind your own swinish little business just for once in your life? Can't you . . . ?" She made a fist and hit him in his half-blind eye. He cried out and covered the eye with both hands. "Can't even fight, can't mind your own rotten little beggar's business, can't stay out of my life. . . ."

Hadad put a bench between them at last and dodged back and forth awkwardly, favoring his bad leg, keeping the bench between himself and her darting, half-naked body. Her claws swung, caught him in the face. He felt fresh blood. He dodged back, looking at her with horror. "Anat! This isn't like you—please—please, if you'd only calm down—"

"Calm down, is it?" Her voice was a catamount's screech, full of hatred and loathing. The once-pretty face was that of a demon, fangs bared. "Calm down, he says! The nasty, snooping little cripple! *Cripple!* Who can't find a woman of his own, and comes sniffing around *my* behind as if it belonged to him! Snooping! You slimy, lousy little weakling! You get out of my house! You hear?"

"But Anat, you don't mean these things—if only you'd let me—"

"You and that self-centered brother of yours! Him with his simpering at the mirror like a woman—and you with your ugly, stomach-turning frog's face, and your crippled leg that sticks out like a cricket's!"

"Please, Anat! Please don't! You'll only be sorry! I—I won't tell Shobai—I just came to see if there was any way I could help. . . ."

"You? Help!" Her laughter was the demon's again; a shrill, vile cackle. "How could *you* help anybody do *anything*? You, that can't do it for himself? That can't make a living? That can't even walk properly? You—"

"Anat, please—please don't say these things—you hurt me so. I don't want to do you any harm. Why should you want to say these cutting, terrible things to me? Anat, I love you—you've been like my sister—"

"Sister, is it? Is it sister that you look up and down as though I were some whore off the streets, every time you come to your brother's house? Look—but don't touch, eh?" She thrust out her chest under the torn cloth, tantalizingly, insultingly. "Well, look—*brother!*" She reached up and tore off the garment and stood naked before him, her hands on her hips, her legs spread slightly, flaunting her body at him.

"Here, Hadad," she said in a hateful voice, her words stinging like acid. "Here's what you *look* at so hungrily every time you come over here to visit that stuck-up brother of yours. Why don't you come *get* some of it? Come, Hadad! I won't hurt you. . . ." But her voice was the same harpy's voice, full of hatred and disdain, and he covered his face with his hands, sobbing.

She picked up a little image of Baal he'd given her for her birthday and heaved it disgustedly at his head. It smashed to a million pieces on the wall behind him. "Just as I thought!" she said in a low rising roar of a voice. "Just as I . . . *thought!*" She let out a humorless croak of a laugh. "As always, he'll look but not touch! Well, now we know what he is! He doesn't like women at all!" she said in a mincing guttersnipe's voice, making an obscene *moue* with her red lips. "Fit for hanging around the schoolyard looking for little boys to fondle, little boys who are too small to defend themselves against the likes of him when he comes by to offer them sweets and ripe figs if they'll let him play with their little . . ."

Hadad covered his ears now. His eyes looked at her and did not see her. His face was a mask of horror, of shock and shame and self-loathing. His eyes brimmed with still unshed tears. "A-Anat," he said in a broken voice.

"Get out," she said in a quiet, controlled little voice, subtle as the serpent. "Get out, you disgusting little—*crippled bastard!* I never want to see your *hog's snout* of a *face* again! *Get out!*"

The two of them picked him up as he sauntered down the street. "That's him," Yadinim said. "Reshef. He doesn't *look* like much, does he?"

Ami-malik gave the soldier a sidelong glance, not turning his head. "Hmm. Not too big or strong. But wiry. Trained down fine. I suppose he'd be quick enough. Looks like he can handle himself."

"He won't look so good in the dark. He won't see so good either."

"Hmmm. Moon's on the wane. Fog bank coming in. Could be quite dark in the back streets."

"There he goes—"

"Right. Now fall in behind him, at a distance. Don't let him out of your sight. I'll follow behind you—but a ways back. We'll just keep after him until the sun goes down. He's sure to wind up going someplace where he'll be—vulnerable."

"Yes. Yes. Easiest thing in the world. I can't wait to get my hands on him."

"Don't be a fool. Never use your hands. Never."

"Right, chief."

IV

Reshef paused by the bridge over the canal. He'd had more than a little to drink by now, and his face was flushed and hot in the warm evening. He stood looking down in the waning light of the moon overhead, and let the soft breeze over the running water cool him.

As his head began to clear, the feeling came back to him, the feeling he'd had all evening. He shook his head as if to clear it, but as he did, he stole a glance to the left, to the right, sweeping the bridge and the areas not in shadow.

He was being watched. He was sure of it.

It had been going on all evening. At one tavern, then another. The strange feeling in the back of his head had alerted him again and again. The only time during the evening when he hadn't had the feeling was in the little twosome he'd shared with the plump little dancer at the Inn of the Lilies, over in the upper-crust quarter. There, in a garden with high walls on all sides (and with the innkeeper bribed to keep everyone else away) he'd had pleasant enough dalliance for a bit, with no prying eyes to bother him.

But before then, and since then, the feeling of being observed had been almost continuous. Ever since—since when? He frowned and thought a bit about the matter. Since when? Perhaps since he'd left Anat's ...

He shook his head again now, from side to side, giving the shadows on the opposite ends of the little bridge the once-over again. And his hand, reaching down to straighten his garment at its thigh-high hem, brushed his scabbard and loosened the sharp sword inside it. Best to be ready for anything.

Anat. His face drew up into a scowl, which softened to a frown. Gods! Women were such perverse creatures! Imagine anyone being treated the way he treated her—and liking it!

The disgust within him rose in his throat; he spat out into the stream. It seemed—why, it seemed that the worse he treated her, the more she liked it. No matter that she grew ever more sullen, more angry; by now she'd learned to keep the anger just below the surface, unexpressed. That kept her from getting her brains scrambled every five blinks of the eye. But knowing that, knowing how he'd react, what a fool she was to provoke him again and again, to beg for his cuffs and curses and for the increasingly more degrading ways in which he chose to take her.

Ah, that was the trouble. She *liked* it. And no matter how gross the pleasures he chose to share with her, some of the salt was missing from the stew if the woman actually liked it, if she actively solicited the entertainment. What made the sexual meal a savory one was the woman's hating and fearing it, begging him to stop, whimpering, pleading. . . .

He smiled his wolfish smile, looking down at the half-moon's reflection in the water, remembering . . . after all, there'd been the little flower-seller over in the Thieves' Quarter, not a month hence . . . *she'd* begged for it too, even with his hands around her throat. And only when she'd finally realized that he meant business, and really *was* going to cut off her breath, had she begun to struggle, to fight him. By that time he'd been inside her, and the feeble fight she'd put up as he increased the pressure had increased his own pleasure, and the passion had built within him, and he'd tightened his grip around her neck and watched, heard, felt her die, felt her slip away from this life at the precise moment when his own passion had burst its bounds and he'd poured his seed into the body of a woman now dead.

He smiled his feral smile again as the thought came back to him, and the fantasy stirred his loins. Ah, there were few pleasures in this world to compare with the feeling of total control as you satisfied yourself just as you were killing. . . .

Yes. Yes, he thought. Anat. It might be something really special. But how? People had seen him coming and going. He'd have to break it off, very publicly, even to the point of embarrassing her in front of friends, just to make sure he had witnesses to his defection. And then in the night, when everyone knew, just knew, that he had finished with her forever, he'd come back, unseen, and let himself in, and . . .

But then, damn it, there was the female servant, the homely one. What was the name? Tanuha? Well, he'd have to do something about her first. No witnesses. None. Perhaps she could be decoyed out into the streets some night, and while she was out there, something could happen to her. . . .

But no. It was all entirely too close to home. Better to choose actors—actresses—for your little scenario at random: people who couldn't be connected with you if there was an investigation.

In his reverie, he let his eyes go again to the wavering, rippling moon-reflection in the water below. For nearly the first time that evening, the sixth sense deserted him. He let caution, sensible caution, slip away . . .

. . . and then they were on him, in a mad rush from both sides of the bridge. The moon glinted on a raised knife; Reshef felt a sharp blade slice through his cheek. His own weapon was out now, parrying a second lunge. But then the other man hit him, and a new blade hacked away at his nape. The blow was dull; it staggered but did not stun him. He swung backhanded, felt the blade connect, heard his attacker groan and felt, rather than saw, him withdraw, the sixth sense back and functioning again.

He turned to the first attacker and went to work on him with the blade, cutting, lunging, parrying, stabbing. The attacker was a large, bearlike man, slow and dull-witted. Reshef beat his blade down and slashed wildly at the man's sword hand. His slash cut through flesh and tendons; the swordsman howled and dropped his blade, his hand ruined. Reshef made a roundhouse swing at him with the sword, slashing the man's face in two. Then he pulled his weapon back, thrust forward, and felt the point go home: deep, deep. . . . The big attacker fell just as Reshef withdrew his blade. He lay and did not move. Reshef, a wild grin on his cut and bleeding face, turned to the other just as the second man came out of the shadows and rushed him, blade held forward like the prow of a ship.

A cold rage running through him, Reshef beat the weapon aside; beat it back; beat the man with the flat of his blade; battered his forearms until, bruised and tired, they relaxed and the assassin's blade fell to the stones. Still he drove his attacker back, punishing him with one brutal blow after the other, as the man howled with pain and fear. Back, back the assassin went, Reshef following, until they both moved into a pool of clear light from the half-moon above. Then, with a master swordsman's skill, Reshef hacked at the man's arms—once, twice. The assassin's arms dangled, useless. Not satisfied with this, Reshef, his hot blood up, crisscrossed an X with his bloody sword on the man's chest, marking with skin-deep cuts the very place he'd thrust to kill. And he went back to work on the useless arms, again: hack, slash . . .

The man screamed and cringed before him. His face was a mask of horror. He held up his arms: bloody stumps, spouting blood. . . . "Please," the man cried. "K-kill me—"

"In a moment," Reshef said through clenched teeth. "It may be more fun to gut you first. Or castrate you—"

"Please. Quick. Kill quick—"

Reshef put his point to the man's groin. "One quick flip with this blade," he said, "and you're a capon. It might be more fun to let you live that way, begging for death."

"For the gods' mercy, please—"

"Ah. Why should I listen?" Reshef laid the flat of his blade against the handless man's genitals. "Why shouldn't I just please myself?" He deftly spun the point up, around, laid it against the side of the assassin's head. Then, with a quick turn of the wrist, he took off the man's ear.

"Gods! Gods! Please—I'll tell everything. It was—it was Shobai who paid us—you'd been cuckolding him with his wife. . . ."

"Ah," Reshef said. He put the blade against the dying man's genitals again and gave his wrist a little feinting flip. "Shall I do the same to your—"

"No—no, please. Shobai told me to—he said 'Cut him up. I want to see him scarred.' "

"Scarred, eh?" For the first time, Reshef felt his face. There was a deep cut running across it. "Why, you bastard! You *have* scarred me!" The blade moved subtly. The handless man held his stumps to his groin, backing away. Reshef followed him, his point touching, feeling, questing.

"He—he said, 'Take out one of his eyes if you can.' He said—"

Reshef steered the bloody, stumbling man around the small pool of light, his blade still held low, feinting, teasing. . . . "Go on," he said. "This is interesting. What else do you know that might interest me? Shobai hired you in Carchemish, did he? What else is happening in Carchemish that it might please me to know . . . ?"

The assassin's legs were weakening. His feet slipped in the slimy blood underfoot. He fell to one knee and only with difficulty scrambled up; he could not use his useless arms. "Manouk," he croaked in a fading voice. "Manouk came to the city. He almost killed me."

"Manouk?" Reshef said, his demonic grin back in the slashed face. "What do you know of Manouk? Manouk of the Shepherd Kings? What was *he* doing in Carchemish? Answer quickly and I may finish you as quickly. *Answer!*"

"Spying—on the city—" the moaning, dying man said. He fell again, this time to both knees. He did not try to rise. He held up the spouting stumps of hands, his life's blood gushing away. His face was drawn now, his eyes glassy. "He—he may be in Haran as I speak. When he rode away, he was heading east. . . ."

"Manouk? Are you sure?" The sword went to the man's face. Casually, almost as if by accident, it blinded an eye. The assassin's face shrank back; he weaved as if he were going to fall. "Ah, but of course you're sure. Who would make up a story like that? And how would you know his name?" He reached up and felt his bleeding face again. "Why, you son of a whore; you've maimed me. I'll bear that scar forever. You scum!"

"P-please," Ami-malik said. But then the first death blow hit him, at the waist, just below the red X. Gutting him. And now he saw the sword raised high for a backhand slash, the one that would take off his head. And, glassy-eyed, he raised his neck to meet it. . . .

"Are you sure you can do it?" Admuniri said.

Danataya fiddled with her veils. "Please," she said. "All I can do is try. . . ." Her face was white as a sheet. "Please, Admuniri—"

The innkeeper's wife looked her up and down. "You're frightened half to death," she said. "But then they all are at first. Yamam was. Well, *damn* Yamam. *Damn* her, anyhow. How could she stand us up like this?" She sighed. "At least she did come up with some kind of replacement. That's better than nothing. Well, all right. I'll tell the musicians." She turned and went away without another word.

Danataya stood in the dark anteroom, shivering despite the many veils. She stepped up to the door's edge and looked around it at the half-lit faces. Where, in all that crowd, would she find a single sympathetic, kind, likable male face to play for as Yamam had suggested? They looked like a bunch of brutal boors. Caravan drivers. Mutton merchants. And—

But just then her heart skipped a beat. Into the doorway came Hadad, the singer. His face still bore the terrible bruises of a few nights before; they distorted his features so much that she could hardly read his expression. But his mouth seemed drawn with care, and his eye showed the same evidence of a troubled mind as before. *Oh, the poor darling.* . . .

And now a little shiver ran through her. Hadad! She'd play to Hadad!

The thought sent goose bumps all over her body; sent shivers through her arms; curled her toes. Hadad! The little singer with the crooked leg, whose singing had given her such a wonderful thrill. Hadad, of whom Jacob had spoken so highly. Hadad, who had, perhaps, never had a woman . . .

. . . Hadad, whose gentle sweetness moved her heart.

In an unconscious motion, she ran her hand over her young body; felt its soft curves, its smooth flesh, all of which she would unveil one step at a time for his soft brown eyes. *Yes*, she thought. *Forget the others.* The secret was to act as though they didn't exist. The secret was to dance for his eyes alone.

Her heart was pounding wildly. And now the music began. . . .

"You can't think of serving him."

"What can I do? Can I turn away the custom of someone in the neighborhood? What would happen when the rumor got around?"

"But Abi-samar—"

"My dear, I can't do it. If you want to control what he drinks, water his wine a bit. But—"

"But husband. He can't hold it. Even watered. Remember what happened last time. A drunken brawl—"

"I'll keep an eye on him. And look, Admuniri. If we don't serve him—we here in the neighborhood, who have his welfare at heart and who can water the drinks if we think he's in for too rough an evening—what do you think he's likely to do? In the mood he's in right now? Why, he'll head for the stews, for the inns of the Thieves' Quarter. And for the love of all that's holy, my dear, think of what *they'll* do to him. Why, they'll drug his drink. They'll dump him in the gutter, picked clean. Abandon the boy to that bunch of vultures? No, thank you—not when I can exercise a bit of control right here in my own inn. I'm going to look out for him. Don't worry. Here. Take him this." He poured wine, half a bowl. Then he poured water. "He won't know the difference. What does a boy like that know of wine?" He patted her ample bottom. "Now go. And tell Danataya to get out there."

"She is out there. She just went on. And, hmm, she's not doing badly so far. Pretty little thing . . ."

"All right. Get moving now. We've a full night ahead of us. And don't worry. About anything. Anything at all."

V

Marsatum opened the door cautiously; it was late for visitors, and her husband was away at a friend's house, negotiating for better terms from the growers. She blinked at the darkness; then she smiled, surprised. "Jacob," she said. "What brings you out so late at night?" She opened the door wide to let him in.

"I would have been home some time back," Jacob said. "But there was a murder—actually, a couple of them—down by the canal. I and one of my sons stumbled across the bodies. I took the boy home and went to call the guards."

"Goodness! So close to our market!"

"Yes. I talked to the guardsman. He said that by the looks of things, the two dead men may have been—may have assaulted someone and then been killed themselves. They were rough types, from what I could see of what was left of them. One of them died cleanly; the other fellow was cut to ribbons."

"Oh, gods! And my husband out in it—"

"I wouldn't worry too much about him. He's at the meeting, isn't he? Well, he'll come home with friends, most likely. And he's a big chap, strong and vigorous even at our age. But look, my dear: I didn't come here to scare you. I'm looking for Hadad. You know, the young—"

"I know Hadad. Why? Isn't he at home resting up from that beating they gave him the other night?"

"Apparently not. I checked. He went out this afternoon, and he hasn't come back. I tried to look in at his brother's, but there was nobody at home. Marsatum, I'm a little worried about the boy. Something's shaken him up terribly. What could it be?"

"I don't know, Jacob. Not for sure. I suspect it may have something to do with Shobai. You know, the boy worships that brother of his. Heaven alone knows why. For my money

255

he's a nasty piece of goods—conceited, self-centered, without a trace of heart in him. Maybe—"

"Maybe the boy's found him out? And can't handle the disillusionment?"

"That may be it. And—you're looking for him?"

"Yes. I've had an eye on him for some time, actually. He's a nice lad, and there's more to him than meets the eye. I'd like to do something for him. If I can."

"Jacob. You've no money—"

"No, I haven't. But sometimes money isn't the only solution to a problem. I do have experience—of life, I mean—and perhaps I can help ease him over the pains of growing up. I mean, I knew his father, and I know what the boys, both of them, must have missed, growing up without Kirta there to guide them."

"You know, Jacob, you've changed. Something's happened to you lately. You used to be the sort who wouldn't get involved."

"You're so right, my dear. I've given my life a new direction, and this time I'm not going to turn back. I've cheated my own sons quite as much as Kirta has cheated his. But no more. From now on I take responsibility for all of my own actions."

"And, no doubt, for a few other people's, too. Bless you, my dear. Anyone who tries to help Hadad is all right by us. I hope you can get through to him. I've tried myself—and failed."

"Well, all we can do is try. But—you haven't seen him? You haven't any idea where he is?"

"No. But if he hasn't turned up by tomorrow, I'll have my husband go looking for him. And I'll put the word out in the community." She led him to the door. "Let us know if you find him."

"I will," Jacob said, and she was once again startled by the serene and mature smile on his face. "And—bless you."

Where was he? Where was he? Danataya struggled to keep the professional smile Yamam had taught her on her face as she danced around the little pool of light, the bells on her ankles jingling. Her eyes scanned the crowd, the avid faces, the brutal grins—the little singer was nowhere to be found. *But he had been sitting right over there . . . he must be behind someone. . . .*

Now: the third veil . . . She threw her shoulders back and let her suddenly bared breasts pick up the light of the flickering torches. She was immediately aware of a change in the climate of the room. The shouts became more coarse, the look on the inner circle of faces more beastlike. Something inside her cringed in shame. But she kept up the steps as Yamam had taught her to do them, kept up the come-hither motions of her slim arms. And a fourth veil followed, and a fifth. . . .

Now the last one was to go, and if her arms had not been so busy going through the sinuous motions Yamam had taught her, she knew her hands would have been trembling. . . . She gulped and put her hands on the waistband . . . she spun once, twice, spun free of the cloth, tossed it to a servant just beyond the door . . .

She was naked—naked before the eyes of a roomful of men: coarse, foul-mouthed, drunken men who wanted her, wanted her not because she was a good person or a gentle and womanly lover—how could they know? How could they have any idea who she was—but who wanted her for a quick brutal tussle in the bushes. Hands reached out to her; she danced free of them, her slim belly undulating, her arms alternately covering her naked breasts and displaying them. Miraculously, her bare feet, the anklets jangling merrily in time with the music, kept up the intricate steps of the dance; her body moved as though it had an independent life of its own; her skin was at once chilled and sweaty; there was almost an erotic feeling about it actually, naked and unprotected in the little room with every eye focused with rapt attention on her, on her. . . .

Then she caught his eye—the singer's, the crippled boy's. She saw the horror, the pity, the sympathy in his open young face as he looked her up and down. She saw him looking through her naked body, right into her naked soul. What he saw there did not make him lust after her at all; it made him pity her and feel for her. A great shudder went through her body, she lost the beat of the music, and her dance faltered. Coins rained at her feet; she slipped and slid on them; she almost fell. The music itself faltered; the drummer missed a beat; the lyrist hit a wrong chord.

She stopped, looked around her, and covered herself with her hands. Sobbing, she dashed off into the dark room next to the kitchen, as the angry shouts followed her and the men out front began pounding on the tables. The band, rattled, struck up a merry tune in desperation; but it was almost blotted out by the noise in the common room, a noise that quickly began to sound like the first stages of a riot.

Hadad reached for his wine bowl and drank, his hand shaking. But the wine didn't dull his own self-knowledge. He knew what had happened. Somehow the girl had looked at him, at him, Hadad—and what she had seen on his face had disconcerted her so badly that she couldn't go on. It was all his fault. And now the customers here at the inn, raw, ill-mannered foreigners just arrived in town with the Carchemish caravan, were threatening to smash up the inn if the girl didn't come back. It was all his fault.

He put down the wine bowl, and now his hand did not shake. He had to find her, and apologize. And apologize to the innkeeper and his wife, too. They were nice people, and didn't deserve any trouble like this, trouble brought upon them by his own stupid, insensitive . . .

He remembered how he had come in; despondent, badly shaken by the experience with Anat. Well, perhaps Anat was right. Perhaps he *was* an inadequate, childish little fool who'd been trying to live a secondhand life through his brother and his sister-in-law all this time. Perhaps he *had* unconsciously lusted after Anat, in default of getting out and trying to find someone of his own. Well, time enough for penance for that. He'd have to sit down and think out all the cruel—but perhaps true?—things she'd said to him, and figure out how to deal with the image of himself that she'd put into his mind. Certainly it was an ugly image. Well, perhaps he *was* ugly—little, skinny, "frog-faced" as she'd said, with his round face and wide mouth, and with (yes! yes!) that ugly, hideous crooked leg that stuck out at such an angle and made him walk like a duck or something. . . .

He struck the table with his own small fist. Whatever he was, it wasn't any excuse for him to come into the lives of innocent people and ruin them this way. Here he'd come into the tavern intending to get drunk, to drown his sorrows and cover his self-loathing—and what had he done? He'd probably lost this poor girl her job. She, who'd been nice to him the night he'd been beaten up. He remembered her, gentle and caring as she'd helped sponge his cuts and wounds. He remembered the soft touch of her hands, her low and pretty voice.

And what had he done to pay her back for her kindness? Why, he'd probably got her fired!

He shook his head free of the last traces of the wine-induced fuzziness he'd spent so much money to attain and stood up, taking care this time to make sure his leg didn't protrude into anyone's path and precipitate another brawl. There was enough rowdiness here already.

He pushed his way gently past the crowd to the room off the kitchen. Admuniri blocked his way. "You can't come in—" she began. Then she recognized him. "Hadad!" she said. "Good, I'm glad you're out of there. Abi-samar is having a hard time cooling them off in there as it is. Here, dear, you go out the side door, I don't want you to get hurt."

"Admuniri," he said, shaking off the hand that sought to guide him. "The girl—what's her name? Danataya? I have to—"

"Ah," she said. "Some girls just can't go through with it. She came out, scrambled into her robe, and took off out into the night. I hope she doesn't run away. Even if she can't dance for the men, she was a good worker. And—it's probably not her fault. It was a rough crowd for a girl's first time."

"First time?" Hadad said. "Oh, dear gods. No wonder. No wonder. It's all *my* fault. She looked me in the eye—I'd had a bad shake-up today, and I was feeling bad. I didn't respond the way she expected me to. I looked at her and thought, 'Poor girl! Why should she have to show herself that way!' It must have showed on my face. That, and the terrible way I was feeling. . . . Oh, her *first* time? No wonder . . ."

She looked at him. He was almost in tears. But on the other hand, there was a bit of firmness, a bit of resolve, about him that hadn't been there when he'd first come into the inn. Maybe something had happened to shake him up. "Hadad," she said. "Go after her. She needs somebody right now. I can't go looking for her, I have to help Abi-samar quiet these people down out front. She needs you. Do you hear? Go to her. Go help her. And tell her—tell her she can have her old job back any time she wants it. Tell her we love her, and—well, you know what to tell her."

"I—I'll think of something," Hadad said. His jaw had a firm line to it for the first time that evening. She smiled nervously at him. He pressed her hand and headed for the door.

But just then Abi-samar stuck his head in. "Admuniri," he said. "Quick. Come help me. I've got to give someone the bounce. He's just brought in a rumor that will sweep through this crowd like wildfire, if I can't shut him up and get rid of him. Quick: he's ordered wine. Give him a drugged bowl. I'll try to keep him quiet in the meantime, and then we can drag him out before he spreads it any further."

"Rumor? Any further? What do you mean?" She looked back and forth from her husband to Hadad, standing in the doorway listening. "What kind of rumor?"

"For heaven's sake, woman, get the wine. The man says there's been a double murder down by the canal. Two men cut to pieces. And, not far away, there's been a rape and murder. Some poor girl was found, raped and dead, not more than a moment or two ago, not fifty paces from our door."

"Raped? Dead?" Admuniri said, her hand to her mouth. "Oh, gods! Danataya—"

"No, no," Abi-samar said. "At least, I don't think so. The guards found her. She seems to have been a taller girl. But quick, my dear. The bowl—"

Hadad hesitated for a moment, his eyes registering his shock and horror. "But—" he said. "But that means—it means Danataya's out there. With a rapist, a killer—and he's still loose!"

"Oh, gods!" Admuniri said. "Go, Hadad! Go! After her! Quickly!"

Reshef stopped at the well and drew a bucket of water to wash his face. The cut on his cheek wouldn't stop bleeding, damn it. Well, the armorer had got his damned revenge for now, even if the assassins he'd paid to do the job hadn't managed to live through it. He, Reshef—he'd bear the damnable scar for the rest of his life. And a damned ugly one it would be—jagged, going from the corner of his eye to the corner of his chin.

Not that he cared a damn about being pretty. He hadn't started out pretty in the first place. It was the principle of the thing that mattered. He had something to remember Shobai for, to hate him for, some day to kill him for. He . . .

Reshef winced at the cold kiss of the water. No, this time killing hadn't done it for him. Not the easy kill of the big assassin or the much more satisfying butchery of the smaller one. Not even the slut who'd wandered along just at the wrong time and seen him as he'd been hacking the little one's head off. He'd backed her against a wall and got her to promise, and then to beg, and then to hoist her skirts for a quick one, and then he'd tried out the little idea he'd thought about earlier in connection with Anat, strangling her just as his climax came to a head . . . but it hadn't been enough to satisfy him. His rage still ran high. His blood still called for stronger pleasures, to get some of his soul back after he'd had it sullied by his wounding, his scarring. . . .

What? Another woman? Another death? Perhaps. But something different this time, something more leisurely, more protracted—something more like the death of the second assassin . . .

He grinned, and winced again at the pain the grin cost him. *Ah!* he thought. *Shobai! Shobai, I'll remember . . . a scar, perhaps? An eye? Maybe both eyes? Maybe your tongue, your manhood, your . . .*

Now, teeth set, he sponged off the last of the blood. It seemed to have stopped bleeding for now. Well, good. That much was all right. But his heart still pounded with rage, and three killings hadn't been enough. Nor had the one rape. His fists clenched; his body shook with a horrid excitement. One more kill, preferably a woman. And this time he wouldn't have his hand forced. This time it would be random, entirely random. The first woman he happened across. Pretty or ugly. And it'd be slow and unhurried, the way he liked it.

The moon shone once, dully, on his twisted grin, and then he was one with the shadows, slipping off into the darkness without a sound.

VI

Jacob, continuing his search, had stopped by his own house to reassure Rachel and his family, and, as a second thought in the matter, had taken a stout shepherd's staff down from the wall on the way out. Now, traversing the streets of the darkened city in the beginnings of a light fog, he held the staff at the ready, bisecting his body diagonally. His keen eyes scanned the dark streets as he moved slowly and purposefully through the quarter.

Now, coming around a corner, he came within an ace of running head-on into the guardsman Ishi-dagan, who had his sword out. Jacob easily parried the sword with his staff and said, "Easy, Ishi-dagan. It's me, Jacob."

"Ah! Jacob! What are you doing out on a night like this?"

"You forget," Jacob said. "I was the one who found the

bodies on the bridge. I'm looking for a friend. I don't want him out in this."

"Ah. I see. Well, it's no night for anyone to be out. You heard about the third body? Right near where the two men were lying?"

"No! Who was it?"

"A girl of another quarter. Raped and strangled. Most likely by the same man—or men."

"Man, my friend. I had a look at the two bodies. I think the same man did both of them in. They—the two he killed—trapped him between them on the footbridge; but he was too good a swordsman. He killed one to each side of him—and with a military blade."

"Military? Are you sure?"

"Of course I'm not sure. But who else has a sword sharp enough to slice a man up with—and strong enough to hack off a man's head?"

"I see. And you're out here with nothing more than that staff?"

"The God of my fathers will take me when He will. In my country we fight lions with these things. I fear no coward who strikes from darkness. Especially against women."

"Well, good luck. But this friend of yours . . . ?"

"Hadad, the sculptor. I think you know him. I can't seem to locate him, and he's not been well. He took a terrible beating the other night—your night off."

"Hadad? What a pity. Well, I hope you find him. We all think the world of him down at the bazaar. But look, Jacob. Take care."

"I will. Rachel has orders to bar the door to anyone but me."

"Good. The gods go with you."

The soldier moved away in the pale glow of the fog. "The One God goes with me," Jacob whispered thoughtfully after him. "I need no others. But thank you."

Reshef sat in shadow, on the far side of the bazaar. He watched the darkness, listening for the little sound he'd heard. There! There it was again—a tiny tinkle, soft and musical. And—yes, there was a second. Coming closer. He leaned forward, the vulpine smile made all the more cruel-looking by the new wound on his thin face.

Yes! That was what the sound was! Bells! Ankle bells—the sort of bells the dancers wore at the inn.

A woman was coming. A woman, alone, into the dark

bazaar. To the well. Now he could see her outline, and the light-colored hue of the short garment which came down to no more than midthigh. She was barefoot; there was no sound of flapping sandal-soles to match the delicate tintinnabulation of the ankle bells. She bent over, and he could see the soft curve of her rump as she leaned over the well. Young; good figure—probably pretty. Only the pretty ones ever got to dance under the flickering lamps, with bells on their ankles.

He stood up, quietly. As he did, she sensed something; sensed, perhaps, his presence. Women could do that. They could tell when a man was looking at them. He stood stock-still. She looked around.

"Who's there?" she said in a tense voice. "Is someone there?"

He did not answer. He stood in shadow, watching her. She dipped one hand in the well water and splashed her face with it. Then she looked around again. Reshef's tight-mouthed smile was as cold as the snows above Lake Van, in the Great Mountains. His eyes narrowed. His hands clenched and unclenched. They were the only part of him that moved.

His body tensed. He gauged the number of steps it would take him to bound to her side, to cup one hand over her mouth, to . . .

"Danataya?" a voice said suddenly. A young man's voice: a light baritone. "Danataya, is that you?"

The girl shrank back—and then she saw the newcomer at the same moment Reshef saw him. He stood in the edge of the same fog-filtered pool of diffused light that she occupied. A young man of middle height, thin-armed. Now the young man moved, and Reshef could see the awkward angle of the leg, the ungainly walk. Reshef's hands clenched and unclenched with a renewed rage. One hand sought the handle of his sheathed sword. . . .

"Danataya," the young man said earnestly, moving forward. "I'm sorry. It was my fault. I've come to apologize, and to tell you—it's all right. Abi-samar and Admuniri understand. It was your first time, and that's always hard. And at a time like that, virtually anything can throw a person off her stride."

"Oh," she said brokenly. "Hadad. Thank you. But—I couldn't—I just couldn't go on—"

"You were doing just fine," he said. He moved closer to her, tried to put one comforting hand on her shoulder; but she shrank away from him. "It's my fault. You looked in my eye, didn't you? And you saw something there that you didn't expect to see. Danataya, I wasn't even thinking of you. I—I had something terrible happen to me today. It shook me up something awful. And when I came into the inn, why, I couldn't think of anything but that. I—I hardly noticed you until—"

"Oh, Hadad. It was awful—"

"Well, maybe that job just wasn't the thing for you. Although—look, don't misunderstand. I—I thought you were the most beautiful thing I'd ever seen. When I finally came out of my stupor, why, I thought—I thought you looked like a goddess."

His hands reached out uncertainly and took one of hers. She did not withdraw it this time; but she would not look him in the eye. "Hadad, how can I—how can I go back and face Admuniri? She was counting on me."

"Danataya, she loves you. Both of them do. Like a daughter. Please. Please come back with me. It's not safe out here. . . ."

Slowly, he drew her away from the well, and they began to move past the stalls of the bazaar.

Reshef, in the darkness, let his smile turn to a sneer, then to a murderous scowl. The cripple! Shobai's brother! The brother of the man who had had him maimed! His hand went to the sword-pommel. What better way to begin paying off the damned bastard for scarring him that way . . .

He moved forward, the sword out now. Stealthily, quietly—skewer the man, then take the woman, take her hard and mean. . . .

But just then, as luck would have it, his arm jogged a stack of wooden crates and one of them fell to the ground. The pair's eyes instantly went his way.

"Danataya!" Hadad said. "Run! Run—quick! Head for the courtyard behind the butcher's! Quick!"

"But Hadad—"

"Somebody's been raped out here!" the boy said. "Raped and murdered—and look! Look at that sword!"

Danataya turned to run—then looked back and saw Hadad, empty-handed, standing facing the armed man. "Hadad!" she screamed. "Come with me! He'll kill you—"

Reshef rushed forward. But Hadad knew his bazaar, perhaps more than any man who frequented it. He was close to Marsatum's stall; his hand went under the counter and pulled out a crate of rancid, rotten vegetables—the sort of thing one

264

sold to the goatherds for swill. He dumped the box between him and the advancing Reshef. Only then did he turn tail and limp awkwardly after Danataya.

Reshef, moving quickly after him, slipped in the swill and fell heavily. He cursed, got to one knee, tried to stand again—and fell once more. His sword clattered on the stones. He reached for it; it slipped from his fingers, smeared as it was with the offal. He saw the two figures recede before him in the street; he cursed bitterly. His hand finally found the sword-pommel; he rose . . .

. . . and as he did, Hadad, up ahead, fell himself, sprawling headlong into the street. The girl reached back for him, helped him to his feet. Reshef, the sword held tightly in his hand now, sprinted after them as they disappeared around a corner. He could hear the boy's hoarse, winded whisper: "In here—quick!"

Reshef rounded the corner himself. They were just pulling closed the door to the little courtyard. "Quick, Danataya," the boy said in a hoarse, gasping voice, "the bolt—"

Reshef bounded to the door. The bolt had not yet been shot. He tugged at it with the muscles of a trained soldier, sheathing his weapon to put both hands into the work. The two of them tugged at the other side, their combined strength less than his own. They gave ground . . . more . . .

And then a powerful blow, something hard, struck Reshef's extended forearms and knocked them down, numbing them. And behind the door to the courtyard the bolt pushed by Danataya and Hadad slid shut with a resounding *bang!*

Reshef turned, holding his forearms together, in great pain. The nerves of both arms were numb; he could not even reach for his sword. He backed away. As he did, something hard struck out of the darkness, quick as a snake; slammed him in the face, bloodying his nose. He backed down the street, trying to get a glimpse of his adversary. Then the moon fell on the man's face and figure through the light fog, and he could see the stout staff in the man's hands. "You—" he said in a hoarse, pained voice. "What—"

But as he spoke, the tip of the staff slammed him in the groin, hard, and bent him over. The dancing tip, as agile as a butterfly, slammed both forearms again: one, two. His numbed hands could not even clutch his privates as he doubled over. And now the staff caught him under the chin and straightened him out again; slammed him in the chest, knocking him back against the brick wall of a house; flattened him out there; and at length came to rest against the tip of his nose. There it remained, forcing his head back against the wall.

"Now," said the staff-wielder for the first time. "Move one muscle, my friend, and the tip of this staff goes through the back of your head, taking your nose with it." The face was in shadow; but somehow the frightened, demoralized Reshef could see the eyes: calm, merciless, firm, unblinking.

"I—know you," Reshef said. "But—from where?"

"No matter," the man said. "Listen to me. You've killed three times tonight. Two of them may have deserved death; I don't know about that. The third? A girl who'd harmed no one? I'd kill you for a copper myself."

"No," Reshef said. "Y-you've got the wrong man."

"No, I haven't. You were going to kill those children just now. Your kind always wants to hurt its betters. But hear me, jackal and worse than jackal. My name is Jacob. My father-in-law is Laban. My wives are Leah and Rachel, and my concubines are Zilpah and Bilhah. I have ten sons. The boy on the other side of the door is Hadad and the girl is Danataya. I—"

"You—I don't know what you're talking about." He tried to flex his hands and found he couldn't. The motion, small as it was, brought pain as the staff pressed hard against his nose.

"Hear me, killer of women. I am giving you these names to advise you. If any of these—yes, or I myself—comes to any harm, or the smallest hint of a suspicion of harm in all the time left to me in Haran, two things will happen. You won't like either of them. You—"

Reshef tried to move again; the staff's tip flattened his nose. The smallest push and it would give. He stopped dead still.

"*Hear* me," the voice said insistently. "The first thing that will happen will be that I—or a friend with whom I have stored certain tablets of sworn testimony—will go to the lord Oshiyahu, commander of the garrison, and give a complete account of the day I brought you vital intelligence of the enemy facing Haran, evidence which you deliberately threw away. *Don't move! Don't speak! Don't answer!*" Now the staff jabbed at him slightly, testing the tensile strength of the cartilage nose-bone. "*Hear me.* The next thing that will happen—later on—will be that I, Jacob, will come after you and show you what I can do with this staff. I—or one of my sons. It doesn't matter. I have neglected the education of my boys in some matters, but these did not include the use of the

266

staff as we of Canaan use it. These aging hands here have killed a lion with a stick much like this. And may again. I have yet to kill a man with it—but I have watched as my brother Esau killed a bandit with one in the Moabite hills, when we were fourteen. Esau taught me all he knew. I can break every bone in your body without breaking the skin. I can take you apart until you have no more bone to give form to your flesh than a child's rag doll has. And what I cannot do, my five eldest sons can do; two of them surpass me with the staff already."

Reshef, trembling, felt his legs give way; but the staff caught him under the neck, at the Adam's apple, and pinned him back against the wall. A steady upward pressure forced strength back into his legs; he stood—and his hand kept its distance from the sword at his side.

"Now," Jacob said. "Haran is doomed. It is doomed because it has traitors like you to guard it. I will leave Haran soon. What you do then is your own business. You will sell it to the nomads for power, or position, or money. This will not matter to me. It is between you and the mercy of the all-powerful God. I will be gone, I and my wives and sons and such of my friends as my good right arm can give shelter to. But until such time—walk softly, Reshef. I know your kind. I know your mind, as I would know the mind of a dog turned coward and eater of offal. Go now, and do what you must do about Haran. But if the smallest harm comes to me or mine, the names I have told you and the names of my sons that I have not—oh, be sure, my friend, that I will know what to do. The God of my fathers has delivered you into my hands. There is no stone that will hide you, no army that will defend you, no fortress that will shelter you. Death will then lie on your eyes every time you lie down to sleep. It will accompany your eating, your sleeping, your lovemaking. You will never know the moment when it will strike. Hear me!"

"Jacob," Reshef croaked hoarsely. But then the pressure on his throat was gone, and Jacob with it. He was alone in the street. He fell to his knees and, trembling in every muscle, vomited up everything inside him. Everything but the lingering, all-pervasive fear . . .

VII

Their escape route was as crooked as a goat's path across a mountain. The moment the door had been barred, Hadad did not stop to congratulate himself; he set out on a complicated path that wound through the back alleys and yards of the town, over fences, through crawl spaces, and at length up the ladder to a storage loft above a commercial building. There they paused for the first time, panting at the rapid pace Hadad had set. He listened carefully for the sound of footfalls below them; then, hearing none, he eased the loft door shut and barred it. "There," he said. "I think we've given him the slip."

Danataya's eyes strained to get some notion of their surroundings. "Hadad," she said. "I can't see a thing."

"That's all right," he said. "I know this loft. I used to play in it when I was a little boy. I know most of this neighborhood like the palm of my hand. You stay put. There used to be a place over here where—why, isn't that nice? They never found it. How many years ago did I put this here? It must have been six years at least."

"What?" she said. "Hadad, come back. I'm frightened."

"Stay where you are," he said. "Please. You could take a nasty spill. Here. Now, let's see if I can get some dry straw—yes, here's . . ."

She sat quietly as he'd recommended. And in a moment she saw a bright flash, another, and a tiny flame. "Oh," she said. She watched the spot. Hadad produced a candle and lit it from the straw; then he stamped on the straw and put out the first blaze. He held up the candle. His friendly, open face smiled at her as he held the candle high.

"Look," he said. "I used to sneak up here to get away from the neighborhood boys when they were making fun of me. I stowed some candles, a bit of flint up in the crevice behind a support beam. Oddly enough, nobody ever found it—and here it is, waiting for me." He overturned a copper tub and set the candle atop it, sticking it to the copper with its own wax.

"Hadad," she said. "You're a wonder."

268

"Me? No—"

"I mean it. You can't run, you say, but you made it through the back paths of the town faster than—"

"Oh, well. One compensates, I guess. My legs are weak. My arms are strong—well, strong enough, anyhow. And I have the advantage of knowing the territory."

She moved closer and sat down cross-legged, looking at him. "Hadad. You—you saved me from that—"

"Oh, well, I mean—"

"You don't know what to do with praise," she said thoughtfully. "You don't think of yourself very much, do you?" He started to answer, but she held up one small hand. "Something—somebody—had hurt you terribly, and you were nursing your hurt. But when you realized *you* might have hurt *me,* you thought of me instead of yourself." She took one of his hands in hers. "That's the way you are, isn't it?"

"I couldn't let you go away thinking—"

She wasn't listening. Instead, she was looking into his eyes, and he could not look away. "It is. Jacob was right. The funny thing is, you don't know how good you are. And you probably believe you're too ugly, too, I mean because of your leg. That's right, isn't it?"

Hadad gulped, and suddenly he remembered Anat, and the terrible things she'd said to him that afternoon. "I—" he said, then found himself weeping, crying like a small child. He tried to pull his hand away, but Danataya would not let him.

"Hadad," she said. "What happened to you? Who did this to you?" Her hand went to his cheek; she guided his whole head to her body, cradling his face against her breasts. "There, my dear. There, now."

Hadad couldn't speak. He felt her arms going around him, at once soft and strong. Holding him to her. Rocking him gently. "If I were—" he began. But he couldn't continue. He shook with hurt and rage and—what? The emotions running through him were too complicated to find release in words.

Finally, he pulled away, gently, and looked at her. He wiped his eyes and nose. He pulled himself together. "I—someone told me today that I was . . ."

"Yes? Please. Won't you tell me, Hadad? You can tell me." She took his hand again. Her eyes were large, warm, caring. She smiled, and the smile had friendship in it, and much regard for him, and—what? Slowly, slowly, he found himself telling the tale of it. Haltingly. Brokenly. But increasingly in control of himself. And while a phrase, a sentence, might be broken by a half-choked sob, he shed no more tears . . . he, who hadn't let himself go this way since his mother had gone mad.

Danataya interrupted him gently here and there at first; but then she realized that what he needed most was to get it all said, and when he said something painful she would only squeeze or caress his hand. At the end she said, "Is that all of it, Hadad? Because—because I want to hear everything, if you really want to tell me. This is a terrible burden to carry if you're trying to carry it alone. If I can help you—"

"Oh, you've helped so much already," he said. "I've been going around for days, unable to talk to anyone. And after today—" But he now smiled a bit and firmed up his jaw a little for her. "It's just that—"

"That you found yourself agreeing with her? Because you had nobody around to help you talk yourself out of it? Goodness, Hadad. Do you know how many people in this town love you, and respect you, and care for you? I think you may not. Why, you should have heard what Jacob said the night you got hurt. He said, 'I wish my sons were more like Hadad.' He went on a long time like that. He wants to be your friend, to be like a second father to you. And—why, Hadad, the whole bazaar loves you. You should have seen their faces when you were singing the other day." She bit her lip and continued. "You should have seen *my* face, Hadad. You wouldn't have thought yourself ugly then. No, nor any of those terrible things your sister-in-law was saying to you today. Hadad, I thought you were beautiful. A beautiful, beautiful man. Straight legs aren't everything. You're kind and sweet and thoughtful, and you have a nice smile, and a person's heart goes out to you from the first—"

But an attack of shyness, or something like it, stopped her for a moment. She pursed her lips, knit her brow. And got the courage to continue from somewhere. "Hadad . . . when I was getting ready to dance tonight, I was *so* afraid, *so* embarrassed. But Yamam—my dancer friend who gave me the job—she told me to choose one pair of eyes and dance for them alone. Forget the rest of the men, she said. Well, Hadad . . . the eyes I chose were yours."

"Danataya—why, you're blushing."

"Well, for goodness' sake, of course I am, silly. This isn't the sort of thing that's easy to say. I mean, what'll you think? After all—"

"You danced for me? For me, Hadad? I can't believe—"

270

There was astonishment on his face, a dawning pleasure, and something else. But then his face fell. "Of course, I let you down terribly, didn't I? Me with my silly self-pity and—oh, Danataya, I'm so sorry. How could I—oh, how I wish I could take it all back ... go back to before I came in. Make it better for you."

He leaned forward. "Look, you haven't lost your job. Really. Admuniri told me to tell you. Come back in the morning, when you feel better. And don't be embarrassed. People have little ups and downs. Little failures along the way to success." Now it was his hands squeezing hers, his voice comforting her. "Besides, if I hadn't been so wrapped up in myself—Danataya, I—I thought you were the loveliest thing I'd ever seen in my whole life. I—why, what's the matter? Did I say something that—?"

"No, no," she said. "I just remembered. I didn't make the money I had to make. I've nowhere to live. I'll be evicted tomorrow. What will I do? Maybe—maybe Admuniri will let me sleep on the floor, in the inn. ..."

"Money? You need money?" Hadad said in a comforting voice. He stroked her hand gently, shyly. "Don't worry. Forget it. Look, I have a little piece of lump gold. We can cash it in, and pay your rent for you." He reached out a timid hand; it touched her hair, ran down the silky length of it, touched her shoulder. "I—I wouldn't let anything happen to you. I can always raise money. I've been raising it for Mother and me all these years. We've never starved. We've never been thrown out into the street. If you need money, I can raise it."

But she was remembering things she'd heard in the bazaar. "You would, wouldn't you?" she said, her eyes wide and soft. "You'd raid the only reserve you have for me? Hadad—dear Hadad." She leaned forward.

Hadad blinked. "I—" But then she put soft lips to his: lips that were first gentle, childlike; then womanly, demanding. She placed her two hands on his two cheeks and guided his face to hers. The one kiss became ten, a dozen. Her lips went to his cheeks, his eyes, his chin. She went to her knees the better to reach him. His hands went awkwardly to her waist, and the feel of her slim body was the most wonderful thing he'd ever felt. Then he let his hands move up her back and down to her hips, as he marveled at the sweet, rounded quality of her body, so different from a man's angular and bony frame. He felt her nakedness beneath the thin shift. His blood stirred, his body responded. Only now there was none of the shame in him that he'd felt when he'd watched Anat. Instead, there was such a powerful new emotion in him, one he'd never felt before. His heart seemed full to overflowing. "Danataya," he said hoarsely.

"Darling Hadad," she said. Her voice was gentle, low-pitched. She knew what she had to do, and there was a delirious happiness inside her that was the absolute opposite of her outward calm. "Hadad, I want you. More than anything I've ever wanted before in my life."

"M-me?" he said. "But—"

"Hush," she said lovingly. Her hands went down, grasped the hem of her shift, and pulled it up over her head in a single neat motion. She still wore the golden stomacher, the ankle bracelets. She wore nothing else, and her skin was golden in the flickering light. "Now you," she said.

In a moment he was as naked as she. "Danataya," he said, "don't look at my—"

"There's nothing wrong with your leg. You're such a handsome fellow, Hadad; I think I'd be attracted to you even if I didn't know what a lovely person you were, or what a beautiful voice you had. Did you know—I've wanted you to make love to me ever since the first time I heard you sing? I was so excited, I could . . ."

But now her eyes, running lovingly up and down his body, took note of his own growing excitement. "Oh, gods," she said. Her hands touched him . . . there. Cupped all of his manhood in her two palms. "How glorious. How beautiful. Oh, what a beautiful man you are. Hadad—please. Now. I need you. Hadad—"

"But—but I don't know how."

"Yes, you do," she said. Her arms drew him down. Gently. Insistently. In the end, passionately. The bells on her ankles jingled merrily, in an accelerating rhythm. She was right. He *did* know what to do. And the joy in his heart was beyond all measure. It was the happiest hour of his life.

There was a time when Reshef was so drunk he could barely stand. Then, as he drank himself through that stage, he got a second wind, and a cold horrible clarity came upon him, and he remembered the thing it was that he'd been drinking to forget. He called for more palm wine, the stronger the better. He'd been found out for a coward, a craven. Armed with his military weapons, he'd been faced down and turned into a yellow dog, a scurrying rat, by a man who bore nothing more lethal than a stick. Afterward, seeking release, he'd gone to the whores—and he'd found the incident had unmanned him. Completely, embarrassingly. "You!" he bellowed at the innkeeper of the nameless, nondescript Thieves' Quarter hostelry. "More palm wine! Quickly!" But his voice was high and squeaky where it had once been the voice of a lion.

After two more bowls of wine, he looked up to see a stranger sitting across from him. When had the man joined him? Had he dozed off for a moment and not noticed? He blinked drunkenly. The eyes looked steadily at him from under beetling brows. "You," the stranger said, "I have—look for you. You—Reshef? No?" He couldn't place the accent. He had a hard time bringing the face in focus. "I ask for you. Here. There. By and by I find. No?"

"Who the hell wants to know?" Reshef said. But the voice was high and shrill again, and he could not meet the stranger's steady gaze. "Who are you?"

But then there was a sudden flash of recognition in him, and he remembered the dying words of the assassin. He blinked up at the stocky stranger with the beard under that strong nose. Somehow, somehow he could never explain—he knew who the stranger was. "You," he said. "You're— Manouk."

The eyes narrowed; the smile did not quite reach them. "Ah," the stranger said. "Better not to put a name. But—you. The man who told me of you—he was wise man. He know who you are, where your heart lie. These—" his hand indicated the faces around the room, in the streets outside, "these not your people. I am right? No one here—yours. Perhaps no one, anywhere, yours. You live for self. Right?"

Reshef looked away from those piercing eyes, forced himself to look again. "Keep talking," he said.

"Ah," said the stranger. "You. Me. We go outside, in street. Here, all ears. We talk. We come to—understanding. No? Come. Air bad here. Think better in street."

Reshef reached for his wine bowl—and his hand knocked it over. He blinked, tried to stand. He steadied himself with both hands on the table, got his feet under him. He stayed there until he stopped swaying, until his legs stopped shaking. Then he looked and saw the stranger standing before him, solid as a granite boulder. Strong, obdurate, patient. Everything he feared. Everything he was not. "Yes, come on," Reshef croaked. "Let's get it over with."

Oh, I know. Said I. But you know my brother could sing, too. When he and I would sing a song together, all the eyes would go to him, and—"

"Hadad, I don't see how your brother—I'm not sure I—"

VIII

Danataya opened one eye in the chill dawn. The light was soft and diffused. She lay on a straw pallet, and both his robe and hers were carefully tucked in around her. She raised her head and looked around, wiping the sleep from her eyes. "Hadad?" she said in a small voice.

Then she saw him. He stood, still naked, his back to her, his body outlined in the open loft door, looking out. His body was thin, but comely. That leg still stuck out at an unusual angle—but now every time she saw it it seemed less a defect to be remarked and more a part of the creature called Hadad who had entered her life and made her feel less alone. She sat up, letting the robes fall away from her, smiling sleepily. "Hadad?" she said again. "What are you doing, darling?"

He turned to her. Suddenly, she thought, he looked older, at once more serious and more happy. His smile was gentle and loving. "Danataya," he said. "The dawn's so lovely—come see it with me." He held his arms out to her. He took a few steps toward her, and as he did so, the awkwardness of his walk became evident again. She took note of it—and then dismissed it. She rose to her knees and embraced his body, her face against his naked belly, her arms coming around to let her hands cup his hard buttocks. His manhood, at rest now, caressed her breast. She touched him there, lovingly, gently; she held her face to his secret parts and kissed them tenderly. Then she stood up and let him embrace her. "Oh, my dear," he said in an altered voice. "I'm so happy. I don't know how to say how much—to say what it is that I feel now."

"I know," she said. A little thrill went through her. She hugged him all the tighter. "I know—"

"Do you?" he said. "I mean, all my life I've felt like ... oh, something nobody wanted, something everyone tossed away. I felt ugly, worthless. The only thing I knew how to do was work with my hands, and few ever found that part of me interesting enough to give me a second glance."

"That and sing," she said. "Hadad, don't you have any idea what effect your singing has?"

"Oh, I know. Sort of. But you know my brother could sing, too. When he and I would sing a song together, all the eyes would go to him, and—"

"Hadad, I don't even know your brother. I'm not sure I would like him if I did. But *I* don't want your brother, and *I* don't care a fig for him. All *I* care about is *you*." She swallowed hard and looked him in the eye. "Hadad—I love you. I think I have since that first day, when you took the minstrel's lyre and sang for the people in the bazaar."

"Me?" he said, his heart full. "Oh, Danataya—I hardly know what to call the way I feel about—about you, and about last night, and about right now. I wonder if 'love' is a strong enough word. I feel as if I'd known you all my life. I feel as if I'd loved you all my life." His hands ran up and down her body, and he shuddered with a delight that was only partly sensual. Then he hugged her hard. "That sweet face of yours, this lovely body . . ."

"Yours, Hadad. And my soul, and my heart, and everything I am and ever will be. Don't you know?"

"I—I think I do. And that's the miracle. That I can hear you say these wonderful things—and that I can believe them." He bent to kiss her now, and his kiss was knowing and authoritative like a man's—and at the same time kept the innocence of his loving half-child's heart. "Come, dearest. Come and look. The dawn's pink and the sky is the loveliest pale blue. The air is clean and new." He bent awkwardly— her heart skipped a beat; already his awkwardness had a sweet grace in her loving eyes—and picked up their garments. He handed her her robe reluctantly. "I hate to cover you. I love you so much as you are."

"Close your eyes, then," she said, reaching up to kiss him as she stepped into her robe. "Imagine me the way you want me. Because that's what I'll be for you." Putting on her single garment, she jingled softly, musically. "Oh, goodness. I'm still wearing Yamam's jewelry."

"I'll always think of you this way. The pretty gold chain around your waist. The jingling bells on your ankles. I swear, Danataya: every time I hear the sound of little bells I'll think of you, and I'll think of the first time. . . ."

She looked down, saw his manhood stir. She helped him into his own garment, smiling, touching him there once more for remembrance. Standing on tiptoe to kiss him again. "Come," she said. "Let's look at the dawn."

In a moment, they stood atop the big building, looking down on the many rooftops of Haran: some flat and spreading, some resembling vaulted beehives. It was as he'd said; it *was* lovely: a soft light bathed everything, and the air was crisp and sweet. He held her hand and squeezed it gently. "Danataya," he said. "You don't think—"

"Think what, Hadad?" She snuggled into the curve of his arm, enjoying the mere touch of his body.

"You wouldn't want to—to stay with me, would you? I mean, I don't have much room, but—"

"Hadad! Why, I—" She tried to think of reasons why it would be a bad idea. But she couldn't think of any. "I never thought of . . ."

"Maybe soon we could find a bigger place—with room for a little table and maybe a stove." He spoke in an earnest voice. "I could probably make more money than I do—it'd just mean taking more temple work. I turn down some of it because it bores me to do it. But if I took all the jobs they handed me—" He stopped, embarrassed, as if he'd asked something reprehensible of her.

"I—I can continue at the inn," she said in a tentative voice. She turned and faced him, and there was excitement in her face. "Oh, Hadad, that'd make me so happy! I can't think of anything I'd like more! Oh, thank you—thank you for asking me, my darling." She hugged him, beside herself with delight. "Yes! Yes!" she said. "Let's do it!"

Admuniri opened the door. She was still in her night-clothes. "Who's that?" she said in a sleepy voice. "Go away!" Then her eyes focused on them. "Oh! Hadad! Danataya! Why, it's hardly time yet for—"

"I'm back to work," Danataya said. "I've come to clean up the common room—if you still want me."

Admuniri looked at them, their happy faces. Then, her face moved slowly into an understanding smile. "Oh, for goodness' sake. So the two of you . . . Well, Hadad, thank you for bringing her back to us. I don't know what we'd do without her." Impulsively, she stepped forward to give the girl an affectionate hug. "Danataya, you gave us such a start! We were so afraid for you, out in the dark like that, especially with someone out there who—" Her face changed. "You didn't run into—?"

"I think we did," Danataya said. Her arm went around Hadad's waist proudly. "But Hadad saved me from him. If it hadn't been for Hadad—"

Admuniri looked into their eager, flushed young faces. Her smile was warm, knowing, accepting. "Well, bless him. And from the looks of you two, I'd say that we'll both be seeing a lot more of Hadad than we have in the past. And not for drinking more wine either, I'll wager."

Hadad left her with a kiss and went back through the just-awakening streets of the morning city. His heart was full to bursting. He'd never felt such delirious joy. Danataya! And she was his, his alone. He wanted to stop strangers in the street and tell them: he, Hadad, had someone to love, someone who loved him and wanted him and had chosen him above all other men in the world! His walk, lopsided and halting, developed a certain spring to it, almost a little skip.

At the well, he stopped and washed his face. His bruises were clearing up, and the cuts on his face were scabbed over. He could see through both eyes now, and what he saw on all sides of him pleased him. His old familiar stall in the bazaar—his nice homey place in the finest bazaar in the finest city in the world . . .

"Hadad!" a much-loved voice said behind him. "So you're back to work!"

He wheeled. "Marsatum!" he said. He reached out impulsively and took both the hands of his astonished old friend. "It's so good to be back! It's so good to see you—and soon I'll be seeing all of you, all my dear friends here." He danced awkwardly around her, holding her hands. She pulled free.

"Hadad," she said. "What's got into you? I've never seen you like this before! I—" She stopped and looked him over. "Although, I have to say, I certainly approve of what I see. Hadad: you seem—different. Something has happened to you. Something for the better . . ."

"Yes! Yes!" he said happily. He took her hands again and leaned forward to kiss her on the cheek. She recoiled, but her expression a moment afterward had as much pleasure as surprise in it. "Something wonderful has happened, Marsatum. Something so wonderful I can't contain myself. I—"

"Hmmm." She snorted, smiling in spite of herself. "There's only one thing that could cause a man to act like that. Yes," she said, remembering, her eyes far away for a moment there. "And a woman, too. Hadad: you've fallen in love."

"Yes!" he said. "Yes, that's just what I've done. And Marsatum, she's the loveliest girl in the world, and—"

"Yes. They all are, aren't they? Well, that's what makes the world work, isn't it? I say, good for you, Hadad. Good for you. We've all been hoping something like that would happen to you one of these days, but we'd almost given up hope.

You've been such a bashful type—why, my little niece—the one who got married last year—she would have given anything to draw your attention. But you wouldn't give her a second glance."

"Her? Me?" Hadad said, dumbfounded. "But Marsatum—" He sighed and shrugged. "Well, nothing I can do about that now," he said. Even his voice seemed to have changed. It had a new maturity in it, for all its boyish fervor and happiness. "I've been forty kinds of fool. But no more: I've learned my lesson. Marsatum: you know who it is, don't you?"

"No. I've been waiting for you to tell me. And you've been taking the devil's own time."

"Danataya—the new girl at the inn."

"Oh, her! Why, she's rather nice! And a pretty little thing, too—"

"Pretty? She's the most beautiful—" But then he grinned at his own callowness. "That's what we all say, isn't it? Well, that's all right. I can't help thinking what I do; I love her so much. . . ."

"Oh, by the way, Hadad. There was a man here to see you. Yesterday. And, yes, the day before too. I wasn't there. Yahila talked to him. You'll have to ask her, but from what she said, I think he'll likely be back."

"What kind of man?" Hadad said. "I suppose it must be someone wanting to offer me some work. Well, I could use some right now. I can use all the work anyone wants to give me. I've got to start getting organized. After all, there'll be two of us now."

"My goodness. It's that serious already?"

"Why, of course. You know what, Marsatum? I think I'm going to try to get rich. I think I'm going to try to get as rich as Shobai."

Marsatum made an incredulous face. She turned as Yahila came into the bazaar. "Yahila!" she said. "Look who's back. He's in love, he's making plans, and now he says he's going to get rich!"

"Hadad!" Yahila said delightedly. "It's good to see you back, son! Wait'll that husband of mine sees you—but did Marsatum tell you? Someone very important-looking was here to see you. Twice. And he said—" She blinked and smiled. "But—here he is again, Hadad. Talk to him yourself."

Hadad turned. Arusian, the man from the merchant Ibalum, stood before him. His expression was a bit different from what it had been before. "Hadad?" he said in the tone one uses to equals. "Good to see you again. I've had an urgent message from Ibalum, in Carchemish. He told me to come straight to you."

"He did?" Hadad half smiled, stunned. He looked at Yahila and Marsatum, shrugging. "But—what did he want?"

"He wanted you to come with me, if you'd be so kind, to the office of the city scribe."

"But—I haven't done anything wrong."

"*Please.*" Arusian smiled, holding one hand up. "Of course you've done nothing. Nothing, that is, except get Ibalum more excited than I've seen him in years. He's shown your work around to a group of merchants west of here. They've gone mad about it. They all want more—and Ibalum wants you. Specifically, he wants your mark on a contractual tablet which will make the two of you partners, so that he can sell your work far and wide. Young man, you won't believe the prices your work is going to be getting."

"Hadad!" Marsatum squeezed his arm. "Did you hear what he said?"

Hadad shot her a thunderstruck smile. "Why—why, this means I'll be able to buy the goods I need for making—"

"No, it doesn't," Arusian said. "It means Ibalum, your partner-to-be, will buy them for you—once we've settled this little matter of the contract. And, oh yes. You're to be advanced any sum you request, within reason, for living expenses. And whenever that runs out, you're to be advanced more. If you need better workspace, let me know about it; we'll rent you a work area that will meet your every need. All you have to do is produce work of your usual quality—and in quantities sufficient to meet an expanding market."

"Hadad! Don't just stand there! Go along with the gentleman! Now, before he changes his mind!"

But Hadad just stood there, looking back and forth from one of them to the other, seeing nothing. An unbelieving smile began to spread slowly across his round face, and a little shudder of joy ran through him. He was thinking: *I'll have to ask the astrologers what kind of day this was.* In one night and morning his whole life had changed completely. Permanently.

CHAPTER NINE

I

"You're sure you won't have need of me?" Kirta said. But as he spoke, his eye wandered out over the little port, over the nest of moored ships, over the rope walk that led down to the water, over the sparse crowds shopping at the market stalls for fish.

Poliwos grinned wryly. "It's a good thing I don't," he said. "Your heart wouldn't be in it anyhow. Go. Ask questions. Find out whatever it is that you need to find out." He seconded his own words of dismissal with a half-impatient motion of his thick hand. "Go, man. What are you waiting for?"

Kirta smiled—and Poliwos quickly forgave him his haste to leave. Kirta had begun the voyage a man who seldom if ever smiled, and Poliwos had first attributed this to Xena's death and to Kirta's self-imposed guilt over this. But it gradually developed that Kirta had for many years been a man who seldom smiled. And it was also equally evident that Kirta was now a man undergoing severe changes. *This* change, Poliwos decided now, was for the good. It was no good for a man to deny his own humanity forever.

"Thank you," Kirta said. "I admit I hadn't been looking forward to spending the rest of the afternoon wrangling with customs people. When do you want me back at the ship?"

"I don't care. Stay until the usual hour to turn in if you like—or if you're learning something. But Kirta—"

"Yes?"

"Watch out. This little town is tougher than it looks. On the other side of the island there's a sheltered cove where pirates anchor sometimes. And when they're, uh, recruiting for one of their raids, well—"

"They press people into service. People who act unwary and who won't be missed too quickly. I understand. I'm armed. The sword I made you—I made another from the same batch for myself."

"Fortunate fellow. The only way one could improve upon that piece you gave me . . ."

". . . would be to make it from the new metal. I've told you: get me ore and I'll make anything you like. Just one little stop on the Lycian coast, where the oremongers come down to the port cities to sell their—"

"You know I haven't any wares they'd want. And besides, I get better prices here on the islands."

Kirta sighed . . . and smiled again. "Very well. As long as you keep your promise."

"I will. Be patient. We have to work our way there. By this fall, we'll make the annual trip to Ugarit and Arvad. I'll let you off wherever you like. You'll have earned it by then. And, Kirta, one more thing—"

"Yes?"

"What if—what if your wife and sons . . . ?"

Kirta's face hardened. His mouth shrank to a narrow line, and his eyes clouded over. "Well, anything can happen. Ever since I decided to return, I've been thinking about that possibility. It's something I'll have to live with. Why, they may reject me. They may all hate me, and send me away. After all, I did abandon them. But who knows? With what I left behind, they may have had a decent sort of life without me. . . ."

Poliwos raised one brow at him. "You're right; for all you know, they're rich and happy, and your sons are strong and healthy and have fathered many sons of their own." He shrugged at the armorer. "Go. You're losing time as it is. And—take care."

But Kirta, once he'd left the trader, hesitated before heading into town. Instead, he walked out to the point, to where the rocky headland came down to the water and a group of fishermen were hauling their boat, its sails now bunched against the yard, into the shallows to unload its catch. It was a good sight, there in the warm sunshine: honest men working up an honest sweat at an honorable trade. In the sunburned nakedness of a fisherman there was nothing to wash off, nothing to rinse out.

As he stood and watched, a bearded giant strode out of the shallow water, balancing on his shoulders a long pole from which hung dripping baskets of high-piled herring. Behind him a younger man, beardless, carried another pole with a big tunny hanging from each end of it. Kirta's eyes ran up and down the younger man's body, seeing the youthfully virile strength of him, untested, unfledged. The boy had a clear eye and curly hair. *Why, my Hadad would perhaps be his age . . . maybe a little older.* There was a catch in his throat as he addressed the boy. "Pardon me," he said haltingly in the language of the islands. "Could you—could you tell me the way to the smith's? I—"

"The smith?" the boy said. He paused. The word was the same as the name Kirta had borne those many years on Crete: *khalkeus.* "I think you'll find him up the hill. See where the smoke is curling from the grove?"

"Oh, yes," Kirta said. "I should have figured it out for myself. Who else would have that big a fire going now . . . ?" But his eyes didn't go up the hill where the boy had pointed. They remained on the boy's face. *Hadad would have a round sort of face, perhaps. Rounder than this boy's. But no. You never know how a little boy's face is going to mature.*

"Thank you," he said and turned away. As he did, he noticed them all looking at him—particularly a brawny, stark-naked man kneeling beneath an olive tree, cleaning fish. The fish-cleaner's eyes were hard. His hand held a stout knife. His expression was cold, suspicious. Kirta beat a hasty retreat up the hill toward the smith's cottage.

The smith was a hefty fellow with a big belly and a red face. Kirta liked him immediately—but wouldn't have given much for his chances of living long. There was already a ruddiness to his big nose, and the veins in it were quite visible. "Well," the smith said, "Eruthros is the name. And from the look of those hands of yours—and from the little burn scars under the skin of your forearms—I'd say you might well be a fellow tradesman."

"I am," Kirta said. "Kirta of Haran. But I've been on Crete for a number of years. Well met, Eruthros." He picked up a sword from a nearby table. "Your work?" he asked. He tried to conceal his distaste for the object; the maker had been no more than a ham-handed fumbler.

"Yes," Eruthros said. "But look here, you're wearing something nice there. Something of your own?" He gestured at Kirta's sword in its scabbard at his side. Kirta shrugged and handed it over. "Gods! You can do work like this? How I'd love to put in six months watching you work, my friend!"

"It's a hereditary knack," Kirta said. "I'm a Child of the Lion. I don't know whether you've heard of us."

"Lion?" The smith's brow knit. "Wait. There was a story. I think I heard it from somebody off a boat. People who bear a certain birthmark, like . . . ?"

"Like this," Kirta said, raising his garment and showing the red mark. "Well, that's interesting. I didn't know our fame—or is it notoriety?—had reached the islands here. What have you heard of us? Bad or good?"

"Why, good. Quite good." The smith turned Kirta's blade this way and that. "But now I see they didn't tell the half of it. You're an artist, my friend, I can tell, a real artist. I fear you're out of my reach altogether. If all of your breed can do this sort of thing . . ."

But then his face fell. "Haran?" he said. "You said you were from Haran?"

"Yes. Why? The family's lived all over. . . ."

But the smith wasn't listening entirely. His face bore first a puzzled look, then a look which shaded off into growing anger and resentment. "Why, that swine! That cheap, chiseling son of a whore. . . ."

"Who?" Kirta said mildly. "I don't understand."

"Why—the dirty bastard. The swindler!" He looked at Kirta, his mouth hanging open. "The man who told me the story—he sold me a sword. It was supposed to have been made by one of you Sons of the Lion, or whatever it is that you call yourself." He put Kirta's sword down hastily and went to the cluttered corner of the room. He began digging into a pile of old metalwork. After a moment he came up with something. "Here. Look at this. Look at this damned thing he swindled me with. And I paid . . ."

The rest of his words were lost in grumbling. Kirta took the sword, held it up to the light. It was clearly not much better than journeyman work. To be sure, it was better than the work of the island smith himself, but . . .

Suddenly, the handle of the sword, long worn, came off in Kirta's hand, and he saw the metal under the wood. Then he saw the stamp of the maker, and his hand shook. He put the sword back down on the table, and then he picked it up once more. "I—" he rasped. "Friend, could I buy this from you? If you were swindled, I'll make it good. Please: what do you want for it?"

"Why—I hadn't thought of it." Eruthros scratched his head

283

with a dirty hand. "Make me an offer. I didn't expect anyone to—"

Kirta reached inside his garment and pulled out a coin at random. "Would this suffice?" he said. The smith gasped and nodded; the coin would have bought twenty such items. "Thank you," Kirta said in a choked voice, and he hurried out of the smith's cottage without another word, holding the dusty sword in one big hand.

Night came; the shadows deepened around him, and the innkeeper lit candles for the little patio that overlooked the harbor and the sea. "Are you sure you don't want to come inside, sir?" he said. "There'll be a chill in the air, and—"

Kirta looked at him through eyes made dull with drink. "What of it?" he said wearily. But then, passively, he stood and followed the innkeeper inside, the tarnished sword sticking out of the ill-wrapped bundle in his hand. As he did, he caught a last glimpse of the lights out on the bay, winking up at him. He scowled and turned his face away from the sea. When the innkeeper had seated him inside, he asked Kirta once again: "Could I bring you something to eat, sir?" And Kirta, his face gray and expressionless in the dim light, said, "No. More wine. More wine, please. . . ."

That was where Poliwos found him an hour later. He sat down across from the smith and put one hand on Kirta's arm. "Kirta," he said. "What's the matter? You don't seem to be yourself. We've hit a dozen ports together since you joined us—and I don't think I can recall your ever doing anything like this. What happened?"

Kirta peered at him, trying to get his face in focus. "Poliwos," he rasped. "Look at this." He unrolled the parcel; the sword spilled out onto the table.

Poliwos looked at his friend; looked at the sword; looked back at Kirta once more. "I don't understand," he said. "An ordinary piece of second-rate work." He half smiled. "Nothing to get all—"

"Pick it up," Kirta said, a note of angry desperation in his voice. "Pick it up, damn you. Look at it."

Poliwos did so. "I still don't see—"

"Here!" Kirta said, and now there was a real note of pain in his strangled voice. He yanked the weapon away and pointed to the broken handle. "Here! Look here!"

"I did," Poliwos said. "But I can't read that language. What does it say?"

"Curses," Kirta said, his tone matching the desolation on his face. "It says *'Shobai of Haran.'* This sword was made by my son. And—and Poliwos. It's—it's shoddy work. Hastily done. Gods! If this is typical of what he does, I've cheated him of everything, do you hear? Everything! If I'd been there to train him, instead of whatever hack he seems to have apprenticed with . . ." He sighed, and seemed visibly to shrink in size. "But I wasn't there. And if my elder son was trained as poorly as this—trained so badly in a trade that is virtually the only reason for being among my line—what have I done to my younger son?" He tried to speak another word or two, but it came out in a half-strangled sob. "I saw someone today—it could have been Hadad. A handsome young man, with a face much like what Hadad's would have grown to be—tall, powerful, with strong arms and legs, looking a little as I must have looked at his age. But a fisherman—a common fisherman . . ."

"Look," Poliwos said. "You don't *know* anything of what's happened with Hadad. You're just speculating. . . ."

But when he saw the look in Kirta's eyes, he knew no words he could utter were going to help. "Ah, well," the seaman said. He stood and looked down at the smith. "You'll have to handle it your own way, I suppose. Perhaps what you really need is to make a night of it. Have you enough money?" Kirta nodded miserably. "All right," the captain said. "Go ahead. Get drunk. Lie with some doxy. But if you're not back by dawn, I'll come after you with a couple of my strongest deck hands. We sail on the morning tide, remember?"

It was a quiet night at the inn. Two whores came in, looked around, and walked back out. Later, one of them came back in and sat down next to Kirta. "Hello," she said. She put one hand on his thigh. He looked at her dully. "Go 'way," he said. "Please." And he reached for the wine bowl again, his eyes on the sword on the table.

The innkeeper threw him out, as gently as he could, some hours before the first pink appeared in the sky. He staggered a bit to one side as he tried to make his way down the street. His sandal strap broke; he kicked it off, and in a moment kicked the other one off to join it. He slipped and fell once, and only with difficulty regained his footing. Ahead of him were voices, quiet, hushed. He headed toward them. Perhaps Poliwos had sent someone after him. But—how many were there? Three? Four? "Poliwos?" he said in a slurred voice. A

285

cloud drifted over the moon, and the faces disappeared. "Poliwos, is that you?"

But his answer was a low snicker. And as he approached them, they drew apart, surrounding him. Then suddenly, before he could reach for the two weapons in his belt, suddenly there was a terrible blinding stabbing pain in his head, on the left side, and he fell to one knee. Then they were upon him. For a moment, the moon came out from behind the cloud, and the faces on which the light fell were those of strangers. He could see the club rise in the air again, and he held up one arm, but the blow fell anyway, with numbing force. He went down on his back; the blows continued to fall, only from several directions now. They came too fast for him to fend them off. . . .

II

Poliwos awoke with the first light. He sat up and looked around. "Kirta?" he called. He blinked away the last vestiges of sleep and stood, yawning and stretching, flexing the stout muscles beneath the outer layer of fat he bore. He shook his head and blinked again. "Kirta," he called again. "Are you there?"

There was no answer. Yawning again, he reached for his loincloth and wrapped it around him. "Hmmm," he said to himself in a husky morning voice. "Didn't make it back." He stepped out on deck. "Paiawon!" he bellowed in a scratchy voice. "Out on deck! On the double!"

His mate was at his side almost before he'd finished the call. "Yes, sir?" he said. "Oh, yes. It's Kirta, isn't it? Yes. By all means. Yes, sir. I'll get someone to go with us." He turned to go, but Poliwos stayed his hand.

"Get Alkinoos," Poliwos said. "Or somebody just as big and strong. And, Paiawon—"

"Yes, sir?"

"Arm yourselves, both of you. I have a strange feeling something's wrong. It's possible that Kirta is just drunk, but I doubt it."

"Yes, sir. He's not the type to pass out in a ditch anywhere. Do you think we ought to take more men with us?"

"No," Poliwos said. "If there's trouble, we'll know before we're far into the city. But Paiawon—"

His mate anticipated him. "Yes, sir. Double guard on the ship. Immediately."

By the time the sun was fully visible, a bright disk above the eastern hills, they had the whole story. The town's streets were full—but the crowd consisted of the old and the very young, and the women of the missing. The pirates had swept down in the middle of the night and raided the village, carrying away fishermen, shepherds, virtually everyone in the town who was male and of the proper age. The women wept; the old men cursed. The city was a wretched shell of itself. And Kirta the smith was one of the missing.

Poliwos and Paiawon searched the village, while Alkinoos went up into the hills. After an hour, Alkinoos returned and reported to Poliwos. "I talked to a peasant in the grove up above, sir," he said. "He told me there were two galleys anchored in the cove on the lee side of the island last night. He went up and hid in the caves; he was used to this sort of thing, and, unlike the villagers, he was able to see trouble coming from his position on the ridge, and to get away."

"I see," Poliwos said. "And the galleys?"

"Left before the first light, sir. Pulling hard on the oars. Well, I don't wonder, sir. They must have taken fifty prisoners this morning."

"I see. And did he say which way they went? Because, well, we're quite vulnerable ourselves—"

"Yes, sir. He wasn't sure, sir. But he guessed north. The pickings are generally better up that way, you know. Up along the coast, to Mukenaian waters."

"Oh." Poliwos's face fell. "I'd had plans to go there myself. But with pirates working those waters, Mukenai can wait. There's money to be made elsewhere, and with less bother— but we're missing the tide. *Paiawon!*" he turned and barked to his mate. "Make ready to lift anchor!" And he watched the seamen scurry back toward the ship, to carry out his command.

In his heart, Poliwos felt a great sadness. He'd come to like Kirta as a friend; the gods alone knew how seldom a ship's captain had a friend to talk to on board, as between equals. You never got a peer's opinion or answers out of subordinates; they were always calculating the effect of their words.

And, besides—Kirta was an unusual man, a man of great learning and intellectual curiosity. One could learn a lot talking with him; one could stretch his mind a bit by marking such a man's replies.

He sighed, watching his crew swing into action. That was a sailor's life, though, wasn't it? Nothing permanent but the damned eternal sea and its sullen moods and fierce rages. Landsmen never quite understood: an old salt's one truly distinguishing characteristic was, more often than not, a deep and abiding hatred of the sea. That, and loneliness . . .

He sighed again. "Kirta, damn you," he said in a soft and despairing undertone, "why did you have to do it? Why couldn't you have just let well enough alone . . . ?"

But the answer came of itself, inside his head, and he didn't even have to listen to it to know what it was. A man had his own *daimon* to contend with. Kirta's was a fierce and demanding one, which tore at his guts constantly, and he moved at its command. No use telling such a man the logical course of action. He couldn't act on it, not with the damned *daimon* roiling inside him. Nothing would ever go well with him again—ever—until he'd set the wicked spirit to rest by finding out, once and for all, what had happened to his wife and children . . .

. . . and what then? Poliwos asked himself now. Would Kirta then find peace, once he'd found them? Or would he waste the rest of his life in a vain attempt to right the "wrongs" he felt he'd done them? For of course, nobody could ever unmake a thing once made. It was a waste.

And what a particular waste! Such a brilliant man! A man on the brink of great things, a man any king would be proud to number among the advisers to his court! And here he was wasting his—

Then he remembered. Gods! Kirta would be a slave now—a chattel manning an oar in a pirate ship. He shivered and let his heavy features slip into a disturbed frown. Ah, yes. The same thing could happen to him, Poliwos, if he didn't step lively and keep an eye out for trouble. And the first thing he could do to that end was to get the devil out to sea, out to where one could spot trouble coming. It was a lucky thing the pirates hadn't decided to come aboard his ship and seek galley-fodder there; they'd have found him grossly unprepared, and they'd likely have taken him and his ship in ten minutes' fighting. Well, it was an omen, a warning. He'd take better care in the future.

He walked down the dock to the slip where his boat lay moored. Paiawon saluted him as he came aboard. "Awaiting orders to sail, sir," the mate said.

"Carry on," Poliwos said. "Weigh anchor." He watched as Paiawon barked orders and the crewmen astern pulled together on the anchor rope. Kirta ... he thought, just once. But then he drove all thought of the smith from his mind.

Salt water in his face awoke him. He lay in the bottom of a boat, a boat that pitched lightly with the motion of the sea beneath. His face lay half-submerged in slops, which lapped against his ear. One of his eyes wouldn't open. He blinked the other and tried to rise. There were shooting pains in several places on his body, and all of his joints were as stiff as his back was.

"Ah," a voice said. "Another one's come alive to join us."

He looked around him. What light there was came from above, from a hatchway. He was in the hold of something, and where he was, it stank beyond belief—rotting, decaying fish, rat manure, the smell of his own rancid sweat as well as other men's. Smells of death ...

"Where—where am I?" he said. And tried for a moment to shake the cobwebs from his brain. The smallest shake, however, led to stabbing pains. He clutched his head and tried to move—and only then noted that one of his ankles was chained to a bulkhead.

"Welcome to number two hold," one of the voices said mockingly. "We hope you'll enjoy your stay here." The voice was sarcastically unctuous.

"Oh, shut up," said another, deeper voice. "Can't you see the poor bastard's hurting? After all, they must have hit him pretty hard to make him stay out that long."

"I—what time is it?" Kirta said. "I've got to get back to the—"

"You don't have to get back to anywhere," the deep voice said. "You're pretty far out to sea by now, I'd say. In case you're wondering, the press gang got you, friend. Just like they got all the rest of us, at one time or another. Only they seem to have hit you too hard. Otherwise, you'd be up on deck raising blisters on your hands and ass, pulling on an oar."

"Oh," Kirta said. "And what kind of ship ... ?" For a heart-stopping moment he thought: *Cretan?* But no. The hold of a Cretan vessel was shaped differently from this. This was a deeper-draft ship. What the origin was, he couldn't say. It was enough that it wasn't Cretan. His life would be worth nothing at all on a Cretan ship now.

"They're pirates," the deep voice said from the dark shadows. "They generally range along the Lycian coast, up into the Inland Sea. They hit the island ships and raid the little island villages."

"I see," Kirta said. "Well, they didn't find much when they found me. Galley slaves my age aren't worth much. I know. I was one once, a dozen years ago. You wouldn't know it to look at my hands these days, of course." He grinned bitterly. "Well, a man's life goes through some odd twists and turns, doesn't it? I was a rich man once. Then I was a slave. Then I was a rich man again, and I lost that again. Now I'm a slave." He felt in the darkness for the cuff around his bare ankle, and only then realized he was naked. "Well, there's one comfort. They won't have much new to show me."

"Don't be too sure," the deep voice said. "I thought something like that myself once. Then I sounded off once too often. Makhawon beat me insensible and threw me down here."

"What is he going to do with you?" Kirta said.

"Sell me, I suppose. He'd have killed me if it weren't for my looks. People like me bring good prices as slaves. Maybe you, too. You're bigger than most, from what I've been able to see of you. Big ones make good, and costly, slaves."

"I remember something like that from the old days. I changed hands a number of times before I won my freedom. But you? You're big like me?"

The man with the deep voice moved into the light. In the pool of sunshine that stabbed its way down into the gloom Kirta could see the speaker's face and his whole bulky, naked body. Both were black: shiny pitch-black, with blue highlights in the sunshine. "I could tell you my slave's valuation almost to the drachma," the big man said. "I've been a slave most of my life. Welcome back to slavery, my once-rich friend. I hope you'll like it better than I do."

The black man's name was something unpronounceable, but the crewmen on a long-forgotten ship had dubbed him "Akhilleus," for his strength. The name, given in derision, had stuck. His companion in the hold was a weasel of a man called Argurios. He was small and weak, and he had attached himself to the strong man, for the protection he would not otherwise have had. Kirta all but dismissed him from the first.

Akhilleus, however, was another matter. The black man was one of the most interesting men Kirta had ever met. He was as strong as a bullock and as gentle as a spring lamb with his friends. And with Kirta, as the first day wore on, he was friendly and understanding. It helped ease the day's transition to Kirta's lowered estate.

More: Akhilleus was, by his own account, perhaps the most traveled man Kirta had ever met. He had gone through many masters in his forty years, after having been sold by his uncle and aunt into slavery with the Egyptian army in his original home, many days' march above the sixth cataract of the great Nile River in imperial Egypt. He'd become a member of a handpicked Nubian troop which had accompanied the Great King on three of his campaigns. Then he'd been captured, and the people who had captured him had sold him months later in Kizzuwatna, and he'd worked for a minor king there, and . . .

They were halfway through that story when they heard a violent commotion on deck. Tramping feet went from port to starboard and back again. Excited voices yelled back and forth. "What's happening?" Kirta said. He peered up through the darkness at the open hatch; but unseen hands above sealed the hatch cover and left the three of them in total darkness, listening to the banging and clatter on deck.

Only after a few minutes had passed did Akhilleus reply. "That horn," he said. "That was the call to battle stations. There's a fight. Whether it's a defensive one or whether we've attacked someone there's no knowing as yet."

"Oh, gods!" Argurios said. "And here we are trapped in the hold like fish in a tank! Akhilleus! What can we do? I—"

But the black giant clapped a hand over his friend's mouth and silenced him. "Easy, now, little one," he said. "I have to listen. Hmmm—they're coming about." Kirta nodded in the dark; you could feel the strain on the ship's timbers as she came to smartly. "There now, my friend," Akhilleus said. "Take it easy. It'll be all right. And if anything happens, I'll get you to safety. I promise."

There was a tremendous wallop on the deck above. Around the spot came the scurrying of feet. "Someone tossed us a little present with the catapult," Akhilleus said. "That's all right. It can't hurt a tub like this—unless what they tossed us was a bundle of faggots soaked in pitch. The only real problem we'll have here will be with fire."

"But—what if we're stove in?" Kirta said. "Won't we be the first to drown?"

"Oh, I can get out of the hold any time I want to," Akhilleus said. "I'll show you, next time there's light to see by. It's what happens when I get up there that keeps me down here. I'd have to fight fifty men to get free. But if the boat's stove, and if they're all bailing out anyhow, I can find my way out. Yes," he said in an affectionate voice to the little man at his side, "and yours, too. But let's hope that doesn't come to pass. I never learned to swim." His deep-voiced chuckle carried over the sounds of fighting on deck.

Kirta sat there for the rest of the fight, his heart beating wildly. It seemed there might well be only two alternatives: freedom, or a quick and merciful death. He prepared his mind for either and tried to set his troubled heart in order.

But when the last sounds had died down topside and the hatch cover was pulled away, he discovered a third possibility. A voice bellowed at them as a rope ladder dangled down in the pool of light. "All right, you three. Up on deck. Make it snappy!"

Kirta looked at Akhilleus's white eyes, glowing in the dark across from him. "Are we to be sold then?" he said.

"No," the giant said. "Most likely a few oarsmen died in the battle. We'll be pressed into service taking their places." And with that, he reached for the ladder, hauling himself up hand over hand, his huge biceps bulging. Kirta tried to follow—but was stopped by his ankle chain. In the end, Akhilleus came back down into the hold and pulled apart the two halves of Kirta's shackle with a single mighty motion of his gigantic hands. "Here," he said. "Come join us on deck. You haven't met Makhawon yet, or the rest of his little friends. Who knows? You may wind up preferring the smell down here. And the company as well. At least a ship's rat can't talk."

III

Kirta stood on the pitching deck, blinking against the sudden bright sunlight. As he did, someone threw a bucket of cold water over him. The water caught him in the face; he spluttered, wiping the salty liquid from his eyes.

"There," Akhilleus said, grinning down at him from his great height. "If we're going to be partners on an oar, at least I won't have to put up with any more of that stink from the hold." He clapped Kirta on the shoulder in friendly fashion and turned him slightly. "Kirta: meet Makhawon, the illustrious commander of this floating pigsty."

"You shut up!" a voice bellowed. Kirta looked down. Makhawon was the broadest man he'd ever seen. He came up perhaps to Kirta's shoulder—no more than midchest on the massive Akhilleus—but must easily have weighed half again as much. There was a layer of fat on the outside, perhaps, but the rest was muscle: rolling, knotted muscle. "Shut up, you insolent black bastard! Get to your oar!"

"Anything you say, Makhawon," Akhilleus grinned, sauntering with insulting slowness toward the pit where the bow oarsmen worked. "Better treat him nice, though. He's a friend of mine."

Makhawon hurled a curse at him. Then, his dark eyes flashing, he turned to Kirta. "Well," he said. "You're big enough, and you look as though you've done a bit of work in your time, for all your aristocratic looks."

"I am—I *was* a smith," Kirta said. It always paid to bring up the subject of any useful trade that you'd held in your free days. Usually it brought better treatment. "An armorer. When your men—picked me up, I was wearing two weapons I was too drunk to use. I made the better of them. But—I see you're wearing it."

"Huh?" Makhawon said. "This?" He pulled the weapon from his belt. "Good work. Better than good work. Look, anyone in the trade can always use a good armsman. I'll put you to work. But right now we need speed. We lost a lot of men in that last little sortie. I'll put you on an oar for now. It won't ruin your hands, don't worry."

"I've pulled an oar before," Kirta said emotionlessly. "Put me across the bay from the black man. Put us opposite one another on the inner aisle. We'll give you speed."

"Huh," Makhawon said. "Well, if you can get an honest day's pull out of that big lump of tar, so much the better. Go join him in the bow." He motioned Kirta away, then added, "When we're in port, I'll see what other work I can find for you."

Kirta nodded and headed for the oarsmen's bays. As he entered the pit, he could see Akhilleus in the bow, turning back to grin at him. "Here!" the black man said. "I saved you a place right next to me."

Kirta, however, seated himself across the center aisle. He sat down behind the shipped oar and held it in his hands tentatively. "Where's the overseer?" he asked. His curt nod indicated the empty seat before the drum, where, ordinarily, the galley slaves' overseer sat and gave the oarsmen their rhythm.

"Same place half the oarsmen went," the Nubian said. "Under the briny. He caught an arrow in the neck. First thing I asked, too. They haven't named a new man yet. Maybe they won't. At least until they've hit port."

"Hmm," Kirta said. "What if you and I set the pace? Are you game?"

"No, please," Argurios said in a high-pitched whine. "The last time he did, he nearly killed me."

"Don't worry, little one," Akhilleus said. "You come up here beside me. I'll pull enough oar for the two of us. And you, Kirta: done! I've been wondering if you could match me on an oar."

"Well," Kirta said, looking at his palms, "I haven't done this for some time. My hands will have it rough for a few days. But there was a time when I pulled a good oar. We'll see. . . ."

"You up there!" Makhawon's raucous voice boomed out. "Enough talk! Full forward! And get your backs into it."

The black giant grinned across at Kirta. "Ready?" he said. And then he bellowed: *"Stro-oke!"* His body uncoiled itself from its doubled-up position, and he pulled back on the mighty beam in his two huge hands, his thick muscles knotting like coils of tar-soaked rope.

Kirta had learned a trick many years before, on the oar. You counted to yourself, in a slow and syncopated rhythm. You filled up all the space between downbeats with some sort of meaningless patter, making the downbeat count coincide with the overseer's slow calling of the stroke: "Fifty-*four* heathen pirate bastards drowning in a pisspot; fifty-*five* heathen pirate bastards drowning in a pisspot. . . ." And although your arms hurt first, and then your chest (you couldn't seem to come up with enough air for each long haul on the oar), and then your behind, and last and worst of all your hands— the rhythm, with its hypnotic quality, tended to get you through. That and closing your eyes, and letting your mind wander . . .

At first, his closed eyes registered the bright sunshine beneath their tightly shut lids. First came the bright colors, drifting back and forth before his mind's eye. Then the bright colors coalesced, and the shapeless forms became a door, half-open, a light shining from beyond it. And in his waking dream, he felt himself walking toward that half-open door. He felt his hand reach for the handle, felt the door give, and saw in the space beyond a world of muted pastel colors, a world of rich greens and soft, warm browns. A land of rolling hills and grassy slopes, with white and brown sheep roaming the heights beneath skies of pale blue. His nose smelled the scents of the spring wild flowers, and as he climbed the hill and looked down, he could see a green valley below, watered by a swift stream that broke in white, bubbly billows over rock outcroppings. . . .

And his mind said: *Padan-aram* . . .

The picture changed now, and he was approaching the tall walls of a city, a city surrounded by gentle hills dotted with olive trees, fig trees, beehives, fruit trees, grape arbors—a city where the homes of the poor were built to look like beehives, vaulted and tapering to a point. . . .

Haran . . .

Now his mind drifted up from the deeper state into which its thoughts had wandered, and Kirta found himself asking for a closer glimpse: *please, please . . . a sight of their faces . . . just one . . .*

But the vision faded, and his dream drifted up from the depths to the surface. And once again, he could feel the aches and pains in his body as he coiled and uncoiled over the large oar. He could hear the black man's deep voice calling effortlessly over and over again: *"Stro-oke . . . stro-oke . . ."*

After perhaps three hours, they shipped oars and waited as another vessel drew alongside them. Akhilleus, with his great height, could peer over the side and see the visitor. But Kirta, dog-tired, preferred to sit and catch his breath, massaging his blistering hands. It was curious, he was thinking: the old knacks came back so quickly. He was now finding that he could with great accuracy determine the approximate time of day by the passage of shadows from one side of the boat to the other. He stretched, yawned, feeling the worn plank beneath his bare behind, twin depressions worn into its polished surface by many pairs of buttocks before his own.

"Huh," Akhilleus said, sitting back down and grinning at him. "They're making a trade with the other ship. They're going to swap some able-bodied men for a good overseer, to replace the man who was killed." The Nubian's speech, in the language of the isles, was really quite free of accent; he

295

sounded like a true Ahhiyawan. Kirta looked at him with interest. What sort of man would he have made, if he had been free? What sort of leader? Chieftain? King? Because there was no doubt in his mind that the big black man had any quality it took to lead men anywhere.

"Well," Kirta said. "That means we'll have to pull harder, I guess. If they're not going to replace the men they'll be trading for the overseer." He looked back to the aft oars: Makhawon was leading two of the starboard oarsmen up onto the deck.

"Doesn't matter to me," Akhilleus said with his nonchalant grin. "You and I could draw this vessel many miles by ourselves. You are a man of much strength, my friend. Not many men could have matched me stroke for stroke that long."

"I'm running out of stamina," Kirta said. "I haven't done this in many years."

"You'll get it back," Akhilleus said. "The oar will kill a weak man, and draw the strength from him as a nurseling draws milk from its mother. To a strong man it feeds strength. You will feel the strength begin to flow into your arms from the oar itself." He clenched and unclenched his mighty hands on the big oar. Then he turned to his diminutive companion. "And you, Argurios? How has the oar treated you?"

"You know how it's treated me," the little man said in a whining voice. "I'm exhausted. I can't make another stroke."

"Listen to him," the big Nubian said. His tone was one of affectionate tolerance. "He's been free riding the whole time. Argurios: did you think I wouldn't be able to tell whether you were actually pulling or not?" His vast, careless shrug dismissed both question and answer. He turned back to Kirta. "But tell me: don't you remember what I'm talking about? From your earlier days on the oar?"

"Somewhat," Kirta said. He crossed his arms and clutched himself by the triceps. They were out of the sun now, and naked and wet from the salt spray. He felt the goose bumps on his arms and shivered a bit. "Actually, I rather wish they'd get back to it and get us moving. At least one doesn't feel cold when one's pulling the oar."

"You're right," the giant said. "Well, what was Makhawon talking to you about back there?"

"He was asking what I used to do for a living," Kirta said. "I told him I was an armorer."

296

"Ahhhh," the black man said. "You won't be an oarsman for long. Well, a pity. I was getting to enjoy your company."

"And I yours," Kirta said. "If he takes me up on deck, I'll see what I can do to get better work for you."

"Hah!" the Nubian said derisively. "Makhawon? He'll see you dead first. I broke his nose for him last time we fought. He's still hurting from it. He had six men hold me down while he beat me with a broken oar. It's not the pain, it's the indignity. He can't stand that a black man did it. His type think black men are an accursed race. Which, I suppose, is about the way my people view him—although I've been away from them so long that I couldn't vouch for the local views and customs anymore."

"Curious thing to think," Kirta said. "Black men, or dark men, rule the whole Nile and half the world. A strange curse, that gives men domination over lands it would take months to march across." He noticed that the Nubian was craning his long neck to look up and over the side. "What's happening?" he asked.

The giant stood up and looked. "I think they've got their man," he said. "He's coming over now. I don't think he was one of the people they captured in the raid—the one they caught you in. He has the air of being a bit more seasoned than that. I think he's been to sea before." He pursed his thick lips. "One of your quiet intense types. Not my favorite, all in all. Although in the long run it doesn't matter. I'll outlast him, as I've outlasted all the rest. He'll keel over in the sun, or get killed in a fight, or get drunk and fall over the side . . . but no, on second thought, this one doesn't look like a drinker."

"You! Blackie! Get your head back down there!" Makhawon bellowed from above. Akhilleus grinned and sat back down. As he did, the new overseer—the man who'd give the oarsmen the stroke, and who'd order them beaten or killed if they rebelled—walked past the end of the pit and Kirta caught his first glimpse of him.

His heart almost stopped. He sat there gaping after the new man, his hands hanging loosely in his lap. He shook his head and bit his lip.

"Here!" Akhilleus said. "You look like a man who's seen a ghost walking. Like a man who's just felt the deathwind blow across his heart."

Kirta didn't answer for a moment. Then he looked the big

297

Nubian in the eye. His face was ashen. "Maybe—maybe you could say both things happened just now," he said. "The new overseer—"

"Yes? Somebody you know?"

"All too well," Kirta said. "His name is Nikos. He's a former slave of mine. And not two seasons ago, I abandoned him to his death. . . ."

IV

After a time, Makhawon appeared at the head of the rowers' pit, fists on hips, a scowl on his face. "All right, you scum," he said. "I've got you some replacements for the missing. You won't have to be pulling for two men every time you haul on the oar. But the first time I hear of any of you leaning on the oar, not pulling his weight, he'll feed the fish within the hour."

He pointed to the end of the rowers' pit. "There they are," he said. The rowers looked back to see a dozen new men file down into the trench and take their places on the benches. "Good, seasoned rowers who can haul all day. The rest of you had better match them, or you're in more trouble than you've ever seen before."

Kirta looked them over. They were "seasoned," all right: naked, brine-soaked, with long oarsmen's muscles. But they hadn't been fed too well, from the looks of them: all the fat—including that needed for sustenance in the winter months to come—had been burned off them by the constant struggle with the sea. He wondered idly—perhaps more than idly—when he and the regulars were to be fed. But he kept silent: that, too, he remembered from his earlier days on the oar.

"Now!" Makhawon said, turning their eyes aft again. "Here is your new overseer." He motioned to a man out of their range of vision. "This is Nikos." Nikos moved into view. He looked them all over—and his eyes changed focus for no more than a blink as he saw Kirta and recognized him. His face bore the same old impassive, unreadable expression Kirta remembered from Nikos's slave days: now, however,

298

Kirta thought he saw in it a coldness he had not seen before. Or was that just his imagination . . . ?

"Nikos was a slave like you," Makhawon said. "He won his freedom rescuing Polydeuces in the raid on Kittim not a month ago. He's a good overseer and a good fighter. He'll probably wind up with a ship of his own one of these days. Polydeuces tells me he gives a good stroke, and he knows the capacity of oarsmen as no other man does. I'd stay on his good side if I were you. After all, when he wins his own ship, he might just decide to buy you . . . if he finds in you any reason for doing so." He scowled at them—and then left Nikos standing on the deck, looking down at them, the drumsticks in his two hands.

Nikos looked them over, his face still expressionless, his impassivity unaffected by the sight of his old master. "You heard Makhawon," he said. "I was a slave like you. I was a slave for years and years." It seemed for a moment that his eye lighted on Kirta—ran up and down Kirta's chattel nakedness, with an especially hard glint in it—for a moment; but then it passed on.

"Until recently," Nikos said. "Then I found freedom. The same can happen to you. I know it hasn't happened often among Makhawon's crew, not in the past at any rate. But he's given me some autonomy. I can recommend men for special treatment if they deserve it. Special treatment like extra rations, or promotion to deck hand status . . . or, in special cases, freedom and full membership in the freedman crew." His eyes went from man to man as he spoke; there was, again, nothing to be read in them at all. "It can happen, but it can only happen to men who pull hard and long—and who fight fiercely when they have to fight."

"You mean they're going to let us fight?" Akhilleus said, astonished. "They'd put a weapon in *my* hand?"

"They might," Nikos said dryly. "Once. To see what you did with it." He looked the big black up and down. "You might decide to use it to kill me, or Makhawon. You wouldn't last long. In the trade, we augmented the ship's complement with a squad of bowmen. You wouldn't look nice with arrows sticking out of you like straws sticking out of a cow turd. You wouldn't feel good, either." He shrugged; his words came out matter-of-factly. "Or you could choose to fight. We'd look on that with favor. We'd look on you with even greater favor if you fought well. For the good fighter, there's freedom ahead. For the better-than-just-good fighter . . . who

299

knows? There may be, some time ahead, not only freedom but a share of the booty we earn. Perhaps even a ship of your own."

"A ship of our own?" a voice called out from the bow seats. "Don't make us laugh too hard, we won't be able to row. . . ."

"Believe or not as you choose," Nikos said in that flat voice. "If you want proof, it stands before you. You can see my slave-brand, and the bar through it. See?" He held up one arm. "But let me tell you: if you believe me, you'll do well to act on that belief. If you do, you'll row like men of bronze. And you'll fight like a pack of demons." He sat down before the drum, the sticks still in his hand. "Now," he said. "Let's try you out. Everyone settled . . . now up oars . . . ready . . . *Stro-oke!*"

But as the oars dipped and the muscles strained, his first call was his last. After that first barked command, he left the stroke to his drum. The sticks in his two hands, he alternated downbeats at a slow, steady rhythm: *one . . . two . . . one . . . two . . .*

Kirta settled into the rhythm easily, feeling the perfect suitability of the tempo Nikos had chosen for the first hard pull from the dead stop. He put his back into the pull and heaved mightily. Out of the corner of one eye, he saw Akhilleus matching him stroke for stroke, his bulging biceps tightening and relaxing with the regularity of a pumping heart.

Now, however, with the boat under way, Nikos gradually increased the rhythm to cruise speed. As the oarsmen settled into the new pulsebeat, Makhawon appeared at Nikos's left, and his scowl turned into a hard grin. "Port rudder!" he bellowed. "Hard to port!" And they felt the ship turn, turn. . . . "Full ahead!" he bellowed. The steersman responded. "Full speed . . . steady as she goes. . . ." Nikos increased the rhythm with a solid pounding of his twin mallets. Now, even the oarsmen could feel the salt spray on the backs of their necks as the galley settled into battle speed.

And now, miraculously, Kirta felt for the first time the phenomenon Akhilleus had told him about: the strength began flowing from the oar into his hands, up his arms. He felt the power coursing through him. His hands tightened around the oar's handle; he felt the powerful wing muscles under his arms bulge with new force.

He turned his head and saw Akhilleus grinning at him. "The islander gives a good beat," he said in a voice unmarked

300

by strain. "I could row all day like this." Then his eye took in Kirta's strong pull at the long oar. "Ah," he said. "You too. It's as I said, isn't it? The power flows up from the sea, through the oar, into your arms."

Kirta didn't answer; but he did find himself smiling at the black giant. As he turned back to his own oar and pulled hard with arms that now seemed tireless, he happened to glance up at Nikos—and found to his surprise that his ex-slave was looking him squarely in the eye as his arms rose and fell over the deep-voiced drum. And again, the expression on Nikos's face was as blank, as unreadable, as a bear's. For the first time an icy wind blew through his heart. *He could have me killed. He could work me to death.* But . . . did Nikos bear him a grudge? Had he, Kirta, unknowingly abused his slave in their years together? More importantly, did Nikos bear him ill will for the scene at the docks at Amnisios, when—however unwillingly—he'd abandoned Nikos to his fate in order to catch Poliwos's boat and escape with Xena?

He looked into the impassive eyes and could find no answers. No answers at all.

Nikos broke off the test run when he had satisfied himself. He stood, put down the drumsticks, and spoke to Akhilleus. "You," he said. "What is your name?"

"Akhilleus," said the black man. "So they call me. You wouldn't be able to say my real name. For that matter I may have forgotten it by now. It doesn't matter. You may call me Akhilleus if you like." His grin was as insolent as ever.

"A good enough name for a strong oarsman," Nikos said. "But I am not fooled. You have not forgotten your real name. You're a proud man, and it matters a great deal to you." He nodded, and fumbled in his garment for something. "As well it might. A man who has forgotten is less than a man. See this?" He held up a shapeless little pebble. "This is from my home earth. I picked it up and put it in my mouth when I was first enslaved and taken away. I have never lost it. If ever I should lose it, I would not know what to call myself. And every one of us who remembers has with him something that is like this stone, even if it's only the memory itself. It's what keeps us from becoming drifters, flotsam on the tide. I won't ask you what your stone is, Akhilleus—but I know you have it with you somewhere."

Kirta looked at Akhilleus. To his astonishment the black man's mouth was closed and his face somber and serious. The giant nodded thoughtfully. Then, himself again, he turned to

Kirta with something like his old grin. "An unusual man," he said. "He reads my mind."

"No," Nikos said. "But I have sat where you sit. Akhilleus: call the stroke for me." And without another word he moved out of their line of vision.

"How do you think they did?" Makhawon asked. He sat in a chair on the upper deck, drinking watered wine. "Am I going to get good work out of them?"

"I think so," Nikos said. "I put them through all the usual changes and maneuvers, and they performed with skill and stamina. I can make a good team of them in a couple of weeks. In a month I could make a racing team of them. You could win money betting on them."

"Hah. And will you?"

"Probably not. There's more money to be made running down a Phoenician trade convoy and picking it clean. Besides—there's the problem of training new lead oarsmen."

"Huh?" Makhawon sat up, looking the cold-eyed islander in the eye. "New lead oarsmen? But I would have thought— the black, and what's his name, the smith—"

"The black is too good to keep on an oar. Anyone can be trained to pull an oar. He's a natural fighter."

"Ah! You're telling me? Why, he broke my nose for me. The last time I threw him in the hold it took half my men—"

"All the more reason to get him out of the hold—and out of the oarsmen's pit as well. Give him some incentive to fight for us, and he'll fight the enemy even better than he's fought us."

"Huh. Trust him with a weapon? I should say—"

"You trust him with an oar. Do you know how much damage a man of his strength can do with an oar?"

"Hmmm. There's merit in what you say. And—I don't like to admit this, but I rather like the big ape. He's got spirit. If he weren't so damned insolent—"

"He won't change, not in that way. But you can still make better use of him than you are right now."

"All right. I'll leave the matter up to you. But what about the other one? I had plans for him—"

"Let's say I—owe him a debt," Nikos said, and the tone of his voice was so startlingly cold that Makhawon shot a quick glance at him. "I've waited long to pay it off. I want him. I'll pay whatever price you name."

"Why—what have you got? If—"

"I haven't anything now. But—look. I'll give you my share of the next raid we make. All of it."

Makhawon motioned to him to sit down. His brow knit. "Gods," he said. "What's your portion?"

"The fiftieth part of the spoils."

"Fiftieth! Why, I get only a seventieth myself, and I'm a ship's captain! Where do you . . . ?" But then his face changed; understanding registered. "Ah. Polydeuces is generous. As I suppose I'd be to a man who did what you did, if I'd been on the receiving end of your loyalty and valor. But—a fiftieth part? Gods! You must want this man a great deal! I gather he's done you ill, eh?"

Nikos reached for the wine bottle, held it high, and, uncorking it, let a stream of red wine flow from the leather bag to his mouth without spilling a drop. "He was my master once," he said simply—and coldly. "You've been a slave," he said. "Wouldn't you give most anything to own your last master, body and soul?"

Makhawon looked at the islander, a strange expression in his eyes. "I might," he said. "I might once, anyhow. Back when I remembered such things better. I've lost some of the ire and the resentment over the years—largely through this stuff." He held up the wine bottle, testing its heft. But as he did, his expression soured. "That's not true," he said. "All it takes is to mention the matter. Then my mind gets to working. My last master once had the skin beaten off my back so badly that I couldn't do anything—sit, stand, lie—without pain for a month. He couldn't have done a better job if he'd taken a knife to me and peeled me as one might peel a plum. And if I had him under my hand right now, for no more than five minutes—why, yes. Yes, I remember. And yes, I know what I'd do."

"Then you agree to my offer?" Nikos said in that dry voice, looking him in the eye.

"Uh—I suppose so." Makhawon looked at him cautiously. "And what will you do? Kill him? Have him tortured? That's an expensive pleasure, for all that one might enjoy it—given the circumstances."

Nikos looked at him for a moment, saying nothing. Then he took another long, thoughtful draught from the wine bottle. He sloshed the wine around in his mouth before swallowing it. "I'm not sure," he said. "My mind is a blank. It's enough to have him, just for now. Time enough for the rest." He looked out to sea—and the expression on his face was, as always, as enigmatic as a basilisk's.

They anchored off a rocky islet south of Samos, in a natural bay that had once been the mouth of a collapsed volcano. The water was as clear as the late afternoon skies; the crew and slaves took turns diving off the stern into the blue water of the caldera. Kirta, breaking the surface after his plunge, looked up into the eyes of Akhilleus, watching him from the ship's deck. "Kirta," the black said. "They want you up for'ard."

Kirta took the black man's outstretched hand and let himself be pulled back onto the deck. The air was chill; dusk was coming on. His naked body, wet from the icy waters of the bay, broke out in goose bumps. "For'ard, you said?"

"Yes." The giant's eyes were concerned, sympathetic. "And . . . Kirta. Watch your step. . . ."

Kirta nodded and padded up the pitched deck. All of a sudden he was acutely aware of his nakedness, of his vulnerability. He was shivering like a half-drowned rat. There was a chill breeze, and the salt water was drying on his body, leaving a briny deposit. His hair hung down in his eyes; feeling miserable, he brushed it aside . . .

. . . and then saw his former slave standing watching him, up in the peaked prow of the vessel. Nikos was warmly dressed against the chill; his hair was neatly arranged. He seemed composed, aloof, at his ease. He looked Kirta up and down. Kirta, clamping down with his back teeth, forced himself to stand erect, to throw his shoulders back, as if he were dressed to meet royalty.

"Kirta," Nikos said. As he did, the last rays of the setting sun fell on his face, and it glowed with a strange red-orange sheen. Kirta shivered in the chill. Aloft, a cold wind sighed through the furled sheets, bunched against the yard.

V

"I used to wonder what I would do if I ever ran across you again," Nikos said. In the fading sunlight Kirta could barely make out his face.

Kirta shivered again. "I often wondered what had happened to you." He blinked, trying to make the adjustment to

304

the sudden darkness. "I might as well have stayed and helped you, for all the good it did me to run."

"Oh?" Nikos said. His face was totally shadowed now. Kirta could make out his outline. "What happened?"

"Xena," Kirta said. "A half-spent arrow from the dock caught her in a vulnerable spot. She died almost instantly."

"Ah," Nikos said, his voice tailing off with a dying fall. "I had a feeling she wouldn't make it. And this freed you to return to your wife and children, then?"

"Freed?" Kirta said. "Look at me. I'm Makhawon's slave. . . ."

"You're *my* slave," Nikos said. There was a trifle more of an edge to his voice. "I purchased you this afternoon."

"Ah," Kirta said. He didn't know what to say.

"You came expensive," Nikos said. "Now we're in reversed positions. I could have you killed. I could kill you myself."

Kirta wished he could see Nikos's eyes. "Was I—was I then so bad a master?" He swallowed. "I'm not being facetious. One doesn't know these things. One doesn't think about them."

"That's the problem, isn't it?" Nikos said. "One doesn't think." He moved forward in the half dark, and Kirta tensed himself, ready for a blow. But the hand that fell on his shoulder fell gently. "Come," Nikos said. "You'll be cold and uncomfortable. And I think you won't have eaten. Come back to my tent and we'll talk."

Kirta followed him aft, and he stood aside as Nikos entered a small tent set up on the aft deck, just forward of Makhawon's larger tent. "Come," Nikos said from within. Kirta entered. Nikos stood before a small table on which he could see wine, bread, cheese. Nikos held out something to him in the flickering light of an oil lamp. "Take this. Rub yourself down. There's a robe on the seat behind you that ought to fit. Then sit here with me and have supper."

Kirta, puzzled, toweled himself down with the rough cloth, wondering what to expect. But he did feel better correctly robed and warm for the first time since his dip in the sea. He sat, taking note of the curious stare that regarded him across the table.

"You asked what kind of master you were," Nikos said, the wine bottle in his hand. He drank and handed the goatskin over. "I hated you at first. I would have hated anyone who stood between me and—and the place I regarded as home." He sat back, his fingertips touching each other. "Home," he

305

said thoughtfully. "We anchored at my home island a week ago. I expected it to be a great experience, a moving experience, peopled with the ghosts of all the people I'd lost or left behind."

Kirta drank deeply—so deeply his head swam. "And—it wasn't as you expected?" he said.

"Kirta," Nikos said, "the thing one leaves behind when one leaves a place is oneself. And the self that I had left there was dead. I was no longer the same person. There was nobody left that I knew. I—" But his voice had a curious catch in it, and he could not continue.

"Nikos," Kirta said. "Forgive me. I failed you, too, didn't I? I could have emancipated you. I could have—"

"And I could free you now. What stays my hand?" Nikos leaned over and took the bottle from Kirta's hand. His eyes were troubled—and Kirta was astonished to see tears in them. "I'll tell you why," Nikos said. "Because we're a couple of fools, just like everyone else. There's a duty lying upon us, a duty to be better men than we are, be we master or slave. But do we do anything about it? Or do we just continue as before, making the same foolish mistakes, being the same fools we were yesterday?" He drank—this time the way a man drinks who intends to get drunk. Then he put the bottle down and motioned toward the table. "Eat," he said. "Eat, for the love of all that's holy. You'll get sick. You can't drink like this on an empty stomach. Eat, damn you!"

Kirta just stared at him. There was already a hurt and vulnerable look on Nikos's face. Him, the master! "Is there—is there something I can do to help?" he said. "I've never seen you like this, Nikos."

"I wanted to kill you," Nikos said, his voice breaking in a sob. "I bought you with that in mind. But now I see you, now I meet you again—Kirta, Kirta, you weren't a bad man. You were preoccupied, forgetful—but you weren't bad. There was much good in you. Particularly at the end, when you'd become aware of yourself. . . ." He reached for the wineskin again. "Something happened to you, the day we destroyed the little fishing town, and you learned the secret of—"

But then he stopped. And the eyes he focused on Kirta now burned with a sudden understanding. "That was it," he said. "That was it after all, wasn't it? You learned the secret you'd spent your life chasing. And that was . . ." His voice trailed off; he looked quizzically at Kirta.

"Ah," Kirta said. He held the sharp knife in his hand, and he looked at Nikos with thoughtful eyes. Then he sliced the cheese before them into rough chunks, and halved the thick rolls. "You know what I learned. That it was all worthless, all of it. It had nothing to do with people. I'd been following some sort of dream, and in order to be true to the damnable dream, I had to be untrue to everyone I knew. You, too, Nikos: I failed you, too, as much as anyone. I probably have no right to ask forgiveness. I—"

"Yes," Nikos said, leaning forward. Again he put a hand on Kirta's shoulder, and again Kirta started; before today, Nikos had never touched his master. But they were not master and slave anymore, were they? Or—but, no, the roles were reversed. "Yes," Nikos said in a tortured voice. "That was it exactly. And—and Kirta. The dream I'd lived for so long, the dream of coming home, that was just as empty as your dream was. Kirta—I *saw* my wife. She couldn't recognize me at all. She had married a rakehell, and she'd turned to wine, and she was old before her time. I looked in her eyes—eyes that I'd dreamed of for years and years—and I could see nothing of what I had loved in her. Because—because, Kirta, I could see in her nothing of myself. It was myself, my own lost self, that I'd been looking for. And when I found it, it meant nothing, because the Nikos who lived then had died a long time ago. . . ." He reached for the bottle again, but Kirta stayed his hand and handed him a chunk of goat cheese. Nikos held it, staring blankly. "Kirta," he said now. "My daughter died in childbirth. It doesn't matter. She would have died that way if I'd been there. Her mother's husband was a wealthy man; he gave her a better marriage portion than I could have provided. Their lives had lost nothing with my disappearance. Nothing but a few memories . . . which faded. They fade as everything fades."

Now it was Kirta's turn to put a hand on Nikos's arm. "I'll tell you what you told me," he said. "You have to eat." But then somehow, the two of them looked in each other's eyes, and Kirta suddenly felt the salt tears rise in his own. He gripped Nikos's arm, watching his once slave, now master, weep uncontrollably like a child.

The moon rose large and full over the islet they'd anchored near. They could hear the crewmen on the spit, singing a bawdy song with hoarse throats. "What can I do with you?" Nikos said at last. "I could free you and set your feet back on the road to—where is it? Padan something or other?"

"Padan-aram. If they're still there. . . ."

"I could do that. But—don't you see? You have a new thing to live for. And it's not your wife and children. Your

307

wife probably won't even remember your face. Your sons probably couldn't care less about you. The world has gone on without you back there. All you'll be doing, going back, will be to break your own heart, learning in Padan-aram the same things I learned on my own isle. No, Kirta. Go forward. You've life left in you to live. . . ."

"Then you're freeing me?"

"Was there ever any doubt? Oh, I cursed you at first, when they picked me off the stones and had me whipped, and when—but none of that matters. When I saw you again, I realized we had more in common than I had against you. I felt sympathy for you. And you bore your slavery, your humiliation, with dignity and grace. I realized that I didn't hate you at all. Forgive? Kirta, there's nothing to forgive. You did your best. Just as I did my best. That's the whole thing about this wretched life, Kirta. All of us—rich, poor, slave and freeman, king and beggar, we're doing the best we can with the situations we inherited. Why, don't you think I'd blamed myself for being taken away, for leaving my wife and child the way I did? But how could I have done otherwise?" He leaned back against the tent pole; there was a look on his face in which Kirta could see the hint of peace. "What use is it to ask myself to be better than I am? I'm a fool. Just as you are. And here you are, torturing yourself with these feelings of guilt over every oversight, every mistake. Can't you see that you're just another fool? One who must come to terms with the fact and accept it? Why waste your life trying to go back and change things? Why . . . ?"

Kirta shook his head slowly from side to side. "You know, my friend, I've *tried* to think things through that way. And the gods alone know how tempting it is. It lets me off the hook, doesn't it? It absolves me of any feeling of responsibility for the kind of world I've helped to create with my foolishness. Oh, yes, I'll admit that I've been a fool—that I still am. But . . . Nikos. What if I *could* do something? Make things better? Give something—I don't know what—to my sons to make up for the neglect they've suffered?"

"How? How, for the love of . . . ?"

"Nikos. My eldest son. I've seen some of his work. It's poor. Oh, not really atrocious, but far below what he should be doing, as a son of mine. Without me to teach him, he must have apprenticed to some hack, and the hack taught him what he knew and that wasn't much. I'm sure Shobai towers over the competition in a backwater like Haran, of course—but for heaven's sake, man, he's a Child of the Lion! He should be an artist, a master craftsman approaching the height of his powers! If I do nothing else, Nikos, I have to find him—yes, and Hadad too; he'll be no better off than his brother—and teach him what I know. . . ."

"Ah," Nikos said. He pursed his lips thoughtfully. "And you're living for this—this family tradition of yours, then? Yes, I can see how that would suggest itself. It has to do with your professional vanity, and—"

"Vanity?" Kirta said. "Is it vanity to—"

"Please! Please! Let's not bandy high-flown sentiments. Not between you and me. We are talking straight, as men who have suffered together. Kirta, let your sons go! They will live out their destinies without you, without remembering you."

"No! No! That's just it! The tradition mustn't die! It's as though my father had passed me a torch that his ancestors had handed down, and I have to keep it lit, because if it goes out . . ."

He let the words trail off. He didn't say anything.

"You see?" said Nikos. "Futility. Vanity. If it goes out, will the sun go out? Will the stars? Will it matter in the slightest to the world? Look—out there." He pointed at the thousands of stars glimmering above the horizon. "Will one of those little pinpoints blink even once if Kirta does not fulfill this mystical destiny of his?"

Kirta stared into the flame of the oil lamp. "All of those things I've been saying to myself, ever since Xena died. But you forget, Nikos. I'm a fool, just as you said I was. And part of my being a fool is continuing to be one. If I accept my past foolishness, am I to reject my present folly? Besides, there's one thing you've forgotten."

"Eh? What could that be?"

"The secret I learned from Turios of Tyre. The secret of smelting the dark metal. The metal that is as hard as the ore that falls from the skies. The metal that would cut through your sword and mine as though they were children's play swords, made of soft wood." His eyes shone in the suffused light of the tent. There was an animated and hopeful look on his face for the first time since they had begun their conversation.

Nikos looked at him. "You—you want to give *that* to your sons. You want to leave it to them, to continue that damned family tradition of yours. . . ." He showed his teeth in a bitterly angry grimace. "Haven't you heard a word I've been saying?"

"Of course I have. But Nikos, Turios of Tyre wasn't the

only man in the world who knew the secret. Nor am I, now that he's dead. He learned it up in Hittite country. And my sons stand in the path of Hittite advancement, the moment the Hittites decide to move south in search of better grazing. They—or any other sort of predator. There was a rumor, back aboard Poliwos's ship. Someone who'd docked at Ugarit told of a great migration from the north—"

"Oh? Of Hittites?"

"No, I don't think so. I think it was from somewhere north of the Valley of the Two Rivers. The man wasn't too sure; he'd heard something second or thirdhand. But . . ."

"Ah. Ah, yes. You want to pass the secret on to your sons, so they can get rich, and—"

"No! No! Don't you see? Whoever arms his men with the new metal will rule the world! And whoever doesn't have it . . ."

Nikos turned to him and looked him in the eye. His expression was one of despair. "All right," he said in a harsh whisper. "Go, then, you damned fool! You're free! Free to do whatever foolish thing occurs to you! Go break your own damned heart and those of all you meet. But remember that I told you first, that I warned you! Vanity! Futility! It's useless, do you hear? Useless!"

CHAPTER TEN

I

"My Lord," said Shobai, bowing deeply. "Shobai of Haran, armorer and Child of the Lion. You wished to see me?"

King Hagirum of Carchemish sat up in his tall seat and looked down at the young man. "I know who you are, Shobai," he said. "Let's not stand on ceremony. Come up here with me. Guard!" he held one hand high. "Wine for the armorer Shobai." He didn't even look to see if his orders were obeyed. He motioned Shobai forward, to the great table on the dais. "Here," he said. "Sit."

Shobai did so, keeping one eye on the dark-browed old man, noting the strength and confidence he still exuded at his age. *What a difference from Shemariah,* he thought. Haran's king was of older and, some said, better blood—but he was king in name only, his every decision or action manipulated or dictated by advisers. This old man wasn't the type to take direction from anybody.

Well, you could tell. The type who insisted on a lot of formality in his dealings with underlings usually had no other way of compelling respect. This man dispensed with ceremony as though it had no purpose at all but to waste his time.

"Now, my friend," Hagirum said. "You say you've finished your work here? That was fairly quick."

"Almost, sir," Shobai said. "The bulk of it is done. What I have set up is a network of armsmakers, all operating from patterns I gave them and all ultimately subordinate to a single supervisor. I've taught your people the systems of assembly. From here on, they can do the work for themselves. There's not a great deal left that you need me for, sir. I worked for a while with the man who's been designing your fortifications—"

"Zuhadiim. Yes."

"Yes, sir. Well, Zuhadiim incorporated some of my suggestions for strengthening the ramparts and making it easier for the bowmen to shoot from cover."

"Ah, good. Well, then. You'll be heading back to Haran? Or perhaps you've other commissions—in Ugarit? Aleppo?"

"I don't know, sir. I hadn't thought about it. Perhaps I'll go back to Haran and await new assignments. I've been working hard here, and I could use a little recreation."

"I see." Hagirum looked up at the guard who brought them bottled wine and a single golden cup. "Thank you," he said. "You can put it down here." He filled the cup and passed it to Shobai. "You first, my friend."

Shobai took the cup, saluted him, drank. He suppressed a smile at the king's mastery of the etiquette that hid the fact that he, Shobai, would taste the king's wine first, and die in his place if someone had poisoned it.

He paused before drinking again and handing the cup back. Where was he going, after all, once the job had been completed and his pay arranged? Would he really go back to Haran? To a straying wife, and—

"Your expression changed a bit for the worse there," the king said, accepting the cup. "Why? Is something wrong with the wine? Because if—"

"Oh, no, sir," Shobai said. "No, indeed. A—an unpleasant thought crossed my mind. Personal business. Family matters. You know."

"Ah, family," the king said. "That reminds me. I didn't know you had a brother."

"Yes, sir," Shobai said, surprised. "His name is Hadad. He's a little younger. Why?"

"He's going to be a rich man, that's why. You should hear what Ibalum of Haran has been telling me. The boy's a genius, he says. Ibalum has signed him to an exclusive contract—"

"Contract, sir?" Shobai said, thunderstruck. "Surely he must be talking about some other Hadad, sir. My brother—contract for what, sir?"

"Why, for sculptures! Golden ornaments! Votive medals and figurines! Surely you've heard?"

"Uh—no, sir, I'm afraid I haven't." Shobai sat back and looked at the king, flabbergasted. Hadad? *His* Hadad? Hadad, the feckless cripple, the failure? "I—I still can't believe you're talking about the same person. When I left Haran—"

"But that was some time back. And—I suppose you and your brother don't correspond much?"

"No, sir. He lets me know when my mother's ill. But other than that—" Then he stopped. There *had* been a tablet from Hadad in the last parcel of mail from Haran. But he'd tossed it aside, meaning to read it later. And then he'd forgotten. "I can't understand, sir," he said. "When I left Haran, my brother was a bottom-level artisan in a second-class bazaar, doing little clay figurines for the temple at piecework rate. How could he attract the attention of a powerful man like Ibalum?"

"Well, I don't know just how they managed to meet. But meet they did. And Ibalum has been singing the young man's praises ever since. He took a trip back to Haran a couple of weeks ago, and when he returned to Carchemish, he could talk of nothing but your brother. He says he has contracts for work from merchants in Aleppo, Byblos, Ugarit, Tyre. . . ."

"Well, I'm glad for him," Shobai said, a bit lamely. "Hadad was slow to get started in life, but perhaps everything will work out for him in the end."

"Work out? He'll wind up richer than you are, I'll wager, if a man like Ibalum gets behind him and pushes. Speaking of which, young man, I've arranged for credit for you in the sum we discussed previously—and there's a small bonus for you as well, thanks to the reports I've heard about your work here. Do you want payment in gold, or—"

"Oh, no, sir," Shobai said. "If credit could be transferred to my accounts in Haran—"

"Done. Stay in touch with us, will you? We may have further need of you. I'm sure we will, if the reports I've heard about the nomads are accurate. I'll be taking no chances. You can tell what I said to Shemariah if you see him. Tell him Hagirum of Carchemish thinks he's in great danger."

"Yes, sir." Shobai kept his face carefully impassive. Hagirum's fears were constantly derided in his own military encampment, and several officers' wives he'd slept with had told him their husbands thought the old man mad. Shobai decided he wasn't ready to concur; there was good sense in this tough old lion. Even if he did seem to tend to err on the side of overprotectiveness . . .

Just then a thought struck Shobai. "On second thought, sir, if my credit could remain in Carchemish . . . I've been thinking of setting up a separate office here, as a point of departure for trips to cities along the Great Sea's coast. Perhaps I could use my earnings here as seed money."

"Splendid. Just as you wish. I'll give the orders. And I approve. Young man, you're beginning to think like a man of affairs, of business. If I were you, with your gift, I'd start taking on apprentices right about now. Bind them to you—but let the journeymen work under your name in the various cities. It'll make you a rich man before you're thirty. That's how Ibalum began."

Yes! Yes! Shobai thought to himself as he strode down the broad steps of Hagirum's palace to the busy street below. He'd keep a separate set of accounts here in Carchemish. Why should he share the money he'd worked so long for with an unfaithful wife, one who'd stoop to playing around with a common soldier, one who'd ...

Hmmm, he thought. What was Haran, after all, but the place he'd used for a base of operations ever since his apprenticeship? Did he need Haran now? And if he could start building up credit here in Carchemish, and squirreling away sums under Anat's nose and sending them to his accounts in Carchemish ...

Yes! The thought struck him with great force—so great that he paused in the middle of the street, and traffic had to reroute itself around him. Why should he even bother to return to a town where his wife had been unfaithful, making him look ridiculous? What did he have there? A madwoman of a mother who didn't even recognize him half the time because he wasn't still the fourteen-year-old she remembered? A brother who ... ?

A brother. He smiled wryly, and when he searched his heart for his true feelings, he was surprised to find a little bit of pride there. Hadad! Well, who would have thought it? Hadad, the eternal loser, the poor wretch who gave his money away to the first person who had a sadder story to tell than his own?

He moved aside as a butcher drove a laden pack-ass past him, then continued down toward the bridge that ran across the river. Standing by the retaining wall that kept the spring floods from inundating the town, he thought to himself: Hadad? Hadad a rich man? Hadad a famous sculptor? He could hardly believe it, but Hagirum had been quite explicit about it being his Hadad, his own younger brother. And the protégé of Ibalum—the richest and most respected merchant of fine goods in all the lands below the Hittite border! Ibalum, whose name was known at the court of the great king of Egypt!

314

Well, that settled something else. He needn't worry about his mother if he just decided to pick up and leave—leave Haran, leave Anat, leave all of them. Leave, once and for all, the embarrassing rumors that were going around, even this far away, about Anat and her whoring ways, about—

He suddenly clenched one huge fist. Come to think of it, he hadn't heard anything from Kihilum, had he? He suddenly straightened up and began walking, very fast, toward the Thieves' Quarter.

It took six inquiries before he located the one-eyed broker. When he did, he was a little surprised to see the man with the eyepatch try to avoid him by slipping away into the crowd at the little bazaar. Shobai pursued him through the knot of people and grabbed him roughly by the arm. "Kihilum!" he said.

The one-eyed man turned his ruined face toward Shobai. "Ah," he said. "Master Shobai. I—I thought it was someone else. I'd meant to send a messenger to you. . . ."

Shobai, his hand still on the man's garment, pulled him aside into an alley. "Look," he said. "Nobody's paying any attention. We can talk here. Why are you avoiding me? I thought you'd be coming after your second payment by now. . . ." Then, seeing the evasiveness in Kihilum's one eye, he stopped and held the man at arm's length. "Don't tell me—your men didn't get him. They didn't do anything about Reshef, did they?" He shook the one-eyed man, and his voice came out in an angry half-whisper between clenched teeth. "Tell me!" he said. "Tell me, damn you, or—"

"I—they got to him," Kihilum said. "I got word only the first of this week. They caught him on the face. A big, ugly scar across his face. He'll be marked for life. But—"

"But? But what? Get it out, damn you. Don't you hold anything back."

"I—I'm trying to tell you. He proved too much for them. He killed them both. That's the word I heard from someone who'd been there, who'd heard the talk in the bazaars. And—"

"And what? What?" He shook the broker again.

"I—I'm afraid one of them talked before he died. Talked to Reshef, I mean." He gulped and rasped out the rest. "He . . . told him who had sent them." The broker cringed, held up one arm to shield his face from Shobai's red rage. "Please!" he said in a whining voice. "I didn't tell them! I didn't! They must have figured it out for themselves! It was all over the bazaars there that it was your wife that he was

315

playing with. He must have forced the truth from them. People tell me they were cut to pieces."

"*You!*" Shobai said, the anger boiling up in him. He picked the broker up by his garment and slammed him against the wall of the nearest building. "You bungled the whole thing, didn't you? Now he knows—and now he'll be waiting for me when I return to Haran!"

"Yes, yes, I didn't have the heart to tell you. I thought: let him keep the second half of the payment. Let him—"

"Second half? And you haven't even earned the first? Why, you little—"

"No! Please! Don't hurt me! Don't hurt me!"

But Shobai had released him; dropped him to the ground. His expression was one of mixed rage and disgust. He spat once into the street's dust beside Kihilum and strode away into the crowd.

Shobai pounded his right fist into his left palm. *The sniveling, cowardly bastards!* he thought. They'd ruined him. Ruined him! He was now the butt of gutter jokes in the bazaars, a many-horned cuckold whose wife was cheating on him with a damned little army opportunist of no family, no background . . . he'd kill her! He'd . . .

Ah, but then what? The penalty for adultery was death, to be sure; but how many of her relatives in Haran could scare up equal charges against him? How much work would he lose there if Anat's brothers organized their not inconsiderable political stock in the city and opposed him, not in the open courts, but in the court of Shemariah?

No! No! The best thing was to leave, just as he'd been thinking of doing. Leave her with the money, the possessions he'd left in Haran. He could always make more elsewhere. After all, he had the foundation of a fortune right here in the credit accounts of Hagirum of Carchemish. It would be no problem turning that into a fortune much larger than the one he'd amassed in Haran. After all, Carchemish was much closer to the middle of things, with its easy connections on the trade routes to everywhere of consequence. From here he could go to Ugarit, or perhaps even one of the cities farther south—Byblos, Tyre, Arvad. Who knew what sort of custom might come his way, working in the seaports where people from every nation around the Great Sea came to call? Why, rumor had it that ships from Egypt, from Kittim, from the far-flung island domain of great Minos of Crete called at

316

these ports. What better place to make his name known the world wide?

But then another thought struck him. Yes, yes—it was so clear! He smiled, and the smile broadened. Then his eyes narrowed in bitter amusement. He'd show the bastards—all of them. The first thing he'd do—before going anywhere else—was ride north and offer his services to the Shepherd Kings. They'd certainly be able to appreciate his work. They'd have use for a good armorer. And with all the conquering they'd done recently, they'd be a sure thing to be as rich as Minos of Crete by now. That was it! He'd ride north in the morning. . . .

II

For hours he stalked through the city streets, his mood growing darker and more defiant as he elbowed people out of his way. *All right, all right,* he thought. *I'll show them. I'll—*

Yes, it was a time for cutting loose. Cutting loose from all of them. Beginning anew . . .

Rounding a corner, he ran into a pushcart and sent both the cart and its owner sprawling. Apples, pears scattered into the street. Shobai, his mind elsewhere, hardly broke step. The tradesman called plaintively after him; his call fell on deaf ears. Shobai's sandals slapped against the stones; his thoughts pounded away at his throbbing temples. He came into his own street now; tradesmen and familiars of the neighborhood saluted him as he passed. He paid no attention to them. His eyes focused briefly on the stairs that led to his top-floor apartment; as for the registering of any awareness on his consciousness, they might well have been blind as any beggar's.

His long legs took the stairs two at a time. As he reached the top he noticed his door was slightly ajar. That damned servant girl again! How many times had he told her to keep the door closed? He kicked the door open. "Asherah!" he bellowed. "Damn it, can't you learn to—"

Then he stopped. The girl, sprawled on his bed, sat up,

clutching the coverlet to her bare breasts. From the tumbled mess of sheets on the bed not two, but three bare feet extended toward him. *Three?* He bellowed with rage. As he did, the owner of the third foot slipped out from under the covers and reached for a garment on the floor.

"Please," the girl said. "I—I didn't know you'd be back this soon—it wasn't his fault—I—"

"You—you slut!" Shobai said in a strangled voice. "And *you*, you slimy bastard—get out right now, or I'll ..." The man in the corner struggled into his robe, half tied it, and edged toward the door, keeping the maximum possible distance from Shobai. Shobai, seeing some hesitation in the man's furtive movements, raised his big arm; the man scuttled out the door, still trying to tie his robe around him.

"Asherah!" Shobai said between clenched teeth. "How could you? When I've treated you so well, and ..." His hands clenched and unclenched.

She had begun to recover her composure, though. Now she stood, skinny and naked, and unhurriedly worked her way into her own robe. "Treated me so well, you say? Worked me half to death is more like it. And then you had the nerve to try to bed me whenever you came home some nights and didn't do as well as usual with the officers' wives. Had the nerve to—"

"You! You damned insolent—"

"*Try* to bed me is right," she said, resentment souring her tone. "No wonder you're not doing so well with the rich folks' wives lately. Can't get it up, can you? And can't keep it up when you get it up, ever since—"

"You! Shut up!"

"Go ahead, hit me! That's all you can do with a woman, isn't it? Ever since you found out your wife was unfaithful to you back in Haran? You—"

"Damn you!" he said in a much diminished voice. "How—how did you find that out? How?"

"Oh, for the love of ... Do you really think you have any secrets around here? Or that anyone who's ever fallen afoul of your high and mighty ways is going to hesitate a moment about passing along a rumor that he hears in the bazaars?"

"You mean ... ?"

"Yes, you fool! Half the town knows you're wearing horns the size of a gazelle's by now. Heaven knows, your little wife seems to have taken few enough pains to hide it from anyone back home. Maybe what she really wants is for everyone

318

there to find out—everyone. Maybe that's her way of paying you back for—"

"But I've given her everything—everything she ever asked for. I've made her rich and sought after ... thanks to me she's well placed in the city."

"And you think that's enough? You think that's what a woman wants? When you spend every waking hour away from her either cheating on her with people like me or scheming about how to get into some rich woman's—"

"Stop! Stop!" he held his hands over his ears. "Get out! Out!"

"You owe me money," she said. "For the past three weeks. Not to mention—"

"There's money in the jar by the door! Take it! And get out!" He shut his eyes to wall himself away from her insulting smile. As she slammed the door behind her, he sank down on the chair beside his disordered bed and, shaking, gave way first to curses, then dry sobs, then to helpless, shameful tears.

The rays of the late sun crept into his window; the shadows lengthened. He still sat there, staring at the wall. The anger had passed; in its place was a hateful feeling of hopelessness, of—yes, impotence. Impotence! Him, Shobai!

She'd been right, of course. It *had* begun with the first knowledge of Anat's treachery, her sluttish and shameless behavior. He'd had two assignations spoiled by his incapacity, and—gods! he thought. Was the word getting around about that, too? If it was, he was ruined as much here as he was in Haran. . . .

Haran. He'd already decided he couldn't possibly return there. Not only was there the absolute assurance that he'd be the laughing stock of all parts of society, from the royal court down to the lowliest bazaar ... there was also the unspeakable Reshef to deal with. And Reshef, knowing now what he knew, wouldn't be held back by the need to challenge Shobai openly, where Shobai might have a chance against him. He could, without the smallest twinge of conscience, hire assassins to do the deed for him. (After all, hadn't Shobai tried to do the same to him?)

And here! Here in Carchemish he was worse than a cuckold. He was a cuckold who died on the doorstep with the wives of some of the most powerful men in the city; women who gossiped with one another—and whose servants passed the gossip along! And of course, now, Asherah would spread the news of his failures with her—to everyone who hadn't already heard. . . .

He shook his head bitterly, shamed, degraded, feeling less than the lowliest coward in town. Him, Shobai . . .

But just then his eye fell on a little pouch on the table beside him. Oh, yes. Hadad's letter. Idly, he reached for it, shook out into his palm the tablet it contained. His eyes strained to read the cuneiform inscription:

Esteemed brother Shobai:
I hope this finds you prosperous and well. All of us here are so proud of you, so famous that kings from foreign courts call for your services.

Hadad, Shobai thought. *If you only knew how I feel just now.* He read on:

The most wonderful thing has happened to me. Ibalum the Merchant has given me a contract and says he intends to make a rich man of me. Me, Hadad! I still can't believe it. But he says he has already taken orders for enough work to keep me busy until year's end. And you wouldn't begin to believe the prices he says he'll be getting for my work.

Shobai's broad shoulders shook with another dry sob. For some reason his heart, already torn apart by the emotions of the past few hours, seemed ready to break now with remorse and shame. He heard in his mind the guileless young voice of his younger brother—his own flesh and blood, whom he'd neglected so long, who loved him so transparently and who'd never had an unkind word for him in all his young life. He wept tears of shame and self-pity from his eyes and read on:

And Shobai, I'm in love. The most wonderful girl has come into my life. Her name is Danataya, and she's the sweetest and most loving person I've ever met. She's beautiful, and she loves me. I didn't think anyone was ever going to love me the way women love other men.

Love, Hadad? How could anyone not love you? With your warm and generous heart and thoughtful ways? How could I,

*the seed of the same seed that made you, have neglected you
all these years? In my damned swinish self-centeredness, how
could I have forgotten you? Abandoned you? Left you, in
your shabby poverty, to care for our mother while I spent my
riches on idle things, on show, on foolishness . . .* The tears
were flowing freely now. He continued:

She isn't going to come to me with a rich dower. But that
doesn't matter. I'm going to be well off enough, Ibalum
says, to do without that. She's an orphan, but her father
was a great man with the army once: a captain named
Nahum.

Nahum? Why, his father—their father—had done work for
Nahum once! Why, sure! A fine soldier, Kirta had said. But
Hadad had been too young to remember. Perhaps Hadad
didn't really remember their father at all. Perhaps he remembered him only in bits and snatches, and had patched together
a shared memory out of his own fragments and of Shobai's
and Tallay's spoken reminiscences.

Mother is all right. She continues to slip away into the
old memories, and I find it harder and harder to bring
her back to herself. Maybe I shouldn't try anymore. The
old memories seem to be happier for her than recent
ones. She seems to have gotten lost back when we were
boys, when you were first starting your apprenticeship.

Yes, she'd be going back to the last time they'd been a
family together, a family that shared and cared. That had
been the point where he, Shobai, had started dreaming his
own dreams, dreams that didn't include his shabby, prematurely aging mother and his awkward-looking, crippled little
brother. No wonder she tried to escape from her present
grubby reality to the fantasy of being a mother with two sons
again, two sons who loved her and cared for her and looked
after her. Because what did she have now? What had she had
all these years when Shobai, the one who'd gotten the education, had deserted the two of them and left them to struggle
by on Hadad's feckless, untutored scratchings in the dirt of
the bazaars? What had she had while he, Shobai, had risen in
the city's meaningless social circles and squandered, often, in
an evening's entertainment enough money to keep Tallay and
Hadad in comfort for an entire winter's season?

Shobai, I'm so happy I wonder if I've ever been happy before in my whole life. If this is what it feels like, I don't think I have been. I hope this finds you happy and well, too. And I hope your work brings you home soon so I can embrace you, dear brother, and introduce you to my darling Danataya. Your affectionate and admiring brother, Hadad.

Shobai heaved a huge sigh, and the tears came again in a great flood. His shoulders shook with shame and pain and self-loathing. There was in this, too, the first stirring in many years of a love he'd forgotten he had ever felt: a strong and protective love for the younger brother whose whole portion, whose life he'd stolen so callously. The simple, warm-hearted young brother who had smiled guilelessly while the other children called him "cripple"—yes, and worse names, too—until Shobai had waded into them and pounded them with fists and feet and left them with lumps to remember him by.

Oddly, there was little feeling for his mother in his present surge of confused and muddled emotions. How could one care for a woman who'd gone mad, who'd retreated into a fantasy world of long ago? But Hadad—Hadad was something else again. It was too late for Tallay. All the love he could give her now would be wasted, like water spilling on a salt desert. She was beyond any help he could send her.

But Hadad . . .

Hadad. How could he make it up to Hadad? How could he make up for years of neglect and beastliness? Of carelessness, thoughtlessness, mindless cruelty? Impulsively, he reached out now for a soft clay tablet, a stylus. He'd write to Hadad, tell him the thoughts that were running through his mind. Congratulate him on his newfound good fortune and on his finding love at last. Open his heart to his brother. . . .

But then he put aside the tablet and the stylus. What was the use? Would Hadad need it now? Would Hadad need *him* now? Now that all his youthful wishes were coming true? No, it was too late, too late, as it was for Tallay. When the moment for reconciliation with Hadad had passed, he'd been looking the other way. Now—now who needed him, Shobai? Who wanted him? *Look: For the first time one of Hadad's letters omits the ritual phrase: "Anat sends her love." Why? Because Hadad has broken with Anat, most likely—and refuses to cover for her anymore. And how long has great-*

hearted Hadad been lying for her—Anat, who never wrote me a letter in all our life together?

He picked up Hadad's tablet again and threw it from him. Then he wished it back in his hand. Too late, too late as always. The tablet smashed against the wall, smashed into a hundred pieces. And smashed all healing trace of the magical draught of love and forgiveness Hadad had sent him.

III

The quarter was one that Shobai had not entered before. He might well have avoided it tonight as well, except for its very remoteness from his usual haunts. Now—now of all moments—he wanted obscurity, a decent obscurity among strangers who did not know him, did not know his name, and most of all did not know the shameful tale of his wife's open and flagrant defiling of his marriage bed. (How, he kept asking himself, could the news have traveled so quickly from Haran to Carchemish?)

Now, under cover of darkness, he sought out this remote district as one might seek out a desirable neighborhood. It was old, shabby, distinctly dangerous. Anyone without Shobai's great size and obvious physical confidence would have been ill-advised indeed to enter the quarter without some form of protection.

Tonight, however, Shobai's air of confidence was illusory indeed. The dark mood that had come upon him had had disastrous consequences for every aspect of his mind—and his body as well. Now, his great shoulders were slumped, his face twisted into a grimace of self-loathing.

Earlier, shortly after the dusk, he had wandered into a tavern in the professional quarter—a place where he had friends and acquaintances. There had been a dancer there, a hot-eyed, buxom little thing with breasts like ripe pears and a dimpled rear end and—well, most of all a roving eye. One which looked the audience over as she danced and stripped, one flashing movement at a time. Finding Shobai's big and well-proportioned body attractive, she focused on him alone. He hadn't felt in the mood, but out of habit he'd let her

323

sweet-talk him into going back upstairs with her after her dance was over. Her own excitement had been greater than his from the first; she'd been hot-blooded, passionate, her sweaty little body smelling deliciously of musk . . .

. . . and, well, there it was. It had ended before it had begun. Her disappointment had become indignation, and her displeasure had been vented at the top of her lungs. He'd crept down the stairs with her yelling at him about his caponish incapacity, of his eunuchlike inability to deliver what his actions had promised. As he slunk out into the crowd, he'd spotted several of his friends, looking at him, hiding amused smiles behind their hands. . . .

He shuddered at the memory. Now! He had to get out of Carchemish now, before he disgraced himself one more time, before he had to face one more knowing smirk! But of course, there wasn't any place to go at night; the great gate of the city was closed and closely guarded, and there was no way to quit the hateful streets of the city before dawn. And he knew—knew for certain—that sleep would elude him again as it had eluded him for several nights in a row. It was no use going back to the apartment, to lie tossing and turning in covers already befouled by his former servant and her grubby lover. . . .

Ahead a door opened; light spilled out into the dusty street, and with it the raucous sounds of a rustic band: the twanging of harplike citharas, the reedy sound of an out-of-tune shawm, the throbbing of a drum. Men's voices, bawling a smutty song. As he watched, a pair of beefy hands appeared, holding a man who'd had too much to drink. The hands raised the drunk well off the ground and tossed him halfway across the alley. " . . . and don't come back!" a voice bellowed in a rude country accent. The door half closed; a beam of light from within still lay across the dirty street.

Very well; that was his kind of place—tonight. Shobai lurched forward toward the light, on leaden legs. When had he slept last—slept long and well, without terrible dreams that woke him in a cold sweat, muttering to himself? He wasn't sure. But—well, he'd tried everything else so far. Perhaps it was time to see what drink could do to chase away the demons that haunted him night and day. . . .

He pushed his way in the door, blinking at the light. The smell inside the place was repellent: the reek of unwashed bodies mingled with the vile breaths and the noxious farts of perhaps half a hundred inebriated men of the lower classes, and over all these lingered the sour and sickening smells of stale palm wine and fresh vomit.

He conquered his rising gorge and elbowed his way to a place at a table, shoving another man out of his way to sit. The man thus displaced snarled at him—and then took note of Shobai's imposing bulk and, prudently, put distance between him and the young armorer.

"What'll you have?" said the burly attendant, turning a hoglike face toward him—a face crisscrossed by scars and pockmarks, a face missing one eye.

"Uh . . . palm wine," Shobai said. "Bring me the jar." He tossed a coin on the table. The coin rang loud and clear; faces perked up, looked his way. Faces filled with cupidity and greed, faces that appraised him, this man who tossed gold about with such prodigality—and calculated the chances of separating him from more of it by more direct means. Shobai tried to stare them down; but his manner lacked its usual authority. No eye turned hastily away from his. Indeed, he fancied he could read disdain in several of the faces, ranging from insolence to outright contempt.

"Right you are," said the proprietor, picking up the coin. "Here, you scum—make way for the gentleman here."

"Uh—that's all right," Shobai said. "And—set up a round for the table, will you? On me." He tried to smile. The faces only regarded him with the curious mock-toleration one might use with a madman.

Once, long ago, he'd known how to handle these types. As a boy he'd made his way among them, lived with them, fought with them—but he'd lost the knack. He'd become something apart from them, and he'd lost the common touch. His attempt now to bridge the gap between them had only alienated them further than before. Nervously, he awaited the return of the proprietor with the big jug in his hands and the bowl perched atop it.

"Here," he said. "Me first." He poured into his bowl and drank deeply. It was meant as a bravura gesture; but Shobai, unused to heavy drinking, swallowed wrong and spluttered. The men around him guffawed. He wiped his lips and poured again. "Now," he said. "All of you—drink up! Drink hearty."

They crowded around him, holding their own bowls forward. Shobai poured; already feeling those first drinks, he slopped the raw stuff onto the table and the floor, and onto his own garments. He laughed raucously above the din. The more gross the evening got, the better. Perhaps in this loud tavern camaraderie there was decent oblivion, and at the end of it the drunken sleep he craved. . . .

Sure enough, forgetfulness came as quickly as his money went. He won a dozen arm-wrestling contests, his huge forearm easily developing enough leverage to outmaneuver the knotted muscles of the shorter, less rangily built men who contended with him. He even arm-wrestled the stocky proprietor and won another jar of vile-smelling, potent palm wine, which he promptly shared with the men around him. In the early morning hours, the night shift of the city guard came off duty, and a dozen soldiers shouldered their way into the thinning crowd of the tavern, ready for trouble.

Shobai was in the proper mood. "Look," he croaked in a wine-slurred voice. "Look at the popinjays in their peacock finery! Are they going to a fight or a ball?" He laughed loudly at his own joke.

The soldiers were unarmed; it was a city law. But their sword-belts bore heavy brass buckles. Off came the belts, most of them to be wrapped around gnarled knuckles with the buckles showing. One of them, however, whirled in the air around its owner's head—and lashed out suddenly, catching Shobai a sharp blow over the eye, a blow that brought blood. Shobai, thoroughly drunk now for the first time in his life, roared with rage and charged the lot of them, alone. The men who had been drinking with him, pleased, looked at each other for a blink's duration—then they dived into action just behind him.

Shobai caught one soldier with a huge fist under the eye; the man staggered back into a row of jars and scattered them as he sprawled on the floor. Another man dug a fist into Shobai's rock-hard gut—and howled with pain, having sprained his wrist. Shobai's big arm went around another man's neck and pinned him, as his other fist pounded the man's face. Then he released his prisoner just in time to evade a flying swan dive at him by a soldier who'd climbed atop a table. Shobai let out a loud laugh and picked up a wine bowl, miraculously unbroken still, and drank it dry before tossing it contemptuously into another soldier's already bloody face. Then he gave a further roar and charged into a pair of the enemy, head down, his giant shoulders catching both men amidships and throwing them against the back wall. . . .

In the end, only a few eyes peered out from the dark places

against the far walls: eyes that belonged to noncombatants who'd prudently managed to avoid getting involved. And in the middle of the room there were only Shobai, weaving drunkenly, and the one-eyed, thickset proprietor of the bar. "You!" the man with the mutilated face said. "You started all this! You'll pay for all the damage, or I'll—"

"You'll *what?*" Shobai said, his voice hoarse and harsh now. He scowled at the owner, trying to get his bulky figure into focus. His expression gave him the appearance—however deceptive it may have been—of a man trying unsuccessfully to master a black rage. The proprietor wavered. Shobai, still trying to focus his eyes, bellowed again, wordlessly. The one-eyed man retreated. Shobai, weaving, picked up a still-unbroken jar and drank from its chipped lip. The wine ran down his jaw and neck and stained his garment. Then, he swung the jar around his head and shied it at the wall, where it smashed into many fragments. The last drops of wine ran down the wall below the point of impact.

"Here!" Shobai bellowed, his eyes still out of focus. "Doesn't anyone else want to fight?" He scanned the thin line of pairs of eyes, off in the far corner. He blinked and finally picked out the dark forms. "Nobody wants to fight," he said. "Suppose enough fighting for tonight. Time to go home. Home to bed . . ."

But as he stood there, trying to get his balance, one of the pairs of eyes resolved into a figure, a figure who stepped quietly out of the dark. "You, sir," the man said. "You're quite a fighter. I could make a lot of money on you."

"Money?" Shobai said. "Who needs money? Got plenty of money. Richest man here, I'll wager. Richest man here. Don't need fight for money. Fight for fun. Fun!"

"I understand," the man said. "But what if one were to show you a way to make even more money? Not fighting. Leading fighters." He began to speak again, but Shobai broke in.

"Fighters?" Shobai scoffed. "Don't make me laugh. Fools. All of them. Fools." He clutched at his throbbing head, conscious for the first time that the many blows he'd absorbed had given him a headache. "Ahhh. Got to go outside. Get fresh air. Wash at the well. . . ."

"Certainly," said the man with the quiet voice. "Here, I'll hold the door. The well's just down there." He made way for Shobai and, one arm under Shobai's, guided the younger man's faltering steps down the dark street. "Here, sir. Don't trip here, now . . . watch the step down. . . ."

He even drew the full bucket up from the well and handed it to Shobai. "Here, you'll want to wash the blood off your head."

"You," Shobai said, after he'd splashed his face and hair, "who are you? And what sort of leader of fighters sits back and watches a brawl? Eh?" He searched the man's face for expression and found none. The face was bearded, impassive, noncommittal.

"I'm a—traveler. I have business here—and in other cities around."

"Oh." Shobai drank, then filled his mouth with water, sloshed the liquid around in his battered mouth, and spat it out into the street. "Well, I'll be traveling myself as soon as it's light. Shake the dust of this town from my shoes." He stood up, threw his shoulders back. He'd regained some of his self-esteem in the fight; at least *that* was something he could do well now. "I'm an armorer," he said. "I just finished a job for the city. I'm heading north to look over these nomads and their Shepherd Kings, the ones who're—well, you know—raising all the hell up to the northeast of here."

"I know who you're talking about," the man said. "You propose to offer your services to them? For pay?" His voice had an added edge of interest now.

"Yes," Shobai said. "Agh! What a taste in my mouth. Well, that'll teach me—Yes, that's what I was going to do. If I can figure out how to get through to them. On the other hand, I should think they wouldn't be hard to find."

"Not hard to find, no," the man said. "But finding the right man among them is another thing. Look, my young friend. You say you're leaving in the morning?"

"Yes—maybe after an hour or so of sleep."

"Very well. But it just so happens I might be able to help you make your contact."

"Contact?" Shobai said. He looked the man up and down: undistinguished, neither rich nor poor, neither fat nor thin. "What do you mean?"

"I mean—I have some dealings, just now, with the man you want to meet. The proper man to speak to if you're thinking of—offering your services. I happen to know he could use a man like you. Yes, very much so. Of course, the matter of pay is up to you. You look like a man who can do his own bargaining."

"Oh? Yes, yes. But—this man you're talking about. What's his name? And where would I find him?"

"Shhh. Please. The streets have ears." The man drew

closer. "He's encamped a day's march north of here, on the fringe of Hittite country. And I virtually guarantee he'll be glad to see you. An armorer? He'd been hoping to strike a bargain with the Hittite smiths, but they're proving hard to deal with. Too argumentative."

"If he has me, he'll need no Hittites," Shobai said. "But, how do I get to him? And—you didn't tell me his name."

"I'll take you, if you wish," the man said simply. "And the name? The name is Manouk. . . ."

CHAPTER ELEVEN

I

The fifty days of harvest came and passed, and only scattered late wheat crops remained in the tilled fields below Haran. Now, the focus of the growers' lives turned to the vineyards on the slopes as the early vintage grapes were gathered and pressed. The heat came on slowly but steadily; husbands and wives, seeking respite from the torrid evenings, brought their bedding out upon the rooftops of their houses in the better quarters of the city. The soil underfoot became parched and impacted; the last traces of subsoil moisture evaporated. The surfaces of the once-rich fields turned to dust, and eddying dust devils swirled in the air.

And still the influx of the refugees from the north and east continued, and the resources of Haran, already stretched in the effort to feed more than its native population, now reached the point of exhaustion. The dispossessed flocked to the fields to work in the harvest and on the threshing floors, displacing native labor, taking shares of the crops that would ordinarily have gone to the poor of Haran.

Yet somehow, the city continued to absorb the migrants; somehow, the easy-going citizens kept the peace, and Haran continued to extend the hand of charity to the starvelings of the steppes. The wheat harvest miraculously managed to provide enough food to avert famine in the town, and the grape harvest proved fat and profitable, even allowing for export to other cities in return for commodities not normally produced in bulk in Padan-aram. The fig trees groaned with provender, and the boughs of the olive trees bowed low with fruit.

And still the refugees poured into the little city—daily, in increasing numbers. . . .

One evening, Jacob and Leah's four eldest sons drove the sheep to their shelters early. Jacob left Simeon, Levi, and Judah to settle among them, by their own means, the question of who would mind the animals on which shift as night drew on; he took Reuben, his eldest, with him and headed in toward town.

"Where are we going, Father?" the boy said. Jacob noted that Reuben's tone, like that of the others, had grown in thoughtfulness and respect when he spoke to his parents now. Jacob looked at him, tall, powerful, clear-eyed; he liked what he saw.

He smiled at the boy. "It's time to confront your grandfather, I think."

Reuben gaped at him, unbelieving. "You mean—face him down? Really? But—"

"You know," Jacob said, "we're paid up. I'm officially a bondman no longer. The last payments were registered through Laban's scribes some days ago."

"Paid up?" the boy said. "You mean . . . ? But you're not really thinking of . . . ?"

"Of course I am," his father said calmly. "And why not? It isn't as if Laban were some sort of fire-eyed demon, after all. I've faced down a lot worse than my father-in-law before, boy." He remembered the incident in the night, with Reshef. "Yes," he added, "and quite recently, too . . ."

Reuben quieted down after that, but there was anxiety in his young face as they approached Laban's house. And when Jacob asked him to summon his grandfather, Reuben hesitated. "Father," he said in a low voice, "don't you think we ought to—?"

"Go get him, boy," his father said, smiling. "I'll be waiting outside here. I think I don't want to face him on his own property. Out here in the common street will be fine."

Laban came out reluctantly at best—and glowering. "What the devil is this, Jacob? I'm busy. Can't it wait?"

"Not too long," Jacob said. "I've waited long enough. Laban, I'm going home."

"Home?" his father-in-law said. "What the blazes are you talking about? You—"

"Home to Canaan. Home to my father. I want to take my wives and concubines and children and return with them to the land I was born in. I've been away too long."

Laban raised one beetling brow at the insolence. "Not while you're a bondman of mine, you won't."

"Ah, but that's it," Jacob said. "I'm paid up. Both in years and in the petty debts I contracted under you. I'm a free man, and so are all my brood. Now: I mean to take what I've earned here as your overseer, and—"

"Earned? What do you mean earned? I'm not prepared yet to accept your wild story about being paid up, much less—"

Jacob pressed on. "Under the laws of Haran you owe me for each year spent as overseer of your herds—"

"Laws!" bellowed Laban. "We'll see who gets to invoke the laws of Haran! I have influence here. You're not leaving me, you and your sons, just as shearing is—"

"Then you deny your debt?" Jacob said. "In public, in front of a witness?"

Laban backtracked a bit. "Deny? Well ... but look, you can't leave just now. I can't spare any—"

"Can't spare?" Jacob said in a voice he might have used to an unruly child. "I've made you a rich man by my care of your flocks. When I took them over, your losses went down by half. Since then your herds have increased by—"

"No!" Laban yelled. "I won't hear of it! You try to slip away and I'll have the Army of Haran down on you too quick to—"

"Father," Reuben said. "Perhaps if we—"

"Quiet, son," Jacob said. "Don't try to step between your father and a man he's bargaining with." He raised his voice again—but stayed in control of himself. "Laban," he said. "Tell you what. I'll make a compromise with you."

"Compromise?" his father-in-law said, suddenly suspicious. "What kind of compromise?"

"We'll stay until the lambing. In the meantime, you'll come out into the fields with me, and we'll remove from your herds all the speckled goats and all the black sheep. These will be mine."

Laban's expression turned crafty. "Speckled goats?" he said. "Hmmmm. And black sheep. Well, there can't be many in either category, even after lambing season. I'll say this for you: you've given me the best wool in Padan-aram, and the best milch goats. . . ."

"All the more reason to let me cull the worst," Jacob said, knowing the darker sheep were little valued in Haran. In Canaan, they would be rarities and would be worth more than the whiter kind. "Tell me, now: is it a deal?"

Laban narrowed his dark eyes. "You won't take any white ones?" he said. "Goats or sheep?"

"My word on it. Any you find with my flocks you can hang me for, for a thief. Me and all my boys—"

"Father!"

"Quiet, son. Your father knows what he's doing. Now, Laban? A deal? Or do I take it to the courts? You'll find I have a friend or two in higher circles myself. I can tie you up for another season or two, even if I lose. Think of the income you'll lose in that time, not being able to sell any stock. . . ."

"Damn you. All right. All right. I'll send someone out right now. I'll send Abihu. You, boy! What's your name? Reuben? Go get Abihu. On the double. I'll call your bluff right now. But just you listen to me. One false move out of you, Jacob, and I'll—"

"Yes, I know. You'll eat me up like an ogre. I think we're done with the bluster, Laban. From this point, we deal as equals. I'll stay through the lambing. Then I go. And I take my—my herd of culls with me. And you won't stop me."

"I won't, eh?" Laban said. His voice was low, tight, and had an edge on it. "We'll see what sort of conditions you'll be laying down when the time comes, my friend. *Abihu!* Where the devil is that man?"

The culls were segregated before nightfall. Jacob sent for Dan and Naphtali; the younger boys helped their elders herd the flocks into a box canyon, and the lot of them settled down for the night, ready to ward off any attack by predator or thief alike. In the end, Jacob sent Naphtali back to tell Rachel where they were. Then he built a roaring campfire, and he and the boys, in a jubilant mood, butchered a young goat and roasted it on a spit.

"You should have seen father with grand—with Laban," Reuben said with a touch of pride in his strong young voice. He stood by the spit, talking with Simeon and Levi. "As glib and cool as an advocate arguing before the king."

"Really?" Levi said. "But how . . . ?"

"Technically, we're free," Jacob said, coming up behind them. "It's just a matter of outflanking Laban and forcing him to let us go. Yes, and outsmarting him." He sniffed the meat and smiled. "I trust you'll allow me to feel pleased with myself. I did a little bluffing back there. . . ."

"I *thought* so," Reuben said with a conspiratorial grin. "It was about your 'influence' at court, wasn't it?"

"Yes," his father said. He sat down before the fire and made room for them to join him. "His friends outrank mine by a dozen levels. But he doesn't *know* that for sure. In point of fact, I probably could tie him up in legal matters, if I had to. But I'd lose more than he would, doing so. Well, it doesn't matter, I suppose. Actually, it worked out about as it was supposed to."

"You mean . . . ?" Reuben gaped at him, then grinned. "Father, you're a fox! A conniving, long-haired, sharp-nosed, red-tailed—"

"What do you mean?" Simeon said.

"Tell him, Reuben," Jacob said. "I'm pleased to see you're onto me." His smile was, indeed, a fox's smile.

"Yes," the boy said. He turned to his brothers, pride in his young voice. "There wasn't any compromise at all. The 'compromise' was a second line of defense father had prepared for himself to retreat to. And when Laban followed him there, the old fox swallowed him whole."

"I don't understand," Judah said. "No compromise?"

"Father *wanted* to stay. If we don't get a part of Laban's flocks, we're penniless. We go back south as paupers. But if we can stay on until the lambing, and take what we choose—"

"What we *choose?*" Simeon said scornfully. "Oh, for heaven's sake, Reuben. You heard the bargain. The culls. The culls."

"But who is left to manage the herds?" Reuben said, poking his brother in the chest with a questing finger. "Answer me that, smart aleck. I'll tell you who. Us. And if we can't maneuver ourselves a majority of the lambs by engineering the matings so as to favor our own ewes, we're a bunch of idiots and deserve to go south in sackcloth."

"Father!" Simeon said. "Is this so?"

Jacob grinned and got up to sniff the meat on the spit. "Gad," he said. "Come up here and turn this thing. It's getting overdone on one side." He turned to the boys around the campfire. "He's right. Good work, Reuben. A smart shepherd like you—or you, or you, or any of us, boys—can figure out ways of making sure Laban's white ewes mate only with our black rams. Right? He'll see at lambing time that we've tricked him out of most of his stock, and it'll all be perfectly legal. And," he said, his eyes going slightly out of focus for a moment as he thought back on his years of servitude, and on all the insults, the slights, the injustices he had suffered at the hands of his father-in-law, "it'll all be richly deserved. For once the biter will have been bitten."

"Reuben!" Simeon said. "He's right. If we just keep an eye out during mating season—"

"Yes, yes," Reuben said. "But Father: what if he does turn out the army when it comes time for us to leave? What if he does have the influence at court that he says he has? Can't he keep us here if he—?"

"Ah," Jacob said. "We'll deal with that when it happens, boys. In the meantime I, who have no powerful friends at court, had better start developing some. And—boys."

"Yes, sir?" Three of them spoke as one, their voices full of a new confidence.

"Reuben and I will be training you in—other things. The staff. The bow. The sword."

"Sword?" Levi said, gulping. "You mean—?"

"Of course, dummy," Reuben said. "Nothing is worth anything at all unless you're willing to fight for it. Anyone knows that. Don't worry. I'll make a master of the sword of you."

"You? What do you know? Don't make me laugh."

"He won't make you laugh," Jacob interjected with quiet confidence, and with more than a hint of pride in his eldest son. "Reuben and Simeon already surpass me with the staff. Reuben reminds me, now and then, of my brother Esau when he was very young. And Reuben's been taking lessons with one of the Lord Oshiyahu's soldiers. At my request. And it's my understanding that he's doing quite well at it."

"Who?" the boys clustered around Reuben now, poking at him. "Are you studying with Reshef? I hear he's the best swordsman in . . ."

Jacob sat back and listened to them. *Reshef,* he thought. The irony of the suggestion made him shake his head. *No, they'd have little of value to learn from Reshef, who strikes in the dark from behind,* he thought. Better the honest young soldier who was teaching him, a stout young fellow named Ilihu. He'd teach them the practical things, the sort of stuff that sneaky fellows like Reshef would steer away from, knowing their own best strokes were a coward's. Ilihu would give them the basics of swordplay, the kind you used on men who attacked you from the front. . . .

Jacob's mind suddenly stopped and dwelt on this. His sons? Fighting for their lives? Would it come down to that in the end? Fighting against bullies and rogues hired by their own grandfather? He scowled. If only he could outflank and outsmart Laban instead when the time came. . . .

And what would happen when Laban's own heirs, his sons

and other kin, learned of Jacob's little trick for increasing his own flocks at Laban's expense—and, by extension, at their own expense as well? Would they join Laban and swell his ranks when the showdown came? And could Jacob's maneuverings then defuse their rage and enable him and his to leave Padan-aram without bloodshed?

He breathed a silent prayer heavenward to the God of his fathers. But, as ever, as always since he'd left the sacred soil of Canaan years before, the God was silent. The thought was like a stabbing pain in his heart. *Oh, God of Abraham! When will You forgive?*

II

The thought preyed on Jacob's mind through the night, and what sleep he got was fitful and troubled. In the morning, he set Reuben to arranging the boys' work schedule and went back to town, crossing the fields while the sun was still no more than halfway to the zenith in the eastern sky.

Pausing atop a ridge he looked across the river valley at Haran, with its heavy walls, its tent village spreading out below the ramparts outside, and the tall towers of its pagan temples rising above the banners on the parapets. It had been his home for twenty years, but he felt no affection for it. He would not be sorry to leave—particularly since his steps were to lead him south to his homeland.

Canaan! The thought was a knife in his heart. How long had he put it from his mind? How long had he deferred thoughts of his native land in his despair? Of his father and mother, who hadn't seen him since . . . why, he had been hardly more than a boy!

And Esau, his brother Esau, on whom he'd played such a cruel, foolish—and in the end irreversible—trick. With his mother's help, he had stolen his father Isaac's blessing as first-born—stolen it from Esau, to whom it rightfully belonged. . . . Would his brother ever forgive him? Would he, now that the two of them were grown men, be able to reconcile their differences? Could he become friends again with his twin?

And would the God again speak to him once his feet had

336

been set on the path to Canaan, once his days of exile were at an end?

This last was the greatest pain of all, the knowledge that the God had deserted him the day he'd left Canaan. It was a problem that would not have occurred to many men. But the God had not spoken to many men. Of all the people that had lived on the earth, Jacob knew of only a handful to whom the God had spoken as He had spoken to him. Perhaps the first had been Terah, his great-grandfather, who'd had the original vision, the one that had told him of the coming fall of Ur to the Elamite invasion, that had told him to take his family and goods and strike north along the Euphrates to resettle in Padan-aram. Then there had been Terah's son Abraham, Jacob's great and legendary grandfather, who had heard the command of the God—the One True God, El-Shaddai—to take his people south to Canaan, which would be given to him and his seed forever.

Yes! Land that was to be Abraham's and that of his descendants, the claims of all other peoples to the contrary! And the God had put mettle into Abraham, put strength into his ancient arm, and had given him dominion over the Promised Land even in the face of a fearful invasion by the kings of Elam and Shinar and their allies. He had steered to Abraham's side the great mercenary warrior Sneferu the Egyptian, who had trained Abraham's people for warfare and led them to victory, dying tragically just before the final victory, victim of a coward's arrow from behind, only moments after he had killed Tidal, King of Goiim, in single combat with his own hand. . . .

Now, however, Jacob's thoughts wandered. His brow knit as he walked slowly down the hill toward the river. The God had also steered to Abraham's side the great armorer Belsunu the Babylonian, great-grandfather of the young sculptor Hadad and a descendant of the line of Cain, the Children of the Lion. What a strange destiny it was that now had drawn him, Jacob, a man of Abraham's line, to friendship with a descendant of Belsunu. . . .

But no. The God worked in His own ways, and perhaps He had some plans for Jacob in which young Hadad figured. Perhaps He had some plans of His own for Hadad as well. Surely the hand of the God lay upon the boy now, with good fortune coming upon him from all sides just as his fate had seemed bleakest. But to what purpose?

Jacob smiled, thinking about his young friend. After the terrible night in which he'd faced down Reshef and made his threat, he'd made it a point to drop by the Bazaar of the Well as often as his footsteps took him into that quarter of the city—drop by and pass a word or two with the boy, or inquire after him if he happened to be away. The friendship had grown strong by stages, and it showed signs of becoming a lasting one. He liked Hadad; the boy had a great heart and, small and weak as he was, had enough spirit for a troop of soldiers.

He had been particularly happy to learn, right after his fight with Reshef, of Hadad's newfound good fortune. The young man had received word that the great merchant Ibalum was offering him a limited partnership and would soon be selling his, Hadad's, wares all over the known world for top prices—Hadad would soon be rich and famous. In addition to that, he had found love and become a man. . . .

Jacob smiled, thinking about Hadad's happy face. He'd become a new man, radiant, dynamic, his heart full of hope and thanksgiving.

Yes, and the boy had not lost that generous heart of his. The moment his fortunes had begun to change, he had set about trying to improve the fortunes of those around him. He had found new and more spacious lodging near the bazaar and had moved his poor mad mother, Tallay, in with him and young Danataya; he'd hired a freedwoman to care for his mother and look after her needs, and . . .

Now Jacob was approaching the ford, and, looking about him, he saw a friend approaching. "Danataya!" he said. "I was just thinking about you and Hadad." He stopped and waited for the girl, and when she reached him, he took her basket of wash from her and put it on one of his own shoulders. "Here," he said. "That's a lot for a little girl like you to be carrying."

"There are three of us now," she said. "And poor Tallay, she's growing incontinent. I think she's ill. But she won't tell us how she feels."

"Ah, poor woman. I have a strange feeling she won't be with us long. Well, her last days will be lived in comfort, thank heaven. How's Hadad?"

"He says he's never been so happy in his life, No, that wasn't the way he said it. He says he never knew before what it was to be happy."

"Ah. How wonderful. And you?"

"Jacob, it's as though all my dreams have come true. Including the ones I didn't have the courage to dream before. I love him so, and—goodness, Jacob, I'd have loved Hadad dirt-poor. I'd have lived with him in squalor. If you put all my girlish visions of a man together, they wouldn't have measured up to anything half as good as what I got when the gods gave me Hadad."

The God, my dear, Jacob thought. *The One True God, who watches over us all.* But he let it pass. "However, there's something wrong? I hear something in your tone—"

"No, no." She shook her pretty young head, a trifle too emphatically, he thought. "I—as I say, I'd have loved Hadad if he were poor. And here he is on his way to being rich. It's just that—well, it's all happening so quickly. It takes my breath away."

There's more to it than that, Jacob thought. He wondered what that something was. He resolved to visit Hadad as soon as the opportunity presented itself and ask around. "Well, look," he said. "Enjoy your good fortune. The both of you deserve it, and Hadad has earned it if anyone has. Have you any plans for the future?"

"I—well, no. Ibalum is calling for more, and it's all Hadad can do to keep up with the orders he has. He may wind up taking on an apprentice. Did you hear the Guild of Artisans has asked him to become a member? Despite all the years of ostracism?"

"No!" Jacob said, smiling. He led her across the shallow ford, one hand out to help her. "I think that's hilarious. It must have taken a lot for them to swallow their pride that way."

"Yes. I told Hadad to let them stew for a month or so. But he isn't that way. He accepted the first day. He says, 'If you can't forgive people for being people . . . ' "

"Yes," Jacob said. "That'd be the way Hadad would handle the matter all right. I'd hang on to that young man if I were you, my dear. Imagine having a spouse who doesn't demand that you be perfect." He smiled; then a stray thought crossed his mind. "Which reminds me, my dear. Rachel was asking about you."

"Oh. I keep meaning to go see her. . . ."

"Would you do that some time? For me? She's so lonely. The other women still tend to avoid her at the ford, when she's washing clothes. If you came down with her—"

"Oh, I'd love to! Tell her I'll be down to see her tomorrow. Would you, please? Or—maybe today?" There was the smallest cloud hovering over the girl's smile. "Yes, today. I'll be over this afternoon. I've just got two errands to do first. . . ."

Afterward, Danataya watched him go, his shoulders thrown back, his gait like that of a man much younger. What a fine man he was! And what a wonderful friend—almost father, for all that the two met only infrequently—he was to Hadad!

If only she could have brought herself to confide in him. . . .

She shook her head. Well, she hadn't, and that was all there was to the matter. What a coward she was!

She picked up her bundle, much lightened by the late morning sun which had dried a lot of the moisture from it. Anyhow, she'd go by and see Rachel today; she'd been meaning to for quite some time now. First it had been diffidence that had stopped her, then business of her own. But now, with the furnishing of their new lodgings almost complete and with Tallay safely provided for, she had the time. And Rachel was a dear woman, warm and sympathetic.

Maybe she would know what to do. . . .

Jacob came upon Hadad in the bazaar. The young man was bent low over a white-hot charcoal fire, blowing through a long tube held in his mouth and snipping off tiny lengths of a very fine gold wire. As he snipped them off, he let them drop onto a glowing piece of charcoal and blew hard on each half-melted fragment. Jacob bent to watch. As Hadad blew on a fragment, its shape altered subtly, contracting from a lozenge shape into a perfect, tiny sphere.

Now Hadad put down shears and wire and took the pipe out of his mouth. "Jacob!" he said with a sunny smile. "What a pleasure to see you!"

"I'm afraid I'm interrupting something important," Jacob said.

"This? I'm doing some granulation work. See?" He indicated a small bronze bowl, its bottom half covered by the tiny balls of gold. "These will go on a golden bracelet ordered by the High King of Ebla. His daughter will wear it during his coronation this fall. I think she'll like it. Not many people north of Egypt know how to do this properly, I think. I picked it up on my own, using some tablets left behind by my father. He learned it from his father, Ahuni, and Ahuni learned it from his adoptive father, Zakir. Zakir, unlike the rest of us, trained in—well, art metalwork, the sort of thing I do. He wasn't an armorer. But he taught my grandfather when they were still working in Mari and Haran, before they came south to work for your grandfather."

"I know these names," Jacob said. "They are famous among my people. Yes, and honored too. So your father wrote down the formulas and procedures for you?"

"Not all of them. I mean, he may have written down more, but I haven't found them yet. Mother doesn't remember much, you know, and for all I know I may have broken some tablets, or scattered them or whatever, when I was a little boy. Or perhaps Shobai has some of them. I haven't asked him."

"What do you hear from Shobai?" Jacob asked.

"I—I'm worried, Jacob. I haven't heard anything. He's overdue home. I wrote him a while back, but Shobai has never been much good for writing letters. It's not his way. However, I met someone from Carchemish. He said Shobai left the city a couple of weeks ago—but he hasn't turned up in Haran, and he hasn't turned up on any caravan manifests either. I paid someone to go ask in Carchemish. Shobai seems to have disappeared off the face of the earth."

"That's odd," Jacob said. "Presumably he finished his job there? And collected his pay?"

"That's another thing. His pay wasn't forwarded here, nor was any document transferring credit to his Haran accounts. Instead, I've learned that the money was placed in an account in Carchemish."

"Perhaps he thinks of—oh, setting up a separate shop there. There would be advantages to that. Carchemish *is* closer to the middle of things. He could answer summonses to other cities much more quickly from there. Besides, taxes are lower in Carchemish."

"I hadn't thought of that."

"Has his wife heard anything?"

"I—I haven't asked. I mean, I sent her a letter, but Anat isn't much for answering either."

"Hadad," Jacob said. "Let's be honest with each other. You don't want to confront Anat, do you?"

"N—no," Hadad said. He pushed back his stool and stood up. Jacob took note of the boy's crooked stance and thought: *a pity the leg couldn't be broken again and reset. . . .* "I—I've tried, really. But after that last scene with her—I mean, Jacob, I used to idolize her. Idolize her! And now—"

"Is she still seeing him? Reshef?"

"Openly. You know, I wonder if Shobai heard about this in Carchemish . . . ? But no. I know his temper. If he were to learn his wife had been trifled with, he'd be back here in a flash. And heaven help Reshef." His face twisted with shame.

"Oh, Jacob—if I could spare him the hurt, the humiliation. . . ."

"Shobai's a big boy, Hadad. He should be able to bear his own pain by now." Jacob changed the subject. "I ran into Danataya. I was coming into town, because I need to see the lord Oshiyahu. We chatted a bit on the way back from the ford where she'd been washing clothes. You've made her very happy, Hadad."

"Me? Make *her* happy?" Hadad's face fairly glowed. "My friend, if I could tell you how I feel—look here." He turned away and reached under one of the new cabinets he'd bought for a parcel wrapped in fine cloth. "It's a surprise for her. It's something she said she wanted, more than just about anything. But that was when we were first getting to know each other. She's probably forgotten she ever mentioned it."

"What is it?" Jacob said, leaning forward, his eyes bright.

"Look," Hadad said. He carefully peeled away the cloth. Inside was a new-made cithara, plainly built and without decoration—but obviously the work of a master craftsman.

"But—does Danataya play?" Jacob said.

"No," Hadad said, beaming. "But I do. And that's what Danataya asked me for. She asked me to buy one, so I could play and sing to her when we're together." There was the clear, brightly burning flame of passion in the lad's gentle young eye. "Ah, Jacob, could I refuse her? If it cost a king's ransom? If I had to bring it from the far side of the earth?"

III

Coming through the bazaar, Oshiyahu ran into the merchant Aqhat. He broke stride, nodded with some cordiality, and moved to go around the speculator; but Aqhat stepped into his path. "Ah, there, Oshiyahu," Aqhat said. "Do you have a moment? I'd like to . . . "

Oshiyahu halted, stood back, looked the heavyset merchant over. "Pardon my haste," he said. "I've just come from another meeting of the king's council, and with the usual results." His wry smile solicited sympathy—but not the kind that hinders. "If I seem brusque . . ."

"I understand exactly," the merchant said. "It takes all day to get agreement on whether the sun came up in the east or the west this morning. I won't keep you long. Unless—unless you could use a drink just now."

"You tempt me," Oshiyahu said. "I've been trying to get more funds for defense. It's like trying to skin a bear while he's still breathing."

"Ah," the dealer in lands said. "I gather nothing much happened. But do you really think you're going to get funds for the army in times like these?"

"Times like which?" Oshiyahu said with some impatience. "Surely you're not going to read me the one about how hard times are upon us. You, of all other. . . ."

"Me?" The merchant's tone rose. "What do you mean?"

"Oh, come on," Oshiyahu said, a conspirator's sardonic grin on his rough face. "Politicians controlled by you land dealers voted against the proposal to limit the number of foreigners allowed within our walls. As a result, the crush of people needing housing has driven prices up. You're in a fine position right now. Why can't you people loosen the purse strings for the army? After all, it's your own properties that will be in trouble when the time comes."

"What time?" Aqhat said. "Oh, yes. Those apocalyptic days of war and pillage and rapine you've been talking about. Do you really believe these nomads will strike at a town the size of Haran? When they've been avoiding all direct contact with Mari to the east?"

"My friend, they'll be here by the spring. And if I don't have the means to drive them away then—"

"Nonsense! You military men always say that around this time of year, when the annual defense appropriations are being decided. It's to your advantage to throw a scare into His Majesty's court."

"Believe it or not as you may," Oshiyahu said. "When the time comes, the present defenses of Haran won't slow them down for long. I and my men will do their—our—best. We'll die magnificently. And then people like you will die, and there won't be anything magnificent about that part of it at all. And let me tell you, your rents won't buy you any solace then. It'll be as if the wrath of all the gods had descended upon you, and there won't be any rock you can hide under."

"That's ridiculous! Hirgab says—"

"Ah," Oshiyahu said, his face breaking out into a smile of

complete understanding. "Hirgab. He's made inroads in the council, hasn't he? He's been removed from the chain of command, removed from a position subordinate to me and put in—what do you call it? This new advisory role. . . ."

"To be sure, he's used his influence. If you had relatives at court you'd use them, too."

"Damned right I would," Oshiyahu said. "But I'd use them for purposes that would benefit the city and its people, not—"

"Hah. You admit the existence of only one point of view. You soldiers are all alike."

"No, we're not. Some are like Hirgab, and want to cut the legs out from under their own men. Gods! I understand he's sent representatives north to talk to the Shepherd Kings himself, on his own initiative. Without consulting me."

"It's a matter of getting adequate intelligence—"

"Intelligence, is it? That's the kind of word he'd use. I see what sort of company you've been keeping lately. Has he reassured you? Has he told you what a lot of sweet-tempered, peace-loving fellows these men up north are?" He snorted. "Gods! What am I doing soldiering, with gulls like you around? I could be selling you fellows raffle tickets on farmland two days' march from the nearest water source. I could be juggling shells and peas, and challenging you to guess which—"

"Hold on, you don't have to get insulting."

"My dear friend," Oshiyahu said, an edge of irony in his rough voice, "I'm not sure I could insult you people if I tried. If you have your way, the streets will be ankle-deep in blood before I'm a year older. When it happens, all I can hope for is that you'll keep your precious innocence all the way to the end, and that when the axe falls it won't just be the poor that it falls upon."

There might have been an answer coming; but Oshiyahu did not wait for it. He turned on one heel and strode away, anger lengthening each one of his brisk steps.

Dushratta met him at the door of his home. The orderly's stance and turnout were impeccable, as always, and his manner was as efficient and unruffled as ever. "Good morning, sir. Did it go well?"

"Don't waste words," Oshiyahu said in a gruff voice. "You know damned well it didn't." He looked at the closed door. "I gather I've visitors. Where is my wife?"

344

"Two visitors, sir. And your wife is at the bazaar. She said not to wait for her. Young Yassib's here, sir."

"Well, that won't take long. Who else?"

"A man named Jacob, sir."

"Oh, yes. We've met. He supplies mutton to the army."

"Yes, sir. I thought you'd remember. And sir . . ."

The orderly's tone was enough to halt Oshiyahu's path up the stairs. There wasn't much of a warning in it, but there was enough, given the complete understanding that existed between master and man, to make the difference. "Yes?" Oshiyahu said. "It's about Reshef, isn't it?"

"Yes, sir. He's been thick as thieves with Hirgab for some time, as you know, and now they've taken him out of the chain of command, along with Hirgab."

"I already got the word about Hirgab. I'm surprised you have. I only just now heard. So Reshef is also out . . . transferred to Hirgab's new staff. Well, good riddance. . . ."

"Very good, sir." The orderly held the door open for him. Oshiyahu strode inside at march pace, taking off his cloak and tossing it onto a bench. His son-in-law stood hastily. His expression was deceptively noncommittal.

"Father," the young man said. "You called for me—"

"Yes," Oshiyahu said. He stood looking at the young man, making no move to embrace or greet him. "How's Halima?"

"Oh, just fine, sir. She—"

"I'll get to the point. You're making friends in some quarters I don't approve of. I'd advise you to watch your step. These are dangerous people to associate with. They're bigger fish than you think they are, and they have a more voracious appetite than you may have bargained for. They can and will chew you up and spit you out."

"I don't understand, sir."

"Don't lie to me, damn it. Do you think I haven't eyes? Ears? I can tell you what kind of soup you ate for supper three nights ago. I can tell you which girls you've cheated on my daughter with in the last month, and when, and where. I can tell you which ones you were impotent with. . . ."

"F-father—"

"Don't 'Father' me, boy. I'll give you one warning, right now. One only. Do you hear me? The message is this: curb that wandering foot of yours. Do it now. Put a hobble on yourself, or by all that's holy, *I'll* put a hobble on you. Stay the hell away from Reshef. He's out of your depth. And"
—his hand reached out to tap the young man on the chest

lightly but meaningfully with one forefinger—"I'd go home nights if I were you. Home. Get nice and domestic. Stay that way. Otherwise, dear son of mine, you may have occasion to learn what the lord Oshiyahu looks and sounds like when he gets mad. Do you understand?" The finger poked once again, this time more stiffly.

"B-but, sir—I don't know what you're talking—"

"That'll be all," Oshiyahu said gently. "You can go now. And Yassib . . ."

"Y-yes, sir?"

"Go home. Go *straight* home."

Oshiyahu shot one glance at Dushratta, his face like stone, his heart full of an icy rage. "I—" he started to say. But there wasn't anything to say. He sighed; his great shoulders slumped. "You said someone else . . ."

"Yes, sir. I'll show him in."

The man the orderly ushered into Oshiyahu's common room, though, was a man much altered from the last time the commander had seen him. His bearing was upright, military; the woes of a subordinate's life had fallen from his shoulders. Oh, yes: there had been some talk. Jacob was a freedman now, with the bondman's yoke gone. Well, it showed. Good for him. "Jacob," he said, extending his hand. "I remember now. Your payment got lost in the records."

"You made up for it with interest," the freedman said. "It's always a pleasure to do business with a responsible man." The two shook hands. "I won't waste time," he said. "I know you're busy. I—I'm planning to leave the city. Not now, next year sometime. I'm—I'm wondering how long I have."

"How long you have?" Oshiyahu said. He raised one brow. "I'm not sure I get your meaning."

"I think you do. The Shepherd Kings. How long will it be before they attack? I want to make my move before the city is destroyed."

Oshiyahu crossed his arms over his broad chest. "Well," he said. "By all the gods, my friend, I do like a man who's direct. And one who is capable as our leaders are not, of figuring out what's happening and making a decision on the basis of this."

"Then I'm right? The city is doomed?"

"It may be. It surely will be, if I can't wake the council up in time. Even then, I'm not sure if we can . . ." He looked Jacob in the eye. "The thing that surprises me, my friend, is that my saying this doesn't seem to surprise you at all. It

346

doesn't, does it? You know something, perhaps? Or are you some sort of seer?"

"I'm no seer. I'm a man to whom the God of my fathers has not spoken since I left my native soil. But I have learned something. I thought to share it with you."

"Dushratta!" Oshiyahu said. "Our guest and I will go into the garden. A little wine, if you would. . . ." He watched his orderly slip silently away and then motioned Jacob out into the walled enclosure behind his house. "Well . . ." he said.

Jacob briefly detailed his meeting with Reshef in the encampment: the soldier's refusal to believe him, the deriding of the news he brought. He did not mention the subsequent meeting. "And, sir—the man I met in the field. I think he was no ordinary nomad. The name—"

"Name? You got his name?"

"Yes, sir. He said his name was Manouk."

"Manouk!"

"Yes. I thought you'd recognize it. He—"

"Why, he's their leader! Or—one of the top men they have! And you met him, talked with him?"

"Yes. He spoke our tongue a little. He acknowledged himself in my debt. He said, 'If I come to Haran, I say, there will be no Haran. Gone. Everything gone—everybody die.'" Jacob expertly mimicked the nomad's thick accent. In his own voice he added, "He said he'd send me a message when the Shepherd Kings' attack was going to fall. When I got the message, I was to leave immediately, I and all my family and possessions. If I did this, I'd be spared."

"And you believed him? How did he say this?"

"Not in jest. I would vouch for his sincerity with my life. I may, in fact, have to."

"Quite true. How extraordinary! What kind of man is he? Honest, you say?"

"Straightforward. I think if he said he was going to kill everyone in Haran, I would take him seriously. Totally seriously. I think he also meant it when he said he'd warn me. But of course, a last-minute warning won't be enough if I'm to get my people and chattels out of town safely and be on the road south toward Canaan before the blow falls. That's why I came to you. That, and the belief that you ought to know all this."

"I thank you. You know, that description you gave—it sounds a lot like something I heard from a friend in Carchemish. Manouk could have been there, scouting the city. If he was, I think he killed somebody."

"I think he would kill in the blink of an eye."

"Gods! He could be in Haran! Right now! I hadn't thought of that!"

"He could. But I haven't seen him. I'll keep my eyes open if you like."

"I wish you would. And Jacob—"

"Yes?"

"About your question. I don't have any idea, just yet, when they plan to be here. My guess is, we've got some months left. And when they come, they'll have a lot of knowledge of the town, and they'll have a good idea when's the best time to hit us."

"Ah. And that would be . . ."

"Late winter? Early spring? Who knows? Think how we're spread out during a planting. During—"

"During the season of the spring lambing."

"Exactly. I'd be out of here by then if I were you. I really think I would."

Dushratta returned with wine bag and cups. Jacob shook his head gently. Oshiyahu drank directly from the skin, holding it high. Then, he wiped his mouth and put the bottle down. "Of course," he said, "I'll rely on you to contact me if you hear anything. Particularly—"

"Particularly if I get my message from Manouk. I understand. You'll hear from me within the hour when that happens."

"Good. And—keep in touch, will you? I don't have many people around me who have your understanding. I need every pair of sharp eyes and ears I can find." He held out his hand again, and his smile was appreciative and welcoming.

But as he watched Jacob go, the thought hit him hard: *Reshef. A traitor! And now out of his control, and favorably placed at court! Along with his boss Hirgab. What damage could he do there?*

IV

Coming through the bazaar, Yassib, his blood still boiling with impotent rage, his mind elsewhere, literally ran into

Zikri, a junior officer of the fourth troop. He was ready to curse and strike out with one heavy hand—and then he recognized his associate. "Oh," he said. "Zikri. I—I'm sorry. I wasn't looking where I was going."

"Huh," Zikri said, brushing himself off. "You sure weren't. And—gods, man, you should see your face. If looks could kill—"

"Yes," Yassib said. "A spat with my father-in-law. Never marry into the higher echelons, let me tell you."

"Ah," Zikri said, an understanding grin crossing his battle-scarred face. "Here," he said in a conciliatory tone. "Let me buy you a drink. You need some calming down before you go back to camp."

"Damned right," Yassib said. "I'll take you up on that. Even if I'm not exactly headed back to camp." He steered Zikri toward a nearby tavern that fronted the Bazaar of the Twin Oaks. "We can talk better in here." He pushed open the door and held it for his friend. "Two," he said to the innkeeper, holding up a pair of fingers. The innkeeper nodded and disappeared into another room.

The two soldiers sat down across from each other at a rough plank table. "You said you're not headed back to camp," Zikri said. "But you're also headed in the wrong direction for home . . ." He let the sentence hang in the air unfinished; one brow went up.

"Home? Back to that shrew I married? Who keeps telling me 'I'll tell my father on you' every time we have an argument? I'd rather sleep in the gutter with a brood sow."

"Ah. The honeymoon is over so soon?"

"Gods!" Yassib looked up, took the wine jug and the two cups from the tavernkeeper, and motioned him away. He poured once, twice; then, tossing his first drink down in a single gulp, he poured himself another before putting the jug down. "Honeymoon? I knew I'd made a mistake before the wedding. I knew by the time I'd posted the banns."

"So soon? Then why . . . ?" But the question was pointless, and Zikri knew it. "I see. This sort of thing always sounds so good. The possibilities stretch out before you endlessly. Only it never quite comes out the way you'd expected it to. Right?"

Yassib sighed bitterly. "You're doing just fine so far. And let me tell you: Oshiyahu is a tough taskmaster. And he has eyes everywhere."

"Ah!" Zikri drank, his eyes on Yassib over the cup. "I take

it there's more to this than just the protective father meddling in your life."

"Right. Now he's telling me where I can go, whom I can see."

"Hmmm. He knows about your friendship with Reshef, then?"

"Reshef?" Yassib said in a harsh tone. "What do you know about—?"

"Oh, come on," Zikri said. "The two of you are thick as thieves. Everybody knows that. And now with Reshef beginning to rise swiftly in the world, riding on the coattails of the lord Hirgab, who has powerful connections at court—"

"Huh. I wish it were that simple. Friends with Reshef? You know better than that. Reshef doesn't have any friends. Not in that sense. But—some of the things he says make such good sense. You look around you—Oshiyahu rattling the saber the way he's been doing—and with the entire council lined up against him, and thoroughly resentful of his views on the subject."

"Ah, yes. I see. And you—you and Reshef, let's say—have figured out where the political power lies right now, and you're rushing to cover yourself just in case there's a big shakeup one of these days. I see."

"You make it all sound so—so crass. For the love of all the gods, my friend, in days like these it pays to look ahead and try to head off trouble. And if you can't turn the cart away from the precipice, it might just pay to get off the cart."

"There's something to what you say. Nevertheless, the idea of crossing Oshiyahu . . ." He drank again, shaking his head. "He may be outnumbered at court now, but the old fox knows his soldiering. He may just know what he's talking about. After all, these nomads—they're a bad lot, from what I hear."

"All the more reason not to want to confront them head on, if that can be avoided. Right?" Yassib's scorn was evident. "I suppose you're in a big hurry to die for your city? To go up against those long knives, that vast sea of bowmen and charioteers?"

"No, but if I do, I hope to heaven I have a tough, wily old devil like your father-in-law commanding me. You know my father served under him, don't you? It was one of those Hittite incursions. My old man said that Oshiyahu turned a clear-cut defeat into victory all by himself. Just by outsmarting the bastards. He knew we'd never be able to handle close-quarter fighting against people armed with the black metal. So he steered them into a box canyon, enfiladed them, and mowed them down with his bowmen."

"Hmmm. This black metal—I'd like to ask your father about it some time. If we could get hold of that stuff—"

"Well, my friend, my father's out of reach. He's been in the underworld, sleeping the sleep of the just, since I was a stripling." He held his cup high. "May he rest in peace!" He drank, and stood up, dropping a coin on the table. "I'll get this one," he said. "I wish I knew what to tell you. It seems to me you're in something of an impossible position. Anything you do just now is going to displease somebody powerful. Please Oshiyahu and you displease the council. Please Reshef and . . ."

"I know," Yassib said, waving him away, a sour look on his face. "I know. . . ."

He had drained the rest of the jug before he stepped out into the street, his face flushed, his eyes red. His mood had elements of anger and despair indissolubly mixed in it, and his step was unsteady. He stopped, looked around . . .

. . . and found himself blinking down into a pair of dark eyes whose expression blended shock, hurt, and sadness. Yes, and something more. Pity, perhaps? "D-Danataya," he said hoarsely.

"Hello, Yassib," she said. Her voice was low, quiet, guarded. Her gaze was unflinching. "I'd thought never to see you again. But—" She tried to smile, but the smile held little of either pleasure or mirth in it. "Well, here we are. How have you been?"

"I—" He blinked, trying to get her face completely in focus. When he succeeded, he blinked again in unbelief. "You look good," he said. "You look lovely. That dress—it's beautiful. And expensive."

"My fortunes have changed," she said. Her tone was matter-of-fact, neither boastful nor spiteful. "I heard you married."

"Y-yes. I—I'd meant to see you—to tell you about it. But—but you'd moved. And no one seemed to know where you'd gone."

"I didn't move until after you'd posted the banns," she said simply. "There was plenty of time for you to tell me." She sighed, dismissing the subject. "It doesn't matter now. I think your feet were set on a different path from mine. I have no regrets. I don't mean to make you feel bad. I'm happy. Happier than I've ever been in my life." There *was* something

351

darker than this, he thought, in her face, in her somber look; perhaps she wasn't telling the whole truth. "Perhaps everything came out for the best after all. . . ."

"You're sure, now?" he said, his voice still hoarse but the words unslurred. "No regrets? None at all?"

She stiffened, and the first sign of anger entered her voice. "None that I'd care to discuss with you, Yassib. And if you've any thoughts of—of our getting back together, you can forget them right now. I've got a man of my own, Yassib. A *real* man. One who acts responsibly, and stands by his word. I wouldn't trade him for—"

"All right, all right," he said. He held up one restraining hand. "I understand." He scowled and turned away. "Good luck to you." As he wove down the street, though, the thought ran through his head: *There's something she's not telling me. It isn't as simple as all that. She's not happy. Not completely. Not through and through. Something's wrong. . . .*

But there was no solace at all in the thought. He'd come off the worst in the exchange, no doubt about it. His scowl returned, and his fists bunched impotently. What he needed, he was thinking, was a short conversation with Reshef. Reshef's cynicism, his unsentimental view, and his clear eye were like a cold bath, cleansing away the murkiness life tended to turn into when you got to thinking about relationships and responsibilities. Yes, he needed a talk with Reshef. Too bad he was out of town. . . .

Danataya stood staring after him for some moments, seeing nothing. How many times had she hoped for a meeting like this, particularly since her life had changed for the better and she could tell him she didn't care, didn't need him, didn't want him! And how empty, how meaningless the meeting had finally been when it had taken place.

She tried to reassure herself now. He'd looked simply awful, with his uniform all disheveled and his face all puffy from drinking. He'd never been a drinker before. Things must not be going well with that rich wife of his.

But the thought carried no sense of victory. Instead, she felt defeated, outmaneuvered, stared down. This despite his own discomfiture. The trouble—yes, the trouble was that he'd seen it in her face. Her own self-doubt, her own fears. Her own insecurity. And when he'd seen it, the fact had changed the meeting totally, changed its character and its outcome. How could she now feel superior to him? Feel that she had repudiated his contemptuous treatment of her? When he'd seen it in her face, and had known . . .

Her hand went to her throat. She could feel the blood pumping there. Her hand trembled.

Rachel, she thought. She had to see Rachel. Rachel would help her. Rachel would reassure her. Rachel knew about these things; she'd been with Jacob a long, long time. Surely Rachel would know what to do. . . .

But when she reached Jacob's house, Rachel was on her way to the bazaar. She showed signs of haste—and of a friendly attempt to hide those signs. "Danataya!" she said, taking the girl's hand between her own two palms. "How nice to see you! But—isn't it awful? You caught me on the way to the bazaar. If only you'd come an hour before. We could have eaten together, and talked. I've been looking forward to seeing you."

"Yes," Danataya said, crestfallen. "I—I'll come by again soon. Maybe I can send a message here and arrange some time when we're not both busy."

"Yes, my dear. Yes! That'd be wonderful. Next week, perhaps? I—but Danataya. I—I'm so glad to see you now, even if only for a moment. I feel so wonderful. I can't wait to share it with . . ." She impulsively hugged the girl and then stepped back, her hands on Danataya's upper arms. "But here I am trying to tell you about me. How are *you?* How is Hadad? Jacob said he was going to try to get by to see him today if he could. You're a lucky girl, you know. Hadad is the salt of the earth. Jacob thinks of him as another son in all but blood. And I think that if he could do so, he'd adopt him." She squeezed the girl's arms affectionately, looking at her with eyes full of joy and love. "And you, my dear? When can we expect to hear that the two of you are getting married? Now that Hadad's doing so well. Come: when are you going to—?"

But then the hesitation, the uncertainty, in Danataya's gaze stopped her, and Rachel's natural sense of decorum took over. "But there I go," she said, "poking my nose into things that are none of my business—forgive me, my dear. It's just that I feel almost as if you were one of the family. Perhaps more so than I ever did with my sister Leah. Although we've made up, we'll never be close, I think. It doesn't matter. But forgive me. I can't help it. I feel so happy today, it's almost as if there weren't any room in my mind for things like—well, you know. Proper manners or whatever. But I'm sure that you'll forgive me. Look, I'll make it up to you, darling. Come over—come over tomorrow, will you? Please? I'll fix something for us to eat, and we can talk to our hearts' content. Do say you'll come."

"Rachel," Danataya said. "Something's happened with you. You're . . . different. You look radiant. I've never seen you this way."

"No, you haven't," Jacob's wife said. "Neither has anyone else. Look, I never could keep a secret from a friend. This morning—this morning I just knew. I *knew*."

"Knew what?"

"Danataya: I missed my time of the month again today. This is the second month. And while this has happened before, and nothing has come of it . . . well, this morning I just knew. I just had the feeling inside, and it was a feeling I've never had with all my false pregnancies before. Ever!" She hugged the girl again, oblivious to the stunned look on Danataya's face. "Imagine! After all these years—I'm pregnant! I'm not barren after all! I'm going to be a mother! I'm going to give Jacob a child of my own!"

Now, however, she noted the look on Danataya's face, and, in her own delirious happiness, misread it. "Oh, but darling. I see you're skeptical. I suppose I'd be too, in your place. But let me tell you. A woman just *knows*. . . ."

Danataya watched her go. Her own heart was as cold as the winter's ice on the tops of the great northern mountains. *"A woman knows,"* Rachel had said. To be sure, one did—but how one reacted to it depended on one's circumstances. The news made Rachel happy. Barren all these years, a disappointment to her husband, she could now hold her head up, look all the other women of the city in the eye proudly, assert her own humanity and femininity.

But her? Danataya? It was a different story. She was just as sure as Rachel was now—sure of the new life that was stirring within her. But she, Danataya, was unmarried. And many a budding marriage had withered when the man was presented with this sort of news. Men didn't like surprises, Yamam had told her again and again. Particularly this kind, above all others.

Oh, Hadad! Was she going to lose him after all?

V

In the narrow street that led into the northern end of the Bazaar of the Well, blind Bahirum had set up his little stand. The street narrowed here almost to the point where a passer-by would have to step over Bahirum's begging bowl, and he had learned that if you could slow the passing foot traffic, the chances were good that they would take pity on you.

Now, in the drowsy quiet of early afternoon, he sat cross-legged in the dust, nodding, trying to stay awake. The warm sun lay heavy on his sightless lids, and he kept dozing off easily, only to shake his head with self-directed anger and force himself back into an erect posture. This could be a good time of the day for a beggar—but no one ever dropped money into the bowl of a sleeping mendicant.

Footfalls down the street shook him awake now: a familiar limping gait. He listened as the sounds came closer. "Master Hadad," he said, his wrinkled old face slipping into a smile.

"Hello, Bahirum," the young man said. "How are you today? How's business?"

"A little slow," the blind man said. "But thanks to your generosity, sir, I won't starve if they pass me by altogether today."

"Ah, well," the young man said, steering the conversation away from the blind man's expressions of gratitude. "Nobody should have to worry about tomorrow the way you had to. And nobody should have to shiver in the chilly air this fall and winter. I'm going to see you've got a decent blanket here."

"Thank you, sir," Bahirum said. "But who will give aid to a beggar with a nice blanket wrapped around him? No, sir. You've done more than enough—what was that sound, now?"

"Oh, that." Hadad followed the soft tinkle with a resounding *thrum!*—a chord that rang powerfully in the soft afternoon air. "I bought a cithara. I've just come back from having it strung. It's a surprise for my girl."

"*Your* girl, sir? Then you're—oh, I'm glad for you. The women of the bazaar used to worry so about you, with no one to look after you."

"Ah. Well, those days are over." There was a note of pleasure, of contentment in the young man's voice. "There's nothing I can do for you, then? Because I'm on my way home, and—"

"No, sir. Thank you, sir. And—the gods be with you, sir." Bahirum inclined his head respectfully and listened to Hadad's unsteady gait as the sound of his footfalls diminished down the street. *You damned fool,* he told himself. *You could have had a nice warm blanket—the best.* Now that the young sculptor had come into comparative affluence, his gifts to his friends were well known and much admired, the more so as Hadad spared no expense. Well, perhaps later he'd make the offer again. . . .

But now he heard another pair of feet approaching. Short, light steps. A child? No, a woman. "Alms?" he said. "Alms, in the name of—"

The steps stopped before him; a coin, very likely of small denomination from its dull clank, clattered in his bowl. "Beggar," a woman's voice said. "I seek Hadad the sculptor."

Bahirum forced his features into a neutral professional smile. "I'm afraid you've just missed him, ma'am. He passed this way"—he motioned down the street with one hand—"not very long ago. He said he was going home. You might catch him if you hurried."

"Very well," the voice said. Bahirum listened for the clank of another coin; listened for some sign of gratitude. Neither was forthcoming. The woman's steps followed Hadad's.

He frowned, picked up the bowl. The coin was the smallest in current use, of base metal. He tucked it in his ragged robe. And he thought about the young woman. Her voice had been patrician, melodious, well placed; but there had been little heart in it. She sounded like a cold bitch. He shook his head sadly. If this was Hadad's girl, so much the worse for the poor fellow. She'd lead him a merry chase, and make his life a sad and rueful one.

Hadad opened the door, looked around. "Danataya?" he said. "Danataya, are you there?"

There was no answer. He stepped inside and went to the door that led to his mother's connecting apartment. He knocked once; then he cracked the door. "Mother?" he said. This call, too, went unanswered. He poked his head inside. Tallay and the nurse were gone; the little room was neat and

356

clean. Then he remembered: this was the day the girl took Tallay to the river to wash clothes. He closed the door behind him and stepped back into his own quarters. The cithara was still in his hand; he'd have to hide it if he were going to surprise Danataya. He stood, deep in thought, for a moment; then he reached up to the overhead beam behind which he customarily kept their loose money. There was a large empty space behind it, where the roof overhang began. He climbed atop a table, holding the precious instrument carefully in one hand, and teetering precariously, he managed to tuck the cithara out of sight. Now, unless her curiosity led her farther afield than usual . . .

"Hadad?" a voice said behind him as he clambered down from the table. He wheeled. A slim figure stood outlined against the light from the open door.

"Anat?" he said. He moved toward her, unsure what to say. He hadn't seen her—or tried to see her—since that terrible day when she'd done her best to destroy him. He wondered what she wanted—and wondered as well how she was going to handle this meeting.

"Hello, Hadad," she said. Her composure was, as always, remarkable. Or was it? He could see her face now. Under the cool surface there was a disturbed look about her. "I—I heard about your good fortune. Congratulations."

"Oh," he said, wondering what to say. "Yes, I'm having to get used to it a little at a time. But—well, I must say affluence is easy to adjust to. Compared to some other things." He winced inwardly at the lameness of his own remarks. "You're looking, uh, well." It was a lie. She looked simply terrible: her natural thinness was now approaching emaciation; her pallor now seemed a sign of recent illness.

"Hadad," she said. "I—I wanted to apologize. I said some very unkind things."

"No, no," he said, holding up one thin hand. "I think you must have been upset. Forget it. Please." He looked nervously around the room. "Can I get you anything? Wine? Food?"

"No, no. Hadad—it's Shobai. I'm worried about him."

"Shobai?" Hadad was instantly alert. "Why? Have you heard from him? Is something wrong?"

"I haven't heard anything. Anything at all. And it's been weeks and weeks."

"Goodness! I would have thought—but he left Carchemish. . . ."

"Yes," she said. Behind the icy restraint of her voice was

357

something very like panic. "I know when he left. And nobody seems to know where he was going. He left with none of the caravans. He may, for all I know, be lying dead out in the brush somewhere. Bandits from the hills—"

"Shobai? Well, it's possible, Anat. There have been some reports—but usually he's so prudent about such things, particularly when there's money involved."

"That's just it. There should have been a transfer of money from Carchemish to our accounts in Haran. There wasn't."

"Ah. I'd forgotten. Yes, I knew that. I—sent someone to Carchemish to ask after him and found out that he'd set up an account there. But I thought—"

"Yes, and now I don't know what to think. He hasn't come home. And—well, remember your father. Picking up and leaving like that, abandoning your mother and you two . . ."

Hadad pursed his lips. Shobai? This was unlike him, to be sure. But Shobai, his mother had always said, had a lot of his father in him: impulsive, headstrong, self-centered. . . . He frowned. There was no use backing away from the hard truths anymore. "It *is* a little peculiar," he said. "But—well, Anat. Your own actions—" He gulped and went on doggedly. "Don't you think they might have got back to him? I mean . . ."

There was the hot flash of anger in her dark eye. "I'll thank you to mind your own business," she said. "If you—"

Hadad sighed. "Anat," he said mildly. "When you came here, you made it my business. Is there something I can do to help? I mean, do you need money or anything? To run the house, or—?"

"No, no." She'd regained her cool front very quickly, he noticed. "But—how do I go about locating him? Or—or establishing once and for all whether he's alive or—or dead? Or whether he's just up and left me for—for some other woman . . . ?"

"I'll have someone look into it," he said. "I don't know the procedures either." Try as he might, he couldn't keep a trace of resentment out of his voice. Here Shobai was only a month or two gone—and she was already trying to have him declared dead or whatever. The better to legitimatize her connection with the fox-faced soldier, no doubt. "In the meantime, Anat—what if he returns? Suddenly, I mean?"

"Why—what do you mean?"

"Well, will he, uh, will he come blundering in on something? Will there be any surprises?"

She shot him a barbed glance. "N-no," she said, her

composure cracking for the first time. "I—I'm by myself now."

Ah, he thought. *So he's moved on....* There was a perverse joy in his understanding of the fact, and he was immediately ashamed of his own malice. "All right," he said. "I'll see what I can do. There's nothing I can get you? You're sure you won't have a—"

"No, no," she said. Then, as an afterthought, she said "Thank you." She looked around, her acute eye evaluating the modest but decent appointments, the touch of taste in their selection and arrangement. "Hadad," she said. "This place shows a woman's hand. Have you . . . ?"

He blushed—and hated himself for it. A hot flash of anger and resentment ran through him again. "I—I was going to tell you it was none of your business, Anat. But yes. I have a girl. She's . . . very nice."

Her eye looked him up and down, evaluating again, finding as always little merit, little worth, in what she saw. "Ah, yes. 'Nice.' I'm sure she is. Good day to you, Hadad."

As he watched her walk away, he wondered for the first time why he had ever found her attractive. Could it have been just because he had had no woman of his own then? And no life of his own? And now, how changed his whole outlook was! Had he grown that much in so short a while?

He sat down behind the table and stared at the door she had closed behind her. He thought of Danataya, and his eye went to the ceiling, to the space behind the beam. Perhaps he'd get the cithara down and practice. How nice it would be to be able to surprise her when she returned! After all, he could spare the rest of the afternoon; the morning's work had gone extraordinarily well and quickly. When she returned, he'd be all tuned up and ready to serenade her, just the way she'd been wanting him to. Yes, he'd get the instrument down again. Those new strings would still be stretching; they'd need some adjusting. . . .

Danataya scanned Yamam's round and pleasant face anxiously. "All that has been running through my mind," she said, "and I can't seem to make any sense of anything. First I think one thing, then another—oh, Yamam, I don't know *what* I think."

"Poor darling," the dancer said. "Now, if it were just any old sort of man, it'd be another thing. But—you know, I never thought you'd convince me he was any sort of catch. He didn't look like much, you know. And when you met him,

359

he was as poor as a beggar, and you certainly didn't need another fish as bad off as yourself, with nothing between the two of you and the winter's cold but—"

"Oh, I love him," Danataya said miserably. "I love him so."

"Yes. Well, that was what I was getting around to. He *is* a sweetheart. You were right. And it really does begin to look as if he were on his way up in the world. You should hear what my rich old merchant says, the old fool. . . ."

"How can I do anything that would—well, would lose him, Yamam? How can I take the chance? He's not ready for—well, for wife and family, for settling down like that."

"Settling? It certainly seems the two of you have been *acting* like an old settled couple. You're home from the bazaars an hour before he leaves work; you rush to get supper on the table—"

"Yamam. It's just—it seems like too big a strain to put on things at this stage. I don't even know if he would—"

"Look, darling, every man wants sons. *Every* man. Why should Hadad be any different?"

"But we're not married."

"True, true," the girl said with a sigh. "And you do have a point. He may just bolt. Some of the steadiest-sounding ones do, when it comes down to things. So what do you want to do?"

Then Yamam's eyes lit up. She sat up, looked at her friend. "I see," she said. "There is, after all, an alternative. And—well, Hadad hasn't much experience of girls. He won't be able to tell the difference. You can say you're going away to visit a sick relative for a few days. And—yes, yes. It might be the best thing after all."

"Then . . . you know someone?"

"The very best," Yamam said. "But he'll be expensive. The worst part is, the expense goes on for a bit. Particularly if he gets the notion that you have money. First you buy his service; then you buy his silence. But it won't go on too long; he's more discreet than most. There's one fellow over on the other side of town who'll milk you forever if you let him. Why, when I used him, I had to get one of my boy friends to beat him up, or he'd still be gouging me for—"

"Yamam: does it—does it hurt?"

"This early? No, not much—not physically, anyhow. You'll feel terrible inside for a while, of course. That's the way it always is. But you're a tough girl. You'll get over it."

* * *

Danataya's hands shook as she opened the door. "Hadad?" she called out softly. There was no answer; still she hesitated. Her heart was pounding. She'd made the appointment for the next day; now it was a matter of keeping it all from Hadad, and working up some plausible cover story.

But then she stepped inside and saw him sitting on the bed, propped against the wall, a look of peace on his gentle face, his eyes closed and his breathing deep. The beautiful cithara still lay cradled in his arms, although his hands had long since slipped away from it. How long had he been waiting there for her this way?

Suddenly, she could not see his face through her hot tears of shame and self-loathing. She stifled a sob with her hand.

VI

"And you, sir? What can I do for you?" the official said. His expression was neither friendly nor forbidding. He looked at Jacob with a neutral eye: Jacob was decently if not expensively dressed, and had an air of solidity, of responsibility, about him. "I—I didn't get the name."

"Jacob, sir," his visitor said, inclining his head slightly in respect. "Sometime bondman to Laban, son of Nahor, a rich pastoralist of the city. Recently freed yet still in the service of Laban as a freedman."

"Ah," the official said. "I've met the noble Laban. A man of substance."

"Yes, sir. I married two of his daughters, who have borne him many grandsons." Jacob leaned on the connection a little, his eyes on the official's face. "Myself, I do business with many merchants of the Bazaar of the Well and other bazaars within the city. I have also done business with the lord Oshiyahu, commander of the—"

But here Jacob stopped. The expression on the official's face had turned to one of extreme displeasure. "Oshiyahu?" the official said. "I wouldn't brag about that, let me tell you. That damned hothead is going to wind up with his neck on the block one of these days if he doesn't come to his senses."

"Neck on the . . . ?" Jacob said, puzzled. "I thought he was—"

"Oshiyahu has made many powerful enemies in recent weeks," the official said. "Myself among their number. And let me tell you, my friend, if you're counting on using his influence, you've got the wrong idea. He'll be out of a job before the next full moon." He held up his hands in a gesture of contemptuous dismissal. "Imagine: he's calling for conscription of the young men of the city. Conscription! In peacetime! Well, let me tell you, he'll get no son of mine. Nor any nephew, or—"

"But I heard—the nomads—" Jacob spoke haltingly, his eyes on the official's fat face, feeling his way.

"Nomads! Bugaboos! Bogeyman to scare the young with! In the first place, they'd never dare attack a major city like Haran. In the second—"

"I defer to your superior understanding," Jacob said. "I may indeed have been misinformed."

The official stopped, looked at him with new eyes. "Well," he said, mollified by Jacob's tone. "That's better. Look you, though: I wouldn't go claiming Oshiyahu for a friend. He's out. Out in the cold. If there were a worse notion to bring up right now, with things tight, than spending vast sums on rearmament and draining off our young men into military service, I wouldn't have any idea what it could be." He rose and came around the table, a patronizing smile on his face. "Now: what can I do for you?"

"Well, sir—I'm sorry, I didn't get your name either."

"Yahadu," the official said. "Assistant to the lord Puzur. I gather your errand has something to do with patronage."

"I shall tell everyone in the bazaar of your wisdom and insight, sir."

"Well. You're in luck, perhaps. Puzur has been hard hit by taxes. He *can* be reached just now. By, ah, someone with the right understanding of how to approach a man in his position."

"I will be guided by you in all things, sir."

"Very well. Nothing must be in writing. Ten silver pieces in a small unmarked bag. And the half of this more, for myself . . ."

"Understood," Jacob said. He flinched inside at the price, but his face showed none of his concern.

". . . and . . . ah, yes, the noble Puzur is fond of mutton. . . ."

"Your words are of crystal clarity. And—a time?"

"Within a week. Shall we say . . . next Tuesday?"

"Yes, sir. Tuesday it will be." Jacob bowed once again, this time more deeply than before, and left the official's presence, backing away, his hands pressed together before his chest.

In the street, he looked up at the darkening sky. *Time to go home,* he thought. He looked around; the street was full of beggars, the blind, the maimed. They gathered here in the street before the apartments of the bureaucrats of the city, where the money was. There were people with missing arms, legs, eyes; a scarred face, a withered limb . . .

But now he took more notice of them. They were not, most of them, from Haran. Their faces, the styles of beards they wore, the cut of their tattered clothing—all these spoke of foreign origins. He stepped forward to stand before a blind man, a man whose eyes had been put out and whose dark sockets gaped at him horribly. "You, my friend," he said. "Where do you come from? You're not of the city, are you?"

"Ah, no, my lord—we all come from afar. From the lands north of Mari, where the devils from the mountains have looted and killed." He indicated his ravaged face. "And, sir, left me as I am." His hand lay palm up before him. "Mercy, sir—take pity on the blind."

Jacob frowned. "You are from one of the sacked cities?" he said. A plan, nebulous still, had begun to suggest itself. "Then you'll know something about the nomads—tell me, do you know one of them named Manouk? A man with a dark—"

"Manouk!" the blind man said, dark rage contorting his gaunt face. "The traitor, the liar, the cheat—yes, I know of Manouk. He came to us with a flag of truce and made us promises of what he would do if we lay down our arms. Yes. And when we opened the gates to the city, the nomad hordes led by the Shepherd Kings swept in and . . ." His words were lost in a sob.

Jacob placed one hand on the beggar's thin shoulder. "Then this Manouk—he's the leader of the Shepherd Kings? Their commander?"

"No, no. There is one higher, a king of kings. He is infinitely worse. Manouk is a snake. The one they call 'the Leader' is to Manouk as the lion to the hind. 'The Leader'—I am persuaded that he may eat all he kills. Women, children, warriors, the old . . ." His voice rose now. "My brothers! My

363

friends! Tell this man about the barbarians, about 'the Leader'!" He turned his sightless face to Jacob again as the voices rose around him. "You see, sir, he . . ."

But his voice was drowned out under the general din that followed. The beggars gathered around Jacob, each shouting to be heard. He caught scraps of it here and there: " . . . killed my wife and daughters, right on the spot . . ." "A giant, an ogre, a monster from Hell . . ." " . . . impaled . . ."

"Here, here!" Jacob said, holding up his two hands. "I believe you. But look, my friends, the people of the city do not believe you. Have you tried to tell them?"

The blind man's reply was full of scorn. "Who listens to a beggar? A foreign one at that? It's all we can do to pry alms loose from tight fingers. If we asked them to listen to what we said as well . . ."

Jacob smiled and dropped a coin into the blind man's bowl. "Look," he said, "I'm a poor man myself. I have no money. But I do have time—some of it, at least. And I'm a good listener. What if I were to find other good listeners and steer them your way? Would you be interested in talking to them? Telling them your story?"

There was shocked silence; then a single voice bellowed "Yes!" His voice was seconded by a dozen others.

There was a thoughtful look on Jacob's face as he strolled through the markets in the gathering chill of evening. The plan that had occurred to him in the street before the house of Puzur was rapidly taking shape.

Whether Oshiyahu's forces, augmented according to his demands before the council, could successfully defend Haran in the event of a nomad attack was an arguable point. It seemed likely that Haran would be unable to withstand much of a siege, bloated as it was with the refugees. Its food reserves were already much depleted, and still the refugees continued to pour into the city, further complicating not only the problem of supply but the problem of maintaining order as well. There had been several minor flare-ups in recent weeks between the refugees and the city's poor, whom they were rapidly displacing; it might be no more than a matter of days before the first major riot broke out.

The question was this: with the level of military preparedness where it was now, could Haran even defend itself at all—either against attack from without or against revolt from within? Jacob, thinking it over now, decided not. In a time of peace and—until now, anyhow—relative affluence, it was difficult to sell the businessmen who ran the city on the notion that present conditions would not remain forever in effect. Oshiyahu's dogged insistence on getting new funds from them for defense had so far only succeeded in branding the commander as a nuisance, a gadfly, an ill-mannered boor. . . .

Well, what if he, Jacob, could help Oshiyahu convince the council and King Shemariah of the seriousness of the threat the Shepherd Kings posed? What if he and Oshiyahu could bring before the nobles of the council a group of the refugees, the most articulate and persuasive among them, and get them to give eyewitness depositions before the assembled city fathers? To tell of the rapacity and treachery of the strangers, of their invincibility in war, their implacability at the bargaining table?

Crossing the bridge, Jacob looked down at the low water of the stream. There was another problem, if siege became fact: the rainy season was still some months in the future, and the city's water reserves were low. Aqueducts from the high hills could easily be cut by a besieging force. Death by starvation was bad enough; death of thirst was horrible in the extreme. The blinded man's tales had drawn terrifying pictures inside his mind: first the children had died, then the old—

Jacob stopped, his hand on the railing of the little bridge. *Why do I concern myself with Haran?* he thought. *I, who long to leave it, more and more with each passing day?* It was, after all, only a home enforced upon him by the bitter terms of his exile; he had only very distant blood kin here. His own land lay far to the south.

He shook his head, his face somber. Ah, but that wasn't all there was to it. He had friends here, friends whom he would be abandoning to their deaths when he left for Canaan. And when the time came, there'd be a wrench at his heart for them, the same as if they were of his blood. . . .

Oh, the ambiguities, the uncertainties of life! The complications, the qualifications that muddied the clear waters! How simple it had all seemed in his youth—and how distressingly complex everything was now!

His mouth tightened. No, he had to keep reminding himself of the priorities, the proper ones. His path lay southward.

Now, closing his eyes for a moment, he found himself remembering for the first time in many years the strange dream he'd had that time on the road north into exile, above Beersheba, before the town of Luz. Yes! It was the last time the God had spoken to him, showing him a vision of the ladder—a golden staircase that rose to the sky above, a staircase on which the shining angels of the Lord moved slowly up and down. . . .

And now the words of the God of his fathers came back to him, words which told him that his descendants would be as the grains of sand on the earth, spreading here and there. . . . *"Remember, I am with you: I will protect you wherever you go and will bring you back to this land. I will not leave you until I have done what I have promised. . . ."*

Jacob's fist closed; he pounded it on the stone rail. A fierce smile spread slowly over his face. The promise! He'd forgotten the promise! And the God had told him he and his would survive and return to the land He had given Abraham and his seed forever. . . .

Yes, but there was a promise he, Jacob, had made, and he had forgotten that one, too. A promise he'd marked with a stone he'd set up, there on the hillside above Luz, in the plain he'd named Bethel: "This stone shall be God's abode, and of all that You give me, I will always set aside a tenth of it to return to You. . . ."

A tithe for the God! And he'd forgotten! In his despair he'd let it slip away and forgotten his own sacred pledge!

Jacob smiled: a slow smile that spread over his face. Had the God spoken to him again just now, reminding him of his forgotten vows? Or was it only his own conscience? Well, it did not matter. The main thing was that he had remembered, at last. And, having remembered, he could do only one thing: renew his pledge, and make the tithing of his goods an accomplished fact before another day had passed. His eyes bright, he lengthened his stride and bent his steps homeward, the heartbeat in his breast, quick and strong.

Half a block down the narrow street from his home he could already smell the rich scents of a festive meal, and his sensitive nose picked out the separate courses by their heady aromas: minced lamb mixed with onions and spices, baked eggplant stuffed with lamb and pine nuts, pastries, the seductive smell of fresh-baked bread. His favorites! And enough for a wedding feast! But who was being married? Certainly none of his blood. . . .

He opened the door and looked inside. "Rachel?" he said pleasantly. "Leah? I'm home!"

But then Rachel came out of the kitchen and looked at him. There was a slow smile on her face, a slow proud smile that set her sweet face aglow. She folded her arms over her breasts and looked at him with pride and love.

"Rachel," Jacob said, looking at her, the door handle still in his hand. "I—I think the God has spoken to me again. Even if it was only for a moment. I had forgotten the promise I made Him years ago, on my way north to find you. But now—now we will renew the sacrifices, reserve a tithe of our goods for Him."

She stood there still, the smile broadening. She did not respond at first. Then she uncrossed her arms and held her hands together. Her voice was low and musky: "Jacob, my darling. The God has spoken to me as well. . . ."

Jacob stared. At first he didn't understand. Then it slowly dawned on him, little by little. And his own smile, when it came, had tears of joy in it as he moved forward to embrace her—gently, tenderly, but passionately withal.

VII

The first rays of the dawn, leaking through the open window above their bed, awoke Hadad. He blinked, stretched, yawned, reached for Danataya. . . .

His hand, outstretched, found no warm, gently rounded form beside him. He paddled in the bedclothes curiously. There was an indentation there, but the cloth was cold to the touch.

"Danataya?" he said. He sat up, rubbing his eyes. "Danataya?" He looked around. In the first thin light he could make out the lines of his furniture, the tables and chairs; but no moving objects broke the stillness of the room. "Danataya!" he said, raising his voice a little.

There was no sound, other than the distant noises of the waking city that carried gently through the window. He rose, wound his loincloth about him, reached for a robe, stepped into sandals. And, the limp as pronounced as ever, he moved across the atriumlike center room of his apartment to the door that led to his mother's rooms. He gently opened the door, looked around. He could see Tallay's gaunt form on the far bed, sleeping soundly; beside her, on a couch, the nurse Nuhama. He closed the door softly behind him as he slipped out.

Where could she be? He opened the front door and looked

367

out into the empty street. The first rays of sunlight were beginning to peep over the rooftops to the east; as he watched, the pink clouds parted to let the morning sun through. High on top of a weathercock a live bird sang.

"Danataya," he said. But it was a whisper this time, one with a dying fall to it.

He stood looking up and down the street for a moment; then, shivering once against the morning chill, he stepped back inside his dwelling. Where could she be? And what could make her leave his bed before the dawn, without explanation? What . . . ?

But now he saw the little tablet on the table. He crossed to pick it up, blinking in the thin light, trying to make out the tiny markings. In the end, he had to light a candle and hold the still moist tablet up to the flame to make out the words: *Darling Hadad: a messenger came in the night. A friend of mine is desperately ill and needs me. I could not bear to wake you. I'll be back in a day or two. I'll try to send you a message.*

There was the affectionate close, followed by the marks that made up her name. Danataya wrote a clean hand; her father had taken pains to give his only daughter skills few princesses could command.

Hadad looked down at the little tablet, biting his lip. It didn't make sense. This was unlike Danataya. In the weeks they'd been together he'd never known her to do anything irresponsible at all; she'd never gone anywhere without giving him exact information as to her whereabouts and the time of her return. It was so unlike her. . . .

He frowned. The more so, he thought, after the lovely, gentle, warm evening they'd had together. He'd awakened from his impromptu afternoon nap to find her sitting above him, looking down at him lovingly. He'd reached for her. . . .

Yes, and she'd found the new cithara he'd bought for her, and she'd insisted he sing while she prepared their dinner. And his songs had brought tears of happiness to her eyes.

Tears? Was something wrong? She had, after all, been uncommonly quick to weep last night. Was there perhaps some shadow over their love, something he didn't know about?

A quick pang of fear ran through him. Danataya had told him little about her earlier life; he'd passed it off, thinking her embarrassed at the poverty to which she'd sunk after her father's death. Yes, and there'd been some sort of episode in which she'd apparently been jilted by some young suitor in

368

favor of a girl with connections, with family and a rich dowry. . . .

A small smile passed over his round face. Dowry? What did a wonderful girl like Danataya need with a dowry? And what sort of man would pass her by because she brought no money, no property to a love match?

He pursed his lips. But—did this have something to do with her sudden disappearance? And who was this "friend" who had so suddenly taken ill and called for her? He pondered the question. Who among her small circle of friends would know? Would her aunt, her uncle? Would Admuniri and Abi-samar . . . ?

Wait. Wait: there was the girl who worked at the Inn of the White Horse. The dancer. What was her name, now?

In the dawn light Reshef strode down the broad street that led to Hirgab's house at the end of the lane. He'd arrived after dark, after the city gates had closed. His rank and position would easily have opened the barred gate to him; but he had been hot and dusty and out of sorts, and in no mood to confront Hirgab with the bad news he'd brought back from Carchemish—that Hagirum's court was of the opposite mind from Shemariah's, and would oppose the Shepherd Kings vigorously.

Instead of entering the city then, he'd gone whoring; there was a fair outside the city, and there had been drink and other rowdy pleasures. There'd even been a rather specialized quarter of bawdy houses, where a man in search of dalliance could find any sort of pleasure he wanted—including the exquisite pleasure of inflicting pain. . . .

His thin smile recorded the memory; but now it was even more crooked and contorted than before; there was a part of his face, around the knife-scar, that did not move when he commanded it to. An icy stab of rage shot through him at the thought, and he remembered now with helpless anger the futile search he'd made in Carchemish for sign of Shobai the Armorer. He'd virtually turned out the dregs of the stews, asking for information about the weaponmaker; but no one had known where the metalworker had gone.

Now, on Hirgab's doorstep, his face retained its resentful scowl as he banged insolently on the door. He barked at the servant who answered, and when he was shown in, he paced like a caged lion until his superior appeared, still dressed in night clothes—but, Reshef noted, freshly scrubbed and combed. "My lord," Reshef said with a bow that barely

369

stopped short of insolence. "You said to call the moment I returned."

"Ah," Hirgab said. "Has my man offered you refreshment?" Reshef shrugged the thought away. "Very well, I gather from the expression on your face that Hagirum won't go along. I expected as much." His own shrug was dismissive, contemptuous. "It doesn't matter. Do you remember the plan we discussed earlier?"

"Yes," Reshef said. He couldn't resist the temptation to add, "You mean the one I suggested."

"Yes," Hirgab said, shrugging this off, too. "Well, I've thought it over and I think we need to put it into practice immediately. This Oshiyahu is getting to be a sore under our saddle. . . ."

"Yes," Reshef said, "and how far are we willing to go in removing the, ah, sore, my lord?" His eyes narrowed as the crooked smile played on his thin lips.

"It depends. We have to do something now. Soon. Are you ready to travel again? I hate to ask you, but . . ."

Reshef's eyes were slits now; his smile was broad. "In the service of such a strategy I'd travel without sleep, my lord," he said. "Then it's—the north?"

"Yes," Hirgab said. "I've a message for you to deliver. A message to—what was his name again? This, ah, friend of yours?"

Reshef, his heart pounding, bowed his head respectfully. He did not answer for a moment. Then he said, "Yes, my lord. A message to Manouk . . ."

"Yamam," Hadad said. "There's something you're not telling me. Please—"

"Hadad. I made a promise." The girl picked nervously at her new robe, the one her rich old man had given her the week before. "I can't go back on it."

"Please." He gripped her hand in his, pressed it. "I have a feeling it's very important. She wouldn't have left me like that if . . ."

Yamam bit her full lip. "Hadad," she said, near despair. "She—she's pregnant. With your child. . . ."

Hadad dropped her hand. His mouth flew open. His eyes widened. "M-my child . . . ?" he said. "But—but I don't understand."

"Oh, Hadad. You men *never* understand. You make babies in our bellies, and then you think it's all our fault, the women's, and then you leave it to us to—"

"To what? To what, Yamam? What has she gone away to ... ?"

And then it hit him. His face fell; the blood drained away from it. "Yamam! She isn't going to ... ?"

"Why, of course," the girl said. "What did you expect? She was afraid the news would drive you away. And she didn't want to lose you."

Hadad stood. He was shaking like a leaf. His voice trembled as he spoke. "Yamam. Yamam! She's going to kill it? Kill my child? Because—because I—" He reached out, grabbed a fold of her robe. "Where? Where has she gone? You must tell me? If I'm too late, I'll—"

Yamam pulled her robe free. "Oh, Hadad! It may well be too late. If only she'd known—" Her voice broke. "Here," she said, handing him a tablet from a table beside her. "The street's a short one. It leads off the Street of the Soothsayers, the one that runs into the Bazaar of the Twin Oaks. But hurry ..."

But she spoke to his retreating back. She would never have believed Hadad the Cripple could move so quickly.

Yassib slammed the door behind him and rushed down the narrow street before his house. There was a trickle of something wet running down the side of his face; he held a hand to it and pulled it away bloody. He cursed under his breath. Halima! She'd nearly brained him with that jug, the little bitch!

He wiped away the trickle of red, his back teeth clamped together. Well, he'd shown *her*. Perhaps she'd think twice before attacking him that way again—once she woke up covered with bruises, her eyes closed by the dark swellings.

But now he stopped dead in the street, and his heart stopped with him for a moment. Gods! Gods! What would happen when Oshiyahu heard of this? What had he said about anyone mistreating his daughter? Gods! Oshiyahu would break him! Literally as well as professionally.

What could he do? Could he go back and—and apologize? Try to get her to hide from her family until the bruises, the black eyes, disappeared? But no; she'd never do that. Not even if he threatened her. Because the one thing their night-long battle had established was that she would no longer respond to his threats the way she had. "I'll tell my father!" she'd screamed at him in that fishwife voice of hers. And she would, she would indeed. She'd bear her lumps and bruises proudly; all she wanted now was revenge. And she'd get it!

What could he do? Panic seized him; he wrung his big hands, his mind rushing from one worthless solution to another. And now the cold sweat on his brow ran down his face as the blood had done. Where could he go? He was ruined, ruined. . . .

"Yassib!" a voice said behind him. He wheeled, his face a mask of fear.

But it was Reshef standing there now, his scarred face twisted in a chilly smile. Reshef took in his fear and panic, and a tiny sneer of condescension lifted one of his thin lips. "Yassib," he said. "I have good news for you."

"G-good news?" the younger man said. "My lord—I'm ruined—it's a matter of hours at best before—"

"Ah," Reshef said. "Trouble with Oshiyahu, I'll bet. Those are nail scratches on that cheek of yours, I'll wager. Fighting with his lordship's daughter again, I suppose, and the old man won't take kindly to that, will he? Well, don't worry. Oshiyahu's days are over. He's—"

"But he'll kill me. I have to—"

"He won't do anything. By noon you'll be on your way north with me, with a detachment of royal guards."

"Northward with . . . ? But that's desertion."

"No it isn't," Reshef said. "You've been separated from the army. This morning. By order of the lord Hirgab. You're on his staff now, not Oshiyahu's. And you and I have a mission to perform, one which will cook Oshiyahu's goose for him before the month is out, or I'm a graybeard."

"Mission?" Yassib said. Then he'd be out of town when Oshiyahu learned of—"Yes! Yes!" He reached for Reshef's hand impulsively. Reshef drew it away, disgusted. "When do we leave?" he said eagerly.

"We already have," Reshef said coldly. "A couple of moments ago. Don't stop for anything; you're in uniform already. But you might wipe off that blood on your cheek."

"But—but if my father-in-law—"

"Forget him," Reshef said. "He's as good as dead."

The leech was an ugly little man with a sty in one eye; his clothes were dirty, and so were his hands. When he touched Danataya's arm, she shrank away from him. "Here, my dear," he said in a wheedling voice. "After all, we're going to have to get—well, better acquainted in a matter of minutes now."

"N-no," she said. "I—I've changed my mind. I don't want to go through with it. I'll—"

"There, now. You've paid for it already. Most of it,

anyway. The rest we can—work out. You're a pretty little thing, you know—"

"Get away from me! I won't—you can't make me—"

"There, now. There, you'll be all right. It's just a matter of a few minutes' discomfort. And then your secret will be safe, you know. Nobody will know."

"Let go of me!" she said. She tried to pull her hand away, but his grip was strong. "You can't—" He reached for her; she slapped his face with her free hand. It jarred loose his grip on the other. She scrambled away to the other side of the dingy room, but he still stood between her and the door. "Now," she said, "just—just let me go and you can keep the money...."

"Well! And a tidy profit that'd make for two minutes of argument with you. I should take you up on it. But I'm thinking. Even if you go to another than me, my dear, you've a secret to keep. And there's one fine way to close my mouth for me, you know. Besides money, I mean. If you were nice to me—"

But now the door was open behind him, and a huge hand descended on his shoulder and spun him around and lifted him high. Danataya's mouth dropped open. "Bunu-ishdar!" she said. The blacksmith paid her no mind, holding the leech high with one hand. His other great paw went around the leech's neck.

Then there was another figure in the doorway, his face dark with concern. His arms spread wide for her; she rushed into them with a sob. "Hadad!" she cried. "I—I thought—"

He held her tight, patting her comfortingly on the back. "I know," he said. "And you thought wrong, my darling. Could you really believe I wouldn't want a child we'd made? Could you really think the news would have made me anything but deliriously happy? Oh, Danataya, my heart is so full! Imagine: a child of my own—"

"Hadad," she said. His arms, thin and short, seemed as strong as the blacksmith's. "Take me back, please. Forgive me. Please. I didn't know...."

"Well," he said, his voice calmer now, "I suppose that means I'll have to spend more time letting you know. And look you: we're posting the banns before nightfall. And I'm going to order up the biggest feast the Bazaar of the Well has ever known. I'm—" But now he stopped, a puzzled look on his face, and held her at arm's length. "You will marry me, won't you? I mean—"

"Oh, Hadad," she said, rushing into his arms again.

CHAPTER TWELVE

I

The major routes of commerce and of war, by this time, had existed for many centuries. They connected the Great Sea, at the Nile Delta, with the Lower Sea below Ur, where the waters of the mighty Tigris and Euphrates finally found their outlet after their long journeys. The main route followed the Euphrates from the fens below Ur northward past Babylon and Akkad before cutting westward, still following the Great River, to Mari, the midpoint on its journey.

From Mari the trade route forked. A minor route worked its way northward toward the sources of the Euphrates and connected with Aleppo, Ebla, and Ugarit. From Aleppo and Tiphsah and smaller watering places along the way, spur routes ran north through the smaller cities such as Carchemish and Haran before heading into Hittite country and the Hurrian highland.

The main route, however, cut across the desert from Mari to Damascus, bypassing all these, bypassing Byblos and Tyre and sea-girt Arvad to connect, at Hazor, with the "way of the sea"—the ancient highway that led along the coast of the Great Sea to Sile and the beginning of the border lands of the venerable Egyptian Empire.

This arching road, from the Valley of the Two Rivers to the wetlands that Jacob's people called Goshen, was the southernmost route known to the great caravans. To be sure, tracks did cut from Babylon to Edom across the dry saltpans and drifting dunes, far to the south of the great trade routes; but the water available on these tracks was barely enough to support the parched bands of Bedouin who guarded them, and would not have given shelter or the chance of life to any caravan, however small.

Along these routes, merchants of a variety of trade commodities wended their way from city to city: vegetables and fruits from the great river valleys; copper, salt, and turquoise from the lands south of Canaan; dried fish, textiles, and fruit from the shore cities on the Great Sea; cedar and other choice woods from the mountains of Lebanon and the Anti-Lebanon; dyes from the cities of the North Coast. There was a brisk trade in camels from Edom and, more recently, in horses from Arabia and from the wild lands north of Nineveh.

Now, however, the traffic along the great bow-shaped paths from the Lower Sea to the Nile Valley was disrupted more and more. To the north and east the nomad band, having crossed the Caucasus in a single column, had broken up into a broad front that stretched most of the way from the Black Sea to the Caspian and advanced in many columns instead of one. These advanced at differing speeds according to the nature of the lands they would have to cross; one column, striking suddenly southward with brutal force, had sliced through the trade route that led from Nineveh, on the Tigris, westward through Hurrian lands to Kanish, in the Hittite country. From here the marauding column's war parties struck again and again at a second route from Nineveh westward to the twin cities of Carchemish and Haran. After a time, Nineveh armed for war, and no new caravans gathered before the city gates to work their way west; on the other hand Nineveh's trade with people to the south, in Asshur and Akkad and the great empires of the Euphrates, doubled almost overnight.

Midway on the now-closed route from Nineveh to Kanish, almost due north of Haran, lay the border city of Melid. It lay on the northernmost fringe of the rich agricultural country that marked the drainage of the upper tributaries of the Euphrates; north of it was semiarid grassland, fit only for pastoralists.

In recent years, however, Melid had made a discovery or two which threatened to change its position in the scheme of things. Not only had copper been discovered in the foothills to the east of the city, but the new ore called iron had also been found, immediately to the west of the little community.

The black metal was useless to the towns on the southern trade routes; none had yet discovered the secret of the smelting of iron. But to the west of Melid lay caravan routes connecting it with Kanish and Hattusas, where Hittite metalworkers had not only mastered the smelting of the heavy ore, but had begun training apprentices in its working. And Melid by now had become one of Kanish's principal sources of supply for iron.

Thus, when one of the surging nomad columns approached Melid from the east and sent out scouting parties, Kanish sent its own messenger to the city to keep an eye on things, with instructions to report back weekly on developments in the mining country. The messenger was unarmed and unaccompanied by a war party of his own; Kanish had its own troubles to the north, where an upstart named Anittas of Kussara was besieging the city of Hattusas and threatening to leave the city in ashes and rubble. Kanish, its own sovereignty threatened by the nomads, was armed and trained for battle; but the focus of its attention remained on events to the north, for the rebels might sweep southward from Hattusas. The few in Melid who understood the workings of the world took note of this and began liquidating their assets and buying pack animals for a hasty move southward. Mighty Kanish, with its attention divided, would be no help at all. For all one could see, Melid was doomed. And there was no sense whatsoever in staying around to watch the inevitable end.

At the nomad encampment to the east of Melid, near what had been the border town of Amida, trumpets sounded, heralding the arrival of someone high in the nomadic hierarchy. Other trumpeters, located on the hills above, had sounded early warnings, and the message had preceded the party's arrival by half a day. The heavy guards posted on the passes were stirred to activity by their officers, and picket posts suddenly began to look more soldierly. By the time the dignitaries' party approached, each detachment stood tall and stiff to welcome the horsemen as they rode past.

Shobai, sitting easily on his Moabite stallion, loomed tall in the saddle above the shorter nomads. He wore his most expensive and impressive robes, and he bore his father's sword in a scabbard and belt made for him by custom leatherworkers in Ugarit. He was conscious of the many eyes on him as he rode slowly through the crowds at the edge of the great encampment, sandwiched between the nomad officers Vahan and Minas.

He had been in the employ of the Shepherd Kings for two months. It was an unusual way for him to hire out; knowing little of his reputation and nothing at all of the legends of the Children of the Lion, the first nomads he'd contacted had insisted that he prove himself before being sent forward to the inner circle where he could meet and make contact with Manouk and his peers.

Grudgingly, he'd agreed. Family pride boiling in his veins, he'd worked like an apprentice for them, putting in long workdays at the forge and training helpers for the easier stages of the work. In the course of arming the party to which he'd been assigned, he'd begun to get some idea of the military strengths and weaknesses of the nomadic force.

Weaknesses? He thought about the matter now, looking around him at the tent city, as precisely laid out as any town made of obdurate stone. He'd seen the sheer size of the encampment from the heights above; perhaps, he was beginning to think, the weight of numbers, coupled with the amazing mobility of so large a force, might well cancel out any weaknesses he'd found.

Now, ahead of him, he saw Vahan dismount and nod curtly to him to do the same. As he did, he saw Minas leap smartly down from the saddle to stand behind him, one hand already on the hilt of his sword. *They still don't trust me,* he thought. Well, good for them, perhaps. After all, he *was* coming into the presence of the second most highly placed man in the entire nomad organization—Manouk, the man who stood as the Leader's right arm and who, some said, was the brains of the entire group.

For the hundredth time, Shobai found himself wondering about this mysterious "Leader," this king of the Shepherd Kings whose name could not be spoken. So far, every attempt he'd made to get someone to give him a physical description of the man had ended in failure. The Leader was simply someone who lay under an unbreakable taboo: to speak of him at all placed the speaker in great danger.

Now this Manouk—he seemed, from all accounts, to be a totally different sort. Both Minas and Vahan spoke of him with some familiarity—if with a deep, hard-won respect that their words made clear the nomads' second-in-command had earned many times over. They spoke of him with the combined awe and affection that old soldiers the world over displayed in speaking of an able and brave commander they'd fought under many times. And yet, Manouk seemed by now to have risen above the status of fighting commander, above the other nomad kings, to a loftier and more strategic role.

Shobai kept his military bearing as the three trooped

through the crowd and then down a long double line of fierce-looking spearsmen. They were approaching a tent larger than the rest, one which bore at its peak a banner of purple hue—a color obtainable only at great expense through trade with Tyre and its sister cities along the coast of the Great Sea: it came from a mollusk found only there, a fact which made it expensive more for its rarity than its beauty.

Following Vahan and Minas into the tent, Shobai braced himself for the distasteful business of bowing and scraping that seemed to be common in the nomad camps; but to his surprise Vahan and Minas, ranged to either side of him, came to a dead stop and did not bow their heads. Vahan barked out something in the nomad tongue—something which seemed to contain his, Shobai's, name—and stood at attention.

On the far side of the tent a stocky man, black-haired, black-bearded, turned to look at them. He said one word in the nomad language and Shobai's companions saluted and withdrew. He looked Shobai up and down. "Greet-ings," he said. "I am Manouk." He waved away Shobai's attempt at a salute. "No," he said. "No—how you say? No ce-remony." His thick hands dismissed the idea. "Come, sit with me. We share wine. We talk."

Shobai followed him to a cushioned dais at the rear of the tent, and sat cross-legged across from the bearded man. Manouk clapped his hands; a dark-haired young slave girl, wearing only a brief skirt, bore a leather bottle and laid it on the cushions before Manouk. Shobai's eye took her in; her body was lithe, graceful, a dancer's. Her breasts were small but exquisitely formed; her legs were long and slender. Her dark eye lit on his face for no more than a second, then she turned away without expression.

"Drink, " Manouk said.

Shobai took the bottle, squeezed it expertly, directing a long plume of red wine into his mouth. He cut off the flow without spilling a drop. Then he handed the bottle to Manouk. The nomad drank and put the bottle down, wiping stray drops from his dark beard. "So," he said. "You are Shobai. Of Haran?"

"Yes," Shobai said. "Shobai, son of Kirta. I have been working in one of the smaller columns. I—"

Manouk cut in. "I . . . am told that you have ideas about our weapons," he said. "You will show me?"

"Well, yes," Shobai said. "But I need a hand. If someone would bring to us the package that I brought on the back of my horse . . . and if you could have one of the spearsmen bring me his spear?"

Manouk clapped his hands again. Someone in the doorway must have been listening to every word; a spearsman entered and laid his weapon down before Shobai, and a moment later another warrior entered to lay down a blue-wrapped parcel on the sand before their feet. The man who had brought the parcel withdrew; the soldier stood at attention before the weapon he'd laid down.

"All right," Shobai said. He took up the spear . . . and suddenly looked around to see a bowman standing in the open doorway, his weapon armed, the shaft pointed straight at Shobai. "No, no," he said. "Please, tell him I'm only trying to show you an improvement here."

Manouk waved a hand; the bowman lowered his bow but remained standing there, the weapon ready to be rearmed at any moment. "Let him proceed," he said in Shobai's own tongue, repeating it in his own language for the unseen watchers.

Shobai balanced the weapon on his hand. "This is a thrusting spear," he said. "As such it is well made. Your infantry can do deadly damage with it at close quarters. But what if they can't come to close quarters with the enemy? Look." He pulled his sword—the one Kirta had made—and stuck it in the sand, point down, by his feet. He hefted the spear again, changing the position of his hand, weighing it. Then he closed one hand over a specific spot on the handle and retrieved his sword. He began hacking away at the wooden shaft and in a moment had removed a handspan's wood from the handle. Now he rebalanced the weapon in his hand.

"Ah," Manouk said. He smiled a cold smile. "I see what you do."

Shobai reached down, took one of the cushions from the raised dais, and threw it backhand across the tent. Then he poised the spear, raised his mighty young arm, and threw. The spear flew as straight as an arrow's flight and hit the cushion precisely in the middle. He turned back to Manouk, this time ignoring the rearmed bow of the archer in the doorway.

Manouk waved the same dismissive hand; the bow lowered again. "I see," he said. "Good. Very good. More chance to kill. And yet the spear is—"

"Is still good for its original purpose," Shobai said. He

379

watched its owner retrieve it and, his curiosity piqued, heft it in his own hand, testing its new balance point. "And now it can kill at far more than arm's length."

"Good, good," Manouk said. "And now—this package in the blue wrapper?"

"Ah," Shobai said. "That's not finished yet. But I thought I'd show it to you anyway. But first—how would you handle a city that made its fortifications as you make your own? With the ramparts bolstered as you—"

"Ahhhh," Manouk said. His eye fixed on Shobai's. Shobai all but quivered under his intense gaze. "As, say, Carchemish arms now? I think I would starve them out."

"Yes," Shobai said. "And waste a season doing so. But if you could breach the defenses of the city at its most vulnerable point?"

"You mean the city gate itself. But—"

"Your people already use a battering ram. But what if you made it this way?"

He pulled back the blue cloth. The model he'd made earlier resembled nothing more than a huge, brutal phallus mounted on a four-wheel truck. Traces led to horses mounted to either side; there were handles for the hands of many men. "Horses mounted to either side help bring it up to speed," he said. "Then the final thrust is accomplished by human hands. Short of the gates of Babylon itself, I think no door made could withstand it."

Manouk looked at him. His smile was inscrutable, joyless, humorless. His eyes bore steadily into Shobai's very soul. "I think we do business," he said in a chilling voice.

II

Afterward, Manouk came out into the thin sunlight with Shobai. His manner was cordial, almost paternal. "You had good journey here?" he said. "No mishap along way?"

"Yes," Shobai said. "How could there be a mishap? Your people control every step of the trail here, and Vahan and Minas could find their way here in the dark." He looked at the long row of spearsmen who stood to either side of them as they ambled easily through the encampment: their faces were expressionless, but this only made for an even more fierce and warlike impression. "Vahan is quite a horseman," he said. "I gather all of your people are."

"Yes," Manouk said. "My people love horse. We train for many, many generation. My father's father and his father as well." He turned to Shobai as they walked. "You like horse?"

"Yes," Shobai said. "I ride a Moabite myself. Come, I'll show him to you if you like." Manouk assented silently; Shobai steered their steps to where the animals were tethered. "Here," he said. He approached his big paint pony and calmed it with one large hand. "His name is Kedar."

"He is big and strong," Manouk said appreciatively. "He is fast? Has—how you say? Stamina?"

"Oh, yes. They breed for that down south of here. Moab is famous for its horses."

"Ah," Manouk said. He patted the animal here and there. "You have . . . bred him? You have let him at mares?"

"Once only," Shobai said with pride. "He fathered a foal who went for the price of two houses. Good blood."

"Yes. Good blood." Manouk's voice took on a covetous tone. "You will . . . sell him? Sell to me?"

Shobai recoiled. "Sell? Sell Kedar? No, no, I'm afraid I—"

Manouk pressed the question. His voice grew sharp edges. "No? Not for much? How much you sell for? What is price?" His hand paddled in the animal's dark mane, almost proprietarily. "I pay any price. Any. You sell?"

"No," Shobai said. "I'm sorry. I couldn't let him go. He's been mine since I—no, I'm afraid I—"

Manouk suddenly stopped, withdrew his hand, glanced sharply at Shobai. His eyes glinted. He looked at the horse once more. "Very well," he said. "Here, I show you where you stay. You work here. Here in camp. What you need—you ask for, I say give to you. All right? This is good?"

"Oh, certainly," Shobai said. "I'll need some helpers. Men to fire the forge, to keep it hot. Men to cut wood. Men to—"

"Whatever you need, you ask, I give. I leave order when I go away, whatever you want, you get. You want men, you get men." His eyes narrowed. "You want women too? Woman for your bed?" Manouk's voice took on a silky insolence now that Shobai could barely abide.

"Perhaps," he said, a little sharply. "Perhaps later. First, I'll get the work laid out and get my forge set up. Incidentally, Vahan showed me one of your war chariots some time back. They're the best thing of their kind I've ever seen. Light and maneuverable . . ."

He let the words trail off with a dying fall. Manouk did not miss his meaning. "But you find flaw?" Manouk said. "You find weakness?"

"I haven't worked it all out. But—well, have you ever seen the Hittite chariot? Or the Egyptian one?"

"Have seen Hittite chariot. But this of Egypt? No. You tell me. You show me."

Shobai smiled, sure of himself, on his own ground now. "Here," he said. He motioned Manouk over to a flat space and drew with his sword. "Now the Egyptian chariot is made like this. The balance is . . . so. The weight rests slightly forward of the axle. Here is the shaft . . . the harness is rather like your own. From this chariot, an archer can ride at full gallop, depending on the ground, and let loose arrows with some accuracy. But in order to do so he has to lash himself to the cart. If the chariot spills over, he can break his neck. Nevertheless, with this single exception it's a good design. I mean, as one-man chariots go. Light, easily steered . . ."

"Ah. But you find flaw with this too?"

"I'd have to work it out with models first. And then with full-scale mockups. But—well, you'll remember the Hittite chariot is a two-man affair, with a driver and a bowman. It allows both to jump free if the chariot goes out of kilter. It goes . . . so." He drew a second chariot beside the first, sketching in bold strokes. "Look," he said. "The weight is equally distributed forward and back of the axle. That way, most of the weight is on the axle itself, and the shaft doesn't lie as heavy on the horses. They'll last longer that way. On the other hand, if one man is hit, the balance goes out of adjustment—"

"Yes, yes," Manouk said. "And you suggest?"

"Well, I'll work on it. It seems to me that a chariot that combined the better features of each of these would be well-nigh invincible. More maneuverable, faster—"

"I see," Manouk said. "You work on this too? Here?"

"I'll need wheelwrights, leatherworkers, carpenters . . ."

"All these you will get. Anything. Anything."

Shobai stood, smiling uncertainly. He was used to having to wheedle and argue for more materials, more workers. This treatment was heady wine indeed. "Well," he said. "I—I'll make a list of what I'll be needing."

"Fine," Manouk said. "Tonight we feast. Tomorrow also. Then business. I leave you to work. Then I go. In—what?

One week? Two? Soon you meet the Leader. He come, he see your work."

"Leader?" Shobai said. "Oh, you mean your, ah, king of kings."

"Yes. Great leader. Bring us all of way from lands to far north, beyond mountains. He will see your work. By and by . . ." His eyes were slits now. Shobai could not decipher his smile for the life of him. "Now," he said. "Now we prepare for feast."

Shobai looked down into the dark eyes, and had the strange sensation of seeing the stocky Manouk, a head shorter than himself, as if the two stood the same height. There was a strength in the man, a power he had never felt in any leader he'd ever worked for. The source of it escaped him—but he wondered idly now if it hadn't something to do with the intense attention Manouk paid to everything he did, with the unblinking scrutiny to which he, Shobai, was subject at this moment. It was an uncomfortable feeling. It made him feel strange, mildly demeaned, somewhat less than he was. It was intensely disconcerting. He wondered what to say; but Manouk cut short his reverie by turning on one heel and walking briskly away.

Shobai stared stupidly after him. Then Manouk stopped, turned, motioned to him. "Your quarters," he said. "You will come?"

The Shepherd Kings' feast took place under the stars, beneath a seamless canopy of white-dotted darkness. At dusk, a gigantic fire-ring was prepared and lit, the space within its great circle left empty. At four places around the great ring, animal carcasses turned on spits over slower fires; the circle itself was meant for light and heat. As Shobai approached it, he could see the nomad kings and their subordinates draw near the fire-ring and arrange themselves in small conversational groups. Robed slaves, male and female, trooped from the food fires to the fringes of the circle, bearing food and wine.

As Shobai neared the circle, a face caught his eye. He stopped, looked, and stood half-smiling, trying to place the face. The girl stood looking at him, her body veiled from head to foot in a long robe that left only hands and feet bare; her hands held a bowl of dates. She said something in a soft voice, offering the fruit. He shook his head, feeling fidgety. Where had he seen her before?

She turned and walked back to the fire-circle, her dark eyes downcast. And watching her swaying, graceful walk told the story for him. Of course! It was the little slave who had served them when he'd first met Manouk that afternoon. Only then she'd been three parts naked, and he'd looked at her with the dismissive view one gave even the comeliest slave. Now, robed and bearing her bowl with the dignity of a free woman, she seemed a vision of grace to him. How lovely! Yet undeniably a slave. . . .

He shook his head; the odd half-smile remained on his lips as he watched her retreat from him. Her slim yet ripe buttocks undulated enticingly under the clinging robe; in a strange way she seemed more naked now, clothed from nape to bare heels, than she had today in nothing more than a skirt. If only . . .

Motion up near the fire-circle caught his eye, though, and broke his train of thought. "Here!" Manouk's deep voice called. "Here, Shobai!" His thick arm waved Shobai forward. The armorer approached, bowed the ritual bow, and seated himself cross-legged next to the dark-bearded leader. "Ah," Manouk said. "You are . . . settled? You have what you need?"

"Thank you," Shobai said, accepting a brimming wine cup from another of the slaves and saluting Manouk with it before he drank lightly from its smooth lip. "I think I've got everything. That is, until I start work tomorrow."

"You have robes? Furs? The night is chill here."

"No, that's quite all right, I brought my own. An armorer travels light, but—"

"You are . . . sure you need no woman? A man sleep warmer with a woman."

Shobai drank again; the raw stuff in the cup burned his throat. "This isn't normal wine," he said.

"It is special. You like? Very strong."

Shobai shook his head, trying to clear it. Well, if it was the nomads' wish that he join in the carousing, perhaps he could unbend a bit. He looked around him; men raised their cups high, drank deep. He caught the eye of a nomad chieftain; it was already red-bordered and indistinct.

"Ah," Manouk said. "Drink very strong. Good. You drink. You and I will drink. Is feast time. Time to be happy. Food, drink, women, fighting. . . ."

"Fighting?" Shobai said. His voice was slurred. "But surely—"

"I show you," Manouk said. He clapped his hands. In a moment, two sturdy warriors, stripped to helmets and loin-

384

cloths, leapt into the ring of fire. Each bore a sword and a small shield. They fenced; the mock fighting grew more spirited. Shobai drank again, feeling the raw liquor coursing down his throat, his head spinning. "See?" Manouk said. "My people love fight. You like?"

Shobai looked—and as quickly looked away. Then he forced his eyes back to the battle inside the fire-ring. This was no sham, it was real! As he looked, one of the near-naked swordsmen caught the other a sharp blow on the chest; blood spurted wildly. The wounded man redoubled his own efforts, ignoring his pain and the red life's blood gushing from his chest. He lashed; the other man fell back, his hand going to the red place where his left ear had been.

Shobai blinked, looked away. As he did, his eye caught that of the slim slave he'd seen earlier; she stood at the elbow of a man in the next party, the bowl still in her slender hands. As he looked, her head turned—and her eye caught his. She looked at him for a moment, her eyes dark and soft, her expression unreadable. Then she looked away.

"Ha!" Manouk bellowed in a gruff undertone, grabbing his arm. "See! See!" He pointed to the ring. The earless man had opened a deep wound on his opponent's upper arm. The other man switched hands with his sword, but could not stop the ferocious assault. The attacker beat him back, back . . . and now he stumbled and fell directly on the flames behind him. He screeched with pain and tried to roll away, to the raucous laughter of the men sitting around the circle; but as he did, he rolled directly into the path of his attacker. A bronze blade gleamed in the dancing firelight; its point found the losing fighter's belly—and ripped.

Shobai looked away. His head swam. His stomach felt queasy. He gritted his teeth against the surging tide of weakness within him and, a low curse in his throat, reached for the drink beside him. He drank deeply this time, ignoring the burning feeling in his throat, ignoring the pounding of his heart. He blinked away the blur in his own vision and drank even more deeply this time.

Then there was a long blank period that he could never remember later. He came to himself, groggy but awake, sitting cross-legged in the same spot, his robe smelling of vomit, his lap strewn with bits and scraps of food that had escaped his lips when he'd eaten. Two overturned cups lay before his feet; a puddle spread from one of them.

He looked around. Manouk was gone; dimly he could see the black-bearded man far across the much-abated fire-circle,

385

talking with a group of men. His eyes swept the crowd, the
bare space within the circle of flame. Later, he recalled seeing
naked bodies dancing in the circle, on the sand: ripe female
forms, wearing only jeweled rings on fingers and toes. . . .

A soft voice broke into his reverie, saying something he
couldn't catch. He turned. The dark-eyed young slave knelt
before him, her eyes concerned, unblinkingly taking in his
disheveled state. She dipped the hem of her robe in wine,
moved forward, and, before Shobai could stop her, had
scrubbed off his forehead. He could see a flash of golden
thigh-flesh where she had pulled up the robe. . . . "No," he
said. "No, don't. I can . . ."

But she couldn't understand him any better than he could
understand her. She half smiled, shyly, and took his arm, mo-
tioning for him to rise. He started to pull away, then thought
better of it. Of course! He was making an absolute swine of
himself. Better let her take him back to his tent and clean up,
perhaps change his robe; then he could reappear among
Manouk's people with some dignity. He let himself be helped
up. . . .

He had fully intended to rejoin the feast. But when he
reached the tent, he was sick again, and head spinning, he
pitched forward on his face. He tried once to rise, but the
strength left him. His eyesight blurred. But before he passed
out, he could see the girl standing, looking down at him, one
hand fingering the brooch that held her robe closed at the
neck. Gods! He'd asked for her, had he? And here she was,
coming to the bed of a drunken swine who—

Here mind and memory grew dim. He slipped off into
a drunken sleep as she stood looking down at him. In the
morning, although he found the now-cold imprint of her little
body beside his own on the bedding, she was gone.

III

His head throbbed; his stomach was queasy; his arms and
legs felt weak and flabby. Yet Shobai's hard-won professional-
ism stood him in good stead now, and aided by two helpers
who understood a little of his tongue, he put in a hard
morning's work supervising the building of his forge. He

interviewed four more prospective workers, settling at last on two men who understood his words and a third who did not; the ones who did could theoretically train the rest. Besides, it would be a good thing for him to learn the nomads' language as quickly as possible, and Shobai had had a good mimic's way with new tongues since his childhood.

From time to time he'd rise from his work and look around, somehow expecting to see some sign of the dark-eyed girl who'd shared his bed the night before, but she stayed away. He wondered whose slave she was. Manouk's? Perhaps the common slave of the camp? But he dismissed the latter conjecture. She was dignified, reserved; most likely she had been of good blood before being enslaved. He sighed, thinking of her. How often it seemed that the slave turned out to be of better breeding than his owner! But that was one of the many injustices of life, and not to be questioned.

At noon, Vahan visited his forge; with him was a strapping, bearded giant in a short kilt, a brawny fellow who stood fully as tall as Shobai. The newcomer, scorning the crisp chill air of autumn, wore nothing on his upper body; Shobai, looking him over, could see the scars of old battles on his chest and arms. His beard was trimmed after the Hittite fashion.

"Shobai," Vahan said in his halting speech, "is visitor to camp." He turned to the newcomer. "Shobai of Haran. Armorer."

Shobai wiped his grimy hands on a wet cloth and saluted the stranger. "Greetings," he said. He tried to think of a welcoming phrase in Hittite, but could not remember any.

It turned out not to be necessary. "Greetings," the stranger said in Shobai's own language, speaking easily and with little accent. "I am Bentesina of Kanish. I arrived during the night for an audience with Manouk." He smiled a wary, benign courtier's smile. "Our friend Vahan tells me you've accepted employment with the, ah, Shepherd Kings."

"Yes," Shobai said. "I armed Carchemish and Haran earlier. I'm sure I won't have to explain the vagaries of the armorer's trade to a Hittite; your people are famous the world over for their work in weaponry."

"Ah, yes," Bentesina said. "I was close friends with the armorer Sarku, who has left Kanish to arm Hattusas against the revolt. You may have heard of him?"

Shobai turned the name over in his mind. It stirred no memory. "I'm sure I have at one time or another. Sarku—I'd like to see some of his work some time."

"Oh, by all means. Be my guest." Bentesina drew his sword

and handed it to Shobai handle first. "This is one of the better samples of his work. Not the best. I couldn't begin to afford his ceremonial work."

Shobai hefted the dark sword—and almost dropped it. It was so heavy! Yet—holding it in his hand, he felt its rightness. The balance, the feel of it—it could have been a sword by Belsunu or Ahuni. But . . . "Why, it's iron," he said. He held it up to the light, feeling the power in it.

"Oh, yes," Bentesina said, not without a little complacency. "If I may say so, Hittite armorers have no peer at the handling of the dark metal."

"Gods!" Shobai said, genuinely awed. "I'd give anything to learn the process. And worked with such sophistication, such skill! I've seen ironwork before—but nothing like this. What my father wouldn't have given to learn to do work of this quality in iron. . . ." He shook his head back and forth. "My father wanted very badly to learn about iron—but when he lived here, your borders were closed to us. It was during the war with—"

"Ah, yes. I was a boy then. Which didn't keep me from seeing my share of fighting, let me tell you. Well, Sarku is no longer with us, as I say. An armorer collects his pay and moves on. I sincerely hope he can do Hattusas some good, although privately I think the revolt will succeed. The leader of the rebels, Anittas of Kussara, is ambitious and able; he may well sack the city as he claims he will. And while he isn't armed by an artist like Sarku, the men he does have do good journeyman work . . . and his forces are half again the strength of the city's."

"A pity, of course," Shobai said, still turning the weapon this way and that. "But that's war. Not much one can do about it. And meanwhile, one has a living to make."

"Ah, yes," Bentesina said, a slight questioning note in his voice. "I understand your city is Haran?"

"Yes. Although I also have a business in Carchemish."

"Haran *and* Carchemish. And you realize that both lie in the path of your, ah, employers?"

"I suppose that's true. But you realize I've armed both cities myself. They'll have the means to defend themselves when and if the time comes . . ."

"Ah. And now you arm their potential enemies." He picked up the little model of the battering ram Shobai had made. "Now *this* is interesting. Ingenious. Does it work the way I think it will? I mean, horses here, and men . . ."

Shobai retrieved the model, not without a trace of anger.

"Pardon me, please. It's very delicate—and it's not quite finished yet." He replaced it on its little pedestal. "Yes," he said. "It's a little improvement on the Shepherd Kings' own version. I'm paid, you understand, to look after the interest of my current employer, whoever he is. That's the way professionals in the trade look at it." He handed back the iron sword, holding it respectfully in both hands.

"I see," Bentesina said. "Professionals. Hmmm, I seem to remember Sarku saying there came a time when a man had to take sides. . . ."

"There are people who look at it that way," Shobai said a little petulantly. "But I'm a Child of the Lion, and—"

"Pardon me," the Hittite said. "A child of the what? I didn't get that last—"

"A Child of the Lion," Shobai said. "We're a hereditary caste of weaponmakers. The legend is that we were given a special mark on our bodies—a mark shaped like a lion's paw print—as a special badge that would allow us to cross all borders to offer our services to all-comers."

"I see. An interesting story. I hadn't heard of it before. I suppose that means you take no partisan interest in who wins a war, a revolution, a siege? You offer your work impartially . . . ?"

"That's the way of it," Shobai said, dismissing the subject. He turned to Vahan. "I think that'll be all for today," he said. "My forge is mostly set up. I can finish tomorrow, I think. Meanwhile, it's a feast day, if I remember properly." He sniffed the air—and noted that the distraction of the conversation had made his headache and his nausea go away. "I think they've already got a couple of oxen turning on spits. Perhaps you'll be joining us for the midday meal, sir?" He looked at Bentesina, and couldn't help glancing at the man's belt, where the splendid sword now hung. "Whatever one may think of my employers, they know how to give a feast. . . ."

His mood changed much for the better now, Shobai clapped the Hittite familiarly on the arm, and was surprised to see the visitor shrink visibly from his touch.

Vahan, however, escorted them all together to Manouk's tent. Inside, Shobai saw laid out before him a sumptuous spread: roast ox, lamb, fresh fruit, dates. Vahan showed him to a seat halfway around the great semicircle from Manouk; he sat down among strangers, who made no effort to introduce themselves. He raised one wry eyebrow at this. Yesterday his status had been that of honored visitor, now it was that of a tradesman in the hire of the Shepherd Kings. Well, no matter. He had more important things to think of than matters of petty politics and his place in the hierarchy. . . .

As he seated himself cross-legged and reached for bread, he saw a slim pair of legs and a pair of slender feet before him. He looked up quickly—and saw the dark-eyed girl again. This time she wore a brief tunic that covered her breasts and left only legs and arms and one dimpled shoulder bare. Her eyes met his; she did not smile, but their eyes remained locked for a moment. What could he read in her glance? he wondered suddenly. Surely little affection. Concern; perhaps even sexual attraction—but a little reserve, a little distance . . . He started to speak to her, but she lowered her eyes and moved away.

Across the circle, Manouk took note of the wordless exchange; his eyes narrowed, but he said nothing. He turned to Minas, on his left. "You leave in the morning, then?" he said in his own tongue.

"Yes, sir. And what shall I tell the commander of the attack forces?"

"Tell Kirakos—" He paused, pursed his thick lips, and knit his dark-haired brow. Then he let his breath out with a shrug. "You say he is deployed all around Melid? The city is surrounded?"

"Yes, sir. The last caravan approaching the city was captured the day before yesterday."

"Good. Tell Kirakos to attack at dawn. From all sides. Then withdraw an hour before sundown. The usual plan. The white flag, everything. They won't give in today. Then he'll do the same thing the next morning. Only the next night have bowmen lob flaming arrows into the city at random, at irregular intervals. The usual thing."

"Yes, sir."

"I give them . . . oh, perhaps a week at most. They've supplies for no more than that. Kirakos knows what to do. Tell him the attack is in his hands, but remind him that the Leader will be here shortly to inspect personally the progress he's made."

"Yes, sir." Minas followed his commander's eyes around the half-circle, to where Shobai and the girl were exchanging enigmatic glances again. "Excuse me, sir, if you don't mind my mentioning it—"

"No, go ahead," Manouk said.

"I—I don't think he knows about—"

"No, he doesn't. If he did, he wouldn't be behaving the way he is. He is not that stupid."

"He means no harm, I think."

"No, but it does not matter. I am offended."

"Yes, sir." Minas caught sight of the look in his commander's eyes and decided to pursue the matter no further.

Vahan had seated Bentesina directly to the nomad captain's right. The Hittite had found his sword got in the way when he sat down, and he had laid it out neatly before him. Now Manouk, turning to him, took note of the weapon. "Your sword, sir," he said in passable Hittite. "It's something I've not seen before. May I?"

"Oh, by all means," the visitor said. He handed it to the heavyset commander. "It happens I'm a collector, you know, on a modest scale, and the weaponmaker is a personal friend."

"Ahhhh," Manouk said, obvious pleasure in his voice as he hefted the sword, holding it first this way, then another. "This metal. I have seen it before. But never have I seen it worked this way."

"No, sir. Sarku's work isn't seen every day."

"Sarku?" Manouk said, his eyes brightening. "And where is this Sarku?" He balanced the sword on one hand appreciatively. "How do I get to see him?"

"I'm afraid that'll be difficult, sir. He's up north, arming Hattusas against a rebellion. He's particularly concerned about that place: he has relatives there, I think. You'd have a hard time of it luring him away from there while the city's still under threat."

"Ah, I understand," Manouk said. "Nevertheless, I will remember the name." His eyes went once again out over the ring of faces and sought out Shobai; they narrowed as he did so. "One would give much to have an army—even a detachment—armed thus." He handed the sword back, not without a certain regret. "And are all Hittites armed so?"

Bentesina did not miss Manouk's meaning. His smile was mild, courteous, understanding. "To the teeth, sir," he said. "It's one of the, ah, faults of my people. We love war. When we've no legitimate reason for conflict, we'll think up an illegitimate one, just to give us a reason for fighting. We're no good at diplomacy, and our art is not highly prized. There are only two things in the world we're good at: fighting—and fortification. We build cities you couldn't breach with the aid

391

of every god from Crete to the Land of the Two Rivers. An attacker would wear himself out invading us."

Manouk caught his meaning and smiled. "On the other hand, I think you said Hattusas might well fall to this Anittas of Kussara? Despite the fortifications . . . ?"

"So I did," Bentesina said. "Anittas has friends inside the city who will weaken its defenses as no foreign invader could do."

"So it often goes," Manouk said. "Many a city has fallen that way. But when this Sarku is once again free, I should much appreciate getting to meet him. Perhaps we can talk business."

"Perhaps," Bentesina said, refusing the wine a servant offered him. "But after all, it's a moot point, isn't it? You've no ambitions toward Hittite soil, as you've assured me—and besides, you've got yourself an armorer. I met him today, this Shobai of Haran. . . ."

"Yes," Manouk said; there was the smallest hint of hardness in his voice now. "But of course, he is no Hittite, and he knows little of the working of the black metal as Hittites do. And—but it's festival time. We will speak of other things." His tone had turned harsh for a moment; now, turning to matters of horse-breeding and trading, his voice regained its earlier equanimity. Bentesina caught the shift and made small talk until Manouk was called away for a moment. Then he turned to Vahan, on his own right. "I gather our new armorer from Haran does not sit well with the commander," he said. "And so early in his employment?"

Vahan shot a glance at the tall young metalworker, down the line. "Shobai is a fool," he said. "A young fool. An older and wiser man might have looked into our customs before making a false step."

"False step?" Bentesina said. Someone offered wine again; this time he took some. "I don't understand."

"Last night, Manouk offered him women."

"Yes? This is common enough."

"Among us, one takes the offering one receives. One does not seek out a particular woman. Not until one knows whose woman is whose."

"Ah." Bentesina saw the girl now; her eyes were on Shobai again, and his on her; but while Shobai's expression was easy to read, the girl's was not. *Pretty little thing,* he thought; but he said nothing. "And Shobai . . . ?"

"The girl is the daughter of Manouk's brother," Vahan said quietly. "Manouk, having offered women, could not refuse her under our custom. But she should not have been asked for."

"I see," Bentesina said. And he thought: *Poor Shobai. And obviously he still doesn't know. . . .*

IV

Shobai waited for Manouk to return, but there was no new sign of the nomad leader. After a time, he excused himself and made his way back to his forge. His assistants had the kiln half constructed; he watched them work, making suggestions here and there.

But as he worked and watched, his mind wandered. The girl—once again she'd paid special attention to him, in Manouk's tent. Her manner toward him was emphatically not that of slave toward free man. Was she, perhaps, free herself? Perhaps a woman of the camp? He'd have to find out. Perhaps when he had more of the nomad tongue. . . .

Now, however, a new thought struck him. It was a notion he hadn't previously considered, and it was sufficiently striking to stop him in his tracks. The girl—she'd slept with him, apparently, even if he couldn't remember any of it. If her interest in him remained, it appeared his attack of impotency had passed. Apparently, he'd performed well with her!

He pounded one big fist into the other palm unconsciously. Why—why, he'd found his manhood again! All it had taken was to get away from the scene, the source, of his shame. All it had taken was for him to get away from places where people knew of Anat's terrible, demeaning treachery.

Well, he thought. *It was the right thing to do after all, coming here.* He smiled. And once again he thought of the girl. What an oaf he was, to make love to a beautiful little thing like that and be so drunk that afterward he couldn't recall anything at all of it! He'd have to make it up to her, really he would!

For the moment, though, he put her from his mind. He'd have to start picking up some of the nomads' tongue, first off. It'd make everything so much easier, all in all, if he didn't have this trouble understanding them or making his own needs and wishes known.

For some reason, now, he found himself thinking about the black metal, iron. He had given the matter of his father's life-long obsession little thought until now. After all, there was plenty of work, everywhere, for an armorer who knew bronze, who could make solid, workmanlike weapons of the traditional materials. And there was peace between the Hittites and the other nations of the area, and the Hittites were the only people in the Great Crescent who understood the working of the dark metal.

But how long would this condition last? he asked himself. How long would the Hittites be content with fighting among themselves, or with raiding the Lycians and Arzawans to the west of their domain, or nibbling away at the edges of the Ahhiyawan settlements north of there? How long before the fierce warriors of the Hatti, seeking new lands to conquer, would swarm across the mountains into Kizzuwatna and strike south and east at Carchemish and Haran? And when they were armed with weapons like those, which would bite through the best bronze swords and shields, who could withstand them?

Well, perhaps the nomads could, just through sheer weight of numbers. Perhaps, in a way, the presence of the Shepherd Kings in the area was a healthy influence on the balance of power in the region. Perhaps . . .

Huh, he thought. *So that's why Bentesina is here.* It was not only a matter of sending a Hittite observer to look into the matter of the nomad invasion and report back to Kanish on their strength and apparent ambitions . . . it was also a matter of showing the nomads that a formidable foe lay in their way if they decided to pursue a westward path. Because it was a sure thing that a sharp-eyed warrior like Manouk would not miss the significance of the Hittites' apparently complete understanding of the dark metal and the secret of its successful smelting and working.

Another thing was certain: the nation which was armed with the black metal would be all but totally invincible in the area. His father, Kirta, had seen this. That was why he'd moved mountains to learn the secret—why he'd even left home, never to return, in search of the elusive secret. He'd understood the importance to the world of the new discovery, and understood how only the learning of this all-important secret could save the nations of the Crescent from being gobbled up, eventually, by the great nations which already had mastered it.

Yes, and after all, who was better qualified to learn it than a Child of the Lion like Kirta? And who would be more likely to understand the need for sharing the knowledge among all nations and not letting it be the private preserve of the rich and powerful, for the sake of the balance of power? Why, a man like Kirta, of course!

For the first time, Shobai understood his father's actions: understood his sacrifice of home, comfort, of his very family, to his unending quest for the secret of the black metal. He'd had a higher end in mind all the time! He'd put the common needs of all the people before mere personal considerations, before mere nationalistic aims.

How wonderful! And now that he, Shobai, could see the sense in his father's design, he could slough off the continuing edge of resentment that had surrounded his picture of his father all these years. Why, his father was a great man! And a great man regardless of whether or not his long quest had finally brought him the secret he'd sought all those years!

The thought was a comforting one, a healing one. His father, Kirta, had not betrayed the ideals of the Children of the Lion after all. He'd held them high to the last. . . .

But just then another thought struck Shobai, and this one was less comforting, less reassuring. *And you, Shobai? How are you upholding the family traditions? The family standards, the ethics of the profession? Will the world be the better for your having made its arms for a generation or so?*

The question was a disquieting one. It disturbed him deeply. He thought of Bentesina's cool questioning of him. *"I seem to remember Sarku saying there came a time when a man had to take sides. . . ."*

He bit his lip, looking down at the workers laying bricks. And looked up just in time to see the girl—*his* girl—standing beside a nearby tent, looking at him, silent as ever. She was wearing her short skirt; her little breasts were bare. Her eyes met his, as an equal's. She stood looking at him, unsmiling. He started to motion to her, to wave her nearer; but by the time his tardy hand had obeyed the order he'd given it, she had gone as quickly as she'd come, leaving, as always, unresolved questions in his mind.

Bentesina came away from the meeting and headed for the area where his horse was tethered, a small smile playing on his thick lips. He'd been called away shortly after Manouk had, and he'd joined the party of visitors a moment later. He'd made the usual moves, but these mattered far less than the ones he'd made earlier that day. What profit in making the usual diplomatic bluster with lesser peoples, when the main thing was to wave the banners of Kanish pointedly under the nose of the real enemy—a man like Manouk, with the armed might of thousands behind him?

No. No use wasting his time on small fry. He'd done what he had come to do—he'd had a look at the Shepherd Kings' forces, what he could see of them. And he'd impressed Manouk with the inadvisability of planning any attack on Kanish. That in itself was a good day's work.

He yawned, stretched. It'd been a long ride, and he had another long ride ahead of him. For a moment he was tempted to stay the night, to take advantage of the festival delights that had been offered him: women, wine, entertainment, a good night's sleep. . . .

But then he'd remembered Shobai of Haran, who had taken what was offered him, chosen of it, and chosen badly. He, an emissary from Kanish, could hardly afford to make a similar mistake. Better, then, to decline respectfully, to make much of his obligations, to thank the commander and promise faithfully to take better advantage of the Shepherd Kings' hospitality later, on some other occasion when his schedule would allow him more leisure, more time to explore the delights of nomad entertainment.

He smiled wryly. And then the smile disappeared and became a rueful, concerned frown. This Shobai: he was so young, so green, so inexperienced. Yes, and so innocently vulnerable. He shook his head, remembering himself at the same age, remembering his own callow, bumbling ways, and remembering, most of all, what they had cost him in his youth. Cost him then, and for a long time afterward. Youth knew so little—particularly of the consequences of its actions.

Imagine, then, someone being willing to go to work for the deadliest enemy his city had. Imagine someone not realizing what this would mean to his friends, his family, his neighbors. Imagine this situation being combined with a deadly interior threat to the city, much like the one Hattusas faced from its own internal traitors—one which virtually assured the city of a certain and horrible death at the hands of Manouk's people. And imagine not having the foggiest idea where one stood oneself in all this.

For a moment his expression became savage, unforgiving. Youth! Damned foolish idiotic youth! Waste! Nonsense! All the unearned pain and loss and death! And for what? Why? Why?

Then he recovered, and damned himself for losing control for a moment, even if no one could see. And put the sad, bad memories from him, and concentrated his thoughts on the long road homeward.

"Then it's settled?" Manouk's visitor said. "You'll join us?" His voice strove to sound confident, powerful; but there was a hollow, uncertain ring to it. His eyes stayed on Manouk's nose, his brows, his cheekbones; they never quite met Manouk's unblinking gaze.

"Yes," Manouk said, unsmiling. "But—must be now? You—not stay for feast? For women, for drink, for . . . ?"

The visitor hesitated. It was obvious he'd have preferred to stay, indulge, seek oblivion among Manouk's tents. But there was a lingering sense of duty—or perhaps something else, something less responsible—in his makeup. He forced himself to say no, the same hesitant half-grin on his thin face. "No, really. Thank you, it's most important that we go now. It'll make all the difference in the world."

Manouk looked the man up and down. It was curious, he was thinking. The dog of middling size, who lorded it over the smaller dogs, would grovel before a wolfhound, a mastiff. This man who stood before him, whose every physical act or motion screamed to him of cowardly self-abasement, whose very voice had in it the echoing emptiness and irresolution of a eunuch's . . . this man was probably a lion before other men. Undoubtedly he was a tyrant before women, before the weak, the crippled, the old. And what was he here? Bah! Manouk kept his face devoid of expression only with a conscious effort of will.

But somehow, he thought now, the gods of war tended to deliver such a man into one's grasp now and then, his mind full of skulking treason and self-interest, the key to something you wanted clutched tight in his sweaty little hands. Best to use him and discard him—but in the meantime, before the discarding, test him, evaluate him, learn just what there was in the using. Perhaps there was more to this coward than met the eye. After all, if the man beneath your own heel could maintain order among the vassals beneath him, why question the means he employed to do so? Very well; he'd test this jackal. Perhaps there were more uses in him than he, Manouk, could think of at the moment. For one thing, the plan he'd outlined was a good one, all in all, given his own needs. It would have cost him, Manouk, months of intrigue to set up an equally advantageous situation on his own—and here this two-faced animal had brought the whole thing to him, bag and baggage, unasked. Truly it was a gift of the gods of war. He rose, stretched, and dismissed his visitor with little more than a wave of the hand. "You wait," he said at the door. "I be here soon."

The same uncertain smile lingering on his thin lips, Reshef shot a silent, resentful coward's curse after him as he watched Manouk go. Damn him! Why did the nomad always seem to have the evil-eye curse on him, so that he couldn't look the filthy black-bearded devil in the eye? Why did the firmness suddenly seem to leave his voice when he spoke to the man? Why couldn't he stand up to—

"My lord." The voice at his elbow startled him; he turned with a scowl.

"What the devil do you want?" Reshef said. "Oh—all right. You gave me a start. Sorry I bellowed at you. He's going to leave with us."

"He's going to . . . ?" Yassib said, mouth agape. "But—but you said it would take a lot of arguing, a lot of—"

"I explained the situation. He agrees it requires his own guiding hand. Well, that's the way he sees it anyway. And all the while he'll be guided by us instead." *Bravado*, he told himself. But it sounded better that way. "You'll be ready to leave too, I hope?" The touch of mockery was back in his tone, but—damn it!—his voice was still the eunuch's alto, with no lion's roar in it. The thought filled him with silent self-loathing which, as always, he camouflaged with his death's-head grin.

"Oh, yes. But I wanted to tell you. I had the damnedest surprise just now."

Reshef guided him by the arm toward the horses, moving him along at a leisurely pace. "Well, look, that will keep. First I want to remind you—"

"But—but this ought to interest you, sir. I mean, it's somebody I think I remember hearing you say you had a grudge against."

"Grudge? What are you talking about? I never hold—"

"It's Shobai, sir. Shobai, the armorer. You know: from Haran. He's here."

Reshef stopped dead. His eyes burned brightly all of a sudden, the old flame back in them again. His voice was taut but there was the hint of the old rasp in it. "Shobai?" he said. He gripped Yassib's upper arms. "Here? I don't believe you."

"But he is, sir. And—and he's working for them. He's set up his forge over by the . . ."

Reshef looked at him; but his eyes went out of focus as his mind went elsewhere. He heard nothing of what Yassib was saying. All he could hear, suddenly, was the low rumble in his mind of his own hatred. His hand released Yassib's arm and, unconsciously, went to the livid scar on his narrow face. And the old smile, the devil's smile, spread slowly over his ferret's face. *Shobai!*

V

Vahan visited Shobai an hour before dusk. He looked over the half-finished forge, the barely begun smelting furnace. His eyes narrowed; he frowned at the complexity of the thing Shobai was constructing. "What is this?" he said.

The armorer wiped his grimy hands and joined him. "I guess you've never seen one like this. Don't worry. It'll be a big improvement over the way you're used to doing things."

Vahan clearly wasn't impressed. "You show me," he said. "I look on. You show."

Shobai smiled, a little indulgently. "Your people are used to smelting furnaces that are allowed to go cold every night and have to be relit every morning. That's wasteful. This is a process my grandfather learned at the Egyptian copper mines at Timna, south of here. It may even have been a process developed, or perhaps improved, by my great-grandfather, Belsunu, who worked there for a long time."

"You mean—furnace run all night?" Vahan shook his head.

"Sure," Shobai said. "It's the best way to keep the temperature high enough to work the ore. This way you never let it cool off. And you don't have to clean it out for more than—oh, maybe four days or so. And while you're cleaning out one furnace"—he pointed to an area nearby where workers were digging a second, parallel, trench—"you put another one in operation. By staggering the cleaning periods, you always have one furnace working ore."

"Ah," Vahan said. He crossed his battle-scarred arms over his chest and regarded the layout with an unreadable eye. "This way you work more ore."

"Yes," Shobai said. "As much as ten times as much ore. You smelt ten times as much copper at one time."

"Ah," Vahan grunted. "How much?"

Shobai tossed weights and measures about in his head. "Say, something like my own weight," he said. He smiled at the incredulous look in the nomad's eye. "Look," he added. "Here's something Belsunu may have devised. At least that's the way my father told it." He pointed to a hole left in the rear of the earthen pot. "There'll be a bellows here, for keeping the fire hot. And these holes will let out the slag—the waste materials—and spill it out into this trough here. The slag will cool fairly quickly, and you can just lift out the solid pieces. This way you can skim the slag again and again and continue to refill the furnace with fuel and ore. The copper collects, white-hot, at the bottom."

"Ah," Vahan said again, a look of comprehension spreading over his dark face. "And—this can be done—big? *Many* furnaces? You can build?"

"Oh, I see," Shobai said. "You're getting greedy. Of course, it could be done. When Belsunu armed the great king Abraham for the Elamite war, down south of here, he did something like that. There were a dozen furnaces going at the same time for smelting copper. He had people working bronze sword-blanks, and he would come along himself and do the finished work. But, Vahan. You haven't got a good enough source of ore for that right now. The two furnaces I'm building here will handle all the ore you have."

"Here," Vahan said. "You build furnaces. Many furnaces. We get ore. We get all ore you want."

"Well, that's fine—but where?"

"Melid. To northwest of here. Already we have plan for Melid. Much copper ore. Much—what is name of dark metal? Heavy? You know. . . ."

"Iron. But look, nobody around here knows how to work that stuff. I—"

"You not know? You learn?"

"I wish I could. My father went off to try to learn it. He never returned. If he had . . ." Shobai's brow knotted for a second; then he shrugged it off. "But that's another story. I've often thought I might head up into Hittite country—since the Hittites have a peace treaty with their neighbors—and learn

400

what I could. But—well, I'm young. There's plenty of time. . . ."

"Is never plenty time," Vahan said contemptuously. "We live today. We die tomorrow." The nomad's face changed now; he dismissed the subject. "We talk about this later. For now you smelt copper. And you make many forges. Ten, twenty . . ."

"Twenty? I don't believe you. There aren't any mines around here capable of supplying—"

"You make furnace. We get ore."

"Look. I'll leave instructions here to start the work if you want me to. But it will take time—the second furnace isn't even finished yet. And as for this story about unlimited ore—I've got to see it for myself."

"You want to see?" Vahan said. "Look. You come tomorrow. We ride west. You see Melid. You see mines. Battle tonight. Tomorrow we win. Tomorrow—Melid no more. You come with me." He looked into Shobai's skeptical eye. "You fear?" he said mockingly. "You afraid to come?"

Shobai stiffened. "Of course not," he said with some indignation. "I'll go anywhere you will. But . . ."

"All right," Vahan said. "Be ready at dawn." A new thought occurred to him now, though. "You speak language of Melid?"

"Uh, that's likely to be some dialect of Hurrian," Shobai said. "I can get by in most dialects of—"

"All right. I have prisoner. I show you. You talk to him. He tell you about mines. And tomorrow we go see for ourselves. But come."

"Wait," Shobai said. He barked out an order to his assistant, the only one with a good command of his own tongue. "All right, show me."

The prisoner was a bit of a shock to Shobai. He was naked, half-starved, hollow-eyed. He sat cross-legged on the bare ground, his hands shackled together to a chain whose other end was fixed to a wagon axle. His face was gaunt; his cheekbones stood out starkly. His ribs showed, too. Shobai looked around, ready to complain to Vahan; but the nomad had disappeared. "Here," he said. "For heaven's sake, hasn't anyone been feeding you?" To his surprise the language came back easily to him; perhaps because he had something meaningful to say.

"Feeding?" the man said dully. Then he shook the cobwebs

401

out of his head and stared at Shobai. "You," he said. "You're not one of them. Who—who are you?" His voice was hollow, hoarse—but there was intelligence in his sunken eyes.

"I'm Shobai, an armorer from Haran. I came to work for them yesterday. But you—"

"Came to *work* for them?" The prisoner tried to spit but could not. "Look, you fool. Get out of here—and fast. You don't know what you're getting into." He sat up, pulled at the chain that restrained his skinny wrists. "Wherever you come from, get back to your town and warn them. Tell them—"

"But I—I couldn't just walk out. I've got a contract."

"Contract? You idiot, those things don't mean anything to people like these—to animals like these. They're no more to be trusted than bears or wolves." Contempt, tinged perhaps with an even darker emotion, soured his hoarse voice. "And here you are, arming the enemies of your family, your friends—"

"Enemies? Oh, they'll never attack Haran. Besides, I armed Haran. Carchemish too."

"It doesn't matter. They'll have traitors inside both cities by now, traitors who'll sell the place out for money, or for a chance at power and prestige. This Manouk—he knows just what their price is, and he goes directly to them and offers it. He has no intention of paying, but he offers it anyhow. He knows they won't be too demanding. They already have themselves convinced they're doing the right thing."

Shobai frowned. *Poor devil,* he thought. He looked over the man's naked body. It was covered with cuts and bruises: the former older, scabbed over; the latter fresh, recent. "I'll bring you some food," he said. "And—it must be cold for you. I'll bring you a robe, a warm one."

"They'll take them away. You're a metalworker. Cut off my manacles. Let me make a run for it. Tonight, after dark. Please. . . ."

"Gods!" Shobai said. "Do you know what they'd do to me if they caught me doing that? Look, I just came to work here."

The prisoner stared at him, his eyes red-rimmed inside the deep sockets. "Ah," he said with a disgusted sigh. "You don't want to get involved. Well, my friend, you *are* involved. You're up to the eyes in it. And do you suppose that for your own treachery you'll be rewarded? Let me tell you—"

"Treachery?" Shobai said indignantly, looking down at the man with anger. "I'm an armorer. Armorers sell to all sides. It's a tradition."

"Tradition?" the man spat at him. "Don't tell me of traditions. You're selling death, friend. Death not only of soldiers, who signed up for it, but of women and children and old people and—"

"Who are you to talk to me like that?" Shobai said, his eyes flashing. "Here I just tried to help you, and—"

"Help? The only way you can help me is by cutting these damned things off." He held up his hands; beneath the shackles Shobai could see the raw flesh on his bony wrists. "Give me a chance at freedom, just a chance. Although heaven knows I don't deserve it." The self-loathing in his voice was thick. "Look, you fool. I know whereof I speak. I was one of the ones who sold out Melid. I was as big a fool as you. Manouk got to me and promised me the world. The world, let me tell you. I was going to be left behind to rule in his place: a viceroy or something. Not that there would have been much left to rule. When they attack the city, they'll burn it to the—" He stopped, horror suddenly in his eyes. "Gods," he said. "Gods." He sat up suddenly, painfully, pulling at the chain again. "Tell me: have they attacked yet? Is the city dead yet? Have they—"

"I—I think the attack was supposed to take place today," Shobai said. "Vahan was going to take me up that way tomorrow to see the mines. He said—he was trying to tell me there was an unlimited supply of copper ore up that way, and I could—"

"Copper! Of course there's copper! As much as anywhere in the world! And iron ore, too! *Gods!*" The prisoner sank back on his heels, his face a mask of anguish. "Of course. They'll need ore for the rest of their campaign. For arming to head south and smash your damned country to hell—that *is* a Padan-aram accent, isn't it? I thought so. And if they control the ore, and you arm them—oh, you blind, thoughtless fool. You stupid, brainless young oaf. They've got you, too, just like they got me. Well, enjoy it while you can. You'll go around here strutting like a peacock, thinking you're some-body. And when they've no further need of you . . ."

"How are they going to have no further need of me?" Shobai said, bristling with wounded pride. "They'll always need an armorer, if there's anything to this nonsense you're feeding me about their grandiose plans for world conquest."

"Can you work iron?" the prisoner said. He saw the effect of his words and pressed on, his voice harsh and cutting. "I thought not. And what happens when they find an armorer who can? Tell me that, my friend. What will you be worth then? With the biggest damned iron deposits in the area in their control? Tell me that, eh? Why, you'll be right here alongside me, bare-assed and in chains. Only I'll be dead by then. Dead or escaped." He leaned forward again, his voice urgent. "Help me. Tonight, when they thin out the pickets. You don't have to take much of a chance. I'm not asking you to get me clothes, or a horse, or weapons. Just cut me loose. I've been trying to slip out of these things, but without dislocating a hand . . ." He held up his raw wrists. "Please," he said. "Do one good thing in your life. One decent thing."

But he could see Shobai drawing away now, and he sank against the great wheel at his back, leaning his head against one of the spokes. "Ah, what's the use?" he said. "You're as blind as I was. Go your way. I won't ask you again. . . ."

Shobai walked away slowly. He looked back once, taking a last look at the gaunt scarecrow of a man leaning against the big wheel, his face impassive now, his eyes unseeing. Then Shobai blinked back tears of indignation and rage and walked on, a little faster now.

How *dare* he say things like these to an armorer? Didn't he know . . . ? He clenched his big fist and pounded his other palm. He quickened his pace.

But then he happened for a moment to look up. And atop the rise to the south of the encampment he could see Manouk's party, mounted and armed, topping the ridge. The pickets saluted the nomad leader; he rode past, looking to neither side. And with him—could those be soldiers in the uniform of Haran?

Haran?

Shobai stopped dead. His face clouded over. And the prisoner's words came back to him: *They'll have traitors inside both cities, traitors who'll sell the place out. . . .*

Could the man have been speaking the truth? And if he was, then was he, Shobai, selling out Haran and Carchemish by working for the nomads? By arming them for war?

The thought was repellent, and it struck at whatever he had learned, in his young life, about loyalty. But what loyalty? Was he not a Child of the Lion, free to come and go everywhere, to arm everyone, without regard for loyalties of nation or tribe? Yes, that was true. Perhaps, then, his mistake had been to settle down in the first place, to adopt a particular city as his permanent home. Traditionally, a Child of the Lion kept moving, didn't stay anywhere for very long. Perhaps the point was that a Child of the Lion shouldn't form attachments, take sides, undermine his own independence by making himself a part of the community he lived in. Yes, that must have been his mistake.

But how could he have helped it? he asked himself indignantly. After all, his father had abandoned him and Tallay and Hadad in the city, abandoned them without much in the way of resources. He hadn't left them much to get trained with. Poor Hadad had had to do without any training at all. Little wonder that they hadn't been able to maintain the traditions properly. So how could anyone blame him for forming attachments, for feeling—well, *guilty* about taking his present job?

"No" he said suddenly under his breath. "I did the right thing. I did. . . ."

But somehow he found himself thinking of the prisoner and his bitter words. And somehow he found himself dreading, ever so slightly, the trip to Melid he'd promised to make in the morning. There were, after all, things to be learned that one didn't really want to know. . . .

VI

Shobai looked for the girl at the evening meal, but there was no sign of her. With Manouk gone and himself seated well away from any place of honor, he found himself curiously isolated around the campfire among people who spoke no language he knew and whose own tongue continued, by and large, to elude him. Vahan and his assistants were gone, preparing for the morning's journey; Minas, the only other person he knew, had gone away with Manouk and the two soldiers of Haran.

In self-defense he drank more than he should, and as the fire died down and the night chill came on, he rose, topheavy, his head reeling, and moved unsteadily back through the rows of tents to his own dwelling.

Distracted, nine parts inebriated, he nearly passed it by. Blinking, he stopped, counted the tents in the row. That was odd; he'd left the tent dark, and now a light burned inside it. He shook his head to clear it and fumbled at his swordbelt for his weapon. It took him a moment to draw, and as he did so, he weathered an attack of nausea and giddiness. Gods! He'd have to watch himself with this rough country brew. You couldn't drink it the way you could wine—even good strong palm wine from the Valley of the Two Rivers.

He poised at the door of the tent—and, when his head had cleared, slipped inside, sword at the ready, eyes blinking at the sudden light. He raised his sword . . .

. . . and put it down again. In the middle of the enclosed space, two candles sat in bronze holders on the sand, flanking her to either side. She regarded him with those big unblinking eyes, her full lips showing, as usual, not the smallest hint of a smile.

She wore the long robe tonight against the chill, and her little feet were in soft boots. Only face and hands showed. The robe was soft and of an expensive cut; above it, her dark hair, unbound, loose, spilled down over those softly rounded shoulders in rich profusion.

Shobai, feeling like a fool, returned his sword to its scabbard. "I—I thought someone had broken in," he said lamely, knowing she still understood nothing. Somehow it didn't seem to matter. She'd come to him, and that was a lot in itself. He looked into her eyes, saw the light of the dancing flames on her soft cheeks with the wide-boned structure. . . . "You're lovely," he said almost involuntarily. "Lovely. I—I think you're the most beautiful thing I've ever seen."

She said nothing. He stepped closer, trying to get her in perfect focus. His hand fell on her shoulder; he started at the rich softness of the material of her garment. "Here," he said. "How do you come by so expensive a. . . ?" Then he stopped. "But—you're a slave. Or are you?" He reached for her sleeve, bared the delicately formed arm underneath. A bronze bracelet circled it at the precise point where a slave-mark would be. He slipped the armlet down her arm and held it in his hand.

"Why—why, there isn't any slave-mark," he said. "I thought you were a slave. But you're not. I don't understand. I asked for you, thinking you were . . ." He put one big hand under her rounded chin, turned her face up to look at him. "But you came to me anyhow. And when you could have gone away, when I was stinking, falling-down drunk, you stayed. I don't understand. . . ." His words trailed off. He sighed and spoke again. "I don't even know your name."

She said something he did not catch. He took her hand and used it to pat himself on the chest. "Shobai," he said. "I am Shobai."

She caught his meaning quickly. She took his hand, touched her breasts. "Sayda," she said. And for the first time there was the barest, faintest hint at a smile. "Sayda."

"Sayda," Shobai repeated after her. "That's a lovely name. Beautiful the way you, yourself, are beautiful. I—look at me, you've sobered me up, coming to me like this. My head's clear again, and—Sayda, you're good for me." He suddenly bent and kissed her lightly on the lips. She tore herself away just as suddenly and stepped back a pace. She stood looking at him, one slender hand touching the lips he'd kissed.

She smiled, and this time the smile reached her eyes. That thin hand touched her lips again—and in a single long lithe movement she was in his arms.

Shobai's heart pounded. He held her close; then he stepped back and looked at her, and the look on her face was the sweetest thing he'd ever seen. He kissed her lips, her eyes; he covered her oval face with kisses. Her hands went to his waist and gently pulled him closer. "Sho-bai," she said in that soft musky voice of hers. "Sho-bai. . . ."

Their lovemaking was passionate, then playful, then peaceful. Shobai marveled again and again at how she managed to retain the precious quality of innocence, of incorruptibility, while matching his own ardor and even surpassing it. His hands went to her body again and again, even when his passion was slaked at last; and when his hands finally lay exhausted at his side on the furs next to her, his eyes continued to look her up and down. She was perfect in every part, a jewel, a ripe fruit at the moment of picking. And she had come to him, simply, undemanding, her every action saying: *"I trust you. I love you. Use me as you will. I'm yours. . . ."*

"Gods," he said in a gentle voice. "And I thought I knew something about women. I knew nothing, nothing at all."

"Sho-bai," she said. Her hand touched him—here, there. The contact wasn't sexual. There was sweet undemanding *caring* in it. He reached for the hand and kissed it.

As he did, he saw the rings on her fingers for the first time. They glinted in the light: bronze rings, not gold. It was not a distinction that mattered; she had looked lovely with no ornaments at all, and now . . .

Something in the glint of the bronze caught his eye. He raised her hand, held it close to his eye. Then he reached for one of the candles and brought it close. "Huh," he said. "Now how do they get that—"

Something else glittered in the dancing light. He reached down, picked up the bronze armlet she'd worn, the one he'd removed from her arm. "Well, I'll be damned," he said, looking it over more closely.

"Shobai?" she said, leaning forward. She reached up, took off the bronze choker she was wearing; then she felt under the furs that covered them for her feet. In a moment she handed him the little bronze toe rings she had been wearing.

He examined all of it, suddenly wide awake, his mind working fast. "Why, this is—for heaven's sake, who could have made this? Surely nobody down south of here. Nobody this side of Shinar, or perhaps Ur. And—you're wearing lots of it, as if it were plentiful where you come from. But—"

"Sho-bai?" she said curiously.

He continued, talking as much to himself as to her. "It's the *other* way of making bronze," he said. "The good way. Using tin instead of arsenic. It's harder, less brittle. You can work it more easily. My master taught me the process, but I never had the chance to work it; tin was too scarce in Haran."

He put the ornaments down and pounded one big fist into the other palm. "But of course, of course! Your people come from the high mountains to the north—and everyone always used to tell me there were big tin deposits there. But the Hurrians controlled the mines, and even if you fought your way through to them, the raiders would pick you clean on the way home. But *your* people—they've *taken* the tin mines, haven't they? And they know the process—or they hired somebody like me who knew it. But—why haven't I heard of any other armorers with the party? Surely they must have some. But where? With one of the other units? Perhaps with the command unit, where this Leader fellow stays . . ."

She smiled, uncomprehending, and kissed his bare shoulder. She had taken to kissing very quickly. It didn't seem to be common among her people.

"Yes!" he said. "What wonderful stuff. It's everything my master said it was. You'd be able to rework this, and make it even harder by hammering, and there wouldn't be that damned trouble we always have with the arsenic fumes during the smelting process." He held up the tiny ring that had circled her toe. "And look at this. Worked so delicately, and yet as hard as iron." The flash hit him, and he almost dropped the little ring. "Why—perhaps one might be able to make weapons of this stuff that *would* deal with iron. That *would* stand up to the black metal. If your people have control of a huge supply of tin like that, if you're about to add to your conquests the copper deposits at Melid, then who needs iron anyhow?" His smile was triumphant. "And here I'd been wondering . . ." He started to hand the little ring back to her, then thought better of it. He reached down and raised her little foot, soft and delicately made. He kissed it gently, replaced the ring. He looked now into dark eyes that regarded him with wonder, astonishment. She touched her instep with one hand. A half-smile trembled on her lips. She reached out to touch him on the cheek; she pulled him closer, as much with her dark eyes as anything, and Shobai, who had thought his passion spent for the evening, suddenly found it returned in force. His heart beat; his breath came in hoarse gasps. He sank with her to the pile of furs, feeling the silken wonder of her skin against him, breast to ankle. . . .

In the morning—in the gray dawn, with the air chill and inhospitable—Vahan shook him out roughly. His eye went to the pallet beside him; she was gone. He breathed a sigh of relief. He sat up. "What. . . ?" he said.

"Time to saddle up," Vahan said. "We ride. We ride to Melid. You come."

They thought of everything. The pony, Kedar, was saddled and ready to go when Shobai, shivering against the morning chill and feeling at last the aftereffects of the amount of drink he'd taken in before Sayda had come to join him, made his way to the open space where the animals stood at tether. He reached up and patted the stout neck of the big paint pony, noting for the first time the difference between his saddle and theirs. "Hmm," he thought aloud. "Cinched just so, and with the rider's weight farther forward like that—why, it might work better at that." He reminded himself to look into the matter of the nomad saddle when he returned. There seemed to be much to learn from them.

But after they had mounted and headed north, his thoughts again went to Sayda, to the evening they'd spent together. Somehow, she'd touched a part of his heart that no woman had ever reached before. Before, women—particularly his wife and his many aristocratic mistresses—had been playthings, fit only for games and—in Anat's case at least—showing off, as one might show off any prized possession: a fine Moabite pony like Kedar, for instance.

But this seemed different. Where, most of the time, he had wished his many women mute to keep from having to listen to their prattle, he now wished he knew Sayda's language better, or she his: he wanted to hear what she had to say—about everything. Her voice was soft and smooth and comforting, and full of passion when the occasion demanded. He sensed the intelligence in her face, wished for greater communion with her. He found himself wanting their union to be total, involving every part of him instead of only his body and the skills it knew and appreciated. . . .

Gods! he told himself. *You're thinking like a man in love. And with a girl who knows nothing about you but your name. . . .* And she? Who was she? Why, another day had passed, and he had once more forgotten to ask. Soft-headed. He was getting soft-headed, no doubt about it.

On the third day, their party met a nomad scouting detachment. Vahan rode out to meet them, while Shobai and the rest waited at the crest of a hill. When the nomad returned, his face, flinty as ever, was softened a trifle by a triumphant glimmer in his eye. "Melid," he said. "Melid fell today. I show you soon. Over hill, maybe hour's ride. But now we turn aside. See copper mines."

Shobai let the nomad captain lead the way for a while. Then he pulled up abreast of Vahan as the path widened. "Vahan," he said. "I've seen some samples of your people's own work in bronze. I mean, well, I guess it's theirs. Unless you hired somebody like me."

"We do both," Vahan said. "Sometimes own people. Sometimes others do better."

"Well, the work is copper-and-tin bronze, not copper-and-arsenic. It's high-grade metal. Where do you get the tin? From the mines at the foot of the Caucasus?"

"Yes, yes," the nomad said. "Much tin. More than can ever use. You want tin? We provide. All you want. All you need. But now—now look."

They had ridden to the top of the hill, and now they looked down on a vast flat valley in which hundreds, perhaps thousands, of naked, sun-blackened men were working at various activities. Digging; crushing the malachite ore others had carved out of the mountainside; smelting . . . the mines of Melid! Shobai let out a little yelp of pleasure in spite of himself. He watched the scene below, noting the uniformed nomads moving among the dark bare bodies. As he watched, one of the nomad overseers barked out an incomprehensible curse and battered a worker to his knees with the flat of his sword. "But—these workers are from Melid?" he said. "The original workers who built the mines?"

"Why not?" Vahan said, shrugging. "Were slave before, slave now. Little difference who owns. Much copper. High grade. You see for yourself. Enough copper to arm half of world. All you want, all you need."

Shobai looked on openmouthed. Yes! He'd never seen a sight like it. It must have resembled the Egyptian workings at Timna, where his ancestors had worked. And with an almost unlimited supply of tin available from the nomads' northern mines ... the Shepherd Kings would be well-nigh invincible! Armed by him, they could even challenge the Hittites for the northern country, iron weapons or no! And maybe—maybe if they saw a way of successfully attacking the Hittites—well, wouldn't they move westward instead of southward?

Might there, in fact, be an outside chance of their sparing Haran? And sparing the conscience Bentesina had awakened in him, Shobai—the conscience which kept telling him, in all his vulnerable moments, the words of Sarku of Kanish: *There comes a time when a man has to take sides.* . . .

VII

Over the hill, in the valley beyond, something was burning. At least three plumes of dark smoke were visible from where Shobai's party wound its way across the flat river plain. A light wind had struck up, and the plumes united higher up, drifting slowly downwind together.

Shobai spurred Kedar forward, pulling even with Vahan. "The smoke," he said. "That's Melid?"

"Yes," the nomad said, matter-of-factly. "I show you, soon."

Shobai held his tongue for a moment. Then he said, "I ... don't understand. You took the city. Now you burn it? But why not just ... take it over? Save it for your own use? Move some of your own people into it?"

Vahan shrugged. "My people not city people," he said.

411

"What we want city for?" But he turned thoughtful and followed up his own comment. "Well, easier to leave people of city, under leader we choose. Sometime leader from city, leader on our side. How you say? Regent?"

"Uh, maybe viceroy would be better. Something like that. I see. But the burning?"

"Oh." The nonchalance was back. "Soldiers fight hard, win battle. When gate come down, soldiers—soldiers act crazy. You know. Women, girls, wine. Better to let soldiers go, for now. You understand. Plenty time to play soldier tomorrow. Soldiers have fun now. Sometimes fun get . . . out of hand. Fires start. People die." He shrugged. But then his brow rose in a sort of understanding. He looked sharply at Shobai. "You," he said. "You make arms for war. You ever . . . *see* war? See battle?"

"No," Shobai said. "Ordinarily, an armorer's job is behind the lines. While the battle's going on, we're still busy making and mending arms. When the battle's over, it's time for us to move on."

Vahan smiled, his eyes mere slits. The smile was indulgent, almost to the point of insult. "Ah," he said knowingly. "Today you see. Maybe you learn something. Is maybe like man who grow cow for others to eat, but eat only bread and cheese himself. No?"

"I suppose so. But of course, one never learns all there is to know of life."

"No. But you—you are young. Very young. Among my people, man who has never fought is boy. Still boy."

"Well, I'm not exactly a stranger to fighting," Shobai said. "I've been in some pretty rough encounters here and there. There was the time robbers attacked when my caravan was—"

"Hah!" Vahan snorted. "Robbers. Bandits. Is not fight. Is not fight at all. You ever use sword?"

"Why, yes. I was about to tell you—"

Vahan turned away contemptuously. "You wait," he said. "You wait. We go across hill, see Melid. You see war. What happen after war. Pretty much same. Only difference people not try to kill you anymore. You, Shobai, you not live in real world. Everything come easy for you. You—" He reached out, felt the rich cloth of Shobai's robe. "You rich man, but you not have to fight for riches. Come too easy. Not understand where money come from, fine houses, slaves, horses. Come from kill. Come from make people dead."

412

"Oh, come now," Shobai said. "I've heard people advance that point of view in taverns. People who envied me, wanted what I had—but who weren't willing to work as hard as I have for it. People like that, who've had a few drinks, will pick you to pieces if you let them. But—"

"Hah," Vahan laughed humorlessly. "You think *Vahan* envy you? You think I want what you have? Shobai, if I want what you have I take." He patted his sword. "You not stop me." He laughed again, dismissing the idea. "Not worry. I want nothing. But—you hear what I say. You remember. You remember when we see Melid."

Shobai threw a resentful glance at Vahan's back as the nomad nudged his horse and pulled ahead. A quick flash of anger ran through him. How dare the nomad bait him so? How dare he patronize a man of his, Shobai's, standing? A rustic barbarian who smelled of sweat and dirt, who made his living cutting up other people?

For a moment he considered what Vahan had said. Well, perhaps he *was* a trifle spoiled, compared to these barbarians who had to hack their way to any sort of affluence at all, and whose chosen way of life forbade them to make any sort of ostentatious display of it. After all, he, Shobai, had been relatively well-to-do since about a year after finishing his apprenticeship; there had always been some sort of border scuffle going on which demanded his services, and as a member of the fabled Children of the Lion he could always command good prices. But, after all, he could still remember poverty, remember days when he and his mother and Hadad had not had the price of a decent meal among them. . . .

At the thought, long since suppressed, Shobai felt a small but real pang of guilt. He *had* neglected them terribly, hadn't he? All the years of irresponsibility, and wild, unchecked spending. And all the while Tallay and Hadad were living shabbily on the far side of town in quarters which by now wouldn't have served a slave of his. If he'd ever given a thought to anyone but himself—

But he shrugged away the thought now. There was time, after all. He'd make it all up to them. Besides, they really didn't need any help from him now, did they? Not with Hadad getting rich, as everyone told him he was doing. No, it would do neither of them any good for Shobai to go around feeling guilty. Things were the way they were, after all. What if the situation had been reversed? Wouldn't Hadad, in his place, have acted as he had? Neglected him, Shobai?

Then the pang returned: a stabbing pain in his heart.

Hadad? Neglect him? Of course he wouldn't have. And Shobai ground his teeth in anguish, remembering his brother as the man he himself should have been: loving, openhearted, generous with what he had to give. . . .

Suddenly his face contorted in anger; with his teeth set, his eyes blazing, he put the whole question from his mind and concentrated his thoughts on the trail that led to the top of the rise.

And then at the top, he looked down into the next valley and saw what remained of Melid. . . .

Back at Manouk's base camp, the runners reached the outer pickets, passed on the news, and continued on their way down into the camp. When they reported to Manouk's lieutenants, the words came out in an exhausted, breathless rush. "Sir," the runner Agasi said. "The Leader . . . an hour outside the pickets, perhaps . . . on his way here." He saluted, but his movements were those of a man exhausted beyond belief.

"An hour away?" said Haigas, Manouk's delegated second-in-command. "You've notified the pickets to shape up?"

"Yes, sir."

"Fine." Haigas nodded to both men. "You've done well. Go get some rest. But report to me this evening." He watched them limp away; then he turned to his assistant, Garapet. "Well," he said with a sigh, "prepare for a reprimand. Because that's what you and I are going to get."

"Are you sure? The camp seems pretty tight to me."

"It *is* tight. But the Leader—he's been on the warpath for some time now. Nobody can please him. He'll find flaws where there aren't any. He'll insult your turnout and mine. He'll find dirt on a spotless sword."

Garapet frowned. "I wish that part of it weren't necessary. It isn't, is it? Really? I mean, if Manouk, say, were Supreme Commander it wouldn't be like that—"

"Hush! You damned fool, don't you know the very shrubs have ears? Do you have any idea how touchy that subject is just now?" His voice was low and guarded.

"Why, no, I—"

"Damn it, there *is* a movement among the chiefs. Don't you dare say you heard me say this or so help me, I'll gut you like a fish. But our Leader—Karakin—has enemies among the tribes. From a king among kings he now conceives himself a king among vassals. And that doesn't sit well with the old chiefs, you understand. They consider him a man like

414

themselves, one whom they raised to his present eminence."

"I can't believe what I'm hearing. Do you really mean—"

"Quiet, you damned fool! Do you want to be turned in as a conspirator? Do you have any idea what'd happen to anyone the Leader heard was involved in something like that? He'd wind up hacked to pieces alive, forced to eat his own tripes."

"Ugh! Don't remind me. But, Haigas—"

"It's as I said," the lieutenant said in a low whisper. "And the chiefs favor Manouk. He—"

"Does he know about this? I mean, is he in on it?"

"That, my friend, I sincerely cannot tell you. I really don't know. You know how closemouthed Manouk is. He keeps his own counsel. But I have this funny feeling that the Leader suspects something, even though he can't put his finger on it. He doesn't act the same toward Manouk. He's suspicious of him. He doesn't show it openly—and he doesn't dare show Manouk any discourtesy, but—"

"Doesn't dare? You sit there bald-faced and say our Leader 'doesn't dare' do this, that, or the other?"

"You know what I mean. He knows Manouk is well connected. He knows Manouk has friends among the chiefs —perhaps more friends than he ever had himself, even before he started taking on so much authority. . . ."

"How is it that it's taken so long for this information to get down to me?" Garapet said disbelievingly. "I mean, I'm not usually this out of touch."

"You've been playing the Great Lover so assiduously with those little twins we captured at the battle of—"

"Oh, come now. That hasn't affected my—"

"Sure it has. Your brains have turned to mush." Haigas reached out and touched the brass fittings on his assistant's belt. "For heaven's sake, polish that! Right now! He'll cut your heart out and eat it raw if he finds anything really reprehensible about your turnout." Haigas frowned. "I'm serious. I wouldn't be surprised at anything he did. After all, this is Manouk's camp, and Manouk isn't here to stick up for it—or for us."

"You really think he'll be like that?" Garapet said, busily buffing the brass on his belt. Then he stopped and looked at his superior, wide-eyed. "But—if that's the way it's going to be—well, the gods help Manouk's niece."

"Young Sayda? Why?"

"You mean you've missed how she's been carrying on with the big foreigner? The armorer?"

415

"Shobai?" Haigas frowned. "Huh. That *is* a problem. You're right. If Karakin finds out about that—"

"You're getting pretty bold, calling him Karakin. I thought the order was always to call him—"

"You're right. Foolish of me. But—what a problem. If he—if the Leader hears about one of our women whoring around with a foreigner—"

"—and a hired hand at that—"

"Yes. *Gods!* He'll have the girl whipped. If he doesn't grab the whip away and do it himself. And—gods! Her a niece of Manouk's!" He sighed, letting the breath out through pursed lips. "If the Leader harms her, you can't begin to imagine the problems that will create between him and Manouk. And remember, my friend, every problem that starts between our superiors will filter down to us, and in a hell of a hurry. The two of them will make our lives miserable. It might even precipitate—"

But here he stopped and looked at his assistant. His eyes were wide, his mouth agape. Both of them knew what the rest of the sentence would have been. And neither of them wanted to frame the words that would complete it. They were still standing there, mute, thunderstruck by the implications, when the trumpet sounded from the high hill above, signaling the arrival of the Leader and his party.

Glassy-eyed, hair tousled, Shobai stumbled through the streets of the dying city, no longer caring whether he stepped in a rank, half-dried puddle of fresh blood or not. He tried to look away from the scene before him, where six soldiers, drunk, gore-bedecked, were taking turns raping a naked young woman, her starveling body covered with bruises. But as he looked away, he could see what was left of her child, a little girl of perhaps six: they'd taken turns with her too, tossing her high in the air and catching her on their spears. Tired of their sport, they'd gutted the child and watched her run, spilling her innards on the ground as she ran. . . .

He felt his gorge rising again, and he vomited into a pool of blood. There wasn't much left in him to vomit up now, and the dry heaves began. He moved away down a narrow cross street; but billowing black smoke once again drove him back into the dreadful town square, where the carnage continued uninterrupted. At his feet, he could see an old man lying in his own gore; they'd hacked off his arms and legs and left him to die. "P-please," the old man said in a weak voice. "Please,

416

sir. Kill me. Don't leave me like this. Please, sir. Now, please. . . ."

Shobai covered his eyes. He was weeping uncontrollably. He ignored the old man, as if he could make him disappear by moving away from him. But in his mind he could hear the thin old voice still; he carried it with him down the filthy street. Perhaps he would carry it with him forever. *"Please, sir, kill me. Don't leave me like this. . . ."*

He stumbled, weeping, into a courtyard, hardly knowing how he had got there. Was this, then, war? Was this what it was like? Was this the industry he had made his living by feeding, by making its terrible tools and toys? Was this the sort of death and destruction his fine handmade weapons had served all this time? Why hadn't anyone told him it was like this?

And the thought seeped unbidden into his mind: *Carchemish . . . Haran. . . .*

VIII

Garapet, puffing slightly with the attempt to keep up with the Leader's enormous strides, followed the nomad king of the Shepherd Kings down the long line of soldiers massed in review formation, his eyes fixed on the commander's grizzled, unruly hair. *It looks like a lion's mane,* he thought.

But place the Leader in the balance with a full-grown lion and he, Garapet, would fear the lion less, he was thinking. Already the Leader, inspecting the pickets above the camp on the way in, had ordered one man lashed to a wagon wheel and beaten to insensibility; another, turned out for inspection with a broken sandal-strap, had felt the direct weight of the Leader's terrible and heavy hand. The commander's huge fist had lashed out and struck the young officer down as if the two were enemies meeting in a street. They'd carried the injured man back to camp on a shield, his collarbone broken in two places.

He himself, though, had already profited from the commander's visit. Haigas, as the man responsible for the allegedly unsoldierly turnout of his troops, had been cursed out slowly, savagely, demeaningly—and banished to an outpost, broken to the ranks. This left him, Garapet, in charge until Vahan returned. And he had every intention of finding some way to capitalize on the fact.

Well, obviously the first thing he'd have to do was stay out of trouble. That wouldn't be easy—although theoretically any problems connected with the present inspection could be laid at Haigas's door. *Gods!* he prayed now. *Just don't let anyone get out of line. . . .*

But as he watched, the Leader's massive shoulders shifted, and he made a sudden right turn. The turn took him away from the massed forces lined up to be inspected; Garapet sighed in relief. The inspection was over. The Leader was heading for the great tent each of the camps always had ready for him, in case of a surprise visit.

Forty paces down the line of tent-rows they passed a place where women were working. The Leader stopped dead. He jerked his head toward Garapet in a peremptory nod. "Here," he said. "What is this?"

Garapet caught up with him. He watched where the commander's hairy paw of a hand pointed—and his heart sank for a moment. "Yes, my Leader," he said, trying to hide his dismay. "Twins. Aren't they lovely? They were captured after the battle of—"

"Send them to my tent," he said. Then he looked at the girls again. A sudden quiet fell over the little group. The women, eight of them, had been grinding corn; now they looked at the bearded giant with apprehension. "Wait," he said. He strode over to where the twins stood, their eyes wide. "You," he said to the one on the left. (What were their names now? Garapet thought. But he realized it didn't matter. Not anymore.)

The girl said something in the heathen tongue. Her tone was supplicatory; her eyes, and her sister's, darted to Garapet for support. He kept his face grim, stony.

Suddenly, the Leader's hand stretched out toward the girl. It took hold of the brief garment she wore—and ripped it all the way down. His hand completed the gesture, tearing the cloth away, leaving her naked. She pulled back, trying to cover herself with her arms and hands. "Ah," the Leader said. He looked her up and down. "The other one is like this too? Then send them along." He turned on one heel and continued his rapid pace down the row of tents. Garapet, gulping, barked an order to one of the aides behind him and struggled to catch up. He did not look at either of the girls, not even when the aide, on his order, tore away the second girl's garment, leaving her as naked as her sister. Somehow, there was something in the air that killed both sexual desire and sexual curiosity in him just now. . . .

Inside, Garapet called for food and drink—and regretted his decision to stay with the Leader when he ate. The nomad commander's manners were those of a rutting hog. But Garapet, having once made his decision to make the most of his chance at preference, forced himself not to look away as his superior gnawed noisily at the half-raw animal bones and tossed his leavings carelessly to the great dog that sat behind him on the sand.

Finally, the Leader wiped his grimy hands on the sand and looked at Garapet, his eyes cold and calculating below beetling brows. "I had hoped to see Manouk," he said. "Where did he go?"

"He had business down south, my Leader," Garapet said. As he spoke, he weighed the cold tone in the Leader's voice when the name Manouk had been spoken. And a small plan stirred timidly in his mind. "He, ah, didn't want to meet you, I think. At least that's the impression I got."

"He didn't?" his commander said, his eye suddenly flashing. "What makes you think so? Has he done something I would not approve of?"

"Well, sir—" Garapet said, mock-deprecatingly.

"Out with it!" the Leader bellowed. "Look. I know about this—this revolt among the other nomad kings. I know what they think of Manouk. Do you think me a fool? Tell me what's on your mind. Don't hold back. You hold back and I'll begin to wonder if you're not perhaps a better friend of Manouk's than—"

"Oh, no, sir. No, not at all. Why, I—"

"Then speak. Get it out!"

Look what you've got yourself into, Garapet told himself despairingly. He cast about wildly for something, anything, to say. "Well, sir," he said. "There's that niece of his. . . ."

"Yes? Yes?"

"Well, sir, uh, we hired a foreigner, from somewhere down south, I think, to make arms, and—"

"Yes? You waste my time."

"Oh, no, sir. I mean—well, the stranger—well, sir, Manouk sent his niece to the stranger's bed, and—"

"He *what?*" The voice was no louder, but the force in it suddenly rose alarmingly. "We *hired* a stranger? And Manouk let his niece whore around with him?"

"Not let, sir." Garapet, seeing his advantage, pressed it in desperation. "He—he initiated the whole thing, sir. He sent the girl to him. . . ." *Gods! Gods! What are you saying?* he thought with a pang of fear. But the ball had already begun to roll down the hill. And besides, he told himself, it wasn't altogether untrue. The foreigner *had* asked for the girl while drunk; and Manouk *had* complied, following the custom. But somehow it hadn't really added up to—

"This girl," the Leader said. "She is . . . experienced? Perhaps a widow? Surely Manouk did not send a virgin to the bed of a—"

"I . . . don't know, sir," Garapet said haltingly. "I—I know the girl hadn't been married yet. But she may not have been a virgin. . . ."

The Leader's huge hand pounded the sand. There was a savage look in his eye. "Strangers," he said. "Foreigners. Manouk. He goes too far. Too far indeed. Perhaps it is time to . . . send him a message."

"Yes, sir," Garapet said apprehensively, wondering what kind of message was intended. "You mean you're going to reprimand him?"

"No," the Leader said. His face was expressionless. His eyes were all but closed. His voice was low and measured when he said, "Bring me the girl. Manouk's niece. Bring her to me!"

Garapet, his heart pounding wildly, took a deep breath. This was it, he was thinking. From here on in there would be no turning back. He'd committed himself. "Y-yes, my Leader," he said in a voice so altered by emotion that he could hardly recognize it as his own.

For a time, for many miles in fact, he was morose, sullen, silent. His head throbbed; his stomach was sour and the taste in his mouth was that of a man who'd eaten raw offal. The slow jouncing gait of Kedar beneath him wasn't much help. He wanted to vomit, but there was no food in him to vomit up; he'd emptied his nagging guts only an hour before. From time to time he glared at Vahan's unperturbed back, up ahead of him.

If only he'd known. . . .

But how could you know without—well, without doing what he'd just done? To be sure, people tried to tell you over the years: that war wasn't just play, that it wasn't just a matter of men with sharp swords testing one another's mettle. But somehow, somehow they never got around to letting you know the whole truth about it all: that war was a game which engaged not only the strong, the armed, the powerful, but the weak and unarmed and innocent as well. That the end result of it was butchery, a vileness unleashed in man which surpassed all his worst imaginings.

And—and it wasn't just bad people who did this, who committed these crimes on the bodies of the weak. It was ordinary people—people you'd eaten and caroused with. People who—before the stresses of war had exposed the beast in their innards—had been human, decent, compassionate men. But if, just once, you let that raving, raging monster loose inside the most reasonable man, he turned into a demon from the darkness.

But no. Even that wasn't true. If that were the whole story, there'd be someone to blame for everything. And the hell of it was that there wasn't. He knew. He knew the men who had rutted and raped the day before, who'd butchered the sick and the lame under the hot-blooded spell of war—these men now skulked about shamefacedly, unable to look each other in the eye, unable to exorcise the terrible memories of what they'd done when the awful spell had been upon them.

And—yes—the worst thing was that he knew that in their shoes he'd have done much the same. He knew himself to be one of them, a man who, below the civilized level of decency, was the same bloodthirsty, self-indulgent monster they all were.

Vahan broke stride, dropped back to join him, the same slightly supercilious smile on his face. "Ah," he said. "You feel effect of much drink. No wonder. You drink enough to kill normal man."

Shobai snarled at him; wouldn't look at him again. "Leave me alone," he said in a hoarse voice. "Just go back to your—"

"Then it is not drink," Vahan said. "You feel bad. You drank last night to stop feel bad."

"I'll never stop feeling bad again," Shobai said bitterly. "And I'll have you to thank for the fact."

Shobai felt, rather than saw, Vahan's shrug. "Why?" the nomad said mildly. "I not invent war. War been with us for ages. What you see—it happen all places."

"You had to show me, didn't you?" Shobai's tone was acid, resentful, desperate. "You just *had* to rub my nose in it. Well, you've had your effect. You've done what you wanted to do. I hope you're happy now."

"Not take everything hard. Shobai, yesterday you learn, as grown man, what I learn when I ten years old. You hear? What make you special? What make you ... above this? What make you manner of man who should not have to know what all men know? Is war. Is part of life."

"Part of life? You mean part of death. Gods, Vahan! Does it have to be this way? I mean, can't you just fight somebody and defeat him and let it go at that? I mean, defeated—he won't bother you anymore. He won't oppose you. You'll have made your point. Why can't it stop there? Why do you have to let the men loose to kill the man's wife and children? Why do you—"

"Ah, Shobai," Vahan said, a touch of sympathy in his voice at last, "wolf kill your sheep. You kill wolf. But he have mate. He have nest, babies. Babies grow to new wolf. Better you kill babies."

"But damn it—"

"Is worse, Shobai. Man worse than wolf. Man remember you kill his father. Man carry memory all his life. By and by he kill you. You see?"

"You—you make it sound as though it were all so simple, like a game children play. But—gods, man! You saw it! You saw what it was like! How can you just sit there and—"

"Shobai. It was not Vahan who thought it big game. It was Shobai. It was Shobai who played at making weapon. It was Shobai, maker of sword."

Shobai put his hands over his ears. "Enough!" he said in a strangled voice. "I don't want to hear any more. I've heard enough, and seen enough, in the last day to last me a lifetime. Just leave me alone. . . ."

But Vahan drew near and put a compassionate hand on Shobai's shoulder, and the words leaked through despite Shobai's attempts to shut them out. "Shobai," he said. "You will forget. Gods are merciful. They erase memory. Little by little. By and by you no remember. By and by pain leave your mind. Shobai—forgive. I do bad thing when I take you to Melid. . . ."

"Bad? No, it was a good thing. Here I've been going through life acting as though actions didn't have consequences." Shobai stiffened his young back and sat high in the saddle, his knuckles white where his hands gripped the reins. "You did me a favor, Vahan," he said in a voice tight with rigid and unyielding self-control. "I thank you for it. Although you've probably cost me a profession in the long run."

"Cost you . . . ?" Vahan looked hard at the young armorer. "No, Shobai. Weapons—they your work. You do good work. Cannot give up for—"

"I can't?" Shobai said. Now his voice had a child's petulance in it, side by side with an adult's resolve. It was a curious combination, and Vahan regarded him with concern. "So I can't quit?" Shobai said. "You just watch, Vahan. You just watch me. . . ."

Vahan looked hard at him again; then he shook his head and spurred his horse forward, drawing ahead of Shobai, the set of his shoulders showing his perplexity. Shobai looked after him, his jaw set. He clung to his newfound resolution with a desperate tenacity; it was all that kept him from slipping back into that desolate mood that had lain so heavily upon him all the way back from Melid. It was his one ray of hope, the one way of getting his pride back. . . .

But then his thoughts went to the girl, Sayda: to her gentle eyes, her soft hands, her low velvety voice. He pictured her in the streets of Melid, and the thought was almost too much for him. He closed his eyes—but succeeded only in making the horrid picture more vivid in his mind. No! This was not for her, this bloody life. He'd take her with him when he went. Surely, there was somewhere safe to take her to, somewhere where he could make a living without contributing to the horror of battle, of combat, of the rapine and pillage and butchery that followed them.

But he had a wife, and he had a place in society, and he could not marry Sayda. Would it be fair to take her along with him, seeing that he—?

Then he thought of Melid again, and his resolve returned in force. Yes! Yes, he'd take her with him!

Sayda!

IX

They straggled into their base camp midway through the third day. By now Shobai's mood was ranging from morose to savage. He barely spoke to Vahan; he spoke to no one else.

His face was wooden, his eyes red-ringed from loss of sleep. He had begun to wonder if he'd ever sleep soundly again. Dreams were supposed to refresh you—but his dreams made him wake screaming, flailing about with his fists, and afterward there was no feeling of self-restoration at all. His dreams diminished him instead.

Disheveled, reeling from fatigue, Shobai dismounted and managed to hobble Kedar in a patch of good grass. Then he made his unsteady way to his forge.

His assistants had done their work well, just as he'd explained it to them. The twin forges were almost complete; the twin smelting-furnaces were built to exacting tolerances. Well, at least the nomads were capable of a certain amount of skill, when they stopped their war and butchery and got down to constructive work. . . .

He looked over his entire operation and took some small pride in it. He'd done a fine job so far, as always. He'd once again shown himself to be a thoroughgoing professional at his work. He doubted if there were a more efficient shop to be found anywhere east of Hittite country.

But then his face twisted in rage and self-loathing, and he became aware of someone standing at his side. He turned, regarded Vahan through bloodshot, weary eyes.

"Good, good, Shobai," Vahan said. "Look very good. Ready to go to work today, tomorrow. Soon as you feel better."

"I feel fine just now," Shobai rasped. "Could you hand me that hammer over there? The big one with the rope on the handle?"

"Yes," Vahan said mildly. He stooped over, retrieved the big armorer's maul, handed it to Shobai. "You change mind, eh? You go to work soon?"

"I go to work right now," Shobai said in a tight, strangled voice. He raised the maul easily in his big hands, spun it once around his head for the momentum—and sent it crashing down on the earthen bowl of the left-hand furnace he'd caused to be built during his absence. The bowl shattered into small pieces; Shobai kicked much of the rubble away with his foot. Then he raised the maul again.

"*No!*" Vahan said, shocked. He put one hand on Shobai's arm; the armorer shook him off. "No, Shobai—you not do this—you stop now—"

"Get out of my way," Shobai said between clenched teeth. And his next swing completed the demolition of the neat little

424

forge he'd built. He stepped to one side and made for the other. Vahan tried to restrain him again; Shobai held up the maul with a snarl. "Vahan," he said in a white-hot rage, "don't lay a hand on me. So help me, I'll kill you. I will."

Vahan stepped back, suddenly subdued—but not, Shobai knew, from fear. "Ah, Shobai," he said. "You take big step. Big step you cannot take back." There was genuine concern in Vahan's voice, and the fact surprised Shobai. "Think, Shobai. Think first. If you do this . . ."

Shobai rested the maul on one shoulder. "Vahan," he said. "You're right about one thing. What I'm doing is irreversible, as you say. But the step was taken back at Melid. And it was from that point that my feet were set on the path. I'll remind you who it was that set them that way."

"Ah, Shobai . . . I do bad thing. I do foolish thing. Forgive. Vahan is fool, stupid fool."

"Forget it. You did me a favor." He put both hands back on the thick handle of the maul. "I'm grateful to you for it. Now stand out of the way and I'll get on with my business." His voice was so taut and phlegmy he could hardly have recognized it as his own.

"Shobai," Vahan said gently. "May gods protect you. . . ." And then, the same sad, withdrawn look on his fighter's face, he went away. Shobai sighed, shook the cobwebs out of his head, and raised the maul again. But it was strange: now the savagery and anger were gone from him. Now there was only the knowledge that the job needed doing, and the cold, sober, single-minded determination to finish it, to smash both forges and furnaces before any more harm could be done through them. His face grim, his heart empty, he set to work.

When he was done, he set the maul down carefully beside the wreckage he'd made, brushed off his dusty hands, and turned to leave. One of his assistants stood behind him, silent, eyes wide, taking in the shattered implements, the rubble-strewn workspace. What was the man's name, now? Ah, yes. Noubar. Shobai looked him in the eye; the man winced. "Noubar," he said. "Do you know the girl Sayda? You know the one: slim, dark—"

"Sayda?" the man said. It was as if a little door had closed off in his face, shutting Shobai out. "You mean niece of Manouk?"

"Manouk's *niece*?" Shobai said, startled. Well, it didn't matter. It didn't matter whose child she was. She was a grown woman, and no slave. "Where would I find her just now?"

"Not know," Noubar said. "But—her tent next to Manouk's tent. One place east of Manouk's tent."

"Thank you," Shobai said, his heart full of purpose again. He ignored the shock and fear in the man's eyes and struck out down the lone row of tents, his strides long and rapid. . . .

"The foreigner did *what*?" the Leader said in his rasping bass, his tone evenly divided between incredulity and rage.

"Ah . . . this hireling of Manouk's . . . he wrecked the furnaces he'd built. The forges, too. One of my men saw him." Garapet, finding the response he'd hoped for, bore onward. "And he apparently gave every sign of getting ready to leave."

"*Leave?*" the Leader stormed. He made a big fist; his eyes flashed under the dark brows. Crooked teeth showed in his bearded face as he smiled a terrible smile. "He will not leave. Alert the pickets. He will not get out of camp alive." He turned to Garapet; but his eyes were out of focus and his mind was far away. "This all is Manouk's doing. He will deal with foreigners. One does not deal with foreigners. One orders them. . . ." The smile was a crocodile's now, the eyes cold as the snows. "I'll be in the command tent," he said. "Have a squad of men sent to me—quickly. And send the foreigner along as soon as you find him."

"Yes, my Leader. Dead or—?"

"Alive, you fool. Alive. Can a dead man work?"

Shobai, almost dragging the girl behind him, ran into Vahan again on the way to the command center. He stopped, letting the young woman catch up with him. "Vahan!" Shobai said in a voice filled with hatred. "Look what they've done! Who—who the devil could have done—?" He bit the words off, indicating the girl with one hand. Vahan looked at her; his eyes narrowed but his face did not change. "Well, look, damn it!" Shobai said. "It wasn't Manouk. He wasn't even here. Who was it?"

"Shobai," Vahan said. "Be calm, now." He looked at the girl again, at the black eye and the bruises on her face and neck and shoulders, at the livid marks of the whip on her bare little breasts and back. "Shobai, is matter for my people. Not matter for you. You go—quick. You leave camp while still time—"

"Not a matter for me?" Shobai's rage was no longer under

426

control. "Gods, man! Look at her! They've beaten her half to death—and all because she came to me. Do you think I'm going to stand here and let them do something like . . . ?" He looked at the girl again. The look on her face changed; she swayed. "Oh . . . gods. . . ." Shobai caught her as she slumped forward. "Vahan, where can I take her? Who takes care of the ill around here?"

"You give her to me," Vahan said. He stepped closer, gently took the battered girl in his arms. "I have my woman look after her. But you, Shobai, you go. Now! Quick!"

Shobai looked at the girl. Then he reached down for his sword—and remembered suddenly that he'd left it on the pommel of Kedar's gaudy saddle. "Damn!" he said, clenching his empty fingers. "Well, it doesn't matter. Take care of her, Vahan. Please. I'm going to . . ."

But the rest of his words were lost, muttered over his shoulder going away. Vahan suppressed a shudder; then he shifted the girl's weight in his arms and set out for his own quarters.

Garapet had joined the Leader again; the two were studying maps of the Melid campaign. Suddenly, a commotion outside broke their train of thought. The Leader looked up. He bellowed to the guard at the tent's door. "What is that?" he said.

"We have the foreigner," the guard said. "It seems that he has come to us, my Leader."

The big nomad stood, beckoned. "Send him in."

The guard held up one hand; then two of his troop marched in, each man holding Shobai by one arm. The armorer looked at the nomad leader; suddenly went limp; just as suddenly shook his arms free. Swords flashed—

"Let him go," the nomad chief said in his own tongue. "You," he said to Shobai in accented Hurrian. "You are—armorer?"

"I was once," Shobai said. "I just came to tell you I'm leaving. I won't do your damned dirty work anymore. We'll settle the matter of the contract later. But—" His voice tightened with the anger still in him. "Did you have to do that to the girl? To Sayda? She didn't do anything to you—"

"Girl is whore. We punish whore," the Leader said, sizing up the large young man before him. The armorer was his own height, but much more lightly built. "What is contract?" he said contemptuously. "Is no contract. . . ."

"I'm glad that you agree," Shobai said. "Very well. There's

no contract. We're quits." He drew a deep breath through his nostrils and spat the words out. "You're scum. All of you. I can't shake the dust of this place from my feet fast enough to—"

The Leader's huge hand struck out, faster than the head of a striking snake, faster than the eye could follow. His great bunched fist caught Shobai over the eye and battered him to his knees. Then the Leader's leg lashed out; his booted foot struck Shobai full in the face. Shobai struggled to one knee, half-blinded by his own blood. "You—"

The Leader's fist came down on the side of his neck now. Shobai fell, rolled, trying to get both legs under him. The Leader, fast for so large a man, leaped to his side and grabbed him by the robe. He lifted, in one quick motion; the robe tore, but he held onto it long enough to throw Shobai out the front door of the tent into the open air. There was an outcry from the massed soldiers outside as they saw the young man hit the ground hard.

"Here, you . . ." It was unclear what it was that Shobai was trying to say. One side of his face was covered with blood; his mouth was a flash of red as well. He rose to one knee, then one leg; the leg buckled under him, but he finally forced himself erect, forced his fists high—

The Leader attacked again. His foot caught Shobai in the stomach. The young man doubled over; a massive fist crashed down on the top of his head. He fell on his face, hard. The Leader moved forward again; kicked him twice in the ribs, the kidneys. Shobai pushed himself to a position where the weight of his upper body rested on his elbows; but the booted foot caught him in the face now and knocked him over on his back, his eyes open but unseeing. One of his hands raised a little from the ground, then fell back. He let out one tiny groan, with no wind behind it; then there was silence for a moment before the Leader's voice broke it: "Take him," he said matter-of-factly.

Shobai awoke in darkness, his whole body full of pain. He tried to move; it hurt, excruciatingly. He tried to breathe deeply, and awakened the same pain in another spot. He blinked his eye, but no light came. Gods! Had he been out that long?

Then, little by little, it started coming back to him. He'd challenged the big man in the rough coat, and he'd . . . But now the memory came back, all of it, in one devastating flash, and fear and nausea shook him. He'd been beaten! Broken and thrown away! And all of it before witnesses!

He raised one tired arm ... and then let it sink back. *Now ... now,* he thought. *Where am I?* He blinked; still the light did not come. . . .

. . . and then again it did. Through the wall of the tent he could see a warm light, growing closer. He could hear voices, saying things in the nomad tongue. He could feel their feet pounding on the ground. . . .

Then the light burst in the door, and there were several of them, big strong types, heavily armed. One of them held the torch high, barked an order. They reached down, lifted him; he howled feebly in pain, the way a child does. They tried to get him to his feet, but his legs wouldn't bear his weight. They were robust, strong, determined; they dragged him by the arms. His bare feet scraped painfully over the rocky ground; then a sudden rush of chill as the cool night air hit his body. He was naked—shivering, miserable.

They approached a brighter light. Dancing flames. Warmth on his battered, goose-pimpled body. They forced him to his knees, held him there. Someone barked an order, sharply. The men immediately grabbed his arms, and another man sank thick fingers in his long hair and held his head steady. The bodies next to him stiffened, as if expecting a blow . . .

. . . and then he knew what it was that was going to happen, and he cried out and tried to pull free. But somehow his strength had left him; he was as weak as a child in their hands. The order came again, louder. There was incomprehensible jabbering in the alien tongue. . . .

Then came the pain: white-hot, searing pain; more pain than he had ever felt at one time in his entire life. It seared into his upper arm, and he could smell the burning flesh, his own flesh, his own . . .

Before he fainted, he looked down and saw the raw blistered flesh of his arm, saw what they had done to him. He was scarred. He was mutilated forever. The mark would heal, but he would bear it the rest of his life. It was the mark of a slave.

CHAPTER THIRTEEN

I

"No, no, please," Hadad said mildly. "It's 'Ibalum.' *I-ba-lum.* You turn the stylus a little this way, and . . ."

The scribe looked up, puzzled. "You read?" he said. "And—and write as well? And yet you hire me?" He looked the young man up and down, his eye not missing the crooked leg that protruded at its awkward angle from the stylish tunic above it.

Hadad shrugged. "My friend," he said with a sheepish grin, "six months ago you could probably have bought and sold me, no matter how poor you consider yourself. I know what it's like to be a small businessman in a time of lean days. Some time back something wonderful happened to me— through this very Ibalum I'm writing to, mind you—and I became wealthy. Should I forget where I came from? Should I withhold my custom from the professionals of the neighborhood to save money? Save it for what?"

"Well, that's very generous of you, sir. I wish a few more people who've come into some money quickly thought your way."

"There's the difference," Hadad said, sitting down opposite the scribe with his wet clay. "It isn't as though I inherited money or anything like that. It's not a onetime thing. What happened to me augmented not just my capital, but my earning power. If the economy holds in this part of the world, I ought to be earning even better money a few years from now." He smiled his friendly smile, widemouthed, crinkly-eyed. "I'll need it, I guess. We're expecting our first child, and we intend to have more."

430

"Ah, yes," the scribe said. "That'll put a strain on your earnings, all right. But you're a tradesman, then? You didn't come by those calluses on your hands in some soft job, I'll wager."

"No. I'm a sculptor, a metalworker. Outside of the guild until recently—which shows you why I was so poor."

"Ah. But . . . you read?"

"Oh. It's a tradition in my family. The father teaches the mother to read—"

"Women? Reading? But—"

"And the mother teaches the children. No, relax. We'll never take the money out of an honest scribe's pocket. We're weaponmakers by trade in my father's line. I just happened to be the second son, and . . ."

His voice trailed off here. His mind wandered. Shobai . . . where could he be? He'd been missing for months now, and there'd still been no word. He hadn't even written to Anat. The thought bothered Hadad: shouldn't he be doing something? Searching for his brother? He bit his lip—and forced his mind back to the matter at hand. What was the man saying now?

". . . don't know if the economy's going to hold, sir, and that's the truth. They keep letting all these foreigners in every day, people who take our jobs away from us because they all work for less than we can afford to. And the guilds—they don't complain, they don't take care of us. I think it's all a conspiracy, sir. They've sold us out, the guild leaders have. They've made their own separate peace with the city fathers and the king."

"Do you really think so?" Hadad said. "Those are strong words. Is it really that bad now?"

"Oh, sir, you wouldn't believe it. If it continues this way—well, so help me, I'm leaving. I'm taking off for Ebla or someplace south of there. I don't know where. Aleppo, maybe. My wife has relatives in Aleppo. . . ." His hand, stylus poised, hung over the clay. "Ah," he said, looking down, "it's drying out."

"Oh," Hadad said. "Oh, yes. Well, where was I? Yes, yes. 'To the honorable Ibalum, from his devoted friend and servant Hadad'—that's *Ha-dad*, please—of Haran. 'To my lord, greetings. Thank you for the gifts and for the payment. My wife sends her gratitude, too. We are well. We expect the child in a matter of months. I have sent through the lord Arusian'—that's *A-ru-si-an*, mind you—'the ornaments and the coronet for the king of Ebla. He is arranging armed guard. I start work tomorrow on the wedding finery you ordered for the Princess Royal of Antioch's wedding. Arusian is purchasing materials. It is difficult. The war to the north and east has closed the trade route to the Assyrian mines. If you can develop new sources of supply it will help me—' "

"Excuse me," the scribe said, working feverishly. "I'm falling behind, sir. . . ."

"Oh. Excuse me." Hadad waved an indulgent hand. He looked up, a bemused half-smile on his round face, and looked around him in the little bazaar. There was some sort of commotion in the next group of buildings—perhaps in the street separating them. The few voices raised in anger seemed to be increasing. He wondered idly at this: in recent days, as the flow of refugees increased, tempers in the city had flared. There had been a small riot in the poorer quarters the day before, one which had required the city guard to put it down; Admuniri, too, had had to hire two stout new men-of-all-work at the inn to keep the peace, particularly since someone had broken Abi-samar's arm in a fight. . . .

"All right, sir?" the scribe said. "It goes, 'If you can develop new sources of supply it will help me. . . .' "

"Oh, yes. 'I am waiting for the turquoise shipment from Egypt.' Hmmm. Is there more? Maybe I should say something about the unrest here, the uncertainty . . . but no. Arusian will have kept him pretty well informed about that."

"I wish someone would inform His Highness, just between you and me, sir. The city fathers—and the king, too, sir—they seem to be the only people who aren't worried. Did you hear about Melid? The nomads razed it to the ground. Now they didn't need to do that. Killing all those people, I mean. They could have taken the mines without the bloodshed."

"They took the mines at Melid? Oh, dear. Well, I hope the lord Ibalum has his own copper sources. I've coronation armor to make for—" He stopped. "They—they massacred the people there?" He looked at the scribe, openmouthed, uncomprehending. "They didn't take prisoners, you mean?"

"Not a one. Killed women and children. I heard from the messenger to Kanish. And—sir, he says the Hittites think the nomads are headed south. South toward Egypt. And look you, sir—we're right in the way. Us with our fat granaries and our big fruit harvest, and our nice green fields for grazing. Do you really think we'd last much longer than Melid did? Why, the siege was no more than a week, some say. Then they just swarmed in and killed everybody."

"Oh, that's terrible," Hadad said. "I've been paying so little attention to all this. I—I should ask Jacob. He knows about all this sort of thing. He's friends with the lord Oshiyahu."

"I'd start paying attention, sir, if I were you. I mean, I know I'm sounding officious, sir. But you say you've a wife, one who's expecting a child soon, and—"

"Yes, that's the first consideration, of course." Hadad, his face troubled, bit his lip again. "Danataya—if it's that bad, if we are in their path . . ." He looked hard at the scribe. "But isn't anybody doing anything? Isn't the lord Oshiyahu arming the city?"

"He can't get any money out of the city government, way I hear it, sir. Can't fight without soldiers. Can't fight without arms."

"But my brother, Shobai, the armorer. He *did* arm the city. Before he went to Carchemish."

"*Shobai?*" The question came sharp and clear. The tone was full of animus at first; then both the scribe's voice and his expression grew guarded. "You said Shobai, sir? Shobai, the Child of the Lion? And he's your brother . . . ?"

"Why, yes. He's been missing for some months now, but before he left for Carchemish, I was sure he said he'd made arms for the whole garrison. Oh, you know, with help, of course. But he'd supervised the whole affair. And . . ."

But now the scribe's face was closed, formal; his smile was no longer a friend's, but a tradesman's, the expression of a worker, secure in his station, speaking to a stranger of another station. "Well, I'm sure you're right, sir. It's none of my business, sir. Is the letter finished, sir?"

"Oh—have I said something wrong?"

"No, sir. It's just that—there are others waiting behind you, with letters to be written."

Hadad wheeled; he blushed. "Oh. Oh, I'm sorry. My apologies to all of you. And—oh, well, sign it 'Your devoted servant, Hadad of Haran.'" He kept his puzzled look as he stood up to look down at the scribe finishing his quickly drying tablet. "But—if you know something about Shobai, please, I—I'll pay for information—any information you have, or can get. . . ."

"Oh, no, sir," the scribe said politely—too politely. "I don't know anything. Just idle hearsay. No more. That'll be two coppers, sir."

"Two? Oh, no, take three. That's much too cheap. You do fine work. But these rumors you say you've heard. If I could just hear anything, anything at all—"

433

"Please, sir, the others are waiting."

"Help me," Hadad said, his voice about to break. "Please help me. I've been so worried. Shobai has never disappeared like this before. He hasn't written to me, his mother, his wife. . . ."

The scribe's lips were a straight line as he looked at Hadad, his eyes flinty, his back straight. "Well, if you must know, sir, the messenger from Kanish said—well, Shobai . . ."

"Yes? Yes?"

"Well, sir, he's taken employment with the nomads. He's gone over to the other side. He's arming our enemies. He's arming, sir," the scribe said with a slow, deliberate emphasis on each word, "the people who are going to come swarming in here one of these days and kill us all."

"No! No! That can't be so!"

"I know this messenger, sir. He doesn't lie. Mind you, sir: these are the people that massacred the people of Melid. With weapons made by your brother—"

Hadad covered his ears. "No!" he cried in a despairing voice. "No! I won't hear any more!"

The refugees whose commotion Hadad had heard earlier were stumbling down the street, their stragglers fighting a bitter battle with the townspeople. Rocks sailed through the air; one of them opened a wound on the head of a woman, staining her headcloth. She almost dropped the small child in her arms, but managed to hold onto him until she could reel weak-legged into a doorway. Behind her, one of her compatriots picked up the rock and sailed it back into the crowd. All around them the din was deafening.

Slowly, the attackers forced the refugees back, back—and now the pursued turned a corner in the crooked little street and found themselves hemmed into a dead end. The attackers surged forward . . .

. . . and suddenly found themselves staring into the eyes of a middle-aged, dark-eyed man of medium height who stepped into their path, armed with nothing more than a shepherd's staff. He was well built, and he held the staff with the air of a man who knew how to use it—but it was something in his eyes, his stance, that stopped them for a moment in their rush forward.

"You!" the man said. "Just stop right there. Just calm down a moment. . . ."

"Better get out of the way, friend," a heavy man in the first rank said. His own hand held a stout club, and he was half again the newcomer's size. "You're of our people, I'd say

434

from your speech. You've no reason to stick up for these foreign scum who come in here from nowhere and—"

"I'm a foreigner here myself," the stranger said, shifting his grasp on the staff. "For all that I've been here twenty years. My grandfather was born in Ur. And from your looks and accent I'd say your own roots didn't go back too far in Haran, either. This is a border town, friend. We don't have the same feelings about penniless strangers in our midst that someone might have in a more benighted city."

"You," the man said. "You're Jacob. Jacob of where is it? Down south in Canaan? Look, you've a good name here. Don't soil it by standing up for these leeches who—"

"Leeches?" Jacob said. "They're just poor folk like the rest of us. I was taking them to the court to testify about the nomads up to the north, and I got too far ahead of them. And what do I see but my own townspeople, my countrymen, attacking them as if they were the nomads themselves."

"That's enough, Jacob," the big man said. "Just stand aside, there, or we'll—" Midway through his speech he brought his club to the ready position. He never got a chance to finish the sentence. Jacob's staff whipped out, feinted at his eyes, cut down to dash the club from his hands and send it spinning away back into the crowd. The staff flashed; it came to rest gently against the troublemaker's cheek.

"See?" Jacob said. "I could have brained you and left you for dead. But I mean you no harm. You've just become ... confused. These people aren't our enemies. They're our fellow victims. The real enemies are the nomads to the north—and the people at court who are starving our army to the point where it won't be able to defend us when the Shepherd Kings strike south."

There was an angry murmur; people in the back of the crowd facing Jacob would have rushed forward. But the staff went once again to the ready position, and Jacob's eyes flashed. "Here!" he said in a voice well suited to command. "The next man who steps forward will have more than my staff to contend with. Look behind you, will you?"

Heads whirled—and they could see the erect spears of a detachment of the city guard. At their head was the burly, glowering figure of Oshiyahu, commander of the city garrison. The murmurs quieted in the blinking of an eye. The soldier walked forward; the crowd parted to make a path for him. "You, there," he said, scorn in his voice. "You'd riot in *my* streets? Knowing what you know about me after all these years?" He spat the next words out. "Get back to your forges and your shops and your hostelries, for heaven's sake. You want to fight? I'll show you some fighting. We'll all be fighting in the streets in a month or two—fighting big, tough nomad troops who can fight back, let me tell you; not poor starveling bastards like these folks you've been pushing around today. You want some practice for that fight? For the fight where we stop them at the city gates or they smash our doors down and rape all our wives and kill all our babies and leave us hacked to pieces in the streets? You want practice for that? Well, I'll give you some. I'm forming a Home Guard. You can all turn up for muster tomorrow morning, down by the river at the second ford." His back teeth were together; his eyes were full of venom. "I'll see you there, you big brave battlers. Every man jack of you." He dismissed them contemptuously with a glance and turned to Jacob. "All right," he said. "Sorry I was late. Let's go. All of you."

Behind him, the crowd dispersed with low murmurs. The small detachment of guards formed around the little group of refugees, and they set out through the streets again, Jacob and Oshiyahu at their head. The pace was swift and purposeful.

II

Hadad went back to his work, but he couldn't keep his mind on what he was doing. He kept picking up the piece he was working on, then putting it back down. His eyes went in and out of focus; even in focus, they didn't seem to light on the silver disk he held in his hands, on the smooth-ground sheep's shankbone that lay beside them on the stone.

Marsatum, the greengrocer's wife, noted his preoccupation and left her stall in her young daughter's care to visit Hadad's area. "Why, that's lovely, Hadad," she said, indicating the disk. "What's it going to be?" It was a stupid question, she knew—but it would serve to start a conversation as well as any.

"I ... what? Excuse me, what did you say?" Hadad blinked and looked up at her, startled. "You said ... ?" Then he noticed the already-concave silver disk in his hand. "Oh. Oh, this. It's going to be a little bowl. I . . . " He shook his head. "My mind was elsewhere."

"Am I bothering you?"

"No, no. Please, I've been neglecting you, I think. And all my old friends. I haven't been over to see you this week, have I? I apologize. I've been working so hard. . . ."

"I was right. Hadad, something *is* the matter. You haven't been like this since Anat . . ."

Hadad blushed, scowled, smiled wanly. "No, no. It's nothing."

"Nonsense. Is it Danataya? Nothing's happened to her, I hope. The baby . . . ?"

"No, no. Everything's fine. The midwife says everything seems to be going perfectly according to schedule. But—"

"Yes?"

"Marsatum—I finally heard some news of Shobai."

"Oh?"

"Well, it may be no more than a rumor. I heard it thirdhand. . . ."

"Gods, Hadad! Where is he?"

"They say . . ." He sighed and stopped, then went on again doggedly. "They say he's up north. Working for the nomads. Arming them."

"Arming them? The enemies of his own people? Oh, Hadad, I can hardly believe that. Even of Shobai." Yet there was that in her tone, almost triumphant, that said *I told you so*. "Where did you hear this?"

"A . . . friend of a friend. The source was a man who had been to the nomad camp quite recently. Someone who had seen what they did to Melid."

"Melid? What happened at Melid?" She was all concern now. "I have a sister in Melid. Don't tell me they—?" She stopped dead. She searched his face. "Hadad, don't tell me. Please. Don't."

He sighed deeply. "You'll know sooner or later. No one was spared. Nobody at all. But—maybe your sister got away before they struck."

"No. No. She'd never leave her home. The poor fool. Oh, the poor fool. She'd be there until the last. Oh, Hadad, don't tell me any more. I can't bear to hear it—"

She stopped now, though, in midsentence. Her hand flew to her mouth. "But Melid—that's—that's north of here. North and slightly to the west . . . why, Hadad, they've come closer. Closer to Haran. And—and Carchemish too. Oh, gods. Hadad, they're coming here. And when they come here, they'll do the same thing they did to Melid, to poor—"

"Oh, Marsatum, I can't think. . . ."

"Hadad! Don't be a fool! Do you think this ragamuffin army of ours could stop them if they decide to head down here? And—and gods alive, Hadad! They'll have to come here. There's nowhere else to go. They won't strike into Hittite country. That would cost them too much. So would striking southeast; they'll leave Mari alone for fear of bringing Shinar and Elam into this. There's no other place for them to move, Hadad. And—why, if what my husband says is right, these nomads—Shepherd Kings, they're called—are carrying such a herd with them they'll have exhausted the last of the northern grazing land by spring. Then they'll be looking for new lands. And here we'll be, underarmed, unprepared—and with our ranks swollen with refugees. We won't last a week under siege. Not with all these extra people to feed—"

"Marsatum. I'm worried about Shobai. He—if he *has* done this thing, he's in way over his head. From what Jacob tells me, he won't be able to handle them. But . . . it could just be a rumor."

"Rumor? Ask Anat. Would he go there without telling his wife? Even if they're not getting along? But look, Hadad. You've got to make plans. You have to get Danataya out of here while she's still fit to travel. When they strike south . . . gods, gods! Oh, I've got to tell my husband about this. I know what he'll say, though. He already wants to sell out and move south. He has an uncle in Damascus. Did you hear? Abirapi and Shapash have already sold their barber franchise. They're moving to Ebla. Not that that'll help them much once the nomads have started to move."

"Abirapi? Shapash? But—"

"Oh, you great dummy. Haven't you seen anything that's been happening around you? Haven't you seen the empty stalls? Haven't you heard that maybe a third of the merchants at the Bazaar of the Twin Oaks, across town, have moved away? Half the bazaar now is manned by foreigners— refugees who can't even speak the common tongue. In a couple of months you won't even recognize the quarter, Hadad. It'll all be a lot of smelly foreigners, jabbering away in outlandish tongues, foreigners with bad manners."

"Leave? Leave Haran? But my mother, Danataya, all my friends are here—I couldn't!"

"Hadad, you fool! In six months you won't have a friend

438

left here! We'll all have moved! And there you'll be with a wife and a sick mother and a swaddling child when they surround the town and—"

"Please! Please!" He held up one hand. With the other he stowed his tools and the little silver disk. "I . . . you had a good idea, Marsatum. I'll ask Anat. That's a good idea. I can't imagine he'd make a move like that without telling her, somehow."

"Get out of town, Hadad! Start making your plans now! Right away—while there's time!"

"You're sure you won't need me?" Jacob said, one hand on Oshiyahu's rugged shoulder. "I mean, I'll wait if you want me to. . . ."

Oshiyahu tolerated the familiarity without comment. He liked and respected Jacob—and there were, after all, those rumors about Jacob having been of high station, high station indeed, back in his homeland. "No, my friend," he said, looking around him in the anteroom of the Great Hall. The refugees clustered near the far wall, talking in hushed, fearful voices in their own tongue. "I'm only going to take a few of them in. Hanunu says His Highness wouldn't tolerate my bringing any more with me. It's all right: I've picked three of the most articulate; they have tales to tell that will curl the royal hair." He smiled with friendship. "No, you go along home. I've enemies here. You don't want to get yourself associated with me in their eyes. I appreciate your courage in helping me thus far, believe me I do. Not many would have stuck with me all the way here. But either I get what I'm asking for today, or I raise a real storm of protest. And when I do, the number of my enemies will increase. I may wind up in serious trouble. I'm not taking any friends with me in that."

"Whatever you wish," Jacob said, concern in his eyes. "But if you need me, you know you have only to ask. Send a message to me, and straightway I'll come to you. Just say the word—"

"No, no. Thanks. And give my best to your wife. Rachel? Is that the name? Ah, yes. You'll be expecting a new one around the family soon, won't you?"

"Yes," Jacob said. "Her first. She's apprehensive, as well she might be at her age. But happy—happier than I've ever seen her." He smiled serenely. "Me, too."

"That's good—good." Oshiyahu's own smile was full of rough masculine affection. "You're a lucky man. Fine sons like that—and such lovely wives . . ." He sighed. "My daughters haven't turned out to my satisfaction, I'll admit, and it's the curse of my life. That and this nomad business. I—I'd had some plans for my son-in-law, Yassib. But he's been a thorn in my side. You know he left my daughter? Left the army? Went over to work for Hirgab and that swine Reshef."

"Yassib?" Jacob said incredulously. "With Reshef? Oh, that's not good news. Not good news at all. Reshef—I think in your place I'd have got rid of him some time back." He stepped back, suddenly abashed. "I'm sorry. I'm being officious."

"No, no. You're right. I've been a complacent fool. Perhaps I've been digging my own political grave. But here I am, and I'll deal with the problems before me as well as I can. You go home. I'll tell you how it came out tomorrow."

"If you insist," Jacob said quietly. "But—you have only to call."

"Thank you. I appreciate it."

The door opened. A brown eye peered out. "Go away, please. My mistress is occupied. You must speak to Mebishum, at the Inn of the Brown Bear, and make an appointment."

But then, as Hadad gaped, the door opened further. "Oh," a familiar voice said in a whisper. "The lord Hadad. I—I didn't mean—"

He could see her face now, her body. Her body was mostly bare; she wore only a tiny loincloth. Her poor homely face was painted like a whore's. "T-Tanuha," Hadad said in a shocked voice. "But—what—why are you—?"

"Please," the girl said. "Go away. Go now. You won't like what you see. It'll just upset you."

"Let me in," Hadad said. He pushed gently past her; she did not resist. He looked around at what remained of Shobai's house, openmouthed. "Tanuha," he said. "What happened?"

"Please," she said, shushing him. "She'll hear. She's just in the room there, with one of her . . . clients."

"Clients . . . ? Oh, Tanuha, it's come to that? But, where is . . . everything? The furniture? The statuary?"

"Sold. Sold for the taxes on the house. There hasn't been a copper of new money in the house since the lord Shobai left. Anat—first she sold everything she could. Then she—" She stopped, held her hands over her bare breasts, her face a mask of shame. "Oh, Hadad . . . she makes *me*, too, when they want two of them. If only—"

440

"Oh, gods! Then . . . she hasn't heard from Shobai at all?" Hadad said.

"N-no. Oh, Hadad, if I could only get away from here. I was the lord Shobai's slave originally, not hers. He wouldn't have wanted me to—"

"Tanuha. What can I do? I have no rights in the matter—and no influence over Anat." She broke up at that, weeping softly. He reached out his arms and held her, patting her back softly. "There, there," he said. "Well, maybe I can do something, although I have no idea what. I'll inquire. Perhaps I can purchase you. Danataya'll need someone to help her with—"

A new thought struck him, though, and he stepped back to hold her at arm's length, looking into her tear-stained eyes with their runny makeup. "Reshef," he said. "Whatever happened to Reshef? Does he still—?"

"Oh, no," she said, pulling her hands free to dab ineffectually at her spoiled makeup. "Oh, I'm such a mess now . . . no, Reshef never came back. And, whatever has happened since then, I'm glad for that. He scared me, always looking at me like . . ."

"Well, that's one good thing," Hadad said, his lips tight, anger in his face. "But these visitors of hers . . . ?"

"I—you heard me say the name. Mebishum. He's her—her procurer." Her poor plain face looked terrible, with the garish makeup smeared all over it by now. Hadad's heart went out to her suddenly; if he *could* purchase her, make her Danataya's helper . . . "And—mine too, I suppose," she said in a voice thick with self-loathing. "Although sometimes she doesn't go through a procurer. I suspect Reshef is sending her his friends, now that he's through with her. Army types. Politicians. His assistant, a young man named Yassib."

"Yassib?" Hadad said, thunderstruck. "Did you say *Yassib?*"

"Oh, look who's here!" Rachel said, looking out the window. She rose and put down her mending, steadying herself, her big belly jutting out before her. As she stood the door opened and Jacob looked in, a warm smile on his face. "Jacob, darling! You're home early."

"Yes," he said. "Oshiyahu sent me back. It was kind of him; he thinks my appearing with him at court will only make me some new enemies. And heaven knows I can't use any of those." He looked at the corner chair. "Why, hello, Danataya! What a pleasant surprise! No, no—don't get up. Please. Take

441

it from a father of ten, soon to be eleven. Your job now is to take it easy, get as much rest and relaxation as you can. . . ."

"Listen to him," Rachel said. "Let them watch one or two births, over the midwife's protests, and they get to be experts. Although he's right, you know. I have to keep reminding myself." She kissed her husband and let him help her back into her chair, winking mischievously at the girl. "See? Take all the help they volunteer. Goodness knows, we women get little enough of that kind of gallantry once we're married to them."

"Oh, I can't believe that, Rachel," the girl said. "Hadad's never stopped being as gallant as an unkissed lad. And in so many ways he and the lord Jacob are one of a piece."

"That they are," Rachel said with pride. "Jacob: what news do you have for us today?" She settled back in the chair, half drawing her feet up beside her.

"Very little that's good," Jacob said. "Melid is no more. Wiped out." He let the words sink in and continued gravely: "Rachel, I'm afraid we're going to have to be prepared to travel on very short notice from now on. Despite any plans I may have made in the past."

Both women caught his somber tone and sat forward. "Jacob!" Rachel said. "But . . . the baby . . . the spring lambing . . ."

"Yes, I know," Jacob said. "But—well, if we can't go back rich with the fruits of the lambing, my dear, we'll have to travel poor. Poor as I was when I came here. Goodness knows, your father will prefer it that way. He'll get what we leave behind—"

"Why do you talk of leaving?" Danataya said. "I still don't understand."

Jacob looked at her for a moment, saying nothing. Then he spoke, softly and slowly. "I see," he said. "Hadad might well have not noticed. He's so caught up in his happy marriage, his impending fatherhood, and perhaps most of all in the new opportunities Ibalum has given him—my dear, we'll be leaving Haran sometime around our baby's birth. I hope we'll be able to wait that long."

"Jacob," Rachel said softly. "You needn't frighten her. . . ."

"She'll have to face it soon enough. And she and Hadad—they've become good and dear friends. What kind of a friend would I be to them if I left without letting them know?"

"I suppose you're right," Rachel said wistfully. "But . . ." She let the words trail off, and now she looked at Danataya with compassion. "Maybe—maybe they can come with us,

442

Jacob," she said. "When the time comes." She looked back at her husband, her face sober and serious. "Then, you don't think the lord Oshiyahu..." she began. Then she stopped again.

"Mind you," Jacob said slowly, even more slowly than before, "I have no overt reason for thinking this. But... I have a feeling. There's a streak of precognition in my family that shows up now and then." He looked at them one at a time, then turned away to the window before he spoke again. "Danataya," he said, "this time next year there'll be no Haran. Not as we've known it. Unless..."

He did not finish his thought. A vision had come upon him suddenly, a vision that saddened him more than any he could remember. And, looking at Danataya now, her eyes bright, her belly high, he could not make himself share it with her.

III

The king and his council faced the newcomers in a semi-circular row of seats, with the king at the center of the row. Oshiyahu, entering the chamber, bowed low, but he let his eyes scan the room as he rose from the bow. The four corners of the room and all entrances and exits were manned by troops of the Royal Guard—troops not under his command in any way.

Missing also from the scene were his own connections at court. Flanking the king were the lord Kazibu and his three fawning satellites—Azirum, Sakirum, and Yakiranu. The rest were neutrals, men who voted with the tide. Looking once again into King Shemariah's washed-out, witless eyes and indistinct smile, Oshiyahu shuddered silently... and for not the first time felt himself horribly alone.

What a well-named lot the members of the peace party were, he thought, looking them over. Kazibu's name, meaningless in the dialect of his parents, meant "liar" in a dialect that began not a league away. "Azirum" meant "helper" in the same tongue, and "Sakirum" meant "hireling"—and that was just what they were. Kazibu, a man whose every statement was suspect, had had Azirum for perhaps no more than the promise of power, but Sakirum, Oshiyahu was sure, had cost good money. Looking the mercenary councilor up and down and not liking what he saw, Oshiyahu idly wondered if, once bought, he would stay bought.

Entering the inner chambers, he had left his own guardsmen behind, as well as his weapons. They had allowed him to bring no more than two of the refugees with him; he had anticipated this, though, and had picked out the two most articulate. These, too, had the most hair-raising stories to tell. He had been composing his prefatory remarks on a tablet ever since this morning; but now, looking them over, he found himself abandoning the formality of the written address.

"We recognize the lord Oshiyahu," Shemariah said in his great overgrown adolescent's alto. "You have business with us, my lord?"

"Yes, sire," Oshiyahu said. "I'll get right to the point. I have reason to suspect the Shepherd Kings are preparing a full-scale assault on the cities of the south—Carchemish and Haran." He ignored the snickers that came from Kazibu's bloc. "They've just finished destroying Melid and taking over the mines there. Now they—"

"Melid?" Shemariah said, interrupting. "But Melid is to the north, my lord. Surely these nomads don't go northward in order to get to the south?" He giggled in a high fluting voice; several of the courtiers echoed him.

"Your Highness understands geography perfectly. Melid is indeed to the north—and beyond Melid, in that direction, lies Hittite country, and the nomads have seen the wisdom of not continuing in that direction. Why indeed should they attack heavily armed and warlike Hittites when they can with infinitely greater ease attack much weaker kingdoms to the south?"

"Much weaker?" Kazibu broke in. "Then your own command is inadequate to protect us?" His sneer was understanding, insulting. "Perhaps we should seek a new commander. . . ."

"You are welcome to do so," Oshiyahu said affably, "if you can find anyone who can successfully defend a Class Two city with a Class Twelve army, manned by dotards and striplings and armed as if the only thing we had to defend against was an occasional bandit attack from the hills."

"Insolence!" Kazibu said. "Look, don't think we aren't on to you, Oshiyahu. All this call for more money, more troops . . . this is nothing more than another one of your empire-building schemes. The military is too expensive already. If

444

anything, we should be considering cutbacks. You're bankrupting us. Once we let you generals spend what you choose—"

Oshiyahu, feeling the black rage stirring within him, held his temper down. He ignored Kazibu and addressed the sad little king beside him. "Your Majesty," he said, "we are in the gravest, direst danger. I have brought with me two refugees from the cities destroyed by the nomads on their way across the northern country. They're here to tell you what kind of enemy we're up against."

"We *have* no enemies," Kazibu broke in again. "It's all a ruse, Your Majesty. The lord Oshiyahu, like all military men, craves power. If we give it to him, he'll just ask for more. I'm sure we can find other and better ways to spend the outrageous sums he asked for in his recent presentation of the military budget for the new year."

The king, his watery eyes blinking, looked from one man to the other. "I don't understand," he said. "One of you says we're in some sort of terrible trouble, and the other . . ." He threw up his weak hands and rolled his eyes skyward.

"Yes, sir," Kazibu said. "I know it sounds confusing. But one of us can prove his assertions, and the other can do no more than drag a couple of raggedy little foreign paupers in here to cast aspersions on—"

"Your Majesty," Oshiyahu said, letting his voice raise itself a trifle for the first time, "if I could just let you listen to what these people have to say—"

"Why don't we bring in the evidence?" Sakirum said from the side, his voice heavy with insinuation. "After all, our case is absurdly easy to prove."

"Prove?" Oshiyahu said. "Prove what? What evidence?"

Kazibu caught Shemariah's eye. "The lord Oshiyahu asks for proof, sire. May I, with your permission?"

"Uh . . . of course," the king said, confusion mirrored on his puffy face. "By all means."

Kazibu waved one hand. Sakirum stood, called to the guards at the side door. "Bring in the lord Hirgab and his party!" he said in a commanding voice.

"Hirgab?" Oshiyahu said. "But—" Turning, he stopped in midsentence. The curtains were pushed wide. A detachment of guards preceded the "evidence"; then he saw Hirgab and Reshef march in, a great mountain of a man between them. He looked at the alien robes and the dark beard . . . and he suddenly remembered Jacob's description of the man he had helped once in the mountains. "Manouk!" he said in a strangled voice. "Manouk of the nomads! Guards! Guards! Seize that man!"

But in the violent confusion that followed, it was not the nomad leader around whom the guards, swords drawn, closed ranks. It was Oshiyahu himself.

Yassib looked the cripple up and down, contempt in his eyes. "So you're what she wound up with," he said. "I shouldn't wonder."

"Please," Hadad said. "I don't know what you think you have against Danataya. You wronged her terribly, and she did the best she could after that. I've tried to make her happy. Let's leave it at that. What I want to know is . . ."

But Yassib had had a couple of drinks an hour before, and the self-loathing had begun to rise in his soul again. It was an itch he could not resist scratching. "I suppose she told you I just left her flat," he said. "Tell me: was she pregnant when you found her?" He chuckled. "I've always been curious."

"N-no," Hadad said, blushing. "Look, I'd really rather get off that subject if we might. I mean—well, she's my wife now, and very dear to me, and . . ."

"Wife?" Yassib said, chuckling. "I hadn't heard. Welcome to my leavings, little man. Now if you'll just let me go. . . ."

Hadad gulped, swallowing his pride, his own rage, his indignation. He had to find out. . . . "Look," he said, "that isn't why I went to the bother of looking you up. It's—"

"Oh, come on, little man. Get it out. You're wasting valuable time I could be spending with the whores down at the—"

"Please," Hadad said, his face red and drawn. "I—I understand you've been up north, to the camp of the Shepherd Kings. I wondered—"

"How did you learn that?" Yassib said, bristling. Then he relaxed. "Oh, well, I suppose by now it'd have got around. Yes, I've been on liaison to the camp for some time. On assignment for the lord Hirgab. I've been up—oh, maybe three times so far. No, four. I just got back, as a matter of fact. Brought a message for Hirgab and for the nomad leader, Manouk, who's at the palace right now talking peace with His Majesty. Why? What did you want to know?"

"P-peace?" Hadad said. "But I thought—" He shook his head and bore on. "I—I wondered if you had heard anything of a local man. A man named Shobai."

"The armorer?" Yassib laughed humorlessly: a half-silent laugh that confirmed his own superiority. "Oh, that damned fool. You can forget him. There's always some idiot like that who can't leave well enough alone, who has to bring ruin down on himself."

Hadad moved forward and grabbed Yassib's tunic with one skinny, surprisingly strong hand. "What are you saying?" he said in a desperate voice. "What's happened to Shobai? Tell me, for heaven's sake!"

"Why?" Yassib said, brushing him off. "Easy, there, little man. Contain yourself. If you did that to the wrong man sometime, you'd wind up getting a broken arm or worse. Besides, what's it to you anyhow? If you . . ." He stopped then. "Oh, for heaven's sake. I clean forgot. You're his brother, aren't you? His little impoverished brother." He took another look at Hadad's clothes. "But you don't seem to be doing too bad just now. You haven't been dipping into the family savings, have you? Taking a little off the top? Heaven knows, no money is reaching that wife of his. She's sold his house down to the bare walls. He didn't send her a dime before he—"

"What's happened to Shobai?" Hadad said, ignoring him. "You know, but you won't tell me. Why? Why?"

"Well, there's no bloody secret," Yassib said scornfully. "The damned fool hired out to arm the Shepherd Kings, and he became a little too arrogant for his own good. He should have known what sort of reaction that would provoke."

"What?" Hadad said, his eyes wild. "Please—what?"

"Well, you don't *try* that sort of thing on these nomads. No, sir. Not for a moment. They won't put up with that sort of nonsense. And they didn't, either. Up and clapped him in irons, just as pretty as can be. Now he's doing for free what they used to pay him well to do—and with a mark on his arm to boot. Damned fool! I'd write him off if I were you, little man. An idiot—and now a slave—"

"Slave?" Hadad said, not fully comprehending. *"Slave?"*

"Jacob," Rachel said, putting one soft hand on his arm. "We've got to take them with us."

Jacob looked at her: at the slim face, radiant with the bloom of approaching motherhood; at the caring in her brown eyes. And he hugged her impulsively to his chest, faint with love like a boy half his age. "I've been thinking about that," he said. "Certainly we can't just abandon them. But how sweet and thoughtful of you to suggest it."

"I feel as though they were blood kin by now. I couldn't love them more if they were."

447

"Nor I. I've given the matter some thought already. I . . ." He let his words trail off, holding her close, and thought about the dread vision he'd had, the one that had shaken him so badly. Should he share it with her? He thought of the fragile life inside her and decided against it for now. The less he could worry her with, the better. "I'm wondering if one should interfere with another person's destiny, even out of love and affection."

"Why, of course we should, Jacob! How could you say for a moment . . . ?" But she looked up and saw his indulgent smile. "Oh, you don't fool me. You don't mean that. You wouldn't dream of just going off and leaving them, when we know what's going to happen to the city."

"Which reminds me: I was wondering if we ought to warn your father."

"Oh, of course. And, of course, he won't believe us. I thought of that myself. If mother were still alive . . . But she isn't. And father—he listens only to what he wants to hear."

"Ah, yes. By the way, Reuben sent one of the boys in to tell me that the ewes have begun coming to term. He expects one or two births over the next few days."

"Already?"

He patted her belly happily. "I'll be saying the same to you one of these days, my dear. These things creep up on one." He took her hand. "Are you ever afraid? I mean, it's your first. . . ."

"Of course I am," she said. She took the hand to her lips and kissed it. "But—I wouldn't be a woman if I weren't also looking forward to it. With joy, Jacob, with more joy than I've ever felt about anything in my life." She smiled. "Except . . . except perhaps that first day at the well, when you rolled the stone away. When you kissed me, and I saw the tears in your eyes, and . . ." She smiled. "Why did you cry, Jacob?"

"A man sometimes cries when he's happy," Jacob said. "Or when he experiences something beyond his control or understanding. I looked at you just once and knew. I knew this was the way my life was going to be, and—"

"Oh, Jacob." She hugged him, a little sob in her own throat. And then she looked up at the window and saw the soldier standing there. "Jacob," she said. "There's someone at the door."

"So there is." He stood and moved to the door and threw it open. "Ah," he said. "Dushratta. Come in, won't you?" He held the door wide for the orderly to enter. "Rachel, this is Dushratta, orderly to the lord Oshiyahu."

448

"Good day, ma'am," the soldier said. "Jacob," he said, "there's an emergency. I've a message. If . . ." He looked at Rachel, smiling; then he looked pointedly into Jacob's eyes.

"No, no," said Jacob. "I've no secrets from Rachel. What emergency? Has there been an attack?"

"It's about that bad," Dushratta said. "Oshiyahu's been arrested. He's been confined to a chamber in the palace."

"Arrested? But . . ."

"Hirgab and Reshef have pushed through the council a verbal agreement toward a peace treaty with the Shepherd Kings. They even brought Manouk down here to negotiate it. When Oshiyahu saw him at court, he said a lot of rash things. Kazibu's faction persuaded the king that he was being insulted. They threw a guard around Oshiyahu and marched him out in disgrace. Now he's under arrest, and they've relieved him of his command."

Jacob stared at him in horror. "The city," he said, "the city's undefended." He clenched his fists. "Is there anything I can do?"

"I'm not sure," Dushratta said. "I'm being allowed in to see him for now. I'll keep you posted. I have other messages for his court contacts when they return to the city. But yes, you're right: for all practical purposes we're laying down what arms we have."

"I can't quite believe it," Jacob said. "Manouk? Manouk's in the city?"

"Yes, sir. And talking peace." The word came out dripping with venom. *"Peace!"*

IV

In the night, Danataya suddenly felt Hadad's hand on her big belly: softly tracing on the distended skin, feeling the great lump within her. Impulsively, she touched his hand, squeezed it to her. "It's still there, darling," she said. "Don't worry. Nothing new has happened since we blew the light out."

He snuggled closer to her, his chest and belly snug against her back. "Just—reassuring myself," he said. "Imagine: it's alive in there. My son. Or my daughter."

449

"Whatever it turns out to be, I'll love it," she said.

"Well, I almost hope it's a girl. A little Danataya. I could enjoy having two of you."

"Well, that would be nice, but I'm sure you'll want a Child of the Lion too. I—I still can't quite believe it, about the birthmark."

"Neither could mother. But it came out on both me and Shobai." He sighed. "Shobai—"

"Don't think about it. You can't do anything."

"I—"

"Shush. Think about our baby instead."

"Danataya, if anything happened to me . . ."

"Hush now! Nothing's going to happen to you. Please. You frighten me, talking like that."

"I have to think about such things. Really. I mean, I talked with Jacob today. . . ."

"I know. Jacob's leaving."

"He'd like to go immediately. I think he will, as soon as the ewes have dropped their lambs. Although he said something about it not being crucial until he gets the word from this Manouk. He really seems to believe Manouk will tell him when to leave."

"Well, he hasn't sent the message. Maybe he won't. You heard they signed the peace treaty today?"

"Yes. But I don't believe it. Neither does Jacob. You know who set it up? Hirgab—and Reshef."

"Reshef! That awful man!"

"Yes. Danataya, I think we ought to give some thought to leaving ourselves. I went to see Arusian today."

"Arusian? Why?"

"He keeps pretty well informed about things. And do you know what he said? He said he's begun moving Ibalum's money south very quietly and circumspectly. And his own money as well. I told him to move ours too. Not to Ebla or Aleppo or any place close by, Danataya, but to Damascus!"

"Damascus? Why, Hadad?"

"He thinks the attack is coming quite soon. Danataya, I think we ought to be thinking about leaving, ourselves. As soon as it's safe for you to travel."

"But Hadad . . . leave Haran? All our friends?"

"Danataya: did you know? Marsatum has gone. Left yesterday. So have Abisuri and Yahila. They left on the morning caravan."

"Hadad! I didn't know! And Shapash and Abirapi are already gone, and—"

"And even Bunu-ishdar is packing his forge. Can you imagine? Bunu-ishdar, a man who hasn't missed a day's work at the Bazaar of the Well, rain or shine, since—"

She turned laboriously to face him, her now-heavy breasts lolling atop the great mound of her belly. "Hadad, this *is* serious. We'll be the only people left."

He patted her bare hip under the coverlet. "Yes, my darling. Now you begin to see. It's serious this time. Unless . . ."

"Unless what? Jacob said the lord Oshiyahu had been arrested! For all practical purposes we don't have anyone running the army."

"Exactly. Danataya, I want to make arrangements for you—for us to go south with Jacob. When he leaves. He'll be glad to have us. Mother, too, of course. He's volunteered to take us numerous times. You and Mother will be safer with Jacob than with—"

"*We'll* be safe? What do you mean? Hadad, you wouldn't send us away without you, would you?"

"Why, no, I . . . look, Danataya. These are dangerous times . . . something could happen to me."

"No! You wouldn't leave me alone, with this—"

"Danataya! Please—please listen. If something did happen to me—and it could, you know, it could—please, please promise me . . . if it's a boy, teach him to—"

"No, Hadad! I won't hear it! Don't tell me!" She covered her ears with her hands. "I won't listen!"

"There, darling, I didn't mean to upset you . . . I won't talk about that any more. Here, my own, my love. . . ." Now Hadad was all tenderness and consideration, his hands softly soothing, his voice low and reassuring. It took many minutes for his words and caresses to begin to relax her, and much longer for her to slip off to sleep again. After she had done so, Hadad lay wide awake until the first rays of dawn, staring at the ceiling, thinking. . . .

In the first hour of light, Jacob arose and rode out to the hills above the city to meet Reuben. The boy came down to greet him, and Jacob noted with pride the tall, commanding seat the boy had on his animal, the broad young shoulders, the clear eye. "Father," Reuben said, "it's working just as you thought. There'll be two mottled lambs to every white one. If it progresses the way I think it will, we'll go south to Canaan as rich as grandfather."

"Yes," Jacob said. "Now all we have to do is get them all away from Haran without a fight."

"You don't really think grandfather would . . . ?"

"Oh, yes, my son. I haven't worked for Laban for all these years for nothing. I know that if he thinks he can trick us, he'll do so. But if he can't . . . Ah. Well, we'll just have to be ready for anything."

"Exactly. But, Father—Rachel—will she be able to travel when. . . ?"

"That is a problem, boy. In the best of worlds, we'd be able to wait and not make her travel until she'd given birth. But these are perilous times. We can't have our first choices. We'll have to do the best we can and trust to the God of our fathers."

"Yes, sir. I—I don't relish being called to strike a blow against my kin, but . . ."

Jacob clapped him on the shoulder, a warm masculine gesture of affection. "Neither do I, boy. And I'll outflank him or fool him if I can, to stave that off. But if the time comes for fighting, I'll strike a good blow for what's mine. And so will you, I'll wager."

"Yes, sir!"

Reshef and Hirgab bade farewell to Manouk's party from the top of the last hill overlooking Haran. They watched the riders wind their way down the trail on the far side of the ridge; neither spoke until they were quite sure the nomad leaders were totally out of earshot.

Then Reshef, a savage grin splitting that ferret face of his, clapped himself on the thigh with an open hand. "Damn!" he said triumphantly. "We did it! We did it!"

"Don't be too hasty about that," Hirgab said. "We still have Oshiyahu to deal with. He's only under house arrest, and his connections will get him off that as soon as they're back in the city. Then we'll have that damned gadfly to contend with, with his apocalyptic talk of 'treason' and 'sellouts.' "

"Oh, he's completely discredited by now. Did you see the way Kazibu handled him in council?"

"Yes, I did. But he wouldn't be able to do that a second time. Besides, Oshiyahu won't bring it before the court again—not without marshaling some forces of his own first. No, he'll take his case to the people. And you may underestimate the strength of his appeal with them, my friend, but I don't. He's very popular in the neighborhoods—even if he

452

does propose to take their damned sons away and make soldiers of them."

"I suppose you're right," Reshef said. "I got carried away with the euphoria of the moment. Yes, we'll have to deal with him. But how?" He looked at Hirgab from under half-closed lids, his mouth set in a wry line. "We can't possibly get him—oh, under sentence of death or anything like that. They'd never stand for it. But banishment . . . ?"

"Huh," Hirgab said, thinking. "It's possible. Insulting the person of the king, something like that. There *were* witnesses. And Kazibu would go along, and bring his group with him." He stared at Reshef. "But Oshiyahu could prove to be just as dangerous out of town as in. Unless, of course, we silence him. . . ."

Reshef laughed: a low, hollow sort of laugh. His face lit up with a demonic smile. "I'll tell you what, my lord. You take care of the banishment part, and I'll take care of the rest."

"You wouldn't—I mean, by yourself . . . ?"

"Soil *my* hands on the old fool? Don't be silly. A plan just occurred to me. Yes, I think it'd kill perhaps more than one bird with the same stone—yes, yes. Not bad, if I do say so myself."

"Well, don't keep it to yourself."

"Ah, yes." Reshef regarded him with the same mocking grin. "I've the perfect person for the job. Someone who owes the lord Oshiyahu a bad turn. Someone who is part of our little play, but who hasn't yet been—well, you might say 'blooded' in our service. It would knit him closer to us, for one thing. There's nothing like shared guilt to make a man cleave close to you, my lord."

"You mean . . . ?"

"The same. I'll even help him find some toughs to help with the job. And—look, we may not need to do the banishment thing, at that. What if I had someone smuggle a fake note to Oshiyahu, a note from Hagirum of Carchemish asking him to come over and assume command there? Do you think the old fool would be able to resist that, eh?"

"Ingenious. No, I don't. He's often expressed envy of the commander of the garrison there. Hagirum spends money on his army—and he's not only been building up the command, he's put in a good six months or more strengthening the walls. The only thing is, you'd have to do it in some believable sort of way. Find just the right courier. And—how are you going to duplicate the royal seal?"

"Easy. I've an old commission from Hagirum, from years back. I know a little old elf down in the Thieves' Quarter who can duplicate any signature, any seal, for a price." He looked significantly at Hirgab. "It'll cost money," he said pointedly.

Hirgab reached in his saddlebag and extracted a purse. He tossed it over to his subordinate. "Here, let me know when that's used up." He looked off into the distance, brows knit. "Gods!" he said. "What if Oshiyahu *were* hired by Carchemish? That'd throw a damper on our plans, wouldn't it?"

"It'd slow down the advance," Reshef said. "Some. But—my lord, those last two times I went north, I had a bit more of a look at their resources. The Shepherd Kings', I mean. I think that even you have no idea how many of the nomads there are."

"Oh?"

"My lord, their present deployment has a front—a *front*, mind you—that stretches from Carchemish to Haran. They could attack both places at the same time and smash them flat. Even if Haran had any heart to fight back—"

"That large? That strong?" Hirgab's brow went up. "But, if that's correct, why go to the bother of—well, I mean, why are you and I . . . ?"

"Manouk is a man of understanding, my lord. Why should he fight when he can get something for free? When he can find able people within the city, people like ourselves, to help him in exchange for their own preferment, once the city has changed hands? The wise man takes the easy way, my lord. Even when the hard way is no harder than this."

"I think I'm going to like being ruler of Carchemish. It's a town that always appealed to me. My middle years were spent there. I told you that, didn't I? When I was twenty-two or twenty-three . . ."

"Yes, my lord," Reshef said. "And—Haran has its own pleasures for a man like myself. There are old debts to settle. . . ." His hand went to the scar on his cheek, and his smile turned into a scowl for a moment. Then, trembling slightly, the hand went to his Adam's apple, touching it tenderly. He was remembering the night when Jacob of Canaan had faced him down, armed with no more than a staff. "Yes," he hissed. "Debts to settle . . ."

"Oh, by the way," Hirgab said. "I talked to Manouk. He has a little present for you. A reward for the services you've done him so far."

"Yes, my lord?" Reshef shot an interested glance at his superior. "Something for me?"

"Why, yes. The day Haran falls ... the armorer Shobai is yours. A little gift."

"Shobai?" Reshef said. "Sho-*bai* ..." He let the words trail off in a singsong. The look on his face went through several changes, from astonishment to calculation to, in the end, deep satisfaction. "Ah, yes, that was nice of him. As I say, Manouk is a man of understanding. A man of understanding indeed. The day Haran falls, you say? Well, let's get to work and do everything we can to hasten that happy hour. ...."

Hadad arrived early, before any of the other regulars at the Bazaar of the Well. He looked around at the now-closed stalls, at the orderly lanes between them. There was a curious, unreal look about the place, so empty, so deserted of the rich life that filled it in the daytime. It looked strange, unfamiliar.

Yet there it was. There was the wretched little stall he had operated from for so long, in the shadow of the greengrocer's booth; there was the new stall he'd taken over when his fortunes had changed, on the far side of Marsatum's. There was the step where he'd sat and played the minstrel's lyre, not knowing dear Danataya was listening. ...

It struck him with a pang that he would be leaving it soon. Leaving something that had been a part of his life for so long that he could have come here in his sleep and taken his proper place, to do his daily chores. ... It would be like leaving a part of himself.

With something like a sob, he let his eyes run slowly over the quiet scene, savoring each detail, committing it to memory. Remember, he thought. Only memory can help you now, help you take a part of it with you, this life you leave behind. ...

Farewell! Farewell!

V

Dushratta found his master sitting back in a chair propped against the wall of his place of confinement. His big, booted feet rested on a table on which were scattered an assortment of writing materials: styli, tablets, the knife used for erasures. There was a wry expression on his roughhewn face, but his whole physical posture was one of complete relaxation. "Ah," he said, "they're still letting you through, I see. That must mean they're not quite ready to cut my head off."

The orderly put down his parcel. "Bread and cheese," he said. "And a leather bottle of the best wine I could get my hands on. These days, sir, that's none too good. You know the wine merchant's left town?"

"Damn," Oshiyahu said, sitting up and dropping his feet to the ground. "Not my old friend Nahbi, from the Bazaar of the Twin Oaks?"

"The same, sir. He said his regular sources of supply are all cut off now anyhow. And—well, sir, he doesn't give this place any longer than you do."

"Gods. Some dog robber you are. All you bring me is excuses." He reached into the parcel, liberated the bottle, and uncorked it to squeeze a red line of wine, arching, into his mouth. He swallowed, wiped his mouth, recorked the bottle. "Well. Not too bad. I take that back." He looked at the bottle. "Of course, *this* fellow will be leaving town next. Leaving nothing drinkable in the damned city at all. I'd better get out of here, if only to find my way to some town where the wine doesn't taste like something dipped out of a sewer." He scowled. "Did my family make it out of town safely?"

"Yes, sir. Everyone but your son-in-law, of course. He—"

"Bah! Don't mention that puppy's name to me. Worst mistake I ever made. I must be losing my grip. So help me, I'm going to ask for an annulment, next city we land in." He belched loudly. "Speaking of which: what's my status now?"

"My information isn't too secure, sir. But it appears there's to be some sort of banishment proceeding. And—oh, yes. This came for you. Apparently from Carchemish." He handed over a clay tablet, his face expressionless.

Oshiyahu read the letter, his face in a scowl. "Huh. Looks authentic enough. The seal and all. But—tell me, old friend. Doesn't this seem a little—convenient? I mean, for an offer from Hagirum to show up just at this moment? Tell me, what sort of channels did this go through, getting to you? Any idea?"

"That was another odd thing, sir. I couldn't seem to find out. There hasn't been a caravan from Carchemish in two days."

"Ah. Our thoughts run in the same channels."

"It would be odd if they didn't after all these years, sir. What are you going to do?"

"I'll bet I have to clear all outgoing messages with the same people who slipped this to you. Wouldn't do to have me sending real, live messages to Hagirum directly right now, would it? I can see the old devil now: 'What's this nonsense from Oshiyahu? When did I write him with any offers?' And he'd heave the tablet at somebody's head. No, no. They'll intercept any messages. And when I've made up my mind to take the job and have packed up and left town—why, I'll just happen to meet with mischance on the high road to Carchemish, won't I? Bandits or something."

"My thought exactly, sir. So you'll be sending a 'No' message then?"

"Heavens, no. I'm going to accept enthusiastically. And I'm going to Carchemish and take a job with Hagirum. Whatever sort of job I can get."

"You are? But—"

"Look, I want to get out of here, don't I? I mean, not only out of this jail, but out of Haran. If I can't have the means to defend it, damned if I'm going to stay in it. Too bad about the citizenry, but I'm a soldier, not a suicide. It'd be a pleasure fighting for Hagirum. He at least understands soldiering."

"But, sir—"

"You think I'm playing into their hands? Look, the difference is that I'll *know* what's coming. I'll be able to prepare for it. And in the meantime, I'll be out of town."

"Yes, sir, but—"

"Don't worry, old friend. I'll have you with me. And I'll hire myself a few strong arms from the Thieves' Quarter to keep us company. Damned if I'll be leaving by myself. They'll let me go . . . and then I'll meet my little 'guard' over the hill. And guess who gets to arrange the details?"

"I see. I do, sir. I'll get right to work on it. How many do I hire?"

"Hmmm. Six. No, eight. Ask around. Get the best. Big bastards who look like they've seen a little fighting. Pay 'em well. They'll probably have to earn whatever we pay them."

"Right, sir. And we'll make arrangements for the meeting as soon as . . ."

". . . as I'm out of here." Oshiyahu smiled. "I haven't asked you if you want to go to Carchemish, have I? Forgive me. You should have some choice in these matters. After all, technically you're unemployed at the moment."

"I'm here as long as you want me, sir. I think it's a matter of habit, sir. If I left your service, I'd have to change all my habits, sir."

"And that'd be too much bother, eh? I understand. I understand more than you think. All right, all right. You're a prince among dog robbers, my friend, and I wouldn't trade you for any two generals I ever served with. Now get on with you, and hire me some muscle. The toughest bastards in town. Don't spare the money. It'll be your hide they'll be protecting, too."

"Right, sir."

Oshiyahu watched him go, an affectionate grin on his rough features. Only when he heard the key turn in the lock, far down the corridor, did he stop and wonder for the first time just who it was that they'd be sending against him. He hoped it would be Reshef. Yes, that would be the best thing that could happen. It would be right in character, too—hiring Reshef to strike from cover, perhaps at dark after his little caravan had bedded down for the night at the oasis. . . .

Yes, they'd actually done well. It was a quite believable ruse—if you didn't look too closely. Unfortunately, he had learned—the hard way—the habit of looking too closely. Well, he'd take the fake offer from Hagirum—and then he'd go ahead and solicit a real one. He couldn't imagine old Hagirum, the sly fox, not wanting another good commander in a time of crisis like the present: Hagirum, who had made clear to all the world his intention to sell Carchemish as dearly as she could be sold. Alone among all the kings of the area, Hagirum had made plain his plan to defend his city to the last man, woman, and child.

Oshiyahu shivered. And what implications had that fact for poor undefended Haran? he thought. *Gods!* Why would the Shepherd Kings bother attacking Carchemish, strong, well defended, when they could have Haran—and their passage through Padan-aram to Canaan and the Nile Delta—for the asking? Poor Haran. In a year it'd be no more than a memory in the minds of the lucky few who had managed to escape its terrible last days.

In the market, Danataya ran into Yamam. Her friend squealed with delight and hugged her close; then she held her at arm's length and looked her up and down. "Oh, Danataya! You've changed so! I almost didn't recognize you. . . ."

Danataya patted her big belly. "Yes, I know. It's this heir of mine in here. I must weigh enough for two of us now."

"No, no, darling. You've positively bloomed! Look at that bosom of yours! You'll be making me look downright skinny! I knew it'd do it for you. Oh, wait until you've had the child. Then you'll have some idea what it's done for your figure. And—and you look so *happy*, darling! I'm so glad for you."

"Oh, Yamam. I am happy. You've no idea. Hadad's such a sweetheart about it. He hovers over me as if I were made of glass, as if I could break into a million pieces at any moment. And lately he's grown so affectionate. More than usually. He'll suddenly come up and hug me, just for nothing, and stand looking at me as if he were trying to—to memorize the sight of me, as if he were going to go blind and would never see me again!"

"Ah, he's in love, my dear. Keep him that way. That's the way my dear old man is about me."

"No, this is something special. There's something poignant about it. I don't know what it is. Yamam: you don't suppose he's afraid I'll die in childbirth?"

"That could be it. But I don't see why that should be any cause for fear. You're a good strong girl; you've a good sturdy woman's pelvis. You ought to come out just fine."

"I'm not afraid. But Hadad—he's so protective."

"Well, although I've no plans for children, my dear, my old man's thinking protective thoughts about me. Did I tell you? We're moving to Carchemish."

"No! But Yamam . . . what'll I do for a friend?"

"Why, darling! Talk Hadad into moving too!"

"Do you know what he's thinking of doing? He's considering an offer from Jacob, our friend, to move south with him to—" She stopped, flustered, and looked around hastily. "Oh, dear. I'm not sure I was supposed to talk about that. Forget that I said it, will you?"

"Certainly. But darling: you're not thinking of going? I mean south? Down to—where did you say?"

"I'm not sure. Jacob comes from someplace south of Damascus. But Hadad's already had our accounts transferred to Damascus. Imagine!"

"Well, it's supposed to be a great city. Although if I were to move that far, I'd prefer to live somewhere near the sea, I think. Tyre. Byblos. Maybe Arvad . . ."

"Goodness. I can't even imagine it. I've never seen the sea. Imagine—water so wide you can't see across it."

"I went to Ugarit with my father when I was a child. It was lovely: this deep, deep blue . . . and I went and splashed in it, at the beach. It's not nice to the taste. It's salty. But it feels wonderful."

"Well, you're rich now, Yamam. Get your old man to take you there."

"Me rich? You're the one. Oh, Danataya, sometimes I envy you. My old man is sweet, but it's not like having a lusty young husband who adores the ground you walk upon."

"Speaking of that, my dear, I'd better finish up and get home. Hadad doesn't like having me out even at dusk these days. It's getting so a woman isn't safe anymore. Did you hear of the horrible thing that happened last night, down by the bridge? There was another girl raped and murdered—just like the night Hadad and I escaped that horrible man with the sword."

"Goodness! I'll watch my step. Although I promised to come in and dance a few times for Admuniri, to help out with the festival crowds. Well, I'll just have somebody walk me home."

"Yamam! You're not *still* dancing. . . ."

"Oh, sure I am. Now and then. Just for fun. It's still a bit of a thrill, really. Watching their faces light up like that, knowing they want you and can't have you. . . . Come now, Danataya, don't turn into a prude on me. Don't tell me you didn't enjoy it at *all*."

"Oh, Yamam. Don't remind me."

"Danataya!" Yamam grinned mischievously. "How soon we turn into staid old housewives!"

"Look, I've got to go. The sun's down to the wall. Goodness, it'll be dark by the time I've got home. Hadad will be furious! I haven't even bought the pears he wanted me to bring home. . . ."

Reshef put down a coin, stood, and looked around. The evening traffic had begun to come in, and from the look of them they'd be a lot of bores. It'd be another hour before the dancer came on. He had a mind for . . . headier fare.

His vulpine smile came out in full now, crinkling the corners of his eyes, baring the sharp canines in his thin-lipped mouth. It had been a long time since he'd felt this good. It was fine to get his manhood back, his old arrogance, his sense of personal power. It had been touch and go there for many months, since that damned Jacob character had faced him down. In all that time, he'd been little more than half a man, and his encounters with women had been a matter of fainting on the doorstep.

460

But now? Now he was, in potential at least, the master of Haran. The fact that the damned stupid inhabitants didn't know it yet didn't bother him at all. It was enough for him, Reshef, to know it, to have the secret locked up inside him, the secret that Haran was his, his, the moment the surrender took place.

It had put heart back in him again. And, better, it had brought back his manhood, his virility. He'd confirmed this with a quick visit to the whores two nights before. And last night, in the darkened streets, by the bridge . . .

He smiled and walked through the crowd to the door. The big oak door opened; he elbowed his way past the incoming patrons and stepped out into the evening air. There was already a low-lying fog in the streets, and the sky was all but totally dark now. The sun went down quickly these days.

He strode down the narrow street, taking a random path. And suddenly, suddenly he felt the urge upon him again, the urge he'd felt the night before. The call to danger, to destruction.

His loins stirred. Yes! The call was strong, irresistible. His newly returned potency craved an outlet. And a trip to the whores wouldn't do much for him now, any more than it would have done last night. No, what he needed was a taste of the real thing. Sex, violent and steeped in another's pain; then the feel of domination, of complete control over the life and death of the feeble creature he held in his hands . . .

Yes! Suddenly he felt the excitement coursing through him like the first few swallows of strong palm wine. His hands itched; his body felt the sudden surge of power, of abnormal strength that he always felt when the urge was upon him. His heart beat wildly; his hands clenched and unclenched. His eyes shone with an unearthly light, their vision enhanced even in the darkness and fog. And as he crossed the bridge, he stopped to look over the side, at the twin quays leading on opposite sides of the stream. Below, on the right bank, a young, pregnant woman, her head veiled against the evening chill, made her way slowly up the quay, her belly heavy. Her dress was expensive; the sway of her ripe buttocks under the high-priced cloth brought a gleam to his eye. . . .

Yes! he thought. Yes! And, his mouth set in a death's-head smile, he vaulted over the bridge rail to land lightly on the quay below.

VI

"Here, I'll take that," Bunu-ishdar said. The giant half-angrily pulled the heavy parcel away from Hadad to place it in his own bulging duffel. "What are you trying to do, Hadad? Break your back?"

Hadad pulled his hands back. "I was just trying to help. You underestimate my strength, old friend. Just because I can't life an anvil the way you can . . ."

"Look," the big man said, "I appreciate your offer of help. But do you realize what my wife would do to me if she heard I'd let you carry the forge tools and you'd hurt yourself?" He grinned a giant's big-jawed grin, slow and gentle. "If you want to help me, take that parcel there. I can't get it into my bag."

"All right," Hadad said, "but . . ." He turned his head; his eyes lit on something. "Goodness," he said. "Who would send a slave out dressed like that in a chilly night like this?"

"Like what? Where?"

"Over there, by the well. And look: she seems to be crying. Goodness! And shivering!"

"Well, she should be, poor thing. She's naked! And in this fog!" The giant looked down at him. "Look, there's a robe in the bottom of that bag—"

Hadad made a dismissing motion with his hand and reached for the collar of his own garment. "No, let me." He walked crooklegged over to the well. "Excuse me," he said. "You look cold and . . ."

But the girl looked up then, and the misery in her face turned to surprise and then shame. "Hadad!" she said. "I—"

"Tanuha!" Hadad answered. "What are you doing out after dark, and with nothing on? Here, take this." He unclasped his outer robe and threw it around her shoulders, fastening it securely at the neck. "There, now let me put the hood up, like so. . . ." He stood back and surveyed his handiwork as the giant approached. "Bunu-ishdar," he called. "It's somebody I know."

"Look, girl," the big man cautioned. "You'd better get

462

home. It's not safe out at night these days for a woman alone."

Tanuha turned her homely, tear-stained face to Hadad. "I was going to run away," she admitted. "But I couldn't get past the gate. Hadad, I can't go back. Not to Anat, not to all the horrible things she makes me do."

"Poor dear," Hadad replied. "I know what you must be going through. Look, I've been thinking about that. I'm going to make Anat an offer for you. I'll buy you from her. She needs money right now; I'll give it to her. You can't go on like this."

"Hadad, if you could do that—I'd work so hard...."

"Well, it's settled," he said, smiling. "I'm going to do it. I'll meet whatever price she asks. Now you just run along home, and don't let her know that you've seen me or talked to me. I'll go over there tomorrow and make her an offer. All right? Just keep it nice and quiet. And look out for trouble on the way, eh? If you see anything odd, just run. Don't be afraid to cry out for help." He turned to the giant. "Ishi-dagan, the guardsman, still works in this quarter, doesn't he?"

"No," the big man said. "He's been transferred to a trouble spot down in the Thieves' Quarter. I'm not sure anybody's working this quarter nights...."

"Well," Hadad said. "All the more reason to run along. Don't worry. I'll talk to Anat in the morning."

"Oh, Hadad! Thank you! Thank you so much!" The girl turned her poor plain face to him, and for a moment the radiance of her smile made it pretty. *Yes,* Hadad thought. *Hope does that sometimes.* "Good-bye," she said, and turned to go, her bare legs flashing under the billowing robe.

The giant shouldered his big bag while Hadad took up the smaller parcel. "You're really going to buy her?" Bunu-ishdar asked.

"It's the least I can do," Hadad said. "She's a good girl, and Danataya will need someone to help with mother and the baby. And—well, I feel some responsibility, after all." They set out on the winding trail down to the riverbank, through streets so narrow even Hadad could have reached out and touched both walls at once.

"Well," the giant said, "it's nice to be able to afford responsible behavior." He cursed as an overhang caught his burden and held it; he freed it and followed Hadad out onto the stone quay that bordered the river. "Gods, it's foggy

463

down here!" he said in his great echoing voice. "You can hardly see the surface of the water at all."

"No, you can't," Hadad said, peering through the gloom ahead. He stopped. "Isn't that . . . ?" Then he ran ahead with his curious lopsided gait, as ungainly as a crab. "Danataya! Is that you, my dear?"

The figure in the fog turned; the dear, familiar face peered out from under the hood of her robe. "Hadad! Here, come across on the footbridge, darling. I'll wait for you."

Hadad turned back to his friend. "Bunu-ishdar! Look who's here! I—" But the giant had stopped and, burden balanced on one huge shoulder, was peering back into the darkness of the quay on the opposite bank, in the path Danataya had taken. "What's the matter?" he said.

"Oh, nothing—just thought I saw something. A flash of light on metal or something like that. I guess it was nothing." The giant shook his head. "Here, Hadad. Give me that package. You go join your wife on the other side. I can handle the rest. Thanks for your help."

Hadad turned it over reluctantly. "Well, all right," he said. "But if you're leaving on the morning caravan, I guess I won't be seeing you again. That—that makes me sad. I'll miss you."

"And I you, friend. But, Hadad, get out yourself. The city is doomed. Take that pretty wife of yours and head south. Don't waste any time doing it." The giant freed one hand to clap Hadad gently on the shoulder, then turned to go. Hadad bit his lip, then hurried to the little footbridge where Danataya stood waiting. Their embrace was quick and impulsive; then they scurried arm in arm down the winding quay toward the warmth and lights of home.

Reshef, his eyes flashing, stifled a low animal growl in the back of his throat. So it had been the cripple's wife after all! What a little coup that would have been!

Even now, looking at the two of them as they hurried along the narrow path by the river, the mad impulse ran through him: to fall on the two of them, slay the cripple with his sword, and bend the girl to his will for the necessary moment or two before he ended her life, too. . . .

Suddenly he choked; grasped his neck with one clawlike hand; fell back against the wall of a quayside building. In his mind he could see the dark, resolute eyes of Jacob boring into his own; could feel the harsh touch of the staff's tip against his neck. . . .

He cursed and, coughing, reeled into an alley that led up the bank. The memory was still fresh in his mind—and prominent in the memory was the inescapable fact that Jacob had thrown his blanket of protection over the boy and girl as well as over his own kin.

The thought clawed at his vitals; unmanned him; filled him with impotent rage. Staggering into the street above, his eyes red with hatred and resentment, he tripped over a child's toy; with a low snarl he picked it up and ripped it apart, scattering the pieces about him with a curse on his lips.

Blind with the madness that lay upon him, he ran headlong into a blank wall. The pain shocked him into a momentary lucidity, and he stood leaning against the wall, his face flat against the bricks, his hands steadying himself to the right and left of his face.

A rational voice spoke in his mind now: it told him there would be time for all things. Time for all manner of killing, for the taking of his pleasure—any kind of pleasure he chose—with any woman left in Haran. Because soon he would be master of Haran: master of a city which would have no defenses left against the satisfaction of his most extravagant whim. The voice told him to forget a momentary setback, to think instead of the unlimited license he would enjoy in the days to come.

But no. The red rage was still upon him, and the urge would not be diverted. His hands balled into fists; he pounded on the stones until his knuckles bled; his shoulders shook with the mad power that was upon him now.

He turned from the wall, let his head roll back, looked up at the starless sky above, obscured by clouds and wisps of fog. The moon was full and round. Its orb cast its cold malevolent light down on him, calling to him, speaking to him in words he could not understand.

Gods? Goddesses? Reshef laughed his hoarse laugh, cold, humorless. He'd left all thought of gods and whatever behind as a child, and trusted to his own wits and manipulative instincts; these had stood him in good stead over the years, and he had never had cause before this to believe in anything but what a man could feel and touch and see. . . .

Ah, but that moon above! That cold, baleful, white, perfect circle, with its ambiguous markings that could be a face or not, depending on how you looked at them . . .

He closed his eyes—and found he could still see it. Only now, its soft edges were hard and its diffused glow was a brightly burning radiance—and from it flowed a power, a strength, that he could feel in his outstretched hands, his upturned face. He kept his eyes tightly shut, but let the crazy grin spread over his face. "Yes!" he hissed. "Yes, yes . . . come into me, whatever you are . . . I'm open to you . . . let me feel you . . . feel your power. . . ."

Others in the city felt it, too. Housewives looked up through open windows at the bright disk, shivered, made the sign against evil, and closed the shutters. Young lovers on the roofs felt the oppressive influence and, chastened, slipped back downstairs two by two. In the army camps outside the city commanders looked up, cursed, spat, and ordered an extra ration of wine divided among the troops. It was the bad time of the month, the time when meek housewives suddenly butchered their husbands in their sleep, when father-and-son squabbles abruptly turned into life-and-death struggles. Innkeepers sighed and called in extra help to put down the fights that would inevitably follow. In the bawdy houses, hulking guards asked incoming guests to leave their weapons at the door. . . .

Tanuha felt it, too, and shivered, hurrying timidly through the side streets to Anat's house. She held the robe close to her otherwise bare body, letting it billow around her legs as she tripped along on silent bare feet. *There, now! There's the Street of the Crescent Moon . . . not much farther now.*

Suddenly, she heard a sound behind her: sharp, clear. A stone clattering on the cobbles. . . . She turned, looked over her shoulder. Nothing—but no! What was that back there, moving from shadow to shadow? Crouched over like a monkey? She pulled the robe tighter about her and shifted her weight to the balls of her feet for more speed. As she did, she could hear the steps behind her—the hard sound of a traveling man's metal-studded sandals on brick. A traveler's, or a soldier's . . . She felt a sudden surge of panic run through her, and impulsively slipped into a side street, breaking into a jog as she did so.

The street was narrow, winding. She stubbed her toe once, painfully, and almost fell; but, keeping her sense of direction about her, she threaded her way through a network of half-familiar alleys and feeder streets, her heart pounding. *Had* she been this way before? Or—

Suddenly, she stopped to catch her breath—and to listen for the tell-tale sounds of pursuing feet. But she could hear

466

nothing but the sound of her own breathing as she gulped deep breaths of air in and tried to still the pounding of her heart. Which way should she go? Ahead, the path forked around an oddly shaped building set in at a sharp angle to the street. If she went to the right now . . .

There was a sound behind her. She whirled and saw, down the corridor, the light fall on a face for a moment: a nightmarish demon-face split by a mad smile. A face somehow familiar, perhaps from her childhood nightmares. . . . She shivered uncontrollably and, the impulse too strong for her, slipped out into the alley again to jog along the winding path, taking the right-hand fork, her bare soles slapping against the worn bricks underfoot.

Up ahead! What was that? An archway? Leading to what? Some sort of bazaar? She gulped and made for it, ducking under the arch despite plenty of room to spare, emerging on the other side. . . .

"Oh, no!" she said. It was a dead end leading to a cluster of barred doors. There were no outlets. She turned . . .

. . . and now she saw him, standing in a half-crouch at the middle of the arch. The light fell upon his smile. "Re-Reshef!" she said in a tremulous voice.

"Ah," he said. "It's the little mouse. The ugly one. Come here, darling, don't be afraid. Let's have a look at you."

She backed away slowly, casting her eyes about for an open door, an alleyway, a way to escape. "No, please, I have to be getting home. . . ."

He lunged; she spun away. But his hand caught the hem of the robe Hadad had given her and now he yanked it away from her. The clasp at her neck broke; the robe fell away from her. She covered her breasts and belly with her hands as best she could. "No, please, Reshef—"

"Ah," he said. "Throw a cloth over your head and you wouldn't be bad, would you?" He twirled the robe around his hand and then threw it aside. "Not a bad little body at all. Well, you never know how a woman's going to be until you've had her. I think you're going to do just fine, little mouse. If you'll just come here, and stop this nonsense, we'll get it all over in a hurry, and then you can be about your business almost as if nothing had happened." The voice sounded almost reasonable, now: sweetly reassuring. But the light fell on his face again, and she saw the mad gleam in his eye.

"No, Reshef," she said. "Let me go. Please. You don't want me. Please, please—"

But then he turned, and she saw the knife for the first time. . . .

Hadad paused at the door. "What was that?" he said.

"I didn't hear anything," Danataya said.

"I thought I heard someone cry out. It was a high-pitched sound, cut off suddenly. . . ."

"I didn't hear anything like that at all. Hadad, come in. You'll catch your death of cold."

VII

It was Jacob who found her, coming into the city after a night spent in the hills with his sons. Mastering the revulsion and then the black anger that grew in him, he summoned the guard and made his report to the magistrates. The little body had been simply used and spoiled and tossed aside, the way a thoughtless child might toss aside a doll. The very idea of such callous disregard for the dignity of a single life sent cold chills through him, but he managed to make his reports and his replies with economy and even with the semblance of equanimity. Then, tired to death in every bone and muscle from the night's labors, he directed his steps homeward again.

There were two additional stops he had to make for business reasons; by the time he reached his home, the sun was high. To his surprise, he found Hadad sitting on his stoop waiting for him, looking fully as bleary-eyed as himself.

The cripple scrambled awkwardly to his feet. "Jacob," he said. "I heard . . . somebody told me you found the body. . . ."

"Yes," Jacob replied, opening the front door. "Come in, Hadad. I gather Rachel isn't here."

"No, sir," the young man answered. "They—they said she had been wearing a robe that looked like mine. Was it . . . ?"

"I think so," Jacob said. "I gather you knew her."

"She was my brother's slave. I met her last night, shivering by the bridge in the fog. I gave her the robe to keep warm on the way home. I—I should have walked with her. I was going to see about purchasing her today, to get her away from Anat. But I put it off. I didn't take the responsibility when I should have, Jacob. I feel it's my fault. And now she's—"

"No, you mustn't think that way, Hadad," Jacob said. "Here, sit down."

"I've been worrying all night. I . . . heard a cry, just as Danataya and I were going inside. I—"

"Hadad, Hadad. Don't torture yourself."

"Jacob, who did it?" The question was rhetorical at first; but Hadad, searching Jacob's face, saw something in his eyes. "Jacob, dear friend. You know so much. You know more than any man I know. Jacob, please, just this once, speak straight with me. Tell me the truth. About everything."

Jacob sighed. But he looked into the young man's eyes, and he knew that there was a time when two friends had, once and for all, to open the last doors that stood between them. There came a time when all reticence had to be put aside. He sat down opposite Hadad and put his hands on the young man's. "Reshef did it," Jacob said.

"R-Reshef?" Hadad's eyes widened. "But—"

"Reshef. Your sister-in-law's lover, Hadad. I'm as sure of that as I am of the fact that the sun came up this morning. Hadad: do you remember the night the man surprised you and Danataya in the bazaar? And gave chase?"

"Why, yes. You—you mean that was . . ."

"Yes. And while he was chasing you, I surprised him in the street. I told him that if any harm came to me or mine—or to you or Danataya—now or at any time in the future, I'd kill him."

Hadad's shock showed in his face. "You, Jacob? But—but you're a man of peace, and Reshef—"

"I would have done it, Hadad. Peace has its uses. So, in the end, does violence. I am wondering now if I should not have killed him then. The girl would be alive today. And the city . . ."

"The city? I don't understand. . . ."

"Hadad. I've been meaning to talk with you. To tell you exactly what's happening to Haran, and why you and Danataya would be well advised to come with me when I go south."

Hadad gulped—but he looked Jacob straight in the eye. "Yes, Jacob," he said in a low but controlled voice. "It's time. I have to know everything. There's a decision I have to make, and very soon."

"Very well." Jacob told him all of it: the meeting with Manouk, the information he'd received from Oshiyahu—everything he knew, right down to Oshiyahu's recent arrest

469

and the decision, announced only yesterday, to banish him from the city. Hadad took it all in, but he was not shaken. Instead, he seemed to gather from the terrible things he was hearing a renewed resolve and a new strength.

"I see," he said in the end. "I've been observing things—talking to people. Marsatum and Bunu-ishdar have been telling me how bad things are." He looked Jacob in the eye suddenly. "You knew I'd given orders to have my money moved south to Damascus?"

"No," Jacob said. "But it was a wise move. Did you plan to set up shop there? It mightn't be a bad choice. Ibalum is sure to have many contacts there—"

"No, no—that is, I don't know what I planned. Jacob, I'm struggling with a decision I—I know I have to make. I don't want to do it. But—but there comes a time when a man has to do things he doesn't want to do."

"Hadad," Jacob said, "I had a dream about you. I don't know whether it was the God of my fathers speaking to me or not. He has not spoken to me since I came north. But, Hadad, it seemed to me prophetic. . . . I saw you—and you were going north, not south; toward danger, not away. Hadad, I think I understand . . . it's Shobai, isn't it? But are you sure that it's for you to do this? Are you the person to go—?"

"Jacob, Jacob, how do I know?" Hadad's face twisted in pain. "Last night I shrank away from a decision to take responsibility for another person's life—and Tanuha is dead. If Shobai is in trouble, I must be there—I was not there to see Tanuha home, and now she is beyond my help."

"Hadad, you can't blame yourself for that. And you can't make a decision like this on the basis of—"

"Jacob. My dear friend. How do you know what decisions I can make?"

That stopped Jacob. He looked Hadad in the eye and shook his head. "No," he said slowly. "You're right. You have to be alone in this, as every man has to be alone in the decisions that count. But, Hadad, if there's any way in the world that I can help you, now or at any time in the future. . . ."

"Oh, Jacob." Hadad squeezed his hands. "I know I can count on you—perhaps more than I've ever been able to count on anyone, since father left. Jacob, if anything happens to me—"

"Look after Danataya and the baby—and your mother? Gladly. As if they were my own."

"And—and if I . . . Jacob, could you, if it's a boy—"

"If Danataya has a boy-child I'll see that he's trained in the craft of your fathers, Hadad. I promise you. But, come back to us, Hadad. Don't make it necessary . . ."

"I'll try, Jacob. You'll be leaving soon?"

"As soon as the ewes are lambed. We'll take the high road south, through Tadmor to Damascus. You can join us at any point. I'll leave messages for you in the major cities. But any place south of Damascus you can mention my name, or my father's. You'll be able to find someone to guide you to where we are." Jacob smiled warmly now. "I keep forgetting. You go down there, Hadad, and all you'll have to do is mention your grandfather's name. Ahuni is still famous in that part of the world, as is Belsunu."

"You're not afraid of trouble with your brother?"

"It's nothing I can't handle. I should have known that years and years ago. But then I would never have met Rachel . . . or you either. A man's destiny is what it is, Hadad." There was a touch of sadness in his tone. "It's a mistake for another to interfere in it, however much one may be tempted by concern, or friendship."

"You understand. You do understand." Hadad's eyes suddenly brimmed with tears, but the tears did not fall. "Jacob. You can't have any idea how good it is to have one friend I can count on. Without that—it's like looking up in the sky each night and seeing a new and strange pattern of stars, with nothing the same. . . ."

"Yes. I understand. You can count on me, Hadad. Find us. Come back safe to us."

"Thank you." Hadad smiled. "My good friend. I—I know what I'm going to do, but I'm not sure how I'm going to do it. Jacob: among your friends down in the refugee community, is there anyone who knows the Shepherd Kings? I mean well?"

"Why, yes. Yes, I know a man who was their prisoner for six months. He can probably tell you as much as anyone. I can take you to him if you like."

Hadad stood up. "Wonderful," he said. "I—"

There was a knock on the door. Jacob walked over to it and opened it. A tall stranger stood there. "Your name is Jacob?" he asked.

"Why, yes," Jacob replied. "You have business with me?"

"Just a message, sir. I was told to memorize it."

"Go ahead, please."

"Yes sir. It just said, 'Tell my friend Jacob it is time.'"

Jacob thought about this for a moment. "Very good," he answered. "I understand. Thank you. And . . . here's something for your trouble."

"Thank you, sir." The stranger wheeled on one heel and left. Jacob closed the door behind him.

"It's a day for decisions," Jacob said. "Come along, I'll take you to the man I told you about."

"Decisions? What was that all about?" Hadad said. "I assumed it had to do with the lambing."

Jacob's eyes had a faraway look in them for a moment. Then he smiled—but the smile did not reach his eyes. "It was from Manouk, telling me to get my wives and sons and all I own out of Haran." He sighed. "Come," he added. "We haven't a moment to waste. Either of us."

Jacob, once again, marveled at the speed Hadad could make through the narrow streets of the poor quarter on that game leg. In a few minutes, their winding street led out into a dreary square where the ragpickers of the city were going through the culls of the closets of the rich. He led Hadad to a dark, hook-nosed man with a withered arm. "Hadad," he said. "This is Surian. He can tell you what you need to know of the Shepherd Kings."

"Thank you," Hadad said. He clasped Jacob's hand. "My friend, if I don't see you again . . . tell her I love her. Tell her I had to do it. . . ." His voice almost broke, but he mastered himself and looked Jacob in the eye. And Jacob, looking at him, saw, magically, a double image of him: Hadad the weak cripple and Hadad the man, the latter standing tall and clear-eyed and fearless, ready to do a man's job in the world.

"I'll do it," Jacob said. "It's curious, my very dear friend. My dream—my vision—showed me days ago a picture of you doing what you are doing right now. I wondered then what I could give you that would help you. Now I think that you have everything that any man could take with him on such a journey."

"You have given me enough already," Hadad said. "Now go. Save your family—and mine!"

Dushratta met him at the palace gate. Oshiyahu blinked at the late afternoon glare. "Damn!" he said. "Only a couple of days shut up in that tiny room and my eyes can't take the sun. That settles it. I may never sleep indoors again."

"Hurry, sir," the orderly said. "We've got to get outside the city gate by nightfall. I think we'll be safer there."

472

"I'll be right along," Oshiyahu said. "I've just got a debt to pay. It's a family tradition never to leave a city with a debt unpaid. It won't take but a few minutes. You go ahead, and I'll join you outside. You've arranged for everything?"

"Yes, sir. And, sir—take this." He tossed over the commander's battered old sword belt.

"I suppose you're right. Now be off with you!" He watched the orderly scurry away as he buckled the belt around his middle. *You've lost a little weight there,* he thought. A good thing too. He'd be back to soldiering in a bit, and he would need to be in something like fighting trim.

He looked up at the late afternoon sky, at the gathering clouds. The sun would be down soon—sooner than he'd thought. He'd better hurry if he wanted to beat the sundown deadline for getting out of town. Settling the sword at his side in its scabbard, he set out into the tangled warren of streets that led off from the Temple of Bel.

Almost immediately, he was aware of being followed. He couldn't have said why; he'd never got around to giving a name to the instinct an old soldier developed over the years, the instinct that warned of danger. He smiled to himself ... and began thinking ahead. Where, if he were the attacker, would he find it easiest to head off his prey and box him in? And where, as prey, could he best forestall this? His mind raced wildly as his eyes scanned the roadway ahead. Yes! Perhaps up there ... Increasing his speed, he made a sudden left turn into a little square someone had laid out around a now dried-up well. He flattened himself against a wall, the drawn sword in his hand. The walls rose high around the little square; the light of the sun had long since left it, and it lay in deep shadow that amounted almost to complete darkness. He squinted at the doorway, every muscle tensed for the effort to come.

Sure enough: footsteps. And in a moment he saw three men slip past him—in single file, the damned fools—and stand looking around, blinded by the sudden darkness. "Looking for me?" he said suddenly—and attacked.

He stabbed hard with the sword's tip and felt it bite deep; there was a low groan and the first man fell forward. Oshiyahu then raised the sword and struck backhand, moving forward in the semidarkness. His blade struck something hard; he slashed again and felt the bronze blade sink into soft flesh. He chuckled and cut hard, twice more, feeling a deep satisfaction when his opponent fell hard to the ground. He crouched, feeling as much as seeing the presence of the third man across the little square. "Come on," he said. "Let's get it over with. . . ."

"F-Father," a broken voice said. "It's Yassib. I—they made me do it. I hadn't any intention of. . . ."

"Oh, it's 'Father,' is it now?" Oshiyahu said in a scornful voice. "Enough of that, boy. You seem to forget that you must take the consequences of your actions. Well, you are about to learn that lesson." He made a circling motion with the sword's tip.

"Father, no, please . . ."

"Defend yourself, damn you! Don't make me any more ashamed of you than I am already." He cut viciously, and he felt the younger man parry forte to forte. "That's better. Congratulations on your raise, incidentally. It'll mean my daughter gets a better pension. That is, if there's any government of Haran to collect it from, a week from now. . . ." He lunged and felt the deft parry again. "Well, good! At least you remember what I taught you in fencing class."

"Father, please . . . I just got in over my head. I had no idea. . . ."

"Say your prayers," Oshiyahu said. His voice was low and purposeful. "Purify yourself if you can." He counted to three, then struck. His powerful swing struck the other's sword down; then he lunged—and felt his point sink in to the hilt.

He let the body, falling away from him, pull itself free from his sword. Then, an icy look on his lined old face, he solemnly saluted the dead, one at a time. . . .

VIII

Jacob and Rachel rose early; there were plans to be made. Jacob lit a candle and sat down opposite her at her little kitchen worktable, taking her hands in his. "Look," he said, "I don't want you getting any ideas about doing heavy work at this late date. I'm going to send two of the boys back. They'll do the packing."

"There isn't that much to be done," she said. "I've known this was coming for some time. I've been putting things by here and there. But thank you for thinking of me."

"Is there a moment in the day when I don't think of you? Well, there may be, one or two. But even then you're in the back of my mind." He smiled proudly. "Then, if most of the work's done here, maybe you can help Leah and the women. They'll spend all their time quarreling otherwise."

"Me tell Leah anything? Well, I'll try. How is she taking the news, anyhow?"

"She started to react . . . oh, well, the way one might expect her to. She doesn't want to leave her home, her friends."

"I can understand that. I have a little of that feeling myself. But Jacob, where you are is home. That's the important thing."

"That's my darling. Besides, both of you will be like minor royalty in Canaan. I don't think either of you has quite understood that yet. I tried to explain to Leah. I think I've got her curiosity aroused, anyway."

"Does she understand . . . what's going to happen here?"

"I told her—but I don't think it's fully registered. She sees her friends leaving, the whole commercial framework of the city coming apart little by little . . . but it's hard for her to accept it." He shrugged. "And there's a way in which I hardly believe it myself. But Rachel, I have to believe it." He squeezed her hands. "And I have to act upon it." His grim face relaxed for a moment into a smile as he looked once again at her fair face, at the big radiant eyes, the soft lips. . . . "Besides, the time has come for me to return to Canaan. And claim my place. Our place."

"It is a little exciting," she admitted, smiling. "If a little frightening." Her face darkened for a moment. "How—how long do you think we have?"

"I've been thinking about that. I think we'll very likely just make it. When Manouk sent the message he meant we should move—now."

"I won't be a burden, Jacob, I promise."

"Of course you won't. Which reminds me, I must get over to see—" There was a knock, timid and quiet. Jacob looked out. "Now that's a coincidence. There she is right now." He threw open the door. "Danataya! I was just about to come see you. . . ."

But he stopped as he saw the girl's haggard face, her red eyes. "What's the matter, my dear? Come in, please."

"It's Hadad," she said. "He didn't come home last night. Or this morning either!"

Jacob exchanged glances with Rachel. Her lips silently formed the words: *He didn't tell her?* "Come in, my dear,"

Jacob said, recovering. "Come sit down right over here. I—I'm afraid I have a message for you. . . ."

Oshiyahu checked the cinch on his saddle, then let it out a notch. He patted the horse's long nose and, having settled the saddlebags to his satisfaction, turned to Dushratta. "I suppose it's about time," he said. "Funny. I never expected to miss the place."

"You've been here a long time, sir."

"Yes. Stupid mistake on my part. Always a mistake for a soldier to put down roots anywhere. The thing to do is keep moving. Don't let a weed grow up your leg." He spat into the road. "The trouble is, a man grows old in spite of himself."

"You're not old, sir."

"Tell that to me some other time of day. This is the first time in six months I've slept outdoors in one of these damned morning fogs. I can hear every joint in my whole body, creaking like an old oak tree in the wind. Well, farewell to civilian pleasures. I'm going to have to go back to earning my living."

"Are you, sir? I mean, we don't *have* to go to Carchemish. . . ."

"I'm surprised at you, Dushratta. Is there another direction I could go right now and keep my good name? My self-respect? Oh, I suppose people wouldn't think badly of me. They'd say the old boy just got too old to fight. And maybe they're right. I *have* been at this business half the age of the earth, it sometimes seems. But maybe that's the problem. You work up the habits of a lifetime, and the first time you're tempted to break one of them, you start looking at yourself and thinking you're ready for the boneyard. What the devil would an old fool like myself do in retirement? Sit around the taverns getting bleary-eyed on palm wine and telling tall tales about the fabulous deeds of my legendary youth? Turn into a flabby-thighed old man who sits around telling the young how to live their lives?" He spat again, this time sour-faced and flinty-eyed. "No, this is better. This way I get to keep some vestige of what I am pleased to call my manhood right up to the end, when I do something stupid and some oaf splits my skull for me. . . ."

"As you wish, sir."

"Which reminds me: if I'm going to commit suicide that's my own damned business, but I haven't any right to go hauling you off to your death. You're still young enough to get another job. Why don't I fire you right now and give you a nice swift kick in the direction of Ebla, or Damascus, or someplace where they pay a decent wage instead of the pittance I've been paying you?"

"Oh, I've done quite well, sir. I've twenty thousand on deposit with a merchant in Aleppo, and . . ."

"Where the devil did you ever pile up that much money on that salary of yours, you scoundrel? Have you been stealing from the commissary?"

"Oh, no, sir. Game of peas and shells, sir. Little trick I picked up in my youth, during the Mari campaign. Now you see it, now you don't. . . ."

"But twenty thousand? How . . . ?"

"Investments, sir. When you bought, I bought. When you sold, I sold. It's worth a lot to have access to good advice, even if you have to get it through eavesdropping. Of course, I wasn't operating on your sort of scale, sir, but I must admit I cleaned up on that textile shipment last winter."

"You had a piece of that too? Why, you old devil!"

"Yes, sir. You've been lucky for me, sir. Lucky enough that I think I'll stick around as far as Carchemish, sir. If you don't mind." Dushratta looked over his master's shoulder. "That's odd, sir. Do you see that?"

Oshiyahu whirled. "Where? Oh—the little fellow with the crooked leg? Why, look at that. He's trying to mount his donkey from the wrong side . . . oh, that's funny. But with that leg I don't suppose he could mount the proper way, could he? At any rate, I doubt if he's ever been in a saddle before. Here, let's give him a hand there. . . ."

But the cripple managed to get into the saddle at last, and to rein in his animal, which was pawing the ground and backing around in circles. Oshiyahu, smiling, walked over to him and took the ass's harness in hand, gentling the animal. "There, there," he said. "That's better." He looked up at the young man on the donkey's back and saw a round face, intelligent eyes, a wide good-humored mouth, curly hair. "It's all right now," he said. "You're supposed to mount them from the other side."

"Oh," the young man said. "Thank you. I'm a little new at this, but I'll catch on. I learn things quickly."

"The pack animal behind you tells me you're headed some ways from here," Oshiyahu said. "We're going to Carchemish. If you're headed that way, perhaps we can travel together. It's not safe for a single rider to travel in these hills, and you'll probably be more secure—"

"Thank you," the young man said. "But I'm not going that way. I'm looking for the track north to Melid."

"Melid?" The old soldier stepped back and looked hard at the young man. "Son, I hate to be the first to tell you this, but Melid—it was destroyed some time ago. Razed to the ground. You don't want to go there, surely. . . ."

"I know, sir. But—well, that's where the Shepherd Kings were. And I have to get through to them."

"Gods above!" Oshiyahu stood, hands on hips, looking up at him. "Look, son, I don't want to meddle in your affairs, but you don't want to go north. Stay away from there. You haven't any idea what you're about. You'd be going to your death."

The young man looked down at him, lower lip between his teeth. "I—I'm aware that may be possible," he said. "But—"

"Possible! Look, son, I can virtually guarantee it. Here, I'll help you dismount. Let's talk this over now."

"I'm grateful for your concern," Hadad said, "but it's something I have to do. My—my brother's up there, in the nomad camp. I talked to someone who had seen him there. He went north to work for them, and now he's a slave. A slave!"

Oshiyahu puzzled for a moment. "I think I know of you," he said. "You're a sculptor, aren't you? A friend of Jacob's, the pastoralist? And your brother is Shobai, the armorer?"

"Yes, sir. I'm Hadad. And—look, sir, my brother's in trouble, and—"

"Hadad, I know your brother. I'm Oshiyahu, formerly commander of the local garrison. And I know something of the situation you're riding into—more than you do. And I really have to say . . ."

"I understand, sir. But—but somebody has to go. And there doesn't seem to be anyone but me."

"For heaven's sake, what is it that you think you're going to do? These people are gathered up there in the hundreds of thousands, perhaps the millions. They're as rapacious as locusts in the field. They'll kill a man too quick to talk about it, out of curiosity or boredom, or just to settle a bet as to which way his guts will poke out of his stomach if you skewer him. They don't give a damn about human life."

"All the more reason to want my brother out of there, sir."

"Look, now that they've disarmed Haran, they'll fall on the city like a bear on a fish. They'll kill everyone there. . . ."

"I know. I know. That's why I've got to do something."

Oshiyahu shook his head exasperatedly. "You? A cripple, unarmed . . ."

"If I bore arms, they'd be *sure* to kill me," Hadad said. "This way, maybe—"

"You're mad! Stark, raving mad! Do you know that? What can you do? Can you do what the armies of Melid couldn't do? What you're trying to do . . . why, I couldn't do it with an army of ten thousand men, and I've been a fighter since I was half your age. What makes you . . . ?"

"But sir, maybe it's something that doesn't call for fighting. Maybe it requires something else."

"Something else! In the name of heaven, what?"

"I don't know, sir. Maybe it'll turn out to be something *I* know how to do. You never know, sir, until you try."

"Gods!" Oshiyahu stepped back now and looked him up and down, the slim body in the nondescript garment, the pitiful crooked leg jutting out grotesquely. "The funny thing is, I don't think you *are* mad."

"I'm not, sir. Not that way."

"And you're a friend of Jacob's, so you probably know what it is that you're going into. You *know* the magnitude of the problem Haran faces. You *know* the city won't be here in a week or ten days. It'll be dust underfoot. You *know* that. And you know what your chances are, too, don't you? You know what the odds are. . . ."

"There aren't any odds, sir. My grandfather was Ahuni, sir, the armorer. Someone asked him once if it was hard to make one of those wonderful swords he used to make, sir. He said that either it was very easy, as it was to him, or it was impossible."

Oshiyahu just stood looking at him. "Gods," he said in a low, still voice. "No odds. And here all of my life . . . The hell of it is, you know you're right. No odds. It's as simple as that. You know, I own one of Ahuni's swords, son. And—yes, it must have been just like that. When I won the battle of Mari, everyone spoke to me of 'odds,' and I knew it was all nonsense. I knew I could win the battle. That was all there was to it. And I went out and did, and afterward everyone ran around quoting odds at me, and I thought they were fools. Fools."

"Right, sir. And I know that I'm doing the right thing. Somebody has to do something right now. . . ."

"You've determined that it's your turn, eh? Yes, yes, I understand that. Well, you're no crazier than I am, are you, young man? Anyone with a groat's worth of sense would call

479

the both of us a couple of lunatics, wouldn't he? You're going into the camp of the Shepherd Kings to try and save your brother—yes, and Haran too for that matter, for all I know—with nothing in your saddlebags but bread and cheese and water. And I'm going to Carchemish to try to win a war with an underequipped army of maybe ten thousand souls against an enemy who probably numbers over a million." He smiled, crinkly-eyed. "Well met, brother lunatic! May the gods smile upon your endeavor and mine!" He stepped forward to clasp Hadad's hand. "Look," he said. "You ride over that hill there, and head west for . . . oh, until the sun is directly overhead. Right? Then you'll see a nice, well-marked trail leading off to the north through a pass marked by two great stones standing in the saddle of a hill. That won't be the track to Melid, but it'll take you to where I think the nomad headquarters is right now. That's where your brother will be; my guess is that they keep an armorer close to the middle of things. If you see him, tell him hello from me. He's a good chap, really. Just a little young. His errors are a young man's errors. Not like the two of us, eh? You and I, we're as old as the hills, aren't we? Well, old enough to know what a couple of damned fools we are, anyway—and old enough to know it's a damned fool's lot to do damned-fool things. Old enough not to question that, eh?"

"Yes, sir," Hadad said. "Thank you, sir. And—good luck!"

"There isn't any luck!" Oshiyahu said as Hadad nudged his mount forward, pulling the pack animal behind it. "Either you make it or you don't!" Hadad waved back at him, smiling mildly. Oshiyahu took a few steps after him, waving one triumphant fist in the air. "There isn't any luck! There aren't any odds! There's only courage, and facing up to your destiny once you've learned what it is! Farewell, young man! Farewell. . . ."

Oshiyahu stood, still waving absentmindedly, for quite some time as Hadad's narrow-shouldered figure, jouncing on the animal's back, receded into the distance. Dushratta joined him after a while, and he was surprised to see tears in the old commander's eyes as he stood watching the two donkeys wind their way down the broad valley to the north.

CHAPTER FOURTEEN

I

Now, all across the Great Crescent of fertile lands that lay south of the great folded mountains, the armies of the invader lay in all their unimaginable strength, deployed in a single line long enough to stretch from the borders of the Hittite lands in the west all the way to the edge of Assyrian dominions in the east. The great herds of the Shepherd Kings roamed the green hills, devastating the grass for farther than the eye could see, cropping it down to the ground and leaving nothing for other livestock, much less for the native wildlife —oryx, addax, mountain sheep, wild goat, deer, gazelle, and wild ass. Even the water table went down under heavy usage; the beasts of the field starved or died of thirst—if they didn't perish in the wholesale hunts that the nomads organized to relieve the tedium of waiting.

Some of the chieftains of the great columns, themselves kings and insubordinate to the iron rule of the Leader, found it difficult to hold their battle-hungry troops in line without giving them a chance to work off their nervous energy. One of these, ignoring explicit instructions, called a raid on Gurgum—a half-Hurrian, half-Hittite city nestled just south of the mountains' fringe on the very edge of the great Plain of Aram—and battered the garrison to its knees. The white flag went up. Nomad troops, entering the city ostensibly on a diplomatic mission, suddenly turned on their escorts and butchered them; then they seized the drawbridge and held the gate against repeated attacks while their fellows poured in through the opened doorway and laid the city waste. In the morning, Gurgum was no more than a black column of smoke and a set of high walls enclosing a charnel house.

The Leader heard of this—and went into a rage. But Manouk and others calmed him down and showed him how the raid had closed off traffic from the Hittite lands all the way south to Egypt, except for the sea trade. He grunted and assented. And he allowed the western garrison to move south into the newly conquered land.

Aleppo, to the south, panicked; for the first time the truth of what Hagirum of Carchemish had been telling them came home to the citizens of that city. They armed hastily. Farther to the south, mighty Ebla strengthened its treaties with Ugarit and Tiphsah and, under terms of the recent agreement with Hamath, was allowed to levy a draft on that city's youth for the mutual protection of the two cities.

The Gurgum raid having succeeded and, in the end, been accorded legitimacy by the Leader's surprising inaction, two of the chieftains of the eastern arm of the great army joined forces and struck south of the mountains to close first the old trade route from Nineveh to Melid, then—unexpectedly—the route north of Gozan. Poised before Gozan, they hung undecided for a day, then struck suddenly south at Gozan. The city held for a day, then fell amid a sickening slaughter.

This put troops of the Shepherd Kings suddenly within a hundred miles of Haran on the east and within the same distance of Carchemish on the north. As if to balance the line, the troops at Gurgum then force-marched to the Great Sea, closing off Carchemish's access to the sea and menacing Aleppo as well. Now the whole area between Haran and Carchemish was threatened on three sides—east, north, and west—by the nomad forces, which stretched in a great half-circle across the Plain of Aram.

Haran suddenly realized the problem facing it; but it had, for all practical purposes, disarmed, trusting in the peaceful motives of the Shepherd Kings. Hastily, it called a levy on the youth of the city—only to find that, for the most part, the city's able-bodied young had long since departed. A new detachment of troops was put together in a ragtag pattern, using mainly men of middle age or more drawn from the city's half-starved refugee population. The search went out for trained commanders, but the best of these had resigned in the wake of Oshiyahu's dismissal and left for other cities— and, with a great show of magnanimity, Hirgab resigned from his civilian position and took over the defense of Haran as commander of its armies. Joining him in the move was his lieutenant, Reshef, who immediately made a great show of training the raggedy defenders of the city in the uses of the sword—when his many absences "on official business" permitted.

Much different was the spirit in Carchemish, where desperation had forced a powerful esprit de corps among civilian and military population alike. Almost daily, King Hagirum appeared personally on a balcony above the city square to announce steps taken to strengthen the city's garrison; when he announced the hiring, as deputy commander, of the lord Oshiyahu, former high commander of the troops at Haran and hero of the great Battle of Mari, the cheers resounded over the rooftops of the whole city. Oshiyahu appeared and made a brief speech, looking confident and serious; the ranks of the army swelled by another two hundred enrollees by nightfall. Daily the troops paraded, looking fit and ready for battle; only the commanders knew how pathetically inadequate their numbers were. The drums beat and the horns blew, and the city made ready to defend its walls to the last man.

Almost as an afterthought, Hagirum banned outgoing traffic from the city except for trade caravans; no one was allowed to emigrate. The same edict went into effect in Haran a day later, and soldiers interrupted Jacob's migration half a day's march south of Haran; but the many bribes he had paid his contacts at court finally stood him in good stead, and he was allowed to pass. And his herds, augmented by hundreds of speckled young lambs, continued their slow progress southward toward the land of his fathers. It was a day or two before the news got through to Laban that his son-in-law had gone, taking with him a herd nearly as large, if nowhere nearly as mature, as his own.

On the march, Bilhah the servant walked alongside the dappled ass on which Rachel rode sidesaddle, gentling the animal, keeping its pace to a slow amble. In the late morning of the second day after their passage from the land of Haran, Rachel spotted Jacob ahead of her, striding along confidently, talking to Reuben. "Bilhah," Rachel said, "let me go to my husband." She took the reins from the servant and spurred the animal forward. She reached Jacob just as Reuben left him to mount his horse and ride ahead to the head of the column.

"Jacob," she said. "I haven't seen you today. . . ."

"Rachel!" he said happily. She looked into his eyes and saw something new there—a power, an authority beyond any he had ever assumed in her presence. "How happy I am to see you!" His hand grasped her bare foot and squeezed it affectionately. "I apologize for my absence. It's been a busy day or two, since the soldiers—"

"Jacob, something else has happened. You're not yourself —but I like the change." Her hand reached down and touched his hair, still dark here and there between the gray streaks that had begun to come upon him in recent days. "What has happened, my husband?"

"I never could keep anything from you, could I?" he said in a voice full of love. "You're right, of course. I'm a new man. Rachel: last night the God spoke to me. Spoke to me, for the first time since I left Canaan! I—I'd thought He would never speak to me again, not until my foot had finally fallen upon the soil of the Promised Land. But He spoke to me, in Padan-aram!"

"This is surely a wonderful sign," Rachel said. "Then— then we are doing what He wishes?"

"Yes! Yes! He gave me His blessing—not only for leaving Laban, but for the taking of the speckled lambs and black kids. He as much as said that the fact that so many of the lambs are speckled—and hence ours—was His own doing, because of the injustice Laban was doing to me. And He said, 'I am the God of Bethel, where you anointed a memorial pillar to Me. Now arise, go forth from this land, and return to the land of your birth. . . .' "

"Jacob!"

"Yes! He has not forgotten me, after all these years. How could I ever have imagined He would? And Rachel—what this means is that He will look out for me in Canaan. He will make peace between me and Esau. Because if it were not the right time for me to make myself known to my brother again, would He send me south just now?"

"I guess not," she said. "Jacob! I'm so happy for you."

"For me! My darling, this is a blessing for all of us. All of us!"

"Yes, Jacob. But—I meant—it means so much to you. I know how desolate you've been, every time you thought of the God deserting you. . . ."

"Rachel, we must begin the sacrifices again. We must go back to all the rituals of my fathers. Only now the God will accept them again. I—I've been remiss. I haven't brought you into my religion—you, or Leah, or Zilpah or Bilhah or the

484

boys. How could I? How could I act as a priest of the God when I believed that He had deserted me? But now—now we shall return to the faith of Abraham. All of us. And you will all share in the blessing He has for us, for all Abraham's seed. Rachel, I must instruct my sons—they know little of their heritage. They do not know the whole story of how the God called first Terah to Haran, then Abraham to Canaan. Rachel, they must know who they are—a people chosen from all others, handpicked by the One God for blessings above all men."

"It's wonderful—and Jacob, that applies to . . ." She smiled and patted her big belly.

"Yes, yes!" He smiled and touched her leg again, a gesture of such warmth and affection that Rachel felt a little thrill run through her. "Now, my dear—I have to ride back to the rear of the column. If there's anything you need send Bilhah for it, will you? I'll be here in—well, as fast as I can get here." He looked at her. "How are you feeling?"

"I'm feeling—close. Close, Jacob. I don't know how long it's going to be now. . . ."

"Well," he smiled, "hang on as long as you can, please. Until we're free of the reach of Laban's long arm, anyhow. It's been touch and go as it is, getting out of Haran just in time. Did you know Gozan had fallen? And the trade route is closed completely?"

"Gozan!" she said. She held one hand over her heart; her mouth hung open. "But, Jacob, that's . . ."

"Yes, I know. When I think of how close we came to—but it's better not thinking about it. How are Danataya and Hadad's mother?"

"As good as can be expected—except that they grieve for Hadad. They think he's dead, or as good as dead."

"Don't tell them I said so, but that may be the truth."

"Oh, Jacob! Hadad? Our gentle little Hadad?"

"Our gentle little Hadad, my darling, is a Child of the Lion, with everything that implies. He may just be the bravest man I've ever known. Braver, perhaps, than our valiant Oshiyahu. I hope the God is with Danataya, and that He gives her a good strong son when her time comes. If He does, I will raise him as the son of a great hero, a man fit to stand beside such heroes as Sneferu the Egyptian, or Abraham, or Eshcol, or Enosh. . . ."

"Jacob! I don't understand."

"You will in time to come, my darling. It has to do with the reason Hadad did not tell Danataya or his mother that he was leaving. He couldn't. He knew how important his mission was, and how impossible it would have been for him to leave if Danataya had asked him not to. I know it seems as though he had abandoned her, Rachel; but Hadad knew what he was doing. He suddenly saw what his destiny was. Perhaps the God spoke to him in some way, Rachel, even if Hadad was an unbeliever. I think the hand of the God is upon him. He has a role for our gentle Hadad to play in the violent and bloody scheme of things. I had a dream about Hadad one night, before he left. It may just be that that was the first time the God spoke to me, in that dream. But He showed me what it was that Hadad was about to do, and—"

"Oh, Jacob!" she said in a voice full of pity and hurt. "What? Tell me. . . ."

"I can't. But I think we will hear soon enough."

"Jacob—will we see Hadad again?"

"I—I didn't see that far. But I'm proceeding as though we won't. For heaven's sake, don't tell Danataya or Hadad's mother."

Rachel didn't answer. She just looked at him, her hand over her mouth, a stricken look in her dark eyes. . . .

She watched Jacob ride away. Her head reeled with the things she had learned, and her heart sank at her own inability to believe in the God in whom Jacob placed such faith. She hoped the belief, the faith, would come; but for now the God had spoken to her husband, not to her. And her own desperation and terror in the face of the threats posed both by Laban and by the great armies of the north, added to her fear of childbirth and her fear of the unknown lands and people to the south, made her reach inside her saddlebag now to caress the little set of household gods she had taken from her father's house a week before their departure. She wasn't sure how much she believed in these either, but somehow the touch of them comforted her; in these chancy days, any comfort she could draw from anything was welcome. Desperately, her hands clutched the little figures; an idle thought came to her suddenly that the little gods were probably made by Hadad, back in his days of poverty and want. Hadad! A pang of pity stabbed her heart. Surely Danataya needed her now, of all times; she'd ride over to see her, talk to her, comfort her; perhaps just the contact would help to comfort Rachel and reassure her. Poor Danataya! Poor Rachel! Surely the earth had never seen such perilous times for bringing one's first child into the world.

Far to the rear of the column, Jacob could see a tiny plume of dust. He stood with Simeon, a little to the west of the path, and watched the dark speck come closer, closer—and resolve itself into a horse and rider, coming at breakneck speed. Simeon suddenly shouted aloud and rushed forward. "Judah!" he cried. And—yes—now Jacob could see the figure of his fourth son astride his stout Hittite charger, galloping at full speed. The boy reined in the animal and dismounted like a Bedouin, in a single graceful motion. "F-Father!" he said. "I rode back, as—as you said. . . ."

"Catch your breath first, son," Jacob said, taking the reins and handing them to Simeon. He put one hand on his son's already broad shoulder and steadied him. "Now—what did you learn?"

"Grandfather—he's right behind us—maybe a day's ride at most. And—and he has all his relatives. There must be twenty of them, all armed. . . ." The boy coughed; his young body shook with the effort to speak. He tried to say something more, but the cough drowned his words.

"It's all right," Jacob said. "We'll be ready for them. And, in the meantime, we'll pick up the pace."

His eyes went to the horizon from which Judah had come, though, and his heart sank. Only a day behind! He forced a confident smile upon his face, but in his heart of hearts confidence was nowhere to be found. *God of my fathers,* he thought, *help me! Help me!*

II

At the campfire that night, Jacob gathered his sons for a council of war. Standing on a little rise, he looked around him, seeing them assembled like stairsteps, some of them no more than children, others full-grown, ready to take their places as men in the community. He smiled, liking what he saw; he'd have to find them good wives in Canaan. . . .

They no longer tended to group themselves according to the mother who had borne them, but mixed freely; they were, for better or for worse, *his* sons now—young men entrusted with various tasks according to their strength, but all working together toward the common goal and fiercely united in their protectiveness toward the women of the party and toward the common property they'd amassed in their last season in Haran.

Who was missing now? Only Levi, who was bringing up the rear, keeping him informed as to Laban's whereabouts and progress. Leah's other sons were there: tall, powerful Reuben and Simeon; fleet Judah; young Issachar and Zebulun. The concubines' sons, younger, had stayed with the herds during the march, but they were ready to help with the fight if it came to fighting. He looked at them all with pride. "Asher," he said, "did you see to the women?"

"Yes, Father," the boy said. "Mother is with Rachel. Bilhah is with Danataya. Everything's all right."

"Good. I purposely kept them away from the campfire. I don't want them hearing what we could be saying. No use in worrying a couple of women so close to bearing children."

"Father," Reuben said, "will Levi be here by bedtime?"

"I hope so, son. I don't like the idea of his being out this late at night. Although, at that, he can take care of himself as well as any. It's just that, like all the rest of you, I think the God has special plans for Levi. Plans having to do, in his case, with religious matters, matters having to do with the worship and honoring of the God Himself. If anything should happen to him . . ." But then he checked himself with a smile. "Listen to me, though. If the God has special plans for him, He will take care of our Levi, won't He?"

"Then you think there's no danger, sir?" Simeon said. "I mean, when Laban gets here?"

"I wouldn't want to go that far." Jacob looked at the fire, now down to fiercely glowing coals. "You know your grandfather and his terrible temper. He's capable of doing something sudden, ill-considered, violent. It's our job to outflank him and make sure that doesn't happen. That is, if we aren't successful in outdistancing him."

"I don't know how that's going to be possible, Father," Reuben said. "After all, we have the animals, and he doesn't have anything like that to slow him down."

"An excellent point, son. So when it does come down to our meeting with him—"

"Father! Listen!" one of the younger boys said. He pointed off into the dark. Jacob stopped in midsentence. He listened . . . and heard hoofbeats, growing closer.

"Reuben," he said. He tossed his eldest son a spear. "Go

have a look." The young man set out in a carefree jog, sure-footed, his young body poised for action. "Now, as I was saying, we have to be prepared for anything Laban will or can do. I want all of you to be armed at all times, not only with the swords I gave you but with your bows and arrows. You younger boys should carry your slings at all times. Incidentally, Dan, I understand you're developing a pretty fearsome reputation with the sling. Judah tells me you killed a fox the other day."

"Oh, Father . . ." The boy twisted his bare toe in the dirt, embarrassed.

"He certainly did," Judah said. "I'll keep him and Naphtali to the rear when trouble comes—but if trouble comes, they'll take their part just like any of us. Dan can put your eye out with the sling at thirty paces. Naphtali isn't as good yet, but he's capable of doing some damage if it comes down to a scrap."

"Good," Jacob said. "I'm proud of all of you. You've comported yourselves in all of this like grown men, like true great-grandsons of Abraham. That old warrior would have taken every one of you to heart. He always said, 'A man's a man, whatever his age.' And this was one who fought valiantly in a major war of conquest when he was twice my age. I can't wait until my father sees you. Well, he can't *see* you, mind you—but he'll be proud of you nonetheless." Jacob paused, smiling at them. "Now, to get down to business . . ."

"Father!" Reuben said. "It's Levi!" Jacob whirled to see his third son climbing the little hill, with Reuben behind him.

"Levi!" Jacob said. "What news?"

"Let him get his breath," Reuben said. "He says grandfather has narrowed the gap between us. He'll be here by morning."

"He's near, Father—I—I think no more than—uh—a few hours' ride. . . ." Levi gasped out between deep breaths.

"What do we do, Father?" Simeon asked. "Can we pack up before dawn and get on the road?"

Jacob pondered. "That might be the only thing we can do. If there were more moon . . . if that cloudbank were to shift, so as to give us more light, perhaps we could travel by night. . . ." He frowned. "But no. We'd lose livestock in the dark that way. And what's the sense in coming this far if we're going to give away livestock to Laban?"

"Well spoken, Father!" Reuben said. "So it's a quick start tomorrow morning, then?"

Jacob was about to reply; but a familiar figure had appeared at the very edge of the circle of light. "Bilhah!" he said. "Dan, bring your mother here, will you, son?"

The concubine hesitated. "I think you'd better come with me instead," she said. "Danataya . . . she's gone into labor!"

Jacob and Reuben rushed to the girl's side. She lay in a bed one of the boys had made, groaning. Bilhah crouched by her side, holding her hand. "When did it begin?" Jacob asked.

"An hour ago," his concubine said. "So far, the pains are pretty far apart, but my guess is she'll bear by morning at the latest."

Jacob sighed. "Well, give her the best of care." He turned to Reuben and motioned him away. "Look," he said to his son, "this changes everything, obviously. We'll have to confront Laban in the morning sometime. We'll leave a couple of the boys with the women and ride back to meet him. We'll have the advantage of knowing the terrain. We should be able to set up some kind of ambush for him. Maybe we can force a standoff. Outflank him. Cover him with our bows, so that he daren't attack."

"Fine," Reuben said. "There was that pass we passed through an hour before we made camp. There are places where five or six well-placed bowmen could slow down an army. If we get up very early, and ride back, we can perhaps be there by dawn. . . ."

"Right," Jacob said. He sighed again. "The workings of the God are strange, but they can't be questioned. If only Danataya had been able to hold out longer. . . ." He shrugged. "But she couldn't, poor darling. And once these things get started, they have their own timetable. Well, we'll have to make the best of things."

"We'll do all right, Father," the boy said, smiling. Jacob thought: *why, he's as tough as a wild boar*. His heart thrilled with pride. Did ever a father have such sons?

After a fitful sleep, he awoke just as the first pink tinge had begun to show in the sky. When he opened his eyes Reuben and Simeon were standing above him, their faces clearly visible in the light of a torch held by Levi. He blinked and grinned up at them. "Boys," he said. "How—how long have you been up?"

"We put on a night watch, Father," Simeon answered. "We took turns standing guard. Judah is taking the watch right now."

490

"Wonderful," Jacob replied. "Are the other boys up?"

"An hour or so ago, I think," Reuben said. "We let you sleep. You were so fatigued we thought you could use another little while asleep." He held his hand down for his father. "Come, it'll be time to ride."

"But—the women," Jacob asked. "They—"

"They'll be all right," Reuben reassured him. "Danataya's pains are still well spaced. This could go on a good while yet. She has three experienced midwives looking on, if you count Rachel. Come," he added, helping Jacob to his feet, "we've got work to do. Issachar rode back during the night. He looked over the pass I mentioned last night at the campfire. The clouds opened up for a bit and he had a good look over the terrain. He thinks it's a perfect place to stop them."

"Excellent," Jacob said. And he thought: *A race of kings, all of them. All of them.* He reached for his bow and quiver. But then he happened to look up. . . .

His heart almost stopped. Three archers stood at intervals around the crest of the little hill, their bows drawn. The bronze points of their arrows pointed squarely at him. With a sinking heart, he recognized one of them, a distant cousin of Rachel's. A fourth, more recognizable, figure stepped into view from behind a dense clump of scrub. Reuben started; Jacob held the boy's arm. "Don't make a fuss," he said as five more bowmen moved into view. "Don't make any false moves, any of you. I don't think he means us harm." He looked at the thick figure coming forward. "Hello, Laban," he said. "We've been expecting you—although not quite so early."

"I figured as much," said his father-in-law. His eyes were squinty slits in the pale predawn light. "We rode all night." His mouth was hard, fixed, a thin line. "We have business, you and I."

"I suppose so," Jacob said. "One thing: my son, who was standing watch. Did you . . . ?"

"He isn't hurt," Laban said. "His pride, perhaps. He's a little new at this. Jacob: why? Why did you do this to me?"

Jacob looked around him, seeing the mute frustration on his sons' faces. "Laban," he said. "I have done nothing to you at all. Have your kin look in the flocks. If you can find one sheep, one goat that does not belong in my share of the accounting, you're welcome to it. I've spent twenty years working for you. Fourteen years working off the marriage-price for Leah and Rachel, six years for the pitiful portion that was mine—and in that time you reduced my wages I don't know how many times. You're a hard taskmaster, and I and my sons have served you well. I—"

"Damn you!" Laban said. "Damn your insolence!"

"Let me speak," Jacob said calmly. "You've done most of the talking for twenty years, and during most of that time, I've sat patiently by and let you. Perhaps it's time you did some of the listening. Laban: what is the situation in Haran just now? Be honest with me."

Laban's face went through an extraordinary change. It became suddenly vulnerable. There was fear and despair in it for the first time since Jacob had known him. "Damn it," he said. "You know what the situation is. I've moved the family a day's ride south. We escaped with hardly more than our nightclothes. The world is coming apart. When I left, the nomads were poised to attack, from two sides. The damned city fathers sold us out! Us, who trusted them! Why, Shemariah himself has fled the city. There's no law in Haran now. There's no food either. People are cutting one another's throats for bread. . . ."

"Exactly, Laban. And here we are arguing over nothing. Instead of comforting one another. What a couple of fools we must be." Jacob looked hard into his father-in-law's eyes. "Laban," he said quietly, "these boys you see are flesh of your flesh. Put down the bows. Put up your swords, for the love of heaven. We're a couple of exiles, you and I, and neither of us has a place to lay his head except what we make for ourselves."

Laban looked at him, his face blank. There was a great hurt in his eyes. "Jacob . . ." he said. He stumbled forward, his hands clutching at nothing. Jacob could not read his expression for a moment; then, when he saw the old man's eyes more clearly, he moved to meet Laban. They embraced with a kind of mutual desperation, as they had never done in the twenty years they had known each other.

As they held each other, Jacob could see the men on the hill lower their weapons. His sons looked at one another, puzzlement on their strong young faces. "It will be all right, boys," Jacob said. "He is our father. Honor him."

Laban clutched at him hard, then stepped back to look at him. "Jacob," he said. "I—I have wronged you. Here we are, as you say, and we have nothing, either of us. I . . ."

"It's all right," Jacob said. "Look, we've still got our strength and vigor. We've still got our intelligence. Each of us has strong sons to carry on his line. For heaven's sake, I didn't have that much when I came north to Padan-aram, a fugitive, a ragamuffin without a copper coin to my name. Compared to what I was, I'm a rich man. . . ."

"Jacob," Laban said through tears, "you've got a streak of your grandfather's understanding about you. You're right, you're right. I started as poor as you, a younger son with no portion of my own—and rebellious at that. What I could do as a stripling I can do now. What I lack in vitality I have gained in knowledge. Here, my son. Let there be peace between us. Now and forever. We'll erect a monument here to mark the peace between you and me. . . ."

"Indeed," Jacob said with pleasure. "And we'll consecrate it to the God of my grandfather Abraham. We'll make the sacrifices, and mark it forever as a holy place."

"Yes!" Laban said. There was joy in his face, behind the tears. "Yes. That's what we'll do." He squeezed Jacob's arms. "Jacob, we . . ."

"Hush!" Jacob said suddenly, his body rigid, his head held oddly to one side. "I heard something—Reuben! What was that sound? I heard a cry—quick, go attend Danataya." The boy nodded and took off at a run. "One of our women is expecting a child within hours, perhaps. Her first pains began during the night."

"Wait," Laban said. "Jacob, I don't know about your other young woman—but that's a voice I recognize. Isn't that . . . ?"

But Jacob, his eyes wide, his mouth hanging open, had come to the same conclusion himself. "Laban," he said in a choked voice, "you're right. That—that wasn't Danataya. That was . . ." He cried out wordlessly and set out after his son. "Rachel!" he said. "Rachel!"

Thus it was that both women came to term on the same day, a day that marked a final and poignant peace between enemies of long standing. Laban and Jacob hovered over Rachel as her labor wore on, until the women drove the two of them away. Five hours after her first pains, her water broke, and the pain grew excruciating as the pangs came more quickly, one after the other. And finally, when instead of anguished screams there was silence, Jacob rushed to her side to learn that he had—miracle of miracles!—an eleventh son, a grave-faced little gnome, delicately made and with hair as red as Esau's. Jacob, weeping with joy, was on the verge of suggesting a name—but Rachel, the pride showing in her face through the pallor, spoke first. "Hush," she said. "His name is Joseph. And Jacob—the God has spoken to me, too. He told me I'll have another son for you one of these years. . . ."

Danataya's labor lasted until the sun was high. Then, to the women's surprise, the birth came quickly, almost easily. Almost immediately, Danataya, seeing the raw red thing hanging by its heels from Bilhah's hands, crying lustily, called out for it. "Give it to me!" she said in a hoarse voice. "I want my baby!" And when she first held it to her bosom, she called for Bilhah to wipe her eyes for her. "I have to see—I have to know. . . ."

Then she did know, and a thrill of fierce pride ran through her, and her thoughts cried out proudly to the absent and sorely missed Hadad: *It's a boy! A man-child! And he bears the mark!*

A Child of the Lion!

CHAPTER FIFTEEN

I

In the first days, he refused to work, refused to rebuild his forges and his smelting furnaces. Manouk rejoined the encampment four days after Shobai's branding, and when he learned of Shobai's rebellion, he called for help from the tribes. A chieftain of the second rank sent him a tall, flinty-eyed soldier named Diran, who reported to Manouk in his tent. "You summoned me?" Diran said without ceremony.

"Yes," Manouk said. "There is a new slave. I need his spirit broken, but not his bones."

"I am a warrior," Diran said, bristling. "There is a fight coming. I have no time for the taming of horses, human or otherwise."

"You'll fight soon enough," Manouk said, looking the big man up and down. "Bend this man's will to my use and you'll be in the front ranks when we take Carchemish. Or perhaps Haran, if you prefer."

Diran thought about the matter. "Haran is full of men who escaped from the cities of the northeast," he said. "One of these killed my brother on the day we took Kurkh. It would be a pleasure to send my father a bagful of skulls. His grief has been great."

"Haran it is, then," Manouk said. "But tame me this mustang, as you say. You'll have a command when we take Haran. You'll avenge your brother twenty-fold."

"Huh," Diran said. "All right. I'll do what you want."

Manouk looked at his huge chest and long arms. "Good. I

495

asked for a large man like yourself. The slave is a man almost as big as you are, strong from years of work at the forge. He is an armsmaker, one of such skills that I would have paid him to work. But he changed his mind and smashed his forge. While I was away, it seems Karakin had him beaten and branded. But now he will not work. I want his skills. I want them whole."

"He is that proficient?" Diran said stolidly. "I might have had him killed. I might have done it myself."

"His work falls short of a Hittite's, but not by much," Manouk said. "Look for yourself." He handed over the sword Shobai had made him in the first days of his work with the Shepherd Kings.

Diran held the weapon this way and that, hefting, balancing. "I see," he said. "It is, of course, hard to make a man work if he would rather die than work, and a slave may not work at his best if he has known freedom. . . ."

Manouk smiled his humorless smile and interrupted him smoothly in midsentence. ". . . but a resourceful man will find a way to do the most difficult things if the stakes are high enough. Don't you agree?" There was a hard edge on his tone; he left little room for doubt that the subject was not one he intended to pursue much further.

Diran's eyes narrowed. Manouk was a better bargainer than he had anticipated, with a sure sense of how far to go. "Very well," he said. "I will give you what you want."

"Good," Manouk said. "When you've brought him around, you'll have your command."

Diran saluted him for the first time and went away. Manouk watched him go; then he called Vahan to his side. "Do you think it'll work?"

"No," Vahan said after a moment's thought. "Not as it stands. Shobai has a stubborn streak. I got to know him a bit before he rebelled. Perhaps I can help here. There are times when the bludgeon alone will not work. One approaches such a man with the bludgeon in one hand and a gift in the other."

"Gift?" Manouk said. "I see. You will act friendly to him from time to time. But—perhaps there's more. Perhaps there's something to be retrieved from the inexcusable behavior of my niece, who has disgraced the family. Have her sent here, won't you?"

Vahan's eyes narrowed; but his smile was one of complete understanding. "It will be done as you wish," he said.

* * *

The assistants they had given Shobai when he had first come to work for the Shepherd Kings had made careful mental notes of the procedures involved in the construction of the multiple forges and smelting furnaces he had built. Now they were busy rebuilding the structures he had destroyed. The first one they had rebuilt, Shobai had destroyed again before he could be subdued; now, until better disposal could be made of him, he sat in the sun, knees up under his chin, one ankle raw from the chafing of the manacle which encircled it. The chain attached to it stretched behind him to a heavy metal stake driven deep into the earth. His beard was unkempt and filthy, his eyes red-rimmed from lack of sleep. He paced naked during the day around his tether, in all weather, sunburned, half-starved, dirty. At night he curled into a fetal ball like an animal, trying desperately to sleep as he shivered. Once a day, they placed food barely within his reach and scurried away before he could get his big hands on them. Failing to catch them, he hurled curses after the men who fed him.

He was learning a bit more of the language now, if only to have a common tongue to curse them in. To his grim amusement, the tongue of the Shepherd Kings contained a greater variety of insults, obscenities, and abuse than any he had ever encountered; in a common garden-variety nomad curse, the gods were called upon to aid in incestuous couplings, anatomical impossibilities, the crudest kind of bestiality. This was the point from which one began to improvise.

After dark, before fatigue came upon him at last, he took advantage of darkness to stand, bent-legged, over the stake which held his chain and to worry at it, trying to turn it, move it, dislodge it. So far, driven deep into the hard and tenacious ground, it had resisted all his efforts to loosen it. So far he had not given up hope. So far . . .

One day, sleeping well into the morning after a night spent in fruitless grunting and sweating over the stake, he awoke with a start as a booted foot smashed into his ribs. He came instantly awake with a snarl and reached for the ankle attached to the offending foot. The ankle in hand, he sank his still-strong teeth into the intruder's leg.

There was a satisfying scream of rage, and a great fist smashed into his temple, knocking him flat again. Instantly, he was on all fours, getting his feet under him; with a growl of animal rage he charged, catching the newcomer at waist level and driving him back, back—only to come up short as his chain stretched tight, dropped him on his face, and a sharp pain shot through his ankle.

Pushing himself up onto his hands, he could look up now and see the newcomer: big, strongly built, lean with a fighter's trim. Sizing up his adversary, he stood erect now, looking at the man who stood just past the reach of his chain. A crafty look on his filthy face, Shobai backed up until he stood with feet straddling the deep-driven stake. "What's the matter, pig-raper?" he said in a voice dripping with contempt. "Afraid to step inside this little circle?" Cursing himself for his forgetfulness, he repeated the insult in a pidgin version of the nomad tongue, gesturing insultingly as he did.

"Time to go to work," the newcomer said. "Back to the forge." The statements were maddeningly matter-of-fact, as if the hiatus since Shobai's last day at labor had been a day or two. "You've lain around long enough."

"Go make love to your father," Shobai said—and again realized he had spoken in his own tongue. Flustered, he struggled with a translation of the phrase into the nomad language. The words wouldn't come; he gritted his teeth and settled for "No. Won't work. No more work. You—you go die."

"Very well," the newcomer said. He reached at his belt for a long, braided whip, which he proceeded to uncoil before him. Shobai, his eyes mere slits, stepped behind the stake and increased the distance between him and the stranger. He dodged to the left and right, feinting, weaving.

It was no good. The stranger cocked the whip back over his head and let fly. With a tremendous *crack!* it licked out at his face and opened a cut over his eye. Blood dripped into the socket, obscuring his vision. He reached up and felt the wound; a flap of skin hung loose where the whip's weighted tip had landed.

Again the lash sang out; this time it slashed at his naked chest, breaking the skin. He bobbed, ducked—but the man wielding the whip was faster than he, more experienced. The lash could even lick around his body and land with piercing stabs of pain on his bare back. And when the fifth lash whipped out at him, it wound around his neck, choking him, dragging him down. His hands clawed at the leather thongs wrapped so tightly around his neck; he couldn't breathe—his eyes grew dim; he fell to the ground, his legs suddenly too weak to hold his weight. . . .

When he awoke, the sun was low in the western sky; the wind had changed direction, and there was a distinct chill in the air. In the northern sky there were clouds—rain clouds. Some of them lay almost overhead. He shivered, hugging his goose-pimpled arms—and cried out suddenly in pain and exasperation at the sharp tinges from the several wounds the lash had made on his face and body. *The filthy bastard,* he thought. *Just let him get within reach again, just once. I'll kill him.*

He looked around. It was long past time for the servants to throw him his usual evening's portion of spoiled food, scraps from the campfire. Were they going to starve him now? Well, all the better. Eventually they'd kill him, and he'd be free of it all. But until then he had every intention of making their lives as miserable as he could, and if there were the bare outside chance of his killing one of them, he'd not hesitate for so much as a moment.

The sky darkened further. He sat down on the cold ground, feeling the hard-packed clay lumpy and painful under his bare buttocks. Now the first drops of rain began to fall, and without further warning there was a deafening thunderclap, and a monstrous bolt of lightning clove the sky from one side to the other, shattering into a dozen streaks. Fear sent shock waves through his body, and before he could stop himself, he cried aloud. Lightning was something he'd feared as a child, and even now a thunderstorm could unman him, sending him in a moment's passing back to a condition of quivering, childish panic.

"N-no," he said under his breath. The rain picked up; the big drops became a flood, battering him. A wind suddenly blew from east to west; the sheets of blinding raindrops became a force that drove him backward until the chain pulled painfully at his leg. And yet another ear-shattering blast of thunder pealed forth, and the sky became as bright as day for the barest ghost of a moment. He cringed, pulling helplessly away from the stake in the middle of his tether— and now, suddenly, he remembered something his father had told him: metal tended to draw the fire from the sky, to attract it. And here he was, with a metal chain around his ankle binding him to a metal stake. "No!" he cried out in a broken voice. "No, please—please. . . ."

The rain was a full-fledged storm now. It drummed on the tent roofs, audibly; puddles became rivulets, rivulets became little streams. When Shobai moved, panic-stricken, away from the stake, stretching his chain to full length, his foot slipped on clay suddenly become sticky, slippery mud; he fell painfully on his back, on the half-healed wound the whip had made; he cried out again in a voice soiled as much by abject fear as by pain. . . .

. . . and then, suddenly, he looked up and saw a figure standing in front of him, and his hatred cast out his fear and discomfort for a moment, and he squinted through the rain, trying to judge how far away the figure stood. He'd just leap forward and grab the bastard by the throat, and hang on come what may.

But now a shock of recognition ran through him. The figure was slim, slight. The bare feet poking out from under the blankets were the delicate feet of a woman, not a man. He peered through the darkness and rain at the hooded face, at the great bulk the figure bore in its heavy-laden arms. And then lightning struck again, and although he cringed again, he could see who it was that stood before him. The figure held something out to him: a great thick rug of some sort, made from an animal's hide, with the fur still on it. "S-Sayda," he said. "Sayda . . . wait. . . ."

But then the next flash, bursting close by, drove him to his knees again. He covered his ears against the clap of thunder that followed it. And when he opened them again, blinking through the driving rain, the girl was gone. At his feet was the heavy animal skin. With a sigh that was close to a groan he clutched at it, held it to his chest. And, shivering uncontrollably, he wrapped it around him and curled up on a high point of land as far from his anchor-stake as he could get, feeling the pounding of rain on the slick side of the hide as he covered all of himself, head and all, with the fur and huddled under it, listening to the ferocious onslaught of the storm until fatigue at last drew him down to healing sleep.

II

In the morning, they shook him awake, rolling him out of the fur and yanking it away from him. Emerging from the first deep sleep he'd had in days, he was lethargic, muddle-headed; the fact saved the two men who uncovered him a broken bone or two, and the best he could manage was muttered curses. Then he was alone again. . . .

The morning was clear and more than a little chilly. Shobai, by now, had learned to ignore the cold, to divert his thoughts into other channels. There was a way, too, in which nakedness was possibly a healthier state in his present condition than rags would have been. Wet clothing took a long time to dry and left you chilled to the bone. Now, damp from the wet mud they had rolled him over into, he found the sun dried his body quickly. He even thought briefly of rolling in the mud again, to see if a layer of dried clay on his body would keep him warm; but in the end he found the warming rays of the sun too comforting to pursue this idea.

To Shobai's surprise, he also found, in spite of lumps and bruises, that he felt better than he had felt in quite some time—perhaps since his imprisonment had begun. He was unable to account for this until it occurred to him to remember how the fur had come to him in the first place. Sayda!

He sat on the ground now and thought of her. As the memories of their earlier times together came back to him, he felt for the first time like weeping. She was the first good thing that had happened to him since—since when? It had been quite a long time. He racked his brains, and to his surprise he could not easily call to mind a time in the past when he had been happy—except for the nights when Sayda had come to his bed, back before his branding and confinement.

Yes! There'd been something simple and unaffected about their relationship. Something warm and uncomplicated, with none of the usual sparring and face-saving and calculating that had gone on with the women before her. She'd simply come to him and given of herself freely and fearlessly, trusting him to treat her well. And he—he had responded in kind, he who had never even had such a relationship with his own wife, much less the dozens of lovers he'd taken while away from her. And somehow, the giving he himself had done, the tender care he'd taken in his lovemaking with Sayda back in those days when they didn't know three words of each other's language—it had done something for him too. He'd felt like a different person, more human, more vulnerable, more—well, more emotionally alive.

Now he looked with new eyes at the passing parade, at the men and women of the camp who came and went, ignoring him. He recalled the people of Haran, of Carchemish, of the other cities where he'd worked, and he saw them in his mind's

501

eye, fresh and new, as if he'd never seen them before. Perhaps he hadn't, really. He'd thought them inferiors, people beneath his notice, as faceless as so many ants grubbing away in an anthill for a mean and comfortless living, breeding and dying meaninglessly.

He closed his eyes and pondered, sifting through the insights that were coming upon him now. Yes! It had been his own life that was meaningless, not theirs. All that time, those people had had something important and powerful that his own shallow way of life had denied him. They'd *cared* about one another. They'd loved, and grown involved with each other, *really* involved. They'd trusted. And it had enriched their lives. And he? What had he had all that time that could make up for the thing those faceless people had had? He'd had baubles, and a pretty wife who didn't give a damn about him, and a richly appointed but empty house that felt about as much like a home as a . . .

What a fool he'd been all those years!

Well, he thought, *you were your father's son, weren't you? Even if you were never a patch on him as a metalworker.* Kirta had been a cold man, lost in his work most of the time. Shobai's relations with him had been as shallow as all his other relationships had been. Quite possibly, little Hadad hadn't remembered much about his father at all. But no: Hadad remembered his father with love, while he, Shobai . . .

Love.

The word seemed strange and new. *That* was what his life had lacked. Not just the love of others, the love people might have borne him, Shobai, if he had been kinder and more open to them. What he had lacked was the love he should have felt for others, shown for others. There had been no giving of himself, ever. Not to Anat, not to his family, not to anyone.

He sighed and blinked back bitter tears. If only one could call time back, relive those days knowing what he knew now! If only he could have a second chance. If only he could revisit those empty years and somehow put love into them. If only he could make up to the people he'd cheated of his love, of himself, for his neglect of them. . . .

How strange it was, that he should learn this now, learn it from a brief contact with a girl whose language was opaque to him! His eyes opened suddenly as he sat erect. Opaque? he thought. Why, perhaps it was the very fact that they *couldn't* communicate in words then that had forced upon him the necessity of communicating by other, perhaps better means. . . .

He sighed again. Here she was, defying authority, risking a beating for him! For him, Shobai, who didn't deserve the tenth part of what she had given him!

And—here a sob shook his big body—it was all too late. Too late . . .

In the late morning, a shadow fell across him. He looked up to see Vahan standing over him. The red rage boiled up in him again, as it did virtually every time one of the nomads moved within reach of his long arms, and he tensed to spring—but then he felt, rather than saw, the difference between Vahan's relaxed stance and the guarded stances of the men who had preceded him. He sat back, leaning against the stake to which he was tethered, and looked up at the nomad warrior. "Vahan," he said in a weary voice. "What . . . you want of me?"

"Ah," the nomad said. "You've learned a bit of our language by now." Shobai realized with a start that he could understand Vahan with ease. It came as a surprise because, from the time he had begun to learn the new tongue in earnest, he had had little or no direct communication with anyone except through the medium of mutual cursing. "Shobai," Vahan said in a voice in which Shobai could make out a certain concern, "it pains me to see you this way. You look like a half-starved lion in a pen."

"Not much to eat," Shobai agreed, tight-lipped. "Not much comfort." He looked up, fire in his eyes. "You—you understand," he said, groping for the words. "Not matter. Not matter with me. Soon I die. Or—soon I escape. Maybe somebody catch me and kill me. Not matter."

"But it does matter," Vahan said. It was curious: in his own language Vahan was a different man. Thoughtful; perhaps even cultivated, in his way. "It matters a great deal. I hate to see this happening to you." His sigh was real, heartfelt. "Particularly since I hold myself in part responsible for what happened to you. The trip to Melid—I thought . . ."

"Not matter," Shobai said. "Forget it. Not—not blame self. Nothing matter."

"Shobai, Shobai," Vahan said. "You mustn't lose heart. You mustn't just give up like this. Don't you see? All you have to do is give in a little. What is it, after all? Just a bunch of banging on metal. Do that much—give in to them no more

503

than that—and I'll see you free again, clothed and fed and with the run of the camp."

"No!" Shobai snarled bitterly. *"Not* just . . . bang on metal. Is—is making things to kill. To kill my kin, my people."

Vahan shrugged. "Haran will fall whether you make the weapons that conquer it or not. Who is to say you will have had a part in that? Who is to reproach you?"

"Me!" Shobai spat out. "Me! *I* . . . reproach me. So nobody else know. *I* know." He shot a resentful glance up at the nomad warrior. "Please," he said. "You . . . not ask this of me. . . ."

"Shobai. It's the principle of the thing. Do you understand? It's not the weapons. Make them badly if you like. Give it only a tenth of your attention. But the thing that keeps you here tethered like an animal, naked in all weather, with nothing to eat—it's the principle. They won't have you defying them. They won't have you refusing to work."

"Not matter," Shobai said stubbornly. "Have . . . own principle. Not work." He looked up, anger in his eyes. "Why they not kill me? Eh? Why not?"

"Shobai, they will," Vahan said. "Soon enough. You haven't much time to come around. Do you know what the disposition of the armies is now?"

"Not know. Not matter."

"Yes, it *does,* damn it! You listen to me! We're poised to fall on Haran like wolves on the flock. The only thing that holds us up is a religious holiday coming up. Tomorrow is a festival day among our people, and we do not fight on the festival day. There'll be a feast, and games and dancing—and on festival days it's our custom to be generous and forgiving whenever possible. A tribal leader will often grant a boon on a festival day that he will refuse on another day. If you've come around by tomorrow, even just a little bit—if you've unbent, and agreed to work at the forge, by then—they'll let up on you."

"Hah!" Shobai snorted. "And—if not?"

Vahan sighed again, a deep and exasperated one. "Shobai, do you know what it'll be like here tomorrow? The tribes will gather here. They'll pull back from the battle lines, leaving only token guards there before Carchemish and Haran. They'll all come, as many of them as possible. Tens of thousands of our people will celebrate together. They will hear of you. And here you'll be, chained like an animal. Like a bear in a pit. They'll pelt you with stones and dung. They'll

504

sic their dogs on you. I don't guarantee they won't kill you, and pretty horribly at that. Just for fun, Shobai: for sport. Particularly after they've been drinking. Have you ever seen a bearbaiting?" He winced as he said it. "Shobai. You'll be the bear. Shobai! I'm talking about tomorrow! Do you understand? Tomorrow!"

Shobai looked at him, his eyes full of loathing. "Not matter, Vahan," he said sourly. "Understand? Not . . . matter. Better to die soon than later."

Vahan waved his balled fists impotently in the air. "Gods!" he said. "How do I go about talking sense to him?"

"Vahan," Shobai said, suddenly calm. "I . . . want to die. You . . . understand. *Want* to die. You . . . think I want to live . . longer than cities I betray?" His voice was patient, almost lifeless. "Day after festival," he said, "what happen then? Haran die. Right? My brother die then? My mother? Yes? Then why *I* live still? Why *I* live, who help kill Haran?" He let the breath out in a shuddering motion. "No good, Vahan. You go tell Manouk. Tell him kill me slow, kill me fast. But kill me before he kill Haran."

"Shobai—"

"You go, Vahan. I . . . forgive. You not . . . bad man. But I not do what you say. You tell Manouk."

Vahan, a great hurt in his eyes, looked at him for some time before speaking. Shobai saw intelligence, compassion in his eyes—and, by and by, understanding of a sort. "All right," he said in a quiet voice. "I won't bother you any more. The gods protect you, Shobai. I wish you and I had known each other in better times, better circumstances. I think we might have been friends. But, you've made your choice. I respect it. I won't try to talk you out of it. I—I have to say I even understand it, and sympathize with it. If it were my family in Haran, I might . . ." He let the words trail off. "Good-bye, Shobai." He nodded gravely and turned on one heel, smart and military. Shobai watched him go, and there was more than a little regret in his own feelings as Vahan marched out of his life forever.

At dusk, they put out water for him—but no food. He shrugged, drank. He had been waiting all day for Diran, the big soldier who had whipped him the day before, to appear. But since Vahan's departure no one had approached him. Perhaps this meant that their tormenting of him had ended— until the festival day commenced and he became the bear in the pit, the target of anyone, large or small, old or young, drunk or sober, who had access to a weapon or a rock, or who owned a dog.

He rose and looked around him. For the first time in his life, he almost wished he were a religious man, a man who believed in the rich and slightly foolish pantheon of gods who governed the gullible in Padan-aram. If he had been, he could be occupying his time now—and perhaps putting his mind at ease to some extent—by undergoing some version of the common purification rituals one underwent when one knew one was going to die. For the first time, he could comprehend the need to impose order on the disorderly and otherwise meaningless experience called death; he could understand the need for belief in a power, an order, a system larger than oneself.

As night fell, he found himself alone. Out of habit he went to the stake and worried at it, struggling, pulling, pushing; but before he did so, he knew it would not budge. The clay had dried after the rain harder than before. The moon rose; he sat looking up at it . . .

. . . and suddenly saw, standing before him, the slight form of Sayda, silent and solemn, her eyes large in the moonlight. As before, she carried a bundle of furs; but this time she came closer, as though to speak. "Sayda," he said, rising. And he almost hesitated before reaching out for her, naked and filthy animal that he had become. But she ignored his hesitation, his reluctance, and rushed into his arms; and the feel of her, crushed against him, came as such a shock to him that he found himself shaking, weeping, sobbing as his love-starved arms held her close and his eager hands roamed over her narrow back, cupped her firm little buttocks, rubbed her gently curving hips. "Sayda," he said. "I—oh, thank the gods you've come to me. Oh, gods, gods . . ."

Now she was speaking for the first time in a tongue he understood. "Shobai," she said. "I had to come. I don't care what they do to me. I—I don't know what will happen tomorrow. Vahan told me about his talk with you. But—I had to come to you. I have to have this night with you. . . ."

Her voice, soft and gentle and alive with emotion, was so dear to him it took the breath out of him. "Sayda," he said. "I must do . . . what I say to Vahan. Must do. But . . ." The sigh that escaped him was more like a shudder than a sigh; it shook his whole body. He turned her lovely face up to him and kissed it, kissed her eyes and cheeks and, again and again, her soft and eager lips. And words would not come to him; there were no words for what he felt.

"Here, my darling," she said, handing him one of the furs. "Oh, gods—the feel of you, so hard and lean and strong—and always so gentle with me. I've missed you so, my own—oh, Shobai, take me, take me now." She stepped back suddenly, untied a drawstring; the robe fell to her feet.

Under a full and velvet-toned moon, the soft evening breeze caressing them, they sank down onto the furs at their feet, and they embraced in the grip of a passion neither of them had ever felt in such strength before. The great void which the absence of hope had left in Shobai seemed suddenly filled with a new, disturbing, and infinitely precious commodity; and as their bodies merged, he *knew* what it was, knew without words in his heart of hearts. In that moment, giving himself up entirely to the new emotion, letting it fill him, permeate him, and flow from him to her, Shobai knew for the first time, on the brink of death, what life was, what it was to be a human being, to be a man.

"I love you," he said. And after a lifetime spent saying the empty words to strangers, to ciphers, he said the words from the heart, to a partner who would be in his heart, in his soul, for the rest of his life. They meant something now; they meant everything, everything. Death, and the morrow, seemed infinitely far away, and the moment and the rapture they shared as a single soul were all that mattered. "I love you," he heard himself saying again and again. . . .

III

The moon was high above the army encampment before Carchemish, where Oshiyahu, now field commander of Hagirum's army, had set up his first line of defense for the beleaguered city. The sky was clear, and the commander, standing atop one of the tall lookout posts Shobai had ordered built when he armed the city, could see quite some distance across the barren wastes that separated the attacking force from his own lines. Puzzled, he called for the captain of the guard.

The order went down the ladder and along the line with lightning speed; it was hardly more than a matter of moments before the commander heard footsteps on the ladder and turned to see standing before him an officer in battle dress. There was something vaguely familiar about the man—and then, as the truth dawned on him, he realized that the only unfamiliar thing about the officer was the uniform. "You?" he said, his eyes narrowing. "You, Danel? This is a surprise."

"Yes, sir," the young officer said, stiffening his back to ramrod straightness and holding his face expressionless. "When I lost my commission, I resigned from the Army of Haran and went to work for Carchemish. At reduced rank, of course. But I've risen two ranks since I enlisted."

"Ah," the commander said, looking him over. "I'm pleased to hear it. And I'm not too surprised. You always had the makings of a damned fine soldier."

"I'm glad the commander thinks so, sir."

"Stand easy, son. You don't have to stay at attention for me. This isn't the parade ground."

"Yes, sir." Relaxation was a microscopic easing of the rigid stance; but his face allowed itself the faintest trace of expression. Oshiyahu still could not read it, though.

"I'll say this once and then we can forget it," the commander said matter-of-factly. "When the troops are ready to move, all debts are paid. Do you understand? No hard feelings on this end. The tablet's wiped clean. I won't be judging you on the old days, but on the new ones."

The young man's face relaxed rather more. "Thank you, sir. And—there's no bitterness on this end. There was at first: it was natural, I suppose. But then I began to see, starting afresh here, just how far I'd slipped at Haran. It was all for the best, sir. I've profited from the experience."

"Splendid," Oshiyahu said. "Now that we've got that over with, let's be easy with each other. We've a battle to win. Has the runner come back yet?"

"No, sir. But I'm to be notified the moment he's spotted."

"Good. I hope he gets back. On an assignment like that, a scout's life isn't worth much. I presume you've got a good man out there."

"The best, sir. Another from the old Haran army. A fellow named Hoshaiah."

"Ahh," Oshiyahu said, and his tone bespoke satisfaction. "I see you haven't lost your eye for soldiering. You're right, he's the best we've got. He may be the best anybody's got." His tone took on a reflective air. "Funny. His was the first report we ever received on the Shepherd Kings—the first worthwhile one, anyway. It was an absolute model of a scout's report. And here he is, in at the end—"

He cut himself off and glanced sharply at Danel, but his subordinate had caught his meaning all too quickly. "Sir—then you think it *is* the end?"

"What do *you* think?" Oshiyahu said, looking out over the wall to sweep the long, long line of campfires facing them. "Look at that. And you know our strength as well as I do, I'll warrant."

"Hmm. Yes, sir. Well, one doesn't want to think in those terms, but eventually it comes down to that, doesn't it?" His sigh was almost inaudible; Oshiyahu felt it more than he heard it. "Well, it's our job. When it comes time, I'll sell my own skin very, very dearly, I think."

"Right. I—Oh, but here comes your man up the stairs. Let's make room for him."

But it was not the guardsman who joined them atop the rampart. It was the scout himself, in plain drab unmilitary garments, his face blackened, his only sidearm a dagger in a stained scabbard. "Hoshaiah reporting, sir." His stance was military without being stiff; he was at peace with himself, and with soldiering.

"Good to see you, son. Report."

"Well, sir, it appears they've halved their strength for the night. Almost precisely half the force in the forward unit has withdrawn to the base camp. The other half will replace them, like a watch changing, tomorrow night. . . ."

"Ah." Oshiyahu traded sharp glances with Danel. "Hmm. And I'll bet you haven't just learned that much and then come back, have you?" He half smiled, saying this.

"No, sir. My curiosity got the best of me."

"Good, good . . ."

"Right, sir. And unless somebody changes things again, I think I have something like the battle plan."

"Ah. And you got this by . . . ?"

"By slipping through and—well, abducting one of their officers." He half frowned, pursed his lips, and continued. "I picked a little chap, I'm afraid. No time for a protracted fight, you understand, sir, and besides he was easier to carry back out with me."

"You *carried* him through the lines?" Danel said incredulously. "With a heavy guard on duty over there?"

"Well, yes, sir. He was out cold or I'd never have been able

509

to do it. And—well, I got him as far as the bank of the stream before deciding I couldn't get him safely across that. So I went to work on him. I'm afraid I got my knife a bit dirty, sir, but I got some information."

Oshiyahu was beaming now. "Yes, go on."

"Very well, sir. It appears there's some sort of religious festival—it begins at sunup. It'll continue until sunup on the day after tomorrow. It's the usual sort of thing: kick up your heels for a day and get it out of your system, and dedicate your hangover to the great god Whoever. Halving the watch allows each unit to get in half a day of drinking and rutting. And then, sir, on the following day, the plan is for the eastern arm of the attack force to move against Haran while the western arm attacks Carchemish. Haran is expected to fall first; then the eastern forces will come over and reinforce the army attacking Carchemish. The man I questioned doesn't know the hour; just the day." He thought a moment, then said, "I think that's it, sir. My memory's usually better than this. But—I had to cut it out of him, one little strip at a time, if you'll pardon the metaphor. I'm a little queasy."

"You've done well," Oshiyahu said. "Very well. If we ever get out of this mess alive, I'll have you up for decoration and a raise in pay." He clapped the young man on one rock-hard bicep. "Now run along and get some rest; you've earned it. That's an order. While you're at it, draw a ration of palm wine. It'll calm your stomach, take it from me. I had to do something like that when I was your age, and it does tend to linger in your head a bit if you let it. Don't let it. That's an order. Get me?"

"Yes, sir!" Hoshaiah said. He withdrew and went down the ladder double-time.

Oshiyahu looked Danel in the eye. "He's a good man. But—are you thinking what I'm thinking just now?"

"I wouldn't be surprised, sir. If they're at half strength, and if they don't know that we know it ... well, I think I'd hit them tonight, with everything I had."

"Good, good ... we ought to be able to do some damage, as much to their morale as to anything. We'll hit them hard and quick—and then get the hell out of there. Hack a bunch of throats, set a bunch of fires—and then get home before they can haul in emergency reinforcements from the base camp." He set his jaw and shook his head, just once. "It'll be costly. We'll lose some men. Even half strength, they outnumber us many times over. We can only do it once, too. By tomorrow night they'll be expecting us. Our only chance now depends upon surprise."

"Right, sir. And sir—you mentioned morale. . . ."

"Yes indeed. Our thoughts run together again. We've a raw, green army, not blooded as yet. Best way to get their toes wet when it comes to battle is to give them an introductory sortie in which they have some chance of success. Make 'em feel good, confident. Get 'em used to killing—and to the sight of seeing their own people fall, too. All the difference in the world between seeing your neighbor die in a battle you've won and seeing it in a battle you've lost."

"Right, sir. And then when the real attack does come, they'll face it better. Good for the backbone."

"We understand each other. You'll be my second-in-command in this. Very well. Now go down and assemble the commanders, as quietly as possible. I'll give 'em a talking to—and then we'll go over—oh, when the moon is high."

"Yes, sir. And—thank you, sir."

"No thanks about it. Look, there's only one thing that pleases an old warhorse like myself more than seeing a new hand prove himself, and that's watching a good soldier who's, well, gone away for a bit and come back. Like yourself. There was a time when I could count on you, and then there was a time when I couldn't."

"Yes, sir. And now?"

"See this arm? I broke it in battle once. My squad leader set it for me—expertly. When it had healed, it was twice as strong as it had been before." He cuffed it with the other hand, roughly. "Now? Now you couldn't break it with an iron mace made by a Hittite. I think you've put yourself back together again, and I think you'll be the better soldier for the experience."

"Yes, sir. I'll make certain that your confidence is well placed."

"Do that. Now—get going! You've work to do."

"Yes, sir!"

Now he was alone on the high perch; but for some reason he could not easily define, he found himself lingering, looking out over the vast forest of blinking campfires in the distance. *Let's see,* he thought. *Multiply each one of those by five hundred men, say . . . and then halve the result . . .* He shivered. Suddenly, he thought of the crooklegged little sculptor, riding off alone toward the enemy lines, unarmed, looking at one and the same time pitiably ridiculous and sublimely heroic, and there was a sudden catch in his throat. He coughed it away. *Poor devil . . . he'll be dead now, lying in a ditch with his throat cut. But gods! what a gesture. . . .*

And here he was, perhaps less heroic but no less ridiculous, riding into the lion's mouth the same damned way. What a way to end a career!

But no—his men would be coming back to camp tonight victorious—some of them at any rate. It would be a costly raid, but in the end—when the final, big battle came—they'd be able to face it knowing they'd made a fight of it and even had appeared to be winning for a while—if you didn't look too closely.

But there was no doubt about it: the end was not far away. The day after the festival, the enemy would sweep down on Carchemish like a pack of wild dogs trapping a rabbit. The end, when it came, would be the farthest thing possible from the glorious strutting and parading a young fool enlisted to do. It would be brutal, and bloody, and grubby, and in the end undignified and degrading. His men would be hacked to pieces.

He gritted his teeth and pounded with one fist on the wall. All the more reason to hit them hard tonight. As hard as possible! And then die the best way you could.

Of course, there was a small chance that they would win. Not much of one. If his men could demoralize half the enemy camp, maybe when the attack came, they'd be able to hold out a bit longer—but, of course, that depended on Haran's putting up some sort of defense and delaying the reinforcement of the line in front of Carchemish. There wasn't much chance of that—but if Haran could hold for a day, say, or perhaps two . . .

Bah! False hopes! And when the Haran force joined the force before Carchemish, and the two wings of the nomad army then attacked in combined force . . . ? He shuddered—then put the thought from his mind. Fight 'em one day at a time, that was the only way to handle it. . . .

As raids go, it was a tremendous success. The element of surprise worked flawlessly, and when they went into the enemy camp they hacked their way, screaming and snarling, all the way to the line of tents. There they came face to face with the full strength of their adversaries, who were terrible to behold: strong, tenacious, fierce, and fearless fighters. Oshiyahu's troops retreated a ways—but they left a trail of nomad bodies behind for every rod of ground they lost. Then they found their footing and counterattacked, driving the nomads back toward their tents again. Advance troops from Danel's command reached the tents and fired them, panicking the nomads' horses and causing great confusion and consternation in the enemy ranks. The nomads fell back even farther, trying to save the animals—and then Oshiyahu, grinning savagely, ordered a strategic retreat to his own lines.

On their way back through the enemy's camp, his men slaughtered all the stragglers they could find; then they double-timed back to their own lines. Once inside their own circle of fires, they laughed, wept, danced with joy. They had fought like men, like heroes. They had hurt the enemy, and badly. They had faced up to death and stared it down; and, poor devils, they thought this meant they could face everything, anything. Their officers sighed—and did not disabuse them of the notion. Instead, they turned to the accounting of their own dead and missing. . . .

To Oshiyahu's regret, one of the latter was Danel. He had led the first unit to go into the evening camp. Men who had fought alongside him said he had fought like three men and killed like a giant among men, charged like an immortal, like a man without fear. He had, in the end, held off a full squad of nomads long enough to let his men fire the tents—and then he had fallen, still fighting like the gallant soldier he was. At the telling of this, Oshiyahu wept; but his tears were the tears of a man whose sadness was alloyed with an almost fatherly pride. "Let us honor him," he said in a husky voice, "and remember him when our own time comes. Perhaps we can meet our own ends with his name on our lips and with a touch of his valor in our hearts." He turned to his officers, new vigor in his voice. "Yes," he said. "Pass the word around. We may go into battle again in a day's time. When we do, we will have a new battle cry." He almost spat the word out in his newfound pride and anger. "Danel! The word is Danel!"

IV

In the night Shobai half awoke to find himself holding her so close they were like one person, her warm naked flesh—nestled, like his, under the heavy furs—pressed so close to his that the smallest motion realigned the whole of both their bodies. His heart suddenly filled to bursting with emotions too strong to classify; he kissed her neck and moved to embrace her—and felt a sharp pain in his ankle as he pulled the chain taut.

His chest shook with a sob of rage and anguish. He rolled back to where he had been, and, half-asleep, she threw one warm arm over him. The arm moved again; its fingers moved over his body; she kissed his shoulder, and slowly, tantalizingly, climbed atop him. They embraced again, under the furs, and gave themselves over to something that, this time, drew more on sensuality than on passion. When the climax came, it grew slowly and built in intensity until, in the end, it came to both of them at precisely the same moment. The gentle dream became starbursts and shivery feelings and then, little by little, a retreat once again into gentle dreaming; fulfilled, their hearts full, they slipped off easily into gentle darkness. Sleep caught Shobai in the middle of the murmured word "love." ...

Pain in his head. Sudden pain in his chest. Bright lights. Sudden freezing cold. And the softness, the warmth, the gentle touch of her flesh suddenly ripped away from him. ...

He blinked, rolled over, got on all fours, blinked again. He rubbed his eyes and tried to look around. ...

She was struggling, little and naked and weak and defenseless, in the arms of a nomad soldier. His face was vaguely familiar; his expression was one of icy rage. He was bellowing at her in the nomad tongue as she struggled. Shobai wiped his eyes again and tried to make out what they were saying as he struggled unsteadily to his feet.

"... said nothing? You mean he didn't agree? He didn't give in? After a night of ... ?"

514

The girl spat out the words. "I didn't ask him! What kind of—of animal do you think I am?" She twisted around and slammed him hard in the groin with her elbow. "Let me go!"

"You!" Shobai howled in a fearsome voice, the tigerish rage welling up in his throat. "You, Diran! You take hands off! Let girl go!" He strained against the chain, stretched his long arm out toward them; but he could not reach them. The growl in his throat became a sob of impotent hatred. He looked around for something to throw; he went back to the stake and pulled at it, grunting and sweating with the effort even in the morning's chill. Only then did he become aware of the other soldiers, standing there, chuckling at him, staring at the girl's nakedness. "Dog-lovers!" he screamed. "Pig-molesters!"

". . . made a bargain, you little bitch. You'll learn what we do to people who give their word and then break it. . . ." Diran's hand grabbed her long hair and held her head; his other hand, a great paw, backhanded her across the face, hard. It snapped her head back and bloodied her nose. Shobai once again rushed them, a snarl in his throat, and again the chain pulled him up short. There was blood on his ankle now. He dived forward, fell on his face, extending his body and his long arms to their fullest length—and his fingers closed on Diran's ankle. He yanked, mightily, and pulled the nomad warrior down to the ground—but one booted foot lashed out and caught him in the face, forcing him to let go. Diran stood, his hand still in the girl's hair, and hauled her to her feet. Then, as Shobai was rising to his knees, he kicked him in the temple again, knocking him down. Shobai's roll again pulled the chain taut and sent a stabbing pain through his leg; he cried out as much in frustrated rage as in pain.

Diran pulled the girl back out of reach. "Bitch!" he said, yanking at her hair, turning her this way and that. "Break your word to me, will you?"

She cried out in pain, but found voice to tell him: "Give your—your word to a dog and—and there's no shame in—in breaking it . . . oh! Oh, stop! Stop!"

He hit her again, this time with his fist, and Shobai dived after them again—and, yet one more time, came up short. Sobbing, cursing, he watched Diran haul her away, down the row of tents, his hand yanking her along by the hair, her little head bent low, her feet stumbling, her little fists pounding away at him impotently. . . .

Now the camp was filling with newcomers. These, he thought, would be visitors from the encampments before Haran and Carchemish. It wasn't long after dawn, yet they'd already begun drinking. Fights broke out; apparently, however, the new troops had had to leave their arms at the gate, and combat between brothers-in-arms became a matter of fist and claw and booted foot.

Some of them took notice of him, too. He was cut and bleeding in a dozen places from a rock-throwing game they'd played an hour before. But when he hadn't cried out for mercy, they'd lost interest. Particularly when the whores showed up and set up their little tents in the middle of the parade ground. He could see the lines forming, growing; fights broke out in the line before one woman's tent, and she stepped out herself, naked except for bangles and a necklace, and cursed them. The crowd howled with laughter.

There was music now, from somewhere. Aimless little tunes that went nowhere, played on some sort of whining shawm whose nasal tones carried a long way. A drum beating behind it, and some sort of stringed instrument tinkling. He could see a young woman dancing down the way, her breasts half-covered by round bronze plates held to her chest by little chains, the bottom half of her body grossly, obscenely naked, her belly undulating in an unbelievable rhythm. As Shobai watched, one hairy hand reached out and grabbed her ankle, hauling her to the ground. There was another roar of laughter. . . .

The sun rose higher in the sky. Shobai sat on the hard ground, his chin on his knees, glaring at them. One of his eyes was half-closed from a bruise; he'd lost a tooth to the rock-throwers. He felt a great hatred brewing in his heart, and he tried not to think of Sayda and of what must have happened to her—if only because he could do nothing about it.

When the sun was high, Diran came to him, soldiers flanking him to the right and left. They bore not swords, but cudgels. Shobai stood, his eyes flashing, his lip curled back over the broken tooth. "Come on," he invited them. "Fight me! Who fight me first? You, son of a dog? You, pig-face?" He beckoned contemptuously to them. "Come kill me! You, Diran? Come! Not be afraid! Not piss for fear! Come!"

Diran ignored him. "Subdue him. I don't care how. Then pound the stake free and release the chain from it. Take him to the parade ground, behind the whores' tents." He turned and started to leave; then he stopped and said over one shoulder, "The pit is already set up. When you have him there, cut his arms and legs free and kick him over the side."

Shobai sneered. "Good-bye, pigs! Good-bye, filth! Good-bye . . ." But just then a bludgeon blow, struck from behind, smashed into the nape of his neck and drove him down. He fell on his face. Other blows rained down upon him; the fourth brought merciful oblivion.

When he came to, in pain, he hung by his trussed arms and legs from a stout pole, and they were bearing him through the crowd like a steer's carcass dangling from the spit. Fists pummeled him as he was carried along, and he stared at his tormentors dully through glazed eyes.

Suddenly, though, there was a commotion, and he was dropped roughly on the ground, still tethered to the pole. He turned his head—painfully—and saw one of the pole-bearers engaged in a fight with one of the drunks in the crowd. The other man who had been carrying him joined in the battle, and suddenly there was a small riot in progress. The fight moved away from him. . . . His senses dulled, he groaned under the weight of the pole across his chest.

There was a burst of laughter near him, and above this a wild, raucous screeching. He struggled out from under the pole and turned his head so he could see out of his one unobstructed eye. He blinked and raised his head a trifle . . .

. . . and saw a strange, bizarre, wild figure dancing idiotically, awkwardly, in a circle. Someone began the drumming again, and the shawm joined in. The figure, wild-eyed, mudbesmeared, half naked, was that of a madman or an epileptic; its limbs jerked crookedly in wild, uncontrolled motions, and its dance was the ungainly dance of an ape. The face was obscured by multicolored mud, smeared on there in great gobs; only the red-rimmed, mad eyes stared out of the filthy face with a madman's intensity. Its arms and legs flew out spastically; it did somersaults, fell stupidly on its face, got back up again to continue its insane, pitiful, brutally comic caricature of human motion. The laughter was cruel, the insults hurled from the sidelines bitter and degrading; but the creature, smiling horribly with that lopsided face, one side of which seemed to be paralyzed, seemed unaware of its effect.

People threw clumps of mud which bounced off the twisted little figure with the monkeylike, deformed limbs; it ignored the pain this must surely have caused, meeting each missile's impact with another head-over-heels caper and an idiot's high-pitched, meaningless laughter. There was something about the mindless cruelty of their assaults on so helpless, so harmless a fool as this that brought bitter tears to Shobai's eyes. And now, his heart sinking, he remembered Melid, remembered the unselective ferocity of the nomad hordes as they had butchered the aged and the infirm alike, with the same beastliness that had moved them to the rape and murder of the women and children. . . .

A voice suddenly stabbed at him, out of the noise; it came from his other side, and he rolled over, pulling the pole atop his chest. "Shobai!"

His eye scanned the crowd—and saw Sayda struggling with one of the soldiers gathered before the whores' tents. "Sho—" But her words were cut off in mid-breath by a great hairy hand clapped over her mouth. Shobai cried out in pain and rage as her naked little form disappeared back into the tent. They'd put her in the whores' tents! They'd put her to whoring for the soldiers . . . !

Now, however, he felt the pole lifted off his chest. The two men pulled it to shoulder height, and, the motion yanking painfully on his bound wrists and ankles, they carried him once again through the crowd. In a while they stopped, and someone slashed at the ropes on his limbs. When he had pulled himself free of the cut ropes, he tried to rise—but someone kicked him to one side, and the earth fell out from under him. He landed hard on one already-bruised side; the fall—a long one—knocked the breath out of him.

When he had managed to pull himself together and got his breath back, he sat up, looked around, and saw the walls of a pit rising around him. He stood, painfully, and looked around again. The pit was slightly deeper than his own height. Looking down on all sides were the drunken faces of his tormentors; as he blinked up at them, someone threw a clod of mud at him. This was followed by another. He retreated across the pit, ducking.

There was a roar of laughter from the crowd, and the faces above turned away from him. He could hear the hideous, pitiful squawk of the madman again, and then he could see him just over the edge of the pit—the dancing madman, his limbs, gruesomely deformed and totally out of control, jerking grotesquely as he danced around the pit. The people stood back to let the idiot caper around the edge . . . and suddenly, Shobai could see no face but the imbecile's. Then the mad fool stumbled and fell on his belly, his head and shoulders hanging precariously over the edge. The laughter was louder than before, reaching the proportions of a roar.

And then something curious—something incredible—happened. And it was over so quickly that Shobai blinked, unsure he had seen what he had seen. The idiot's hand lightly tossed a flat clump of mud down at him. It landed at his feet. He stared up at the suddenly altered face ...

... and then the strange figure was gone, pulling itself back up off the edge, dancing away into the crowd which followed him down the line of whores' tents. It left Shobai to gape up at the deserted lip of the pit in which he stood, and to reach down, at last, and pick up the little clump of hard clay, look at both sides of it, and stand holding it, thunderstruck at the recognition of what he had just seen.

For one split second, the idiot face had relaxed into a semblance of humanity, recognizable under the coating of mud. The face had become a face. A finger had gone to the now normal lips; the no-longer-mad eye had winked at him. Winked at him! And now his heart almost stopped as he realized why there had been something vaguely familiar about the idiot's deformed body.

The crooked leg. Just like Hadad's.

The eyes and the face has been those of his brother.

The deliberately crooked arms had had a purpose—to hide the fact that one of his limbs was deformed.

Shobai, gasping, held one hand over his heart, listening to the crowd's screams of cruel laughter above.

He lifted the little clay tablet again and read the familiar hand.

It said, *"Courage! I'm here to get you out. Don't let on you know me."*

V

The officers' feast was lavish to the point of prodigality. Ox and lamb roasted on spits side by side; from these, the cooks carved great dripping slices. There were brimming bowls of *boombar*—stuffed lamb casings—and skewers of *shawerma*—marinated beef. There was *jigerr,* or lamb liver, and dishes of *turlu guevej,* a savory stew made with lamb and mixed carrots, onions, and okra. Finally, there was *tutumov,* or pumpkin candy. The smells were enchanting. This was the rich fare of leaders, of wealthy owners of large herds, of Shepherd Kings; mere soldiers, whatever their rank, did not see such fare often.

For some reason, however, Vahan found himself wandering among the fires and the heavy-laden tables, growing less interested with every passing moment. His mood had turned sour, and with it his stomach. Whereas, an hour or two before, he might have turned to the immense feast with gusto, with a light heart—now, without palpable reason, he found the rich array of sights and smells repulsive. When one of the slaves preparing the feast offered him a skewer of *khorovadzh*—lamb and onions roasted low over the coals, a dish he ordinarily ate with delight—he made a face and turned away.

Something was eating at his soul.

The worst part of it was that he knew what was bothering him. And he didn't want to face it. Still less did he want to face the necessity of doing something about it, knowing the turmoil that would result from this.

He sighed, turning eyes and nose away from the row of cooks and their food. If only the problem would go away! But . . .

He scowled and clenched his fists spasmodically. But, of course, the problem *would* go away, and soon enough. His problem was Shobai, and the unfamiliar and thoroughly unpleasant sense of guilt he, Vahan, felt over his part in Shobai's present torment and impending death. And the problem wouldn't last long, because Shobai wouldn't last long. It was highly unlikely he'd outlive the passage of the sun across the daytime sky, much less the night. In a while he'd be dead, and that would be the end of it.

Damn! he thought bitterly, his stomach punctuating his thoughts with another violent pang of pain. Of course, the trouble wouldn't be over then. Not for Vahan, it wouldn't. There was a way in which the trouble would only be beginning with Shobai's violent and degrading death. Because, of course, that would be the point where choice had passed away from him. Where recrimination for a past, not a present, error began—an error now irremediable.

Another pang of pain. He bent slightly forward, his face barely kept expressionless by a powerful effort of will. His hand pressed his lower side.

Vahan, you've got to do it. You've got to try....

He cursed silently, stopped dead, pressed his hand to his side again. Well, there was nothing for it but to do what his heart—and his damned aching belly—kept telling him to do. He moved forward, rounded a roped-off area where a girl was dancing to a shawm and drum, and headed for Manouk's tent.

Manouk, like himself, was staying away from the food today. He sat, silent, watching the others around his fire-circle eat and converse. His face was somber. He looked up to see Vahan standing over him, noted the nod Vahan gave him which said clearly: *Let's talk.* He rose from his cross-legged position and followed Vahan to the far side of the tent. "You want me?" he said.

"Yes. Shobai, the armorer . . ."

"Ah." Manouk's hand waved the subject away. "Don't talk to me of Shobai. The matter's in Diran's hands. He has to prove something to me. If I intervene . . ."

"But if you don't, the armorer will be dead by the time the sun is over that hill across the plain there. . . ."

"Without doubt. But either he will work or he will deal with whatever Diran has to offer. The business about the girl backfired. My niece—"

"Diran has given your niece to the soldiers."

Manouk's eyes narrowed. "And he did not inquire as to whose child she was? Ah, that is bad judgment. I will have my brother and sister-in-law to deal with. Although the girl asked for it herself."

"See? Diran has failed. He has also offended a powerful chieftain, your brother."

Manouk sighed. "There is something to what you say. Diran is a fool, more muscles than brains. He would have made a bad commander anyway. There are men who fight well but are fit only to be led. He has just done himself out of a position in the front ranks before Haran tomorrow. If indeed I put him in the army before Haran. We may need every free hand for Carchemish. You heard what happened during the night?"

"No. What . . . ?"

"With our garrison before Carchemish reduced to half strength and our defenses lax, Oshiyahu organized a midnight raid. He lost many men, including some captains. But the raid was a successful one, destructive and demoralizing. The tents were fired, the animals driven away. We lost a great number of men—and the ones who remain are low in spirit, beaten, scarcely fit to spearhead an attack in the morning."

"Gods! What are you going to do?"

"What else can I do? I'll move in a fresh command—the troop from Melid, who are well rested by now and well disciplined—and mix them with the garrison there. When young, demoralized troops see the men next to them standing their ground, fearless and unaffected by it all, they'll hold their water themselves."

"The Melid troop? Then you won't pull troops from the Haran front? They're closer . . ."

"No. Karakin, in his wisdom"—the irony was thick on Manouk's tongue now—"has decreed that Haran will be reduced to rubble. An example to the cities of the south. I have to admit it's a good terrorist tactic. But the order is that not one man will be pulled out of the Haran force."

"Very well. Incidentally, our Haran turncoats are in camp. I saw one of them. The rat-faced one. I heard that the other, his superior, stayed behind in the city."

"He'll be along soon. He's staying on to maintain the fiction that he's going to lead the battle against us." He snorted. "Battle." He looked Vahan in the eye now. "The rat-faced one has not reported to me. Well, it does not matter because he does not matter, any more than the other one does. They think they'll rule Haran and Carchemish for us. There'll be nothing and nobody to rule. I'd have them put to death except . . . somehow, I think the rat-faced one will come in handy some time in the future. He's resourceful."

"Yes, and treacherous. He'd stab us in the back in a moment if we were weaker, more vulnerable. If there were an enemy to betray us to."

"Of course. He's that type. But such men sometimes prove useful. When he stops being useful—" He made a sudden, grossly terminal motion with one hand. "Of course, you know we have a visit scheduled today, from the divinely appointed Karakin."

"Ah. The, ah, Leader won't like what he'll hear about Carchemish."

"Well, that can't be helped. Vahan: I'll speak straight to you. There is talk among the border kings. . . ."

"I've heard it, sir. And I have to say I understand it. These are proud men, used to thinking themselves the equals of any man, whatever his station."

"Yes, and there are a lot of them. Enough to sway the rest,

if it came down to— Well, we understand one another, I think."

"Yes. Enough to know where we'll stand when the time for choice comes."

"Yes. But that is not now. Not before the walls of Haran and Carchemish. Not unless the Leader precipitates something himself, and in a manner we cannot ignore or forgive."

"I understand. He's popular with the troops."

"He is. Particularly after he's made one of his rabble-rousing speeches, stirring up their blood. And I have an idea that's what he'll be up to today." His expression showed his distaste only by the set of one nostril, lifted, flared.

"Well, that's out of our hands just now," Vahan said. "But—I was going to lead the subject back to Shobai. Could we . . . ?"

"Vahan. Don't ask me about Shobai. He has until dawn to change his ways, if he is allowed to last that long. . . ."

"But . . . Diran will throw the dogs into the pit with him. He'll not survive five minutes of that."

"All right. That much you can advise him against. That and the usual little games. We'll not go burying him in the sand up to his neck and playing pig-sticking games with his head."

"If he dies, it must be of natural causes?"

"I won't go that far. If Diran wants to put men in to wrestle him, that's a legitimate diversion as long as they're both unarmed—or both armed."

Vahan sighed. This was a major concession. No matter that it was not the one he had wanted. "All right," he said. "I'll tell Diran." He started toward the door, but stopped dead, listening to the faraway sound of the crowd. "Hark! That's a different kind of noise."

"Of course it is," Manouk said. His mouth hardened, his eyes narrowed again. "That'll be our invincible Leader, coming in to make one of his grand entrances. Well, be off with you—before Diran has your friend skewered and turned on a spit like *shawerma*."

And it was, in fact, the coming of the Leader which spared Shobai for an hour. He had been the butt of one of Diran's diversions for the better part of the early afternoon; three of Diran's biggest and most bellicose warriors, having drunk sufficient palm wine, had dropped one at a time into the pit to

523

wrestle Shobai, and bets had been placed right and left by the drunken onlookers at the pit's edge. Shobai, the spark of hope faint but alive in his heart, had something to live for now, and he fought for his life. In the pit one man lay dead, strangled by Shobai's powerful metalworker's hands. Another, a gigantic man half again Shobai's weight, had been felled by Shobai's leg-chain swung around his head and let loose to slam hard against his attacker's temple; Shobai had then broken his neck—and paralyzed him from the neck down. From time to time he whimpered like a child, immobile on his back in the bottom of the deep pit.

As the third man was about to leap down and do battle with the fatigued Shobai, the commotion surrounding Karakin's arrival drew him and his audience away. Shobai listened to the cheering in the distance and calculated whether, when darkness came, he could pile the two bodies one on top of the other and, climbing atop them, get out of the pit. But the speech droned on, off in the distance, and the cheers continued, and he grew impatient as the sun lowered in the western sky. He looked down at the paralyzed man, biting his lip, thinking.

"Please," the man said in a small voice. "Please help me."

"Shut up," Shobai said. "You wanted to kill me. You got what you had coming. Take your death like a man."

"Please . . ." the man said. Shobai scowled. There was a way or two to shut him up. He pulled the other body over and laid its huge bulk atop the paralyzed man. The sudden weight on his chest made it virtually impossible for the man to breathe, much less get air for speech. Shobai made an expression of distaste and stepped on top of the two bodies, stepped up . . .

. . . but when he reached above the pit's edge, there was nothing but slick clay to get his hands on; they slipped and slipped again. If only there were something near the edge to hold on to.

He tried and tried again, as the sun sank lower and lower. His efforts only made the lip of the pit slicker and slicker. Discouraged, he went back to the far side of the pit and sat down, trying to catch his breath after the effort. He was dog-tired, bone-tired; but he knew he could not rest. In a while, whoever was speaking over there—he presumed it must be the Leader—would finish, and they'd all be back. And then it would be too late. . . .

He awoke suddenly, a stab of fear shooting through him. It was dark, and the cheers were resounding over the little valley that held the camp. The speechmaking was over! They'd be back soon! And he'd dozed off—and lost his opportunity.

The moon, still nearly full, crept over the edge of the pit. Shobai climbed to the lip again, struggled with the eroded clay; but he sank back again, frustrated. And just as he stepped down, he heard a voice above him. He looked up to see moonlight falling on a familiar face. "Hadad!" he said in a hoarse whisper.

"Quiet, for heaven's sake," his brother said. "Here, take this. It's tied to a tree on the other end. If you can, use it to climb up to where I can catch your hand . . ."

Shobai took the rope, mounted the piled bodies, and in a moment held his brother's slim but strong hand. Hadad pulled him up, up . . . and soon Shobai was standing in the moonlight, embracing him, the emotions thick and wildly mixed in his heart. . . .

"Here," Hadad said in a businesslike voice Shobai had never heard from him, a voice full of resolve and purpose. "No time for that. There's no time to lose. Come this way. I've a place we can hide until the wee hours when they'll all be drunk."

Shobai followed him as Hadad struck out in that curiously efficient, crooklegged waddle of his down a dark row of tents. "Hadad," he said, "the second shift'll be along—the other shift still has its feasting to do. . . ."

"No they won't," Hadad said. "I talked to one of the cooks who spoke Hurrian. The army of Carchemish staged a raid last night. It was so effective the leave has been canceled for the second shifts from both Carchemish and Haran. Now quiet, please; there are soldiers near here. . . ."

Shobai obeyed. And in a moment Hadad steered him past a half-drunken watchman to the great plain, just past the horsepens, where the war wagons and chariots were stored. "Up there," Hadad said in a cautious whisper. "That one there, with the cover over it. Slip under quickly—and keep it quiet, now."

Shobai had walked all this way holding the chain still attached to his ankle. It clanked once, softly but audibly, as he climbed into the wagon. But then he was inside, and Hadad was slipping in behind him. The space under the wagon cover was warm and dark; the many-layered cloth admitted no light. Shobai sat back, leaning his tired back against the side of the wagon, catching his breath for the first time, barely able to believe what was happening.

525

Hadad had freed him! Timid Hadad! Hadad the weakling!

VI

Diran stood before Manouk, weaving slightly on his feet. The commander looked him up and down, his face wooden. "Report," he said.

"Sir," the big man said, "the prisoner Shobai..." He cleared his dry throat, covering his mouth with one large hand.

"Go on," Manouk said, his voice flinty and chill. "He's gone, isn't he? And you've waited most of the evening to tell me?" He glared up at the giant tribesman, the corners of his mouth stretched tight by the sour expression on his face. Then, ominously, his eyes darted to the two guards who flanked him. Instantly, the two stiffened; their hands went to their sword-hilts; the atmosphere in the big tent grew appreciably more tense.

"I—I was going to report earlier. But I thought I could have found him by now," Diran said hoarsely.

"But you didn't. And since you didn't notify anyone, none of the rest of us could be mobilized to help you find him. And in the meantime, he may have gotten through our lines."

"Oh, no, sir. I'm sure he can't have—"

"You're drunk." Manouk spat the words out in disgust. "Moreover, it's quite likely that our camp security is very lax just now. I've already received reports that someone smuggled palm wine out to the second watch. One man has been broken in rank and will be whipped before the entire encampment when we stand to in the morning. No; most likely the armorer's gone. And who should have been watching him? Who was responsible for him?" He glared at Diran; at the guards at his two sides; at the crude design his own sword had been scratching in the hard-packed dirt before him—the mark of a lion's paw print.

"Sir, I'll have him by morning. I—" Diran began. He was valiantly trying to hold himself together, to keep his body on an even keel. His words came out slurred. His eyes blinked away the double images they kept trying to show him. "I'll have him . . ."

"No, you won't," Manouk said. Suddenly, he nodded curtly to one of the guards, and huge, powerful hands closed on Diran's arms. "The reason is, you'll have replaced him in the pit." He spoke past Diran to the guard. "I'm done with him," he said. "Put him where the prisoner was." A refinement occurred to him, and after a moment's reflection he acted on it. "Only—manacle his hands behind his back. And then . . ."

"No!" Diran said, struggling. "No! Please!"

"And then push the dogs into the pit." He smiled icily.

"No!" Diran screamed. "No, Manouk! Please . . ." But the butt of a sword slammed into the side of his head and weakened his knees for him; the two dragged him outside.

Manouk listened to his weakened, receding cries for a moment; then he nodded to no one in particular. In one blink of an eye a third guardsman had stepped forward. "Reinforce the outer perimeter," Manouk commanded. "I think he's right, actually. I don't think the armorer has made it that far. He's still somewhere in camp. Scour every cubit of ground. Find him."

"Yes, sir. And report here?"

"That, or send someone after me. I'm going over and have some words with Karakin. Might as well get it over with."

"Sir," said the captain of guards, "not a confrontation? Because—"

"I know the danger. Thank you for your concern. I won't let it get that far if I can help it. But there is an issue of priorities. You heard him with the troops?"

"Secondhand, sir. He wants to send the relief troops from Melid to Haran, not Carchemish. He wants to make Haran an example."

"Yes. It's that little turncoat, Reshef. He's in camp, and he went to Karakin behind my back. He wants Haran leveled for reasons of his own." Manouk scowled. "Sneaky little bastard . . ." But he waved it away. "Enough. He does not matter, except as he influences Karakin."

" 'Karakin,' sir?" the captain said. "Is it wise to call him that when he demands . . . ?"

"The hell with his demands. All those imposing titles. I knew Karakin when he hadn't hair on his loins, when he went into battle with snot dripping from his nose." He scowled. "Don't worry, I won't openly antagonize His Leadership. I'll just say, 'Your Leadership, if you don't relieve the Car-

527

chemish force by dawn—and with seasoned war-wise troops at that—so help me heaven, I'll string you to a tree and let the Fifth Archers loose on you for target practice until you look like the grandfather of all hedgehogs.'" He looked the captain in the eye. "That ought to be indirect enough, without going to the other extreme and going right over his head."

"Yes, sir." But the look in the captain's eye left no doubt that he thought Manouk was treading far out into dangerous territory. . . .

Shobai blinked, opened his one good eye. "Wha—?" he said, sitting up, his voice still thick with sleep. "H-Hadad," he said, holding his chest with one battered hand. He tried to open the second eye, but it was swollen shut by now. "I—I must have slipped off. R-right after we arrived . . ."

Hadad, sitting across from him, his round face shining with happiness in the light of the little candle he'd placed in the middle of the wagon, held one finger over his lips. "Shhh!" he said. "Whisper, and quietly. The covering is opaque enough to allow us a little light, but we daren't make much noise. They've been by here a couple of times already, looking for us." He smiled and put one fist on Shobai's knee in a gesture of rough masculine affection. "Oh, Shobai, it's so good to see you. I wasn't sure I'd be able to find you."

Shobai stared at him, his expression deformed by the beatings he'd taken in the past few days. "Hadad," he said, unbelieving, "how did you get here?"

Hadad smiled his guileless smile. "For goodness' sake, did you think I could abandon you after I'd heard you were here—when there might be something I could do to help?"

"But—but the odds . . . you could have been killed, every bit of the way. And—and you may not survive the day as it is. Getting out of here . . ."

"Well, it is taking a chance. I admit that much. But—why, it was a chance I had to take. My brother a slave?" His eyes suddenly turned to Shobai's bicep. "Oh, dear—oh, your poor arm. The slave mark . . ."

"It's nothing. I could have it struck through if we got to a city. But, Hadad, we're doomed. There's no way we can get out of here. And escape to where? Haran and Carchemish will be rubble by this time tomorrow night. They're poised to attack."

"I thought of that. And—well, maybe, I thought, there was something I could do to help Haran. You know, to save it. And as long as there was anything I could conceivably do, how could I possibly fail to try it?" He tried to turn the subject away. "Here. I stole you some clothing. It's not fancy, but it'll be warm enough. Heavens! You've scratches and bruises all over. What have they been doing to you?"

Shobai, taking the proffered robe, ignored this line of thought. "Help Haran? Save it? Hadad, are you mad?"

Hadad smiled his infectious smile. "Don't give up on me too quickly, my brother. I got this far, didn't I? Despite what kind of odds?" He chuckled softly, reaching for a parcel behind him. "Here: when you're dressed I've got some food, and a little wine. I don't want you to eat too quickly, now; I suspect they haven't been feeding you much." He stopped, his eyes wide. "You're so skinny . . . *have* they been feeding you?"

"They stopped yesterday," Shobai said. "It doesn't matter. After a time you don't notice, as long as you've a little water to drink." He rose to his knees, pulling the robe around him and securing it at the shoulder with the plain clasp Hadad had brought. Then he sat back on his heels. "Hadad," he said, "I can't tell you what it means to me to see you. I—I've had time to think about the way I wasted my life all those years, about the great wrongs I've done you and mother."

"Hush, now!" Hadad whispered. "Don't talk about . . ."

"It's your time to hush," Shobai said gently. He was looking at Hadad as though he'd never seen him before. "Hadad, Hadad . . . primogeniture is a cruel custom, but it needn't be if the father is there to make sure the second son is taken care of and esteemed in his own right. But we didn't have that. Our father, may he some day find peace, left us and went into foreign lands. He may be dead now for all I know. That left it up to me. But . . . with mother losing her reason like that, there was nobody to show me what I should do. I mean, about you. I was left to my own devices, to my own egoism and selfishness. I—"

"Please, Shobai!" Hadad said. "Here, eat. Save your strength for—"

"Don't interrupt me, Hadad. I'm—I'm saying things that may sound foolish to you, but if I die without saying them—well, they're important to me. I have to tell you. . . ."

Hadad stared at him. Then the understanding dawned, and his eyes softened. He reached over and took his brother's larger, stronger hand, holding it as tenderly as he might hold Danataya's. "I understand," he said. "You've come so close to death . . . yes, yes. I understand. For the good of your soul. Yes. Go ahead, Shobai. I'm listening."

529

Shobai's eyes brimmed with tears. He wiped them away from the eye that could still see. "Hadad, I've been a callous and thoughtless fool. I've ruined many lives besides my own, and I've done you such wrong. No, hush, don't interrupt me or deny what I'm saying. That can wait. My own foolish, self-centered life has robbed you of your youth, your childhood. I've lived as a rich man while you and mother lived shabby, grubby lives, poor, underfed, clothed in rags often as not. . . ." He held up the other hand. "I know, I know. You'll tell me that it wasn't that bad for you, that you always got by, that there was much happiness in your life. I suppose you'd be right to say so, too. That's the way you are. Drop you in a sea of woes and you'll create yourself a little cove of happiness and kindness and thoughtfulness, just because that beautiful, self-renewing spirit of yours is so forgiving."

He looked at Hadad's blushing and dissembling for a moment, still holding his brother's hand. "No," he said quietly. "Just once before we're dead, brother, hear what and who you are, from someone who knows. You're probably the only truly good man I've ever known, and if what the priests of Bel say is at all correct and there's another life ahead for us, I doubt that I'll ever meet another such soul as yourself there, either. You look small, Hadad, but you're big. Big! Bigger than I, or father, or any of us. You . . ."

His eye lit on a gold chain around Hadad's neck. He reached out and grasped it, pulling from under Hadad's robe the medallion he had made for his and Danataya's wedding; she had worn its mate. "Look at this! It's yours, isn't it? What work! What beauty! What understanding of the spirit of the metal! Hadad, *I* never understood metal like this. Neither, for all his eminence, did father. Maybe Belsunu and Ahuni did, in their way. But you—you're the *real* Child of the Lion. You, not me. The genius of the family went underground for a generation, and then it landed on you. And because father wasn't here to judge between us, the mantle fell upon me, and I didn't deserve it, couldn't live up to it. Perhaps I always knew that. Perhaps that's why I always led such a shallow life, heaping expensive rewards on myself and ignoring you. Because it was you, not me. Always, Hadad. You. You, whose untutored fingers could make beauty out of anything you ever touched, even out of the cheap clay they gave you to make the votive images for the temple. You, with your great, gentle heart and everlasting sweetness—"

"Shobai, no! You wrong yourself—"

"There you go! The only fault you ever had, Hadad, was

530

that you didn't know how to judge your worth. You didn't know you were better than I, better than father, better than any of us. You didn't know you were a great artist, or a great man. Why—look at you! Look at you, who can forgive me for all I've done to you. . . . No, more! Who could leave the happiness you wrote me about, with that new wife of yours, and come up here, single-handed, unarmed, into this—this dragon's mouth—and to save me, who doesn't deserve even to call myself a member of the same race with you, much less to call myself your brother—"

"Shobai!"

"Hush. Hush, little brother. Great brother. Brave brother. Here. Ever-faithful friend. Valiant, gentle man, who marches into darkness to save a brother, who stands half again your height, who's six times as strong as you, and who doesn't deserve you for a moment. Hadad, you're a man. You honor the very word. You honor the name of humanity. Hadad: if we live, I'm going to make it up to you for my years of neglect. No, I know you're richer than I am already. I heard stories on the road. I heard about Ibalum. I heard about your wedding. I heard—is her name Danataya?—I heard she was with child. True to form, it's you and not I who father a Child of the Lion. That's as it should be. The line should go through you—" He stopped for a moment. "I take it Danataya's safe? And mother?"

"They're on the road south with—"

"Good, good. Then it's up to you to get out of here, to get back to them. But Hadad—I'll make it up to you, I swear I will."

"There's nothing to make up, Shobai. I'm your brother. I love you."

"I . . . you do, don't you? You always have. And it's taken me this long—it's taken me to the brink of death—even to begin to understand what the word means. Perhaps—perhaps it isn't too late, even for a fool like me. . . ."

He squeezed Hadad's hand. He had no more words. The feelings in his heart were too strong for words. He tried to speak and could not. Instead, he watched the happiness, the warm glow, growing on Hadad's round face, with its crinkly-eyed, widemouthed, infinitely loving smile.

"Oh, Shobai!" Hadad said. "I'm so happy!" He wiped the tears from his eyes with the back of his hand, smiling as he wept. "I've got you back again!"

VII

Inside the tent, the battle was raging. The Leader's angry bellow boomed forth, drowning out, for the most part, Manouk's quiet but steadfast replies. Reshef, a dark and secret smile playing on his thin lips, stood just outside the entrance to the tent, inside the ring of guards, his arms crossed, the fingers of one hand drumming on the bicep of the other.

An idea had just begun to occur to him.

There was a bellow louder than the others from inside. He cocked one ear toward the sound, picking up some of it: "... question my authority? *My* authority? You go too far. ..."

"Not your authority, my, uh, 'Leader.' " The irony was thick on Manouk's tongue, and his voice was raised a trifle from its normal level. "Your judgment, perhaps. Haran, just now, is unimportant. We can come back and destroy Haran with half a troop of soldiers. It will wait. But Carchemish is another matter altogether—"

"Haran first! No compromise!"

"Hear me, Karakin. Hear me. And don't play me that infallible leader tune again, please. I knew you when we were boys, and I remember. Gods! Could I forget? You're impetuous. Your first thoughts on virtually any subject are terrible. You—"

"Manouk!"

"Oh, stop blustering. Save it for the foreigners, who don't know you the way I do. Listen to me, now. What I was going to add was that if anyone could ever get you calmed down—and that was my role many times, as you recall—if anyone could get you to reconsider, your second thoughts on every subject were always superb. That's what made you a good leader. ..."

"Well, Manouk ..."

Reshef's smile showed his uneven teeth now. *Why, the sly fox. Manouk! He's a man after my own heart. Listen to him, now, applying the oil. In a moment or two he'll have Karakin convinced he thought the whole thing up.*

He turned away, turned to the young soldier guarding the tent door. "Quite an argument going on there," he said in a passable nomad tongue. "Are they always this way together?"

The guard looked sharply at him, wondering whether to trust him—and, if so, how much. "Sometimes, sir," he said. "It's the way of commanders."

"Ah. Well, I'm sure they're both very good."

"The best, sir. I've served under both. Manouk, if you'll pardon my saying so, sir—he's the man for a long haul, for a siege. Steady as they come, and smart. The Leader, now—he's the man for a charge. Fires you up, he does."

"Splendid. Now if they'd only work in harness together . . . I hear there's some dissatisfaction among the chiefs. Frankly, I heard some prefer Manouk to the Leader."

The soldier glanced at him again, his eyes wary. "I . . . don't know anything about that, sir. But if I heard seditious talk, I think I'd report it."

"Oh, to be sure I have," Reshef lied. "Through channels. At the present rate it'll take six months for the news to reach the top. You know how that is."

"Yes, sir," the soldier said, relaxing a bit. He even yawned. "Excuse me, sir. I wish the morning would come. I'd hoped to see some action by now."

"Patience," Reshef said. "Plenty of time for that." He faked a yawn himself. "Well, I think I'll go take a short nap. Get nice and fresh for the morning. See you later. . . ." He nodded good-bye and strolled away. The idea that had come to him earlier was beginning to take shape in his mind.

Poor stupid Diran, he thought. The clumsy bastard had let Shobai, his—Reshef's—prize, get away. And he hadn't been able to figure out any way to find him. But perhaps . . .

What was it that Diran had been telling him in his drunken outburst, an hour before they'd stripped him and tossed him into the pit with the dogs? There was something about a girl Shobai had been taken with, a girl who'd been told to worm assent out of Shobai and who'd refused. Diran had had her beaten, and had given her to the soldiers as a whore.

But her name? Her name? Damn it, there were fifty girls working in the tents just now. There were maybe fifty more in reserve, for when the first fifty wore out. And he had perhaps until dawn to find the right one.

Yes, the girl. That was the ticket. Find her, and you'd find Shobai. If the soldiers had left anything of her to find. . . .

"There!" Hadad said, his voice tight after the strain. He pulled the metal bar free and held up the link of chain he'd twisted and broken. Shobai rubbed his ankle. The ankle manacle was intact, but the chain was down to a single link. "Sorry if I hurt you," Hadad said. "But at least this won't make noise or trip you up. If I'd had better tools . . ."

"You did just fine," Shobai said. "Besides, I've lived with this damned ankle bracelet so long I wouldn't know what to do without it." Still, he rubbed the sore spot ruefully. "Now: what's the plan?"

"It's maybe an hour before the dawn," Hadad said. "We'll want to move in a few minutes. If I can get another few moments' light out of this last candle before it gutters out . . ." He opened a little parcel and laid its contents before him: a paintpot, a little water, brushes. Then he opened the front of his garment.

"What the devil are you doing?" Shobai said.

"Never you mind," Hadad said, mixing the water with the dry pigments. "Here's a pair of sandals. I don't think they're quite big enough for you. Best I could steal. Now let me be for a moment or two."

"Hadad, what are you up to?"

"Never mind, brother of mine. It's just a sort of last-resort idea I had." He mixed, painted here and there. "Shobai, I couldn't steal any swords. Too chancy. Besides, they have them stacked at the gates, for everyone but guards. They didn't want any pitched battles starting up after a few drinks. But there's a cudgel over there by your leg. You might be able to do some damage with that." He turned to his brother. "Now," he said, putting the little paintpots aside and closing his tattered robe. "This way"—he pointed with one finger—"is north. Keep that in mind. You'll be a little disoriented when we step outside, with the sun not yet up and few stars overhead. That way"—he pointed to the southeast—"is the way I got in. There's a little dry wash. I found a trail the mountain goats used to use. I marked the entrance to the wash with a broken branch from a tree. I hope it's still there."

"Aren't you coming with me?" Shobai said.

"I can't. They'll surely spot two of us. I'm going to do my idiot act, and see if it won't get me out the front gate. That's not far from the place where your little arroyo lets out. I'll meet you down by the river, under a terebinth which has been struck by lightning. You'll recognize it in a moment. It was split right down the middle. Half the remaining tree died; the rest is in bud now. If I'm not there by the time the sun is high—if either of us isn't there . . ."

"I get you. One of us has to escape anyhow—if only to care for Danataya and the baby."

"Yes," Hadad said. Then, for a moment, a faraway look came into his eyes. "Baby," he said softly. "Last night, before I came into the camp, I dreamed Danataya had a baby. A boy-child, Shobai! A Child of the Lion! It was so vivid, so real. . . ."

Shobai squeezed his shoulder. "The more reason to get you through safely to see it," he said. "Time to go. Do you want me to go first?"

"Yes. I'll be right behind. And Shobai: the gods watch over you. May they protect you . . . I love you, brother."

"And I you. And if I'm spared, you'll never have cause to worry over me again. Not if I have anything to say about the matter. And Hadad . . . your child'll have a second father. We'll raise him rich and loved, you and I and Danataya."

"Yes. Yes! Now go!"

Shobai lifted the cover cautiously, looked around, slipped to the ground. There was only the first beginning of light in the eastern sky. He kept low, close to the ground, and headed past the long row of wagons toward the place Hadad had pointed out to him. He paused at a low-lying bush to look around.

His heart almost stopped. A patrol! He backed up quickly, as quietly as he could, slipped inside a high-sided wagon, flattened himself on its floor. He listened, hardly daring to breathe, as the voices came nearer.

There was a woman with them! He could hear her high-pitched, muffled voice; someone had gagged her. But it was not a man's voice; he was sure of that.

". . . for heaven's sake, pick the little bitch up if she can't walk; it's easier than dragging her. Come on, now! The morning watch'll be out in a bit. They could use a little diversion too."

"I don't know. She's pretty beat-up by now. Look at her eyes. Look at her . . . uh, oh. Look, Surik. I think she's choking. For heaven's sake get the gag out. Her eyes are rolled back."

"Here. Here, girlie." Shobai could hear the sound of a face being gently slapped. "Here, come to, won't you? Damn it all, now. . . ."

Shobai cursed silently. They'd stopped dead, not three

paces from the wagon in which he lay. And now he could hear the girl's voice, sick and faint and woebegone. ". . . please—please let me go. My . . . my father is Baitsar, of the Fifth Light Horse . . . he'll reward you. . . ."

"Hah!" one of the soldiers said. "A soldiers' whore, daughter of a commander? Don't make me laugh. Besides, Baitsar is dead. They got him in the raid at Carchemish last night. Think up another one, sweetheart."

"Father . . . dead? But—look, call Manouk. I'm his niece. There's been some terrible mistake. Tell him it's Sayda. . . ."

Sayda? Shobai's eyes widened. His muscles tensed. He took a firm grip on the cudgel Hadad had given him. Sayda? Here? He set his teeth in a snarl. There were two of them, from what he could hear . . . only two . . .

"Look, tell it to the gods, eh? In your prayers. Don't waste it on us, darling. Now come along with me, won't you? There's a good girl . . . just one foot before the other."

Shobai crouched in the wagon bottom . . . and charged. Silently. Swinging the cudgel. It caught the first soldier over the temple and felled him, his skull crushed. On the backswing, Shobai smashed the other in the ribs. Sayda fell to the ground, her poor face bruised and covered with scratches.

A sudden *whirr!* sounded by his ear. And Shobai saw a bronze-tipped arrow bury itself with a *thunk!* in the tall sides of the wagon.

He whirled.

Six sharp arrows poised on strung bows, pointed at his heart. The bowmen's faces were hard as flint. An officer stepped forward from behind them. "Good work, men," he said. "We've got him. You: take the girl. Sergeant: send for Reshef. He'll be happy to hear this. There may even be a little reward."

Shobai's face fell. "R-Reshef?" he said.

Hadad swallowed the lump in his throat, set his face in the idiot grin, and waddled out into the path toward the guard post, his legs wobbling spastically, his arms twitching. When the guards spotted him, he giggled insanely and did a backflip, purposely landing wrong in a comic pratfall.

There was no laughter. "You," the first guard said. "Approach. Now. Get a move on there."

Hadad's heart skipped a beat. And he fixed the lopsided smirk on his face again, one eye twitching. "My masters like?" he said. "I do funny dance?"

"You stay right where you are," a harsh voice said behind

him. He turned his head, staying in character, a bolt of fear running through him.

There in the path stood Reshef! Behind him, four stout guardsmen! And—and the expression on Reshef's face . . . it was changing, as those sharp eyes looked him up and down. "Why, look at this," Reshef said, that horrible smile on his face. He stepped forward, grabbed Hadad by the hair, yanked him to full height. "I saw him doing his little act earlier and never suspected. It's Hadad, isn't it? Anat's brother-in-law. And I didn't even recognize that crooked leg at first. You did a fine job of misdirection, there, my friend. But a fat lot of good it'll do you now." He grinned, and his grin was worse even than his smile. "So *that's* how Shobai got out. I'll be damned." His glance moved away from Hadad, dismissing him. "Take him to Manouk," he barked. "The other one will be there by now."

Other one? Hadad thought, his heart sinking. *Shobai?*

But when they dragged him before the heavily guarded command tent, Shobai was nowhere to be found. He heard voices inside as they stood him up, then stepped to one side of him, swords drawn. He glanced around—but saw no means of escape.

Two men came out of the tent behind Reshef. One was dark, bearded, intelligent-looking. This would be Jacob's friend—friend?—Manouk. Hadad blinked, trying to see a mass murderer in this stern but basically just-looking man. And then his eyes went to the other one, and he had no trouble seeing mass murderer in this one at all. He was huge, unkempt, with shoulders the width of a door. His expression was one of barely contained rage, and his eyes were terrible.

"This is Hadad, of Haran," Reshef said. He repeated this in the nomad tongue for the Leader's benefit.

"So," Manouk said. "You came to rescue your brother?"

Hadad gulped . . . and managed to speak, dry throat and all. "No," he said. "I came to your camp to kill you. All of you."

There was raucous laughter—none of it louder than the laughter of the giant at Manouk's side. *So,* Hadad thought. *Both of them understand a little of my speech.* He swallowed hard and went on, desperation overriding the abject fear in his heart. "You're laughing," he said. "You—you mean Reshef, over there, hasn't told you? About Haran?"

"Told us . . . about what?" Manouk said, his voice neutral.

"You come weaponless, small, crippled, and you say you have come to kill us. What could Reshef know that would make such a statement anything but the idle chatter of a fool?"

Hadad started. This was no pidgin Hurrian Manouk was speaking! "He—he's bluffing, Manouk," said Reshef. "He's not worth considering. There's nothing wrong."

"Nothing is wrong in Haran?" Hadad pressed on, too afraid to stop. "How would you know, Reshef, come to think of it? You haven't been in Haran in a week. You've been over here selling us out." He held up one hand; it shook. "See that? See that hand of mine shaking? That hand is my weapon, Reshef. That hand—and this breath of mine."

"Don't listen to him," Reshef said. But Manouk waved his hand. Motioned to Hadad to continue.

"My very weakness is a weapon," Hadad said. "And I may already have killed you with it. Haran is half empty, full of the dregs of the earth, refugees, the old, the sick. The sick. Do you hear me? And it's full of rats. Rats which come out of the cellars, now that the ratcatchers have left in fear of you. Rats who bite men and women."

"No!" Reshef screamed. "He's lying! He's lying!"

"Believe what you will," Hadad said. "Do you know the symptoms? Chills and fever. Quick, erratic heartbeat. Stupor. Spastic motions like the ones I was making when you caught me. I haven't really reached that stage yet—but I studied it enough, nursing my friends and neighbors to their deaths. I can mimic it. Soon I won't need to, will I? Will I, Manouk?"

Now he saw the doubt in Manouk's eyes. And he pressed on, his voice rising. "You're not sure whether to believe me, are you?" he said. "Well, I wish it weren't so. But it is. It's the only weapon I have, and I came to fight you to the death with it. All of you. You may kill me, but I'll win. Do you understand? Perhaps a dozen of your guards have touched me. Even more manhandled me when I was doing my idiot act in the square. And how many of you have breathed this infected breath of mine? How many of you have—like you, Manouk!—drawn death into your lungs from my lips as I spoke?"

"I—I don't believe . . ." Manouk began.

"Then look," Hadad said quietly, ominously.

He threw off his tattered robe.

Even the giant beside Manouk gasped. And Manouk's hard face turned white for a moment in the pale morning light.

538

They could see the red blotches now, all over his chest. They could see the bulging buboes, the size of a baby's fist, on Hadad's naked groin.

Hadad's voice became a hateful, insinuating stage whisper. "Yes," he hissed. "You understand now. It's all right. I'm just giving you a little scare. Put me to death if you like. Forget what I've told you. And come. Come attack Haran. It won't put up much of a fight, mind you. Not many able-bodied people left." As they looked, aghast, Hadad, standing naked in the dawn chill, went into a fit of uncontrollable shaking. He reached down for his rags and pulled them on, his hands shaking as he did. But he could still speak.

"Come on," he said, "who'll be f-first? Touch me! Kill me! We're all going to die soon—all of us!"

There was a stunned silence. And then Manouk spoke. "Plague," he said. "I should have remembered. It nearly wiped out Haran two generations ago. *Plague . . .*"

VIII

Amid the confusion that followed, the soldiers drove Hadad from the camp at spear's point, and he retired to a low hill above the river, overlooking the camp. From his vantage point, he could see both the rendezvous where he had promised to meet Shobai and the growing chaos in the command camp on the other side of the hill.

Below, hundreds—perhaps thousands—of tents were being struck as the nomads made haste to pick up all their chattels and possessions and leave as quickly as possible. Apparently, the word had spread already, and the evacuation of the nomad encampment, begun in an orderly fashion, had begun to degenerate into a full-scale panic.

Nevertheless, the Shepherd Kings *were* nomads, and they traveled light. For the most part, they had no more goods to pack than each man could carry on his horse's back, although the big command tents had to be taken down in stages and packed in the wagons. Sectional tent poles, lashed together when in use, were dismantled now and their components loaded on top of the wagons.

Now, however, as the troops mustered in formation and began marching away, the somber thought came to Hadad: *Why, they're marching to Carchemish.* Carchemish, where the kind and sympathetic soldier Oshiyahu had been going . . .

Gods! he thought. *I've saved Haran . . . but I've doomed Carchemish. . . .* He thought of Oshiyahu, of their strange and poignant meeting outside the walls of Haran. And his heart sank as he remembered the soldier's words, tinged alike with bravery and despair: *"Well met, brother lunatic! You and I, we're old as the hills, aren't we? Well, old enough to know what a couple of damned fools we are, anyway—and old enough to know it's a damned fool's lot to do damned-fool things. Old enough not to question that, eh?"*

Hadad sighed, and the sadness caught at his heart. *Oshiyahu,* he thought, *forgive. Forgive.*

How wise the soldier had been! Yes, a man had to do what he had to do because of what he was. A man had to act in accord with his nature, and that nature never matched anyone else's. And because of the discrepancy, one man was bound to appear a fool to any other, if he acted according to his nature. The sin was in backing away from what it was in your nature to do, to be.

And—yes—Oshiyahu would now die, fighting as he had always fought, knowing how little winning or losing meant, surviving or dying. And the main thing was for him to die the way he had lived—strong, resolute, facing down his fear and making little of it.

He turned now and looked down the hill to the little grove by the river, with the blasted terebinth. There was no sign of Shobai still. Hadad's brow knit; his mouth twisted. *Shobai,* he thought, *please make it through. Please.*

Of course, there were those like Shobai who discovered only late in their years just who they were, what was the inner nature they must follow. His brother was at an important crossroads in his life, making new choices. . . .

Hadad smiled in spite of himself. Late in his years? No, not at all. Every man had his own rhythm. It would be sufficient if a man learned his true nature on his deathbed, at a hundred years of age. And Shobai was young by anybody's standards. Oshiyahu had known this, understood it. *"A good chap, really. Just a little young. His errors are a young man's errors."*

He sighed. But—if only Shobai would come . . .

Patience, he told himself, *patience.* And he thought: *I'll give him until the sun comes above . . . above that hill right over there.*

And then what, Hadad? Then what will you do?

He frowned. And his mind raced. But try as he might, he could think of nothing.

Reshef cursed, watching the wagons roll away. There was a cold spot in his heart that nothing seemed to be able to drive away. He'd been outflanked, outwitted, his plan turned into rubbish by the cripple's bluff. And the bluff had worked, magnificently. Damn him!

His clawlike hands clutched each other spasmodically. *The little bastard!* He'd no more had the plague than—

Ah, if only I could get that scrawny neck between these hands. If only . . .

Idly, his hand went to his cheek, as it always did these days in times of stress; his fingers ran up and down the still-livid scar that halved his face. There was in his heart a touch of the humiliation he had felt when Jacob had faced him down in the streets of Haran, armed only with a staff. He felt weakened, diminished, less of a man than . . .

There was a sudden blank spot in his mind, as if a great hand had wiped clean a wet tablet on which he had been writing. And the blankness was replaced with a single thought, one which gave him heart again, which he greeted with an almost sexual pleasure, the blood flowing hot both in his extremities—his feet and his clutching hands—and in his loins. It was the same feeling he would sometimes have when prowling the streets at night, looking for a woman to . . .

Shobai.

He'd forgotten. They'd captured him. He'd got the word. But apparently someone had gotten his signals crossed and taken him someplace other than Manouk's tent. But where?

It was a good question. And—well, look. The camp was breaking up. Had the armorer been loaded on one of the wagons and taken away? Had someone—someone else, damn him—ventured to kill him? And rob him, Reshef, of his one remaining pleasure in the present painful and demeaning situation?

He spotted a figure he recognized, set out at a jog after him. "Captain!" he said. "Captain of the guards!"

The soldier turned, nodded, but did not break stride. Reshef pulled up alongside him. "Captain," he said, puffing at the sudden exertion, "about the armorer Shobai—do you know what happened to him?"

"The prisoner? The big one?" The captain ran his tongue along the lower edge of his upper teeth. "I think the men had some trouble subduing him. Do you know the big cage where Manouk used to keep that young pet lion of his, before it died?"

"Uh, yes," Reshef said, his mind racing. *Where? Where?*

"All right. Well, you won't know where it is now. They moved it after the animal died. They used it for confining animals for the slaughter; it's in the tent they used for the officers' mess. We're not taking that one along. It mildewed after the last rain."

"I see," Reshef said. "And the prisoner's there?"

"If he's anywhere, just now." He turned and looked at Reshef. "With Haran removed from the list of priorities, will you be joining us in the Carchemish campaign?"

"Uh, I think perhaps later," Reshef said. "I'm mainly here as an observer and adviser," he said. "But I'll be in at the kill." He smiled his oily smile. "Thank you for the information." He ignored the expression of distaste in the captain's face and struck out in a northeasterly direction through the confusion and dust.

Hadad had given up on meeting Shobai, and he had moved closer to the camp to look down from one of the now-deserted guard posts high above the parade ground. He peered through the dust, hoping for some sign, watching the pack animals being driven away, watching the last structures being taken down.

There was one tent—a big one—which no one was apparently much interested in. Hadad idly wondered why. All the other major tents, the ones with more than one pole, had been struck and loaded, yet this one had attracted little attention. . . . His eyes roamed away from it, but the question remained in his mind.

Then his heart almost stopped. There was a figure, a vaguely familiar one, in military dress—but not the dress of the nomads. It seemed to be heading toward the big tent.

Reshef!

Hadad gulped—and, reluctantly, started down the hill, his descent made more ungainly by his crooked leg. His hands sweated; his heart pounded fast. He wished he had a weapon of some kind. He felt sure he'd need it, and soon. . . .

The cage was big, strong, solidly built; it had been raised to accommodate a lion. It stretched nearly to the top of the big tent. Beside it, the white-hot coals of the morning's cooking fire still glowed. The place had been abandoned in such haste that some of the cooks' tools still lay on the ground. A skewer—the kind used to cook *khorovadzh* over the coals—lay on the fire, its tip glowing like the coals.

Reshef looked at the far side of the cage, past the open door—and smiled.

The big armorer had apparently put up a fight—and no one had taken any chances after subduing him. He was spread-eagled against the bars of the cage, his hands tied to the crossbars high above his head, his legs spread as wide as his arms, and his ankles lashed securely to the crossbars a foot from the ground. His whole weight hung from his wrists; his eyes were closed now, but Reshef could hear a soft groan escape from his open lips.

Reshef smiled. A little shiver of anticipation ran through him. "Shobai," he said, reaching down to pick up the white-hot skewer by its wooden handle. "Shobai, wake up. I have a little surprise for you. . . ."

Hadad hurried forward. Strangely, no one seemed to be paying the smallest attention to him. The soldiers, the hangers-on, all were too intent on their own pressing problems even to take notice of the real source of them.

Still, he felt himself in danger, and he winced whenever one of them, alert or not, passed too close to him. More and more, he wished he had a weapon of some kind.

Suddenly he stopped dead.

Up ahead was a wagon. On the wagon stood a wooden weapon rack—a rack full of swords, and only the one man to guard it . . .

He slipped forward, keeping quiet. His eyes turned this way, that. He edged up to the wagon, behind the guard. His hand stole out. . . .

The guard shifted his feet.

Hadad froze.

Then the guard relaxed. But Hadad's hand moved out, slipping the nearest of the swords free, slowly, slowly . . .

And now it was loose, and in his hand. He withdrew his arm through the opening in the side of the wagon. The guard bellowed to someone far away: "Hey, you! Get those damned horses up here! On the double!"

And Hadad was away, the precious weapon hot in his sweaty hand. He speeded up his awkward but oddly efficient gait almost to a trot; he could see the tent right ahead now.

Suddenly, there was a piercing, shuddering animal scream of abject pain.

Hadad's heart skipped a beat. His eyes widened, his mouth flew open.

The cry had come from the tent up ahead. Now there were other cries . . . almost whimpers: a child's cry in an adult's voice. And—just as Hadad caught his breath and moved forward in an ungainly jog, tightening his grip on the sword in his right hand—a great deafening screech, a soul-wrenching cry that shook him to the soles of his feet, a howl of torment that would echo in his ears for the rest of his life . . .

Hadad burst through the doorway of the tent. "Shobai?" he cried. "Shobai!"

He stopped. Stared in horror. The sword hung lose from his inert fingers. His knees shook.

Reshef turned to look at him, a hideous smile on his rat's face. The white-hot skewer dangled from his hand.

"Oh, there you are, Crook-leg," he said in a mockery of friendly greeting. "I'm just finishing up some business here. Paying off some old bills." He stepped aside to indicate Shobai's hanging body.

Shobai's clothing was in rags, torn away from his body. Now he hung mostly naked, his wrists bleeding from his struggles; red welts crisscrossed his chest. His head hung forward, his hair hanging over his face. Hadad could not see his face. "Shobai," he said. "Are—are you alive?"

"Oh, he's alive," Reshef said. "Sorry about the chest. I was practicing. Just checking on whether the iron was hot enough. Then—well, I thought of—well, cooking his masculine equipment." Reshef waved the still-hot skewer at Shobai's naked genitals. At the approach of the heat Shobai's body stirred, but his head still hung low, covered by his hanging hair. He groaned in a low, rasping, tormented voice.

"Shobai," Hadad said, gripping the sword in his hand. "It's Hadad. I—I won't let him do it. I . . ."

Reshef ignored him. "But then I thought of something better. He hired roughs to scar my face. I thought: why not trade his face for mine? And what better place to start than . . . ?" But his smile returned, and his eyes were on Hadad's, cold as a basilisk's, and Hadad felt the cruelty and power in him and shivered visibly. Reshef's hand went to Shobai's hair, and his fingers grabbed the hanging locks and forced the prisoner's head back, back, so Hadad could see his face.

This time it was Hadad who screamed. *"Shobai!"*

Reshef had spared Shobai's cheeks. But the searing, burning point of the white-hot, razor-sharp skewer had reached out with a touch as deadly as a dragon's kiss, to each of Shobai's eyes. . . .

"See?" Reshef said over Shobai's low moans. "A trade. His face for mine. Only I always repay my debts with interest. Isn't it pretty?"

Shobai was blind. Blind!

The sword dropped with a clatter at Hadad's feet. His hands covered his mouth. He stared, his face white with shock. "Shobai," he said in a small, broken voice.

IX

The tortured face of the hanging man turned his way, its seared eyes seeing nothing. The weight of the big body tore at the mutilated wrists. "Hadad," the agonized voice croaked almost inaudibly. "Go. Run. He'll kill you. . . ."

Reshef's face took on that terrible smile. "He's right, you know, Crook-leg. I'd run if I were you. Or hop, or whatever it is that you do. I'd get well away. Forget this trussed ox up here on his spit. He's none of your business—nothing to die for. Besides, if you stay here, I may add you to the agenda for my afternoon's entertainment. . . ."

Hadad, trembling, his heart empty, looked at the poor ravaged body hanging from the cage. And, his hands shaking, he bent over to pick up the sword he'd dropped.

"Ah, there, now—" Reshef said softly, insinuatingly. "So you're going to be a fool. . . ."

"No," Shobai said from his rack, his voice rasping, painful. "No, Reshef. Leave him alone. He—he's never struck a blow in anger in his life. He doesn't know how to fight."

"I won't leave you, Shobai," Hadad said. "I—I've got a sword. He won't touch you again. . . ."

"No," the ghastly figure lashed to the cage said. Hadad looked away from the charred eyes. "Reshef's a master of the sword . . . don't fight him. . . ."

"So," Reshef said, ignoring him. "The little frog with the crooked leg won't let me touch his brother again? Won't *let* me?" He glanced down at the skewer, cooling in his hand.

"Ah, well," he said lightly. "Perhaps I won't at that. Not until this thing has been reheated." He made as if to toss it aside; but then he changed his mind. "No," he said. "No, I'll keep it, even if it *has* cooled off." He felt the point. "Good enough. What do I need with a hacking blade? A sharp point will do."

"G-get away from my brother," Hadad said. "You move— over there." He stood awkwardly holding the sword, pointing with his free hand. "Go."

"Ah, Shobai," Reshef said. "What a pity you'll be missing this. A real, live duel, the way they used to do them down on the quays by the river in my wicked youth." He snickered. "Two gallants fighting over a matter of honor, or whatever. Or over the honor of a lady." He made a mock-sour face. "Well, there's no lady here. Although when I'm done I've plans to make a lady of *you*, dear boy. Or whatever you call someone who isn't a man any more . . ."

Hadad swallowed. His hands moved with a life of their own. With a wild cry, far beyond any control of his own, he sprang forward, with an agility even a man without his handicap might have envied, swinging the sword over his head. Reshef, taken by surprise, feebly tried to parry Hadad's clumsy swing with the skewer; but he only succeeded in partially deflecting the blow. The flat of Hadad's blade caught him on the side of the head and knocked him cold; his legs became rubber underneath him and he fell in a heap and did not move.

"Shobai," Hadad said, "I think I've—I've hurt him. His head is bleeding. He isn't moving." He hesitated for a beat; then he moved to Shobai's side, slashing first the ropes on his ankles, then that on one wrist. As he cut the other wrist free, he stepped under his brother and helped ease his heavy weight down. "There, now—can you stand?"

"I—I don't know." He tried his legs, leaning on Hadad. "I think so. Hadad: is he . . . is he dead?"

Hadad began to answer; but the question was answered for him. With a growl Reshef, coming off the floor, his sword and not the skewer in his hand, lunged mightily. The sword point missed Hadad's unprotected back by a hair's breadth as Hadad moved. Hadad, reacting quickly, felt the cold metal under his arm—and slammed the arm into his side, trapping the sword between his arm and his body. He twisted—and almost dislodged the weapon from Reshef's grasp.

With an audible snarl Reshef pulled the sword away and stepped back. "By hell," he said. "I think I *will* kill you. I'll cut your damned heart out. I'll pull out your guts and string them around your neck."

Hadad stood his ground. "Shobai," he said. "Please. Feel your way to the door of the tent. Feel your way by the wall . . . it's to your left. Get outside, where someone can see you. Where someone can help you . . ."

"Don't!" Shobai said, groping behind him for the wall. "Don't fight him, Hadad. . . ."

"Shobai, please. If you don't get away—get free of him— everything I'm doing will be wasted."

"Come on, Crook-leg," Reshef said tauntingly. He waggled the dancing point of the sword before Hadad. "I'll give you a little lesson in fencing. Just come at me. Any old way . . ."

Hadad backed away from him, slowly, carefully leading him away from Shobai and the open tent-flap. "Shobai," he said quietly, "just slip outside. I think I can delay him until you're free. Call out to someone. Get someone to help. They can't see the slave mark. They won't know the difference. The camp's full of foreigners anyhow."

"Hadad?" Shobai said. "Oh, Hadad, if you'd only come with me. Don't fight him. . . ."

"Too late, Shobai," his brother said. "Now go, please. Remember me—to mother and Danataya. And find my child. Find my child and help it. Whatever it turns out to be."

There was a terrible clash of metal against metal. Shobai, hearing, winced—and, his heart in ashes, he stumbled out of the tent into bright sunshine that he could feel on his half-bare body—but would never see again.

Reshef cut, slashed on the backswing, drove Hadad backward. "Well, you've bought him a moment or two," he said. "But it doesn't matter. How far can a blind man get? Oh, don't fear. I'll catch up to him after a hundred steps. That is, after I've finished carving you like a goose."

Hadad gritted his teeth—and attacked, holding the sword in both hands. There was strength to spare in his two united arms; the blow caught Reshef's blade forte against forte and jarred his hands; the sword fell to the ground. Reshef started to bend over to retrieve it; but Hadad raised his own weapon head-high, poised for a mighty blow. "You—you reach for that," Hadad said in a timid little voice, "and—and I'll cut your head off."

Reshef stood, backed away a step, saluting him as if he held a weapon in his hand still. "Why, so you might," he said. "My compliments, Crook-leg. You've a trifling amount of mettle after all. Anat always described you as such a sniveling milksop." He smiled in a mockery of graciousness. "Now I'm at your mercy," he said. "What are you going to do?"

"I . . . look, you," Hadad said, swallowing hard. "You just get inside that cage over there. I'm going to lock you up, long enough to make sure we get free of you. You'll be able to find your way out sooner or later . . . but by that time we'll be able to get away from here. We can get to Haran, perhaps. And by the time I've finished telling everyone in Haran about your part in all this, you won't dare show your face there again." He spoke through clenched teeth, as much to keep his teeth from chattering as anything.

"Why—why, yes," Reshef said, that mock-ingratiating smile on his face, letting himself be herded slowly toward the open gate of the big cage. "Incidentally, that was quite a blow you struck there. You've more strength than I thought. Clumsy, but strong. It's funny: sometimes the very clumsiness of a beginner can be his strength. I mean, one expects such and such a move on his opponent's part—and then when it doesn't come and instead someone lets go a big wild swing like that . . ."

"Enough t-talking," Hadad said unsteadily. "Just back right in there . . ."

"Certainly," Reshef said. "Whatever you say, dear boy."

He swung the gate wide as if to enter—but when Hadad edged closer to him he swung the door suddenly the other way. The door caught Hadad in the face; he staggered backward . . . and dropped his sword.

Quick as a flash, Reshef was upon him, battering him to his knees with fists made hard by many years of fighting. Hadad clawed impotently at the ground for his sword; but it was two steps away at least. Reshef, snarling, kicked him in the face—and dived for the sword.

He was up in a rolling motion, his feet under him, the sword at the ready; but to his surprise Reshef now saw Hadad, who had fallen and done a somersault to land on his own feet, come to rest not a step from his own—Reshef's—abandoned weapon. Hadad stooped and picked it up. And, using the same odd two-handed grip, he faced Reshef again.

"Wonderful!" Reshef said. "But I'm afraid I'm growing tired of this. Time to end it all, Crook-leg. Time to put you to sleep, dear boy. Time to go back out and find your brother, the Mole, groping his way through the scrub, and put *him* to sleep, too. No sense leaving any witnesses, you know."

"You—you didn't leave any witnesses when you killed the

women, did you? When you killed poor little Tanuha?" Hadad backed away, one ungainly step at a time.

"Tanuha? Oh, you mean Anat's homely little slave? Oh, no." He lunged, withdrew; Hadad barely managed to get out of his way. He feinted again, throwing Hadad off balance. Hadad recovered—but bumped against the tent wall. Panic-stricken, he jumped to one side, ending in the center of the tent after a frantic scramble. "No," Reshef said. "I'm not one of your exhibition-minded types when I'm taking my pleasure." He feinted again; Hadad jumped, awkwardly. "I *told* Anat I was going to get myself a piece of that one day. Serves her right for encouraging the little slut to go around bare-assed that way, you know. And a nice little piece she was, too, boy. Soft and tender—she cried out so piteously...."

"You—you filthy animal!" Hadad said. He swung the sword again, as powerfully and as wildly as before; but this time Reshef was ready and waiting for him. The blow was parried easily ...

... and now, suddenly, definitively, Hadad knew it was all over. It was the end of the game. The mad glint was in Reshef's eye, the glint that must have been there when he murdered the girls he had raped. The glint that Hadad had seen in the rat-faced man's eye when he had first burst into the tent and seen Shobai's poor battered body hanging from the crossbar of the cage, his pitiful, sightless eyes hidden by his long hair.

Reshef smiled. There was pleasure in the smile now. His breathing was low and regular, his attitude relaxed. His point danced back and forth, darting out here, there—and little cuts opened on Hadad's chest, his forehead. "Point," Reshef said softly. "Point again."

Hadad raised his own sword—and Reshef's blade moved almost too quickly for the eye to see. Two blindingly rapid slashes—and deep cuts opened on Hadad's forearms. The one on his left arm was a stab of excruciating pain; his grip on his sword became a one-handed one. He parried another slash clumsily, backing slowly toward the open tent-flap. And, his eyes on Reshef but his voice not addressing Reshef at all, he said plaintively but with an undertone of calm, "Good-bye, Danataya. Good-bye, Shobai. Good-bye, Mother. Farewell, Jacob...."

"What are you saying, Crook-leg?" Reshef said derisively, his point licking out like a snake's tongue to pink Hadad painfully in the chest, the upper arm. "Praying?"

Hadad ignored his words, concentrating on trying to parry

the quick lunges Reshef made with the point of that sword of his, too quick to see. "Farewell, my darling child whom I've never seen. I love you all. I'm sorry I failed. I did the best I could. But I couldn't find my way home to you. I miss you all, and if there's a next life in which I can see you again . . ."

"Here," Reshef said. "Enough of this." He engaged Hadad's sword, made a quick powerful twist of the wrist, and disarmed his opponent. Hadad's sword flew out of his hand, landing at Reshef's feet. Reshef poised, on guard. "Damn you!" he said. "Defend yourself!"

But Hadad stood now, hands at his sides. There was something like a smile on his face; a look of peace, a look of acceptance, a look of understanding. "Farewell," he said again, not speaking to Reshef at all. "My love goes with you always. . . ."

It was the peace in his face that Reshef could not stand. *Peace!* With a snarl he drew back his sword and ran Hadad through the body, once, twice. He withdrew his sword that second time, viciously, looking at the dying of the light in the boy's eyes. Watching the life leave him. Watching his unmatched legs, one of them already grotesquely out of line, lose their strength in a sudden rush as the breath of existence slipped easily out of him and the discarded body, void of the evanescent thing that had made it move, tumbled in an ungainly heap at his feet.

Reshef stared.

He felt empty, empty.

There was no feeling of victory. Again! Again! Cheated! Cheated of his triumph! Always! Always!

A red rage rushed into the void in his insides. He stepped out into the sunshine and bellowed: *"Shobai! Shobai! He's dead! Do you hear? Dead! I killed him! I killed your brother!"*

But his words echoed through an empty camp. All around him there was nothing to be seen but the worthless leavings of an army that had marched away in tall columns of dust. While he fought, the encampment had emptied of life, leaving behind only the messiness of an abandoned kitchen midden.

"Shobai!" he screamed again. But his voice trailed off into nothingness. The warm sun beat down mercilessly. The sky was rich and blue and cloudless. Far in the distance he could hear the muffled beating of a drum, as the army of the Shepherd Kings marched off to war.

Overhead, a lone vulture circled lazily. . . .

X

Shobai, too—face and body racked with unimaginable pain—heard the drums as he lay in the back of the wagon which rattled slowly over the uneven ground, taking him step by plodding step out of the nomads' now-deserted encampment. Over the creaking of the wheels, Reshef's fading words carried to him across the valley: "Shobai . . . I killed him! I killed your brother. . . ."

It was too much. His hands clawed impotently at his cheeks, avoiding his seared and ruined sockets. "No," he said. "No, please . . . let it not be so . . . let him be lying. . . ."

The man up front in the driver's seat called back to him: "Easy, there. Try to relax a little. There's water in the bag by your hand, if you need it."

Shobai groaned. "If only I had died earlier. If I'd had the courage to kill myself."

"Courage, son?" the driver said in his slow, patient voice. "Courage is what it takes to stay alive, not to die. And certainly not to throw away the gift of life itself. Lie still, there, won't you? I'll get you to help as soon as I can. I know you're in terrible pain. Look: there's wine in the other bag. It's right by your foot, there."

"Oh, gods! Gods! If I'd died first, he wouldn't have risked his life to save me—and now it's all wasted, wasted." He sobbed, pounding his big fists on the floorboards of the wagon.

"Well, it's there if you want it," the kindly voice said. "Suit yourself, son. If I had anything stronger, I'd give it to you." He clucked softly at the asses drawing the wagon. "Come on there, now, Blackie. You, too, One-Ear. Up the hill now. . . ."

Shobai rolled over on his back, feeling the warm sun on his face, incongruous in the absolute night of his tortured mind. It was no use calling on any gods to help, he was thinking. The plain fact was that there weren't any. It was all a sham, a charade, a bad joke. A cruel joke, indeed, to play on poor devils who grunted and sweated their way through a comfortless life. Would a god, a god to whom you spoke and offered tribute and prayers, let such things happen? Would a god offer absolute and crushing defeat to the good and reward the evil with such universal triumph?

Look what had happened. Now he, Shobai, didn't count. He'd richly earned his own present woes—yes, and worse— many times over by the thoughtless and foolish life he'd led. What did a shallow fool like himself matter?

But—Hadad . . . Haran . . . all the innocent people who didn't deserve the terrible fate that lay ahead for the city. Peaceful, easy-going Haran! Proud Carchemish! Beautiful cities which would be rubble on the morrow, their citizens dead, mutilated . . .

And Hadad, with his great heart and guileless, generous, brave, and loving soul . . .

He sobbed, biting into his clenched hand. And—and who had won? Reshef? The nomads! The Leader!

He remembered Hadad's last words to him now: "Remember me—to mother and Danataya. And find my child. Find my child and help it. . . ." He groaned in anguish again. Help? Him? A blind pauper? A slave? A man without a city? A man who, even if the slave mark were to be obliterated, would then find himself beggared and helpless? Fit only to squat in the street and solicit alms? And—yes—in what city? Haran and Carchemish were gone, gone. The funds he'd had on deposit there would be rubbish. His richly appointed house in Haran would be a burnt-out hulk, if indeed it still stood at all. Anat—faithless Anat—would be raped, impaled, dead in a gutter somewhere. He was empty-handed, a cipher, a man without a name or an identity anymore . . .

. . . and blind! Blind! Blind!

They stopped late in the day by a little stream; Shobai could hear it gushing down the hillside, dancing over rocks. The driver of the cart helped him down, sat him on a rock by the brook, and washed his face tenderly.

"You—you could just leave me," Shobai said. "I can die here as well as anywhere. Is the stream deep? I can drown in water a handspan deep—"

"Hush. Hush. I won't have you talking like that. Now let me clean this off here."

"Who are you?" Shobai said suddenly. "And why won't you leave me alone? Let me die? Who—?"

"Me?" the driver said. "The name is Yadiri. I'm a trader, purveying foods to the Shepherd Kings for their little festival. And now I'm going home to Hamath, after a stop in Haran."

"Haran?" Shobai said with a despairing, anguished snarl. "You fool, don't you know Haran is dead? Haran will be ruins, garbage, rubble by now! If you go to Haran, you go to your death!"

"Well, no," the man said, washing the caked blood from Shobai's cheeks gently. "You obviously haven't heard. The raid on Haran—it's been called off. I don't know why. It seems to have been a very sudden decision on someone's part. That was the reason for the quick mobilization, you know. Suddenly, somebody gave the order, and everyone started forming to march to Carchemish." He sighed audibly. "Poor Carchemish! A nice town. I did a lot of business there."

"But—Haran? Haran has been spared?" Shobai said, putting a hand on his arm, his face tense and unbelieving. "I—I don't understand. . . ."

"Neither do I, my boy. But if the gods are going to spare Haran for whatever reasons, I'll give thanks to them and count my blessings. Haran was always one of my best markets. I'll admit it comes as a surprise. I had expected the nomads to wipe the city from the earth."

"B-but—but—" Shobai gulped. "Look, how fast can you get me to Haran? Because . . . look, I'll give you money. I'm a rich man in Haran. This slave mark—it was put on me by the nomads. It won't be valid in Haran. Not if the city has escaped, not if the nomads have decided to spare it. I have a big house, property, credit. . . ."

The trader looked at Shobai's rags, and when he spoke his voice, however gently, reflected his disbelief. "That's all right, son. I don't want your, uh, money. We'll be in Haran soon enough, I suppose. This road leads to a midpoint on the caravan route between the two cities."

"I know the spot," Shobai said. "And that's maybe a half day from Haran. We should be in the city by—look, how far are we from the place where we pick up the caravan route?"

"We'll pick it up early tomorrow. I made camp north of the crossroads to avoid bandits—though I doubt if they're much in evidence these days, come to think of it."

"Then—then we could be in Haran by evening tomorrow, couldn't we? Couldn't we?"

"Conceivably. I'll try. I must say it's good to see you perking up like this." He clapped Shobai on the shoulder. "Courage. I'll have you back among your friends and kin by tomorrow night. And don't ever give up hope. Never!"

* * *

"Gods!" said Hoshaiah. "Just look at them, sir."

Oshiyahu scanned the great horde before him. "You think that's a lot of them, son? Well, there are more on the way."

"More, sir? But—"

"A messenger came an hour ago, and he said that the nomad troops that were poised for an attack on Haran are being shifted over here. Even the Shepherd Kings' command camp has been broken up, and everyone is marching on Carchemish."

"Ah." The breath let itself out slowly, audibly.

"Yes, it appears that, for some reason, Haran's been spared—for now, anyway. As for Carchemish—" He stopped abruptly, squinting into the distance. He held one hand over his eyes to shield them from the afternoon sun. "Well, I'll be damned," he said. "Isn't that . . . ?" He mumbled to himself, his words indistinct. "They must have ridden at top speed all the way from—"

"What is it, sir?" Hoshaiah said.

"The two men down there who just rode up. See? The ones up ahead of the guard unit accompanying them?"

"Uh—yes, sir. Why?"

"Well, that one in the red robe is Manouk, or I'm a walleyed idiot. And that monster next to him must be . . . oh, yes. There couldn't be anyone else like that. That has to be the one they call the Leader."

"Their supreme commander?"

"Yes. Gods! Look at him! How do they find a horse that can hold him? He'd break the back of any charger I ever put a saddle on. And—why, they're both here! Both of them! What an opportunity!"

"Opportunity, sir?"

"Yes, boy!" Oshiyahu grinned. "Imagine—if we were to hit them right now, before they bring the other reserves up . . ."

"Attack, sir? Attack? Sir, that's impossible!"

Oshiyahu looked at him—and Hoshaiah blinked, seeing the expression on his face. He did not say anything for a moment. Neither did his commander. Then the younger man spoke. "Then . . . it's come down to that, sir?"

"Of course it has. The moment they freed the troops to come over from Haran . . ." Oshiyahu flashed a tight grin at him, his eyes resolute and hard. "Think, son. Which would you prefer? Waiting for them to hit us? Waiting for that incredible force to sweep over us in wave after wave? Or . . . a nice quick charge? A glorious assault on their front line, with both their supreme commanders facing us—and a chance to kill off a few of their finest before they . . . ?"

He left the question unfinished. And, his eyes, his face bearing a new and changed expression of his own, Hoshaiah slowly nodded. "I'll form the men, sir. May I suggest that you and I go in with the first detachment of foot troops, after the cavalry has charged. Bowmen to the rear, and a volley for each wave as we hit them."

"Very good. Incidentally, from this moment, you're a captain of guards—Danel's old position. You've earned it."

"Thank you, sir," the young man said, clear-eyed, strong-voiced, his choice made, his mind set, his backbone strong and straight. "I'll try not to disgrace myself."

Again the element of surprise worked its wonders. The Carchemish archers cut down a row of infantry, and Oshiyahu's light horse cavalry, screaming themselves hoarse, swooped down on the second rank, spears flashing. They withdrew and regrouped for another charge; by then Oshiyahu's foot soldiers, with the old warrior himself at their head, were wading into the nomad lines, hacking and stabbing, bellowing their lungs out with the new war cry Oshiyahu had given them: "For Danel! For Danel!"

Oshiyahu, his heart pounding, a fierce grin on his face, took on two nomad swordsmen at the same time. He disarmed the first with a single twist of his still-powerful wrists. The second lunged and grazed his upper arm. "Why, you son of a bitch!" Oshiyahu said, hacking mightily; his blade felled the nomad in a single, backhand blow. He turned just in time to parry a wild blow from another warrior—and, eyes flashing, bellowed with laughter to see Hoshaiah stab the man in the side and bring him to his knees before braining him with the flat of his sword.

He looked around, smiling a fierce and terrible smile. "Manouk! Where are you?" he bellowed. "Send me your Leader! Your Leader! I am Oshiyahu of Haran!"

Then—he saw what he was looking for. The gigantic form of the nomad commander stood a head taller than the men he was fighting. As Oshiyahu hacked his way through the crowd toward his prey, he saw the big man virtually behead a Carchemish warrior with a single sweep of his blade. "Here!" Oshiyahu said, gesturing with his blade to make clear his intentions, "You! Leader! Fight me! Stand and fight me!"

The big man looked his way—and those mad eyes flashed,

comprehending the challenge. He pushed his way toward Oshiyahu, calling out to him in a voice that carried like a lion's. "You—come! Die!"

"I am Oshiyahu of Haran!" his adversary shouted. "Oshiyahu of the Battle of Mari! Stand and fight!" A single man barred his way; he hacked at that soldier's face and beat him to one side—onto another man's sword. "Stand!"

The Leader growled, low in his throat—and attacked.

His first swing caught Oshiyahu's sword just above the handle; the power of the stroke was immense, and almost jarred the weapon from his hands. But Oshiyahu gave ground, just enough to draw his opponent in—and then lunged, stabbing the Leader high in the chest. He withdrew like lightning and saluted the big man sardonically. "Point!" he said. And attacked again.

This time the Leader was waiting for him. Oshiyahu felt his blade turned, ducked as a vicious lunge just missed his neck. He parried, disengaged; feinted high—and hacked low, catching the big man in one ankle. He bellowed with uncontrollable laughter; the hit had been a good one. Lame a big bastard like that, and—

The Leader charged. He lunged at Oshiyahu's face—and Oshiyahu gave ground, one step, two steps. Then Oshiyahu held ground, engaged, beat his opponent's sword aside, lunged, missed, and feinted with his body as if to give ground again. The Leader lunged, once, twice . . .

. . . and on the second lunge impaled himself on Oshiyahu's blade, to the hilt. His dark eyes widened; his mouth flew open; he dropped his sword. . . .

Oshiyahu tugged at his own weapon, pulling it free with difficulty. His smile faded. There was a look almost of disbelief on his face as the giant staggered forward and fell on his face. "The Leader!" someone called out. "He's killed the Leader. . . ."

Oshiyahu let his guard down for a moment, for no more than the blink of an eye—and a spearman, coming up from the side, buried the point of his heavy weapon in the commander's belly. Oshiyahu dropped his sword, clawing at his side. Then the strength left him, and he was down. There were three of them, stabbing away at him as he tried to rise, and then after a time he could rise no more. Through dim eyes he saw Hoshaiah fighting his way toward him . . . and then Hoshaiah fell, struck down by a dozen hands. Then the breath began slipping away from him, and he could not breathe. And presently life slipped away from him as well, and the sounds of battle became a great echoing quiet. . . .

In the aftermath, as the nomad soldiers moved from body to body, killing, hacking off heads, Manouk found the bodies of Oshiyahu and the Leader, lying not an arm's length from each other. A nomad soldier was bent over Oshiyahu's body, his sword drawn. Manouk snarled, stepped forward, grabbed the soldier by the hair and dragged him away. "Touch his body and I'll kill you. Do you hear? With these two hands. Karakin, whom no man could kill, lies dead by this soldier's hand. Would you then dishonor the body of such a warrior?"

"N-no, sir," the soldier said, backing away from the icy rage in his commander's eye.

"Very well," Manouk said. "Guard his body until it can be taken away, and let no man lay hand upon it. If I find a new mark upon him when the horses come to bear him and Karakin away, you won't live to eat another meal. Believe me."

"Yes, sir." And as Manouk moved away, the soldier cursed his ill luck. The rest of the army would move into Carchemish within the hour, and there he'd be, stuck guarding a couple of corpses. What an injustice! What a disappointment!

There was a roar from the army up ahead as the great battering-ram moved toward the gate. Soon it would be up to the old, the feeble, the sick to defend the dying city. . . .

CHAPTER SIXTEEN

I

Three times Shobai awoke screaming in the night. Each time, Yadiri patiently rose and tried to comfort him. To him, it seemed inexpressibly poignant for so young a man to lose so much and have so little in the way of defense against what had happened to him, and he sat up for long hours trying to help Shobai get back to sleep.

He awoke, however, in the morning to see Shobai sitting up, his sleeping-furs neatly rolled beside him, his head held high, ears cocked for any sound. When he heard Yadiri's first rustling motions, rising, he spoke, softly. "Good morning," he said.

"Ah," Yadiri greeted him, stretching, sitting up, finally standing, his hand on his back. "I grow old for this business of sleeping on the ground," he added, yawning. "My back's stiff." He yawned again: once, twice.

"Look," Shobai said. "I apologize for—for keeping you up last night. And . . . thanks. You are a kind man. I—I'm too much bother. Perhaps you'd really do best leaving me somewhere. . . ."

Yadiri bent to roll his own sleeping-rugs. "Nonsense, my boy. You're no trouble, really. And how could I hold my head up again—me, Yadiri the trader—if I abandoned a fine young fellow like yourself without getting him to safety? To a place where people could help?" He tied the rugs with a thong and carried them, along with Shobai's own borrowed furs, to the wagon again. "Look, I have some idea of what you must be going through—but no, I suppose I don't, do I? I've been trying to imagine. . . ."

Shobai sighed. "My spirits lift a bit now and then . . . and then a chance thought can send me once again into the depths. The worst times may be going to sleep—and waking again. Waking to eternal night. . . ."

"That's a terrible thought, I'll admit," the trader said. "Here, I'll make a little fire. I could use some herb tea before we leave."

"But—the hardest thing," Shobai said, ignoring him, "I think the hardest thing isn't the pain or the shock. It's the feeling of worthlessness." His voice faded to a near-whisper; he was talking more to himself now than to Yadiri. "And the feeling that . . . that . . . why, everything's lost. Evil has conquered good. If I had my eyes back . . . if I were rich and powerful once again, with all the strength that I wasted for so long . . . could I bring back Carchemish? Could I bring back H-Hadad?"

His brother's name brought back a rush of feeling; with a sob, he covered his mouth with both hands. "Hadad," he mumbled.

"There, now, son," the trader said, putting a comforting hand on the young man's head. "Don't give up hope. Don't sell life short. When something terrible happens, you think all is lost, all is irremediable. It always looks that way. But when you look around you—"

" 'Look'?" Shobai said bitterly. " 'Look' is hardly a word to use to me any more, I'm afraid. Look with what?" Then his face twisted in self-loathing. "I—I'm sorry, that just slipped out. And I'm in pain from all this. My—my eyes hurt —as if they were still there to hurt. . . ."

"Look, son," the trader said. "Why don't I fix you a soft bed in the back of the wagon? I can spread the furs underneath you; that'll cushion your ride. And these blankets on top . . . There's wine here, too, plenty of it. Take it for the pain. Don't be too proud to accept help. It just isolates you. . . ."

"I—thank you, Yadiri," Shobai said. "Maybe I will. I didn't get much sleep last night. I—I know that sounds lame. I know I kept you up, too. But—"

"Don't be proud. Your body has undergone a great shock. You've been beaten, too, from the look of you. You've had a bad time of it. Look, I'll leave you a little bread and cheese. Just reach for it; it'll be up front, right next to the wine bottle. You can't have eaten much lately."

"It doesn't matter," Shobai said. "I couldn't eat much now anyhow; it'd make me sick. But—thank you. Thank you for all your kindnesses."

"Quite all right. Look, son, we'll sleep in Haran tonight. There's a ford outside the city where you can wash up, take away the dust of the road. I can lend you a fresh robe. It won't be much, but it'll be better than those rags you're wearing, even if it won't fit too well . . ."

"The ford," Shobai said, his tone softening. "I know the place. Yes. The women of the city used to wash clothes there—and bathe while they did it. There was a whole section, down where the trees grew close to the river, where no man was allowed. But when you rode past, you could hear them giggling, and when you rode across the river at the low point, on the flats, you could look over in the patch of sunshine between the trees and see them, standing naked in the knee-deep water, laughing at you." His tone grew more nostalgic, reminiscent. "I can see them in my mind's eye right now, flaunting their bodies without shame. Now, mind you," he said, turning that sightless face to the trader, "these were women who, any other time, would blush at the thought of a man seeing them that way."

Yadiri watched him, kept looking at him, as he prepared herb tea for the two of them. The memory seemed to have softened the bitterness and defeat and despair in that gaunt young face, with its horrid scars and the terrifying burn marks around the empty eye sockets. The pain must have been terrible. He must in fact be in horrible pain even now. . . .

And then the moment passed. Shobai's voice broke off abruptly. His face fell. "Imagine," he said. "I'll never see a woman naked again. Never!" He showed white teeth—one of them was broken—in a bitter smile. "Never touch one either, I'll wager. What woman—what whore, in the lowest crib in the worst quarter of the meanest town—would willingly lie with a blind man with a face like mine?" He started to raise one hand to his still-painful eyes, then pulled the hand back. "No. No, it's all gone. Farewell to all joys, then. All the ones I knew, anyhow. That time of life has passed. How strange: I knew that I would grow old, and that the pleasures would pass away from me. I didn't know it would happen before I reached my twenty-fifth year."

His face changed, darkened. It was curious how expressive a face without eyes could be. "Hadad," he said. "Hadad died when he was hardly more than a child. He'll never know his woman again, see his baby. All the good things of life will pass him by, all the things he had never had a chance to have as a boy—and all because of me. Of me." His sigh was a sob, an echoing cry of anguish. "And—and no one will know where he lies. He dies unburied, unmourned, with no one to sing his soul across to that next land they're always telling us about. He'll be meat for vultures. Just another dead body. And it's all so meaningless, so wasteful. And all the evil ones—Reshef, Manouk—they go free. They triumph. Their victory banners fly by on the high road, on the way to new murders and new wretchedness, while Hadad—"

"Here," Yadiri said gently, "here's your tea. Try to drink some now. It's good for you."

Once they were on the road, the gentle jiggling of the wagon beneath him finally lulled Shobai off to a fitful sleep, from which he half woke from time to time only to slip back into sleep again. His dreams were a mixed lot: some were horrid nightmares; some, gentler than the rest, took him back to happier times in his youth . . . and then the wagon would hit a rough spot and jog him awake, and he would come to life, only to know that he lay in a darkness from which he could never emerge. He cried out . . . and in time slipped off again. . . .

Having gone to sleep with the sun low in the east, Shobai awoke when it was at its zenith, and its rays were warm and soothing. He mumbled something and kicked off one of the blankets that covered him; and, waiting for sleep to come on him again, he listened to the voices. Yadiri had apparently picked up a couple of travelers and given them a ride. From the way they talked, the two strangers obviously had traveled far together. Drowsily, Shobai listened to the voices:

". . . barely got out of Carchemish in time," one man was saying, in an accent that seemed utterly foreign to any city Shobai had visited. "Of course, a lot of others were getting out, too, but most of them seemed to be heading south, to Ebla or someplace else."

"Yes," the second man said. "We couldn't find a caravan, hire pack animals, anything. We finally bought two horses, the oldest and worst I've ever seen. There simply wasn't anything else. The first one gave out on the first day. We went a while on the second one, together—but he died not far from where you picked us up."

The second man's accent, Shobai thought, was that of Haran. And as he drifted to the edge of sleep, there was something extraordinarily comforting about the fact. The voice was not one blessed with a natural warmth; but its hominess and matter-of-factness made it sound soothing to his ears, starved as they were for the familiar, the everyday, the homely after his months of captivity and mistreatment among men of strange tongues. The words continued in an undertone:

". . . certainly glad to hear Haran's been spared," the man with the Haran accent was saying. "From what they told us in Carchemish . . ."

"It was a miracle," Yadiri replied, "I mean, I was there, right in the middle of their base camp, and I still couldn't tell you why the sudden change of heart. Of course, it means the end of poor Carchemish. . . ."

"A great pity. But Haran: it'll be good to see Haran after so many years."

"You may not recognize it. Most of the people are said to have left in panic. It'll be full of foreigners: poor ragtag rabble from the northern cities, escaping from the nomads themselves."

"Well, we'll just be visiting. And after all, cities have a way of changing, you know."

"Not Hamath," Yadiri chuckled. "Not a backwater like my town." He added ruefully. "It'd take destroying it to change it."

"Let's hope that doesn't happen," said the other stranger, the one with the foreign accent.

"Yes," Yadiri replied. "I gather you two are old experienced travelers—men who have seen many lands."

"Yes," the man with the Haran accent said. "It is no big thing. In the end, one place is much like another. Unless you've kin there, or close friends, people you're on the closest terms with. Without that, a place won't mean much to you."

"I wouldn't know," the trader said. "I'm a small-time trader, one who seldom travels more than three days to a new market. I did see Damascus once, when my father was alive. It was big and dirty. I didn't like it."

"I didn't, either," the Haran man said. He paused a moment, following his memories—then took up the conversation again. "Who's this poor devil in the back? I didn't get much of a look at him, but those burns around the eyes . . ."

"Ah. That's a sad story. I found him wandering in the nomad camp after the Shepherd Kings had moved their men out. He'd apparently been working for them in some capacity but had offended them somehow. They branded him, blinded him, beat him. . . . I'm taking him to Haran. Perhaps someone will care for him there. He had some sort of story about having money there. But you see him—no, I guess you don't, though. Well, dirty, in rags, with the slave mark on his arm—it's hard to believe him."

"Hmmm. The slave mark has defaced many an aristocratic arm in years past. Particularly where barbarians like these nomads are concerned."

"True. I'll try to steer him to some help of some kind. He's had a bad time of it. He was half starved, bruised, covered with fresh wounds. He must have a rugged constitution to have survived all that—and the blinding, too. What a terrible thing to do."

"Yes, yes. One sees so much suffering, so much cruelty in this life. Look: if you can't find any of his kin or whatever, we've got a bit of money to spare, I think. I'll give it to you. You seem a thoughtful and honorable man. Give it to the boy. Help him find a place to lay his head. You know. . . ."

"Thank you," the trader said, sincerely touched. "I thank you for his mother and father. Whoever they are."

II

"There we are," Yadiri said as the wagon rounded a low rise and the walls of the town could at least be seen. "Haran." He shook his head sadly. "A year ago we wouldn't have come this far without someone stopping us. There was an army here then. There was a guard post right back there, not fifty steps down the road. Look, see the clearing?"

"Yes," the man from Haran said. "Then, the army has been disbanded?"

"Sad to say, yes. There are those who claim the city was sold out—sold to the nomads. That someone in a high place made a deal. Frankly, I like the theory. Particularly since I saw Reshef in the nomad camp. He was there the whole time. He'd sell out his mother, if he'd had one."

"All the more reason," said the man with the foreign accent, "to wonder why the attack did not take place. Why the—what did you call them? The Shepherd Kings? Why they did not take an undefended city, but instead chose to besiege a city mobilized for war. It is passing strange."

Shobai, in the back, lay on his pallet and chewed at his lip. Well, the city stood, he thought. That was the important thing. If it still stood, he might be able to touch some of the funds he had on deposit. And then . . .

The bitter thought came back again, as it always did: *And then . . . what?* What good would money do him? What good would it do anybody? What pleasures could it buy a man who no longer had any reason to live? Who had lived through what he'd lived through, seen what he'd seen before they put him where he could see no more, lost what he'd lost?

And in point of fact hadn't he lost everything? Everything but his life? And what was that worth, with nothing left to live for? Perhaps—perhaps the best thing would be to end it. Just end it. There were, after all, a lot of ways to die. The river, for instance. At the bridge that ran by the Bazaar of the Well—Hadad's old bazaar (Hadad! Hadad!)—the water was swift and deep, running its course along a path lined by man-made stones, man-made paths, between man-made quays. A man could drown easily enough there.

Or—there was the Temple of Bel. The ziggurat. There was a place where the wall was breached, where rains had weakened the wall and the stones had slid free and fallen to the ground, far below. If he could . . . say, hire an urchin from the streets to guide him to the place . . .

It would be a kindness to Yadiri, of course, for him to wait until the trader had good-heartedly brought him into the city and helped him find his way to the offices of the merchants who held his funds on call. No use in saddling the trader with his heavy burden of self-loathing and sorrow any longer. He'd wait a bit, and then . . .

The wagon was jostling to a halt, though, and now came to a dead stop. He could feel the wagon's load grow lighter by a man's weight, and in a moment he heard Yadiri's voice right beside him, the trader standing by the wagon, putting a gentle hand on his arm. "Son," he said. "We're here. We're in Haran. Well, at least we're outside the walls. We're at the ford. I thought you might like to go down to the water with me and freshen up, and perhaps change clothes."

Shobai sat up, facing no particular direction. It was strange: with your sight gone, it didn't seem to matter which way you faced. Or what you said or did either, for that matter. "Yes," he said. "Perhaps that would be best." He put one hand on the wagon's tall side and pulled himself forward feet first until he could slip to the ground. "If you could give me a hand. . . ."

"Certainly," the trader said. "I've spare clothing here under my arm. You can bathe at the ford, and I'll hand this to you when you're done."

"Thank you," Shobai said. "I—I hear voices. We're not alone, I gather."

"No, there seem to be a number of other travelers here, doing the same thing we're doing. And—oh, yes. There's a pair of travelers I picked up on the road. They've been riding up front with me. Their horses gave out on the road from Carchemish."

"I gathered that. But—could you take me a little farther downstream? If I'm going to take my clothes off, what's left of them—well, I'm not a pretty sight now. I don't want to offend. I . . ."

"Of course, if you like. But it seems to me you're too concerned, if you'll forgive my saying so. People have certainly seen worse wounds than your own in this terrible day and age."

"Yes. I realize it's ridiculous. But—in the nomad camp they put me on display, wounds and all, like an animal in a pit. I—I could face this with barbarians, with strangers. But these—these may be some of my own people. I . . ."

"I think I understand. I'll do as you ask. But, look, I see a friend of mine over there. A fellow trader. If I take you to a shallow spot in the stream, over here away from everyone, could you perhaps—well, call out for me when you're done? I'll come get you and help you. But I would like to talk with my friend for a moment. Maybe he knows something about . . ."

"Oh, certainly. Yes, here; I feel my feet in the water. Yes, here's the little pool. And when I'm done, I can sit on this flat rock. By all means. Don't trouble yourself over me. I'll—I'll call you when I'm ready."

"Right. Right. Just sing out, nice and loud."

Shobai could hear him splashing away. He hesitated; then he stripped away the rags he had been wearing, balled them up in his hand, and heaved them mightily downstream. The water felt good. He hadn't had anything but rainwater touch his skin in . . . how long? He was filthy, mud-caked; the cool touch of the mountain water would wash the grime away. If only it would wash his mind clean as it washed his body ...

Then, suddenly, he realized he knew the spot he stood in. Yes! He'd stood on this very flat rock when he was a seven-year-old, when the water, now thigh-deep, had been up to his chest. And he'd dived off headfirst, and ...

Yes! Just out there was a deep spot, and the main channel of the river was there, and the current was strong. ...

But no. That would be unfair to Yadiri. He would wait. There was no hurry. No hurry about anything. Ever, ever again. He slowly slipped down to a squat in the cool water, feeling it rush by his bare body. He ducked his head, wet his filthy hair. When he arose, the water stung the sore place where his eyes had been. He bit his lip, trying to keep from crying out. And he listened to the voices, their words drifting downstream toward him on the late afternoon breeze. Yadiri was speaking to one of his trader friends.

"... why, Ila-salim! I didn't think to find you here! You were going to head straight for Ebla. ..."

"... so I was. But when Haran was saved, I realized that Haran was safer than Ebla right now. Perhaps forever. Or for as long as the Shepherd Kings are in the area."

"I don't understand. They're still in the area. They could ride over here in a moment and wipe the town from the face of the earth. I don't intend to stay here long."

"I do, my friend. To hell with Ebla. Ebla will be a wet spot in the road in six months. Haran will be here for another generation. I'll take my chances in Haran from now on."

"Excuse me," said one of the travelers who'd shared the road from Carchemish with Yadiri and Shobai. "You were saying ... Haran is safe? I'd like to hear more if I might ..."

"Me, too," Yadiri said. "What happened? You were there. But you seem to have heard more than I did."

"Heard more? Why, I was present when the city was saved. Right there. I saw it all with these two eyes. Heard every word. It was a miracle! A miracle! There's no other word for it."

"A miracle! For heaven's sake go on, man!"

"Well, they were all ready to go. And then up come the guards, and Karakin—their 'Leader,' you know—and Man-ouk are there, now, and the guards say 'We caught this man trying to get out, sir,' and—but no, it was the traitor talking, now I think of it, the one they call Reshef. The traitor from Haran ..."

Reshef? Shobai perked up his ears. And he stood facing the voices upstream, straining not to miss a word.

"Anyhow, they're about to order this fellow's execution, the one Reshef caught. And all of a sudden he steps up and says, 'No, you're not. But it doesn't matter if you do or not, because you're all dead men anyway.' I mean, here he is, all dressed in rags like a mountebank, his face smeared with mud, and he's telling these monsters—these murderers—something like that. And the Leader—why, he could break the fellow in half with one hand . . ."

"Please, go on. . . ."

"Right. Well, anyhow they ask him why. What does he mean, they're all dead? And he up and says, 'Why, I've got the plague! I've brought you the plague, you so-and-sos! Haran has the plague, and everybody's dying there, and I've brought it to your camp!' "

"But—but that's a lie!" a strange voice said nearby. It was echoed by several others. "There hasn't been any plague in Haran since my grandfather's time."

"True. You and I know that. But the nomads didn't. And cool as a cucumber, the little fellow says, 'You don't believe me, eh? Well, take a look at this!' And he shucks his robe and stands before 'em, bare as an egg, naked as you're standing here yourself, and say, 'Take a look, boys. Just take a look. And that's what you're going to look like in a week or so. You'll get the chills first, and then you'll get a fever.' "

"That's the most amazing thing I ever heard," said the traveler from Haran, the one who had accompanied Yadiri's wagon. "Whoever this fellow is, he's got to be the bravest man I ever heard of. That's marvelous. Single-handed, without a weapon, he steps forward and saves a city. I—I'm deeply moved by this, really I am. It restores your faith in humanity. . . . Do you know what happened to him?"

"Well, I'm afraid that I do. Of course, the first thing that happened was that the Shepherd Kings panicked. They ordered the men to strike the camp, to form for a forced march to Carchemish. All of 'em, every man and boy." He let a note of sadness creep into his voice for a moment. "Poor Carchemish . . ."

"Excuse me," the traveler with the Haran accent said. "We know about Carchemish. You were saying. This heroic young man—what happened to him?"

Shobai moved toward them, one fumbling blind step at a time. His heart was beating wildly. His foot slid on the slippery pebbles at the bottom of the stream and he fell face-first in the water; when he recovered and found his footing again, they were talking once more:

". . . poor devil. I'd packed my cart and was on my way out of the camp, and I almost ran over him. He was lying in the road, dead as you could ask. I stopped and checked on him. He'd been run through once or twice, and he'd apparently died pretty quickly, without lingering pain. Thank the heavens for that, at least. But imagine! A hero. A hero, the likes of which they'll be singing about over the campfires for a hundred years to come. A real hero, in this age of traitors and cowards. And where does he lie now? No one will ever know. His bones are probably scattered to the four winds by now, picked to pieces by jackals and vultures and . . ."

"Picked to pieces?" Yadiri said. "You mean . . . you saw it all—you knew who he was, the man who saved Haran—and you let him lie there? You didn't bring his body back to Haran for us to honor and sing over into the next world? You let him lie there and you rode away?"

"I didn't have any choice. The traitor Reshef—it was him all the time—he came up on me and he says, 'You get out of here, or you'll get the same.' Boiling mad he was, as if the boy had got away instead of getting killed by his sword. Because he'd been hollering a moment before, like he'd done something fine instead of something cowardly: 'It was me! Me, Reshef! I killed him!' "

Shobai stumbled and fell again, this time into a pool that was chin-high. He came up coughing, spitting out water; he tried to move forward again, but fell once more, floundering, his arms waving. *"Hadad,"* he tried to say, but the word was buried under a coughing fit. He struggled to get his footing, but his feet slid out from under him.

"Look," the man with the accent said. "The blind boy—he's in trouble. Over there . . ."

Splashing. Coughing. Couldn't swim. Couldn't seem to get any air. Couldn't seem to get his head above water. No air. Breathing water now. All of it going. Going away. Slipping off. Was this death? Death now? No breath. No air. Eyes gone, ears going too. Arms, legs growing weak. . . .

It was Ila-salim, the trader, who reached him first, with Yadiri close behind. Between the two of them, they managed to get his head above water—but he wasn't breathing when they did. Fighting the eddying current, they carried him to shore—and Yadiri, seeing the blue coloring of his skin and the goose bumps, immediately wrapped him in his own robe before laying him out on his belly. Ila-salim sat down atop the boy's buttocks and pounded his back—and, miracle of miracles, the reaction was quick: vomiting; weak groans; breath. . . .

"For heaven's sake," Ila-salim said, rolling the gasping boy onto his back. "Do you know who this is? Yadiri, do you know who it was that you brought back? It's the boy's brother. The hero's, you know. And—Gods! They've blinded him! How horrible!"

"The hero's? His brother? Then—you know who our nameless hero was?" Yadiri said.

"Know him? My friend, it's certainly apparent that you don't know Haran. If you did, really, you'd have recognized this boy here, scars, starvation and all. I wonder what they did to him, now I think of it. Why, he used to be half again this heavy, this strong. They . . ."

"Excuse me," the traveler from Carchemish said, a note of urgency in his voice. "You were saying. You knew who the hero of Haran was? The boy who saved the city?"

"Why, yes. Everybody in Haran knew him, just about. The nicest little fellow you ever met in all your life. He was a gentle little chap with a crooked leg. He had a little shop in the Bazaar of the Well, where he did little statues and things like that. I heard he'd come into some money recently. All the more reason to wonder what brought him up to the enemy camp to try to save the town. And—imagine. He gave up everything! Everything!"

"For the love of heaven, my friend—who was it?"

"Why, Hadad the sculptor, of course! Hadad the metal-worker! And this poor devil is his brother, the rich one who—here now! Here! What are you doing? You can't do that?"

But the stranger's hands were tearing at the robe Yadiri had thrown over the half-drowned young man. His eyes were fixed with horror on the seared, useless eyes, the scarred face, the broken tooth in the open mouth that gaped up at him. There was as much gentleness as insistence in his motions as he pulled the cloth away and rolled Shobai on his side.

As he did he let out a gasp of surprise. And after a split-second's pause there came from his throat a long, drawn-out moan of pain and anguish and fear and despair, one which every listener who stood anxiously by his side would remember for the rest of his life. . . . "Nikos!" he said brokenly. "Nikos, look at the mark on his side! Look at the mark!"

"What's the matter?" Yadiri said.

"Shobai," said Kirta of Haran, sobbing. "My son, my son . . ."

CHAPTER SEVENTEEN

I

Behind the men's advance posts but ahead of the slow-moving herds, the women rode: Jacob had purchased two wagons in a border town called Edrei, just northeast of Ramoth-gilead, and the two young mothers rode in these, attended by Leah and the concubines—and by poor mad Tallay, who seemed actually to have taken to traveling. The women, seeing the change in her—she had put on weight, and even begun to take some small pride in her appearance—even trusted her with the babies from time to time; she seemed happiest when she could somehow manage to pretend she was back in her own child-bearing days.

Now she sat cross-legged in the first of the two wagons, holding Rachel's infant, Joseph, in her arms and cooing to him. Bilhah slept beside her, snoring lightly, and Rachel sat in the extreme rear of the wagon as it jounced along, dangling her feet over the back.

The sound of hoofbeats awakened her from her reverie, and she half turned to see Jacob guiding his horse up alongside the slow-moving wagon. He dismounted and, still holding the reins, jumped easily up onto the tailgate beside her. He tied the reins to the back of the wagon and turned to smile at her. "Rachel," he said. "You're the loveliest sight I've seen all day. It's downright sinful for a woman to be so pretty so soon after her child's birth."

She stroked his thigh affectionately. "How lovely of you to say so," she said, "When we reach Canaan—"

"Pardon me," Jacob said smiling. "I don't mean to interrupt you, my dear, but we're *in* Canaan. We've been on the

571

soil of my fathers for . . . oh, ever since we approached Ramoth-gilead. Across those hills over there is the Valley of the Jordan. We're already some distance south of Lake Chinnereth."

"We—we are?" she said, one hand over her heart. "Why—why didn't someone tell me?"

"I've been busy. And no one else has ever been here. How would any of the rest know when we'd entered the Land of Abraham?"

"Goodness," she said. "I'd thought it was going to be a longer journey. Then—then you're home. . . ."

"Well, I'd have to say that was a little premature. The land we're in now is occupied by the descendants of friends and allies of my grandfather's. One of Eshcol's grandchildren rules here. There are some members of the tribes founded by my uncle Ishmael. Now there are some interesting people. Tough as wildcats, and the finest horsemen in the world. They could give riding lessons to the Shepherd Kings." Ruefully he added, "I'm just hoping they won't have to."

"Indeed," Rachel said. "Is that who's been following us for the last day? Spying on us?"

"Ah, what a sharp eye you have, my darling! No, I'm afraid those are—well, emissaries of my brother Esau."

Rachel stared at him, her mouth open. "Esau! But, Jacob—there are so many of them."

"You don't know the half of it," Jacob said. "I sent one of the boys ahead two days ago with a message for Esau. You know, something like 'I've been in the north with Laban, and I'm coming home with my wives, chattels, and possessions. I hope you're disposed to be friendly.' Something like that." He shook his head. "I was expecting Simeon to have to ride all the way to Edom. But Esau doesn't miss much that goes on in Canaan. He was halfway here already, alerted by his scouts."

"And?"

"And Levi—he's just now—he just sent word back by Asher that Simeon had returned. Simeon says Esau is coming to meet us in person. . . ."

"In person!"

"With four hundred men." Jacob lifted one eyebrow expressively. "Four hundred! That's an army, my dear. And they're armed like one. Did you know Abraham did not have that many men under his direct command when he routed and slaughtered the Armies of the Four Kings?"

"Jacob—does he mean trouble?"

"I have no idea. But—Rachel. The God is with us. No

harm will come to us. I had a dream last night. In it not Esau's men, but the angels of the One God rode flanking us. I said to myself: 'This is the army of the God!' And then I felt better. Safer. And I prayed to the God, and I thanked Him for the favor He's shown us. Why, I came to Haran without anything in my hand but a staff, and—well, look at us. We're affluent, as pastoralists go." He looked up at the hillsides above and spotted another one of them, riding slowly just below the crest of the ridge, looking down at him. "I received no answer, but when I awoke I felt better than I've felt in days."

"How long do you think it'll be before he shows up with this army of his?"

"Not long. And—look, I know I've just got finished telling you I was feeling confident, that the God was watching out for us. But, I've dreaded the confrontation with Esau for twenty years. After all, I wronged him terribly. It was the sort of thing you do when you're a boy, young and thoughtless. But I hurt him terribly. And Esau—even when we were children he was a fearless and terrible fighter, and he had a terrifying temper. I once watched him kill a bandit in the hills with nothing but his shepherd's staff. And the bandit was armed with a sword. Why—Esau must have been about fourteen at the time. Yes, we'd turned fourteen two months before, as I remember. . . ."

"Heavens! I'd be apprehensive myself."

"Yes. So what I've done—I just now got finished doing it—was to set two of the boys to cutting a certain number of the animals out of the herd."

"Jacob! What for?"

"They'll be a present for Esau. I'll camp soon, by the ford up ahead. Then I'll send a couple of the boys ahead with Esau's gifts. And I'll tell him to meet me on the far bank of the river."

He sighed. And Rachel, looking at him, could see signs of care on his face. "Jacob," she said. "You haven't been sleeping nights, have you? All this worry, this responsibility . . ."

He sat, brow knit, lips pursed, and did not say anything for a moment. "My feelings are a mixture," he said. "They keep me awake even when I'm almost too exhausted to stay awake."

"Oh, Jacob," she replied softly. "I can cure that. Come to my bed tonight. . . ."

"So soon?" he answered, a little startled—but pleased.

"Jacob, I'm fine. I'm a very healthy woman. And I've missed you all these nights. As I'm sure you've missed me. . . ."

He carried her hand to his lips. "Rachel," he said in a husky voice. . . .

Danataya held her child to her breast, feeling the tiny lips draw powerfully on her nipple. "There, darling," she said. "There, my little sweetheart. There, baby mine. . . ."

Leah watched her, watched the soft and maternal smile on her face, and wondered once again if this could be the same skinny, woebegone girl she'd seen in the streets of Haran, carrying water for the inn, her face smudged, her garments filthy. Motherhood became the girl, that was certain.

And it was a fine child she'd had, poor thing. A lot like his father, if she remembered him properly: the face was round and the little mouth generous. The eyes were big and brown and warm. He looked a bright little thing, all alert like that. "Danataya," she said. "We were wondering last night—when are you going to get around to naming him?"

Danataya didn't answer for a moment, but continued her soft cooing at her little son. Leah was almost persuaded the girl hadn't heard her, and began repeating her question; but Danataya looked up and smiled. "I'm sorry. I—I was thinking." Gently, she disengaged the baby and moved him to the other breast. His tiny fingers flexed and grasped at nothing, and he made a wry face until she guided the nipple to his mouth. "What? Name him? But it's his father's place to name him. Hadad will pick out a name for him. Most likely a fine Sumerian name, I suppose. Something from his grandfather's land . . ."

"Danataya," Leah said almost reprovingly. "He can't go unnamed until then. Who knows if—who knows when Hadad will come down to join us? Please, dear, let us help you."

"But I'm telling you. Hadad will be along. . . ."

"Danataya. You must face the possibility that . . ."

Danataya looked her directly in the eye for the first time. "Eventually, perhaps, I will," she said in a very calm voice. "Do you think I don't know how likely it is that Hadad—my gentle Hadad—has been ki—?" She gulped and tried again, but could not get the word out. Leah's heart sank, and she cursed herself silently when she saw the sudden tears in Danataya's eyes. "B-but Leah . . . I'm not giving up hope, not for so much as a moment, until—until . . ."

574

"I'm sorry," Leah said. "I shouldn't have brought it up. I tend to be officious. It's a curse with me."

"It's all right. You're talking sense. But—but I don't want to talk that kind of sense just yet. You understand, don't you? And—and as for the baby, look—it can wait. Can't it?"

"How about a name having to do with metalworking? He'll be a great metalworker like his father and grandfather. Jacob said so. He said Hadad told him if anything happened to him, Jacob should see about getting him apprenticed to . . ." Leah stopped, hand over her mouth. "Oh, I've done it again. I'm so sorry. . . ."

"It's all right. It is, really. Don't fret."

"We could just call him Ben-Hadad. That means 'son of Hadad' in the tongue they speak down here."

"Oh, that's fine. That's a good name for now. When Hadad comes, he can think up something better. But what better name for a stout, healthy little boy than his father's? Ben-Hadad. I like it. Thank you, Leah." She smiled tenderly down at the tiny face. Its eyes were closed, and the strong little draughts on her body's milk were beginning to come slower and farther between. "Look," she whispered, almost inaudibly under the creaking of the wagon. "He's slipping off to sleep. So nicely. So sweetly. Hadad goes off to sleep like that. I watch him sometimes."

"Oh, darling. I'm so sorry. I just can't keep my big mouth shut. And every time I open it I hurt you."

"It's all right," Danataya said in an even softer whisper. "Look. His little face is relaxing. His little hands keep clutching, but his face is just—oh, look. He's let go. He's almost asleep. Oh, won't Hadad have fun singing him to sleep. My lucky baby! My lucky little Ben-Hadad! You'll have a sweet father with a beautiful voice who can sing you lovely lullabies. And he'll make you little toys of clay and of metal, and play with you. . . ."

She ignored Leah's soft sob. "Leah," she said, her eyes still on the baby. "Did I ever tell you how I fell in love with Hadad? I was getting water from the well, and all of a sudden I heard a lyre playing, and here came this absolutely heavenly, beautiful, gorgeous voice drifting across the bazaar to my ears. I fell in love with Hadad before I ever had any idea who he was. Before I'd even seen him. I just knew that nobody who could sing like that could be anything but a beautiful spirit.

"Lo and behold, that was what he turned out to be. Sweet

575

and honest and loving and caring, as gentle as a lamb. Everything I ever wanted in a man, although I didn't know it. I started out wanting what the girls all say they want: a strong athletic type, with big powerful thighs and—but look at us, here I wound up with a man with a crooked leg, and . . ." She sighed. "He always thought it was ugly. I felt sorry for him at first because he obviously hated it so. But from the moment I heard that lovely voice of his, I knew he was beautiful, and never again after that could I find his body anything but lovely. Even the leg. The leg was part of my Hadad, and it was beautiful. I had a hard time getting my girl friend Yamam to understand; but when she got to know him better . . ."

She freed one hand to wipe the tears from Leah's cheek. "Oh, don't cry, Leah," she said. "Look, I'm not. I—I think I'm done with crying. Can you understand that? I cried and cried, both before the baby was born and after. When I knew there was a good chance my Hadad wasn't coming back, that there was a chance he'd never see his child, never hold me again. . . . But Leah, you can cry only so much. You can mourn only so much. You can hurt only so much. Then you realize you have others to live for . . . like my little one here." She smiled at the baby again, and the smile alone was enough to set Leah off to weeping again. "Hush now!" Danataya said. "You'll wake him. Hush, let me try to sing him a little song Hadad taught me. I can't sing it as well as Hadad could; I've no voice to speak of. But maybe the baby won't mind. It was a little lullaby the great king Shulgi of Ur wrote for his own firstborn. It goes like this:

> *Ua! Aua!*
> In my song of joy, he'll grow stout as an *irina*-tree,
> In my song of joy, he'll grow strong as a *sakir*-plant.

The baby stirred; the mock-yawn that spread across his round little face looked for anything like a smile, a happy smile. Danataya shivered with happiness and went on, softly:

> Come Sleep, come gentle Sleep,
> Come to this my son,
> Hurry, Sleep, to my much-loved boy,
> And put to sleep his restless eyes.

I'll find a wife for my darling son,
She'll sit on his lap and kiss his eyes;
She'll bear him a son as sweet as mine,
To make him happy all of his days.

And the wife who loves him will feed his heart,
And the son who loves him will feed his soul,
And he'll be happy to the end of his days,
His days made bright by joy and feasting.

Come Sleep, come gentle Sleep,
Come to this my son,
Hurry, Sleep, to my much-loved boy,
And put to sleep his restless eyes.

Danataya looked down at the tiny face, at peace now, the little chest rising and falling rhythmically. "No, Leah," she said softly. "I haven't lost Hadad. Not even if—if he doesn't make it back to me. That's the thing about having an artist to love. Could I ever lose a man altogether who could give me a song like that? No, no. He's with me right now. I can almost feel him. He'll always be with me, that way. He's given me so much already that they can never take away. I can't lose him. Not ever, my dear. And—see? He lives on in this tiny body here. In these strong, straight little arms and legs. Only—only this time he won't have a weak, crooked body to hold him down. No! He'll grow as strong and confident as Shobai." She smiled gently. "Thank you, Leah. Thank you for the lovely name. I couldn't ask for a better. Ben-Hadad . . ."

II

That evening, Jacob cut short the great advance of his caravan and, posting his sons as guards on the perimeters of the herds, camped just north of the great gorge through which the Jabbok River flowed down to the Jordan. Leaving the women with Reuben, he rode down to the river and looked across it. *It's been a long time*, he thought. *A long, long time . . .*

The region was well watered—better than the land he'd

lived in as a boy. It was green and lush. There could be worse places to settle. . . .

But no. The walls of the cleft were too steep here. Better to settle, if one were disposed to settle, a little to the west—perhaps where the two rivers joined, or on the point of land between them, just north of the place where they came together. . . .

Yes. There was some sense in that. There'd be good graze there for goats and sheep alike. The weather was mild. The mountains to either side of the Ghor stood effective watch over the narrow valley, here before the valley of the Jordan broadened out to flatlands, as the river flowed toward the great sink of Siddim. The place would be defensible, even when the Shepherd Kings moved south . . .

. . . and yes! Yes! There was even a little metalworkers' colony on the banks of the Jordan just above where the Jabbok joined it. At this spot, the banks of the Jordan spawned a marvelously smooth variety of clay which was perfect for the casting of bronze, and the area had become famous among the workers in the trade. The colony had been founded originally by workers who had apprenticed under the great Belsunu and who had migrated northward after helping the legendary armorer arm Abraham's people for the war against the Four Kings.

The thought sobered Jacob. Arms. Metalwork. War. He sighed. Well, that had been one of his reasons for coming south in the first place, hadn't it? To arm his father's people, to unify them against the common foe—and to make sure his hot-headed brother Esau didn't lead them into a half-cocked, suicidal war that they couldn't possibly win. . . .

Well, then, what better place to settle than here, where he could buy arms—and where he could act as an early warning for the advance of the Shepherd Kings? Esau, from what he'd learned, had settled far to the south, in Edom. By the time the war advanced that far, the nomads would have rolled right over Isaac's domain, in the peaceful Oaks of Mamre. Unless he, Jacob, could somehow stop, or at worst divert, their advance . . .

Stop them here, then. Stop them before they even entered the great valley itself. Or die trying.

He thought of the armorers' colony again, and the thought led him inevitably back to Hadad—Hadad and his incredible act of selfless bravery.

Bravery, yes. Some might have called it foolhardiness. Imagine: a gentle young dreamer who'd never struck a blow in anger in his life, taking off single-handed into the mouth of the dragon like that, unarmed, with the crazy notion that he could save his brother, perhaps save Haran all by himself. . . .

Jacob could almost think him mad himself. But he remembered his dream: the one in which he'd learned of Hadad's mission—and of its likely outcome. In his dream he'd wept and prayed for Hadad to survive the encounter—but the Voice in his mind had said, "Would you rob a man of his destiny?" And, weeping, he'd sat in silence, unable to find words for the thoughts in his mind.

He sighed again. Well, he'd made Hadad a promise. And the boy had fathered a stout and strapping Child of the Lion to carry on his forefathers' illustrious line. What better place to keep his promise and have the child, when his time came, apprenticed to masters in the trade?

Yes. There was even a little community there, a cluster of houses on the land above the river: a place with an undistinguished name—Succoth. Well, names meant little. An eminent name would not put mettle in a coward. A nondescript name would not hold back a hero. Succoth. Very well. Let it be here. He'd stand here—or fall here, as the God chose—when the time came.

This settled in his mind, he rode down to the ford and crossed the little river. Then his horse wound its way up the cliffs to a vantage point on the far side. He turned and looked back in the fading rays of sunlight. Yes: this would make a good outpost for guards to stand on, keeping watch over his eastern flank. . . .

The sun faded; darkness came on. *Well*, he thought, *no time for making it down the cliffs tonight. I'll sleep here.* He dismounted and guided the animal to a small grove of trees in the lee of a rock outcropping. He had a merry little campfire going by the time the last rays of light had faded in the west. From a leather bag that hung from his saddle, he took a small portion of lamb, some onions. He arranged these on a skewer and cooked them after the fashion of Haran: *lahum mishwi*, he'd called it for twenty years. He'd have to use another name for it now. What had his family called it?

Then, as he sat cross-legged before the fire, his thoughts began to drift. And—why, he must have dozed off! He looked around him, blinking—and looked straight into the eyes of a stranger. . . .

He started—but as he reached for his sword, he took note of the stranger's face and thought better of the move. The face was clear-eyed, open, trusting, the face of a man past his youth but not yet old. A likeable face. "I . . . forgive me," Jacob said. "You gave me a shock. I'm afraid I must have been sleeping when you came."

"I didn't want to disturb you," the man said in a mellow and friendly voice. "Please be at your ease, Jacob."

"Jacob?" Jacob said. "You . . . know me, somehow?"

"I know all men. I know all things. I know whence you come and where you are going." The man sat easily, his face distorted slightly by the rising currents from the fire that lay between them, flickering flames playing on the smooth part of his face above the thick beard. "I know the past and the future. I know the thought in your mind at this moment. You . . ." He chuckled, and Jacob noted the kind light in his eye. "You think I'm mad."

Jacob grinned back at him. "A touch," he said. "That's exactly what was running through my mind. It's all right. Don't mind me. I'm not quite awake yet. Would you like something to eat?"

"No, thank you." The amused expression was still there. "You don't believe me about knowing the future either, do you?" he said good-naturedly. "Ask me a question and find out. Ask me what was in your mind before you dozed off. Ask me about Hadad. Ask me about Haran."

"Had—?" Jacob sat up, rubbing the sleep from his eyes. "How do you know about . . . ?"

"I know all things," the stranger said simply. "Put your mind at ease. Hadad lies with his fathers. Haran is saved, by Hadad's hand. His name will be honored for many generations. In time to come, you yourself will bear great honor there for having befriended him."

Jacob stared—and suddenly found himself breaking into tears. "I—I believe you, somehow. I haven't any idea why—but—somehow I knew. . . ."

"The wise man weeps. The fool forgets. Your tears do you honor as well. Hadad left a son, one you must raise for his father's sake. Stand by the child, Jacob—and in time to come he will stand by you and yours in your time of need."

"T-time of need?" Jacob said. "Then—that sounds as though my present problems will be solved. . . ."

"You speak as though there were something to fear. But you haven't felt fear in a long, long time, Jacob. You've forgotten your fear in the course of becoming the man you've become: resolute, responsible, caring. You're not the frightened boy who fled his brother twenty years ago."

"I—so I'm not. But—but I fear Esau. I fear him now."

"No you don't. Look, Jacob, look at me."

Jacob stared. The stranger's face, suddenly, was the teen-aged face of his twin, Esau—the way he'd looked in their youth, before Jacob had run away to Haran. He gulped—then gasped as he happened to notice his own hand.

It was the hand not of a man in his forties, but of a boy not yet twenty. He felt his face, felt the clear unwrinkled skin. "I—but what have you done to me? To us? How could that . . . ?"

"You're a boy again, Jacob—for a time. And I'm your brother. Your stronger, hot-headed, vengeful brother. Neither brother has changed—except that your heart has changed, and so has his. You're older and wiser. Only the body is what it was. Come: wrestle with me as you used to do when you and Esau were boys. I'll show you. You used to fear . . ."

As the stranger spoke, he stood unhurriedly and threw off his clothing. Blinking, Jacob did the same, not knowing why, looking at his brother's still vividly remembered body with its red hair on the chest and loins, at the chest deeper than his, the arms stronger. . . .

"Come," the stranger said, crouching, circling. His smile was Esau's now: challenging, daring. He feinted with one hand—and the other reached out, lightning-fast in the flickering firelight, and caught his arm. Jacob pulled free—but he pulled the stranger forward as he did so and abruptly rolled onto his back, sticking out a foot. The stranger came forward, balanced on Jacob's foot, and did a somersault over Jacob's body to land in the underbrush beneath the trees.

Jacob was on his feet in a moment, facing the stranger, marveling at the half-forgotten lines of Esau's ruddy face, at his freckled body. . . . "See?" the stranger said. "Once you'd have quaked with fear. But now . . ." Smiling, he charged. Those strong arms went around Jacob's chest. But Jacob's hands went to the stranger's face, shoving his head back. And suddenly his thumbs went to the arteries on the stranger's neck, and pressed down . . . down. . . . The stranger sank to the ground, then rose, smiling. "See, Jacob. You've come into your manhood. Fear has been left behind, and with it the weakness it engendered. Come. Come at me."

Somehow the mock struggle between them seemed to stretch out now. Time passed; Jacob could not say how much. He felt the power in the stranger's arms and legs, the stamina . . . but he was amazed to find that his own matched these, more than matched them. He went through the motions, through holds, feinting moves. . . .

. . . and then stopped, astonished. "How . . . how long have we been doing this?" he said, incredulous. "I—I don't believe what's happening."

"Believe what you will," the stranger said, pointing to the light in the eastern sky. "It'll be sunup within the hour. And time for me to leave you." He smiled—and suddenly the face, the body, were no longer Esau's. And he, Jacob, was a man of forty-odd years again, breathing hard after strenuous exercise. "What . . . ?" he said.

But then the stranger attacked. And Jacob fell, and a stabbing, blinding pain shot through his hip, and he lay moaning as the stranger stepped back, still smiling benignly, and began putting on his clothing. "Ahhhh," Jacob groaned. "What—what did you do? It hurts . . . it hurts. . . ."

"Life hurts, Jacob," the man said. "But a man—he ignores the hurt. He fights to win. He prevails."

Jacob found his way to one knee, gritting his teeth. The pain was excruciating, but so was the anger in his heart.

He charged, feeling the stabbing pain—and then, suddenly, feeling other things more: anger, indignation, the wish to win, the wish to avenge himself for this last indignity.

The stranger, caught by surprise, went down. Jacob, ignoring the agony in his hip joint, pinned him. He looked down at the mild, bearded face, rage in his eyes. "Look, you," he said, "I don't know who you are. Some sort of magus, perhaps. Some sort of magician who can cloud people's minds somehow. But you're going to tell me what's been happening here, or . . ."

The stranger looked up at him. He smiled peacefully, in the same friendly fashion; then—then suddenly Jacob was kneeling atop nothingness. Nothing was in his hands. He was alone in his little camp. He looked around, startled. . . .

. . . but no. He stood, shivering, pulling his own robe about him, trying to ignore the pain in his hip. "W-where are you?" he said. "Who . . . ?"

There was a Presence with him in the campsite, in the little clearing under the grove of trees. He could feel it; he could see nothing. And now the stranger's voice, still soft and gentle, boomed out a dozen times louder than he had heard it last: *"Jacob,"* it said slowly. *"Be no longer Jacob. . . ."*

"What do you mean?" Jacob said, his hands held to his heart. "Jacob is my name. . . ."

"No more," the voice said. *"You are one who has tested his strength with Me . . . and prevailed. . . ."*

Jacob, shivering, his mind reeling, fell to his knees. It didn't seem to matter which way he faced when he spoke: the voice was everywhere. "I meant no harm, Lord. . . ."

"Rise," said the voice. *"Kneel no more. From this moment you have a new name. Your name is Israel—one who has power with the God. . . .*

"Be fruitful and multiply. A mighty nation springs from your line, and your descendants will be kings. Kings of the land of Abraham, which I give to you and yours forever. . . ."

Then the Presence was gone. And Jacob shivered in the dawn chill, watching the pink tinge in the sky.

His hip hurt him all the way back to camp, with the horse he had so painfully mounted jogging along beneath him. But in camp he refused treatment, even though resourceful Reuben claimed to know how to set a dislocated hip joint. "But Father," the boy said, "if you don't set it now you may never be able to. Do you want to hurt the rest of your life?"

Jacob looked at him, his eyes so intense in their mixture of resolution and pain that Reuben blinked and almost looked away. "I have looked upon the face of the Almighty God," he said in a quiet voice. "He put His mark on me to help me remember the moment. He gave me His blessing—and a new name. Well, I don't intend to forget. You won't either. And neither will any one of the sons and daughters we father, from now until the last days of the world. Not if I have anything to say about the matter." He blinked away the pain on his face and smiled at his strapping young son. "Come on, boy. Let's go meet that brother of mine."

III

On the third day Yadiri, after some haggling, managed to rent a stall for trade in one of the bazaars of Haran and, offering credit on one of the better financial houses in his home city, set up shop trading in textiles. It was not one of the richer bazaars; the walk-past trade was mostly half-solvent exiles from the north, and for this and other reasons most of the regular merchants had deserted their stalls and moved south. It was several days before he learned that this was the bazaar of Hadad, the unsung hero of the city.

By now, Hadad's close friends and confidants were all gone; but there still remained a few who had known him distantly and who remembered his cheerful and friendly manner, his generosity both in poverty and in the wealth that had attended his last days. A passing stranger's chance remark about "that little gimp-leg who used to work here" sparked a near-riot one afternoon; it was the first break in the gloom that had settled over the little square since news of the saving of Haran, and the reasons for it, had trickled back into the demoralized city.

Finally, after a week, Yadiri located someone who knew the name of the inn where Kirta had rented rooms. Leaving his stall in the hands of a friend, he made his way through the quarter to the Inn of the White Horse. Climbing the stairs, he knocked at the second door.

Nikos—the faithful friend who had been both slave and master to Kirta—answered the door. "Yadiri," he said, "this is a pleasant surprise. Come in—but quietly, please. I finally got him to sleep, with the aid of some nostrums from the bazaar."

Yadiri entered, sat down. "I've been wanting to look you up, but I couldn't find you until now. How is the boy?"

"Well—depressed. Manic. His state of mind goes up and down like a puppet on a string. There's still some pain, you know. But the main thing with Shobai is that—well, it's been a shock. Several kinds of shock." He frowned. "Frankly, I'm not worried about the boy that much. He's strong—and there's mettle in him. You know, he was right: he is rich. Very well-to-do, even if that wife of his has possession of the house." He lowered his voice a trifle, one eye on the closed door behind him. "I went past it. The urchins of the neighborhood have defaced it with all sorts of lurid pictures depicting what seems to be going on inside these days. His wife—well, she won't be his wife long. A thoroughly bad case. Quite flagrant about it. Well, as I say, there are laws about that sort of thing. But I haven't told the boy yet."

"I gather the real problem is Kirta."

"It is. The whole thing—it's broken him. And I don't seem to be able to put back the pieces. He's lived for a year or more, now, for nothing else but to return to Haran and right all the wrongs he fancies he's done his family. And now it's too late: Tallay's gone—the gods alone know where—and

Shobai is blind, and little Hadad, who perhaps suffered most from Kirta's absence all those years, is dead. And for all we know the line of the Children of the Lion has come to a dead end—although Hadad apparently had a pregnant wife somewhere. She seems to have disappeared off the face of the earth, though. And Kirta . . . he blames himself for everything."

"Poor devil. And nothing you can say to him can . . . ?"

"He listens, but he does not hear. 'The gods gave me a precious garden to tend,' he says, 'and what did I do? Look at it. Blighted. Dead . . .' "

He stopped. He cocked one ear at the door behind him. "Sorry," he said. "I thought I heard something. Maybe the boy was stirring. I'm trying to get him to eat something these days. Sometimes he will, sometimes he won't. It depends on his mood. But frankly, I think he'll break his depression before Kirta breaks his own. Right now Kirta is out wandering the streets, asking people about Hadad. You should have seen him downstairs with our innkeeper, listening to stories about his son. 'Right here, at this table, Hadad fell in love with the girl,' he says. 'We were trying her out as a dancer. She'd already gone sweet on *him*, a little, after hearing him sing in the bazaar one day. She came back cooing about it. . . .' " He sighed; when he spoke again there was a touch of hoarseness in his voice. "It appears the boy was some sort of saint. Everyone loved him. Everyone mourns him."

"I know. I rented a stall in his old bazaar."

"Then you understand. And Kirta hears all this—hears of the desperate poverty to which Hadad and Tallay were reduced, and of the way the boy provided, and stayed cheerful, and didn't complain—and it breaks his heart. Yadiri, I don't know what to . . ."

There were footsteps on the stairs, though, and he held up one hand. "That sounds like him," he said. He rose and went to the door just as Kirta opened it and stood framed in the doorway. "Kirta," he said. "Here's Yadiri come to see us."

The armorer looked around, nodded at their visitor, and came inside. "It's cool outside today. I've a chill in my bones that just won't go away." He rubbed his arms. His face was drawn and his expression that of a man stunned. "Yadiri," he said. "I've been—I've been to see a man named Arusian. He was the Haran representative of the merchant Ibalum. . . ."

"I know both of them slightly. Ibalum's a bit out of my league."

"Yes. Well, Arusian showed me some examples of Hadad's

work. Yadiri, the boy was an artist! A great artist! Ibalum called him a genius—and the word is no exaggeration. I've seldom, if ever, seen work of comparable quality. It had already begun to command sizable prices. Now, Arusian says, the price will go sky-high."

"I understand he had accumulated some money," Nikos said. "Did you . . . ?"

"Yes. It's in an account in his name. Ibalum has been scrupulous in his managing of Hadad's funds. But . . ." Now the despair came back in force; the great shoulders drooped. He sat, his back slumped over, his whole body showing his fatigue and desperation. "Hadad," he said. "I wish I'd known him. My son, my little boy . . ."

Nikos reached out a hand to the sobbing man on the chair—and then pulled it back. Biting his lip, he looked to Yadiri for help but found none. "Kirta, what's past is past. You have to start thinking about what to do; what to do *now*, Kirta. . . ."

He stopped again. His head turned; he listened. "That's Shobai in there," he said. "I'll go see what's going on. Come to think of it, he's probably slept long enough. Yadiri—could you be a good fellow and make a fire there? Maybe the boy will take some food. . . ."

"I—I'll make it," Kirta said. He knelt by the fireplace and stacked fagots beneath a dry log. "Do you know what I ruined all these dear people's lives for, Yadiri? What I missed the loveliest years of my own life for?" He almost spat the words out as he rubbed dry sticks together over a pile of shavings. "What I missed knowing my sons for?" His voice took on a savage edge. "I told myself it was all for knowledge. I made it all sound high-minded. Altruistic. 'For the good of mankind . . .' Bah! It was nothing more than the secret of how to build a fire in an oven."

"A fire?" Yadiri said. "I don't understand."

"That's all it was. Twelve years of experimenting, twelve years of the riches of Minos of Crete being thrown down a bottomless well, twelve years of devastating whole forests at a time. And all for the secret of how to make a fire." He almost choked on the words. "Twelve years of cheating myself and others. Lying to myself—and *most* effectively, let me tell you. The half-truths, the fabrications I erected to excuse my behavior, Yadiri! And all for what?" He pulled back a burnt finger, sucked on it. "For the secret of making a better stove."

"A better stove? But I thought you were a smith. . . ."

"A stove, my dear Yadiri, for making a commodity called iron. For smelting a metal that will cut through bronze, a metal that will make weapons for the killing of more innocents like my—my son. Oh, how proud I thought I'd be! I'd be the first—well, no, the second man in the world other than a Hittite to learn how to do this arcane trick of prestidigitation. I'd be famous. I'd be an adept of the craft. I'd be taking knowledge, sacred knowledge, a little farther. . . ." He turned and looked at Yadiri through red-rimmed eyes that showed graphically the pain and sorrow he'd lived with for a week now. "Twelve years. Twelve years of nothingness. Twelve years I'd trade for a day of Hadad's precious life . . ."

There was a noise. Kirta looked up—to see Shobai, standing in the doorway. He was clad only in a loincloth; his gaunt, ravaged body was pale. His face had that unreadable expression the blind develop. "F-Father," he said in a rasping voice. "I—I couldn't help overhearing. You—you *learned* how to do it? To make iron?"

"Why, yes. But—"

"You *solved* the problem of the constancy of the heat? You actually learned how to make the furnace? I tried so hard myself, again and again, three or four years ago, when I was first a journeyman here in Haran. . . . Then, when I learned what the Hittites could do with ease, I abandoned my damned inadequate furnace."

Yadiri looked at Kirta—and started. He looked at Nikos quickly and caught the expression on his face. Nikos put one finger over his mouth. "Yes," Kirta said slowly, his voice much changed. "I did that myself a dozen times. And since you've tried to work on iron, you know the attendant problems. The fire has to be fed with a blast of air, and the ore has to be completely surrounded with charcoal. But if you expose the ore to carbon too much, the iron is hard and brittle, and you can't work it properly. On the other hand, if you expose the ore to air it'll reoxidize. And even if you do it right, you have to hammer the hell out of that spongy mass you get from it, to force out the impurities."

"Yes, yes. Go on." Shobai's dead face was beginning to come alive, little by little. Nikos held one hand over his heart, half smiling, his eyes abrim with tears as Shobai spoke. "I figured out that it took two furnaces: one for smelting, and another for reheating it for the hammering, to soften it. But when I did it, all that came out was garbage. . . ."

"Yes! That's the part I couldn't figure out for myself, either. I had to learn it from Turios of Tyre, on his deathbed.

And even Turios—a genius, a great metalworker if one ever drew breath on this earth—even Turios didn't figure it out by himself. He said he learned it from a Hittite slave who'd been blinded in a war—"

He stopped suddenly, shocked at what he'd said. "I—I'm sorry. I . . ."

"It's all right, Father," Shobai said, groping his way to a chair opposite his father's, facing him, his face animated, his voice vital for the first time. "It's all right. A blind man can work a forge, can't he? I've been thinking about that. There are parts of the process that require sight—but all one needs for those parts is a knowledgeable partner. And, Father. I have you, don't I?"

"Shobai . . ." The words wouldn't come. Only tears. Shobai, his voice resonant, spoke, one hand on his father's knee.

"Father," he said. "Teach me to make the dark metal. Teach me to make iron. . . ."

Kirta, sobbing, shook his head. "Useless," he said. "Worthless. What good would it . . . ?"

"Father!" The boy's powerful young voice boomed out. "Worthless? Useless? A weapon the nomads don't have? A weapon the Hittites would rather eat hog-meat than give to them? A secret that will make the enemies of the Shepherd Kings strong enough to fight them? To hold them off? To prevail against them? Father, I *know*—perhaps better than any man alive knows—what their strengths and weaknesses are. And I know what can beat them. Or, at worst, scare them away."

Kirta stared at him, saying nothing. Shobai reached out blindly and took his father's hands, gripping them hard. "Father," he said, "when they attacked Carchemish, they could not have breached the walls, because I had fortified them the way the Shepherd Kings fortify their own towns. . . . If they battered down the gates—it was only with the battering ram *I* made for them.

"I know all their secrets, their weapons. . . ." He ticked them off, his voice strong and insistent, squeezing Kirta's hands in a powerful grip. "Body armor—made of bronze! Swords and spears—with bronze blades! A chariot design I perfected for them—and which I, blind or sighted, can teach anyone else to build! True, they have numbers. But they're not invincible. Hadad showed that. They can be outflanked, outsmarted. And with iron weapons, in the hands of men of mettle, they can be faced down. They can!"

"Shobai," his father said. "You give me courage. That's more than I've ever given you, heaven knows."

"No! Not so!" Shobai bared his broken teeth in a fierce smile. "Look what you've just done! You've given me a reason for living again. . . ."

"I—I don't understand."

"I wanted to die, Father! I wanted to die because it seemed to me that evil had won over good! That this had robbed life of all meaning! But—the good *can* win, Father! The nomads *can* be defeated! They *can* be stopped! Father—teach me the making of iron. You and I. We can do it. We'll move south, arm the cities, unify them against the kings. . . ."

"South! But you mean Ebla, or Ugarit, or . . . why, they're doomed already. It's too late for them."

"Perhaps. But, Father—there's one other thing. Somewhere down there—somewhere, we'll just have to find out where— Hadad has a wife, and perhaps mother is with her. And— Father: Hadad's wife should have had his child by now, with any luck. Somewhere in the world there's a new Child of the Lion. I feel it in my bones. Hadad did too, before he died. He *knew* he had a son. Somewhere we'll find him. And in the meantime we'll warn—and arm—the cities of the coast, and Damascus, and the other lands Belsunu armed against the Elamite invasion. You and me, Father!" His voice throbbed with emotion now; his face colored; there was new vigor in his gaunt form. Watching him, Nikos and Yadiri exchanged smiles below tears, deeply moved. "Father—I used to wish it had been you that I'd apprenticed to."

"I know," Kirta said bitterly. "But—"

"Father, will you take me on as an apprentice now? This moment? And teach me the making of the black metal? Even if I'm a bit clumsy at first, and need as much supervision as a child? I'm a fast learner, Father. And now I have a reason to learn. A reason, Father? Several reasons. I want to help stop the nomads. I want to find Hadad's child . . ." He hesitated, smiling. The smile was a bitter one, and there was a resolute set to Shobai's strong jaw. "Father?" he said.

"Yes, son. Yes! Oh, gods—I don't know what to say."

"I'll tell you what to say," Shobai said. "Tell me, 'Yes, Shobai: I'll teach you the craft. Yes, Shobai: I'll go south with you and arm the free people against the kings. Yes, Shobai: I'll help you look for Hadad's child. And . . .'" He drew in a deep breath, and the strength flowed back into his gaunt frame visibly as he spoke. "Say to me, 'Yes, Shobai:

some day, before we're much older, I'll help place Reshef's neck between these hands of yours. Some day . . .' "

And now the vigor, the resolution seemed to pass from Shobai's big hands into his father's large frame. And Kirta's expression changed. The light came back into his eyes. "Oh, yes," he said fervently, in a low, thrilling voice. "Oh, *yes*. Yes, indeed, my son. That's one I'll swear to. If it's in my power to give it to you, you'll have that pleasure." He squeezed his son's hands, and Shobai beamed with joy at the sudden feel of his father's great physical strength. "I'm at your disposal. Now and forever. When do you want to start?"

"Father," Shobai said, "We've already started. And, Father . . ."

"Yes, son? Yes?"

"Welcome home."

IV

There on the hills above the gorge of the Jabbok they finally met: on the one side, Jacob and his wives and concubines and his children; on the other, his brother Esau, flanked by a host of armed men who seemed to stretch out as far as the eye could see.

Jacob nodded at Reuben. "Well, it's time," he said.

"Father," the boy asked. "What do you want me to do?"

"Nothing," Jacob replied. And, smiling, he rode slowly out to meet his brother in the middle of the field. As he rode forward, he could see Esau, his stout body sitting high in the saddle of a big, high-spirited Edomite charger, looking like a part of the horse.

Six paces apart the two men reined their animals and looked each other up and down. "Who the devil are all these?" Esau said in a gruff, grown man's voice, his face as fierce as ever, waving one hand at Jacob's entourage.

"I've been in Haran," Jacob said. "And—as you can see, I've been busy. Fathering children, mostly." He smiled wryly.

"Someone brought me a bribe from you. Keep your damned sheep and goats. I'm richer than Sesostris of Egypt. What the devil do I need more for?"

"As you wish." Jacob looked him over. "We don't look much alike any more," he said, dismounting. "You've lost a little hair. And . . . put on a little weight."

"Huh. And you're a graybeard. Look at us. A couple of old fools." Esau snorted, getting down from his horse in one easy, fluid movement. "Although, damn it, you seem to have done well enough for yourself. Well, you always were the type to land on your feet."

"A point well made. I owe you an apology. Perhaps more than that. I've wronged you terribly. And I can sincerely say—"

"Oh, the hell with that noise. I'm too damned dumb to run a country this size, and it didn't take me a year to find that out. It needs a sharp operator like you, finagling with the chieftains, flattering them, getting around them the way you could always get around people. I haven't the patience for that. You're the rightful heir. Who the devil says primogeniture is always just?"

"Esau, I'll have to talk to you about something. Immediately. There's a lot of danger up north. A tribal migration by a giant army of nomads—and they're heading—"

"I've heard something about it. Nothing the two of us can't lick together, I suspect." He looked Jacob up and down, hands on hips, shaking his head. "Jacob. Old Jacob. You know what pleases me most about seeing you again after all this time?"

"No. What?"

"You're not afraid of me any more. You look me right in the eye like a man. When we were kids, you used to pussyfoot around me if you thought I was mad. Now—damn, Jacob! You're a sight for sore eyes. . . ."

"You too. But—what are these boys doing here? This army of yours?"

"That?" Esau said. "That's your honor guard. Look, if you're going to come into Canaan, the least we can do is put on a bit of show. After all, it's not every day when we can welcome a king of the blood."

"King? Me? But . . ."

"Look, Jacob. The people need a king. They need a father. At best I've been a regent, waiting for you to come back and take over. And I don't like the job. Too much responsibility. You can't imagine how it bores me, adjudicating disputes between the chieftains when my mind's a million leagues away. And father's too old for—"

"Father! How is he?"

"Too weak to travel. But he'll be waiting at Mamre's Grove. Will you be settling down there? Near us?"

"I think not. We'll talk about that later. But—" Jacob could hold it in no longer. He stepped forward and embraced his twin. "Esau! Brother! It's so good to see you!"

Esau happily pounded him on the back. "Yes! Yes! I've missed you so. . . ."

But it wasn't Esau's style to lose his emotions in public—not the tenderer ones, anyhow. He stepped back now, red-faced. "Here," he said, "let me introduce you to Canaan. Most of these fellows were hardly more than a gleam in their old man's eye when you left. But they've heard about you."

He stepped back, hands on hips again, and bellowed to the host before him: "Here he is! Welcome him, all of you! And remember this day as something special! We've got a king again! A king in Canaan!"

The roar rose from many throats, swelled, and rose again. The assembled host held swords, spears high, waving them in triumph. Still in formation, they broke ranks to either side and rode around to flank Jacob's little entourage. Slowly, the great assemblage moved forward into the land of their fathers.

As Esau rode out proudly to lead the escort down the hillside to the junction of the two rivers, his brother suddenly saw in his mind's eye the face of the stranger who had contended with him the night before, who had lamed him and blessed him. And words once again came into his mind: *"Be no longer Jacob . . . from this moment you have a new name. Your name is Israel—one who has power with the God. . . ."*

Yes, he thought. Israel. And the stranger's words came to him again, as they had come to him on the hilltop in that magical dawn: *"Be fruitful and multiply. A mighty nation springs from your line, and your descendants will be kings. Kings of the land of Abraham, which I give to you and yours forever. . . ."*

He looked out over the green land below, at the mighty river flowing forth to bring life to the waterless land, at the lovely wisps of fog still lying over the wadis, at the broad expanse of the valley beyond, and the sight stirred his heart as no other sight could have done.

Yes, he thought. *This land is mine. Mine and my people's. The land of the Children of Israel. And the name the God has given me will lie upon the land of my fathers forever, until the last rocks on the hillsides crumble, until the stars and moon fade from the sky, until the seas run dry. . . .*

But then, riding slowly down the hill after his brother, Jacob smiled at the high-flown splendor of his words. And his affectionate gaze went out over the land below him, and a deeper thrill than this ran through him.

What need of grandiose words to describe it? It was less than this—and more, infinitely more, immeasurably more. It was home.

EPILOGUE

*Now, beyond the small circle of light around the guttering
fire and the twin torches, it was totally dark. The light of the
flickering flames fell on no more than the first row of faces as
the old man's words died out and his sorcerer's hands wove
the last strands of the story's tapestry to their completion.*

*Bright eyes still caught the fire's glow out there in the dark,
though. Unblinking, they followed the movements of the
tale-teller's hands now as the old man waved them to silence
and straightened his ancient body to its full height to speak
again.*

*"Now ends one night's telling of a tale, my children," he
said. "Now comes the time for sleep, and with the light the
time for work, for the greater glory of God. . . ."*

*There was an audible sigh from the younger members of
the crowd before him. He raised one hand again and the
silken texture of his voice once again rose above them. "But
on the morrow I will return. And then you shall hear a new
tale of the Sons of the Lion. . . .*

*"You shall hear of how the Shepherd Kings came to the
Land of Israel, and of how its king and leader, once Jacob of
Haran, met the danger. . . .*

*"You shall hear of the travels of the blind armorer Shobai,
who with his father brought the making of iron to the Lands
of the Covenant. You shall hear of his long search for the son
of his brother, for the lost Child of the Lion. You shall hear
of his search for the false and treacherous Reshef, betrayer of
his own city, slayer of the gentle Hadad. . . .*

*"You shall hear of the sons of Rachel and Danataya, boys
whose fortunes and souls were linked from birth, and of how
fate separated them in their youth, sending Joseph into
bondage in a distant land. . . ."*

His words trailed off now, in the winds of evening, spinning out the promise of new tales to come: tales of love and loss, famine and plenty, courage and failure, treason and self-sacrifice. And, almost in midsentence, they stopped abruptly, leaving the people hanging. One hand clasped the other, and he bowed simply. "Tomorrow," he said, backing slowly into the darkness. "Tomorrow . . ."

"FROM THE PRODUCER OF WAGONS WEST COMES YET ANOTHER EXPLOSIVE SAGA OF LEGENDARY COURAGE AND UNFORGETTABLE LOVE"

CHILDREN OF THE LION

☐ 26912	Children of the Lion #1	$4.50
☐ 26971	The Shepherd Kings #2	$4.50
☐ 26769	Vengeance of the Lion #3	$4.50
☐ 26594	The Lion In Egypt #4	$4.50
☐ 26885	The Golden Pharaoh #5	$4.50
☐ 27187	Lord of the Nile #6	$4.50
☐ 26325	The Prophecy #7	$4.50
☐ 26800	Sword of Glory #8	$4.50

Prices and availability subject to change without notice.

Buy them at your local bookstore or use this handy page for ordering:

- -

Bantam Books, Dept. LE5, 414 East Golf Road, Des Plaines, IL 60016

Please send me the books I have checked above. I am enclosing $_____ (please add $2.00 to cover postage and handling). Send check or money order—no cash or C.O.D.s please.

Mr/Ms _____

Address _____

City/State _____ Zip _____

LE5—11/88

Please allow four to six weeks for delivery. This offer expires 5/89.

**FROM THE PRODUCER OF WAGONS WEST
AND THE KENT FAMILY CHRONICLES—
A SWEEPING SAGA OF WAR AND HEROISM
AT THE BIRTH OF A NATION.**

THE WHITE INDIAN SERIES

Filled with the glory and adventure of the colonization of America, here
is the thrilling saga of the new frontier's boldest hero and his family.
Renno, born to white parents but raised by Seneca Indians, becomes a
leader in both worlds. THE WHITE INDIAN SERIES chronicles the
adventures of Renno, his son Ja-gonh, and his grandson Ghonkaba, from
the colonies to Canada, from the South to the turbulent West. Through
their struggles to tame a savage continent and their encounters with the
powerful men and passionate women in the early battles for America, we
witness the events that shaped our future and forged our great heritage.

☐	24650	White Indian #1	$3.95
☐	25020	The Renegade #2	$3.95
☐	24751	War Chief #3	$3.95
☐	24476	The Sachem #4	$3.95
☐	25154	Renno #5	$3.95
☐	25039	Tomahawk #6	$3.95
☐	25589	War Cry #7	$3.95
☐	25202	Ambush #8	$3.95
☐	23986	Seneca #9	$3.95
☐	24492	Cherokee #10	$3.95
☐	24950	Choctaw #11	$3.95
☐	25353	Seminole #12	$3.95
☐	25868	War Drums #13	$3.95
☐	26206	Apache #14	$3.95
☐	27161	Spirit Knife #15	$3.95
☐	27264	Manitou #16	$3.95
☐	27841	Seneca Warrior #17	$3.95

Prices and availability subject to change without notice.

Bantam Books, Dept. LE3, 414 East Golf Road, Des Plaines, IL 60016

Please send me the books I have checked above. I am enclosing $_____
(please add $2.00 to cover postage and handling). Send check or money
order—no cash or C.O.D.s please.

Mr/Ms _____

Address _____

City/State _____ Zip _____

LE3—4/89

Please allow four to six weeks for delivery. This offer expires 10/89.

BANTAM
SHOP-AT-HOME
C·A·T·A·L·O·G

Special Offer
Buy a Bantam Book
for only 50¢.

Now you can have Bantam's catalog filled with hundreds of titles plus take advantage of our unique and exciting bonus book offer. A special offer which gives you the opportunity to purchase a Bantam book for only 50¢. Here's how!

By ordering any five books at the regular price per order, you can also choose any other single book listed (up to a $5.95 value) for just 50¢. Some restrictions do apply, but for further details why not send for Bantam's catalog of titles today!

Just send us your name and address and we will send you a catalog!

BANTAM BOOKS, INC.
P.O. Box 1006, South Holland, Ill. 60473

Mr./Mrs./Ms. _____
                    (please print)

Address _____
City _____ State _____ Zip _____
                                          FC(A)—10/87
Please allow four to six weeks for delivery.